Song Of
The
Second Son

Book 3

Of The Warrior Series

By

Sandra J Yearman

Seraphim Publishing LLC

We Will Bring Light To All The Dark Places

Registered trademark-Sandra J Yearman

Seraphim Publishing
438 Water St
Cambridge, WI 53523
sandrajyearman@gmail.com

Library of Congress Catalog Number: 2014913974

ISBN: 978-0-9890263-1-4

First Edition

About The Author

Sandra J Yearman is a native of Wisconsin, where she currently resides. She graduated from the University of Wisconsin with a Bachelor of Arts degree in Journalism. Sandra was a member of the United States Army Reserves for over twenty years. She retired from the Dane County Sheriff's Office in Madison Wisconsin as a sergeant.

Sandra is a cancer survivor. And it is on this journey that she says she found her voice and began to write. She established Seraphim Publishing LLC in 2008. Sandra has spent decades supporting and working with rescued domestic animals.

Books written by Sandra:

Novels

Brother Kings
The Scroll And The Sword
Song Of The Second Son
The Faces Of The Damned
A Single Lion Roars
Stand Before The Children
Tyrants, Dictators And Kings

Politicians And Kings
Armada Of The Dead

Poetry

A Gathering Of Angels
I AM Who You Seek
A Celebration Of Angels
The Time Of Angels Is At Hand
The Warrior On Bended Knees
Celebration of God
On His Wings
The Voice Of An Angel
If I Had Wings
Souls On Fire
As Angels Hover Over
From The Mist The Angels Came
You Are The Song
Be Still
Walking With Angels
When Angels Smile
Angel Dreams
An Angel's Touch
Dancing With Angels

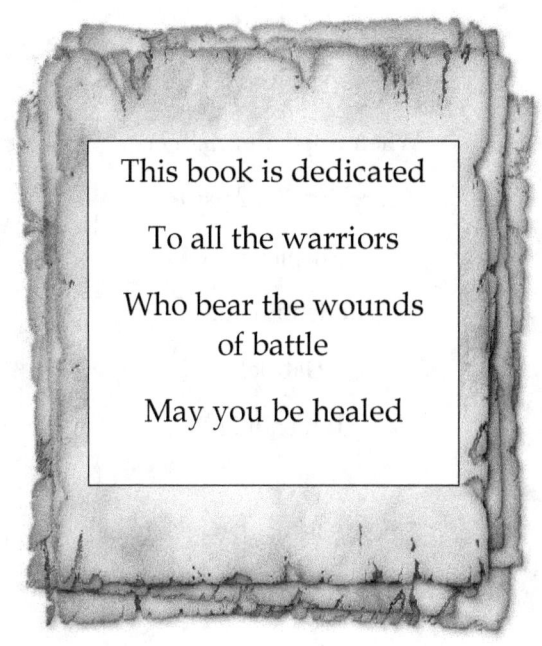

This book is dedicated

To all the warriors

Who bear the wounds
of battle

May you be healed

Contents

Contents

Chapter I
The Song

The second son

Of the second son

Of the second son

Wants to be praised

But beware

He will bring darkness all his days

The madness burns within him

The anger and the pain

The people fled before him

For his wrath not to gain

The masters shrieked in horror

At the evil they created

The world called to darkness

Holy altars desecrated

The doors to hell were opened

The monsters, the insane

Were set upon the children

What was to be gained?

"Thedes, Thedes," called Ratri loudly as he ran through the forest.

Hearing his name, Thedes stopped his practice of Shesone, an ancient fighting discipline of the Shettee Tribe. He grabbed his shirt from the ground and started to run towards the voice. "I am coming Ratri, what is wrong?" The two warriors ran towards each other's voices until they met near a small creek.

"Thedes, Ibula sent me for you. She wants you to come home right away."

"Is someone hurt?"

"I do not know; Ibula did not appear hurt but she did look worried when she called to me," Ratri said as the Ruala and the Shettee turned and started to run to Thedes' house.

"Ibula," yelled Thedes as he opened the door to their home. "What has happened?" As Ibula walked into the kitchen Thedes continued, "Are the children alright? What is wrong?"

"Oh, Thedes I am sorry to worry you so, we are all fine," said Ibula. "But we received a letter from Simon, I opened it thinking it contained the date of the christenings but as I read it I knew I had to show it to you right away." Ibula handed a folded piece of paper to Thedes; who read the letter out loud.

Dear Thedes and Ibula,

I am writing to tell you the celebration of the christenings has been put on hold. Petra; was kidnapped five weeks ago and we have been searching diligently for him. Our family has received threats from the dark lords as well as the Insidiae; we fear the worse. Please do not think we have forgotten about you.

As Always,

Simon

Ibula spoke as soon as Thedes stopped reading, "Thedes, Petra saved your people and they are family now; I think we should join in the search."

"As do I," Thedes said as he walked towards the door. "I am going to call a meeting of the Grand Council to see if others would like to join us."

"My Lord, we have just returned with Malus, would you have me show him in?" asked the Taperian soldier.

"Well it is about time," growled Cerephus. "What took so long?"

"We were attacked by small bands of Hutas twice, My Lord."

"How many men did you lose?"

"Three, My Lord."

"Yes show him in and have one of the soldiers get Erebus."

Cerephus stood up from his desk as a tall, thin man entered the room. Malus had long gray hair down to his waist with a scraggly gray beard almost the same length. Both his hair and beard had thick stripes of black in them. Cerephus thought that the stripes almost looked painted on. As Malus crossed the room to shake Cerephus' hand, his thick red robes seemed to glide across the floor. There was something very pleasant in his demeanor, which Cerephus thought odd, as Malus was a dark sorcerer.

"Thank you for coming; Erebus should be here momentarily," Cerephus said. "Would you like a drink?"

"Actually I would like a meal, I am starving," replied Malus. Cerephus walked across the room and opened the door. "Have Martha bring lunch for three, we will eat here in the war room," Cerephus said to one of the guards who were standing in the hallway.

"I take it Erebus has explained the seriousness of the situation we face here," Cerephus said as he returned to his chair behind the massive desk. "I will pay well for your services but I do expect results."

"Actually Erebus has not explained a lot. But the underworlds are changing," Malus said.

"What do you mean they are changing?" Erebus asked as he entered the room.

"Actually I was hoping you could explain some of it to me," Malus said as he sat down on one of the chairs surrounding the table. "Worlds are opening up that have been closed for centuries. Doors are opening, doors to worlds of great darkness. It is as if the zoo keepers are opening the cages."

"It is as if he disappeared off the face of the world," Sudfad said with frustration.

"That boy is precious to me too," said the Sanuri. "I am finding it most curious that I have not had one vision about Petra's kidnapping; it is almost as if I am blocked from seeing."

"But how can that be?" asked Sudfad who was riding in the lead of one of the search parties.

"I did not want to say anything before," said the Sanuri with concern in his voice. "But I believe there are some great magics at work here. Even the Enrops were blocked from seeing the abduction."

"So are you saying you do not think it was men who took him?" Sudfad asked fearfully.

"Oh no, from what Kyra said I believe they were men."

"But the child said they wore masks."

"Yes but she also said that Petra's dog bit one of the men in the leg and it bled and she bit another in the wrist and that too bled. They would not have bled red blood if they were demons. And there is something else; for Petra's last birthday I gave him a necklace, a very special necklace and I told him to wear it always. I showed Petra how he should place his hand over the crystal and call my name and I would be able to find him, no matter where he was."

"Just after we left, I sent Marie a note asking her to search through Petra's room. Renya sent a note today. She said that not only did they search the bedroom but the entire castle and Kyra searched every location that she and Petra played and it has not been found."

"Well that is a good thing, isn't it?" Sudfad asked. "If his hands are bound he may just not have been able to use it yet." The Sanuri did not comment as neither man wanted to verbalize the possibilities of the situation. Both men rode in silence for some time before Sudfad spoke again. "I cannot even tell you how it feels," he said. "I protect the largest Kingdom in Opots yet my own child is abducted from our back yard."

"My dear friend, we have discussed this before," said the Sanuri compassionately. "You cannot blame yourself for this, you need to remain focused. Have you any ideas how these men got past your soldiers?"

"Not yet, Raul is looking into it. That is why I want one of us to stay at the castle at all times."

"I too can share in that responsibility; I feel as if your family is mine also."

"You are part of the family, my wife adopted you a long time ago," Sudfad said with a laugh. "What has been weighing on my mind is that a ransom has not been asked for. Whoever took Petra did not do it for the money."

Erebus stopped talking as Martha finished setting the table with platters of food. "Thank you Martha," Cerephus said as he started to fill his plate. "This smells wonderful."

Erebus waited until Martha closed the door behind her before he spoke again. "Several generations ago a pact was made between some of the members of the Insidiae and the demon Omnibus to help Omnibus escape from The Abyss. Tributes were paid to set into motion a human blood line of evil proportions because the Insidiae feared the essence of Omnibus could not be contained in the body of a normal human. So this, I don't know what you want to call it, demon seed was passed down through the second sons for several generations, stopping at King Roch."

"So that song is true?" Malus said in disbelief. "I thought that was just a fable. Where is Roch now?"

"Things are a bit complicated," Erebus continued. "Months ago The Lion of The Great Ruler put an affliction on Roch. He still walked and talked but Roch looked and smelled as if he were dead. Then he went into a state of unconsciousness and appeared to be transforming"

"Into Omnibus?" Malus asked.

"We weren't sure," Erebus said. "A member of the Insidiae came here to check on Roch. Apparently they have great details about how the transformation is to take place and the changes we were seeing in Roch didn't seem to fit. But no one has ever used a human as a vessel for a demon before so who really knows."

"Erebus, you mean no one has successfully used a human as a vessel for a demon before," Malus said. "I have read of ancient attempts of such acts."

"Malus, do you have those writings with you?"

"No but we can locate them."

Just tell him why he is here," Cerephus interrupted. "You can fill him in on the details later."

"This member of the Insidiae was greatly concerned that Roch might not be strong enough to fulfill his role as the Vessel as the energies have already been put into motion for the ascension. He paid Cerephus to care for Roch until his return. And somehow Roch just disappeared a few weeks ago."

"What do you mean disappeared?" Malus asked.

"He just plain vanished," Cerephus said. "None of the guards saw anyone come into the castle or saw Roch leave, not that he could walk on his own."

"The Insidiae are looking for him," Erebus said. "And every spell I do is being blocked by something or someone. I want you to help me get information; I think our combined powers can break through whatever is blocking me."

"I am a little confused," Malus said as he stared at Erebus. "What is Roch to you, I mean why do you care what happens to him?"

"Because this is Roch's castle," Cerephus said. "Erebus and I have taken over Roch's kingdom. As a man he was a monster. We want to know if we are going to be dealing with that monster or a demon."

"Omnibus isn't just any demon, he is one of the Old Ones, you know that Erebus," Malus said. "The Insidiae must have some powerful magics if they think they can raise a demon from Solv; it's never been done to my knowledge."

"What is Solv?" asked Cerephus.

"It is one of the locations in The Great Abyss, where The Great Ruler sends demons to imprison them," Malus said.

"So you mean it is hell?"

"No, the demons dwell in hell dimensions," Malus explained. "From what I have heard The Abyss is like a vast emptiness, the demons lose their powers there. Which is why I find it curious that the Insidiae could make a pact with Omnibus; how would they communicate with him?"

"Something smells good," Thaos said as he entered his chambers.

"I'm making cookies," Nikki called out from the kitchen. "And Ryan is here to see you."

Thaos entered the kitchen and kissed Nikki then patted her pregnant stomach. "I'll take what he is having," Thaos said when he saw a glass of milk and a large plate of cookies in front of Ryan. Before Ryan could speak Nikki said, "We need to invite Ryan and Sonja over for dinner."

"We need to?" Thaos asked with curiosity.

"Yes, Ryan wants to get to know her better and he's kind of shy," Nikki said as she set a plate of cookies and a glass of milk in front of Thaos, who was now seated at the table. Nikki leaned against Thaos and put her arm around him.

"Thaos how did you get Nikki to spend time with you?" Ryan asked seriously.

Thaos grinned, "I asked her to my bed and she never left."

"Thaos," Nikki said with a scolding tone to her voice then she started to laugh. "Actually he is right. Ryan you are so red, did we embarrass you?"

"Not exactly," Ryan said shyly. "I have, it's just that." Ryan glanced at Nikki then looked back at Thaos and said in a low voice, "It's just that I have never been with a girl like that."

"Well you are going to have to talk to Thaos then instead of me," Nikki said with a laugh and returned to her baking.

"When you finish your milk and cookies we will go for a walk," Thaos said.

"Come on in," said Stephan to Thaos and Ryan. "Ingr we have company."

"Here, Nikki sent these," Thaos said as he handed Stephan a plate of cookies.

Ryan stared at Ingr as she walked out of the kitchen. Ingr saw the look on his face and started to laugh, "I know Ryan, one day I didn't have a stomach and look at me now. I'm going to have to get bigger clothes. I just finished frosting a chocolate cake do you want some?"

"Honey we will all take some," said Stephan as he handed her the plate of cookies. "And I think you look beautiful," Stephan said and kissed Ingr on the forehead.

"We came here for some man talk," Thaos told Stephan as the three men took seats at the kitchen table.

"Man talk?" Stephan repeated with a grin.

15

Thaos winked at Ryan and said jokingly, "Rumor has it that Stephan dated every girl in this kingdom and maybe some of the surrounding ones." Ingr looked at Thaos and laughed as she knew he was saying this for her benefit.

"Oh, that kind of man talk," Stephan said and laughed.

"This is really good cake," Ryan said as he was trying to change the subject.

"Ingr what can you tell us about your friend Sonja?" Thaos asked. Ingr saw how red Ryan got as Thaos spoke.

"She's a very capable warrior. She didn't start training until she was ten, but she is a fast learner," Ingr said as she was filling the men's cups with coffee. She is really nice but very shy and she's never had a boyfriend, if that is what you are asking."

"Ryan would like to get to know her better," Thaos said as he reached for a second piece of cake.

"Ryan you will have to make the first move because Sonja is too shy to," Ingr said.

"What if she doesn't like me?"

"Ryan you will never know if you don't talk to her."

"Ingr I have never really had a girlfriend before," Ryan said shyly. "How do I get her to want to spend time with me?"

Ingr looked at Stephan and Thaos then laughed, "Well, you could do like these two did; they never left our sides for a moment until we fell in love with them."

"She's right," Stephan said. "I was damned if I was going to let another guy get her attention. But Ingr is really shy also. So we spent a lot of time doing things that we were both comfortable with like riding and shooting competitions."

"Ryan if Sonja is interested in you she will want to spend time with you," Ingr said kindly. "And if she isn't, there are a lot of other girls in our tribe that Nikki and I can introduce you to. I know you don't really know anyone around here but us."

Ingr paused for a moment then said, "I have an idea. Every week Nikki, Angelina and I visit our families why don't you come with us and we can introduce you to our tribe. That way you can meet more people and make some friends too."

Ryan turned dark red and asked, "Will Elexas be there?"

"Ryan you never did tell us what happened with her the night of our wedding celebration," Thaos said with a grin. Ryan glanced at Ingr.

"You can tell them," Ingr said.

"Elexas is awful pretty but I don't even know how to explain it," Ryan was becoming more embarrassed as he spoke. "She wanted to take a walk in the gardens and as soon as we got outside she started kissing me." Ryan paused, "And she started taking my clothes off. I don't know what I would have done if Ingr, Nikki and Angelina hadn't come upon us."

Stephan and Thaos were trying very hard not to laugh. Stephan looked at Ingr and said, "And I suppose it was an accident that you girls came upon them."

"Not at all," Ingr said defiantly. "We were watching them and saw Elexas pull Ryan out of the Great Hall. We followed them to see if Ryan needed help and he did. Ryan is like my little brother, I watch out for him."

"Ryan's older than you," Stephan joked.

"It doesn't matter," Ingr said then she turned to Ryan. "Don't worry about Elexas." Both Stephan and Thaos roared with laughter.

"Tomorrow morning take me to the caverns where the transformation was to take place," Malus said. "I will bet we can get some information in there."

"What do you mean? What kind of information?" asked Cerephus.

"Cerephus think of it like this; you ride onto a battlefield where two powerful armies once fought. They are both gone now but they always leave things behind. You as an experienced soldier would probably be able to tell a great deal about the battle by the tracks and objects left behind. Don't you agree?" Malus asked.

"Yes."

"Erebus and I are experienced in reading the signs left behind by beings of other worlds. We may not get the answers you are looking for but I am sure we will find some information."

"I find this all very interesting. Erebus and I have already been to the caverns. What will be different if we go again with you?"

"First of all Erebus is being blocked from contacting his sources in other worlds. So far I am not being blocked but if I was; by Erebus and I combining our powers we can create an energy so powerful that only the most powerful demons can stop it. And if that happens, then you will know it is the Old Ones who are stopping you from getting your answers. And that in of itself will give us a direction to go."

"This has been the longest and the worse trip of my life," Sophie complained out loud to herself. Since leaving Roch's castle Sophie's journey had been plagued with one mishap after another. Twice the carriage had broken down, for different reasons.

The third day a great storm washed out the road they had originally been travelling on and a few nights later the sounds of a lion disturbed their camp. The horses became so terrified by the roars' of the lion that they broke away from their tethers and escaped. One of her drivers had to walk to the nearest village and purchase more horses.

"This ordeal should be over soon," Sophie said as she continued to talk to herself. "I should be at the monastery in two days."

Chapter II
When Good Men Gather

"My Lord, the soldiers said you need to come to the front lawn right away," Marie said as she entered Sudfad's study.

Raul was sitting at his father's desk. "Did they say why?" Raul asked as he put down the papers he was reading and stood up.

"No My Lord, they just said to come quickly."

Raul grabbed a sword from the wall and ran past Marie and down the hallway to the front doors of the castle. He opened the massive wooded doors and stopped abruptly; for standing before him was an army of Ruala and Shettee warriors. A broad smile came across Raul's face as he called to Marie, "Marie please gather all the women and tell them we have most welcomed guests. I will take everyone to the Great Hall, please bring refreshments."

"Yes My Lord," replied Marie before she hurried away.

Raul quickly walked down the steps. At the bottom of the staircase Thedes extended his hand to shake with Raul but Raul grabbed Thedes and hugged him instead. Then Raul turned and kissed Ibula on the cheek.

"We came as soon as we got Simon's letter," Ibula said.

"Simon's letter?" repeated Raul.

"Yes, he wrote to us telling us the christenings had been postponed and when he told us why, we knew we had to help," Thedes said.

"Please have everyone gather in the Great Hall, I will brief you on what we know and where the search parties are," before Raul could finish speaking Renya ran up to Ibula and hugged her, then she hugged Thedes.

"Oh!" Renya exclaimed when she saw the hundreds of warriors on the front lawn. "Thank you so much," Renya said then started to cry. Ibula put her arm around Renya's shoulders.

"We are here to help Renya," Ibula said soothingly. "We will find him."

Vitomas and Annabelle were overjoyed to hear that the Rualas and Shettees had come to help search for Petra. Even though Marie had told them; the Princesses were still surprised when they entered the Great Hall and found it filled with warriors. The two women worked their way through the crowd until they found Ibula and Thedes, who were standing with Renya and Raul.

"We are so glad you are here," Vitomas said as she hugged Ibula first and then Thedes.

"Honey, Thedes and Ibula will stay in our chambers," Raul said.

"I'm staying there too," Annabelle said with a smile as she also hugged their guests. "I know it's silly but I just can't stand to be by myself. So when Simon is gone I stay with Vitomas and Raul."

"Well, actually we planned to be out with the search parties," Thedes said then he looked at Raul. "So how did those men get past your soldiers?"

"We still have not found out," Raul said gravely. Thedes and Raul looked at each other in silence for a few moments, both men knowing what the other was thinking. "Yes Thedes, we fear we have a traitor among us," Raul said.

"My Lord," said the soldier.

"I see them," said Simon with a smile. He signaled the men behind him to stop their horses. The soldiers from Wetpr led by Prince Simon sat on their horses and watched as fifty Ruala and Shettee warriors landed in front of them. One of the Ruala warriors walked towards Simon; who dismounted to meet his ally.

"Betu it is good to see you," said Simon as the two warriors shook hands. "What brings you here?"

"When Thedes and Ibula received your letter, they presented it to the Grand Council and many of us volunteered to help you find your brother."

"What!" said Simon with surprise.

"This boy helped our Shettee brothers to escape the Hutas; we feel as if we owe him," Betu said. "We arrived at your castle yesterday. Some of our warriors will be joining your father and the Sanuri, others are joining Matthew and his men and the remainder are staying at the castle to protect your family and to find the traitors among your men," Betu said in a lowered voice.

"I don't know what to say; I am overwhelmed by your generosity. Did Raul tell you of the information we have so far?"

"Yes and he sent this for you," said Betu as he handed a folded paper to Simon.

Simon unfolded the note and read it. Betu could see the look of concern on Simon's face. "Raul says two of our soldiers bodies were found buried in shallow graves in the lands near the castle. They were stripped of their uniforms and the bodies were fresh, so they were killed recently," Simon said.

"I know," Betu replied. "That is why some of our warriors are staying at the castle."

"I don't understand this," Meekos said as he turned from the window of his hotel room in the City of Nora, in the Kingdom of Stordt. "Something is wrong."

"How long has it been since you heard from Sophie?" Pravis asked.

"It's been weeks and you know we have feared that someone is intercepting our messages," Meekos said nervously. "I can feel it in my bones, something is very wrong. Where is Tenebrae anyways? He is late."

"He said it might take a while. Meekos, I have never seen you act like this before, you are usually the one who is so calm."

"I don't like any of this," Meekos said with disgust as he paced back and forth. "Now we owe great debts to two powerful demons and we are setting a trap for an emissary of The Great Ruler. I don't know whose wrath I fear more."

"Well look at it this way; you threatened many times to get the Sanuri for interfering with our plans, so now we are doing it."

"Pravis do you really think it is going to be that simple?" Meekos yelled. "And further more do you really trust Ahriman?"

"What do you mean?"

"Pravis think about it, Ahriman has done nothing but ridicule us and take our riches. I suspect he has his own agendas not only regarding Omnibus but the Sanuri as well. I would feel better if I just knew what he was up to."

Both of the high priests looked up as they heard a knock at the door. "Well, it's about time," Meekos snapped as Tenebrae entered the hotel room.

"Don't yell at me I told you the paperwork would take time. But everything went as planned," Tenebrae said. "As soon as I told Endleson that King Roch wanted to buy a small area of his family's gold mines, Endleson couldn't sign the papers fast enough. Seems like the folks around here are terrified of Roch and his men."

"Good, tonight we start preparing the chamber for the ascension," Meekos said with relief. "Pravis you have the list of what we need. Tenebrae will get the Hutas. While I hire some workers. Then when they are done with our projects, they will be our first gathering of food for Omnibus."

"When do you want to get Roch?" Pravis asked as he stood up to leave.

"Hopefully we will have a place to put him by the end of the week," Meekos said. "We need to get him here before the Sanuri shows up."

As Sudfad and the Sanuri led a company of soldiers westward; the Sanuri's attention was drawn to shadows forming on the ground. He looked up and said with a grin, "We have company." Sudfad gave the order to 'halt'. The soldiers stopped near a clearing by the monastery near Philiste in the Kingdom of Wetpr and watched as dozens of Ruala and Shettee warriors landed before them.

Both Sudfad and the Sanuri dismounted and greeted their friends. "Misha, so good to see you," said the Sanuri as he gave the warrior a hug. Then turning to Sudfad, the Sanuri said, "King Sudfad this is Misha, a lieutenant in the Ruala forces, Misha this is King Sudfad of Wetpr."

"My Lord this is for you, from Raul," said Misha as he handed Sudfad a folded piece of paper.

Sudfad read the paper, then said, "They found the bodies of two of our soldiers buried in the woods on our lands. The soldiers had been stripped of their uniforms." Sudfad paused then said, "And the bodies were fresh which means that even now we have spies among us."

"The search parties left weeks ago," the Sanuri said. "So the spies must be at the castle."

"My Lord," explained Misha. "We are here to help you find the boy. After the bodies were found; some of our warriors are staying at the castle to protect your family and to search for the traitors. The rest of us have divided up and are joining the search parties."

"We are ever so grateful for the help," said Sudfad. "But please tell me how did you hear about Petra's abduction?"

"Simon wrote a letter to Thedes and Ibula telling them the christenings would be postponed and the reason. Thedes presented the letter to the Grand Council and within hours we were flying towards your castle."

The Sanuri got a proud smile on his face as he listened to Misha speak. "The Lion told me there would be a time when good men would come together; breaking down the barriers of race and cultures to stand up against darkness. I did not think I would live to see that day," said the Sanuri.

23

"I hope you aren't getting sick of me," Angelina said as she carried Jacob into the parlor where Mathas, Rosa and Margarit were sitting. "It's just too quiet with Matthew gone."

"Nonsense my dear," Rosa said as she put down her embroidery work. "You are part of this family too. Here let me hold little Jacob."

"I realized this is the first time that Matthew and I have been separated for more than a few hours," Angelina said as she sat on the floor near Margarit who was playing with dolls. "It's amazing; I never before realized how much time Matthew and I spend together."

Mathas and Rosa smiled at Angelina's comments. "It doesn't matter how long you are married, you will always miss him when he is gone," Mathas said. "And I am sure that he misses you and Jacob just as much."

"I've also realized now that we are starting a family that I won't be able to go to battle anymore," Angelina said sadly.

Rosa looked at Mathas waiting for him to speak. "Angelina hopefully there won't be any battles for you to go to, but that doesn't mean you aren't still a warrior and it doesn't mean you can't keep training," Mathas said. "Did Matthew tell you that you couldn't be a warrior anymore?"

"No," Angelina said. "He made me promise not to do anything dangerous while I was pregnant." Angelina started to smile. "The problem is that we have two different meanings of 'dangerous.'"

"Do you regret that you are starting a family?" Rosa asked.

"Oh no, Matthew and I both want lots of children, I guess I was thinking that we could continue to have the same lives and a big family too. I just didn't think some of this through."

"My Lord look to the skies," said a soldier to Matthew. Looking up, Matthew was surprised and pleased to see Ruala and Shettee warriors circling overhead. "Halt," ordered Matthew. "We have friends joining us."

For the many Wetprian soldiers who had not seen the Ruala and Shettee warriors before this was an unbelievable experience. Matthew and his men watched as dozens of Ruala warriors, both male and female, landed on the ground before them. Some of the Rualas carried Shettee warriors. Matthew dismounted and walked up to them.

"I am Gael, brother of Ibula," said a handsome Ruala warrior as he extended his hand to Matthew.

"I am Matthew one of the adopted sons of King Sudfad and Queen Renya; I am glad to meet you."

"The boy that was taken helped to save our Shettee brothers, we have come to help. Also I have a letter for you from Raul."

"Do you know what this says?" Matthew asked as he took the letter.

"Yes, I saw the bodies."

"Gael this says the bodies of those two soldiers were fresh; Petra was taken over five weeks ago," Matthew said in disbelief.

"I know that is why some of our people are staying at the castle to protect Sudfad's family."

Sudfad and his men made camp late into the evening. The Sanuri and Sudfad always shared a campsite; on this night they asked Misha to join them.

"I have never seen a king cook before," said Misha as he watched Sudfad preparing their meal.

"I've been a soldier all my life, had to learn to cook or starve," Sudfad said and laughed.

"And a fine cook he is," said the Sanuri as he dropped an armload of wood near the fire. "From what I hear he is a much better cook than the Queen," the Sanuri said chuckling.

"Misha, my wife has fought in battle and believe me when I say she could lead an army. A natural leader, she is a generous and compassionate queen, a wonderful mother and wife but please don't let her near a kitchen," Sudfad said with a laugh as he was putting steaks onto the plates. "Truly the first time she cooked for me I was sick for two days."

Misha took his plate and started eating, "This is very good," he said then paused. "I don't know if I should tell you this but your wife started to cry when she saw that we came to help."

"She is utterly heartbroken," Sudfad said sadly. "As are we all."

"In my culture warriors do not harm children; they fight other warriors," Misha said with contempt. "We are proud to be warriors."

"I too am proud to be a warrior and have tried to raise my sons with integrity. But like with anything else in this world there are those who act without honor, a disgrace they are to all mankind," Sudfad said then paused. "I guess I am not really that hungry," he said and set his plate on the ground. "Sanuri you are being awfully quiet tonight."

"I am going to take a walk," the Sanuri said as he stood up. "I will eat my dinner later."

"Do you want company?" Misha asked.

"No Misha; this I need to do alone."

Chapter III
Searching For Answers

The Sanuri walked out into the wilderness. The huge trees of the forest blocked the starlight. In the darkness he walked alone. "Are you here?" the Sanuri called into the night. "I need to speak with you." The area of the forest where the Sanuri was standing became illuminated with a great light. The Sanuri turned around and saw The Lion standing behind him.

"Why am I being blocked?" asked the Sanuri with frustration. "I keep asking for guidance and nothing comes."

"It is not the heavens that is blocking you but your own fears," replied The Lion.

"My own fears," the Sanuri repeated incredulously.

"My old friend you are so close to this family that your emotions are out of your control and that is very dangerous for one as powerful as you. And you know that fears are often a wedge between man and The Great Ruler."

"No, you are right. Please where is Petra?"

"For weeks you have been asking us to show you were the boy is. You are not asking the right questions."

"What should I be asking?"

"You should be asking why. Why was he taken?"

"This is a trap," uttered the Sanuri as he started to grasp the reality of the situation.

"Yes, and if you had not been so blinded by your emotions, you of all people would have realized that by now."

"Tell me is Petra still alive?" the Sanuri asked fearfully.

"Yes, the boy is scared but fine for the moment."

"Oh, thank The Great Ruler. I must warn Sudfad and his sons."

"The trap is not for them."

The Sanuri stared at The Lion for several moments. "The trap is for me?"

"Yes and Ahriman himself has put it into motion."

"Ahriman, I have not heard that name for many generations. Why is he setting a trap for me?"

"Members of the Insidiae have Petra. They think they can force you to reverse the mark I left upon Roch."

"I do not have the power to do that."

"And Ahriman knows that. He has other plans for you. Why do you act so surprised that the demons are trying to destroy you?"

"I don't know. I realize you are right and I have not been thinking any of this through. Please give me what I need so I can rescue the boy."

"Now you are asking for the right things," The Lion said. "The boy is being held captive in the Kingdom of Stordt. The Insidiae know that if Sudfad brings his army into that land it will be considered an act of war. But you, the Rualas and Shettees can enter those lands. Tell Sudfad to take his family home and we will bring his son back to him."

"We," repeated the Sanuri.

"Have I ever let you face powerful demons alone?"

"Is the King of Stordt involved in this scheme?"

"No, he has no knowledge of it, nor would he get involved as he has enough of his own concerns now. You do not know the men who were hired to kidnap Petra but you know the men who are paying them."

"Is it Meekos, Pravis and Tenebrae?" the Sanuri asked with disgust.

"Yes and they are just now beginning to set up another chamber for the ascension. Go now and speak with Sudfad. Send messages to the other search parties because you will leave at dawn."

"What is the meaning of this?" shrieked Sophie. "I demand to see my brother at once. My brother is High Priest Meekos, you will be sorry you are treating me like this," Sophie yelled at the two priests who were escorting her down several long hallways. Suddenly they stopped before two massive wooden doors.

One of the priests knocked on the door and they could hear the hinges squeaking as the door opened. There was a large table in the room that Sophie and the two priests entered. Sophie did not take the time to count but figured there were at least twenty priests in the room and they all wore green bands on their robes.

"I am High Priest Raphael," a handsome dark haired man said. "Please have a seat."

As Sophie sat down at the table she explained, "My brother is High Priest Meekos, I am here to visit him. Please tell me is something wrong or has something happened to him?"

"Why do you ask?"

"Well, it has been a long time since I have visited this monastery but the last time I was here I was allowed to walk around freely."

"You are not a prisoner here," Raphael said gently. "What is your name My Lady?"

"Sophie, my name is Sophie I am Meekos younger sister." Sophie's untrusting nature was being softened by Raphael's gentle charm.

"Sophie, may I call you Sophie?"

"Yes."

"Sophie you were brought here because we too are curious as to the whereabouts of your brother, he and two other high priests have been missing for weeks."

"Missing! Are you sure?"

"Sophie you do not think I would lie to you?" Raphael asked. "As you can imagine we are all quite concerned that something horrible may have happened to them. No one at the monastery has received word from any of them. Tell me when was the last time you spoke with your brother?"

Taken back by the words of Raphael; Sophie stopped to think about the last time she had received a message from Meekos. "He visited me in Stordt a couple of months ago and after that I think I might have received one or two letters from him." Sophie's eyes grew wide at the realization that Meekos had not contacted her in weeks. "Your Eminence, now that I think about it I have not heard from my brother in weeks."

"Sophie, would you like my men to take you to Meekos' chambers? You must be exhausted from your trip."

"Why yes, that would be kind of you," Sophie said as she stood up.

"Sophie, please if you can remember anything that will help us find our brethren, come and tell me."

"Of course," said Sophie as she turned and started to walk towards the door.

After the door closed, High Priest Raphael said to the other priests in the room. "I want her watched at all times. There is more to that woman than first appears; did you see that dark aura around her?"

"What do you mean we have to go home?" Sudfad yelled. "Sanuri I don't understand what you are saying."

"I just met with The Lion," the Sanuri explained. "And Sudfad I am so sorry to tell you this but Petra was kidnapped to set a trap for me. He is alright but he is being held in Stordt. You know you cannot take your army into that kingdom, it would be considered an act of war. The Lion said that the Rualas and Shettees can accompany me as I go after Petra."

"I don't like this at all," Sudfad said angrily.

"Sudfad, these are the orders of The Lion, you cannot go against them. He will help me get Petra. We must send messages to the other search parties tonight, telling your men to return home and telling the Rualas and Shettees to join me. I must leave at sunrise."

Sophie started to search Meekos chambers as the housekeeper was preparing dinner. Sophie was becoming increasingly afraid that something horrible had happened to her brother which meant that she might be next. Sophie was becoming frustrated and agitated as she searched Meekos' study, suddenly Sophie had a realization. She left the study and marched into the kitchen.

"Marla, has anyone else been in my brother's chambers since he disappeared?"

"Why yes My Lady," Marla said innocently. "Those other priests were here looking for clues as to what could have happened to High Priest Meekos."

"Did they take anything?"

"That I do not know," Marla said. "Is something missing?"

"I don't know yet. Tell me Marla who are the other priests who are missing?"

"High Priest Pravis and High Priest Tenebrae."

"Marla what is it? You have a strange look on your face."

"I don't know if I should tell you; but some months ago three priests were found dead in one of the gardens. They were here visiting your brother."

"He didn't tell me about that. How did they die?"

"All I know is there were prints of a great lion found near their bodies."

"What!" Sophie said fearfully.

Sophie waited until after midnight before she left Meekos' chambers. She carried a small lantern and walked the desolate halls of the monastery. The only priests who were not sleeping at this late hour were some of the members of the Patronus, those who were keeping guard and those who were watching Sophie. High Priest Raphael and some of the other leaders of the organization were having a late night meeting.

Although a large woman, Sophie moved quietly and gingerly as she deliberately turned down many different hallways in an attempt to confuse anyone who might be following her. Sophie walked down to the first floor of the monastery. Near the front entrance was a long hallway which contained many large, framed paintings hung on both sides of the corridor.

At the very end of the hallway, Sophie reached behind a painting of High Priest Meekos; her fingers grasped onto a large brass ring which she turned to the right, within moments a secret door in the stone wall started to open.

Sophie walked through the door and immediately came upon an old stone stairway. She walked down narrow stone steps for almost twenty minutes before she touched ground. There were four corridors before her; Sophie new that the number of corridors was meant to confuse people for they all led to the same place.

She walked down one long damp corridor until it opened into the large caverns that Meekos had built under the monastery. Sophie had hoped to find Meekos or some sign of him in the caverns. She found the large pit were the sacrifices to Ahriman had been killed. She found the altars and saw the bloody symbols painted on the walls.

Lost in her despair Sophie did not hear the movement within the caverns. "Let go of me!" screamed Sophie as two priests grabbed her arms.

"Sophie I must thank you, we thought that such a place existed but we could not find it," said Raphael as he walked up to her. Some of the men started to light the torches that were affixed along the walls. Soon the dancing light of the fires exposed the grizzly slaughter area before them.

"Your Eminence, this pit is filled with bones," announced one of the horrified priests.

"We will need to examine them," Raphael said then he turned to Sophie again. "Has your brother been sacrificing people as well as animals down here?"

"I don't know what you are talking about," Sophie replied with indignation.

"How did you know this place existed?"

"I will not tell you anything," Sophie said defiantly.

"Lock her up," Raphael ordered the priests who were restraining Sophie's arms. "But wait a moment." Raphael walked close to Sophie and stared into her eyes, then he closed his eyes and prayed. When he opened his eyes he placed his hand on Sophie's arm, which immediately began to smoke. She screamed in pain. "Just as I thought you are a witch," Raphael said.

Suddenly the chambers were filled with Ahriman's loud maniacal laughter. Everyone, including Sophie jumped at the sound of the unseen demon. Raphael told his men to stay where they were standing as he walked alone into the center of the huge cavern.

"I claim this entire monastery for The Great Ruler," Raphael said in a loud and commanding voice. "Be gone demon you are no longer welcomed here."

Ahriman started to curse in an ancient language and he caused a great wind to rage through the cavern. Raphael stood his ground as the force of the wind beat against him. Raphael stood his ground as he felt the presence of evil descending upon him. Raphael stood his ground and yelled into the darkness of hell, "You no longer have power here." Ahriman's voice echoed through the caverns as he cursed the high priest who would not bow before him.

Suddenly the roar of a single lion echoed in the caverns; a roar that terrified the great demon himself. Ahriman's voice could no longer be heard. The raging wind stopped and the caverns were silent again.

"The demon is gone," Raphael said as he walked back to his men.

"He will be back," Sophie warned.

"Not as long as I have anything to do with it," said Raphael.

"You fool; people will always be bartering with him," Sophie said with conviction.

After the freshly killed bodies of the two Wetprian soldiers were discovered; Thedes and Ibula decided to stay at the castle and help to find the killers. The soldiers who were killed held low rank, so anyone wearing their uniforms would blend in with the vast majority of soldiers.

Raul was not happy that so much of his time was consumed with Sudfad's duties and meetings. Raul would have preferred to lead the investigation into the murders but instead he turned the investigation over to Thedes, who formed six groups.

Thedes led group one, Ibula group two, Hadar, one of Ibula's brothers led group three, Alma a female lieutenant led group four, Riftca a male lieutenant in the Ruala military led group five and Naal, a Shettee warrior led group six. Raul provided Thedes with the names of the hundreds of thousands of troops who were stationed at Fort Salar.

"This is going to be like finding a needle in a haystack," Raul said as he handed the stacks of rosters to Thedes. "How do you think you will find them?"

"First we will look for signs of injuries, those dead soldiers looked like they put up a fight," Thedes said. "And I can't imagine stolen uniforms fit properly, to say nothing about blood stains and their behavior."

"You might have more than two intruders," Ibula warned.

Raul's eyes suddenly widen, "Ibula talk with Gala. She made a wonderful potion that made a prisoner tell us the truth once. I don't know if you want to give the potion to all of the men, maybe your lead suspects."

"I like that idea," Ibula said as she looked at Thedes, "You know there might be some other potions that we can make that might be of assistance. Thedes I might have to send some warriors back to the caves to retrieve some plants."

"That is your area of knowledge," Thedes said. "Do whatever you need to do. We certainly could use the help. In fact if you send some warriors back why don't they ask Mateo to join us since he is the Chief Healer; besides he kept saying he wanted to visit Sudfad again?"

"The Enrops are watching over the soldiers," Raul said. "Apparently they can tell if a demon is disguised as a human."

"I don't think demons killed those soldiers, the bodies would have been more damaged," Ibula said.

"What do you mean?" Raul asked as he remembered Matthew describing the bodies they found in a cabin weeks before."

"Demons have incredible strength and they like to inflict great pain," Ibula said. "It is not unusual for demons to tear bodies apart."

"Then there is something I must tell you," Raul said. "A few days after Ariel was born, Matthew and Angelina were returning to Lentz. Angelina found a small boy in the woods; he was very sick and covered in dried blood. Matthew took some men and they searched for the boy's parents."

"They found the bodies of a man and a woman torn to shreds in an old hunting cabin on our land. Matthew had the bodies buried. Simon and I went to the cabin. The walls and ceiling were coated in blood, in fact there was so much blood that we could see the outlines of two chests that must have been taken."

"How long ago was this?" Thedes asked.

"Six or seven weeks."

"Did the boy tell them anything?" Ibula asked.

"He is only about two years old."

"And where is this boy now?" asked Ibula.

"Matthew and Angelina adopted him," Raul said. "Why?"

"There is a possibility that boy may still be in danger," Ibula said. "Please draw us a map so we can see this cabin ourselves."

"One other thing," Raul added. "Someone took the time to wipe the ground clean of tracks."

By sunrise the next morning all of the Ruala and Shettee warriors had left the search parties and joined the Sanuri. The group headed south towards the Kingdom of Stordt; their route would take them east of the Rodite Forest. King Sudfad, Prince Simon and Prince Matthew dejectedly led their search parties back to the castle in Salar. None of them wanted to stop searching for Petra but none of them would disobey the orders of The Lion, the emissary of The Great Ruler.

Sudfad sent an Enrop to the castle to tell Renya and the others that they were returning home and the reason. Sudfad knew that his wife was heartbroken over the kidnapping of Petra and to return home without the boy would only intensify her grief. As he led his men eastward, Sudfad tried to focus on the yet unknown threats that could still be near his castle; for thinking about Petra's fate was too painful for him.

Neither Simon nor Matthew were the type of men to give up on a mission; especially one so dear to their hearts. They understood that both the Sanuri and The Lion were right; they could not take their men into the Kingdom of Stordt, even to rescue their brother for the risk of war was too great. Yet both Princes felt it was their duty to be the ones who rescued Petra. The journey home for all three search parties was long and solemn.

With the first light of dawn, Ibula carried Thedes as she and twelve other Ruala warriors flew to Langa Woods in search of the cabin where the two bodies had been found. Langa Woods was an old forest that covered hundreds of acres in both the Kingdoms of Wetpr and Lentz.

Thedes always marveled that his tiny wife could carry him in flight but then he marveled at many things with the Ruala people.

Before their Kingdom of Xepoltr was destroyed by the Hutas, the Shettees were an isolated race. Over generations their kingdom had become very self-sufficient; a goal their people sought so they would not have to interact with other races.

The Shettees were a race unlike any other; their ancestry was said to have evolved from lions and humans. They were a mighty race; strong and fast. The Shettees walked on two legs and their bodies resembled humans except for their superior strength. The great manes that surrounded their heads distinguished them from other creatures.

There was not a day that went by that Thedes did not think about the glory Xepoltr once had. But now his life had taken him on adventures that he never before would have dreamed about. He had a Ruala wife who he adored and he was bonded with a family of humans; such things would not have been possible in his life as it was.

And now Thedes' highest honor was that he was friends with the powerful Sanuri, a holy man, who Thedes had never heard of before the destruction of his kingdom. Now that Thedes was the leader of the Shettees who resided in the Ice Caves of Mordv; he questioned if the Shettees' former quest for isolation had harmed his people more than protected them.

"I see it," Hadu called as she pointed to a small clearing. The Ruala warriors circled the area around the cabin, looking for adversaries before they landed. Half of the warriors entered the small hunting cabin to examine the murder scene while the others searched the surrounding land.

"Raul was right," Thedes said as he inspected the blood spatter patterns on the inside of the hunting cabin. You can see the outlines of two small chests and something else. What do you think this is Ibula?"

Ibula walked over to the dimly lit wall and stared at the unusual outline. "I'll bet they were carrying some bags that they stacked on top of each other. After all, they were traveling because this place looks like it has been deserted for some time. What I can't understand," Ibula continued. "Is how the child escaped. What do you think Thedes?"

37

Thedes walked over to the only bed in the cabin and picked up the mattress. "There is no place to hide a child in here, except maybe under the bed, there is enough room here. But you would think the child would cry while his parents were being butchered. Except for the blood there is little here," Thedes said with disappointment.

"Perhaps they have had better luck outside," Ibula said as she opened the door. "Thedes did you notice this before?" Ibula said as she picked up a small object that was hanging on a tree branch, which was close to the door. "What do you think it is?"

Thedes examined the object which was made from small bones and jute and painted with designs. "I don't know but let's take it with us."

Thedes and Ibula joined the three other Ruala warriors who had been examining the outside walls of the cabin. "Looks like something came in the two small side windows," said Odam. "There are deep claw markings on the windowsills and the wood directly under the windows."

Ibula looked around as if she felt someone watching them. "There is a presence of evil here, can anyone else feel it?"

"We found nothing in the forest that was out of the ordinary," said Hadu as the two groups of Rualas rejoined each other in front of the cabin. "Except the child's bloody footprints; which we followed to an old campsite and saw the ground where the child must have collapsed."

"That must have been where Angelina found the boy," Ibula said. "It is still hard to believe that a two year old could not only survive in the wild but walk a mile to help. Something must have been protecting that child."

"In more ways than one," said Karta. "There are tracks of a great panther that appears to have walked through the abandoned campsite."

"Thedes I would very much like to see this child," Ibula said suspiciously. "Demons can take any form."

"You think the child is the killer?" Thedes asked with astonishment.

"Either something very good or something very evil was protecting that child," Ibula said. "Either way it was something powerful."

"Put a gag on that kid," Rodgers yelled. "I'm sick of listening to him."

Polgate reached for Petra but the boy rolled to his right, stood up and began to run. Petra only got about ten feet before Vardin caught him. Vardin pinned Petra's arms behind him as Polgate walked towards Petra holding a gag and ropes.

"You little bastard," Polgate yelled after Petra kicked him in the shin.

"Hold still," Vardin hollered. "Tratz help us."

"So how many men does it take to tie up one little boy?" Zac asked sarcastically as he watched the fracas.

Tratz grabbed Petra's face with the hand that was still bandaged from Kyra's bites. Petra was unable to move as the three men bound and gagged him.

"I'll be glad when we can kill the little monster," Tratz said as he returned to the table and his hand of cards.

Chapter IV
Suspicions

"I should be giving you a back rub instead of you giving me one," Stephan said as he melted into relaxation from Ingr's massage. "But this feels so good."

"I don't like to lie on my stomach anymore," Ingr said and laughed.

"Well, I am sure we can think of something," Stephan said with a suggestive tone to his voice.

Ingr didn't say anything for several minutes as she was trying to decide if she should share Bella's secret. "Stephan, I want to tell you something that your mother told Nikki and me; she said it was a family secret but I think you should know."

"A family secret? I didn't know we had any family secrets," Stephan said kiddingly.

"Stephan this is sad and I hope Bella doesn't get mad at me for telling you."

Stephan had been lying on his stomach but now he rose up and looked at Ingr. He could see the look of concern on her face. "You have my attention, go on."

"Bella said that she and Claudius had always planned to have a large family," Ingr explained. "She got pregnant with a second child when you were around two. She said the kingdom was fighting invaders from across the sea and Claudius was off to war. Bella said that in those days Claudius and Fahron did not have these big castles so they sent word that their families should go to the King's castle for safety."

"Bella was taking you to Mathas' castle; you were riding in a small boca when there was some kind of accident. The boca rolled down a rocky hill. She was trying to protect you, which she did, but she broke her leg and several other bones and a few days later she lost the baby. Bella could never get pregnant after that and she said your father has always felt guilty because he wasn't here to prevent the accident. Did you know any of this?"

40

"No, I wonder why they didn't tell me."

"Bella said she didn't have the heart to tell you. I think both of your parents are still really sad about it. I like Bella so much; I hate to see her sad. I hope we have a baby girl so we can name her after your mother."

Stephan leaned forward and kissed Ingr on the lips, "I would like that very much and I am glad you told me this secret. It kind of explains some things."

"Are you going to tell Bella I told you?"

"Not if you don't want me to," Stephan said as he turned and lay on his stomach again.

"I don't think she would mad," Ingr said as she put more lotion on Stephan's back.

"Ingr you know we have never talked about how many children we would like to have."

Ingr laughed, "I am still in shock that I am pregnant with this one."

"Seriously how many children would you like?"

"I hadn't really thought about it but I would like a big family. I don't really care about the number but I would like to have both boys and girls," Ingr paused for a moment then said with determination. "And I would like them all trained as warriors."

"Good, because I want a big family too and I like the idea of training them all as warriors." Stephan said with a warm smile. "We will have them go through Sorren's training." This comment brought a brief smile to Ingr's face.

"You know my father spent all the money on whiskey so there was never enough food for the family," Ingr said sadly. "And even now my mother would not be able to feed them all if it wasn't for you. Stephan I just feel so grateful. Our children will have such good lives. Everyone in the family wants children, so they will be loved and have enough food to eat and won't have to live in fear."

Stephan sat up and turned around so he faced Ingr. "What did you fear?" Ingr didn't respond. "Was it Thaddies?" he asked sternly.

"Yes," Ingr whispered.

"Why?"

Again Ingr did not answer. "Nikki told me that the reason Sorren and Shara took you in was because Thaddies tried to rape you. Is that true?" Stephan asked as his anger towards Thaddies rose within him.

"Yes," Ingr said in a soft voice.

"Honey did he ever hurt you?"

"He beat me."

"I mean sexually."

"No, he tried many times; usually when he was drunk," Ingr said with shame. "One time Angelina came home with me so I could visit my mother and well, Thaddies was really drunk and said some awful things and grabbed me. Angelina threw him against the wall and put a knife to his throat. After that Sorren would go with me when I went home."

Stephan hugged Ingr tightly. "If Thaddies wasn't already dead I would kill him."

Stephan lay on his back. Sleep did not come easily to him this night. Ingr was sleeping next to him with her head on his chest. Stephan stroked her long silky hair as thoughts were racing through his mind. He remembered the first time he saw Ingr; her incredible beauty made him stop breathing for a moment and that memory made him smile now.

Ingr was one of the most beautiful women Stephan had ever seen. Her bright blue eyes seemed to dance and they were all the more set off by her tan skin and white blonde hair. Ingr had the body of an athlete which she carried with grace.

Ingr was a well-trained and fierce warrior yet she had an innocence and vulnerability about her that stirred Stephan's protective nature. And now that she was his wife and carrying his child he was having feelings that he had never experienced before. Stephan knew he was too over protective at times; but the times they lived in were harsh and they had already seen so much darkness and violence.

Stephan looked at Ingr's sleeping face and thought of the dolls that Lazo had found in the remnants of Juleta's castle. "Were they a warning?" he wondered. "Or has some evil plan already been set into motion?" Stephan hated Juleta and the horror she had brought upon so many. "We are not going to wait around to be attacked," Stephan thought with conviction. "I will speak with Thaos in the morning and we can work out some plans that we can present to the others."

High Priest Raphael called Padres Darius and Lucas into what was now his office in the monastery at Malga. "Keep the witch Sophie confided to her room for four days then allow her to escape. She is not stupid; you will have to make it appear that she escaped by her own means," Raphael said as he poured himself a cup of coffee.

"But Your Eminence, why would we allow her to escape?" Darius asked in astonishment.

"She will never give us the information we are seeking," Raphael said. "But if we let her go she may lead us to Meekos."

"Do you think Meekos knows we are here?" Padre Lucas asked.

"It is difficult to know. It appears they have a finely intertwined network of spies. At this point I am expecting anything." Raphael stopped speaking because there was a knock at the door.

"Your Excellency I have a letter for you from King Tobias of Puntd," Padre Joseph said as he handed an envelope to High Priest Raphael, who turned it over and saw the golden seal of the King on the back. The three priests watched a smile come across Raphael's face as he read the letter.

"The Sanuri sent a letter to King Tobias telling him of some of the problems we are dealing with. The King has graciously offered any assistance that we might need including his military," Raphael said as he put the letter back into the ivory envelope. "We may very well have to take him up on his offer."

"My Lord, the soldiers asked that I bring you to the front entrance," Marie said as she stood in the doorway of Sudfad's study. "There is a group of priests here asking for the King."

"Thank you Marie," Raul said as he stood up from the desk. Marie accompanied Raul as he walked to the front door of the castle. Raul saw twelve priests on horseback wearing the robes of the Patronus and two older priests wearing the traditional brown robes. "I am Prince Raul, my father King Sudfad is not here; can I be of service to you?"

One of the Patronus dismounted and walked up to Raul, extending his hand. "I am High Priest Gabriel. The Sanuri requested that we bring Padre Bartholomew and Padre Thomas here. He feared they were in great danger at the monastery in Malga."

"Please all of you come in," Raul said after he shook the hand of the high priest. "Of course we have heard the Sanuri speak often of Padre Bartholomew and Padre Thomas." Raul motioned for the men to enter the castle. "Marie would you prepare breakfast for our guests? We will eat in the family dining room."

"We also have some manuscripts and scrolls that the Sanuri requested," Gabriel said as he motioned for his men to bring the items into the castle.

"We will take those to Father's study," Raul said to Gabriel. As Raul led the men down a hallway towards the study, he stopped before the door to the dining room. "Please make yourselves comfortable," Raul said as all but the men carrying the manuscripts and scrolls entered the dining room.

Marie prided herself on always being prepared for unexpected guests. Now that the Royal Family had increased in size, Marie supervised a staff of six cooks. Within minutes Marie had trays of beverages and place settings on the dining room table.

"My Lady you have guests," Marie said when she saw Queen Renya in the hallway. By the time Raul returned to the dining room, Renya had already been introduced to all of the priests and was making preparations for them to spend the night.

"You make us feel most welcomed," High Priest Gabriel said as he took a seat at the table.

"You certainly are welcomed here," said Renya sweetly as she walked out of the dining room.

"Is the Sanuri here?" Gabriel asked Raul.

"You have not heard?" Raul asked but he did not wait for Gabriel to answer. "Our adopted brother Petra was kidnapped some weeks back. The Sanuri, the King and others are searching for him."

"Petra," gasped Padre Bartholomew. "He is such a dear boy." Padre Bartholomew looked at Gabriel. "That is the boy who warned the Shettee refugees and who saved my life."

Before Raul could finish telling the priests about Petra, Renya quickly reentered the room, her face was pale as she handed a note to Raul. Raul read the note then handed it to Gabriel. "All the search parties are returning to the castle per the orders of The Lion. Petra was kidnapped to set a trap for the Sanuri and is being held in the Kingdom of Stordt. The Rualas and Shettees are accompanying the Sanuri in the search for Petra."

"Forgive me but I do not understand why The Lion would send the search parties home," Padre Thomas said as his voice was shaking.

"It would be considered an act of war for our troops to enter Stordt," Raul said.

Gabriel could see how distraught Renya and Raul were over the news. "The Lion himself is now involved in rescuing the boy, have faith, he will be returned safely," Gabriel said soothingly.

Stephan and Thaos were unusually quiet as they rode to the morning meeting with Claudius. "Is something the matter boys?" Claudius asked. "You both are so quiet and Stephan you look like you haven't slept in a while. Is everything alright with Ingr?"

"Ingr is fine, Father. Thaos and I are worried about those dolls that were found in Juleta's castle," Stephan said with frustration. "I feel like we are sitting around just waiting for the next attack."

"So what do you propose?" Claudius asked.

"Thaos and I want to talk to the Sanuri and see if he can give us some help. Father if it was just me I wouldn't care but I have a wife and a baby coming and I am really worried about them."

"Isn't it amazing how your perspective about life changes when you are about to become a father." Claudius said as he looked at the worried expressions on the faces of the two young men.

"Claudius do you have any thoughts about this?" Thaos asked.

"The Sanuri told us that Juleta had set a bounty on our heads. If we eliminated the means of payment there would be no reason for demons or dark lords to come after our families," Claudius said. "We need to find out how she was going to pay the demons and where the payment is stored."

"She was sleeping with an advisor to King Zorta. His name was George and he was always giving her money," Thaos explained. "The poor bastard was older than Mathas and from the looks of him I will bet he never had a girl flirt with him until Juleta got him in her snare. George would have done anything for her."

"Perhaps the two of you should pay George a visit?" Claudius suggested.

"Lazo told me once that she wanted him to rob a gold shipment from the mines in Ganz," Thaos said. "I think I will have another talk with Lazo." Thaos looked at Stephan. "Want to come along?"

"Try and keep me away" Stephan said. "I don't trust Lazo as far as I can spit. Something about that guy reminds me of a snake."

"Lazo is devious but he is also cunning," Thaos said. "He didn't trust Juleta either, so he was always spying on her. He might have some information that can help us."

"Father I like your idea about talking to George. Will you watch out for the girls while we are gone?" Stephan asked.

"Stephan those two girls are like my own daughters, of course I will take care of them while you are gone. But perhaps you should bring this issue up at the meeting. Mathas might be able to help you with George. I believe he is friends with King Fahra."

"Oh, I am so sorry," said Gala with embarrassment as she entered the dining room. "I did not realize you had guests."

"No Gala, please join us," said Renya. "These priests are friends of the Sanuri's."

"King Sudfad had asked me to try and find out what one of those objects was that Angelina and Matthew found," Gala said as she was walking towards Raul with the object in her hands. "I have been doing research for weeks and the best that I can come up with is they are some type of talisman to keep demons away."

"May I have a look?" asked High Priest Gabriel. Gala handed him the object which was made of small bones with jute woven around them.

"I have never before seen designs like those painted on the jute," Gala said as she stood next to Gabriel's chair. "I looked through several books on ancient languages and couldn't find any words or symbols that were similar."

"That's because these blasphemous words are not uttered in this world," said Gabriel as he examined the object. "These are the words of the Old Ones, the oldest and most powerful demons in existence. How did this come to you?"

"My cousin and his wife, both of whom are warriors, were leaving this castle and returning to the Kingdom of Lentz. Angelina found two of those things hanging on tree limbs. That same night she found a small boy near death in the woods."

"The child was covered in blood but it was not his. The next day Matthew found the bodies of two people who had been torn to shreds in an abandoned hunting cabin in our kingdom," Raul explained. "I have some friends searching that cabin as we speak."

"What are they looking for?" Gabriel asked.

"They suspect a demon tore those people apart. They wanted to see if there were any clues left at the cabin."

"Your friends might be in great danger," Gabriel said. "This is called an aboultis it is a type of calling card for demons."

"I don't understand," Padre Thomas said.

"There are all levels and types of demons," Gabriel explained. "Just like with humans, demons will often hire others to do their dirty work for them. I would guess that multiple demons or groups of demons were hired for a job, possibly the deaths of those people you mentioned. The demon or demons who actually completed the job left these behind as a way of telling other demons the job is done and the owners of these aboultis' will be collecting the bounty."

"Here," said Mathas as he handed a sealed envelope to Stephan. "This letter tells King Fahra of Juleta's deeds and the threat she still poses to our families. I have requested that he give you any assistance he can."

"Thank you," Stephan said as he put the envelope in an inside pocket of his leather jacket. "I wish Matthew was back, I bet he would want to come along."

"You and Thaos aren't planning on going by yourselves, are you?" Claudius asked.

"Father we can take care of ourselves," Stephan said with a grin as he looked at Thaos.

"You know how cunning Juleta was," Mathas said earnestly. "She could have all kinds of traps set up for you. Take some troops with you. And that is an order!"

"Boys we all know that you are superior warriors but you are going to have to change the way you do things," Claudius said. "You both have pregnant wives at home. You're going to have to stop charging into battle by yourselves."

Neither Stephan nor Thaos said anything; they both knew that Claudius was right. This would be the first time that either of the men would be leaving their wives. Both Stephan and Thaos had only been married for months, a time frame not long enough for them to change their thinking and behavior.

"How many men do you want us to take?" Stephan asked.

"Take a company," Mathas said. "Who knows what you could run into?"

Rodgers, Polgate, Tratz and Zac sat at the table in their small cabin playing cards, a daily distraction for them. The men all jumped from the table and grabbed weapons when they heard a horse outside of the window.

"My, you boys are jumpy," said Vardin through teeth that were clenching a cigar. "Vardin carried four cloth bags of food and whiskey, which he set on one of the tables. "Kid still alive?" Vardin asked as he looked at Petra who was bound and gagged; lying on a mattress on the floor.

"He wouldn't be if I had anything to do with it," Rodgers said contemptuously as he threw down his hand of cards.

"Well, we don't get paid until the job is done," Vardin said as he walked over to Petra. "The boss wants the kid fed and cared for until then." Vardin shook Petra, who instantly woke up and started squirming. "He's alive," Vardin said as he turned and walked to the table containing the bags. "I'll fix us something to eat."

Matthew's group was the first search party to return to the castle at Salar. After dismissing his men, Matthew took care of his horse, taking his time as he did not want to face Renya.

Walking slowly Matthew walked up the front steps to the castle, the door opened; Raul, Vitomas, Annabelle and Renya were standing in the doorway. They all saw the sadness in Matthew's face and demeanor.

"I am sorry Aunt Renya," Matthew said as he hugged the Queen.

"Sudfad sent a message, I know The Lion told you all to return home," Renya said soothingly, "Matthew there is nothing else you could have done."

"I promised you I would bring Petra back," Matthew said dejectedly.

Vitomas and Annabelle each kissed Matthew as Marie walked up to the group.

"Matthew have you eaten?" Marie asked. Matthew did not speak but shook his head from side to side, to indicate he had not. "I will fix you something," Marie said then she looked at Raul. "Should I serve him in the dining room or the study?"

"In the study," Raul replied. "We have some things to discuss."

Matthew and Raul talked in Sudfad's study, as Matthew ate his meal. "I didn't want to face your mother," Matthew said as he poured himself another cup of coffee.

"She isn't happy but she understands," Raul said. "But I have some other things to speak with you about. Some of the priests from the Patronus stayed here a few days. They escorted two priests, who are friends of the Sanuri, and will be our guests for a while. One of the high priests recognized the object that Angelina found in the forest. He said it is an aboultis, a sort of calling card for demons."

"I don't understand."

"The priest said that it is likely that multiple demons or groups of demons were hired for some sort of job, possibly the deaths of those people. The demon or demons who actually completed the job left the aboultis behind as a way of telling other demons the job is done and the owners of those aboultis' will be collecting the bounty." Raul was interrupted by a knock on the door.

"Raul, its Thedes and Ibula."

"Come in," Raul called out. "I asked them to join us," Raul said as Ibula and Thedes entered the study. "Thedes and Ibula examined the cabin where you found the dead bodies and they found another aboultis hanging over the door. They saw claw marks on the outside of the two windows to the cabin and they followed the boy's trail to your campsite."

"Matthew we could not figure out where they could have hidden the boy," Thedes said. "And if the parents were unable to hide him, why was he spared? And how did he make it to your campsite?"

"Angelina and I have wondered the same things," Matthew said.

"Matthew we would like to come home with you and meet this boy," Ibula said.

"Why?" asked Matthew suspiciously.

"If the demons truly did not find the boy he might still be in danger and well," Ibula hesitated. "There is another possibility."

"Ibula what is it?" Matthew asked.

"Demons can take any form; perhaps it was the child who killed those people."

"The Sanuri has not only seen Jacob but christened him. I think he would have noticed if the child was a demon," Matthew said.

"Well something very powerful was protecting that child Matthew; either something very good or something very dark. And if it was the darkness protecting him, you have to ask why," Ibula said.

Simon led the second search party home. Like Matthew, Simon felt that he had let Renya down. Rarely did Simon fail at anything but on this day as he walked into the castle he felt like a failure. Annabelle ran to the front entrance and flew into Simon's arms. They kissed passionately for several minutes as the rest of the family gathered.

51

"I'm sorry Mother," Simon said as he hugged Renya.

"Simon I am telling you the same thing I told Matthew," Renya said lovingly. "You had no choice."

"Is Matthew here?" Simon asked Raul.

"First give me a hug," Vitomas said. "We really missed you."

"Matthew returned a couple of days ago but he left right away for Lentz," Raul said. "Thedes and Ibula and a few other Rualas went with him."

"Why?" asked Simon

"There is some concern about the boy they found. I will fill you in on the details later," Raul said.

"Raul let him spend some time with us before you talk business," Annabelle said as she put her arm around Simon's waist. Raul smiled and nodded as Simon and Annabelle walked down the hallway with their arms around each other.

King Sudfad and his troops returned to Salar the following day. Like Matthew and Simon; Sudfad was depressed and dejected at the thought of returning home without rescuing Petra. Although Renya had been strong for both Matthew and Simon; she cried when she saw the look of sorrow on her husband's face.

Both Renya and Sudfad had fallen in love with that courageous little orphan when the Sanuri brought Petra to their home. It wasn't long before Petra won over the hearts of the entire family with his good natured and comical ways.

"You look exhausted," Renya said as she hugged Sudfad. "Let me get you something to eat and I will draw you a hot bath."

"I really need to keep working," Sudfad said sadly and kissed Renya on the forehead. "Is Raul in the study?"

"Sudfad, work can wait; you need to eat something," Renya scolded. "Raul and Simon are with the teams investigating the deaths of our men; they should return soon."

"Where are the girls?"

"They're shopping."

Sudfad's eyes grew wide, "With guards I hope."

"Yes, of course dear," Renya said soothingly. "Now please, take a seat and I will bring you a glass of whiskey and a meal."

Sophie was watching her captors very carefully. The Patronus had locked her in a room that was once the quarters of a priest. She had a bed, several tables and chairs, a dresser and a small bookcase. The room was small and very crowded. Sophie noticed that the bars in the two windows had been recently installed. Raphael allowed Sophie to have some of her clothing but he would not allow her to have her books or other items in the prison room; for fear she would practice black magics.

Three times a day, the Patronus brought Sophie large trays of food, pitchers of water and pots of coffee. They even brought her wine for her evening meal. Her captors were ever courteous although they would take her from her room at odd hours to interrogate her. Sophie knew the layout of the monastery very well as she had spent much time there with her brother Meekos. Sophie searched the room carefully for any hidden compartments or objects she could use in her escape.

When Sophie moved the dresser she found an old leather pouch that was stuck between the wall and the back of the dresser. Sophie retrieved the pouch which was very dusty; when she opened it she found a variety of small tools, the type used for leather work.

Quickly Sophie moved to the door and using two of the tools was able to open the lock. Sophie slowly opened the door and peered into the hallway. She did not see anyone but she could hear voices and smell food. Sophie shut and locked the door. No sooner had she hidden the leather pouch, when one of the Patronus brought a tray of food into her room and set it on the table.

"Your Eminence, the witch has moved the dresser," said Padre Tobias. "I saw it when I delivered her lunch."

"Well, it looks like we may have an escape tonight," Raphael said to the priests who were seated around the large table, eating their midday meal. "Now remember, follow her to the stable and once she starts to ride the Rualas will follow her."

"Don't you think she will see those warriors flying overhead?" asked Padre Augustus.

"They are going to alternate with Enrops," Raphael said assuredly. "The last letter I got from the Sanuri said that Meekos, Pravis and Tenebrae are also involved with the abduction of King Sudfad's son. The Sanuri is hoping that Sophie will lead us to the boy. I suspect she will go straight to the stable but if not, I want a few of you in Meekos' chambers, don't stop her just watch her."

Sophie waited until darkness enveloped the monastery before she unlocked the door to her room. She quietly made her way through the deserted hallways. "Unless the Patronus plan to interrogate me this night, they won't know I am gone until morning," Sophie thought as she walked towards Meekos' chambers. She hid in a storage closet across the hall from the door to Meekos' chambers, watching and listening. When Sophie was convinced that she was alone, she entered Meekos' parlor.

Sophie was afraid to light any candles so she felt her way along the walls as she headed to the room where her things were. So fearful was Sophie of being found that her senses were heightened, Sophie could hear her own breathing and heart beating. Meekos' chambers were dark and silent; Sophie took small steps as she felt her way around the rooms.

She walked from the front parlor to the study, then to the hallway which led to the bedrooms. Sophie carefully placed each foot on the floor for fear she would knock something over. "What the hell," Sophie gasped as she placed her foot into a puddle. "Sticky what would be?" Sophie did not complete her thought before she fell over the body of the dead Patronus priest.

Sophie picked herself up and ran down the hallway to her bedroom. She lit a candle on the dresser then reached into one of her bags and pulled out a dagger. Grabbing the candle Sophie returned to the hallway. She found the body of the priest she had tripped over. His robe was soaked with blood from his multiple wounds.

Sophie turned and ran back to her bedroom. She changed her clothes and grabbed a small suitcase. Sophie quickly packed her jewels, money, two books and some clothing then left Meekos' chambers. Sophie was starting to limp as she made her way towards the stable; she had bruised both of her knees and hurt her wrist when she tripped over the body of the priest. Unaware of the many eyes that were upon her, Sophie saddled a horse that was in a stall closest to the front of the stable and rode out into the night.

"Your Eminence," called Padre Philips as he burst into the office of High Priest Raphael. "Edward and Sorben are dead."

"What!" exclaimed Raphael as he jumped out of his chair.

"I saw bloody foot prints in a hallway and followed them to the chambers of High Priest Meekos; I found the two bodies in there."

"Come," yelled Raphael as he ran out of the room and down a hallway towards Meekos' chambers. Raphael slowed down when he came upon bloody footprints on the carpet of one of the hallways. He momentarily examined the footprints then followed them into Meekos' quarters. Padre Philips had lit some candles when he first entered Meekos' chambers, now he was lighting many more, to give them enough light to examine the scene.

"Padre Sorben is in the bedroom to the left," Philips said as he carried a candle to Raphael, who was standing over Padre Edward's body in the hallway. Raphael carefully examined the body, the floor and the walls.

"I don't believe the witch killed him," Raphael explained. "Look, she tripped over his body and slid in the blood, then as she stood up she balanced against the wall." As Raphael spoke he pointed out the various prints from the blood. The two men followed Sophie's bloody foot prints into one of the bedrooms.

55

They saw a blood stained dress on the floor and opened dresser drawers. They walked out of that room and into the room across the hallway where they found Padre Sorben's body.

"The wounds look similar," Raphael said as he examined the body.

"What do you think killed them?"

"I don't know who killed them but they used a dagger."

High Priest Raphael had his men wake all of the priests in the monastery and take them to the Great Hall for an emergency meeting. Raphael told his men to tell the priests of Malga that the meeting was going to be held to give them information about two bodies that were recently discovered. Although Raphael had no intention of divulging the reasons that the Patronus had arrived at the monastery, he understood that giving the priests some information would ensure their cooperation with his men.

"I am putting High Priest Josiah in charge of the murder investigation," Raphael said at the meeting. "I have locked down the monastery, no one leaves and no one enters without my personal approval. I know that most of you are not members of the Patronus but I am asking for your assistance in this investigation and in the security of this monastery. Honestly I fear there may be more victims."

The Great Hall of the monastery at Malga was filled with priests, the majority of whom had been assigned to that monastery for many years. As High Priest Raphael stood in front of the crowd of hundreds, not a sound could be heard. Slowly an old man stood up.

"Your Eminence, I am High Priest Zophar and before I joined the order I was trained as a healer. I have maintained my skills in the service of The Great Ruler and the monastery. Perhaps I can be of service to you."

A warm smile crossed Raphael's face, "I would very much appreciate your assistance. In fact, will you meet with Josiah after this meeting?"

The priests at Malga had maintained a great distance from the members of the Patronus as they did not understand the reason this elite group within the church had suddenly assumed control of the monastery.

High Priest Raphael had no intentions of exposing the behaviors of High Priests Meekos, Pravis and Tenebrae until his investigation was completed. But once High Priest Zophar crossed the invisible barrier of fear and suspicion and extended his hand to the Patronus; the other priests followed his lead. One by one the priests stood up and identified themselves and offered their services to High Priest Raphael.

Sophie headed north towards the Kingdom of Stordt. Escaping the monastery made her feel both exhilarated and fearful. She kept thinking about the dead priest she saw in Meekos' chambers and questioned who could have killed him. Sophie didn't want to go to Erebus' castle until she found out what happened to Meekos. And if Meekos was hurt, Erebus could be in danger also. Sophie decided to go to Taperia.

Sophie rode all night although she had to go slowly because of the thick darkness. Finally exhaustion overtook her as the first rays of the sun were rising in the eastern sky. She spied a small thicket of trees and decided to take refuge in it. No sooner had Sophie lay down and covered herself with a blanket than she fell asleep.

Sophie did not wake as the Ruala warriors landed in the thicket and watched her. Nor did she wake when a flock of Enrops did battle with a flock of Ravens that were carrying a message for Sophie. The Enrops gave the message to the Ruala warriors who read it and sent it to High Priest Raphael.

Sophie did not wake as Meekos was performing a spell to find her. He called her name into the darkness and told her where he was. Meekos' message resounded through different worlds. Sophie did not respond, but Meekos' message was heard by others; too many others, something he would later regret.

Chapter V
Hidden Enemies

"Still here," Thaos said to Lazo as he and Stephan sat down at Lazo's table in Nates Tavern in Langer.

Lazo smiled exposing his brown and broken teeth. "Want to play a little cards boys?" Lazo asked as he dealt three hands of five cards.

"Not really," Stephan said as he poured whiskey into the three glasses he had carried to the table.

"Thaos your friend here isn't used to being watched," Lazo said. "I believe there are a lot of ears in here, so let's not make it look like ya joined me just to get information."

Thaos took a fist full of coins out of his pocket and laid them on the table. Stephan did the same and the three men started to play cards. "I was wondering how long it would take ya to come back with questions," Lazo said as he threw a gold coin into the middle of the table.

"We are wondering where Juleta got her money and where she may have hidden it," Thaos said as he took another card.

Lazo grinned as he clenched a cigarette between his teeth, "Let me guess, ya are trying to figure out how she is going to pay the bounties she put on your families."

Stephan looked at Lazo with surprise, because he had figured out their intentions. Thaos laughed when he saw the look on Stephan's face, "He's a lot smarter than he looks," Thaos said about Lazo.

"If I help ya, I want part of the cut," Lazo said.

"Hell, you can have it all," Stephan said as he poured more whiskey into their glasses. "We just want the bounties off our families."

"Thaos, I do like your friend more every time I meet him," Lazo said.

"Lazo, the bounties are most likely to pay demons," Thaos said. "You could be making a whole lot more enemies."

"Witches, demons, what is this world coming too?" asked Lazo with a laugh.

"I will take two," Thaos said as Lazo handed him two more cards. "There's two men by the door who seem pretty interested in this table."

"Yeah, and those three standing at the bar, were in the other two taverns I was in tonight," said Lazo without taking his eyes off from his cards.

"Why would they be following you?" Stephan asked.

"Oh for any number of reasons," Lazo said with a smirk. "But who says they are after me? Thaos here has pissed off more people than he can count and ya rich boy, do ya have any enemies? Are ya sure those bounties are only for demons to collect?"

"Where's your horse?" Thaos asked nonchalantly.

"Tied out front," Lazo responded.

"They won't jump us until we leave," Thaos commented.

"Well, on the bright side, if they are after the bounty perhaps they can give us some information," Stephan said. "I'll take one."

Lazo dealt a single card to Stephan, "So ya want to have a little talk with those boys?" Lazo asked with a grin. "Then let's have some fun." Lazo put the deck of cards on the table, looked at the three men standing at the bar and let out a loud whistle, then he waved his hand for the men to approach the table. Thaos smiled as he watched the men walk towards them. "Care for a friendly game of poker?" Lazo asked.

The three men looked surprised and confused, then one of them said "sure," and they grabbed chairs from other tables and sat down.

"Been seeing ya boys everywhere I go," Lazo said as he dealt cards to all the men. "A fella might think ya were following him."

One of the men smiled as he looked at his hand of cards, "Or a fella might be a little paranoid."

"How many more men have you got outside?" Thaos asked as he threw down a card.

"Enough," the man replied.

"And what would you be called?" Thaos asked.

"Prescott."

"Well Prescott, we're looking for some information," Thaos said as he watched the two men standing near the door move a few steps closer to the table. "What's your price?" One of Prescott's men was sitting to the left of Thaos; Prescott was sitting to the left of that man and across from Lazo. The third man was sitting next to Stephan and across the table from Thaos.

"Don't know if you've got that much money," Prescott said wryly.

Thaos looked into Stephan's eyes then looked towards the men approaching the table, Stephan got the message.

"Have a drink fellas?" Lazo said as he started to fill everyone's glasses with the bottle of whiskey on the table.

The man sitting next to Thaos screamed in pain as Thaos rammed one of his knives through the man's right hand, pinning it to the table. Thaos lunged across the table and grabbed the man next to Stephan by the hair and cut his throat. Stephan jumped up and thrust his sword through the stomach of one of the men who was charging at them.

The second man punch Stephan in the jaw as Stephan was pulling his sword out of the first attacker. Then the man punched Stephan in the kidneys as Stephan swung around with his sword, slicing the ribcage of his attacker; who screamed and fell to the floor. Stephan plunged his sword through the man's heart; then he quickly looked at the door but did not see any more threats; so Stephan turned his attention back to the table. Thaos was standing behind Prescott holding a knife to his throat.

"Ya boys sure are handy," Lazo said with a grin. He had not moved from his chair during the fight.

"Who sent you?" Thaos asked through clenched teeth.

Stephan shoved the blade of his sword against the neck of the man who pulled Thaos' knife out of his hand and was now approaching Thaos with it.

"Do you want to die?" Stephan asked.

The man looked at Stephan for a moment, trying to read the look in Stephan's eyes; then the man dropped the knife and grabbed his wounded hand.

"I asked you a question," Thaos said as he pushed the knife harder against Prescott's throat.

"Ok, ok, I will tell you," Prescott gasped. Thaos relaxed his hold on Prescott but did not let go of him.

"I don't know who hired us." Prescott said. Thaos grabbed Prescott by the hair and pressed his knife against Prescott's throat again. Prescott raised his hands into the air as if to signal he was surrendering. "No, really we don't know their name."

"Then how did you get hired?" Thaos demanded.

"Boys I think we have company," Lazo said as he watched three more men walk into the tavern.

"You know what to say," Thaos said as the pressure he was applying to Prescott's throat was starting to draw blood.

"Stay back," yelled Prescott.

"Now tell me," Thaos said angrily.

"It's a draw," Prescott said. "Me and the boys entered a draw."

"What is he talking about?" Stephan asked.

"Tell him," demanded Thaos.

61

"It's like a game; each man throws in two hundred dollars and receives a note. The note tells you what you need to do and how much money you will earn," Prescott explained.

"Do you have the note?" Thaos asked.

"It's in my right shirt pocket."

Stephan reached into Prescott's pocket and pulled out a piece of paper. He quickly unfolded it and became enraged as he read the note. "Do all of the notes say the same thing?" Stephan growled.

"All I know is that the ones my boys and I got are the same," Prescott said.

"Where is this draw being held?" Thaos asked.

"There are some caves outside of Sendra, in the Kingdom of Zorta. The caves are two miles east of the town, there is a series of hills with three peaks; the peak to the left has several caverns with passageways that connect them. Walk through the first two caverns and take the path to the right, you can't miss it." Prescott said with a sneer.

"What do you mean?" Stephan snapped.

"The room is full of demons," Prescott said. "And an ugly bunch they are."

"Those hills are close to the witch's castle," Lazo said. "Watch out!" Lazo shouted as he jumped out of his chair. A knife flew through the air and struck the wall across from Stephan. Suddenly the man who threw it fell to the floor; exposing a knife in his back, as his two partners quickly turned towards the door they each fell to the floor as Sorren's knives penetrated their throats.

"There might be others," Stephan called as Sorren was pulling his knives out of the dead bodies.

"My men have them," Sorren said as he walked towards the table.

"It's started," Stephan said as he handed the note to Sorren.

"What are you supposed to bring back to prove you've made the kills?" Thaos demanded.

Prescott hesitated, "Ears, but those demons said they can tell if the ears are from the right people."

"Who is Lazo?" asked Sorren as he read the names written on the note.

"I guess I am in good company," Lazo grinned. "So Prescott, what is the signal to tell you all that the game is over?"

"They said they would send messengers."

"What sort of messengers?" Thaos asked.

"They said we would know when we saw them."

"Is there a reason I shouldn't kill you now?" Thaos asked as he again pressed the blade of his knife against Prescott's throat.

"Wait, there is something else," Prescott said. "If I give you this information will you let me and the boys go?"

"Well your boys are gone," Sorren said dryly. "It's just the two of you at this table."

"Is it a deal?" Prescott asked and nervously gulped.

"If we let you go, how do we know you won't come after us?" Thaos asked.

"We will leave and not come back," Prescott said fearfully.

"Talk," Thaos said.

"In my left shirt pocket there is a map with information."

Stephan put his hand into Prescott's left shirt pocket and pulled out another folded paper; Stephan's face went white as he read it. Sorren grabbed the paper out of Stephan's hand and read it, then he handed it to Thaos, who let go of Prescott's hair to take it.

"Is there more?" Stephan demanded.

"No, no," Prescott said. "Honestly."

63

Thaos let go of Prescott. "Go!" Thaos said angrily.

"You cannot trust them," Sorren said then he whistled loudly as Prescott and his partner ran out of the tavern. Both men screamed as they were grabbed by Nordes warriors and killed.

"Sorren why are you here?" Stephan asked.

"I was visiting Angelina and Mathas told me of your plans. And honestly I like them, I too do not like the idea of waiting to be attacked," Sorren said. "So I gathered some warriors and came looking for you."

"And we are glad to see you," Thaos said. "I think we should leave here. Lazo you will need to come with us, you're on that hit list too." The men left the tavern and started the ride back to Claudius' castle.

"Sorren we haven't told any of the women about these threats," Stephan said.

"Well, you are going to have to now," Sorren said. "That map has all the paths they normally travel; which means someone is watching them. I don't understand your involvement," said Sorren as he looked at Lazo.

"Lazo and I worked for Juleta," Thaos said. "Lazo this is Sorren the Chief of the Nordes Tribe and basically family; our wives are Nordes warriors."

"Warrior women?" Lazo said. "I've never met any before. But to answer your question; Thaos and I would stand up to Juleta and have some fun at her expense. Guess she doesn't have much of a sense of humor," Lazo said with a grin.

Sorren looked at the fear on the faces of Thaos and Stephan. "Boys, those girls can take care of themselves, they are powerful warriors. It is only natural that you want to protect them but you are doing them a great disservice by not being honest with them. How would you feel if the roles were reversed?"

"Sorren they are both pregnant, have you seen Ingr lately?" Stephan asked.

"That doesn't make them any less dangerous," Sorren said then laughed. "Every time Shara got pregnant she was mean as a hornet; no one wanted to get on her bad side."

"He's right," Thaos said as he looked at Stephan.

"Well then, when we get home we will have a family meeting," Stephan said with dread.

Lazo kissed both Nikki's and Ingr's hands when he was introduced to them. "I will say ya boys did well for yourselves," Lazo said as he looked at the girls admiringly.

Jealousy surged through Stephan as he took Lazo by the arm and turned him around. "And this is my father Claudius and my mother Bella," Stephan said. Stephan found himself wanting to punch Lazo as he watched him kiss Bella's hand.

"Sorren," Ingr said excitedly as she quickly walked up and gave him a hug.

"When is that baby due?" Sorren asked as he looked at Ingr's stomach.

"You can say it, I know I am as big as a house," Ingr said with a smile. "I'm not really sure but within the next few weeks. Stephan's hoping for twins. You know my mother had two sets of twins." Sorren looked at Stephan and winked. Nikki walked up to Sorren and hugged him also.

"And look at you," Sorren said as he looked at her pregnant stomach. "You girls are like such daughters to me that I feel like I am going to be a grandfather," he said sincerely. Nikki kissed the old warrior on the cheek.

Claudius handed out glasses of whiskey and wine as everyone took seats in the parlor. "Thaos I think you should be the one to start the story."

Thaos slowly stood up and walked to the center of the room. "Lazo and I both worked for Juleta and she tried to kill us both. Lazo was attacked by demons several times until he almost died. He took shelter in a monastery as he healed."

"About a month ago he left the monastery and spied on Juleta's castle. When he saw it was deserted he went in it and found a group of dolls that were arranged on a table in her parlor. The dolls resembled everyone in this room except for Sorren. There were also dolls that represented Mathas' family and the Sanuri. Lazo gave Stephan and me the dolls and we gave them to the Sanuri."

"Thaos I don't understand the significance of the dolls," Bella said.

"We believe they are used to put curses on people," Stephan replied.

"Thaos why didn't you tell us any of this?" asked Nikki angrily.

"Because we wanted to protect you," Stephan answered before Thaos could say anything.

Nikki stood up from her chair, "You two make me so mad; all the time you are trying to protect us like we are a couple of china dolls. But what you really are doing is blinding us to our enemies. Don't you understand you are putting us in more danger? We are warriors too!"

Lazo grinned as he watched Thaos walk up to Nikki and put his massive arms around her. "Nikki you are right and I won't do it again," Thaos said then kissed her on the forehead.

"We already know Juleta may have put bounties on our heads," Ingr snapped. "The Sanuri told us."

Claudius could see how angry Ingr and Nikki were. "In their defense the boys have been losing sleep over this. Just this morning they spoke with Mathas and Fahron and devised a plan. They are going to Zorta to try and find out the details of how Juleta planned to pay the bounties and to find the money, so no one would try to collect it. And earlier this evening they went into Langer to speak with Lazo again."

"We were attacked by a group of men," Stephan said as he watched the look of horror taking over Ingr's face. "With Sorren's help they are all dead but Thaos got some good information from them first."

"There's some caves near Juleta's castle where a group of demons are having a draw. Combatants pay to take part and then are given notes telling them what they must do and what they will be paid when the job is done," Thaos said. "These are the notes the men were carrying." Thaos handed the note to Claudius first, who then passed it around the room. Everyone was quiet as the horror of their situation struck their realities.

"A chest of jewels and a chest of gold coins," Ingr said out loud as she read the note. "Stephan why does my name have two marks by it?"

"Probably because you are the one who cut her and forced her into the fire."

"What?" asked Lazo in amazement.

"Ingr is a hell of a shot throwing knives," Sorren said. "She hit Juleta several times before Juleta backed into a ditch of fire."

"There is more," Stephan said solemnly.

"The men were also carrying this," Thaos said and handed the second note to Claudius.

Claudius' face was turning red from anger, "Why this means we have spies watching our every move."

"You have to warn Angelina and Matthew," Ingr said as she looked at the map that Thaos had taken from Prescott.

"We were planning on going to Mathas' after we told you," Stephan said.

Ingr handed the map to Nikki, "I understand why you want to go to Zorta," Ingr said. "And I think it is a good plan but Stephan this baby is coming in the next few weeks; I would really like you here."

Stephan walked over to Ingr who was sitting in a chair. He knelt in front of her, "Honey I want to be here too but I would also like to stop this madness before our child is born." Stephan took Ingr's hand and kissed it. "If we leave first thing in the morning I think that should give us enough time."

Ingr stared at Stephan and for a moment; he thought she was going to cry but to his surprise Ingr said, "I understand, I would do the same thing." Stephan hugged and kissed his beloved wife.

"Nikki how do you feel about all this?" Thaos asked.

"I only wish I could go with you; Juleta is like a plague that we cannot cleanse from."

Thaos walked over to Nikki and kissed her. Then he looked at Lazo and said proudly, "We have fought in battle with our wives and they are fine warriors."

Lazo shook his head and smiled, "Why can't I ever find a girl like that?" Then Lazo turned to Claudius. "Thaos may have told you that neither he or I trusted Juleta. I was around the castle a lot more than he was, so I bided my time by spying on her. I never saw her ride to the caverns where the draw is being held but I saw her take a whole lot of trips to the bank in Toman, that's a village across the river from her place. Now she was always telling us she had no money, so ya got to wonder why she was at the bank so often."

"Didn't she want you to rob the gold shipments from the mines in Ganz?" Thaos asked.

"Yeah she talked about that a lot but I don't know if she actually went through with her plans. But at the end there when she hired Hector, she had him doing secret jobs."

"Who is Hector?" Ingr asked.

Lazo looked at Thaos, who said, "You can tell them."

"It wasn't a secret to anyone in the camp that Juleta had it bad for both of your husbands. I think about the time she decided to kill Thaos and me she hires this new guy and damn if he doesn't look enough like Thaos to be his brother."

"What!" gasped Nikki.

"It's true, I saw him myself," Thaos said.

"I hate her even more now," Nikki said.

Lazo laughed then continued, "Her boyfriend George always came in a carriage and he often had his driver carry in all sorts of boxes and parcels. So I am willing to bet he gave her a lot of money, whether it was his to give, I don't know."

"You mean he may have been stealing from King Fahra?" Claudius asked.

"I wouldn't put it past him," said Lazo.

"Neither would I," Thaos added. "Lazo also watched her when she had several suspicious meetings, so if we can't find the bounty in the caverns; Lazo might be able to point us in the right direction."

Stephan cringed when he heard his father tell Lazo to stay at the castle. Stephan did not like or trust Lazo but he believed they needed Lazo's help finding the bounty.

"Sorren what do you think?" Claudius asked.

"I have a few things that I want to say," Sorren said sternly. "You have all been talking like this is a private matter. My pregnant daughter and son-in-law are two of the people who have bounties on their heads. And as Thaos said earlier we, I mean all of us are family now. Don't think I am going to sit by while you get picked off one by one. Claudius you know you wouldn't just stand by."

"Sorren you are right," Claudius said apologetically. "I am sorry; I did not mean to exclude you."

"Sorren and his men saved our butts tonight," Stephan said. "We were damn glad to have them show up."

"This is what I have been thinking," Sorren said. "We all know there could be problems with the boys taking your troops into another kingdom. Now Stephan told me about the letter that Mathas wrote to King Fahra but how do we know he isn't part of this too. You have a fort near the border between Lentz and Zorta, have soldiers there ready to move if you send them word, while we enter Zorta with my warriors."

Claudius's face broke into a grin, he grabbed a bottle of fine whiskey and filled Sorren's glass first then those belonging to the other men.

"I like it," Stephan said.

"Thaos what do you think?" Claudius asked.

"No disrespect but the Nordes warriors are a lot better fighters than some of our troops. I would welcome them along."

"I greatly like the idea," Claudius said and raised his glass. "To family." Everyone in the room raised their glass, including Lazo, "To family," they all repeated.

"Boy's it is getting late. I think we should discuss all of this with Mathas before you think about leaving for Zorta. Why doesn't everyone get a good night's sleep and we will all attend the morning meeting," Claudius said then he turned to Sorren. "Sorren you and your men are welcome to spend the night."

Chapter VI
Gabriel

The following morning Stephan, Thaos, Sorren and Lazo told King Mathas the information they had gotten from Prescott and their plans to go to Sendra. The King approved their plans but asked them not to leave until the following morning."

"I understand you want to take care of this as soon as possible," Mathas said. "But I am expecting Matthew home after lunch. Last night I received a message from him that was vague but Matthew also talked about threats to the family. I would like all of you to return later this afternoon and we will have another meeting with Matthew.

Sophie slept until the sun was high in the sky. She awoke both hungry and thirsty. Born a lady of standing she had never learned the necessary skills of caring for herself in the wilderness. Sophie mounted her horse and resumed her journey northward, unaware of the enemies that watched her.

The hot sun beat down on Sophie as she rode along an old and dusty road. She regretted that she did not take the time to take one of her hats; as the sweat ran down Sophie's face and stung her eyes.

After another hour of traveling, Sophie began to feel faint. She saw a small grove of trees to the side of the road and rode over to it. Sophie dismounted and sat under one of the trees. Both Sophie and her horse enjoyed the cool shade that the trees provided. The warm breeze and the soft buzzing of bees soon lulled her into a deep sleep.

"If you can act civilized, we don't have to tie you up," Vardin said to Petra as he untied the boys' hands so he could eat. "I understand why you are fighting us but it would be a lot easier if you just went along with the plans."

"What plans?" Petra asked suspiciously.

Vardin smiled. "Just eat your lunch," He said and walked across the cabin to the table where the other men were sitting.

"I don't know why you bother," Tratz said with disgust. "We will never be able to trust that brat."

"Well, our payday depends on the welfare of that brat; something the rest of you seem to forget," Vardin said.

"We have been held up here for weeks," complained Polgate. "When is that priest coming for the boy?"

"I assume they are working out a ransom," Vardin said. "But I agree I didn't think it would take this long."

"What if something happened?" Rogers said. "Don't we have some way to contact him? Because if we aren't getting paid I don't want to spend any more time stuck here with this kid."

"My Lady are you alright?" Sophie jumped, startled from her sleep by a strange man who was standing over her. "Are you lost?" the man asked.

"Kind Sir, I was travelling to Stordt when my carriage was attacked by bandits. They let me go but I have no food or water," Sophie said.

"Well come with me," the man said as he helped Sophie to her feet. "Our home is but a few miles from here. We have a modest life but my wife and I can certainly give you a meal and a night's lodging." The man helped Sophie mount her horse.

"I thank you," Sophie said kindly. "Might I ask your name?"

"Gabriel," the handsome man said with a smile.

"Impressive," Meekos said as he inspected the new chambers for Omnibus' transformation. "I really did not expect the work to progress so quickly."

"If the workmen don't work fast enough, we give them to the Hutas," Pravis said with a laugh. "That seems to motivate them greatly."

"The stone tank that I ordered should be completed at the end of next week," Meekos said. "Of course we will have to carve the inscriptions into it. But after that is complete I will travel to the castle and retrieve Roch." Meekos was quiet for a moment.

"Does it still bother you that you have not heard from Sophie?" Pravis asked.

"Yes, something is wrong I can feel it in the pit of my stomach. Every time I send ravens to her, they do not return; something is interfering with us."

"Do you think it is the Sanuri? Because as long as we have the boy we can control him."

"Don't be so naïve," Meekos snapped. "The Sanuri is a powerful being; he doesn't have to do anything so that is why I am working on a backup plan."

"A backup plan? What is it?"

"I haven't worked out all of the details yet; but when I do I will tell you and Tenebrae."

"Why this is a lovely home," said Sophie as Gabriel held the door so she could enter. "Please take a seat. I believe my wife is in back in the garden. I will tend to your horse."

Sophie was grateful and relieved to have been found by this kind stranger. She was starving and the smell of baking bread awakened her cravings for food. Soon the door opened and a beautiful young woman entered with a basket of freshly picked vegetables.

"Hello," the woman said. "Gabriel told me we had company. I am sorry I look a sight I have been working in the garden."

"Nonsense you look fine," Sophie said. "I am just very grateful that your husband stopped to help me."

"Would you like something to eat?"

"Oh my yes, I am starving. And would you have a glass of water?"

73

"Of course," said the woman as she put down the basket and turned to get the water.

"What is your name?" asked Sophie.

"Natasha."

"Natasha, it is very nice to meet you," Sophie said as she took the glass of water and started to drink.

"This is a fine meal; thank you both so much," Sophie said as she hungrily devoured a plate of stew and fresh bread.

"Gabriel said you were attacked by bandits," Natasha said. "Certainly you don't plan to continue to travel alone on horseback?"

"I will hire another carriage as soon as I find a town," Sophie said.

"Danner is but a few miles north of here," Gabriel said. "You should be able to get a carriage and driver there. I could escort you there myself."

"Why, thank you so much for your kindness," Sophie said appreciatively.

"Will you have to travel far?" Natasha asked as she poured more coffee into Sophie's cup.

"I am traveling to Taperia, I plan to stay there for a while," Sophie said as she eyed an apple pie that Natasha was carrying to the table.

"Do you have family there?" Natasha asked.

"No, in fact that is why I am travelling. I am trying to find my brother. He has failed to contact me for the past few months, which is not like him at all," Sophie said as she started to eat a piece of warm pie. "You may have heard of him, High Priest Meekos. He was working at the monastery in Malga but when I went there to visit him, they told me he was gone. I will admit I am quite worried. He is the only family I have left and we are very close."

"I certainly hope you find him," Natasha said soothingly. "Do you think he will be in Taperia?"

"I don't really know. But he had work he was doing near there for a while; perhaps he has returned to that location."

"I don't mean to scare you," Natasha said sweetly. "But a woman travelling alone into the Kingdom of Stordt.; why I have heard such awful things about King Roch. Are you sure it is safe for you to go there?"

"I used to live there; I will be alright," Sophie said as she took a second piece of pie. "Besides King Roch became quite ill and another is leading that kingdom."

"I had not heard that," said Gabriel. "Who is King there now?"

"His name is Cerephus, he was a general in King Roch's army."

"Is Roch dead?" Gabriel asked.

Sophie hesitated before she spoke again. "I really don't know; I had heard he was awfully sick with a mysterious affliction; some say he got it from a messenger of The Great Ruler."

"What such affliction would that be?" asked Gabriel in surprise.

"I heard that his skin was rotting from his bones," Sophie said. "He looked and smelled as if he was long dead but he was very much alive."

"Oh that sounds awful," Natasha said as she cleared dishes from the table. "I will prepare a room for you."

"My dear you have done so much already," Sophie said now that she was feeling better after eating. "If Danner is only a few miles away I will leave now. I am anxious to find my brother."

Gabriel left the kitchen to saddle the horses, while Natasha packed some food for Sophie. "Thank you so much for your kindness," Sophie said again to Natasha as she and Gabriel walked towards the door. When Natasha cleared Sophie's dishes she found two gold coins under her plate.

Gabriel and Sophie made pleasant conversation about the weather and Natasha's fine cooking before he asked. "My Lady, Stordt is such a huge kingdom, how do you plan to find your brother?"

"I have been thinking about that," said Sophie thoughtfully. "And that is a very good question because he has not responded to any of the messages I have sent to him. King Cerephus is allowing the publication of books and papers again, although under King Roch few people were allowed to learn to read. Perhaps I will put something in the papers and hope that he sees it."

"Here we are," Gabriel said as they stopped their horses in front of the stable. "I will bid you good day My Lady, may The Great Ruler travel with you." Gabriel turned and rode back towards his house.

"Can I help you," asked an older man as he walked out of the stable; wearing dirty overalls.

"Why yes, those kind people who live down the road said I could hire a carriage and a driver here, is that true?"

"Yes My Lady but I am a little confused. What people told you to come here?"

"Gabriel and Natasha, certainly you know them. They live in that little farm house just three miles south on this road."

"The man looked at Sophie as if he was confused by her words. "My Lady I know the house you speak of. I travel past it every day and no one has lived there for years."

Sophie felt a sense of relief as her carriage started the journey to Taperia. This carriage was not as fancy as the one she had previously rented but it was much better than riding on horseback. "That filthy old man," Sophie thought about the owner of the stable. "He kept looking at me like I was crazy. I'll bet he was drinking. He thought I imagined Natasha and Gabriel."

Sophie huffed in anger as she thought about the man's demeaning attitude. Then she thought about Natasha and Gabriel. It had been a long time since Sophie realized how kind people could be. And for just a moment, a very brief moment, Sophie felt a pang of remorse as she thought about the devastation that Omnibus would bring to this world.

After High Priest Gabriel left Sophie at the stable he returned to the farmhouse. "Do you think she suspected who you were?" Natasha asked when Gabriel walked into the kitchen.

"No, and I want to tell you how proud I am of you Natasha. You got more information out of her then they did during all the interrogations."

"Well, I am just so happy that you allowed me to participate with this mission," Natasha said as she smiled proudly. "I started two letters, one to Raphael and the other to the Sanuri. I wrote down all of Sophie's words. How would you like me to end them?"

"Tell them that my little sister and I are going to Taperia."

"Taperia, but how will we get past the border guards?"

"I was thinking of asking our Ruala friends to give us a lift; I always wanted to fly," Gabriel said and gave Natasha a wink.

"Angelina," called Matthew as he entered their chambers. "We have company."

"Matthew you're home," squealed Angelina as she ran to the front door carrying Jacob. Although she saw Thedes, Ibula and four other Ruala warriors in the doorway, Angelina's focus was on Matthew. "I missed you so much," Angelina said as she jumped into Matthew's arms. The others smiled as they watched the young couple kiss.

"Ibula, Thedes it is so good to see you," Angelina said as she hugged each of them.

"This is Hadar, Bac, Asher and Calla," Thedes said as he introduced the Ruala warriors to Angelina.

"They will be staying with us for a few days," Matthew said.

"Wonderful," said Angelina as she gave Matthew another hug. Then she looked at their visitors and said, "Please excuse me but this is the first time that Matthew and I have been separated since we met and I am just so excited to have him home."

"Believe me, we understand," said Ibula warmly. "Is this Jacob?"

"Yes, would you like to hold him?" Angelina asked as she handed the child to Ibula. Jacob was a good natured child who smiled and cuddled with Ibula.

Angelina jumped up and kissed Matthew again then turned and saw the way Ibula and the others were looking at Jacob. "From the looks on your faces something is going on here," Angelina said. "What is it?"

"Honey, those things you found hanging in the trees are called aboultis, they are like calling cards used by demons. There is a great likelihood that some type of bounty was put on the heads of the people we believe were Jacob's parents. Thedes and Ibula visited the cabin and found another aboultis hanging over the door. They found claw marks going into the windows of the cabin, but they could not find any place where Jacob could have been hidden. They followed his trail to our old campsite and well..."

"What Matthew is having difficulty saying is that it is hard to believe a demon would show such mercy as to spare this child's life. So if they did, there must have been a reason," Ibula said. "And if the child truly escaped the detection of the demons, something very powerful was protecting him until you found him. Angelina, I asked Matthew if we could see the boy. Demons can take any shape. But I can see there is no demon in this child. But if there was a bounty on this boy's family he might still be in danger."

Angelina took Jacob from Ibula, "I didn't know what the aboultis were but I have been thinking many of the same things that you have. That is why I was so eager for the Sanuri to christen him. I thought the Sanuri would be able to tell if there was evil in him."

78

"What did the Sanuri say?" Thedes asked.

"He said Jacob was meant to be with us but he did not yet know why," Angelina said. Jacob held his arms up for Matthew to take him. As Matthew hugged Jacob Ibula said, "He seems like a sweet child."

A soldier walked up to the group, which was still standing in the open doorway. "My Lord, I have a message for you," said the young man as he handed a note to Matthew.

"How did anyone know I was here?"

"My Lord the message was delivered yesterday and I was told to give it to you personally upon your return home."

Before Matthew was able to open his message a second soldier appeared in the doorway, "My Lord the King wants to speak with you now."

Matthew looked at Angelina wearily. "I'm sorry; I will return as soon as I can," he said as he handed Jacob to her.

Angelina looked disappointed. "I will get our guests settled in while we wait for you," she said trying to sound cheerful. Matthew kissed Angelina and disappeared into the hallway. Angelina looked at their visitors and said, "This will be fun; you're our first guests in this home. Come I will show you to your rooms."

The visiting warriors had brought few possessions with them, so they had little to unpack. "Ibula would you mind watching Jacob while I make us some refreshments?" Angelina asked as she handed Ibula the boy. "Tell the others to meet in the parlor," Angelina said as she sped out of the chambers that Thedes and Ibula would stay in.

Calla was a beautiful young Ruala warrior, graceful and athletic; she looked like she was gliding on air when she walked into the kitchen where Angelina was preparing food. "You have a beautiful home Angelina. I have never been to this kingdom before so I was honored when Ibula asked me to come."

"Please make yourself at home here," Angelina said as she was slicing fruit and putting it on a platter. "Calla would you mind taking those three trays into the parlor and ask Thedes if he would pour the wine and whiskey." Angelina nodded towards three large trays that held glasses, bottles of wine and whiskey and platters of cheeses, sausages, bread and honey.

"You are making so much," Calla said as she picked up the first tray.

Angelina carried the last tray of food into the parlor, which consisted of platters of smoked fish, fruits and nuts. "I feel so embarrassed," Angelina said. "If I would have known you were coming I would have fixed something a little nicer."

"Don't be silly," Ibula said warmly. "This is wonderful and they certainly seem to like it." Ibula smiled and nodded towards her brother and the other two male Ruala warriors who had heaped their plates with food."

Angelina noticed how Bac, a handsome young warrior was watching Calla, who seemed oblivious to his admiring looks. Angelina smiled and was about to speak when there was a knock at the door. As Angelina opened the door a soldier said, "I am sorry to bother you My Lady but Prince Matthew has requested that I escort all of you to their meeting."

"What the..." Lazo did not finish his statement as he watched Angelina, Ibula, Thedes and the rest of the Ruala warriors walk into Mathas' study. Lazo turned to Thaos and whispered, "Are those Angels?"

"No, more family," Thaos said with a laugh. Thaos was enjoying the look of utter confusion on Lazo's face. Lazo was a man who felt that he had seen and done everything, a thought he often expressed to others. Thaos had never seen Lazo look like he was surprised by anything; that is until now.

"Father," Angelina called out happily when she saw Sorren. Angelina walked up to Sorren and kissed him on the cheek.

"Let me take Jacob," Sorren said as he put the boy on his lap.

80

Matthew stood up and said, "I believe everyone here has met before, except for Lazo. Lazo this is my wife Angelina. Angelina this is Lazo, he and Thaos worked for Juleta at the same time." Lazo stood up and took Angelina's hand and kissed it; a move that made her cringe.

"This is Thedes, leader of the Shettee Tribe."

Lazo walked up to Thedes and shook his hand. "Nothing personal but I had heard your tribe was wiped out by the Hutas."

Thedes smiled, "Unfortunately that was almost the truth."

"And this is his wife Ibula, she is a princess of the Ruala Tribe," Matthew said.

Lazo found Ibula's beauty intoxicating. He kissed her hand and said, "Please excuse me for staring but I have never seen people with wings before."

Ibula laughed, "We hear that often."

"This is her brother Prince Hadar, Bac, Asher and Calla."

Lazo was on his best behavior as he shook hands with the male warriors. He could see that Calla was younger than the rest. Her long dark, curly hair and bright blue eyes took Lazo's breath away. Lazo kissed her hand. "And are ya married?" he asked. A question which made Calla blush and filled Bac with jealously.

"Oh, he is going to get himself in so much trouble," Stephan whispered to Thaos as they watched Bac's reaction.

"Please take seats," Matthew said to the visitors then he turned to Mathas, Claudius, Stephan, Thaos and Lazo, who had returned to his seat. "As you know King Sudfad's son was abducted. Thedes and Ibula brought a small army of warriors to help in the search of the boy. After the search parties had left the castle, the freshly killed bodies of two Wetprian soldiers were found partially buried near the castle. The uniforms of the soldiers had been stolen."

"Raul put Thedes in charge of the investigation into their deaths and the quest to find any spies among the soldiers. Without going into a lot of detail now, Thedes and Ibula also searched the cabin where I found the bodies of the people we believe were Jacob's parents. Thaos after listening to what you just said, I believe both of you have information that may be related to each other's investigations; which is why I asked them to join us."

Thaos looked at Matthew and asked, "Do you want to talk to Angelina in private before I tell them our story?"

"Matthew what is he talking about?" Angelina asked.

"He is suggesting I talk to you in private because you are going to get mad but Thedes and the others need to hear this also," Matthew said. "So I am going to let Thaos repeat his story then I will explain why we took the actions we did."

Everyone in the room sat in silence as Thaos told them about his and Lazo's involvement with Juleta, the battle at her castle, the Sanuri casting Juleta into The Abyss and his warnings that she had put bounties on their heads. Thaos continued to tell the group about Lazo's narrow escape from death, the dolls that Lazo found and the fight that had taken place in Nates Tavern. Thaos paused at this point in the story.

Matthew looked at Angelina, "Before you yell at me for not telling you about the dolls, we had our reasons. Thaos and Stephan gave the dolls to the Sanuri, who was going to find out information about them. All of us in this room decided not to tell our wives about the dolls until we had more information because we didn't want to worry you." Matthew watched as Angelina's face was growing increasingly redder from her anger.

"Then Petra was abducted and the Sanuri has not gotten back to us; so Sorren, Claudius, Stephan and Thaos came up with a plan to try to find the bounty so there would be no reason for anyone to come after us. Thaos and Stephan met Lazo to get more information." Matthew turned to Thaos, "Do you want to explain the rest of the story?"

Thaos repeated the information that Prescott had given them about the manner and location of the draw. Then he handed the two notes that he had gotten from Prescott to Matthew. "First I want Thedes and Ibula to read these," Matthew said as he handed them the notes.

"A chest of jewels and a chest of gold," Ibula remarked.

"Why don't we let everyone read these notes then you can tell your findings," Matthew said as he handed the notes to Angelina. When she saw the maps Angelina could no longer contain her anger.

"Matthew we have unseen enemies and you blinded us to them," Angelina said angrily.

Angelina was interrupted by Sorren, "Angelina perhaps it would be better if you and Matthew had that discussion at a later time."

Angelina was silent for a moment as she tried to compose herself. "You are right Father." Then Angelina looked at Matthew, "I am sorry," she said angrily. Angelina handed the notes back to Matthew, who handed them to the remaining Ruala warriors.

Thedes stood up and told the group about the murdered soldiers, the aboultis, their search of the cabin which revealed the outlines of two small chests in the blood spatter and their concerns for the safety of Jacob.

Mathas shook his head and said, "This horror just has no end. So are we suspecting that Jacob's parents may have stolen those chests of bounty and the demons killed them?"

"Perhaps they didn't steal the chests but were merely transporting them," Ibula offered. "The demons found out about their cargo and killed them for it."

"Either theory does not explain why they spared Jacob's life," Angelina said fearfully.

"I am beginning to think that is a question that only the Sanuri will be able to answer for us," Mathas said. "Sorren would you please tell everyone about your plans?"

"Stephan and Thaos were planning on leaving tomorrow morning for Zorta to try and find the bounty," Sorren explained. "Mathas gave Stephan a letter to present to King Fahra explaining why they were in his kingdom and asking for his help. Mathas told the boys to take military troops into Zorta."

"I proposed that Nordes warriors, including myself, replace the soldiers which would stop any possible political problems of an invading army. Mathas has a fort near the border between Lentz and Zorta; he will have soldiers ready to assist us if we need them. Honestly I don't know if we can trust Fahra since his close adviser was Juleta's boyfriend."

"I have approved Sorren's plan and appreciate the help," Mathas said. "They will leave at first light tomorrow. Now Matthew I know you just returned home but you may join them if you want."

Matthew looked at Angelina, "I would like to go but if Jacob is in danger I should stay here."

"Matthew go," Angelina said. "I can take care of Jacob. This nightmare that has been placed upon us has to end. We all have children coming; we cannot spend our lives hiding from darkness. I just wish so badly that I could go with you."

"I know you do," Matthew said as he hugged and kissed Angelina.

Thedes and Ibula talked between themselves then Thedes stood up again. "We would like to offer our services. I have to get back and help Raul but Ibula will stay with Angelina and we have other warriors at the castle who can join you."

"Splendid," said Sorren with a big smile.

"Thedes, Simon and Sudfad should be back at the castle by now, perhaps you can join us after all," Matthew said.

"I still need to speak with Raul first," said Thedes.

"Of course," Mathas replied.

"I will fly Thedes back," Hadar offered. "But I would like to return and join them."

"My Lady may I stay here and help?" Calla asked.

"As well as I?" asked Bac

"And I?" Asher asked.

Ibula looked at Thedes and smiled. "Yes you may all stay, although I don't know if you are more interested in the battle or Angelina's hospitality," Ibula said with a laugh.

Chapter VII
Impending

"What is this?" Matthew asked, as Angelina led him into the castle garden and to a small table that was surrounded with candles.

"Ibula is watching Jacob for us," Angelina said. "So we can spend some time together before you have to leave again."

Matthew bent down and kissed his wife. "I am sorry I didn't tell you about the dolls before."

"And I am sorry I yelled at you in front of the others," Angelina said as she handed him a bottle of wine to open. "But let's forget about all that tonight."

Everyone was unusually quiet at the dinner table in Claudius' castle. After the meal was finished Stephan and Ingr and Thaos and Nikki all returned to their chambers. Stephan and Thaos were planning on leaving at sunrise for Zorta and it was the first time they would be leaving their wives.

"I will help you pack," Ingr said.

"Maybe you can pack some food for us," Stephan said. As determined as he was to stop the bounties that had been placed upon his family; Stephan now felt guilty and sad to leave Ingr when she was so close to giving birth to their first child.

Ingr left the room but Stephan kept talking to her; he talked louder so she could hear. "Ingr I was thinking that perhaps you and Nikki should stay together while we are gone."

"Why?" she called back.

"Just in case something happens to one of you, especially in the middle of the night," Stephan kept talking loudly so he did not hear Ingr return to his study where he was packing his weapons and maps. "We really don't know when the baby is coming, what if you go into labor early."

Ingr giggled, "I will talk with her."

Stephan turned around and his eyes grew wide as he looked at Ingr who was wearing a black lace nightgown. "You look beautiful," he said admiringly.

"I know it's hard to look sexy when you are as big as a house."

"Honey you always look sexy to me. And you don't seem to have gained weight; that is all baby."

"Stephan can you stop for a minute I want to give you something."

Stephan now realized that Ingr was holding three objects that were wrapped in silk. "You know it is so hard to buy anything for you because you have everything," Ingr said with a smile. "Vitomas and Annabelle told us of something they had made for their husbands and they said Raul and Simon really liked them. So Nikki and I had some made for you and Thaos but we weren't planning on giving them to you until after the first baby was born." Ingr handed Stephan one of the gifts.

Stephan unwrapped the silk material and looked at a golden locket with the family crest made out of inlaid jewels. "This is beautiful."

"Turn it over," Ingr said. Engraved on the back of the locket were the words *With all our love*. Before Stephan could say anything Ingr explained the significance of the gift. "I have a small lock of my hair in there and will add some of each babies' so we will always be with you; no matter where you are."

Stephan was lost for words momentarily as he opened the locket and saw a wisp of Ingr's hair with the tiniest of pink ribbon. "I love it," he said and hugged Ingr tightly.

"Yours and Thaos' lockets are just a little different in design," Ingr continued. "We showed them to Bella and Claudius and they really liked them. So Nikki and I had two made up for your parents." Ingr explained as she unfolded the silk cloths from the other two lockets. "We made Bella's more feminine and with a longer chain so she could wear it around her neck. Read the back," Ingr said as she handed the two lockets to Stephan. "Do you think they will like them?"

Stephan smiled warmly when he read the inscriptions, "I know they will love them."

"We will wait until you and Thaos are home, so we all can give them to your parents."

Roch's nightmare lingered for what seemed like an eternity to him; trapped inside a dead body, his mind racing always. The songs and whispering that he kept hearing were tormenting him constantly. His insanity grew as he feared he would never escape from this hell. Roch tried to sleep as a reprieve from his reality but sleep was not a gift that came to him often.

Roch had no idea of where he was, he believed he had been moved from the castle because he remembered feeling as if he was being moved. His bed at the castle was warm, Roch felt as if he was lying on ice. He was so disorientated; Roch had lost all conception of time. And that whispering was making him insane, if he could only understand what they were saying.

That evening as the Sanuri sat near his fire he prayed to have an audience with The Lion. Before the Sanuri had completed his prayer the powerful Angel appeared in his guise of a lion.

"I am sorry to bother you," the Sanuri said. "But I do not understand why we are travelling so slowly, Petra's life is at risk."

"I know you are anxious to find the child but he is alright for now," The Lion replied. "There are many things in motion and timing is important. You have always followed me before. I ask that you show the same faith as you have in the past."

"I am sorry old friend," said the Sanuri then he smiled. "I don't think it is my faith as much as my patience that is being tested here."

"Petra too is being tested as are others in this situation. Remember what I told you before; every one chosen to fulfill the prophesies will have to conquer darkness in some form. Fears of all kinds create and perpetuate darkness. In a time like this when you and Sudfad's family are shaken with fear; your faith is what will lead you out of the darkness."

Thaos had ridden in silence since their small army started its journey eastward earlier in the morning. He was surprised at his own emotions; it was much harder for him to leave Nikki behind than he would have imagined. Thaos kept thinking about the night before when she came to their bed dressed in a pale pink lace nightgown; he thought she looked even more beautiful than usual. Thaos was not prepared for the emotions that the gift of the locket evoked within him. Thaos' harsh life and adventures had so pushed his desires for a family to the background that they were all but forgotten; until he came to Claudius' home.

Claudius and Bella had treated Thaos like their son almost as soon as he met them. Thaos both respected and admired Claudius and he cared deeply for Bella. Both Stephan and Ingr seemed like his brother and sister. Thaos and Stephan realized how much they were a like, which they both admitted was not always a good thing.

No sooner had Thaos found a home, then he met the love of his life. At first he was not sure if he really loved Nikki. Thaos knew he wanted her as his wife; but he had not opened his heart to anyone for so long that Thaos wasn't sure if he was capable of love. Last night Thaos realized how much he did love his wife.

Sorren, Thaos, Stephan and Matthew all rode side by side. Lazo rode farther back, so he could watch Calla, who was flying with the new group of Ruala warriors who had joined them. Thedes was among this group. Hadar, Thedes' brother-in-law, carried him as they flew over the Nordes warriors. Stephan noticed that Thaos kept touching his shirt pocket as they rode.

"Your locket?" Stephan asked as he nodded towards Thaos right shirt pocket. Thaos did not answer but simply nodded. "Did Nikki tell you about the ones the girls had made for Mother and Father?" Stephan asked.

"No."

"Ingr said that Mother and Father liked our lockets so much that the girls had some designed for them. She showed me last night. Father's is similar to ours and Mother's is much more fancy with a long chain so she can wear it around her neck.

89

On the back they had inscribed *With love from all your children and their children."*

Thaos noticed that Stephan sounded a little emotional as he was talking. "The girls want all four of us to be together when we give them the gifts." Neither Thaos nor Stephan spoke for a few minutes.

Both Sorren and Matthew overheard Stephan's words. "You boys are doing the right thing," Sorren said. "It's hard to leave your families but you have to protect them. And you think your lives are crazy now, just wait until your babies are born."

"You're right," Matthew said as he tried to force a smile. And the group rode eastward in silence.

Although Padre Bartholomew and Padre Thomas found their accommodations and acceptance by Sudfad's family beyond their imaginations; they felt useless. The two priests had spent so much time doing research for the Sanuri that they now felt without purpose. They both started to spend more time with Gala so she could teach them the art of healing. They were fascinated by the Ruala and Shettee warriors who were staying with the Royal Family and sought to learn more about these cultures.

"I feel like we could be doing so much more," Padre Thomas complained to Padre Bartholomew as they took their morning walk through the castle gardens.

"Perhaps we should request an audience with the King and Queen and ask them if they have projects for us," Padre Bartholomew suggested. "I know there is an orphanage in Salar perhaps we could be of some assistance there."

"High Priest Gabriel said that the Sanuri was very explicit in his orders, that we do not leave the castle until his return."

"Then let us speak with the King and Queen this morning, before we both go crazy from boredom," Padre Bartholomew said. The two old men returned to the castle and found King Sudfad and Queen Renya in the dining room finishing their breakfast.

"We are sorry My Lord," Padre Bartholomew said apologetically. "We did not mean to interrupt your meal. We will come back."

"Nonsense," said Sudfad with a smile. "Please join us. Have you eaten?"

"No," replied Padre Thomas. Marie was clearing the dishes from the table that had been left by the other family members. "I will be back in just a moment." Marie said and left the room.

"I am sorry that I have not had much time to speak with you since my return," Sudfad said. "Renya and Raul told me about the visit by the Patronus. The Sanuri and I are close friends; he has spoken of you often, I am glad to finally get the chance to meet you."

"We are both very honored to be here," Padre Thomas said respectfully. "Your family has welcomed us with open arms and made our stay of the upmost pleasure." Padre Thomas nodded to Renya as he said these words. "But, well, we don't want to sound ungrateful. But Padre Bartholomew and I have spent so much time doing research and helping the Sanuri that we are finding ourselves feeling quite useless now that we have so much time on our hands. We were wondering if you had some projects that we could assist with."

"I hear you have been spending time with Gala learning the arts of a healer," Renya said.

"Yes," Padre Bartholomew said. "She is a remarkable woman and we are learning a great deal. She confided to us that she has talked to The Lion and that he told her to come to you."

"That is true," Sudfad said. Sudfad stopped talking as Marie placed several plates of food and a pot of coffee in front of the priests.

Both of the priests thanked Marie. "We are not used to being served," Padre Bartholomew confided.

"Padre Thomas and Padre Bartholomew you are both loyal servants of The Great Ruler," Sudfad said as he and Renya both smiled at the priests. "I am sure that I am not telling you anything new when I say there are no coincidences in this life."

91

Padre Thomas stared at Sudfad and Renya. "From the moment we walked into this room you both acted like you were expecting us, why?"

"Well we were," Sudfad said with a knowing smile. "We received a letter from the Sanuri a couple of days ago. In it he explained that The Lion said you would come to us and we were told the project to give you."

After they had all finished their morning meals, Sudfad and Renya led Padre Thomas and Padre Bartholomew into the King's study. "Please have a seat," Sudfad said. "What I am about to tell you cannot under any circumstances leave this room. You must swear an oath to The Great Ruler."

Both priests looked at each other in confused amazement then they both made the promise. "What I am about to tell you may sound crazy but I can assure you that the Sanuri will testify to my words. Many generations ago my forefathers made a covenant with The Great Ruler. They swore to protect His Word and His children to their greatest abilities and for that my family has been blessed."

Sudfad continued, "My family is the Keepers of The Holy Scrolls of The Great Ruler. Until now, only certain family members were told the truth; other than the Sanuri you are the first outsiders who we have been allowed to share the secret with. You must be very faithful men for The Lion to direct me to tell you these things."

"I have heard stories but I thought they were only old myths," said Padre Thomas as he stared at Sudfad in disbelief.

"I have been a friend of the Sanuri's for most of my life and your words now help to clarify a great many things," said Padre Bartholomew reflectively.

"And there is more," Sudfad said. "Have you ever heard of the Prophesy of The Seven Sons?"

"Yes," replied both priests almost in unison.

"The prophesy does not mean seven sons of a human father," Sudfad said. "So far there are six of us, the seventh has not yet been revealed to our group. Does all of this surprise you?"

"Yes and no," said Padre Bartholomew. "Actually I am more surprised that you have been allowed to tell us these things."

"You do understand that this knowledge puts you in even greater danger than you already have been, so it is imperative to us all that you uphold your oath to The Great Ruler."

"What do you need us to do?" Padre Thomas asked.

"I am not sure how you are going to feel about your first projects," Sudfad said. "But I am sure The Lion has his reasons for assigning them." Sudfad turned to Renya who rotated the lever hidden behind the bookcase, thus opening a secret door in the wall of the study. "Please follow us," Sudfad said.

As the four walked down the many steps to the Holy Vault, Sudfad explained to the priests what they were about to see. Renya walked into the vault first and started to light candles. "Sudfad it is very dusty down here," she said with disgust. "I must come down here and clean."

"Padre Thomas and Padre Bartholomew, the Holy Vault of The Great Ruler," Sudfad said as he waved his hand towards the many shelves of scrolls, books and holy gifts. "Kings and demons of all manner have killed to try and set their eyes upon this room. My family has sworn an oath to The Great Ruler to protect these items until such time that The Lion tells us to return them to the outside world."

The two priests slowly walked around the room looking at things. "This reminds me of the Hall of Antiquities," Padre Thomas said.

"The Lion would like the two of you to be the caretakers of this vault. Because of the madness at your monastery, the Sanuri as well as the Patronus have brought many more items here, as you can see by all of these baskets that are set around the floor. The Lion would like you to organize and document all of the items here, then I believe he has some research for you to do."

"This is certainly right up our alley," said Padre Bartholomew happily.

"Does the Patronus know about this vault?" Padre Thomas asked.

"No, besides all of us in this room and the Sanuri, Raul, Simon, Matthew and their wives know about it and they are all sworn to secrecy. Do you accept this trusted position that The Great Ruler is requesting of you?" Sudfad asked.

"Yes," both priests answered as one voice.

"Then you have now entered into the covenant we have with The Great Ruler," Sudfad said. "Now this does mean that you will be living here. Renya will take you around and show you the choices of chambers within the castle or a cottage on the grounds."

"Are any of the cottages big enough for two to live in?" Padre Bartholomew asked.

"Yes, the largest one is close to Gala's," Renya said.

Padre Bartholomew looked at Padre Thomas, who smiled and nodded. "We are simple men," Padre Thomas explained. "We would be quite content in a cottage with a little garden and some chickens like Gala has."

"Then that cottage is your new home," Sudfad said. "Renya will help you get settled in."

Chapter VIII
Truth

"My Lord, Ryan is here to see you."

"Thank you Sarah; please show him in," Claudius said.

Ryan walked into the parlor, shyly standing in the doorway, "I am sorry to bother you but Thaos asked me to check on Nikki and Ingr while they were gone."

"Ryan come in and sit down," Claudius said cheerfully. "We are just having a glass of wine before dinner. Would you like wine or whiskey?"

"Wine," Ryan said as he took a seat.

"Can you stay for dinner?" Bella asked.

"Yes, thank you."

Ingr started laughing, "Ryan your eyes almost pop out of your head every time you look at how big my stomach is."

"I don't mean to insult, Ingr."

"I just think it is funny," Ingr replied.

"Are you sure you are just having one baby?" Ryan asked innocently. "I've met your twin brothers and sisters. Maybe your family is prone to such things."

Ingr smiled at Ryan's comment. "Ryan I am not sure about anything except that I am really ready for this baby to come; everything is becoming so difficult."

"If either of you need help with anything, I'm here," Ryan said. "I brought you both gifts. Well, gifts for the babies. You have always been so kind to me. They are in a boca outside I will go get them."

"He is such a sweet boy," Bella said as soon as Ryan left the room.

"We are trying to find him a girlfriend," Nikki said. "But he is so shy he never talks to anyone we introduce him to."

"Ryan it's beautiful," gushed Bella as she got out of her chair to look at the cradle.

"I will be right back with the other one," Ryan said and quickly left the room. The entire family looked at the fine detail and intricate carvings of Angels on the top of the cradle.

"Ryan this is so beautiful," Ingr said as he carried the second cradle into the parlor.

"My grandfather was a very talented man. He taught me many things including wood carving."

"Ryan we love them, thank you," said Nikki and kissed him on the cheek. Ingr was standing next to Ryan and kissed him on his other cheek. Ryan turned red and was unable to speak.

Thedes and Sorren were doing most of the talking in the group of men who were sitting around the evening campfire. Lazo joined the group; as he grabbed a bottle of whiskey to fill his cup he said, "Yes sir that Calla sure is a pretty little thing."

Thaos looked at Lazo, then at Thedes to see his reaction to Lazo's words. Thaos looked back at Lazo and warned, "The Rualas are vicious warriors and that girl is not like the women you usually spend time with; you should tread carefully."

"Boy ya sure have changed since you settled down," Lazo said sarcastically.

"Yes I have."

"We all have," Matthew added.

"Well, what if I just want what ya all have. A pretty little warrior girl to take care of my needs," Lazo said with a salacious grin.

Stephan stared at Lazo. Every comment that Lazo made seemed to irritate Stephan and this one was certainly no exception.

"Stephan don't look at me like ya want to cut my throat," Lazo said. "I am serious. I'm happy for ya boys and I'm thinking that I am ready to settle down too."

No one said a word for several minutes then Stephan spoke, "Sorry, guess I am just touchy. Leaving Ingr when she could give birth any day is harder than I thought." Stephan paused for a few moments then continued, "Ingr is always joking around but I think she is scared of going into labor and I have never seen her scared of anything before. I just don't want her to go through that alone."

"Shara and Angelina will be with her as well as your family," Sorren said. "I know it's not the same but Stephan you know she will be with people who love her."

"I've never seen anything like this before," Henry commented as he drove a team of horses towards the Nora gold mines. In the back of the boca that Henry was driving sat a large stone tub; which was so heavy that the boca had to be reinforced. Eight horses pulled the boca, while five men rode along side.

"What in the world do you think it's used for?" asked Sam as he rode next to the driver's side of the boca.

"Looks like a damn big bathing tub to me," Henry said. "But why in the world would they want to put it into a cave?"

Sam started to laugh, "Must be a bathing tub for a damn giant; that thing is huge."

Although it was but a few miles from the Nora Stone Works site to the gold mines, the travel was slow because of the weight of the cargo. The sun was high in the sky when the men stopped in front of the mine opening indicated on the delivery map. As Henry stopped the horses he looked around the vacant landscape. "Awfully quiet around here for a working mine. Jay look at that map again we might be in the wrong place."

"You're in the right place," High Priest Tenebrae said as he walked out of the darkness of the mine. "Some of my men are bringing a cart to put that on."

"We had to reinforce the boca," Henry said. "Can't imagine you would have a cart strong enough to hold this thing. Mind me asking what this is?" Henry asked as he climbed down from the boca.

Tenebrae did not answer Henry's question; he just watched the six men loosen the tethers on the tub. A loud sound of chains banging against stone could be heard as the cart was being pushed through the mine.

"Sounds like they are almost here," Henry commented without turning back towards the opening of the mine.

"What the hell!" yelped Jay as he felt the sharp blade of a Huta warrior's knife against his throat.

"What's going on here?" demanded Henry as their group was surrounded by Huta warriors.

"These are my men," replied Tenebrae with an evil grin. "They will help you unload."

"Unload, they're Hutas," Henry yelled as a Huta nudged him with the tip of a spear.

High Priest Pravis walked out of the shadows of the mine and stood next to Tenebrae. The two watched as the Hutas and the men from Nora carefully moved the tank from the boca to the cart, which was made from strong timbers. As they watched the men push the cart into the mine Pravis laughed and said to Tenebrae," I'll bet when they got up this morning they never thought this would be the day they died."

"Gala this is fascinating," said Padre Thomas as he and Padre Bartholomew helped Gala carry baskets of potions to the castle.

"Do you think the Princes would allow us to observe the effects of this potion?" Padre Bartholomew asked.

"Raul and Simon are very nice, if you asked them; I am sure they would let you," Gala said.

98

Although Padre Thomas and Padre Bartholomew had only known Gala for a few weeks the three were becoming close friends. The Priests had moved into the cottage that was but yards away from Gala's. She helped them organize their home and gave them plants from her gardens so they could start their own gardens. Both priests were very interested in learning about herbs and medicines and Gala enjoyed their company.

"Princess Ibula was going to send for some special plants from the Ice Caves of Mordv but she left for Lentz and has not returned," Gala said. "Ibula is a healer among her people and I am very excited to learn of her medicines."

The three were walking through the castle gardens when two soldiers passed them. "Good day," Padre Thomas said to the soldiers, then he stopped abruptly.

"What is it?" asked Gala.

"Bartholomew did you see them?" Padre Thomas asked as he turned to look at the soldiers. One of the soldiers heard what Padre Thomas said and turned and looked at the priests. "They are Meekos' men," whispered Padre Thomas. "Quickly get to the castle." The two old priests and Gala quickened their pace.

"They are behind us," gasped Padre Bartholomew. The three started to run but they were no match for the much younger men who chased them.

"Help! Help!" screamed Gala as they ran towards the castle. "Help us, please help us."

One of the men tackled Padre Bartholomew. The priest fell on his stomach but the soldier turned him over and started to punch the old priest in the face. The second soldier grabbed Padre Thomas and spun him around then he punched the priest in the stomach.

"Help! Help!" screamed Gala as she dropped her basked and picked up a piece of a tree limb that she saw on the ground. "Help us! Help us!" Gala screamed as she started to hit first one and then the other attacker over the head. What seemed like an eternity was but seconds before Ruala warriors, Wetprian soldiers and Enrops came to the rescue.

The two attackers were pulled off the priests. The man who was beating Padre Bartholomew pulled a large knife out of his boot and lunged at one of the Wetprian soldiers. A Ruala warrior quickly grabbed the attacker from behind and placed a knife against his throat until the man dropped his knife. The second assailant tried to punch one of the Ruala warriors but three Wetprian soldiers grabbed him and wrestled him to the ground.

"They aren't your soldiers," Padre Thomas gasped as two Wetprian soldiers were helping him to his feet. "They work for High Priest Meekos, I have seen them at the monastery in Malga."

"And you are sure of this?" Sudfad asked as he, Raul and Simon ran up to the group.

"Yes My Lord," Padre Thomas said. "They attacked us because I recognized them."

"Take them to the dungeons," ordered Sudfad.

"Are you alright?" Raul asked Padre Bartholomew, who had blood running down his robe.

Before Padre Bartholomew could answer, Gala said, "I will take care of them, but My Lord these baskets are filled with the potions Raul requested."

"The same potion I had you make for the Taperian soldier?" Sudfad asked.

"Yes, My Lord."

"Excellent," Sudfad said. "Raul, Simon you know what to do."

Raul and Simon had the soldiers take the two intruders to the dungeons and put them into separate cells. After an hour one of the prisoners was taken from his cell and escorted to an empty cottage on the royal grounds. The Wetprian soldiers tied the prisoner to a chair and waited for the Princes to arrive.

Gala had tended to the minor wounds that both Padre Thomas and Padre Bartholomew received during the attacks.

100

Although Gala advised both men to go to bed and rest, the priests begged Raul and Simon to allow them to view the interrogations. Both Padre Thomas and Padre Bartholomew were fascinated with the truth potion that Gala had made and wanted to see its results.

When Raul and Simon arrived at the cottage they told the soldiers to wait outside; although they allowed both of the priests to stand in the back of the room. Simon held the first prisoner's head so Raul could pour a small bottle of the potion down his throat.

"What is that crap?" yelled the prisoner after Simon had released the hold on his head. "Did you just poison me?"

"No," Raul replied as they stood in silence waiting for the potion to take hold.

"What the hell is going on here?" demanded the prisoner. "What was that stuff you poured down my throat?"

Neither Simon nor Raul answered the man's questions. After almost five minutes they started to see visible changes in the prisoner; his eyes appeared heavy and he started to weave back and forth in his chair.

"What is your name?" Raul asked.

"Odell," the prisoner responded in a slurred manner.

"Who do you work for?" Raul asked.

"Meekos."

"Who is he?"

"A high priest at the monastery at Malga."

"Did you and your partner kill our two soldiers and steal their uniforms?"

"Yes, could I have some water?"

Simon nodded at the priests and Padre Thomas left the cottage to get water. "We are getting water for you, but first tell us why you were sent here?"

"To keep an eye on the Royal Family."

"Why?"

"That I don't know."

"How do you get messages to Meekos?"

"Ravens."

Raul looked intently at Simon who nodded; the Princes did not want to ask any questions about Petra's kidnapping until they were convinced the prisoner was under the influence of the potion.

"Were you involved in Petra's kidnapping?"

"No, we came after that."

"Is he alive?"

"I don't know."

"Do you know where he was taken?"

"Some place in Stordt, I think a cabin."

"Do you know where this cabin is?"

"No."

"Do you know why he was kidnapped?"

"No."

"Do you know who kidnapped him?"

"Yes."

"What are their names?"

Padre Thomas entered the cottage with a pitcher of water but Simon motioned for him to stand back. Padre Bartholomew was writing down everything the prisoner was saying.

"Rodgers, Polgate, Tratz, Zac and Vardin."

"How do you know these men?"

"They work for Meekos too."

"Do you know what they intend to do to Petra?"

"No."

"Do you know how they were able to get past our guards?"

"Yes."

"Tell me how, all the details."

"Campbell and Denton let them through the gates."

"Who are Denton and Campbell?"

"More of Meekos' men.

Raul looked at Simon, then asked. "Are they posing as our soldiers also?"

"Yes."

"How many of Meekos' men are at our castle?"

"Well, counting me and Hanger, there are nine here?"

"Are they all posing as soldiers?"

"Yes."

"Is Hanger the man who was taken to the dungeons with you?"

"Yes."

"Can you give us descriptions of the rest of Meekos' men who are at our castle?"

Padre Bartholomew wrote down the descriptions and names of the seven other spies who were impersonating Wetprian soldiers. Simon assigned soldiers and Ruala warriors to start searching for the men, after he warned the members of his family that they were in danger.

Raul stayed in the cottage as soldiers took Odell back to the dungeons and brought Hanger, the other spy to him. Raul waited until Simon returned and the two men forced the truth potion down Hanger's throat just as they had done with Odell. The potion took effect on Hanger sooner and Hanger appeared much more intoxicated from the potion than Odell had been. Hanger gave Simon and Raul very similar answers to Odell's until Raul asked a new question.

"Why is Meekos spying on us and kidnapping our brother?"

"I think everything he does has something to do with that demon they are trying to raise. I think that old boy is afraid something is going to go wrong and the demons will burn him in hell."

"When you said old boy, you meant Meekos?"

"Yeah, him and those other two high priests. They act so hoity toity like they are better than the rest of us. We all know they bewitched those Hutas and sacrifice people to the demons. They are just liars and murderers like the rest of us," Hanger laughed. "Yeah I wouldn't mind seeing those priests get what they deserve."

Sudfad had entered the cottage as Hanger was talking. "Put him back in the dungeons. Don't kill them as we may be able to get more information from them. We need to send a message to the Sanuri with this information," Sudfad said.

Sorren rode up next to Thaos and said quietly, "It's not really my business but if your friend was acting around my daughter the way he is around that young Ruala girl, I would break both his legs."

"Lazo is not my friend," Thaos said with disgust. "And I agree with you. These people came to help us and I think he is going to start trouble."

"One of the Ruala warriors keeps looking at that girl like he is in love with her; why doesn't he do something?"

"I don't know."

"I think we should talk to Thedes before something bad happens," Sorren said. "This evening you distract Lazo and I will talk with Thedes."

"Gabriel is that you?" Natasha called out as she was taking a pan of biscuits out of the oven.

"Yes and we have company," Gabriel said as he and Calen walked into the kitchen.

Natasha finished putting the biscuits on a plate before she looked up at Gabriel. Standing next to her brother was a Ruala warrior who was so handsome Natasha could do little but stare at him. A large man with blonde hair and brilliant blue eyes was staring at Natasha just as intensely.

"Gabriel you never told me your sister was so beautiful," Calen said admiringly as he looked at Natasha's long black curly hair and violet eyes. Natasha was curvaceous but slender and when she smiled at Calen and revealed her dimples, Calen's heart melted.

Gabriel looked at the way Natasha and Calen were looking at each other and smiled. "There may have been a reason for that," Gabriel said with a laugh. "Natasha this is Calen, Calen my sister Natasha." Gabriel said.

When Natasha realized she was staring at Calen, she blushed and looked down. "How many others are with you, I only have three chickens in the oven, but they are large," she said shyly.

"That is more than enough," Calen replied. "There are four others, they are checking the area before they come in." Calen turned to Gabriel and handed him a set of saddlebags. "Raphael said there is money, identification papers and maps in one bag. He put a large envelope in the second bag, which he wants you to read right away and respond to him."

Gabriel took the saddlebags, "I am going to read these papers," he said and started to walk towards one of the bedrooms. Gabriel turned and asked with a smile, "Will you two be alright if I leave you alone?"

"Gabriel!" Natasha gasped with embarrassment.

"I will watch over your sister," Calen said and smiled as he took a seat at the kitchen table.

"I'm sure you will," Gabriel said with a sarcastic grin. Then as an afterthought he added. "When the others come, tell them to settle in. Whoever lived here before must have had a large family because there are plenty of beds." Gabriel walked into a bedroom and closed the door.

"Would you like some coffee?" Natasha asked nervously.

"Yes and one of those biscuits too," Calen said as he boldly stared at her. "We brought different clothes for the two of you and weapons for two. Do you know how to use weapons?"

"Yes, Gabriel taught me," Natasha said as she put a plate with biscuits and a jar of honey in front of Calen.

"So you are a warrior?"

"Me a warrior, no," Natasha replied with a laugh.

"You are hunting demons and you know how to use weapons; why do you not call yourself a warrior?"

"I guess I never thought about it like that."

"All the women in my tribe are warriors and yet they are also wives and mothers."

"Really," Natasha said with fascination. "You will have to tell me about your people."

"Are you married?"

"No." Natasha was so shocked by Calen's question that she could barely answer.

"Are you spoken for?"

Natasha composed herself and looked Calen in the eyes, "You certainly are bold; are all Rualas so bold?"

"Rualas are as different as humans."

"Well, you look human to me, except for the wings," Natasha said. She hesitated for a few moments then asked, "May I touch one?"

"Yes," Calen said with a grin.

Natasha walked behind Calen and gently touched one of the large wings that protruded from his back. "They feel like a bird's wings."

"What did you expect?"

"I don't know," Natasha said as she noticed that Calen had drank all of his coffee and eaten his biscuits. "Would you like some more?"

"Yes please," Calen said as he handed her his plate. "Are you a member of the Patronus?" He asked as he watched Natasha preparing their meal.

"I am not a priest but there are a group of us who work with them," Natasha explained as she tossed a salad. "All members of the Patronus look like warriors. Sometimes they need others who don't look like warriors to gather information, do research, watch people and such things; and that is what I do. Our parents died when I was young, I have been helping Gabriel since I was a child." Then Natasha's voice softened. "Gabriel is a great man, I am very proud of him."

"You never answered my question, are you spoken for?"

"No," was all Natasha said before the bedroom door opened and Gabriel walked into the kitchen. "Gabriel do you want some coffee and biscuits?" Natasha asked.

"Yes but I will take them in the other room. Raphael has sent me a lot to study."

"Gabriel how is it that a woman as beautiful as your sister is not spoken for?"

Gabriel laughed, "Because she spends all of her time asking to join me on missions."

"And he scares all of the boys away," Natasha said with a laugh as she prepared a plate for Gabriel.

"That I do," Gabriel said. "Natasha would you take that into my room?" After Natasha left the room Gabriel walked closer to Calen. "Did Raphael tell you what was in the envelope?"

"No."

"He has received information that the three priests we seek are preparing a place for the transformation of Omnibus. And that they have kidnapped Sudfad's son in an attempt to force the Sanuri to somehow assist them. I believe that the witch does not know where her brother is, but if she is going to Taperia she must expect him to be in that area."

"We will be with you for the entire mission," Calen said. "Do you want to send for more warriors?"

"We might need them. I have not told Natasha everything about this mission but I will have to now. This mission may be too dangerous for her."

"I believe your sister would follow you into hell if you asked."

"And that may be exactly where we are going," Gabriel said solemnly. "Calen if something happens to me I want you to protect her."

"Of course."

"And Calen, you are a good man but my sister is pretty naïve when it comes to men; don't lead her on if you aren't interested."

"I'm interested."

"What are you two whispering about?" Natasha asked but before they could answer four more Ruala warriors walked into the kitchen.

"Natasha this is Dagon, Rabi, Koby and Luca," Gabriel said. "Gentlemen this is my sister Natasha."

"I can have a meal ready soon if you are hungry," Natasha offered.

"That would be fine," Koby said. "I know I am starving."

"Where should we put these things?" asked Luca as he held up one of the packs they had been carrying.

"Why don't you put them in my room and I will sort through them," Gabriel said as he pointed towards the door to his bedroom.

"You are a good cook," Luca said to Natasha as they were all seated at the kitchen table eating. "Of course Calen hasn't noticed because he can't stop staring at you," Luca added kiddingly.

"I've noticed," Calen said with a smile as he watched Natasha blush.

"Gabriel does it bother you that my cousin is acting so bold?" Luca asked only partially joking.

Gabriel was quiet for a moment as a sly smile came across his face. "Well, from what I can see she is staring at him too."

"Gabriel, I am not," Natasha scolded; which made all of the men at the table laugh. Natasha became very embarrassed and was quiet for a few minutes; then she tried to change the subject. "So, you all seem to know each other, how did you meet?"

"What, this is the fifth mission that we have assisted Gabriel with," Luca said. "The Sanuri sent us to him the first time."

"Our world in the Ice Caves is very peaceful. The Sanuri took us there to save our race, as he has done with the Shettees," Calen explained. "We owe The Great Ruler and the Sanuri our existence; so we offer to be of service whenever we can."

"I thought the Shettees had been wiped out," Natasha said.

"They almost were," Calen replied. "But now they live among us as our brethren."

"And you all get along?" asked Natasha.

"Yes, we have had no problems," Calen continued. "In fact our Princess is married to the leader of the Shettees."

"Really," Natasha said with sincere interest.

"You and Gabriel will have to visit the Ice Caves some time," Calen suggested. "A more beautiful place you will not see."

Natasha's eyes grew wide and she quickly looked at her brother, "Gabriel could we?"

"I would like that too," Gabriel said. "But for now we have to focus on this mission. Luca you said we should travel at night, why?"

"For two reasons, one so we won't be seen and two so we don't have to fly during the heat of the day," Luca explained. "Our robes are made of a special material that keeps us cool when it is hot and vice versa. They also repel water. Your clothing is very different, you would become too hot flying in the sunlight for a long distance."

"How long do you think it will take us to get to Taperia?" Gabriel asked.

"We should look over the maps, Calen said. "But I would guess three days."

"When do you want to leave?" Luca asked Gabriel.

"I was hoping for tonight but I have some work to do for Raphael and I will need to brief you all on some new developments." Gabriel turned and looked at Natasha. "After the briefing if any of you want to pull out of this mission; that would be understandable."

"Why are you looking at me?" Natasha asked. "I begged you to bring me on this mission. I'm not going home."

"Even if I tell you that a powerful demon may be trying to escape his prison and enter this world?" Gabriel asked.

"And you think I am going to let you face that demon by yourself?" Natasha asked with indignation.

Calen turned to Gabriel and said with a grin, "Told you."

Later that evening, after dinner, Sorren, Stephan and Matthew met with Thedes. Thaos was to keep Lazo busy and unaware of the meeting. It was decided that Matthew should do the talking since he knew Thedes better than the others.

"Thedes, we want to talk with you because all of us have concerns about how Lazo is acting towards that young Ruala girl," Matthew said. "I will admit that we don't understand all of your customs or the customs of the Rualas but Lazo is not a good man and well, we are surprised no one has tried to stop him."

Thedes looked at the concern on the faces of the three men and broke into a smile. "I am so glad to hear your words. None of us wanted to insult your families and we too are not aware of all of your customs or how close you are to that man."

"Personally I hate him," Stephan said. "But he is necessary to this mission. Thedes if he acted towards my wife like that, I would kill him. Do you want me to have a talk with him?"

"I think Bac should be the one to talk to him," Thedes replied.

"Is that the young warrior who looks so in love with that girl?" Sorren asked.

"Yes, but she does not seem to be aware of him or his feelings for her," Thedes said.

"Well, I am the oldest one here and I have raised both of your wives," Sorren said as he looked at Matthew and Stephan. "Thedes mind if I have a fatherly talk with that girl. She needs to know we will protect her and that she doesn't have to be treated like that. Frankly I'm afraid he is going to try to rape her."

"Then we will just kill him," Stephan said angrily. "We will do this mission without him."

"I would prefer to stop the problem before it gets that far," Sorren said.

"Thedes would it be alright if Stephan and I talked to Bac?" Matthew asked. "Thaos is keeping Lazo busy so he is unaware of what is going on."

"I think Bac would be comfortable speaking with you," Thedes said. "If you need me, let me know."

After Sorren had a talk with Calla, he looked for Matthew, Stephan and Bac. Sorren found the three men walking in an area of the woods.

"What did you tell him?" Sorren asked.

"We gave him permission to do anything but kill Lazo, unless he really had to," Matthew said.

Sorren had a fatherly tone to his voice as he spoke to Bac. "I just talked to Calla. Now Bac you need to know that I raised both Matthew's and Stephan's wives and I have other children. Calla told me some of the same things I have heard from my own daughters."

"She is so worried about proving herself a strong warrior on this mission that she has been afraid to ask for help. And that girl is young and naïve, she did not truly understand Lazo's intentions before I told her," Sorren continued. "Now we will gladly intervene with Lazo but if you love that girl, she should know that you are protecting her. But first you need to talk to her about your feelings."

"Does she care for Lazo?"

"Of course not," Sorren said. "He scares and disgusts her but she has been afraid to say anything. I told her she had other admirers and she was surprised that it was you."

"What did she say?"

"Calla said she was surprised you would be interested in a girl like her."

"What did she mean?" asked Bac with confusion.

"Hell if I know. She is a teenage girl and trust me they see the world differently."

"Where is she?"

112

"I left her with Thedes. I wasn't sure how long Thaos could keep Lazo distracted."

"Thank you all," Bac said. "I have been wanting to kill that man but I thought she cared for him."

Thedes and Calla were sitting by his campfire when Bac walked up to them. "Calla can I speak with you in private?"

Calla looked at Bac then at Thedes with embarrassment, "I am sorry I have been so much trouble."

"You haven't been any trouble," Bac said as he held his hand out to her. Calla stood up and took Bac's hand and the two walked into the forest.

"Calla I should have talked to you before now but I guess I was scared."

"Why would you be scared Bac, you are such a brave warrior?"

"Because you act like I don't exist and honestly I thought you liked Lazo."

"Bac!" Calla said loudly. "How could you or any of you think such a thing?"

"Because you never said 'no' or did anything to discourage him."

"Bac I didn't know what to do; I have never met anyone like him before."

"Do you want him to leave you alone?"

"Yes," Calla said softly. "I feel so embarrassed; I am a warrior I should be able to handle this."

"Calla I will deal with Lazo but you must promise me that you will tell me if he bothers you again. Do you promise?"

"Yes," she whispered. "Bac what are you going to do to him?"

"That depends on him," Bac said then he moved closer to Calla. "I have another question for you. Will you spend time with me so we can get to know each other?"

Calla looked up into Bac's large brown eyes. "I would like that," she said sweetly.

"Calla I need to know, are you saying that because you really would like to spend time with me or because I am helping you with Lazo?"

"Because I really would like to get to know you better."

"Why did you tell Sorren you didn't think I would be interested in a girl like you?"

Calla looked at Bac with surprise. "Because you are well known for your skill and bravery as a warrior." Calla's voice grew softer, "And I have seen how other girls watch you. Bac you could have any girl you want."

Bac looked at Calla with confusion as the two walked to his campsite. "Calla I don't understand why my skill as a warrior has anything to do with my attraction to you. You are a very beautiful and sweet girl, whose attention I have been trying to get for a longtime. And none of this explains that comment you made to Sorren."

Calla was quiet for a while as she was thinking of how to answer his question. "Calla will you answer my question?" Bac asked with frustration.

"Bac I am trying to figure out what to say that you won't laugh at me," Calla said self-consciously.

"I won't laugh, I promise."

"Bac you said you have been trying to get my attention but you have had my attention for a long time. You are so handsome that when I am around you I can't talk and I get embarrassed so I just don't say anything." Bac stopped walking and faced Calla as she spoke. "I see all those pretty girls flirting with you and I wish I could act like that but when I am around you I get so nervous, I don't know, I feel like I make a fool out of myself."

114

"Calla are you saying that you have been interested in me?"

"Yes, for a very long time," Calla said shyly. "But I didn't know what to do or say. I know you must think I am such a fool," Calla said with frustration.

"I am beginning to think we are both fools, if we have had feelings for each other but have been too afraid to act on them."

Chapter IX
Lazo

Bac and Calla sat at his campsite talking and laughing for hours. "Bac, I..." Calla did not finish her sentence.

"You what?"

"I have really enjoyed spending time with you," Calla said shyly.

"I have too," Bac said as he watched how the firelight made her large eyes sparkle. They had been sitting close to each other, on the ground. "You're shivering," Bac said and put his arm around Calla pulling her closer to him. Calla eagerly snuggled against Bac.

"I feel so foolish; for years I have had a crush on you and have been too afraid to talk to you. And here you are so nice and so easy to talk to."

"Years," he repeated with astonishment. "You've had a crush on me for years?"

"Well, a couple."

"I never would have guessed and believe me I have been watching you for a long time."

"Do you remember when Ibula and Thedes got married and everyone celebrated for a week?"

Bac smiled. "Yes and every day there were tournaments and competitions and dances; I really enjoyed them."

"And you did so well. I hadn't really watched you in any fighting competitions before those ceremonies. Do you remember that competition you were in where twenty warriors start fighting until there is only one standing. You beat them all. Of course I was so afraid you were going to get hurt. I couldn't keep my eyes off from you. After that I followed you to every competition. I was so proud of you."

"If I remember right, I got my butt kicked a couple of times during those tournaments. Why didn't you ever come up to me afterwards?"

"Oh and be one of the many girls who were standing in line waiting to congratulate you. I really don't think you would have noticed me if I had," Calla said with a grin.

"So what you are really saying is that you were jealous," Bac said teasingly.

"Perhaps a little."

"Calla I would have noticed you." Bac leaned forward and softly kissed her on the lips. Bac pulled his head back so he could look at Calla's face; then he leaned forward and kissed her again. Calla was nervous at first but she slowly put her arms around Bac's neck as they kissed again and again. "Lay down," he whispered as he shifted his position.

Calla did as he said. "Bac I have never, I mean..." she started to say nervously.

"Calla we are just going to kiss, I promise," Bac said as he moved on top of her. Their kisses became more and more intense as their passions surged within them. Abruptly Bac stood up and said "It's getting late, I will walk you back to your campsite."

Calla sat up but did not stand. She suddenly looked like she could cry. "Bac would it be bold of me if I asked to sleep by your fire?"

Bac kneeled down and looked into her eyes. "Calla you look really upset, what is the matter? Did I do something?"

Calla hesitated for several moments then said, "Last night Lazo came to my campfire."

"He did what?" Bac asked angrily. "What did he do?"

"He tried to kiss me but I stopped him," she said haltingly.

"Calla how did you stop him?"

"I put a knife to his throat."

Bac stood up and pulled Calla to a standing position. "Let's get your things. Calla for the rest of this mission you will sleep by my fire."

117

Natasha shot up in bed when she felt a hand on her shoulder. "It's just me," Gabriel said.

"Is something wrong?" Natasha asked as she tried to clear her head.

"We will be leaving soon," Gabriel said. "You will need to get dressed. Pack your things and some food."

Natasha jumped out of bed as Gabriel was walking towards the door. He turned and said, "You should probably wear your riding pants."

"Why?" Natasha asked in bewilderment.

"Because your skirts will likely fly up in the wind."

Gabriel was more than an older brother to Natasha. He had raised her since their parents died when she was nine. Natasha adored Gabriel; she thought he was the wisest and bravest man she had ever met. Natasha knew Gabriel's integrity was above reproach and his faith in The Great Ruler unshakable. Natasha tried to emulate these characteristics that she so valued in her brother. When Natasha walked out of her bedroom she saw that all of the Ruala warriors were already up.

"I made coffee," Gabriel said.

"You should have woken me up sooner," Natasha said as she hurried into the kitchen. "Do we have time for me to at least make you some eggs?"

"Yes," Gabriel replied.

The smell of fried eggs and ham filled the small farm house as Gabriel and the Rualas studied the maps that Raphael had sent along. Natasha called them to the breakfast table as she was slicing several loafs of bread. "I know it's not fancy," Natasha apologized as she filled their cups with coffee.

"It's just fine," Gabriel said.

"Gabriel I will carry you," Luca said. "I'm sure Calen wants to carry Natasha. It's easier for us if you do not carry any packs on your backs, we will carry them. And don't be surprised if you get dizzy, although it is easier at night because you are less likely to watch the ground."

The group ate their midnight breakfast, finished packing and were ready to leave in less than an hour. Natasha watched as Luca stepped behind Gabriel, put his arms around Gabriel's waist and ascended into the night sky.

"Are you ready?" Calen asked.

"I will admit that I am a little scared."

"I will hold you tightly against me to prevent extra movement of your body. You will be fine," Calen said reassuringly.

Natasha caught her breath when Calen put his arms around her; she was not sure if it was because she was nervous about flying or because she was nervous about being so close to him. Natasha squealed when they took flight.

"Are you alright?"

"Yes, this is exciting," Natasha replied. After a few minutes she said, "Calen tell me about your world."

The night air was cool and the sky was illuminated by the moon and the stars. The five Ruala warriors flew effortlessly in the night sky as they started their journey northward. Calen and Natasha talked for several hours before she became quiet. "Are you alright?" he asked again.

"I'm just really dizzy and I'm afraid I might get sick."

"It might help if we changed your position," Calen suggested.

"How?"

"Well, you could turn around and face me."

Natasha was quiet as she thought about his suggestion. "I don't think that is such a good idea."

"Why?"

119

"As tight as you are holding me and if I was facing you, I just don't think that would be a good idea."

"Natasha are you saying you are afraid you would kiss me?" Calen asked teasingly.

"Calen!"

Calen laughed, "I could hold you like I was carrying you and walking."

"Ok, let's try that."

"Natasha," Calen said with a seriousness she had not heard in his voice before. "If you change your position during flight, you must listen to me carefully and do exactly as I say. Do you promise?"

"Yes."

"First I will tell you what we are going to do. When I tell you, I will help you turn towards me. I want you to put your arms around my neck and hang on as tight as you can. Then I am going to let go of your waist with my left arm and I am going to grab your legs. Do you still want to do this?"

"I think so." The change of position only took a few seconds but they were terrifying seconds for Natasha.

"Just lean against me and close your eyes, it should help," Calen said as he cradled Natasha in his arms.

Natasha did as Calen said. Their bodies were pressed tightly against each other; Natasha could feel Calen's muscular frame through his warrior's robe. She found herself soaking up his smell; she felt embarrassed when she realized what she was doing. All of the Rualas smelled different from humans, they almost smelled like flowers Natasha thought as they soared through the night sky.

Natasha had never met a man who made her have such feelings. She felt both excited and a little afraid around him. There was something about Calen that made her feel like she had known him all of her life instead of just a few hours.

As she lay in Calen's arms she was thinking about her feelings for him and wondering why she felt a tinge of fear. It was then that Natasha realized she could become lost in Calen and that is what scared her.

When Bac and Calla walked into her small campsite they found Lazo stretched out in front of the fire, drinking whiskey. "Well it's about time ya came home," Lazo said as he turned and stared at both Calla and Bac. Calla let go of Bac's hand and walked boldly forward.

"Lazo I have chosen Bac."

"Well I guess I didn't realize there was a competition," Lazo said wryly as he slowly stood up, all the while eyeing his rival. Bac did not say a word as he and Lazo stared and started to circle each other. They reminded Calla of two stallions she had once seen fighting for dominance.

"Lazo go, I do not want you," Calla said loudly.

Lazo stopped, "If that's how ya feel Honey," he said and turned to leave the campsite. Lazo took two steps and quickly turn back towards Bac, throwing a knife at the Ruala warrior. Bac grabbed Calla and moved them both to the left; the knife whizzed past them. Bac lunged forward hitting Lazo in the stomach with all of his weight; knocking them both to the ground. Bac was on top of Lazo and punched him in the face with his right fist, then his left fist and again with his right fist before Lazo was able to push Bac off from him.

Others could hear the commotion and soon everyone was leaving their campsites to see the fight. Lazo picked up a piece of fire wood and swung it at Bac's head. Bac blocked it with his left forearm. The wood cut into Bac's skin and blood started to gush from the wound. Unfazed by his injury Bac quickly did a roundhouse kick to Lazo's stomach; as powerful as it was, the kick did not knock Lazo off his feet.

Both men quickly recovered their balance and Bac did a high sweeping kick, with his foot landing on the side of Lazo's head. Lazo fell to the ground, stunned by the blow. Bac jumped on top of Lazo and started to punch him in the face again.

121

Thaos was stepping forward from the crowd to stop the fight, when Sorren stopped him. "Let the kid get a few more blows in first," Sorren said.

Blood was gushing from Lazo's nose and Bac's arm as Bac landed blow after blow on Lazo's face. Lazo suddenly used all of his power to throw Bac off from him. Lazo took two steps backwards to put some distance between him and his opponent; then pulled a large knife out of his boot. Bac also pulled a knife out of the sheath on his belt.

"Stop them!" screamed Calla.

"Ok that's enough," Sorren said loudly and as one; warriors from all tribes subdued the fighters. With multiple people restraining them, the two fighters stopped.

"He's been coming to her campsite; she had to pull a knife on him last night," Bac said as he faced Sorren and Thedes.

"Is that true?" Thedes asked as he looked at Calla.

"Yes," she said as tears flowed down her face.

"Thedes he is our problem now," Sorren said. "Take him to my campsite," Sorren ordered the warriors who were restraining Lazo.

The warriors who were restraining Bac let go of him as Calla ran up to Bac crying. "Your arm, let me look at it."

"Wait until we get to my campsite," Bac said as he put his right arm around her shoulders. Then he turned and said to the many warriors standing around them. "She is not safe here, she will stay at my campsite; will some of you help move her things?" Calla had few belongings with her, so only two warriors helped to carry her things. One warrior a Ruala and the other a Nordes.

"A warrior shouldn't cry," Calla said as they walked to Bac's campsite. Bac still had his arm around Calla and now pulled her closer to him and kissed her on top of her head. "Whoever told you that warriors can't cry?" he asked with a smile. Calla put her arm around Bac's waist and leaned into him as they walked.

122

"This is it," said Bac as they reached his campsite. "You can just put her things anywhere."

"Let's look at that arm," the Nordes warrior said. "Calla can you get me some water and a cloth?"

"Thank you," said Bac as he sat down near the fire. What are you called?"

"I am Galen and it's about time someone took Lazo out," Galen said with disgust as he cleaned Bac's wound. "Some of us have been watching him and we knew it was just a matter of time before he started trouble." Then Galen turned to Calla and said, "I know we are all strangers but know that if you or anyone else in your tribe needs help you can come to us."

"Thank you," Calla said. "Is his arm broken?"

"No but he will need stitches," as Galen spoke another Nordes warrior walked into Bac's camp. She carried towels, bandages, a medical bag and a bottle of whiskey. "Galen, I thought you would need these," Sasha said.

"Bac, I would like you to meet my wife Sasha," Galen said. "Sasha this is Bac, Calla and I'm sorry I don't know your name," Galen said as he looked at the Ruala warrior standing near Bac.

"I am Gael."

"His father is the Chief of the Grand Council and the King of our people," Calla said with pride.

"It's nice to meet you," Galen said as he sterilized a needle in the campfire. "Bac I want you to drink some of that whiskey, actually a lot of that whiskey. And Gael would you hold his arm still."

"I don't want to get drunk in case Lazo returns," Bac said.

Galen looked at Sasha then said, "We will stay with you."

"As will I," Gael said.

"Start drinking," ordered Galen.

Bac was getting very drowsy from all the whiskey he drank. Calla quickly laid her blankets near the fire, since she did not know where Bac had put his. "Lay him down here," Calla said as Galen finished bandaging Bac's arm. Bac fell asleep as soon as he lay down.

"Sasha you stay here," Galen said. "I will get our bedding."

Gael looked at Galen, "I will wait until you return before I get mine." Galen nodded at Gael and walked away.

Both Sasha and Calla were sitting near Bac. Sasha lovingly moved some of Calla's hair from her eyes. "We have a daughter almost your age," Sasha said. "If you get scared or anyone bothers you, come and stay with us."

"Thank you," Calla said appreciatively.

It was late when Galen, Sasha and Gael brought their bedding to the campsite and went to sleep. Calla slipped under the blankets and cuddled close to Bac. Calla lay on her side with her head propped up on her arm and watched him sleep. Calla still couldn't believe that Bac had feelings for her. She thought he was so handsome and brave. Calla's heart swelled as she watched Bac sleep. She started to play with the dark curls that framed his rugged face. Then she leaned forward and softly kissed Bac on the lips.

"Am I dreaming or are you in bed with me?" Bac asked as he opened his eyes and turned towards Calla.

"Actually you are in my bed," she whispered. "I didn't know where your blankets were."

"Well I like it," Bac said softly. "You know you can kiss me again."

Calla giggled and kissed Bac on the lips. Bac was lying on his right side facing Calla, when he moved his left arm to hold her he winced in pain. "Oh Bac, don't hurt yourself. How can we do this so it won't hurt you?" she asked emotionally.

Bac thought about her question for a moment. "Well, maybe you can lie on top of me for a while."

"But won't that hurt you?"

"If you keep me distracted I won't feel the pain," Bac said with a grin as he rolled onto his back. "Just slide on top of me." They kissed for several minutes before Bac whispered, "Take your robe off."

"I can't, there are others here."

"Aren't you wearing anything under it?"

"Of course I am."

"What?"

"A camisole and panties," Calla whispered.

"You can take the robe off then."

"You still have your robe on."

Bac started to laugh, "Calla if I take my robe off we will be making love; are you ready for that?"

"No," she whispered. Calla sat up while she was still on top of Bac and untied her golden belt and laid it to the side of the blankets then she removed her warrior's robe and placed it next to the belt. The robe concealed her curvaceous figure which was now accented by a tight fitting camisole.

"You have a beautiful body," Bac whispered as desire surged through him.

Calla lowered herself on top of Bac and kissed him. As they kissed, he gently started to explore her womanly body.

Chapter X
Loved Ones

The first rays of the morning sun were just protruding into the darkness of the night when Gabriel's group landed at their first campsite.

"What was all of that fancy maneuvering you were doing?" Koby asked Calen.

Calen was holding Natasha until she was steady on her feet. "She was getting sick, so we changed positions."

"Are you alright?" Gabriel asked.

"Yes but I feel silly," Natasha said as she looked at Calen. "I am sorry I was so much trouble."

"You weren't any trouble," Calen said with a grin. "In fact you were very pleasant company when you weren't thinking about puking on me." Natasha shot Calen an angry look, as the others laughed.

"Calen, from the look on her face, I would not turn my back on her," Luca joked.

"Tonight we will start off like this," Calen said as they started their second night of flight. Calen picked Natasha up and cradled her in his arms, like he had done the night before. When he started to ascend into the sky, Natasha felt a thrill run through her but she was not afraid.

"How can you hold me so long? Don't your arms get tired?"

"I guess we are just built for this because this is how we carry everything when we fly."

Neither of them spoke for several minutes as they soared through the cool night air. "So last night when you were afraid of me holding you so that you faced me..."

Calen did not finish his question before Natasha interrupted, "I was not afraid!"

"Ok, last night when you didn't want me to hold you so you were facing me; was that because you were afraid you would kiss me?" Calen asked with a grin.

"I like how you ask me these questions when we are flying and I cannot leave."

"I'm not stupid," Calen said with a laugh.

"I don't want to answer your question."

"Why?" Natasha did not respond. "Are you afraid of hurting my feelings?"

"No, it's just embarrassing."

"Then you do want to kiss me," Calen teased.

Natasha was feeling embarrassed because she really did want to kiss Calen and wondered if he could tell. Natasha had wanted to kiss Calen since that first moment she saw him in the kitchen of the farmhouse.

Natasha had always focused on training and education so she could work with Gabriel on his missions. She had met boys that she would be mildly interested in for short periods of time, then she would forget about them. Calen on the other hand made her body feel alive. Natasha didn't understand it but somehow she felt like a woman around Calen and she desired him greatly.

"Calen why are you even asking me this?"

"Because I want to kiss you," he said softly. "And I have wanted to kiss you since the first moment I saw you."

Calen and Natasha were looking at each other as they spoke. Natasha was both thrilled and surprised when she heard Calen's words. She stared into his eyes, searching for a sign of his sincerity; what Natasha saw warmed her heart. She leaned up and softly kissed Calen on the lips, once, twice, three times they gently kissed. Then Calen brought her up closer to his face and kissed her passionately on the lips; a kiss that set them both on fire, a kiss that lasted too long, a kiss that almost made them fall from the sky.

The night after Lazo's and Bac's fight, Calla was cooking dinner for Bac at his campsite. Their visitors had left and it was the first time Bac and Calla were alone since the fight. Bac sat on a large log near the fire as Calla prepared their meal.

"As swollen as your arm is, does it hurt?" Calla asked.

"Yes."

Calla poured some whiskey into a cup and handed it to Bac. "Here this might help," she said and returned to her cooking.

"I really don't want to drink this," Bac said and put the cup down.

"You don't have to worry about Lazo," Calla said. "Sorren has him tied to a tree."

Bac laughed, "I like Sorren, he is a good man. In fact I like all of the Nordes tribesmen we have met."

"So do I," Calla said.

Bac watched as Calla was cutting his meat into small pieces, "I could probably do that," he said with a grin.

"You're hurt, I can do it. Galen and Sasha told me I could stay at their campsite too."

Bac was quiet for a moment before he spoke, "Are you going to?"

"I want to stay with you," Calla said as she put a plate of food on the log next to Bac. "I want to take care of you."

Bac lifted her hand to his mouth and kissed it. "Stay with me Calla. I have been in love with you for a very long time. We could make a life together."

Calla was standing in front of Bac and now knelt in front of him. "Bac I love you so much," she whispered then put her arms around his neck. "This is my dreams coming true. I can't believe you are really saying this."

Bac cradled Calla's face in his hands then kissed her passionately. "Why don't you lay the bedding out," Bac said as he stood up and started to remove his robe.

Luca and Gabriel were already making their second camp of the journey, when Calen and Natasha landed. Gabriel watched as the young couple walked towards him hand in hand. "You are holding hands and you both look more enamored now then you did before; what has changed?" Gabriel asked sternly.

"We kissed," Calen replied. "Gabriel we will not lie to you and I promise you, on my honor, that you have nothing to worry about."

"I will hold you to that, Calen."

"Gabriel I kissed him first," Natasha said. "If you want to be mad at any one, be mad at me."

"I'm not mad Natasha; just concerned."

"I know and I love you," Natasha said and kissed Gabriel on the cheek. "Now gentlemen I am going to prepare our breakfast." Both Gabriel and Natasha walked towards the packs that had been placed on the ground. Rabi walked up to Calen and whispered, "That must have been some kiss because I saw you falling."

"It was," Calen said with a grin. "It was."

The haze of love making still clung to the young couple as they walked hand in hand to Sorren's campsite. Bac and Calla were all smiles when they approached Sorren, Matthew, Stephan, Thaos and Thedes, all of whom were sitting near the campfire eating breakfast. Lazo was tied to a tree a few feet away.

"Sorren we would like to talk with you," Bac said cheerfully. Sorren stood up and walked closer to the young couple.

"We wanted to tell you that we will be getting married and we wanted to thank you for everything," Bac said as he let go of Calla's hand so he could extend his hand to Sorren.

129

As Sorren and Bac shook hands, Calla walked closer to Sorren, stretched up and kissed the old warrior on the cheek. "Thank you," she said, then returned to Bac's side.

"When are you getting married?" Sorren asked.

"As soon as we can make arrangements with the Sanuri," Bac replied.

"Bac, you and Calla can marry at our castle if you would like. It might be easier for you to meet up with the Sanuri there, than at the Ice Caves," Matthew offered.

Bac and Calla looked lovingly at each other. "Thank you Matthew," Bac said and the two Ruala warriors turned and walked back to their campsite. When Sorren turned back towards the campfire, the others were all looking at him and grinning.

"Sorren you are a hero again," Matthew said teasingly. "I can see it now, soon there will be a little Ruala baby named Sorren flying around."

"I like them, they are nice kids," Sorren said with a smile as he took his seat near the fire.

"Yes sir, she is a pretty thing," Lazo said.

Stephan quickly swung around and yelled, "Lazo I am about ready to kill you myself; will you just forget about the girl."

"She is going to be hard to forget," Lazo said with a malicious laugh.

"Is it true she put a knife to your throat?" Thaos asked Lazo.

"Sure is."

"Then why did you go back for more?" asked Thaos.

"Thaos ya know me," Lazo said with a salacious grin. "I like a girl with spunk."

After everyone had finished eating breakfast Gabriel looked at Calen and Natasha, "I would like to speak to both of you in private." Gabriel walked about ten yards from the campsite and Calen and Natasha followed him.

"You are both intelligent people so what I am about to say should not come as a surprise. Both of you look and act like you are in love." Natasha attempted to speak but Gabriel held his hand up and said, "Let me finish. If the two of you decide you want a relationship together that is your matter to work out. I will not stand in the way. Calen is a good man and I trust he would give you a good life. And Calen my sister would be a good wife to you."

"But we all know that emotions cloud thinking. If the two of you are considering a serious relationship you must discuss your future. Calen, I don't want my sister to feel like a prisoner in the Ice Caves. And Natasha I don't want my friend to be unhappy living in a world he does not want to be in." Both Calen and Natasha looked at each other with fear in their eyes for they had not considered these things.

"To say nothing about motherhood becoming more complicated because your babies have wings and you don't," Gabriel smiled and winked at them as he said these words. "But my responsibility is this mission. We are but a few and we have no idea what we are going to face. You both are experienced fighters but you know that if you cannot keep focused on the tasks at hand that you can get hurt or get someone else hurt."

"So I have a question for you and I want you both to think about your answer before you give it," Gabriel continued. "Can you keep your focus on this mission? Because if you cannot I will send you home. Now that doesn't mean you can't see each other anymore."

Natasha's face was filled with guilt. "Gabriel as usual you are right about everything. I am so sorry. But I took an oath to you and to The Great Ruler and I don't want to leave."

"Nor do I," Calen said.

"Then the two of you must work out a way to stay focused," Gabriel said.

"Gabriel we will, I promise," Natasha said. "But I have a question about something you said. Were you telling us that if we decided to have a serious relationship that you would give us your blessing?"

"Actually I believe I already did," Gabriel said with a grin.

Natasha suddenly turned around and walked back to the pile of packs. She started to take the weapons from the packs, inspect them and organize them. "Why did she leave so suddenly?" Calen asked.

"She's upset, you may want to talk with her," Gabriel said.

Calen walked over to Natasha and watched her as she inspected the blades, the fastenings and the straps of the weapons and sheaths. She pulled a bullwhip out of one of the packs and placed it on the ground.

"Whose whip is that?" Calen asked.

"Mine."

"Really?"

"Yes, it is a very useful tool," Natasha said. She would not look at Calen as she worked.

"Well girl, I guess there is a whole other side of you I need to get to know," Calen said kiddingly. She did not respond. "Natasha are you crying?"

"No," Natasha said as her voice was choking up and tears were flowing down her cheeks.

"Natasha why are you crying?"

Natasha continued to look only at the weapons as she spoke. "I feel so bad, Gabriel is right. I can't stop thinking about you and I don't want to get anyone hurt and I don't want to go home. And, and I love Gabriel and owe him everything. I don't want to lose him from my life."

"Why would you lose him?" Natasha didn't respond. After Calen thought about her words he said, "Oh, you're thinking that if we become serious you might not see your brother again." Natasha was kneeling on the ground and continued to work on the weapons without looking up but she nodded her head. "Natasha come here please."

Natasha stood up and walked up to Calen, who put his arms around her waist and pulled her close to him. "Honey we will work this out," Calen said as he moved a strand of her black curly hair out of her eyes.

"Honey, you called me Honey," Natasha said as she was crying.

Calen laughed and gave her a hug. "I have spent as much time in your world as in mine this year and most of it was working with your brother. If we decide to take this relationship slow, I can visit you and you can visit me in the Ice Caves. And if things work out that you and I make a commitment to each other and you come home with me, we can visit Gabriel and he can visit us. He is my friend and I want to keep him in my life too."

Calen and Natasha continued to hug each other as he spoke. She was crying on his shoulder and not speaking. "So, you can't stop thinking about me. What are you thinking?" Calen asked.

Natasha lifted her head so she could look Calen in the face. "Calen all I can think about is how much I want to kiss you. I have never felt like this before. I don't know, I think I am falling in love with you."

"Why are you making it sound like a bad thing?"

"I don't know if it is a good thing or maybe it is just not a good time."

"Well young lady, I find myself thinking about kissing you all of the time too. I think we just have to kiss more so we don't think about it so much." Natasha started to giggle and Calen leaned down and kissed her on the lips. "I think I'm falling in love with you too," he whispered into her ear.

Luca and Gabriel stood a few feet away watching the young couple. "Perhaps I should have waited to give them that talk," Gabriel joked.

133

"What did you tell them?" Luca asked.

"That whatever they decided, they had my blessing but they have to start focusing on this mission or I am going to send them home."

"That was generous of you," Luca said. "Gabriel, Calen and I grew up together and I have never seen him like this. He really does have feelings for her."

"I realize that," Gabriel said. "But she is inexperienced and he is her first love. Do you remember your first love; didn't you kind of go crazy?" Gabriel asked. Luca smiled. "If I would have told them they couldn't see each other that is all they would have thought about. I told them they have to work out something together so they can focus."

Luca was quiet for a few moments then he said, "You know that might really backfire on you."

"What do you mean?"

"They might decide to go for it, just to get all that sexual tension out of their systems."

"Oh, believe me I thought about that too," Gabriel said.

Gabriel and his group were preparing for their final flight to Taperia. As Natasha was preparing the evening meal; Gabriel asked The Great Ruler to send Enrops to their campsite. Within twenty minutes a large flock circled their camp and started to land. As the leader of the flock walked towards the campfire; Gabriel called out, "Fengu it is good to see you."

"You as well, Gabriel," replied the large bird. "What do you need?"

"We are headed to Taperia," Gabriel explained. "There are three high priests from Malga who we believe are trying to raise Omnibus from Solv and have kidnapped King Sudfad's son."

"I am aware of these things," Fengu replied.

"First we need a place to stay that is close to the city but remote enough that our Ruala friends will not be detected."

"That I may already be able to help with," Fengu said. "There is an old hotel on the outskirts of the city, on the north side. It was greatly damaged during the last Huta attack and it appears that the owners have abandoned it. But we will go there tonight and tell you if it is a safe place for you. What time are you planning to leave?"

"It is only a couple of hours from here to Taperia; we can wait for your return," Gabriel said. "Also, there are caves near King Roch's castle that were the original site chosen for the ascension of Omnibus. Do you know where they are?"

"Yes, we can take you there."

"Very good. Do you also know where the Sanuri is?"

"The Sanuri has many Ruala warriors with him. They entered Stordt a day ago and are travelling west towards Nora."

"Why Nora?"

"That I don't know."

"Would some of your flock fly to the Sanuri and tell him that we are here and what we are doing?"

"What exactly are you doing?" asked Fengu.

"We are going to try and stop the ascension of Omnibus. If the Sanuri has any information for us, we would appreciate it."

The following night, Natasha was in her room in the old abandoned hotel. She had just changed into a nightgown when she heard a sound on the balcony. Quietly Natasha stepped over to the table in the center of the room, pulled her sword from its sheath and swung around. Calen jumped back and started to laugh, "You are dangerous with that."

"I can be," Natasha said with a coy smile, then her tone changed. "Calen why are you coming through the balcony?"

"Honestly I wanted to see how easy it would be to break into your room. Did you know there are no locks on those doors?"

"I know; there isn't a lock on the front door either."

"What!" Calen said angrily. "I am not letting you stay in here alone."

"I am not sure any of the other rooms are much better."

"Then I will stay with you," Calen said with determination, then his voice softened. "How would you feel about that?"

As Calen spoke, Natasha returned the sword to its sheath and walked up to Calen. "I would like that. I haven't seen you all day and I missed you," Natasha said then kissed him. "Does Gabriel know you are here?"

"I told him that I wanted to say good night to my girl but he doesn't know yet that I will be spending the night."

"Your girl, am I your girl?"

"Do you want to be?"

"Yes," Natasha replied and kissed Calen again.

"Do you know what I mean when I ask you to be my girl?"

Natasha got a confused look on her face. She realized she was not familiar with Ruala customs. "Perhaps you should tell me."

"You and I will only see each other and no one else."

"Oh I like that," Natasha said and kissed Calen again. He could feel the curves of her body underneath the thin material of the nightgown. After they had kissed for several minutes, Calen removed his bow and quiver of arrows from his back. He unfastened a belt around his waist that held two knife sheaths. Then he walked over to the bed and sat down, as he unfastened another knife sheath that was on his lower leg.

"I bought you something," Natasha said with excitement. Calen watched Natasha as she walked towards him; her thin white nightgown clung to her body and flattered her womanly shape.

"Bought me something, why?"

"Because I wanted to." Calen gave Natasha a quizzical look. "Because I can't stop thinking about you and I wanted to do something nice for you. While I was shopping I realized I don't know what kind of things you like or even what your favorite color is," Natasha said as she handed Calen a small pouch. "If you don't like it tell me and I will get you something else."

Calen pulled a heavy golden chain from the pouch. The chain was made up from many strands of gold braided together. From the chain hung a pendant, which held a large ruby stone. The ruby was not polished and had a very rugged look. Calen was both surprised and overwhelmed by such an extravagant gift."

"Turn it over," Natasha said with excitement still in her voice.

Engraved on the back of the pendant was a circle. Inside of the circle were two horizontal lines and between the lines was a flame. "Do you know what that is?" Natasha asked.

"No."

"Many, many years ago there was a time when the followers of The Great Ruler were persecuted greatly, much more than they are now. This was the symbol that they would use so they could recognize each other. Calen you are so quiet, you don't like it do you?"

"Natasha I am so touched I just don't know what to say."

"Please try it on so I can see if it is large enough," Natasha laughed. "You do have a big neck."

"Why don't you put it on me," Calen said and shifted his position on the bed so she could stand behind him.

"Calen you have to do something with this collar, I can't get the necklace on you."

Calen was wearing the traditional white robe of the Ruala warriors. A belt of spun gold was wrapped around his waist and he wore sandals that strapped up his lower legs and were a golden color.

Calen stood up and removed his robe. Natasha knew Calen was muscular but now she caught her breath as she looked at Calen's powerful body that was clothed in only a pair of short white pants.

Calen sat back down so Natasha could reach his neck. She fastened the chain, then walked around him so she could view it from the front. "Calen I like it but please if you don't, tell me." Natasha took Calen's hand and attempted to pull him up. "Look in the mirror," she said.

The two walked over to a mirror that was hanging on the wall. "Natasha I love it, thank you," Calen said then leaned down and kissed her. "Natasha we have to talk."

Calen took Natasha's hand and the two walked over to the bed and sat down. "Honey did you buy this here?"

"Yes, when all of you were gone today I went shopping."

"By yourself?"

"Yes Calen, I can go shopping by myself," Natasha said with a laugh.

"Did you tell Gabriel or anyone you were going?"

"No."

"Natasha, Taperia has a reputation throughout all kingdoms for being an evil place. I don't want you walking alone around here."

"Calen I can take care of myself."

"Well, that does depend on how many attackers you are fighting and what if Sophie saw you? The mission would be compromised."

Natasha's eyes grew wide, "Calen I didn't think about that. I didn't see her but I wasn't really paying attention. Oh what was I thinking? I have to tell Gabriel." Natasha quickly stood up.

Calen grabbed Natasha's hand, "First you have to change; the others are with him. I will go with you."

Natasha quickly grabbed a dress and put it on over her nightgown while Calen put his warrior's robe back on. The two left her room and walked down the hallway to Gabriel's room.

When Calen and Natasha entered Gabriel's room, they saw only Gabriel and Luca sitting at a table drinking whiskey. Before Calen could close the door, Natasha was confessing. "Gabriel, I did something very stupid and may have jeopardized our mission. I went into Taperia to buy a gift for Calen and I didn't think that Sophie might see me."

"Did she?" Gabriel asked.

"Not that I know."

"Did you tell anyone you were going?"

"No."

"So we would not have known where you were if something happened?"

"That is true Gabriel and I am so sorry. Calen said this is exactly what you were talking about when you said we could be blinded by our emotions. I just didn't think it would happen to me. I swear I will never do it again, please don't send me home."

Gabriel looked at the young couple who were standing before him holding hands. "Tell me Natasha did you speak to everyone you met, like you usually do?"

"Yes," she answered with concern in her voice.

"We might be able to use this to our advantage. You always carry Mother's wedding rings, do you have them here?"

"Yes."

"Good, put them on and tomorrow I want you to return to Taperia, go shopping and talk with people. Tell them that you and your husband are new here and are looking for a home. Find out the local gossip. The Sanuri said they found many bodies in that cave; so people were being taken from someplace. And make it look convincing; really buy things so people don't think you were just after information."

"Gabriel," Calen said angrily. "I don't want her walking the streets of Taperia alone, it is too dangerous?"

"We will have Enrops follow her." Gabriel saw the angry look on Calen's face. "Calen you know you cannot go with her, we can't risk having any of you seen. Natasha fights like a man and she is so sweet and charming that people just open up and tell her everything. She is our best chance for getting information."

"I still don't like it," Calen's face was red as he spoke.

Natasha turned to Calen and said soothingly, "I will be alright; I do things like this all of the time."

Calen was so angry he did not speak for a few moments, then he said. "Gabriel you should know that Natasha and I have made a commitment to each other there will be no others in our lives." When Gabriel did not speak Calen continued. "There are no locks on any of her doors; I do not want her to stay alone in that room, so I am staying with her." Calen's voice was challenging as he said these words. But then he added, "But I will still keep my promise to you."

Natasha could see how angry Calen was becoming. She did not want Calen and Gabriel to fight, so Natasha quickly tried to change the subject. She let go of Calen's hand and walked closer to Gabriel, handing him a small pouch.

"Gabriel I know it does not excuse my poor judgment but this is what I bought for you."

"Thank you," Gabriel said as he watched Calen take Natasha's hand and walk her out of the room.

"Gabriel you know Calen didn't mean anything," Luca said after the door closed.

"How can I be mad at him, he is trying to protect my sister."

"Those two will end up getting married," Luca commented as he filled their glasses with more whiskey.

"They already are they just haven't realized it."

"I don't understand what you mean."

"Luca look at how protective Calen is of Natasha and how he is doing all of these little things to take care of her. And you don't know Natasha well, but she is very headstrong. My sister has devoted her entire life to the missions and taking care of me. If someone else would have said he didn't want Natasha to go to Taperia and get information there would be hell to pay; but she just smiled and held his hand. I am glad that she is falling in love with a good man. They are already defining their relationship."

"You didn't seem too mad about what she did," Luca said.

"Honestly, thinking about buying her boyfriend a gift instead of hunting a demon; it's the first time she started acting like a girl her age."

"Open yours," Luca said as he nodded towards the pouch.

Gabriel pulled a golden chain out of the pouch; at the end of the chain was a beautifully decorated gold pocket watch. Gabriel opened the cover on the watch and saw an inscription. *"With all my love, Natasha."* Without speaking, Gabriel handed the watch to Luca to look at.

"This is very beautiful," Luca said admiringly.

"Yes it is," Gabriel said softly.

Chapter XI
Planning

Calen was visibly angry as he and Natasha walked down the hallway from Gabriel's room to hers. Natasha could feel the tension coming off Calen and decided not to speak until they were behind closed doors. Calen held the door for Natasha, who walked to the table in the middle of the room without speaking. Earlier in the day Natasha had brought a variety of items from the abandoned hotel to her room, including glasses, a bottle of wine and a bottle of whiskey.

Natasha poured a small glass of wine for herself and a larger glass of whiskey for Calen. When she turned around she saw that Calen had removed his warrior's robe and sandals and was sitting on the bed wearing only his short white pants and the necklace she had given him.

Natasha walked up to Calen and handed him the glass of whiskey, while setting her glass on the bedside table. "I am moving my things in here tomorrow," Calen said almost confrontationally.

"I would like that," Natasha said softly as she stroked Calen's hair and kissed him on the forehead. Natasha sat down on the bed next to him. "Calen don't be mad at Gabriel. I have been training for these missions since I was a child and I beg him constantly to let me participate. If you want to be angry at anyone, be angry at me," she said soothingly.

Calen stared at Natasha without speaking; he was not prone to fits of anger but now he felt like he had hundreds of emotions surging through him and colliding.

"Calen, during our very first conversation you and I both said that we wanted to continue to work on these missions. Has something changed since then?" Calen still did not speak so Natasha continued to try to reason with him. "You have told me that all the women in your tribe are warriors and you have even told me a little about some of your former girlfriends. Would you be this angry if one of them was on this mission? Or Calen is something else going on that I am not seeing?"

142

"Honesty Natasha, right now I feel like I have a million thoughts running through me and I don't know what the answers are."

"I can accept that," Natasha said as she stood up and took off her dress, exposing the thin, white nightgown that draped off from both of her shoulders. She saw that Calen's glass was empty and picked it up. As Natasha walked to the table, to refill his glass; Calen realized that he could see through the material of her nightgown in the candlelight.

"Calen, I don't want the two men who I love, fighting," Natasha said as she poured his drink. Her back was turned to Calen and she was waiting for him to speak, but he did not. Natasha walked back to Calen, who took the drink and set it on the bedside table and pulled Natasha onto his lap.

"So you love me?" Calen asked.

"Yes," she said softly.

"Are you sure Natasha?"

"Calen I know things are moving so fast between us, sometimes I feel like my head is spinning. Maybe I am crazy to fall in love so fast but I do love you, I am convinced of that."

Calen let out a soft laugh. "Well I think we are both a little crazy but I love you too. It's like I have been enchanted since the moment I laid eyes on you." Calen kissed Natasha's forehead, then the tip of her nose, then her lips. "You aren't a witch are you?" he asked kiddingly.

"No," Natasha laughed. "But maybe that witch we are following put a spell on both of us." The two young lovers laughed and kissed again.

Calen pulled his head back so he could look into her eyes. "Natasha," Calen said very seriously. "We have a lot of decisions to make and we need to learn each other's customs but I am convinced that we can work through all of that." Calen cleared his throat and asked, "Natasha will you be my wife?"

Natasha suddenly realized that she was crying. Her face lit up in a warm and loving smile. "Yes Calen I will marry you." They kissed passionately for several moments.

"I was thinking that we could have Gabriel marry us," Calen said. "What would you think about getting married tomorrow, then having the celebrations after we complete this mission?"

"You have already been thinking about this, haven't you?" Natasha asked and laughed.

"What do you think?"

"Yes, I like that idea," Natasha said and kissed Calen on the cheek.

"Do you want to wear your mother's rings until we can have ours made?"

Natasha's eyes started to well up with tears again. "Actually I would like that a lot."

"You know Gabriel is going to want to make sure that we have thought this through," Calen said and laughed again. "So we may be up all night talking. You know Luca is my cousin; his parents were killed in battle when he was young and my parents raised the two of us as brothers. I have another cousin Misha who came to live with us when he was a small boy, and I have three older sisters who are all married and have children."

"Koby and Dagon spent so much time at our house when they were small that Father built them a room and they never left after that. Luca and I live together in a cabin in one of the forests of the Ice Caves. I will build a larger house for us." As Calen was telling Natasha about his life, she could see the tension leaving him. It was like a great weight was lifting from his shoulders. Calen's infectious smile had returned. While Natasha listened to Calen, she felt like her heart was swelling and about to burst through her chest.

Sophie was filled with relief when her carriage arrived in Taperia. They had been traveling all night and although Sophie tried to lay down on the seats of the carriage she could not sleep.

Sophie's aching body made her realize her age; almost five days in a carriage was more than she could deal with. Sophie had the driver stop at the Taperian Imperial Hotel which offered the most lavish lodging in the city. The hotel was located in the middle of the business section of Taperia, just buildings away from the General Store and a seamstress.

Many of the shopkeepers closed their doors and moved from Taperia after the second Huta attack. Among this exodus was the owner of the only woman's clothing store. Sophie planned to treat herself. She was going to the General Store and buy yard goods then have the seamstress make her some new dresses. But first she needed a hot bath and a meal.

Sophie entered the lobby of the hotel and walked directly to the clerk. "I need a room but first I need to know if some of my family are staying here. Do you have a man named Meekos as a guest?"

The young clerk looked over the register which was lying open on the counter. "No My Lady," the young boy said with a stutter.

"Well I have two cousins, who I am also expecting; their names are Tenebrae and Pravis." Sophie peered at the ledger as the boy read the names. "No My Lady, they have not arrived yet. Would you like to leave a message for them?"

"Actually I may be staying with you for quite a while. I would like your finest room and I would like to be notified when my family arrives." Sophie looked at the young boy sternly. "No matter what time of day or night, I want to be notified immediately."

"Yes My Lady."

"Also, when does your kitchen open for breakfast? I am starving and exhausted."

"My Lady, the cooks are already at work. I am sure that if you come back down in half of an hour the dining room will be open."

"Thank you," Sophie said wearily as she started to ascend the stairs.

Natasha and Calen got little sleep that night. They were both up before sunrise. Natasha was making breakfast as the Ruala warriors came down to the kitchen of the abandoned hotel.

"Flowers on the table," Rabi said. "Is today something special?" Natasha smiled, walked up and kissed Rabi on the cheek then returned to the stove. "Ok, what is going on?" he asked. "Where is Calen?"

"He will be back soon," Natasha replied. "Rabi would you pour the coffee?"

"Something smells really good," Koby said as he entered the kitchen.

"I have a morning cake and biscuits in the oven," Natasha said.

Dagon and Luca entered the kitchen together, "Are we having steaks for breakfast?" Dagon asked with surprise.

"Yes, I went shopping while you were all gone yesterday," Natasha said. "You are also having pancakes, potatoes and eggs."

"Are these wine glasses on the table for breakfast?" Luca asked.

"Something strange is going on here," Rabi said with a laugh.

"Well I don't care what it is," said Dagon as he took a seat at the table. "This food looks great and I am starving."

Just as Natasha finished putting all the food on the table, Gabriel and Calen walked into the kitchen; both men were smiling.

"Ok, what is going on here?" Rabi asked again. "You all look like a cat that ate a bird."

"Calen and Natasha are getting married right after breakfast," Gabriel said proudly and took a seat at the table. All of the Ruala warriors smiled and each congratulated the couple, as Calen poured a fine wine into their glasses.

"I honestly don't know why they waited so long," Koby said sarcastically.

146

"Trust me, we have talked at length about how fast this is going," Calen said. "And we think we have worked most of the issues out. We are going to have two homes, one here and the other in the Ice Caves." Then Calen looked at Luca. "You can have the cabin; I will build a bigger home for us."

"Good, I will move in with you, Luca," Koby said with a mouthful of food. "Your cabin is much nicer than mine."

"Gabriel, I hope you support me on this but I don't want Natasha working on any missions when she is pregnant," Calen said.

"I agree," Gabriel said with a big smile.

"And we are going to hire a Ruala nurse to chase the kids around since Natasha doesn't have wings." Everyone laughed at Calen's statement.

Luca looked at Natasha and said, "You just wait, they start flying before they walk."

"Really?" Natasha said with amazement. Calen's face was beaming as he looked at her and nodded.

"There was really only one thing we couldn't decide on," Calen said. "Gabriel do you want your own home in the Ice Caves or are you going to stay with us?"

Gabriel paused for a second as emotions flooded through him, "Well I will have to think about that," he said smiling.

"Gabriel, well both of you will love the Ice Caves; they are so beautiful," Dagon said as he stacked pancakes on his plate. "Calen what I want to know is, can we come over to your house to eat, I am really going to miss Natasha's cooking."

"Yes," Natasha replied as she was flattered by the comment.

"It's up to the two of you," Gabriel said. "But instead of building a home here, you could just move into the castle, it certainly is big enough."

"Castle!" Calen said. "You live in a castle?"

"Well you don't think I was going to raise a little girl in a monastery with all of those men, do you?" Gabriel asked.

"Calen, wait until you see our weapons room," Natasha whispered.

The wedding service was short. Natasha and Calen stood in front of Gabriel in the middle of the hotel's dining room, which Natasha had filled with bouquets of wild flowers she found near the building. The four Ruala warriors stood near the young couple as they said their vows.

"You may kiss the bride," Gabriel said at the conclusion of the service. Calen and Natasha kissed as the warriors clapped. Natasha threw her arms around Gabriel and kissed him, before she received a kiss from each of the Ruala warriors.

"I should get ready to go into town," Natasha said smiling.

"Natasha you just got married," Gabriel said with a grin. "The work can wait, take the day off."

Natasha smiled and looked at Calen. "What do you want to do?" she asked sweetly.

Calen gave her an incredulous look. "You mean you have to ask?"

Natasha suddenly blushed and started to smile. Calen put his arm around the shoulders of his bride and said to the others, "We will be in our room." As the newlyweds were walking through the dining room, Natasha could be heard saying, "Well Calen, I didn't know, it's daytime." Calen's laughter echoed through the large room.

"Gabriel are you alright?" Luca asked as he noticed the look of sadness on his friend's face.

"Yes, just a little sentimental," Gabriel said. "I've taken care of her my entire life, now it's up to Calen."

"I suspect the two of them are going to be spending more time with you than you realize," Luca said. "They were serious about you living with them in the Ice Caves."

"Yes I can just see it now," teased Dagon. "Uncle Gabriel trying to catch the babies with a butterfly net." The old hotel was filled with laughter.

"Pravis are you about done?" snapped Meekos irritably.

"Yelling at us doesn't do any good," Tenebrae said calmly as he read a newspaper in the sitting room of Meekos' hotel chambers.

"I am just anxious to be going," Meekos said as he carried another small suitcase into the sitting room. "Never have Sophie and I gone so long without communicating. And now of all times, at such a crucial time, it is making me very nervous."

"You know that if something was wrong she would have let you know," Tenebrae said in an effort to calm his friend.

"And what if she is unable to contact me?"

Before Tenebrae could respond, Pravis entered the sitting room with a handful of papers. "Meekos, you can't hurry this," Pravis growled. "The ink has to dry completely or people will be able to detect these papers are forgeries."

"Now you are sure you don't want one of us to go with you?" Tenebrae asked.

"I don't believe it is necessary," Meekos replied. "I believe Cerephus and Erebus will be so relieved to rid themselves of Roch that they will help me load his body into the coffin."

"Now remember you have to say he is your cousin," Pravis said. "All of the papers state he is your cousin."

"I'm not stupid!" Meekos growled. "It's you two I have to worry about."

"What do you mean?" asked Tenebrae who was clearly offended by the remark.

"I mean, who knows when the Sanuri will show up and if we don't have the boy in place and Roch in place; well, who knows what could happen."

149

"He does have a point," Pravis said.

"It's time for you to contact Vardin and tell him to bring the boy here," Meekos said as he walked out the door.

Later that evening Gabriel and Luca followed the smell of a baking roast to the kitchen of the hotel. Both men stood in the doorway and grinned as they watched Natasha dancing around the kitchen and singing.

"For a girl without wings, wouldn't you say she is floating Luca?" Gabriel asked.

"Natasha you look radiant," Luca said as he sat down at the kitchen table.

Natasha removed a towel that was covering a platter of sliced cheeses and sausages and put the platter on the table. "Would either of you like coffee?" she asked almost singing.

Both men were laughing as they watched Natasha gaily moving around the kitchen. She set two cups of steaming coffee in front of Gabriel and Luca. "I never realized that love making was so wonderful," Natasha said then her voice became a little more serious as she looked at Gabriel. "You have devoted your life to taking care of me Gabriel. I think you should think about yourself now. Perhaps you should look for a wife. You are young and so handsome, any woman would be darn lucky to have you."

Gabriel laughed loudly, "And what woman wants to be married to a demon hunter."

Without hesitating Natasha replied "I would. And besides there are female warriors." As Natasha put a plate of hot biscuits in front of Luca she asked. "Luca are there any Ruala women you think Gabriel could be interested in?"

"Boy, your little sister doesn't waste any time, does she?" Luca asked as he grabbed for the biscuits.

At that moment Calen walked into the kitchen grinning. He winked at Gabriel and Luca then walked up to Natasha who was standing at the stove with her back to the men. Calen put his arms around Natasha's waist and kissed the back of her neck.

"Natasha don't get mad but the guys think we should move to a different room."

Natasha turned around still holding the wooden spoon that she was stirring the gravy with. "Why?" she asked innocently.

Calen looked at his bride with a big grin on his face. "Because we are a little noisy and they are afraid they won't be able to sleep."

Natasha's eyes grew wide as she realized what Calen was saying. She buried her head in his chest and gasped, "I am so embarrassed."

Calen put his arms around Natasha and hugged her tightly, "There is nothing to be embarrassed about Honey." Suddenly he could feel her shoulders quivering. "Natasha are you crying or laughing."

"Laughing," Natasha said as she turned back to the stove, deliberately avoiding eye contact with any of the men in the room. After a brief moment she said, "Gabriel, I suppose this means Calen and I will have to move to a different room in the castle."

"Natasha, your chambers are too small for the two of you to live in," Gabriel said. "Actually I was thinking you should take a wing of the castle; that way you will have room for babies and guests."

"Really?" Natasha asked as she quickly turned and looked at her brother.

"Yes."

Natasha looked at Calen, who said, "Sounds fine to me."

Natasha ran over to Gabriel and hugged him and kissed him on the cheek. "Thank you, you are so generous."

"How long before dinner?" Calen asked as he grabbed some slices of cheese from the platter.

"At least twenty minutes," Natasha replied.

"I am going to start moving our things," Calen said and started towards the door.

"You might want to consider moving down to the first floor," Luca kidded.

Meekos started his journey to Cerephus' castle to retrieve the body of Roch. He had never received the messages that Sophie sent to him saying that Roch was missing; nor had she received any of his messages for several months. It was no coincidence that flocks of Enrops attacked each of the evil messengers and brought the messages to High Priest Raphael. But unfortunately for Raphael, Meekos and Sophie had started writing their messages in code. Raphael and some of the other priests were working diligently on trying to break the code.

The Patronus were still investigating the murders of the two priests discovered in Meekos' chambers as well as the crimes committed by High Priests Meekos, Tenebrae and Pravis. High Priest Josiah was leading the investigation into the murders. After the bodies were examined; Josiah and Raphael were convinced that Padres Sorben and Edwards were not killed by demons but by men.

Both Josiah and Raphael knew the implications of their findings. With so many of the Patronus keeping watch for Sophie the night of the murders; intruders into the monastery would have been detected. Both high priests feared the worse, that there were spies either among the priests assigned to the monastery or among the Patronus themselves.

Natasha was humming to herself as she walked around the streets of Taperia. Gabriel had bought a small uncovered boca for her to use as she posed as a curious newcomer to the area. The boca was pulled by only two horses. Natasha tied the boca in front of the General Store and walked up and down the street shopping and speaking with people. Natasha would periodically return to the boca to put the goods that she purchased in the back of the wagon.

Natasha spent a great deal of time in the General Store, since it was filled with women and she was listening to their conversations. She bought bags of flour, sugar, coffee, vegetables and all manner of canned goods. The store clerk helped Natasha carry these items to the boca; just as Natasha was walking out of the store she overheard a comment which made her turn around.

"My I am so absent minded today," Natasha said to the store clerk. "I forgot my shopping list and I just now remembered I need some more items."

"Well, you just holler if you need help finding anything missy," the old man said and walked behind a counter. The two women who got Natasha's attention were looking at clothing items so she joined them in that small area of the store.

"Why it is just the scariest thing," a woman in a blue bonnet was speaking. "My sister Alice, you've met Alice." An older woman with a white scarf on her head; nodded in agreement but did not speak. "Alice said that in the last few weeks over twenty men have gone missing from Nora. They are all thinking that Rogetts are hiding in the mines; not that anyone has lived to say they saw one. Now everyone is scared to work in the mines; can't say I blame them. I wouldn't want my Frank facing those horrid devils."

Natasha picked out a blouse for herself and a shirt for Gabriel, so she would not look conspicuous as she followed the two women in the store. "Are they sure it's Rogetts?" asked the woman wearing the scarf.

"What else could it be?" the woman in the bonnet replied.

"Well maybe there was a cave-in in the mines."

"Those men weren't together, well I take that back; Alice told me six men did go missing from the Nora Stone Works in the same day." The women changed the subject so Natasha paid for her items and walked to the boca. Across the street from the General Store was a tavern, as Natasha put her packages in the back of the boca she saw two men watching her from the doorway of the tavern.

153

Natasha shopped in a couple more stores but it wasn't until she walked into the butcher shop that she heard anything of interest. The shop was filled with people so Natasha took her time looking around; waiting for her turn at the counter. As Natasha listened to the conversations it was obvious to her that the old butcher seemed to know everything that was going on in the city. Ten customers left the store before Natasha approached the counter. She placed a very large order, hoping to have enough time to talk with the butcher.

"Mine you I am not complaining but are you feeding an army?" the butcher asked with a laugh.

Natasha batted her eyes at him and smiled, "No my husband's family is coming to visit. We haven't seen them since we got married and he has seven brothers. Believe me they will eat us out of house and home," Natasha said as she rolled her eyes. "We are new to Taperia and I couldn't help but hear you talking with some of your customers; you certainly sound knowledgeable about this area."

"Yep, you just ask me anything," the butcher said as he was wrapping two hams.

"Are you sure you wouldn't mind?" Natasha asked sweetly.

"No, just try me," the butcher said with pride. "You are going to need help carrying all of this, where is your boca?"

"In front of the General Store," Natasha replied. "I will move it up here. My husband and I are staying just outside of town in an abandoned farmhouse."

"There's a lot of them around here," the butcher said. "Ever since the Hutas started attacking us, people are moving out in groves. And some of the people that are moving in are not the kind you want for neighbors if you know what I mean. It's good to see a nice young couple move here."

"We want to buy a little place of our own but since we have been here I have heard about Huta's and Rogetts. Is it safe to live here?"

"It has never been really safe to live here; when King Roch was around, his men would terrorize this place. But no one has seen him of late. And like I said there are some pretty dangerous strangers arriving in town, more lately than usual."

"Why do you think that is?"

"Don't really know, but some of them are peculiar. Like this one fellar, I think he is a little touched in the head, myself. About two months ago he starts coming in the store. He comes in every Wednesday morning like clockwork. He said he's staying in one of those abandoned farmhouses but I know he's not alone because of the amount of food he buys. Every time he walks in here he keeps looking over his shoulder like he is expecting to get attacked. He pays then asks me if someone named the Sanuri has come into town. I still don't know who he is talking about."

Natasha felt like her heart leaped in her chest as the butcher was talking. "I am going to get the boca I will be right back."

"I ain't going nowhere," the butcher said with a laugh.

As Natasha climbed into the driver's seat of the boca she saw the two men from the tavern start walking towards her. Natasha flicked the lines hard as she said, "Gid up." The horses lunged forward forcing the men to jump back.

Natasha drove down the two blocks to the butcher shop and stopped the team in front of the shop. The butcher carried three big loads of packages to Natasha's boca, the last load she walked with him. When they walked out of the butcher shop they saw the two men from the tavern standing near her boca.

"Go back into your shop old man," one of the men ordered. The butcher did not move but looked terrified.

"Do as he says," Natasha said sweetly. "I will be alright." The butcher turned and ran back into his shop as Natasha walked around the front of the boca towards the driver's seat.

"You almost ran me over," said one of the men as he followed closely behind Natasha.

"Guess you shouldn't stand in front of my horses then," Natasha said as she turned her back to climb onto the boca. The man roughly grabbed her left arm; Natasha quickly swung around and pushed the tip of a knife against his crotch.

"I suggest you back off," Natasha said as she stared him in the eyes.

The man let go of her arm and backed up several steps. Natasha climbed onto the boca and flicked the lines, the horses sped off. About five minutes later an Enrop landed on the seat next to her. "Those men that were bothering you got four more with them and they are all riding this way."

"I can't lead them to the hotel," Natasha said as she started to unbutton the short jacket she was wearing. "Will you get Calen and Gabriel?"

"The road splits soon, take the right that way you will stay in the open so we can find you," the Enrop said and flew off. Natasha's jacket had numerous sheaths sewn into the lining, each sheath held a five inch knife with a three inch double blade. Natasha took two of the knives out and laid them on the front seat of the boca, she covered them with her skirt. She reached under the front seat and grabbed her bullwhip, which she placed beside her.

Although she had a five minute head start, the horses pulling the boca where no match for the riders following her. As Natasha got further from the city, the men quicken their pace.

Babu, the Enrop, flew through a broken window into the hotel and yelled, "Calen, Gabriel, Natasha needs you." All of the men came running out of the kitchen. "Quickly," yelled the large bird. "There are six men after her and she is leading them away from the hotel." Babu flew outside and towards the road he knew Natasha would be on. Rabi grabbed Gabriel as all of the Ruala warriors took to the sky.

In all of his years of combat, Calen had never known terror; now it filled his being. Calen's heart was racing and the adrenaline surging through him made him fly faster than he thought possible. Calen shot past the other Rualas, following Babu closely.

Within minutes two men rode on each side of Natasha's team of horses and grabbed the lines; forcing the horses to stop. Before the boca came to a complete stop Natasha stood up, grabbing her bullwhip. She whipped both of the men around their heads and faces multiple times before a third man jumped on the back of the boca and grabbed from behind.

Natasha turned quickly, while grabbing a knife from her jacket. She plunged the knife into the man's stomach and pushed him off the boca. Instinctively Natasha turned around to face the two men who had stopped the horses. She grabbed the two knives she had placed on the front seat. The first knife hit the man on her right in the throat. The second knife pierced the heart of the man on her left.

A fourth man climbed onto the back of the boca and grabbed Natasha from behind in a bear-hug fashion. Natasha stopped struggling and quickly dropped her center of gravity. She slid under his arms and jumped off from the boca; landing on her feet. Natasha turned to face her three attackers. One of the men started to work his way behind Natasha as the other two lunged at her. Natasha grabbed another knife from her jacket as the man closest to her lowered himself to pounce. He screamed for just a moment as the knife impaled his eye and entered his brain.

One of the men grabbed Natasha from behind and started to laugh. "You're a little wild thing," he said. As the second man walked towards her saying, "This is going to be more fun than I thought." Natasha lifted both of her legs off the ground and kicked the man in front of her in the groin. The man holding her was so distracted and aroused by her struggling that he was never aware of the young Ruala warrior who landed behind him and broke his neck.

Calen stepped over the body simultaneously grabbing Natasha and pushing her behind him. Calen pulled a knife from his sheath as he faced Natasha's last attacker. The man took two steps back as he pulled a large knife from a sheath on his belt. "Well what have we here?" the man asked as he stared at Calen.

"She is my wife," Calen growled.

The man seemed unfazed at seeing the Ruala warrior. He grinned maliciously and spit a wad of tobacco on the ground. "Well Angel boy, she was your wife." As the man lunged at Calen, Rabi dangled Gabriel over the attacker. Gabriel kicked the man in the head, knocking him out.

"Calen you can have him later," Gabriel yelled. "I want him alive, he may be of use to us."

Calen swung around and grabbed Natasha, "Are you alright?"

Natasha's heart melted when she saw the fear in his eyes. "I'm fine, I knew you would come for me," she said and kissed him on the lips. Calen hugged his wife tightly as he proudly said to the others, "She killed four before I got here."

Gabriel took a rope from one of the assailant's horses and used it to bind the still unconscious man. "Go through their pockets," he ordered. "We may find something useful."

"What do you want done with their horses?" Dagon asked.

"Free them. But we need to hide these bodies."

Dagon started to unsaddle the horses as Luca and Rabi searched the men's pockets. Koby pulled the knives out of the corpses and wiped them off. He walked up to Natasha and Calen. "Where did you have all of these knives?" Koby asked. Natasha held the sides of her jacket open so he could see the sheaths.

"Damn, Natasha," Koby said as he handed the knives to her.

"Gabriel I got some important information," Natasha said.

"Is that why these men were after you," he asked.

"No they were watching me from a tavern. I pulled a knife on one of them when they tried to stop me from leaving Taperia," Natasha replied.

"Gabriel I said it was too dangerous for her to go in there alone," Calen said angrily.

"But it was worth it," Natasha said. "I have information, possibly about the kidnappers and the location of the ascension."

Gabriel gave his sister a proud look. "Natasha I will ride back with you. Calen would you carry him and tie him up in the basement of the hotel, remember I want him alive for now."

Calen kissed Natasha again, then walked over and picked up the prisoner and soared into the sky. The other Ruala warriors dumped the bodies in a wooded area about one hundred yards from the roadway. Gabriel helped Natasha into the front passenger's seat of the boca then climbed into the driver's seat and headed the team towards the old hotel.

Sudfad was surprised that he had not received any messages from the Sanuri for some time. He started to worry, that perhaps the Sanuri had found Petra dead and wanted to give them the news in person. The days seemed like weeks as time took on a life of its own while the Royal Family waited for news about their son.

Raul and Simon were always protective of their families but this horrid intrusion into their lives caused them great fears. And the knowledge that spies had dwelled among them for so long without detection only increased their anxieties.

Petra was beloved by all the staff and the atmosphere in the castle was that of mourning. Maries' little sister Kyra was consumed with guilt that she was not able to save her friend from his kidnappers. Renya tried to be strong for the family but her heart was broken by the loss and uncertainty of Petra's situation. Her dear friend and companion Laurel tried to console the Queen but Petra's loss affected Laurel greatly also.

As a form of relaxation Sudfad had asked Alexander to teach him the craft of carpentry. The two men spent countless hours together in the shop that Sudfad had built for his friend. After Sudfad was sent home from his quest for Petra, he found himself spending more time in the workshop as a distraction from his pain; that was when an idea came to him.

Two nights later Gala, Padre Thomas and Padre Bartholomew were invited to join the Royal Family for dinner. The mood was solemn as Sudfad stood up to address his family and guests.

Sudfad was waiting for Marie to finish serving before he spoke, but to Marie's surprise Sudfad asked her to stay in the dining room.

"Our hearts are broken by the kidnapping of Petra, and fears consume us all about the safety of our children and grandchildren. It breaks my heart to see my family shattered and sad. We know that the Sanuri will find Petra and return him to us but until that time I believe we need some distractions from our grief."

"I have decided to build a learning center on the royal grounds. Our children and grandchildren will not only learn the disciplines of the sciences, mathematics and languages but will learn other skills and crafts as well."

"Both Padre Thomas and Padre Bartholomew are well educated men who have taught in schools and Padre Thomas has also taught at a university. They have both agreed to be teachers at this center. Gala will teach the knowledge of a healer. Alexander will teach carpentry and Raul and Simon I hope you come up with classes for the science of military arts as well as fighting skills and horse riding."

"I want to have classes for our children at every age of their lives. Vitomas and Annabelle you both have artistic talents and work diligently with your children; perhaps you would like to work on the lessons you want the small children to learn. This school is for our family so there is no limit as to what can be taught. Simon and Raul I would like you to locate a building site."

The family sat quietly as Sudfad spoke, all of them surprised and pleased by his plans. Sudfad turned to Renya. "And do you know anyone who can plan and organize immense projects like Renya and Laurel. Ladies the school is now in your capable hands."

"What a wonderful idea," Renya said and stood up so she could kiss Sudfad on the cheek.

"There is more," Sudfad said. "Marie members of your family have become part of ours and little Kyra risked her life trying to save Petra. If you or any of your family would like to attend classes at our learning center you are all more than welcomed."

Marie was visibly overwhelmed, before she could speak Annabelle said, "Marie should teach cooking classes."

"I agree," said Vitomas with delight.

"My Lord I am so overwhelmed I don't know what to say, except for thank you," Marie blurted out as she started to cry.

"I will not force anyone to be a part of this project," Sudfad said as he looked at the faces around the table. Is there anyone here who does not want to participate, there is nothing wrong if you don't?" No one raised their hands or said a word they all smiled at Sudfad.

"I am envisioning a large center that will fulfill our future needs. So please consider this as you plan and design the classrooms. Raul and Simon you have both attended universities, I believe your experience would be most helpful here."

"Sudfad when you say you are envisioning a large center," Renya asked. "Are you planning on including Mathas' family?"

"Yes," Sudfad said, "And Thedes and Ibula also; they are part of our family now. And honestly I feel there will be more."

"This is exciting," Renya said and kissed Sudfad on the cheek again.

"I want a learning center where our children will receive excellent educations while being safe from the darkness that attacks us," Sudfad said.

It took two more days for Sudfad's men to locate the seven remaining spies who were hiding among the thousands of Wetprian troops stationed at Fort Salar. The last two were caught as they tried to flee the fort; a patrol of Ruala warriors captured them. Simon and Raul administered Gala's truth potion to each man individually but little if any new information was obtained. It was clear to the Royal Family that the spies were nothing more than dangerous minions.

The nine spies were locked in the dungeons of Fort Salar. Each man was locked in a separate cell. Timothy, son of Fahron, laughed as each spy was escorted down the dismal hallway to their cells. Timothy would call out taunts and laugh at the prisoners as they were locked up. A large man named Thronson stopped before he entered the cell, he turned and yelled at Timothy, "You little bastard, if you don't shut up I'm coming over there and pulling that tongue out of your head."

"Keep moving," one of the guards growled as he pushed Thronson into a cell and locked the door behind him. Then the guard walked over to Timothy's cell. "We're all getting sick of that mouth of yours. I have half a mind to open a few doors around here and let those guys kill you, the King certainly won't mind."

Timothy had been jumping around the cell door on his haunches. Now he stopped and sat down on the floor without speaking.

Chapter XI
Discoveries

Gabriel threw a bucket of cold water on the Taperian man they had tied to a chair in the basement of the abandoned hotel.

"What the hell!" yelled the man as he was forced into consciousness. "Who the hell are you?" he growled.

Gabriel backhanded the man across the face. The blow was so powerful that it knocked the man and the chair over. Calen and Luca righted the chair back up as Gabriel said with great intensity, "I am the brother of the girl you tried to rape."

The Taperian man looked at both Calen and Luca and clearly saw that all three of the men in the room wanted him dead. "What do you want?" the man asked.

"Information," Gabriel growled.

"What kind of information?" Gabriel did not answer. "Can I make a deal?" the man asked as he was looking around the room for exits and weapons.

"What kind of deal?" Gabriel asked.

"If I can find a way to help you with what you are looking for, will you let me go?"

"I guess that depends on you," said Gabriel.

Natasha told Gabriel all of the things she had heard and observed in Taperia as they rode back to the hotel. Upon their return to the hotel, Gabriel went directly to the basement for his first interrogation of the Taperian prisoner. Now, hours later he shared Natasha's information with the Ruala warriors as they ate their dinner.

"This is Monday," Gabriel said. "Early Wednesday morning I will go to the butcher's shop and wait for the man asking about the Sanuri. If he shows I will have a flock of Enrops here to follow him."

"I would like you close behind," Gabriel said to the Rualas. "If indeed this man is one of the kidnappers, who knows what you will find when you get there."

"We have all seen this boy," Luca said. "King Sudfad and Queen Renya invited all the Rualas and Shettees to their castle to thank us for saving their sons. Some months ago the Sanuri had asked the Rualas to protect Raul and Simon. But when our warriors found the Princes, they had been battling a small army of Hutas and were almost dead. I wasn't in the group that found them but Calen and Dagon were."

"Those two men were hacked to pieces," Dagon said. "The Sanuri himself came to the Ice Caves to heal them and even after that they lived in the Ice Caves for several months. Princess Ibula and Thedes cared for Raul and Simon in their own home. Later King Sudfad and Queen Renya adopted Ibula and Thedes into their family."

"So Petra would recognize Ruala warriors, this is good," Gabriel said. "I sent a message to the Sanuri with the information that Natasha provided. I ask that he send some of the Ruala warriors to assist us."

"Good," Calen said as he hungrily devoured his dinner. "I was going to suggest that. We might only get one good chance to save the boy and we should be prepared."

"My thoughts exactly," Gabriel said. "I also sent a letter to Sudfad telling him that we are following a lead on the kidnappers."

"Did you get any information from that horrible man in the basement?" Natasha asked as she walked around the table filling coffee cups.

"He wants to bargain for his life, but so far he hasn't given us any useful information," Gabriel said.

"Let him get really hungry then entice him with some of Natasha's good cooking, he might be a little more willing to cooperate," Koby suggested.

"That's not a bad idea," Gabriel said. "It might be more effective if I send new faces down to him. Koby, Dagon and Rabi you get the next turn with him."

"Maybe you should let Natasha at him," Koby said teasingly. Then he looked at the other Ruala warriors. "Did you see that jacket she was wearing the entire lining was nothing but knife sheaths?"

"Oh Koby I have more surprises than that," Natasha said kiddingly.

"I don't want you anywhere near that man," Calen said sternly as he looked at Natasha.

"Calen we were only joking around, I don't plan to go near him," Natasha said as she walked up and kissed Calen on the cheek. Natasha knew how scared Calen was for her and she did not want to make an issue of her participation in the missions now.

The Sanuri always made his camp separate from the other warriors so The Lion could visit him; for The Lion did not show himself to the others.

"I just received a message from Gabriel," the Sanuri said as The Lion walked towards the campfire. "Natasha got information about some men who might be Petra's kidnappers. Gabriel plans to set a trap and is requesting some Ruala warriors."

"A lot of good people are helping us and many will lose their lives before this is over. Send Gabriel at least one hundred warriors; he will need them. Also, as we speak Sudfad is telling his family that he plans to build a great learning center on their property. He has no idea of the energies he has just put into motion. Sudfad proposed this project to help his family heal, yet his plans will help to heal this world. When the time is right, I want you to teach of The Great Ruler at this school."

"Of course. I am quite pleased with his idea."

"As are we. What is the matter my friend?"

"I feel like I could be doing so much more," the Sanuri said with frustration. "There is such darkness on the horizon, I could stop it; we could stop it."

"If a father never allows a child to learn to walk for fear that child will fall and hurt itself; what is that father doing?"

"The father is using his fears to cripple his child," the answer is obvious but I do not understand the significance here."

"People cripple themselves with their fears, the power they give to their fears cause the fears to grow and to magnify. Soon the fears of the fathers are crippling the children, then their kingdoms, then their worlds. And where there is fear there is hatred; this is the darkness you see on the horizon."

"And these are also some of the tests of these worlds," The Lion continued. "Can the beings rise above the fear and hatred and return to the powerful, loving beings The Great Ruler created. Sanuri you have walked in these worlds for hundreds of years and you look upon the beings here as your children. As a father there is a time to protect them and a time to give them wings. How will they ever conquer the tests if you do not allow the tests to be taken?"

The next few days were uneventful for Sorren, Stephan, Matthew, Thaos and the others who traveled to Zorta. Sorren kept Lazo tied up much of the time, as he did not trust the man; nor should Sorren have. Lazo was a patient man, one of the few good qualities he possessed. Lazo knew he could not steal the treasures that the demons were using as bounties by himself. This small army of warriors that was traveling to Zorta would fight the demons, allowing Lazo the distraction that he needed.

Lazo could tolerate being tied up for a few days because ultimately he would get what he wanted. And one of the things he wanted was Calla. His lust for her was overwhelming him. Calla was becoming an obsession in his mind. It did not matter to Lazo that Calla did not want him; he would take her for his own, of that he was sure. Lazo spent countless hours planning different scenarios of how he could kill Bac and escape with Calla.

"Lazo you're awfully quiet over there," Thaos said. "Are you still alive?"

"Yep, just sitting her fantasizing about that little Ruala girl." Lazo knew that his remarks irritated Stephan, which caused Lazo amusement.

"We will be at Fort Castor tomorrow," Matthew said. "Lazo if you are not going to be a useful member of this group, I will have you locked up at the fort; because you are more trouble than you are worth right now."

The possibility of being locked up at the fort was not something that Lazo had anticipated. He knew he had to work his way into their good graces if he had a chance of getting the treasure and the girl. "Aw fellas, ya are so busy holding my actions with Calla against me that you haven't given me a chance to be useful."

"We might have forgotten about your actions if you weren't making disgusting remarks every ten minutes," Stephan said as he put another log on the campfire.

"Perhaps it's time for Lazo to prove his worth on this mission," Sorren said. "Lazo what can you offer us that no one else here can?" Sorren asked seriously.

"Aw Sorren, you're making me pull my ace out," Lazo said with a grin. "I had hoped to keep it for a rainy day." Stephan looked at Matthew and rolled his eyes at Lazo's comment.

"Well we're waiting," Sorren said.

"I always got a kick out of watching George come to visit Juleta, that poor bastard probably never had sex before he met her. Juleta had him wrapped around her finger and knowing how ruthless she was, I wondered what she was setting him up for," Lazo said. "Ya know I can talk better with a little whiskey." Sorren filled a cup with whiskey and gave it to Lazo. Lazo's hands were tied in front so he could eat and drink.

"George always brought Juleta gifts, at first flowers and such, but it wasn't long before he was hauling boxes and bags from his carriage. That's when I realized that his behavior had changed."

"When his driver would let George out of the carriage, George would look around guilty-like before he brought things into the castle. The old boy started to act more and more like he was afraid he was being watched, that's when I started to wonder what he was hiding."

"I sneaked inside the castle one night and watched George's driver carrying things into the castle, some of the things he was carrying looked damn heavy. Juleta was telling the driver to put everything down by a wall in the parlor. Thaos ya know the wall, it had a big mirror that she was always looking at. Well after George gets his rocks off and leaves, Juleta goes into the parlor. She took the mirror off the wall and damn if there wasn't a lever hidden behind the mirror. I saw her turn the lever and heard a sound like something heavy was moving."

"Suddenly Juleta stops and looks in my direction like she could sense I was there. I beat it out of there. The real reason I went back to the castle was to see what was in that hidden room; that's when I found the dolls."

"So what was in there?" Thaos asked impatiently.

Lazo laughed, "Not a damn thing but ya could see the outlines of what was on the shelves and floor. The outlines were made from ash from that fire, so someone came in after your battle and removed the stuff."

"What did the outlines look like?" Matthew asked.

"On the floor there were outlines of five good sized chests. On the shelves the outlines were strange, didn't know what made them until I found a few gold nuggets on one of the shelves."

"So she did rob the mines," Thaos said.

"That's what those outlines looked like, bags of gold."

"So your ace up your sleeve; is that Juleta had more treasure than we thought," Stephan said contemptuously.

"Stephan you are always so tetchy, don't know how that pretty little wife of yours puts up with you."

"Don't let him get to you," Matthew said to his friend.

168

"Well, I figured if someone was careless enough to leave a couple of gold nuggets behind they might have left something else, so I tore that room apart. If one of ya wants to look in my right shirt pocket you will see what else I found." No one moved from the campfire so Sorren stood up and walked over to Lazo. "It's the envelope." Lazo said as Sorren put his hand in the pocket and felt several different pieces of paper. As Sorren was taking the envelope from Lazo, Thedes joined Thaos, Matthew and Stephan at the camp fire.

"What's going on?" Thedes asked.

"Lazo here is trying to prove to us that he is worth keeping around and not locking up at the fort," said Stephan.

Sorren returned to the fire and pulled a letter out of the already opened envelope. Sorren read the first page of the letter in silence then handed it to Matthew who was sitting closet to him. The second page was a map.

"I have never heard of King Douma or the Kingdom of Ogg," said Matthew as he passed the letter to the next man.

"I have," Thedes said, "I will tell you when we have all read this letter."

"I have too," said Sorren as he handed the map to Matthew. "But honestly I thought it was just an ancient myth. I mean who can live under water?"

Calen was patiently waiting for Natasha to finish preparing the dough for the morning's biscuits. Although the abandoned hotel was a huge building, the group of demon hunters tended to congregate in the small kitchen. Natasha always had a pot of coffee on the fire and usually had treats of some kind for her newly acquired family.

Natasha took great pride in her cooking. Even before their parents died Gabriel took care of his little sister. Natasha loved Gabriel with all her heart and could never figure out a way to repay him for all he was doing for her. Until one day Natasha overheard some women talk about cooking and how it pleased their families.

Natasha was ten at the time and immersed herself in learning the skills of cooking and baking. It did not take long before Gabriel was praising her meals and inviting others over for dinner. For Natasha cooking a great meal; was the one way she felt like she was both taking care of Gabriel and doing something for him.

The only reason Gabriel allowed Natasha to accompany him on her first mission was because Natasha asked to come along as the cook. When Natasha saw what her brother really did on his missions she was both horrified and thrilled.

Determined to help and to protect the brother who she idolized, Natasha became obsessed with learning every skill necessary to work on the missions. When other girls her age were playing with dolls or thinking of boys; Natasha was taking sword lessons and learning how to climb rock walls and how to fight.

"I'm done," Natasha announced as she placed a towel over the dough, which would rise during the night.

Calen quickly stood up from his chair, took Natasha's hand and announced that they were going to bed. The men at the table laughed. "Calen it seems like you two retire earlier every night," Luca said teasingly. "Pretty soon it's going to be after lunch."

Calen laughed as he escorted his bride through the kitchen. "When we are done with this mission, Natasha and I are spending a week in bed."

When all of the men had finished reading the letter Sorren turned to Thedes, "Sounds like you know more about this kingdom, why don't you go first."

"As you know my people lived in the Kingdom of Xepoltr for hundreds of years. To the west of our kingdom is the Waste Lands of Manod. They are called the Waste Lands because nothing can survive there. The land is barren of all vegetation. There are tar pits and quicksand pits everywhere. Water is scarce in the Waste Lands and it is said that anyone who travels through them is never seen again."

"Have you actually seen the Waste Lands?" Thaos asked.

"Oh yes, there is a ritual of manhood that each Shettee boy must complete to become a warrior. When we lived in Xepoltr part of that ritual was to survive in the Waste Lands for a week," Thedes said. "To the west of the Waste Lands is the Schenomi Sea. Legends say that at one time the Waste Lands were lush and beautiful and inhabited by a tribe of humans called the Valdees.

It is believed that the Valdees were such a cruel people that they displeased their gods, who punished them by turning their lands into the Waste Lands. The Valdees are said to have declared war against their gods and after several battles the Valdees knew they would be defeated. Their people had no place to go, so their king ordered them into the sea.

Their king was named Douma. It is said that he formed an alliance with a powerful demon who cast a spell on Douma's people allowing them to breath in water. Douma is said to have built an entire kingdom on the floor of the Schenomi Sea; which he named Ogg."

"That sounds like a bunch of crap to me," Lazo said as he was starting to feel his whiskey.

"And yet there is a letter, signed by King Douma of the Kingdom of Ogg, telling Juleta where to bury his payment," Sorren said. "My people have heard these same legends about the Waste Lands and the Schenomi Sea. The only difference is that we have heard that the Valdees are still paying tribute to the demon that saved them, so at times they sneak into the kingdoms and do his bidding."

"I would take this letter very seriously," Thedes said.

"I just wish it said what services she paid for," said Sorren.

"Unfortunately, knowing how full of hatred my sister was, it is probably a threat against one of our families," Matthew said sadly. "It's like this never ends."

"Thaos look at that map," Lazo called over. "Recognize anything?"

Thaos studied the map, which did not have the names of any towns or cities on it. "Thedes is this where the Schenomi Sea is?" Thaos asked as he pointed to the left lower corner of the map.

171

Thedes scrutinized the map for several minutes then both he and Thaos looked at each other.

"What is it?" Matthew asked.

"This appears to be a map of all the water ways from the Schenomi Sea to the Kingdoms, of Zorta, Lentz and Wetpr," Thedes said.

"Well, that would make sense if the Valdees live in water," Sorren said. "They don't need information about roads."

"Keep looking Thaos," Lazo said. "Every time we went into the castle what was our girl doing?"

"Staring out of the parlor windows at the River Toba," Thaos said as he held the map closer to the light of the fire. "It's very faint but there is an 'X' by the river behind her castle."

"I suspect that is where the payment is buried," Lazo said.

As Thaos, Matthew, Stephan, Sorren and Thedes sat around their campfire studying the map and letter that Lazo had taken from Juleta's castle; Thedes opened up and for the first time told them of the destruction of his kingdom. Even Lazo stopped making comments as he listened to Thedes describe the horrors of the war between the Hutas and the Shettees that lasted for centuries.

Thedes was not one to show his emotions, a trait shared by most Shettees but as he described the eleven day siege that ended in the destruction of the Kingdom of Xepoltr, his voice trembled. "The sky would darken as thousands of arrows rained upon my people. The Hutas soaked the tips of their arrows in the venom of the Atha serpent," Thedes hesitated for a moment. "That venom is very strong and usually paralyzes and kills instantly but the Hutas mixed it with something to make my people endure horrible deaths."

"The children would instantly go into convulsions. They would bleed from their eyes and nose and puke up blood. At the very end their skin would turn black. Adults had the same reactions but it took longer for them to die."

"Our leader was King Neputa, he was a fierce warrior," Thedes continued. "None of us could believe that we would ever lose to those demons, but Neputa in his wisdom saw the truth. He ordered me and five other warriors to take all of the women and children to the monastery at Avaide and to stay there until he came for us."

"We did not want to leave but now I realize that if we had not, our race would have been wiped off the face of this world. The priests took us in for many months; they treated us well, even though we were not of their race or faith. Then one day a little human boy rode to the monastery to warn us that the Hutas were coming to the monastery for us, that boy was Petra, the adopted son of King Sudfad."

Thedes paused as Sorren filled everyone's cups with whiskey, including Lazo's. "I am sure you have all heard the story. Six priests led us through six long tunnels to the base of the Safer Mountains. The Hutas tortured and killed the priests who stayed behind at the monastery. Petra was hiding in the woods and managed to pull an injured priest to safety. While Petra was helping us; the Hutas destroyed his village and killed his family."

"So how did Petra end up being adopted by Sudfad?" Sorren asked.

"The Sanuri found Petra and Padre Bartholomew and took care of them. Eventually the Sanuri brought Petra with him to Sudfad's castle and according to Simon; Renya adopted the boy the next day."

"Thedes I worked for a man named Tafer for a while," Thaos said. "Tafer has a castle northwest of the monastery at Avaide. I was hired to protect his family from the Hutas. Almost two years after the fall of your kingdom, Shettees were again seen in the Kingdom of Norkv. People were talking about a group of Shettees who had escaped the Huta death camps and were looking for their people."

Thedes stared at Thaos in utter disbelief, "Thaos are you saying some of my people still live?"

"Thedes I don't know where they are now; but many people in Norkv were talking about them and giving them shelter and food."

"I bet they came to the monastery and when they saw that it had been destroyed they started to search for us," Thedes said in almost a whisper.

"Thedes," Lazo said seriously. "I have spent a great deal of time in the Kingdom of Ganz, especially Port Friada. One night I was in a tavern playing cards and some men at the bar were talking about running into a group of Shettees. Everyone in the tavern started listening to them because of course everyone thought your tribe had been wiped out. These men said they talked with the leader of the group, a one armed fella named Trit, I think."

"Tristt," Thedes said with jubilation. "He was a friend of mine."

"Well these guys said that Tristt said he was heading north and another group of Shettees was heading west, trying to find their people."

"West, that would be the Waste Lands," Thedes said. "But it would make sense, because Marba is to the east, which is where they escaped from and the Rosu Mountains border our kingdom on the south." Thedes paused as he allowed himself to consider the idea that some of his tribe might still be alive. "You two have given me hope that I will see my kind again; I have not felt that in a very long time. Thank you."

Natasha got up early to start the bread and biscuits. As she was walking in the kitchen towards the stove she glanced out of the window and jumped. Natasha ran back into her bedroom, "Calen wake up."

Calen jumped up, "Are you alright?" He blurted out although he was not completely awake.

"Calen, there is an army of Ruala warriors outside. I don't know how I am going to feed them all," Natasha said as she pulled back the curtains and let the rays of the rising sun into their small room.

"Honey wake Gabriel," Calen said as he got out of bed and started to dress. "I'm going outside." Then as an afterthought Calen added, "Don't worry about feeding them all, our troops do cook their own food in the field."

174

As Natasha started to walk out of the bedroom Calen called out, "On no you don't, come back here." Natasha giggled and walked up to Calen, who grabbed her and kissed her passionately. "You think I am kidding about us spending a week in bed, don't you?"

"Oh no I don't," Natasha replied. "And I am looking forward to it too." Calen kissed Natasha again and did not want to let go of her.

"Honey we can't do this now," Natasha said with a laugh.

Calen let out a loud sigh, "I know, you better leave now while I still have some willpower."

By the time Gabriel and Natasha walked outside, Calen was already talking with the Rualas' leader.

"This is Prince Lakin the leader of these warriors," Calen said. "And this is Gabriel and my beautiful wife Natasha," Calen said and put his arm around Natasha's waist.

"Calen your wife," Lakin said with surprise. "Congratulations." Lakin stepped forward and kissed Natasha on the cheek. "Your husband is a fierce warrior and a good man and also my cousin."

Natasha smiled, "If you will excuse me I am going to start breakfast, Prince Lakin I hope you will join us."

"Thank you and you can just call me Lakin, after all we are family now."

"You are just in time," Gabriel said.

By the time Luca, Dagon, Rabi and Koby came down to the kitchen, Gabriel and Calen had briefed Lakin about their mission and the information that Natasha had discovered. Natasha started serving breakfast as the Ruala warriors greeted their Prince.

"After some of you retired last night, I received word that the witch had arrived in Taperia," Gabriel said. "She is staying in the Taperian Imperial Hotel on the top floor with a balcony window that faces the street. So far she is alone."

175

"Do you think she had anything to do with the attack on Natasha?" Calen asked.

"At this point no," Gabriel replied. "It appears that those pigs were acting on their own."

"What happened?" Lakin asked.

Luca looked at Calen who was getting red in the face, so Luca decided to explain. "Six men followed Natasha from Taperia and attacked her."

Lakin quickly looked at Natasha. "Are you alright?" he asked with concern.

"She killed four of them before Calen got to her," Koby said with admiration. "And our little sister doesn't call herself a warrior."

Natasha smiled at Koby's comment. "We still have one alive," Gabriel said. "He is tied in the basement. I thought we might get some information from him, but so far nothing useful."

"Mind if I try?" Lakin asked.

"Oh that's right," Luca said. "You can do that hocus pocus thing."

"What's he talking about?" Gabriel asked.

"It's something my father taught me," Lakin said. "It's hard to describe. It's like putting people to sleep on a certain level of their brain; so they appear to be awake and talking but they really aren't. People are more likely to tell the truth in this condition."

"Have at him," Gabriel said. "But first we have business in Taperia."

Lakin turned to Natasha, "I must say it has been a long time since I have eaten such delicious food, thank you."

"She always cooks like this," Rabi said with a grin. "Calen doesn't know it yet but we're all moving in with them."

Calen laughed, "Oh we know it."

Gabriel walked into the butcher shop in Taperia as soon as the doors opened. He sat at one of the tables and read a newspaper, while the butcher performed his daily routine. The congenial butcher gave Gabriel a cup of coffee and struck up a conversation. At least an hour passed before customers started to enter the shop. Two more hours passed before Vardin walked in. Just as the butcher had described to Natasha, Vardin suspiciously looked at everything.

Vardin had tied his horse in front of the window of the butcher shop so Gabriel could see that it appeared Vardin had come into the city alone. Being a creature of habit; Vardin inquired about the Sanuri before he exited the building. Gabriel waited until Vardin was on his horse before he walked out of the shop and stood on the wooden sidewalk in front of the butcher shop. Gabriel nodded to two Enrops who were perched on the hitching post in front of the shop. The birds proceeded to follow Vardin.

Vardin was a paranoid man who was always looking over his shoulder; but on this morning the feeling that he was being watched gnawed at him. Vardin traveled for ten miles on the main road leading westward out of Taperia, he crossed the River Nebu and entered a thick old forest.

It was in the forest that the Ruala warriors flew lower and joined the flock of Enrops who were following Vardin. The canopy formed by the old trees prevented the sunlight from reaching the forest floor as well as providing concealment for the Ruala warriors and the passengers they carried. Luca carried Gabriel while Calen carried Natasha, who brought a pack of medical supplies and food along as she did not know what condition Petra might be in, if they found him.

Vardin traveled in the forest for several miles before he tied his horse in front of an old cabin. There were no roads or paths that led to this cabin. Some of the Rualas landed several hundred feet away from the small building; Gabriel and Natasha were among them.

"I do not want to storm that cabin until we know where Petra is, we have not come this far to cause the boy's death," Gabriel said.

177

"Let me walk up to the cabin, I will say I am lost and need help," Natasha offered. "I will get them to let me inside."

"Natasha, I don't like that idea," Calen said sternly.

"Petra is a friend of mine," said an Enrop who stepped up to Gabriel. "He will recognize me. I will look in the window."

"And what is your name?" Gabriel asked.

"I am Nica and my flock protects King Sudfad's family. The boy should never have been taken, that is why we are all here now."

"Very well," Gabriel said. "We will wait until you return."

Six Enrops flew to the cabin and looked in the various windows. Petra's eyes grew wide when he recognized Nica sitting on the windowsill directly across from where he was lying bound on a mattress. "I have to go to the bathroom," Petra said. The men playing cards ignored him. "I really have to go," Petra pleaded.

"If I take you outside you won't try to run away again will you?" Vardin asked.

"My legs are asleep," Petra replied. "I couldn't run if I wanted to."

"Let me put these supplies away and I will take you out," said Vardin.

Nica quickly flew to Gabriel, "Petra is tied up on a mattress on the west wall of the cabin. Near the east wall four men are sitting at a table playing cards and the man we followed is near the back of the cabin putting away the things he bought. When Petra saw me he told the men he had to go to the bathroom and one of them said they would take him out in a couple of minutes."

"Smart boy," Gabriel said and quickly devised a plan.

Vardin had a rope tied around Petra's waist when he opened the door of the cabin. They walked a few feet from the cabin when Luca and Rabi swept down and attacked Vardin. Calen quickly grabbed Petra and took him back to Natasha.

Simultaneously the flock of Enrops flew into the cabin and attacked the eyes and faces of the kidnappers, who were so occupied fending off the birds they never saw the Rualas swarming in. All of the kidnappers were captured alive as Gabriel had ordered.

"Petra we are friends," Natasha said as she examined the boy for injuries.

"I know, thanks," said Petra with a smile that exploded on his face.

"Tell me are you hurt anywhere," Natasha asked as she looked at Petra's filthy clothes and skin.

"No, where's Nica?"

"In the cabin fighting with your kidnappers," Calen said. "Are you hungry Petra because my wife brought a bag of cookies along?"

Petra's eyes lit up; "Cookies, yes." Natasha laughed as she took the bag of cookies from her pack and gave them to Petra, who could not eat them fast enough.

"I wish I would have brought some clean clothes for him," Natasha said.

"I just want to go home," said Petra.

"We will be taking you home soon," Calen assured him.

"Nica," cried Petra and threw his arms around the bird, hugging him tightly. "I was so happy when I saw you, I knew you were going to save me." Nica leaned into Petra and the two seemed to embrace for several minutes.

Gabriel walked back to Calen and Natasha. "I have sent messages telling both King Sudfad and the Sanuri that we have Petra and will return him home soon. I also told them that we have the kidnappers. I want to interrogate them before we do anything else."

"I am staying with Petra," Nica said.

Prince Lakin walked up to the group. "Petra I don't know if you remember me but I am Ibula's brother. I am assigning twenty warriors to take you home. Have you ever flown before?"

"Only with him," Petra said and pointed to Calen. "It was fun."

"Well, I am glad you enjoyed it because you will be flying for a couple of hours," Lakin explained.

Petra broke off a piece of his cookie and offered it to Nica. "Nica now I will know how you feel when you fly."

Chapter XIII
Another Sword

Sudfad and Renya were finishing their coffee at the breakfast table and talking. The rest of the family left the dining room after breakfast; leaving the King and Queen to enjoy a few moments of peace and solitude.

"Sudfad what on earth is that noise?" Renya asked as she stood up, "It's coming from outside." Renya walked to one of the dining room windows and pushed the window open. "Sudfad there are Enrops flying over the yard and screeching. Something must be wrong." Sudfad quickly walked to the front foyer of the castle and opened the door; Renya followed behind him and they both walked out on the stone stairway. "Sudfad do you hear what they are saying?" Renya asked as she started to cry. Renya turned around and called for Marie to get the rest of the family.

"Petra's coming home," screamed the four Enrops repeatedly as they flew up to Sudfad and Renya. The birds appeared to be excited at the message they were bearing. "Gabriel saved him and the Rualas are bringing him home now," one of the birds said as it landed near Sudfad's foot.

"When will they get here?" Sudfad asked as the meaning of their words had not yet pierced his grieving heart.

"An hour, maybe two," the same Enrop answered. "They don't fly as fast as we do."

"Please tell us, is he alright? Is he hurt in any way," Renya could barely get the words out.

"He looked to be alright," a second Enrop said. "But he is very dirty; if he had cuts we could not see them."

"Nica is staying with him," the first Enrop said as the other family members started to join Sudfad and Renya on the top of the stairs to the castle. Tears were flowing as the Royal Family of Wetpr started to realize their nightmare was over.

The five kidnappers had their wrists and legs bound and were sitting on the ground outside of the cabin as four Ruala warriors searched the small hunting lodge.

"Gabriel," screamed an Enrop that suddenly soared upwards into the morning sky. Gabriel could not see why the bird screamed until he saw six more Enrops join their comrade as he started to battle with five ravens. More Enrops quickly joined the fight as the people watched from below. The birds loudly screeched as they tore at each other with their beaks and their talons.

Feathers were raining down upon the spectators. Although the ravens fought viciously they were outnumbered by the Enrops and soon lost the battle. Within minutes Sar, one of the Enrops, brought Gabriel the message that the ravens were carrying. Gabriel read the note and handed it to Luca, who was standing the closest to him. The note contained one short message, *Its time, bring the boy to Nora.*

One by one, Gabriel had the kidnappers taken into the cabin so he could interrogate them. Calen and Luca joined Gabriel, while Rabi, Koby and Dagon assisted the eighty other Ruala warriors with watching the prisoners and guarding against an attack. Natasha stood outside with Rabi. Prince Lakin and twenty other Ruala warriors were escorting Petra home. Petra squealed with delight as he and Lakin soared through the sky.

For the next two hours members of the Royal Family and staff had their eyes glued to the sky; awaiting any sign of the Rualas and Petra.

"I see them," called out Annabelle excitedly as she stood in the front doorway of the castle. Annabelle turned and ran through the castle gathering the family. As the Royal Family was walking down the front steps of the castle Lakin was the first Ruala to land. He held Petra for a moment to steady the boy then let him run to his parents.

Petra was running and crying when he jumped into Sudfad's arms. Sudfad could not speak and simply hugged and kissed his son before handing him to Renya.

"Why I'm crying so hard I can't see you," Renya said as she kissed and hugged Petra, who was crying and did not speak. As the Ruala warriors landed they watched the emotional reunion in silence. Petra hugged and kissed his parents, Alexander, Laurel, Simon, Annabelle, Vitomas and Raul. As soon as Raul put the boy down, Petra saw Marie walking towards them; Petra ran and jumped into her arms.

While Petra was hugging Marie, he looked over her shoulder and saw Kyra slowly walking towards him with Petra's German shepherd puppy, Argus at her side.

"Kyra," Petra said and Marie set him on the ground. Kyra had been consumed with guilt since Petra's kidnapping; when she saw him the words did not come easily. The two playmates faced each other.

"I took care of your dog for you, while you were gone," Kyra said before she started to cry. "Petra I am so sorry that I couldn't stop them." Petra put his arms around Kyra and the two hugged for a few moments.

"It's ok Kyra, you tried." Then Petra turned towards his family and the Ruala warriors and said in his normally exuberant style, "She bit one of them really good, his hand swelled up and turned colors and everything."

Laughter rang through the courtyard as Sudfad and Renya turned to Lakin. "How can we ever thank you?" Sudfad asked.

"It was our pleasure but the real thanks should go to Gabriel and his team; they have been searching for Petra and the priests behind his kidnapping," Lakin replied with modesty.

"Please come in and tell us everything," Sudfad requested.

"We really should go," Lakin said. "We have all of the kidnappers alive and Gabriel is interrogating them, when he is done what do you want us to do with them?"

"Bring them to me," Sudfad said angrily. "I will make an example out of them. No one hurts my family."

Renya walked closer to Lakin and put her hand on his forearm. "Certainly you and your men could share a meal with us."

Lakin smiled, "I think that would be fine."

Sudfad's family and the twenty-one Ruala warriors ate lunch in the Great Hall because the family dining room was not large enough. Petra told the family about his time with the kidnappers as he hungrily devoured his food.

"So why did they keep you tied up all of the time?" Kyra asked as she sat next to Petra at the table.

"Because I kept kicking and biting them," Petra said nonchalantly.

Lakin explained the events of Petra's rescue. "Gabriel didn't say anything about going after Petra when he was here," Renya said.

Lakin paused for a second and looked at Petra and Kyra before he continued speaking, "Gabriel and his sister Natasha are" Lakin spelled out the word "d e m o n hunters."

"Why is he spelling out demon?" Kyra asked Petra in a loud whisper.

"I don't know," Petra said and shrugged his shoulders.

Lakin chuckled, "Well, I guess I don't know why I spelled it out either." Lakin talked for the next thirty minutes, telling Sudfad's family about Gabriel, Natasha, Calen, Luca, Koby, Rabi and Dagon.

"Lakin you said they didn't have time to prepare for their wedding didn't you?" Annabelle asked.

"Yes."

"Come on, I have some ideas," Annabelle said to Vitomas. When both Princesses stood up, "Annabelle asked, "Lakin about what size is Natasha compared to us?"

Lakin looked at both of the Princesses and smiled, "She's close to the same height as you two, but she is built a little more like Vitomas."

"Thanks," Annabelle said and grabbed Vitomas' hand and the two young women left the Great Hall.

184

"Why don't you two go to Petra's room and play," Sudfad suggested. Kyra and Petra started to walk out of the room, when Petra suddenly turned and asked excitedly, "Lakin will you give Kyra a ride so she can see what it is like to fly?"

"I will," offered one of the Ruala warriors and walked out of the Great Hall with the children.

When Renya was convinced that Kyra and Petra could not hear her, she asked. "Why in the world was Natasha in Taperia by herself? Such a young girl in that dangerous place."

"Natasha is a fine warrior," Lakin replied.

"But there were six of them," Renya said referring to the men who attacked Natasha.

"Gabriel and Natasha are the only two humans in the group," Lakin explained. "We cannot let the Taperians know there are Ruala warriors in their kingdom, so my warriors cannot be seen."

Simon and Raul looked at each other then Raul asked, "Could you use a couple more swords?"

"You would be very welcomed," Lakin said with a smile.

"Raul!" Renya scolded. "Vitomas and Annabelle will be furious. You two haven't been home that long since the last mission."

"Mother you heard Lakin. The same priests were behind the attacks on me and Simon and Petra's kidnapping; they have declared war on our family and when does it stop. And besides if they are able to help that demon escape from his prison, our world will be devastated," Raul said.

Simon looked at Lakin and asked, "Can you wait until we pack a few things and talk to our wives?"

"Of course."

"Lakin, The Lion did not want me to take troops into Stordt, when we searched for Petra. I don't know if he still feels the same. But if you need my armies; let me know," Sudfad offered.

185

Although Matthew, Thaos, Stephan, Sorren, Thedes and the others had been gone less than two weeks; it seemed like months for the families left behind in Lentz. Angelina and Ibula became very close friends, as they realized how much they were alike and how much they had in common. To the relief of both of them; there had been no threats against Jacob, at least not yet.

Ryan kept his word to Thaos and visited Nikki and Ingr every day. Both girls realized Ryan was lonely and wanted to feel useful; so they started to make up projects for him to work on. When Nikki and Ingr shared this information with Bella, she hired Ryan to build a large weapons armoire as a gift for Claudius. Since Ryan was living in an army barracks, Bella fixed up a woodworking shop for him in one of the large sheds behind the castle.

"Nikki will you tell Ryan we expect him for lunch," Bella said as she was arranging a large bouquet of flowers. "I don't believe he has eaten with us on the nights that you girls cook, so tell him to stay for dinner also. I am sure he will enjoy it."

"Is he in back?" Nikki asked as she put down the knife she was using to cut vegetables.

"Yes," Bella said.

"Bella, that was the nicest thing you did for Ryan," Ingr said as she sat in a chair in the kitchen and cleaned shrimp. "Making that workshop for him."

"He is a very talented boy," Bella said. "He could easily make a living selling his woodworking."

"Have you seen him when he works?" Ingr asked. "It's like he comes alive."

Bella lowered her voice, "Girls I am going to ask you something and I want an honest answer. Do you think Ryan is cut out to be a soldier?" Nikki and Ingr looked at each other but neither spoke. "He is just so different from Stephan and Thaos, he's so sensitive and artistic; I worry about him," Bella said. "Why aren't you girls answering me?"

"Because we like Ryan and don't want to get him into trouble," Nikki said.

"Oh my dear, you are not going to get him into trouble," Bella said. "But you are both trained as warriors, I simply want your opinions."

"Bella, Ryan is the kindest person and he has many talents but he is not a warrior. I don't think he has what it takes," Ingr said.

"I agree with Ingr," Nikki said. "No matter how much training Ryan has, well, he just isn't a fighter. I am going to find him now." Nikki said and walked out of the kitchen.

"Bella why are you asking about Ryan?" Ingr asked.

"Well, don't say anything to the men, but I have been thinking about asking Claudius to release Ryan from the military and to help him set up a business in woodworking."

"That would be wonderful for Ryan," Ingr said. "But do you think Claudius would allow it?"

"I was going to wait until after I gave him the armoire as a gift," Bella said; suddenly she lowered her voice. "Here they come."

Nikki walked into the kitchen first and had a big smile on her face. "Ryan made you something Bella and it's so nice I told him to give it to you now. Bella close your eyes."

Bella did as Nikki requested, she could hear movement in the kitchen and Ingr whispering. "You can open them now," Nikki said. On the kitchen table was a large wooden jewelry chest, with intricate carvings. "Ryan this is beautiful," Bella gasped as she ran her fingers over the detailed carvings.

"Open it," Nikki said. Inside of the chest were tiny draws, each lined with velvet material. Bella pulled the lid up farther and music started to play.

"Ryan this is delightful, what a wonderful gift," Bella gushed.

"I wanted to do something for you as a way to thank you for the workshop," said Ryan.

"I love it," Bella said as she walked across the kitchen and kissed Ryan on the cheek.

"Ryan," Ingr said then she repeated his name louder. "Ryan, I think it's time for you to get Angelina."

"Is the baby coming?" Bella asked excitedly.

"I think my water just broke."

When Ryan reached Angelina's home, he was still so shaken all he could say was 'Ingr.'

"Is the baby coming?" Angelina asked. Ryan nodded. "Ibula, Ingr's having her baby, I have to go."

"I am a healer too, I will come with you," Ibula said.

"What about Jacob?" Angelina asked as she ran to the bedroom to get her medicine bag.

"You hold him and I will carry you," Ibula replied as she lifted Jacob from the floor where he had been playing with toys.

"What should I do?" Ryan asked nervously.

"Will you go to my village and get my mother?" Angelina asked. "She raised Ingr, she will want to be there."

A few minutes after Ryan left, Ibula soared into the air; she had the medicine bag draped over her back and Angelina in her arms. Angelina was holding Jacob, who was getting used to flying and did not cry. After a few moments in the air, Angelina started to giggle. "Poor Ryan, he is so nervous I hope he doesn't get lost."

By midafternoon Lakin and his men were landing at the kidnappers' cabin.

"What took you so long? Was there trouble?" asked Calen. When he saw Raul and Simon walking up to them, Calen smiled and extended his hand.

"We have some old friends joining us," Lakin said with pleasure. Raul and Simon shook hands with several Ruala warriors as Calen brought Natasha to meet the Princes.

"Simon, Raul, this is my wife Natasha," Calen said with obvious pride. "Natasha these are the Princes of Wetpr, Raul and Simon."

Both Raul and Simon kissed Natasha on the cheek. "We have heard a great deal about you from Lakin and Petra," Raul said. "Petra calls you the pretty lady with the cookies." Both Natasha and Calen smiled at this comment.

"Gabriel is in the cabin interrogating the kidnappers," Calen said.

The looks on the faces of both Raul and Simon suddenly became very grave. "We want to join him," Raul said. Simon and Raul turned and started to walk towards the cabin. Raul stopped and turned back to Calen, "Keep Natasha out of the cabin."

"What are they going to do?" Natasha asked.

Calen put his arm round Natasha's shoulders and asked, "Honey what do you think Gabriel and I would do if someone kidnapped you?"

"Kill them."

"No," Lakin said. "King Sudfad wants them alive; he wants to make an example of them. But I am sure Raul and Simon will let the kidnappers know how they feel about them."

Raul and Simon knew Lakin, Calen, Koby, Dagon, Luca and Rabi from their stay in the Ice Caves. The warriors reunited over dinner. Wine flowed freely and the kitchen was filled with laughter. Gabriel waited until the end of the meal to talk business. "We will have to split into two groups," Gabriel explained. "One group will have to stay here and watch the witch, while the other goes to Nora."

"I should stay here," said Natasha as she put three pies and two bottles of whiskey on the table. "I know her and I am getting to know some of the town's people, they trust me and give me information."

"Natasha remember what happened the last time you went into Taperia," Calen said angrily.

"Calen, you know we can't let the Taperians see any of your warriors, we need Natasha's help," Gabriel said. "Of course you will stay here with her."

"Gabriel I can't believe you are allowing her to take such risks again," Calen said with his voice raising.

"I will stay with Calen and Natasha," Simon said. "Raul cannot because the last time he was here he was marked for a dead man. But I am not known here and I can let my beard grow out and disguise myself if needed."

"Very good," Gabriel said. "Natasha has been using the story that she and her husband have recently moved to the area and are living in an abandoned farmhouse until they can find land and build their own home. You may have to pretend to be her husband at times."

"That's fine with me as long as Calen approves," Simon said as he looked at Calen.

"Simon, I am putting my trust in you to protect her," Calen said as the anger was draining from his face.

"Calen you have my word that I will do everything to protect her," Simon promised.

"Thank you Simon, I feel better about this now," said Calen. Then he turned to Natasha, "Please do what Simon tells you, he is a very experienced warrior."

"Calen we would not want our wives to walk the streets of Taperia either," Raul said. "Natasha is very courageous."

"I have already sent some Enrops and Ruala warriors to Nora. They will locate a place for us to stay and scout the area," Gabriel said. "It would take the kidnappers four days to ride to Nora; we will need only two since we will be flying; so we have some time. Lakin let's leave twenty-five of your warriors here and the rest will accompany us to Nora."

Raul and Simon waited until everyone was done eating their pie. Natasha was clearing the dishes from the table when Raul said, "We have some things to say."

190

As Raul spoke, Simon walked over to the kitchen door and picked up two large packs that were lying on the floor. "Our family is overwhelmed with gratitude that you have brought Petra back to us. Especially after hearing the dangers you have faced. The King and Queen have ordered your presence at the castle after this mission is completed so our family can thank you properly."

"All of us?" Dagon asked.

"Yes," Raul said. "But they know this mission might take a while so they sent some gifts for you now." Simon opened one of the packs and he and Raul walked around the table and handed every warrior a sheathed sword. We have one for you also Natasha since you are a warrior," Raul said. The gifts brought many comments of appreciation from the warriors.

"Each sword has engravings on the hilt. A sword and a scroll; they are our family symbols. The scroll represents our work for The Great Ruler," Simon explained. Raul opened the second pack and pulled out daggers that matched the swords, each warrior also received one of these. Raul then pulled a small carrying case out of the pack.

"Lakin told us that you and Calen did not have time to prepare for your wedding or to celebrate it," Raul said as he handed the case to Natasha. "So our wives sent you this."

"What is it?" Natasha asked as she grasped the handle.

"We don't know," Raul said with a laugh.

Natasha reached into the case and pulled out a lilac colored nightgown made completely of lace. "This is beautiful," she gasped as she unrolled it and held the nightgown up for Calen to see.

"You will have to thank your wives from me," Calen joked as he touched the fine lace.

"There's more," Natasha said as she reached into the bag. The men watched as Natasha pulled each new gift out of the case with the awe of a child. She passed the jars of scented lotions and perfumes around the table for everyone to smell.

"What is this? It's warm to the touch," Natasha asked as she dipped her finger into a small jar of oil.

"Massage oil," Raul said with a grin. Natasha quickly looked at Calen and smiled.

"Natasha we have to warn you," Simon said kiddingly. "Our wives like to use those oils and we have lots of babies."

"They are telling me that Ruala babies fly before they walk, can you believe that?" Natasha asked Simon and Raul. Both men laughed.

"I think it is time for my bride and me to try out some of these gifts," Calen said as he started to put the jars back into the case.

"Oh there is more," Simon said.

"More," Natasha repeated in astonishment.

"Remember our family did not have much time to prepare gifts for you. Mother has sent you something, but she realizes the gift is very personal and if you don't like them she will not be offended." Simon handed a very full pouch to Calen, who poured its contents on the table. All eyes grew wide as they looked upon a large collection of exquisite rings. "Mother would like you to choose your engagement and wedding rings from these, but as I said she will understand if you had something else in mind."

"Calen can we even accept such extravagant gifts?" Natasha asked.

"The King and Queen can afford to give them," Raul said assuredly.

"When Mother told Father what she was sending, he said she could not send rings for just two of you; so he chose an assortment of rings from the royal vault and is sending them as tokens of our appreciation," Simon said as he poured the contents of another large pouch onto the table.

"Are you serious?" asked Koby in amazement as he looked at the fine jewels lying before them.

"These gifts are nothing in comparison to what you have given to us," Raul said. "Please accept them."

"Gabriel try on that emerald ring, the one surrounded by diamonds, it looks like something you would like," Natasha said.

"My sister knows me so well," Gabriel said as he looked at the ring admiringly. "This is very beautiful. But I was waiting for Prince Lakin to choose his ring first."

"Nonsense," Lakin said. "Gabriel your team has faced the dangers, I have done little. Choose your gifts."

Calen picked up a ring with a golden band and a large ruby stone that was surrounded by diamonds. "I like this," he said as he handed it to Natasha. "Try it on."

"The rings should be close to your size," Raul said. "Lakin said you were about the same size as our wives."

Natasha started to cry as she looked at the beautiful ring on her finger. "I guess you found your engagement ring," Simon said with a warm smile.

"Calen make sure you pick out a ring from both pouches," Raul said as he poured more whiskey into everyone's glasses.

Calen and Natasha chose gold wedding bands with rubies and diamonds in them. The other warriors each chose a ring and proudly placed their gifts on their fingers. Natasha stood up and walked over to Raul kissing him on the cheek, then she kissed Simon. "How are we ever going to repay you?" she asked.

"You already have," Raul said.

Calen stood up, "Thank you again for the fine gifts; you and your family are most generous and I look forward to thanking them also in person. But I think Natasha and I will retire." Natasha kissed Gabriel on the cheek and the two newlyweds walked out of the kitchen.

"They certainly look in love," Simon said.

"I'm rather jealous," Dagon said and grinned. "I wish I could find a girl like Natasha." Then he looked across the table. "Gabriel you don't have any more sisters hidden away do you?"

"No, wish I did," Gabriel replied. Everyone at the table could hear the sadness in his voice. Gabriel paused for a moment as if lost in thought, then he looked at the others and said, "Now that they are gone I want to talk about the prisoner in the basement." Gabriel looked at Raul and Simon, "He is one of the men who attacked Natasha. Understandably I have to keep Calen away from him."

"I don't believe he and his men attacked Natasha from any orders from the priests or the witch but something Natasha said keeps gnawing at the back of my mind. She said the butcher told her that in the last few weeks lots of dangerous men were coming to Taperia and staying. I don't know if it is related to Omnibus but I would like to know what is going on," Gabriel continued.

"There is one more thing Gabriel" Luca said. "Calen said that the prisoner was surprised at being interrupted but did not seem surprised to see a Ruala. It has been my experience that most humans are a bit shocked when they first see us."

"Luca that is a good observation," said Gabriel.

"Simon and Raul have brought along a potion that their healer makes, they say it forces someone to tell the truth," Lakin said.

"Well let's see if it works," said Gabriel and all of the men left the kitchen.

When Calen and Natasha entered their room, she took the lace nightgown from the case and quickly walked into the closet.

"Why are you changing in there?" Calen asked as he lit candles and poured two glasses of wine.

"Because I want it to be a surprise," Natasha said through the closed door. "I really hope this fits." Calen took the bottles of massage oil from the case and placed them on the small table next to the bed.

"Well what do you think?"

Calen smiled as he looked at his beautiful bride. Natasha' black curly hair cascaded down her back. The lilac material made her violet eyes dance. The shear lace nightgown clung to her womanly curves. "You are so beautiful," Calen said and walked the distance of the two steps that separated them. "My Lady may I have this dance?" Calen asked as he placed his left hand on the small of Natasha's back and took her hand in his.

"I have never danced with a naked man before," Natasha said and giggled.

"I certainly hope not," Calen said and kissed her passionately. For the two young lovers, time seemed to stop as they laughed and danced to their own music.

Chapter XIV
Nora

With the exception of one very unusual statement; Gala's truth potion revealed little as Gabriel and the others interrogated the prisoner in the basement of the abandoned hotel. As Gabriel suspected it was lust that motivated the attack on Natasha, not orders from the three high priests or Sophie. Although the prisoner had not previously seen a Ruala warrior, he had heard of them which is why he was not shocked to see Calen. But when Gabriel asked the man why he and his gang had recently come to Taperia; the prisoner gave them an unexpected answer.

"A few weeks ago, we had no intentions of coming to Taperia, but I know it sounds crazy; it was almost like something was calling to us."

Gabriel started to fear that Omnibus was calling all that was evil to Stordt in preparation for his ascension. The next morning Gabriel, Raul, Luca, Rabi, Lakin and others left for Nora. Leaving Koby, Dagon and twenty-five other Ruala warriors with Simon, Calen and Natasha. Before Gabriel left he told Calen the prisoner was his. Calen asked Simon to take Natasha into Taperia because Calen didn't want her at the hotel when he killed the prisoner.

Simon drove the boca as Natasha sat in the passenger's seat. "I want to buy a hat and some different clothes," Simon said. "I think I need to look more like a farmer or rancher."

"You do look like a soldier, even in Gabriel's clothes," Natasha said. "We can go to the General Store for your things. People congregate there, so we may overhear something of interest."

"After I change my clothes I was thinking of going over to the Taperian Imperial Hotel and do a little spying on the witch," Simon said. "I don't believe she has ever seen me. But she has seen you hasn't she?"

"Yes and fairly recently so she would recognize me."

Simon was quiet for a moment, then he looked at Natasha with a grin on his face. "I've got an idea. We will buy you a black dress and a hat with a veil. We will tell people that we are in mourning."

"I was thinking of getting a room at the hotel that we could use when needed. If you are disguised we can walk around the hotel without fear of being discovered."

Natasha laughed, "I like it Simon."

Simon and Natasha bought their disguises and got a room on the top floor of the Taperian Imperial Hotel; the same floor where Sophie's room was located. Simon chose a room with the balcony on the back of the building in case Calen or any of the other Ruala warriors joined them.

Simon had never seen Sophie so he needed Natasha to point her out to him. Simon and Natasha decided to spend the afternoon sitting in the dining room of the hotel, which was just off from the main lobby. They chose a table that gave them the best view of the lobby and the front door.

"There she is," Natasha whispered. "She's the older woman wearing the red dress, carrying a lot of packages." Although the lobby was crowded, Sophie was easy to identify. They watched as Sophie walked up to the desk clerk, although they could not hear what she was saying. After a few words with the clerk, Sophie walked up the stairs to her room.

"Ok, now that I know what she looks like I am taking you home," Simon said.

"No you aren't, this is just getting fun."

"Natasha what am I going to say to Calen?"

"You promised to protect me; not stop me from working on the mission, Simon."

"Well then, if you aren't leaving, I think we should go upstairs and see what she is doing."

"What are you wearing?" Calen asked when Natasha and Simon entered the kitchen of the abandoned hotel. Natasha laughed and pulled up her veil so she could kiss Calen.

"Simon bought it for me so the witch wouldn't recognize me," Natasha said gleefully. "We sat in the dining room of her hotel and watched her, it was great fun. Let me change and I will start dinner. We bought a lot of food also."

"I just wanted Natasha to point the witch out to me then I wanted to bring her home," Simon explained.

"But I refused to come back so soon," Natasha said and kissed Calen again. "And it's a good thing I didn't." Natasha handed Calen a large ring of keys.

"What's this?"

"Keys to all of the rooms in that hotel. I pretended like I was crying and while one of the maids tried to console me I took her keys," Natasha said. "And Simon got a room in the hotel with a balcony at the back of the building so you and the others can go there."

Calen looked at Simon and shook his head in amazement. "Your wife is very good at these missions," Simon said then he looked at Koby and Dagon, "Would you mind helping me bring the supplies in?"

Calen followed Natasha into their bedroom. He helped her unbutton the back of her dress then he put his arms around her waist and kissed the back of her neck.

"We got a letter from my parents today," Calen said happily. "They can't wait to meet you and Gabriel. Natasha you know I told you I was going to build a house for us."

"Yes," Natasha said as she put another dress on.

"As a gift, Mother and Father would like to build the house for us and furnish it, so we have a place to go to after the mission. What do you think about that?"

"I think it is wonderfully generous of them," Natasha said excitedly.

"Good I am glad you like the idea. The letter they sent has two pages of questions they want us to answer," Calen said with a laugh.

"Do you want to read them to me while I fix dinner?" Natasha asked. "Or would you rather go over them when we are alone?"

"Now would be fine. My parents will be pleased that we accepted their offer."

"Calen I am so excited, our first home," Natasha said and threw her arms around his neck. Calen put his hands around Natasha's waist and picked her off the floor. The two kissed until they heard voices in the kitchen.

"Simon this came for you," Koby said and handed Simon a small envelope. "It must be from your wife because it smells like perfume," Koby added with a grin. Simon sat down at the kitchen table and opened the envelope. As he read the letter a concerned look came across his face.

"Simon is something wrong?" Natasha asked.

"Annabelle, that's my wife, thinks she is pregnant again. She says it's too early to be sure but she wants me to know so I make it home for the birth." Simon put the letter down. "Raul and I were on a mission that took us from home for many months; then we were attacked by Hutas and almost died. The Rualas saved us and healed us in the Ice Caves. We have only been reunited with our families for a few months before we decided to join you. Neither my wife or Raul's wife are happy that we are gone again." Simon paused. "I missed the birth of my daughter; which tore me apart."

Natasha walked up to Simon, put her hand on his shoulder and looked him in the eyes. "Simon," Natasha said in a scolding manner. "You are not going to miss the birth of this child; you can go home anytime you want, we will not think badly of it."

"I want to go home but I need to stay here, at least for a while."

"Well, one way or another we will make sure you get home for the birth of that baby," Natasha said with authority.

"Someone is following us," Gabriel whispered as he and Raul walked down a wooden sidewalk in the City of Nora.

"I hear them too," Raul said about the rapidly approaching footsteps.

Both men quickly turned and saw a beautiful young woman a few feet behind them. She wore an expensive light blue dress with a purple hooded cloak over it. The hood was down, exposing her blonde hair which she wore up. The woman stopped when they turned and faced her. She stared both men boldly in the eyes for a moment, then smiled and walked in between them.

"There are eyes watching," the woman said as she stretched up to kiss Gabriel on the cheek. "Act as if we know each other." Gabriel smiled and kissed the woman on the cheek. She then turned to Raul and they exchanged kisses. The woman took Raul's right arm and Gabriel's left arm in hers.

"You are asking too many questions, we need to get off the street," she said with a sweet smile. "I will take you to my office."

"Who are you?" Raul asked

"My name is Hannah, I am a physician here. If anyone stops us, you are old friends of mine from collage and wanted to surprise me with a visit."

Gabriel smiled at the woman's ingenuity. "And what collage would that be, My Lady?" he asked.

"Cicero College," the woman said as she smiled at a man and woman who passed them on the street.

"You went to college in Wetpr?" Raul asked with surprise.

"Yes, I know who you are," she whispered. "And it is not safe for you here."

An older man wearing an expensive suit walked up to them. He stopped and bowed before Hannah who let go of Gabriel's and Raul's arms and held her hand out for the man to kiss. Knowing that Hannah did not know their names, Gabriel quickly stepped forward and extended his hand to the man. "Hello, I am Gabriel and this is my cousin Raul."

"This is Lloyd; he is one of the prominent bankers in this city. Lloyd these are friends of mine from college who just surprised me with an unexpected visit," Hannah said as she smiled happily.

"How long will you be staying?" Lloyd asked.

Gabriel took Hannah's hand in his own and gave her a flirtatious look, "I don't know yet, that may depend on Hannah."

Lloyd chuckled, "Oh I see. Well if you remain in Nora, let me invite you to a ball we are having at the Endleson Hotel in two weeks; only the best people with be in attendance."

Hannah's voice became cold as she said, "Yes I am sure only the best."

"Hannah you must let go of your anger," said Lloyd.

"That Kind Sir I do not have to do," Hannah replied angrily.

"Please Hannah, for your own good," Lloyd said gently.

"If you will excuse us, we have much to catch up on," Hannah said and once again took the arms of Raul and Gabriel. They walked past Lloyd and down the street for several hundred feet before Hannah told them to take a right turn. They walked through an alley that opened into another street. They stopped at a building with a sign that read, *Hannah Marcus Physician*. After they entered the front door, Hannah hung a sign out that read *Closed*.

"There are a lot of weapons in here for a physician's office," Raul commented as he looked around the room. Hannah did not reply.

"Tell me Hannah," Gabriel asked suspiciously. "Why is it that a beautiful young woman as yourself shows no fear running up to two strange men?"

Hannah smiled, "Because I am prepared," she said as she removed her cloak and took the small crossbow off that was hung by a sling over her back. "And unlike the others here, I am not afraid to use weapons. Please let's go into the sitting room," Hannah suggested and nodded towards a door at the opposite side of the office.

"After you," Gabriel said, not trusting Hannah.

"Marcia," Hannah called out as they entered the parlor. "We have guests." Hannah noticed that both Raul and Gabriel acted guarded for attack.

"You do not trust me," Hannah said. "That is wise; you should not trust anyone in this godforsaken kingdom. Please have a seat."

A beautiful young girl with golden brown skin and long straight black hair walked into the parlor. "Marcia this is Raul and Gabriel, they are guests and may be staying with us for a while," Hannah said as she gave Marcia a knowing look. "Would you please bring us some coffee and biscuits?"

"Yes Hannah," Marcia replied and turned and walked from the parlor.

"Now My Lords what would bring the Prince of Wetpr to Nora?" Hannah asked boldly. Neither man answered her question so Hannah continued. "Prince Raul, I was in the crowd when you and your family introduced yours and Simon's first born sons to the citizens of Wetpr. Your wife Vitomas is a woman of extraordinary beauty. Has she ever told you of the horrors you took her from?"

"She rarely speaks of her life here but she still has nightmares," Raul said as he was trying to determine Hannah's intentions.

Hannah became visibly angry as she started to speak, "Less than a year ago, while I was still in Wetpr Roch brought his men to Nora. The Endleson family pays Roch for protection but mind you that protection is not from invaders but from Roch and his men. Roch walked into a ball in the Endleson Hotel and I am told that as soon as he entered the ballroom he focused on my baby sister. She was but a child, beautiful with long curly blonde hair like Vitomas."

"Even though Endleson paid Roch, that monster dragged my little sister out of the hotel and raped her and killed her in the street and not one of the good people of Nora lifted a finger to help her. Then Roch let his men have the city; by morning one third of the city was in flames and seventy-four men, women and children were raped and killed, and no one tried to stop them."

Hannah was shaking from anger as she spoke. "Marcia's family was killed. Thank The Great Ruler, her father hid her from those monsters." Hannah stopped speaking as Marcia served coffee and biscuits to their guests. Hannah waited for Marcia to leave the room before she continued speaking, "Prince Raul there must be something extraordinarily important for you to be here. I am at your service; please let me know what I can do."

"How did you know we were here?" Gabriel asked.

"My hatred of the King and his men is not a secret. There are others who feel as I but they fear for their families."

"So are you saying you have a small army?" Raul asked.

"No," Hannah said with a laugh. "I wish I did. But I have many who are loyal to me and they are my eyes and ears."

"Spies," Gabriel said.

"That is a more unpleasant term; but yes." Hannah replied. "And My Lord, you have not yet revealed your identity."

"I am High Priest Gabriel with the Patronus."

"I am not familiar with the Patronus but a man of The Great Ruler is in just as much danger here as Prince Raul."

"The Patronus is a special faction of the Church. You might say we are an army," Gabriel said then smiled warmly. "And Hannah I am beginning to think you might be the answer to a prayer. Did anyone else recognize Raul?"

"No, not to my knowledge. I was in the General Store when two different people pointed you out as strangers who were asking questions about the disappearances that have been occurring around here. When I saw Prince Raul I realized I had to get you both off from the streets."

"You keep referring to Roch as the King but we had received word another man named Cerephus is King," Raul said. "And you can call me Raul."

"We have heard that too but no one around here believes that. We think Roch is up to something."

203

"Why do you say that?" asked Gabriel.

"Because there has been no word of Roch's death or even a battle. Roch is many things but he is not a coward; he would not give up his throne without a fight. And Cerephus was one of Roch's generals. Little has changed since Cerephus announced he was King; perhaps that is because Roch is still in charge. At any rate it is as if Roch disappeared off the face of this world."

"Do you live here alone?" Gabriel asked.

"Marcia and I stay here some times. These are just my chambers connected to my office. My family's home is outside of Nora."

"And does your family live there still?" asked Gabriel.

"No, my parents are both dead now," Hannah said sadly. "My father killed himself from grief and shame after Laurabelle was murdered by Roch. My mother died of a broken heart shortly afterwards." Hannah paused for several moments. "You see my parents were in that crowd watching what Roch did to Laurabelle."

Neither Gabriel nor Raul spoke for a few moments as they could see the intense emotions that Hannah was experiencing as she talked about her family.

"Please do not think this is inappropriate," Raul said seriously. "But are you telling us that you live by yourself in this place?"

"I have hired people at the big home sometimes, but yes."

Gabriel smiled, "There is something about you that reminds me of my sister; she too is a courageous warrior. We are not alone; would it be possible for us to stay at your family's home?"

"Of course. We can go out there after you finish your coffee."

"Won't it be suspicious if you close your office?" Raul asked.

"I am not the only physician here and by now everyone knows that two handsome college men came to visit me. They will not think anything of it." Hannah started to laugh. "Some of the people may hope you are suitors and will pacify me."

"Some of the good people of Nora are afraid I may cause trouble with the King."

Raul smiled, "And would you?"

"Just give me an opportunity."

Hannah and Marcia rode in a small boca, while Raul and Gabriel rode on horseback. The women did not take notice of the six Enrops that were flying overhead. They rode for almost an hour before Hannah led them down a smaller roadway to her home. The house was large and well built. There were barns and sheds on the property, all of which looked well cared for. Flower and vegetable gardens surrounded the house, but no people were seen as they hitched their horses.

"I thought you said you had hired people," Gabriel said as he helped the women down from the boca.

"I do hire two men to take care of the grounds and the animals but they do not come every day."

"I am going to look around," Raul said as Gabriel entered the house with the women.

"Forgive us but we must be careful," said Gabriel.

"I understand; search the house," Hannah said. "I will make some coffee."

Twenty minutes later Raul entered the house, just as Gabriel was walking into the kitchen from the cellar. "There is an empty barracks," Raul said to Gabriel.

"Yes, my father raised cattle and horses: he had many hired men working for him."

"This is a large house, there are seven bedrooms," said Gabriel.

"How many men do you have?" Hannah asked as she poured four cups of coffee.

"Counting me and Gabriel about eighty," Raul said.

"Eighty!" Hannah repeated with astonishment. "I don't have that much room in the buildings."

"But could they camp in the woods behind your house?" Gabriel asked.

"Of course," Hannah said. "Marcia and I can share a room that will open up another for your men."

"You are most gracious," said Raul. "There is one more thing; the warriors that are with us are Rualas."

"Really, how exciting, I have never met a Ruala," Hannah said then turned to Marcia. "They are people with wings."

"Wings? I have never heard of such a thing," Marcia said.

Less than twenty minutes later Gabriel and Raul took the women outside so they could watch the Rualas land. Both Hannah and Marcia were speechless at the sight.

"This is so thrilling," Hannah said after a few moments.

"Hannah and Marcia, this is Prince Lakin of the Ruala Tribe," Raul said. "Hannah has opened her home to us."

Lakin kissed both women on the cheek, "It is my pleasure and thank you for your kindness."

"Please forgive us, we are acting like schoolgirls but we have never met Rualas before and watching you fly was very exciting," Hannah gushed.

"We can always take you up so you can experience it," Lakin offered.

"Oh really," Hannah said with excitement and turned to Marcia who looked scared by the idea. "Well, perhaps we should wait on that. Please come into the house."

The next two hours were spent with the women helping their guests to settle in. Raul and Gabriel were to share a room in the house. Prince Lakin and Luca shared a room, Rabi had also come, he was going to camp in the woods until he saw Marcia, he then decided to stay in the house.

The women were preparing lunch for those who were staying in the house, as Lakin told them his warriors were prepared to fix their own meals.

"I could certainly buy more food," Hannah said as she was setting the dining room table.

"If you suddenly purchased food for eighty men wouldn't that look suspicious?" Gabriel asked.

"You are right, it has just been me and Marcia here for a long time," Hannah said, then as and after thought she added. "But the smoke house is filled with meats and there is a great deal of canned foods in the cellar, you certainly are welcome to what we have."

"You are most generous," said Lakin. "I am sorry we are putting you to so much trouble."

"This is no trouble and actually it is nice to have guests," Hannah said. As they ate lunch Hannah answered the men's questions about Nora and the disappearances. "I really doubt if Roch or his men are behind the disappearances because only men are missing, no women or children."

"We heard some believe Rogetts are responsible for the disappearances," Gabriel said.

"That is always a possibility," Hannah explained. "But the disappearances have occurred from a variety of places not just the mines. It is my understanding that Rogetts usually attack close to mines or caves because they cannot tolerate sunlight yet one of the cooks at the hotel disappeared during the day. If Rogetts travel in packs, how could they come to a busy hotel in the middle of the day without being seen?"

"What hotel?" asked Gabriel.

"The Endleson," Hannah replied.

"Isn't that the same hotel where the ball is being held?" Gabriel asked.

"Yes, why?"

"Tomorrow I will go to that hotel and look around but I think I would like to attend the ball," Gabriel said. "I believe that is the type of function that the men we seek would attend. Hannah would you accompany me or would that be too traumatic for you?"

"No, I will go with you but you will need some clothes. Tomorrow I can take you to a tailor and buy you a suit."

"My Lady, you may accompany me to a tailor but I will certainly buy my own clothes," Gabriel said with some indignation.

"I am sorry I did not mean to offend you," Hannah apologized.

"I'll start looking around the mines tomorrow," Raul said. "Hopefully I will be less likely to be recognized there."

Gabriel was driving Hannah's small boca as she sat in the passenger seat. They were heading to the tailor's shop in Nora.

"I am sorry that I offended you yesterday," Hannah said. "That was not my intent."

"I know," Gabriel said. "And I am sorry that I snapped at you."

"I still don't understand what bothered you?"

"I am a wealthy man; I do not need your charity."

Hannah gave Gabriel an incredulous look. "You certainly aren't humble for a priest."

Gabriel looked at Hannah and laughed, "Perhaps that is a lesson I need to learn."

"In fact you don't seem very much like a priest at all."

"And you have met many other priests?" Gabriel asked.

"Actually I have, when I lived in Wetpr," Hannah said. "I helped out at the orphanage in Salar, which is run by priests."

"Those priests were old and stodgy but you are well educated. You speak and carry yourself like a nobleman and you look like a warrior. Gabriel what are you?"

"I am all those things," he said with a soft smile.

"Well my noble, warrior priest; why are you in this godforsaken place?"

"I am hunting three men who are leading a group of people who are trying to help a powerful demon escape from its prison in The Abyss. Roch has a part to play, although I do not understand it yet." Gabriel saw the shocked look on Hannah's face. "So do you still want to help us?" he asked.

"Yes, of course."

"I find it curious that you are so willing to help total strangers when it is such a risk for you?"

"I guess I don't feel like Prince Raul is a stranger," Hannah said. "When I lived in Wetpr it was like a dream; that is the most wonderful place and it's like that because of King Sudfad and his family. They are such noble and generous people; I am proud to be of service."

"I once met Queen Renya at the orphanage. She brought money and supplies and stayed to play with the children. She is the most gracious woman I have ever met." Hannah paused for a few moments. "Being here is like living in a nightmare that I cannot escape from." Hannah turned her head so Gabriel could not see the tears that were coming to her eyes.

"What keeps you here Hannah?" She did not answer Gabriel's question. "When this mission is over why don't you return to Wetpr with us? Raul and I can find you a place to live and you could open your medical practice anywhere in the kingdom."

Hannah continued to look away as she spoke to Gabriel, "Sometimes I feel like my hatred for Roch and his men is the only reason I get up in the morning."

"So what are you saying?"

"I guess I don't know," Hannah turned and looked at Gabriel. "Could we please change the subject?"

"Of course."

"Tell me, what do you and Raul need me to do?"

"Hannah I want you to take me around the city and to introduce me to people; would you be willing to do that?"

"Of course but you do realize that people here are so terrified of Roch that they will not answer your questions."

"I seek information about many things," Gabriel said. "And trust me I have been working on missions for many years, I can be very discrete."

"I didn't mean anything against you I was just going to say that perhaps you should tell me some of the things you are looking for and I can speak with my friends, or as you call them my spies," Hannah said.

"Actually those are some of the people who I want to meet."

Chapter XV
The Caves of Sendra

Lazo gave a sigh of relief when they rode past Fort Castor; for he could not afford to be locked up during this mission. By midday this small army from Lentz had crossed the border into the Kingdom of Zorta. That evening they made camp east of the eastern fork of the River Toba. They would have to travel southwest for almost two days to reach the caves where the demons were holding the draw and hopefully the bounty.

It was after dark when Sorren walked back to the campsite. He walked up to Lazo and pulled a large knife from his sheath. "Don't make me regret this Lazo," Sorren said as he cut Lazo's restraints. "I talked with Bac and Calla and announced to the others that you were being untied. Trust me if you try anything you are a dead man."

"Thanks Sorren," Lazo said with his usual wryly smile. Lazo stood up, stretched then walked over to the campfire and poured himself a cup of whiskey. "Stephan don't look at me like that, I'll play nice," Lazo said sarcastically.

"Bac don't be so angry," Calla pleaded after Sorren left their campsite.

"That man does not deserve to live," Bac said. "I have to admit I am surprised that Sorren unleashed him."

"Sorren said they need him and we are most likely going into battle," Calla reminded Bac.

"I just don't want him anywhere near you," Bac said as he took Calla's hand. "I will kill him after this mission." Both Bac and Calla turned suddenly as they heard someone approaching their campsite. Galen and Sasha walked up to Bac and Calla smiling.

"Didn't mean to startle you," Galen said.

"Please sit by the fire," Bac offered. "We were just talking about Lazo, Sorren untied him."

"We know," Galen said as he took a cup of whiskey that Bac was handing him. "That's why we are here. Sorren told everyone that Lazo is being set free and if he does anything wrong, well, justice is in our hands. So Sasha and I are moving our camp over here by yours, and from the sounds of it, so are about another dozen Nordes warriors."

"Thank you," Bac said. "But we don't need your protection."

"Think of it more as we don't want to miss the fireworks," Galen said and laughed.

Three Enrops returned to Matthew and his men as they hid in the shadows of the hills that contained the caverns where the draw was being held.

"There are no signs of life around the hills," Jatu said. "I don't mean it is just quiet, there is no life other than the plants."

"What does that mean?" asked Sorren.

"Many times creatures will leave an area that is inhabited by demons," Jatu explained.

"There is plenty of vegetation and water here, so there should be animals and insects," Matthew said. "Must mean we have the right place."

"Let us go into the caverns and check for any alarms the demons may have created," Jatu the Enrop said.

"Alarms, damn," Lazo said. "If that draw is still going on, our best bet might be for a couple of us to go up there and act like we want to sign up."

"I was thinking the same thing," Thaos said. "Lazo and I should go; we look like criminals."

"Thaos, you can't go, you're one of the people on the hit list," Matthew said. "I think we should wait until Jatu returns before we decide if someone is going to act a part."

"I will go with Lazo," Sorren said. "I can make those demons believe I am a criminal."

Jatu and four other Enrops were gone for almost thirty minutes, before they returned to Matthew and the others.

"We were starting to get worried about you," Matthew said.

"We found the demons exactly where that man told you they would be. We could see eighteen of them but there could have been more in other areas of the caverns. They didn't have any guards or alarms," Jatu explained. "Which means they fear nothing."

"We could not enter the small cavern they were in without being seen but we could see in from one of the tunnels. There are several tables and stools in the cavern. It looks like the demons are playing cards and drinking. There are shackles connected to the stone walls, but they are empty. We saw two chests but could not see what was in them."

"Is there only one entrance into that cavern?" Stephan asked.

"No, there are three tunnels that lead into it," Jatu said. "Others of the flock are exploring the tunnels now."

"I still think Sorren and I need to go in first and try to do business with them," Lazo said. "It's the best way to get information."

"I agree," said Sorren.

"First I want to get warriors in place, so if things go bad you aren't in there alone," Matthew said. "We will wait for the rest of the Enrops to return."

"There's one thing about demons," Lazo said as he and Sorren boldly walked through the caverns looking for the place the draw was being conducted. "Ya can always smell them before ya see them."

213

"You might not want to say that so loudly," Sorren warned as they made their way through the dark passageways. But Sorren too, could smell the putrid odor that emanated from the hell beings.

"Well fellas, ya ain't easy to find," Lazo said as he and Sorren faced a cavern full of demons. Most of the demons were sitting at tables gambling, they remained silent as they sized up the two human intruders. "Now don't be looking at us like that," Lazo said. "We're here to join the draw; that is unless our money ain't good here."

One of the demons stood up and walked towards Lazo and Sorren, "How did you hear about the draw?" he asked suspiciously.

"Prescott and his boys," Lazo said. "We got to playing cards and drinking and Prescott started talking. And ya know he's probably talked to more than me and Sorren here."

"Humans," the demon said with a disapproving grunt.

"Well hell fellas, can we get in on the action or not?" Lazo asked.

"The price is two hundred dollars a note," the demon said.

"Sorren I told ya it would still be going on," Lazo said with a grin.

"We need a note each," said Lazo as they watched the demon walk over to one of the tables and pick up a large wooden bowl, which he now brought to them.

"Let's see your money first," the demon said.

Lazo and Sorren each pulled out two hundred dollars' worth of gold coins and handed them to the demon, who then extended the bowl to them. As Sorren and Lazo each picked a folded piece of paper out of the bowl Lazo said. "This bowl is still pretty full, so ya haven't had many takers?"

"What do you care?" asked one of the demons sitting at a table near the front entrance.

Lazo scratched his head, "Well actually I care a lot because everyone who bought a note is my competition." A couple of the demons laughed loudly at Lazo's remark.

"So how do we let you know when we've accomplished the tasks?" Sorren asked as he continuously looked around the cavern.

"Bring us back their ears," the demon who was holding the bowl said.

"Now don't ya guys think that I would be wanting to cheat ya or nothing," Lazo said with a grin. "But how do ya know if we bring you the right ears?"

A large demon with horns protruding from his cheeks started to laugh, "I like this guy," the demon said. "Have a drink with us."

"Don't mind if we do," Lazo said as he and Sorren walked over to the table where the demon was sitting.

"Thanks," Sorren said as he picked up a glass of whiskey. "You gotta name?"

"Ulger," the demon said as he filled their glasses again.

"Thanks," Lazo said as he downed his glass of whiskey in one swallow.

"The witch who set this up was brilliant for a human," Ulger said. "We've never seen anything like this. Follow me."

Ulger stood up and walked across the cavern. As Lazo and Sorren followed, they were trying to determine Ulger's size; they guessed him as over eight feet tall. Ulger picked up a large covered basket and set it on the nearest table. When Ulger removed the lid, Lazo and Sorren were staring at another set of the same dolls that Lazo had found in Juleta's castle. "These are your targets," Ulger said with a laugh. "If we place the ear of the victim against the doll with their likeness; the doll will burst into flames."

"Well I'll be damned," Lazo said. "I'm impressed."

215

"So how will we know if someone beats us to the prize?" Sorren asked.

"Trust us, you will know," Ulger said with a loud laugh.

"Kinda don't like the way ya are laughing when ya say that," Lazo said still grinning.

"It will be a surprise, humans like surprises don't they?" Ulger asked.

"I'm not a surprise type of guy," Lazo replied. "How long do we have to get this done?"

"That is up to you. The witch said these people may be hard to kill. But remember there are others with a head start on you," Ulger said as he walked back to his table and his hand of cards.

"Been nice doing business with ya," Lazo said. "Don't cha know that me and Sorren will be back claiming that treasure."

The Ruala warriors who were standing in two of the three tunnels that led to the cavern that the demons were in, now silently backed out of the tunnels. The Ruala's as well as Lazo and Sorren realized they could not kill the demons now, because there were too many unanswered questions.

"My Lord, there is a man here requesting to see you and Erebus," the Taperian soldier announced as he stood in the doorway of the war room.

"Did you get his name?" Cerephus asked as he looked up from his desk.

"High Priest Meekos."

"Show him in, then go get Erebus," Cerephus ordered.

"Being a king suits you," Meekos said with a grin as he entered the war room. Cerephus stood up and poured three glasses of whiskey, handing one to Meekos. "It's a little early for me," Meekos said as he declined the drink.

"You had better take it; you might need it."

"What are you talking about?" Meekos demanded.

"Erebus will be here in a few minutes. It would be better if the three of us spoke."

"Would you call Sophie?"

Cerephus stared at Meekos in disbelief. "Sophie left here weeks ago, Meekos. She said she had sent you messages."

"Messages, I never received any messages," Meekos said as fear slowly started to rise within him. "And why would she leave? That does not sound like Sophie at all?"

"You mean you don't know?" Erebus asked as he walked into the war room and closed the door behind him.

"Know what?" Meekos demanded angrily. "All I do know is that I have been sending Sophie messages for weeks and she has not answered any of them." Erebus took a seat where he could look at both Meekos and Cerephus.

"Actually we were hoping you could tell us what the hell is going on," Cerephus said. "After your last visit, I had Roch moved to the center wing of the castle so I could have his chambers. Sophie stayed by his side."

"One day she runs in here screaming at Erebus and me and accusing us of taking Roch. We had no idea what she was talking about, so we ran to his room and he was gone. We searched the castle and interrogated the staff; no one saw Roch or any strangers. You saw him yourself; Roch could not have walked out of this castle."

Meekos now drank his glass of whiskey in one gulp. "Then Sophie just ups and leaves for several days, when she returns she walks in here dressed like a lady of nobility and says she is leaving and going to stay with you in Malga."

"What!" gasped Meekos.

"She said she had been in the caves that were prepared for the ascension and they had been destroyed by holiness," Erebus explained. "But it sounded like she had talked to someone in the caves who knew where Roch might be."

217

"I have been trying spells to speak with the underworld; to get answers about all of this," Erebus said. "But something is blocking me. So I sent for another powerful sorcerer to help; thinking that we could combine our powers but we have accomplished little except to be told to stop asking questions."

"Who is this other sorcerer?" Meekos asked in almost a whisper.

"Malus, from Ryed," Erebus replied.

"I have heard of him," Meekos said. "He is said to be very powerful."

"Meekos I will be honest, I will sleep better once we know what has happened to Roch," Cerephus said. "As a man or a demon he is very dangerous and I will probably be the first person he tries to kill. Do you know what is going on?"

"No," Meekos said as the sweat ran down his face. "I feared something was wrong when I had not heard from Sophie. You say she is at the monastery in Malga?"

"She said that with Roch gone, her work here was completed and she was going to you," Cerephus explained. "She did not look or act like the Sophie we had known all these years."

"She is a woman of wealth who was playing a role," Meekos admitted. "Would you mind if I stayed here for a few days while we try to figure this out?"

"Meekos I don't particularly like you but you can stay here as long as you want," Cerephus said. "I want to get to the bottom of this."

Meekos looked at Erebus, "Perhaps if you, Malus and I combine our powers we can get some answers."

Sorren and Lazo turned and started walking out of the cavern; the hair on the back of Sorren's neck started to rise. "Something's not right here," he whispered to Lazo as Sorren grabbed the hilt of one of his knives.

"Just keep walking," Lazo said.

Suddenly a blood curdling scream filled the cavern. Enrops flew to Matthew and his men who were divided into two groups; each group was waiting outside of one of the exterior entrances of the tunnels.

"It's a trap, it's a trap screamed the birds. Meanwhile the Ruala warriors who were already in the tunnels turned and ran back to the cavern that Sorren and Lazo were in.

Matthew was leading one group of warriors and Stephan the second group; both groups ran into the dark tunnels following the sounds of the Enrops. Part of the flock of Enrops had been hovering outside of the front entrance to the cavern, when they heard Lazo scream they flew in and attacked the demons.

When Lazo screamed Sorren quickly turned and threw his first knife before the turn was complete. The knife hit the demon who was closest to Sorren in the throat. Sorren's second knife landed between Ulger's eyes, and penetrated his brain. The huge demon continued to stand although he was already dead, Ulger started to sway and fell forward.

As Sorren was grabbing another knife he glanced down at Lazo and saw that he was still alive but his head was covered in blood. A huge demon was running towards Lazo, Sorren quickly stepped in front of Lazo and took the full force of the demon's weight as the demon knocked Sorren to the ground. Sorren and the demon were punching each other; powerful blows that might have broken weaker beings.

Suddenly Sorren thrust his right thumb under the demon's left eye and gouge the eye from the socket. The demon screamed in pain and for a split second loosened his grip on Sorren who used his body weight to roll on top of the demon. Sorren punched the demon in the face three more times before the demon threw Sorren off from him.

Sorren was so focused on his fight that he did not see the Nordes and Ruala warriors who now filled the cavern. Screams echoed in the caves from both the men and the demons, the screeching of the Enrops was deafening. The sounds of battle alerted demons in other caverns, who now ran to join the fight.

Matthew thrust his sword through the stomach of a nine foot demon. The demon did not go down. Matthew pulled his sword out and thrust it into the demon's chest. The demon stumbled back a couple of steps then swung his battle axe at Matthew. Matthew ducked and the battle axe missed him. Matthew thrust his sword into the demon's crotch. The demon screamed and fell onto its knees. Matthew swung his sword and the demon's head rolled onto the floor.

Thaos was the first to see other demons running into the cavern; Thaos yelled to Stephan as he charged towards the demons. Stephan grabbed a fiery torch which was fastened to the wall and plunged it into the face of a demon he was fighting with. The demon was covered with long black hair which quickly ignited. Stephan turned and saw Thaos running towards an onslaught of demons. "Demons coming in the front," Stephan yelled and ran towards Thaos. Nordes and Ruala warriors now ran to the front of the cavern to battle those demons.

Thaos held a sword in each hand as he charged towards the demons; he took the demons by surprise by running through their group instead of battling with one demon. Thaos stabbed and sliced demon flesh as he was running among them. Many of the demons who were now focusing on Thaos were attacked from behind by Stephan and the other warriors.

Lazo's vision was blurred by the blow to his head. As he stood, nausea filled his being and his head started to spin. Lazo staggered to a spear that was propped up against the wall, he grabbed the spear and moved as quickly as he could towards Sorren, who was still battling the giant demon. The demon had Sorren pinned against the stone wall as he was choking the Nordes Chief.

Sorren was starting to lose consciousness when suddenly the demon's hands released his throat. Sorren opened his eyes and looked at the demon standing before him. Green bile and foam spurted out of the demon's mouth as he started to stagger backwards. Lazo had run the spear completely through the monster puncturing its lungs and heart. Lazo pushed the demon, who collapsed on the floor.

Lazo was regaining his sense of balance as he looked through the battling mob. A sadistic smile started to form on Lazo's face when he saw Bac at the far end of the cavern fighting with a demon. Lazo grabbed his knife from his boot sheath and pushed his way through the combatants towards Bac.

Sorren was catching his breath and wiping blood out of his eyes when he realized that Lazo was heading towards Bac. Sorren pulled one of his knives from the dead body of a demon and ran after Lazo.

Bac was fighting with a demon of tremendous proportions. Both Bac and the demon were bleeding from multiple wounds and the fury of their battle was exhausting them. Bac had his back to Lazo and never saw him coming. The din and chaos of the battle prevented Bac from hearing Calla's screams.

Calla separated from the demon she was fighting with and flew towards Lazo. She already had a dagger in her hand as she grabbed Lazo's hair, which was soaked in blood and slippery, so that Calla lost her grip. She reached for Lazo's head a second time when an explosion filled the cavern and Calla was blinded by the light.

Meekos sat before the fireplace in his chambers in the castle of King Cerephus, drinking whiskey. Meekos' hand shook as he put the glass to his mouth. He grew up a sickly and weak child, who was routinely tormented and bullied by others. That is until he turned to black magics.

Meekos' covenants with the demons gave him the power and retribution that his heart desired. Once he tasted power, Meekos appetite could not be satisfied. He became a leader, not because he possessed the strengths of character of a leader or had the integrity of a warrior but because he demanded ultimate control.

Now Meekos realized he was scared; the fear shook him to his very core. Meekos felt like he was not in control of anything anymore. For over three hundred years Meekos had been systematically putting the pieces together to prepare for the ascension of Omnibus.

Now at the eleventh hour everything seemed to be falling apart and he did not understand how or why. The punishment for failing at this mission was horrors beyond comprehension. Meekos would not allow himself to think about that possibility. He realized he must gain control of the mission again.

And Sophie, his beloved sister, where was she and why hadn't he heard from her. As these thoughts swirled in Meekos' mind he had a realization. Sophie would know he would return to Taperia, she must have left him a message of some kind. Meekos walked out of his chambers and back down to the war room where he found Cerephus and Erebus.

"I have been thinking deeply about this situation and I believe that Sophie would know I would return here and thus try to leave me a message. I want to search her room and then search the caves."

"Be my guest," Cerephus said. "We have not touched anything in her room since she left."

"I have never been in her room, so I would not know if anything was out of the ordinary," Meekos said. "Would you accompany me?"

"Actually I haven't been in her room since she left," Cerephus said as the three men walked out of the war room and down a long hallway to the room Sophie lived in for over twenty years. The three men walked into the relatively small room which was near the kitchen. The barren room was clean and orderly.

Erebus stood in the hallway as Meekos and Cerephus looked around the room. "Found something," Cerephus announced as he bent down and picked up a small envelope that had fallen from the nightstand. "It has your name on it." Cerephus said as he handed the envelope to Meekos; who sat down on the edge of the bed and opened it.

My dearest Meekos,

There is so much to say but you have not responded to any of my messages for months; this concerns me greatly. Roch simply disappeared without a sign or trace. I believe that Cerephus and Erebus had nothing to do with his disappearance. They both fear the wrath of Roch the man and Roch the demon.

*I sent you four messages after his disappearance and when I
did not hear from you I went to the caves. I rebuilt the altar and
replenished the offerings.*

*I stayed in the cave for three days, working, dancing and
summoning any spirit that could give me answers. My last
night there I feel asleep from sheer exhaustion. I awoke because
the giant snake that we worship was choking the life out of me.
The snake was being controlled by a very powerful demon that
I was not familiar with. I begged him to help me find Roch.*

*The demon talked as if he had great contempt for our plans to
raise Omnibus. He ridiculed me greatly, but he finally told me
that Roch was in a place where I could not go. When I asked if
Roch was alright, the demon laughed and said Roch was in a
place that he deserved. I asked if we could still complete the
ascension of Omnibus. And the demon gave me an answer I did
not understand.*

*He told me to go to my brother the hypocrite and that you
would tell me all I need to know. I have packed my things and
am awaiting a carriage as I write this letter. Hopefully I will
see you in a few days. But if our paths do not cross, I have faith
that you will return to the castle looking for me and find this
letter.*

As always your Sophie.

The roar of The Lion echoed through the Caves of Sendra. All of
the combatants were blinded by a white light of an intensity not
known to their worlds. The battle between the demons and the
humans, Shettees and Rualas stopped as the battle between the
powerful emissary of The Great Ruler and the Old Ones
commenced. The hills began to shake and tremble from the
power of the combatants in the caves. Worlds collided as five of
the oldest demons in time attacked The Lion.

The demons that had been conducting the draw were mere
minions compared to the Old Ones. Rock walls collapsed and
smoke filled the caverns. Snakes of all manner suddenly covered
the floors of the caves and deafening shrieks filled the tunnels.
The warriors of Sendra suddenly realized that the Sanuri was in
their midst as he was running up to them.

223

"Leave this place now," the Sanuri yelled. "There are powerful demons here and The Lion is doing battle."

"Give us our sight back and we will battle with him," Matthew yelled through the din.

"We will stay," hollered Stephan but we cannot see.

The voice of the Sanuri now rose above the screams and the turmoil, above the sounds of the collapsing hills. And as he spoke tears came to the Sanuri's eyes; tears of pride. "All who will stand by The Lion your sight has been restored; everyone else leave these caverns quickly."

The Old Ones sent snakes and armies of demons and monsters into those caverns. The screams and war cries of the combatants penetrated the barriers between the worlds; announcing that the war between the Forces of Light and the Ancient Evils was long from over. Three days and three nights the worlds shook. The Old Ones sent plagues and fire. They tried to cripple the warriors of Sendra with their greatest weapon: fear. But the choices had been made and the covenants sealed.

Natasha and Simon returned to the Taperian Imperial Hotel every day. They would arrive in the morning and watch Sophie. When Sophie left the hotel one or both of them would follow her; soon they recognized a routine to her behavior. Sophie would get up at dawn, have breakfast in the dining room of the hotel; then go shopping.

Sophie would return to the hotel for lunch, take a two hour nap in her room, go shopping, return to the hotel for dinner and retire to her room. Every time Sophie entered the hotel she would walk up to the desk clerk and ask if she had any messages or if her family had registered for rooms.

Both Natasha and Simon realized that Sophie was doing nothing more than waiting for word from her brother. But they knew they had to search her room. After four days of watching Sophie they decided to search her room the following morning when she was shopping.

"Ahriman," whispered Meekos as he folded the letter and put it into the pocket of his robe.

"What is it?" asked Erebus. "You look like you've seen a ghost."

"Much worse than a ghost," Meekos said in a hoarse voice. "I really could use a drink. Let's return to your war room and I will explain."

After all three men were seated Meekos said, "Over three hundred years ago I and others made a pact with the demon Omnibus to help him escape his prison in The Abyss; where he had been sent by The Lion of The Great Ruler. For our servitude we received wealth and power in this world."

"But we soon discovered that beings cannot travel between the different worlds easily and Omnibus needed a form, or vessel in this world that was strong enough to contain his power and energy. If you do not know already, Omnibus is one of the Old Ones and his powers are incredible." Meekos drank down his glass of whiskey and Cerephus poured him more.

Meekos continued, "We were given orders by dark lords to create a vessel for Omnibus. But the Vessel not only had to be strong it had to be conceived of pure evil. King Sharonne, a King of Stordt also was part of this pact. Sharonne volunteered to originate the evil linage needed to create the Vessel."

"The darkness that already existed in Sharonne was greatly intensified by the dark lords until evil totally consumed him. That evil was passed through Sharonne's family for generations, through the second sons. King Roch is the Vessel for Omnibus. The evil he possesses is beyond the world of man. When I saw what The Lion had done to Roch, I knew The Great Ruler knew of our plans."

"Do you know what it was that The Lion did to him?" Erebus asked.

"It was no affliction, at least not in the sense of a sickness like everyone assumed," Meekos answered. "I have read about such things. I guess the best way to try and describe it." Meekos paused. "Think of it as if The Lion held a great mirror before Roch and all of the evil that Roch sent into this world was reflected back upon him. He was attacked by his own evil."

225

Neither Cerephus nor Erebus spoke as they listened intently to Meekos' words. "I have been working closely with two other high priests, one is named Pravis and the other Tenebrae," Meekos said. "In our desperation we called to another of the Old Ones to get answers about how we could still complete this mission; because if this mission fails, we will be punished horribly. The demon we called to, is named Ahriman."

"We never should have gotten involved with him," Meekos said with a shaky voice. "Now we owe debts to both Ahriman and Omnibus. Sophie wrote in her letter that she went to the cave and resurrected the altar and called forth to any being that could give her answers. She describes having an encounter with a powerful demon, who was aware of Roch's location. I believe that the demon she encountered was Ahriman."

"Where is Roch?" Cerephus asked fearfully.

"The demon told Sophie that Roch was in a place where she could not go. I would imagine that means in one of the hell dimensions," Meekos said.

"So he is gone?" asked Cerephus.

"Or he is becoming more powerful?" Malus asked sharply as he entered the room.

"Where have you been?" Erebus asked. "I have looked everywhere for you."

"I have been to the caves and there is something I need to show all of you," Malus said gravely.

Consumed with fear, Lazo tripped and fell many times as he ran through the darkness. It wasn't until he fell into the water of the River Toba that Lazo realized he was no longer in the caverns. Lazo stood up on the shore of the river and attempted to get his bearings. The fear that had filled him now turned to horror as Lazo realized he could not see. The darkness of the caverns had been immense prohibiting any sight at all. But now that Lazo realized he was outside he knew he should be able to see more than complete and total darkness.

Malus led Erebus, Meekos and Cerephus to the caves near the River Nebu. "Even with our combined powers," Malus explained as the four men entered the caves. "Erebus and I have been blocked by some powerful force, every time we try even the simplest spells. All we really are doing is trying to get answers and we have been repeatedly warned to stop asking questions." The four men now entered the cavern where Sophie had resurrected the unholy altar.

"As you all know," Malus continued. "We suspect that The Lion of The Great Ruler was here some time ago. But more recently something very powerful must have been in here."

"Sophie encountered a powerful demon here, before she left," Meekos said. "I believe it was Ahriman."

"That may explain what I am about to show you," Malus said as he walked behind the altar and into the tunnel that led to the room where the ascension of Omnibus was originally planned to take place. "Although I don't know why he would do such a thing."

"Do what?" Meekos asked irritably.

"I think this is something I just have to show you," Malus replied.

As the four men neared the cavern where the large stone tub and a second altar still stood; they started to hear voices, more like screams but unusual in nature. All four men were carrying lit torches. "Put the torches in the holders," Malus said then come back and stand by me. As Cerephus was putting his torch in the metal holder affixed to the stone wall, he suddenly ducked as he felt a presence near him. Turning Cerephus saw nothing. He returned to the area where Malus was standing.

All four men were quiet, trying to discern the voices they were hearing. Suddenly they saw something that resembled lightening in the middle of the cavern. The lightning flashed several times and a deafening sound like thunder echoed off the stone walls. Smoke started to billow out of the area where the lightning was seen, then something flew out of the smoke and around the ceiling of the cavern.

227

The creature appeared to be a type of bird but not like anything any of the men had seen before. It was somewhat similar to a raven but had a huge elongated beak with large teeth. The creature flew over the heads of the men several times then suddenly disappeared.

"That is not the only creature I have seen in here," Malus said. "And I didn't recognize the others either."

"What are you saying?" Cerephus asked.

"These creatures are not of this world," Erebus replied with obvious concern in his voice. "It appears we have an opening of some kind to a hell dimension."

"What! How can that be?" asked Cerephus.

"My friends and I did not realize just how powerful Ahriman was when we summoned him," Meekos said. "I believe he is powerful enough to do something like this."

"Well, do you think he deliberately left this opening?" Malus asked of Meekos.

"I don't think he makes mistakes," Meekos said. "We summoned him to give us answers because we feared the wrath of Omnibus. Ahriman's ego was very insulted that we did not fear him more than Omnibus. He could be showing us how powerful he is."

"Let's hope that is the only reason," Erebus said then walked over to the stone tub and attempted to touch it. As Erebus was lowering his hand to the stone, he screamed in pain and quickly pulled his hand back. "That's why the creatures aren't coming farther into our world," Erebus said as he walked back to the others. "There is still holiness in this place."

Malus, Meekos, Erebus and Cerephus left the caves and returned to the war room in Cerephus' castle. These four unlikely companions now came together out of fear. "What does all this mean?" Cerephus asked as he poured four glasses of whiskey.

"I don't trust Ahriman," Meekos said fearfully. "I strongly suspect he is going to sabotage the ascension of Omnibus."

"Why would he do that?" asked Erebus.

"I don't know, maybe to prove that he can," Meekos said. "I suspect he has Roch and I don't know what that means for any of us. If Roch returns as either a man or a demon he will probably try to kill us all."

"Is there a way we can kill him first?" Cerephus asked.

"You mean while Ahriman still has him?" asked Meekos. "I believe that is highly unlikely" Meekos paused. Since it appears we are now in this together there are some things I probably should tell you. Ahriman wants us to lure the Sanuri into a trap. This concerns me greatly because in so doing I will be calling the wrath of The Great Ruler upon us also."

"Who are you referring to when you say us?" Erebus asked.

"Me, Pravis and Tenebrae."

Malus sat quietly while the others talked as he was pondering their situation. "Perhaps we are looking at this in the wrong light," Malus said. "We have been complaining that we are being blocked from speaking with beings from the underworlds. Now it appears that we have an open door to the underworld. I think we need to go back to the caves and try to get the answers we seek.

Chapter XVI
Exposed

Calen and Koby entered the Taperian Imperial Hotel by the balcony of the room that Simon rented. Their plan was to search Sophie's room while Simon and Natasha followed her. Several Enrops took positions outside of the hotel so they could warn the Ruala warriors if Sophie returned.

The room Simon rented was two doors down the hallway from Sophie's, with a view of her door. Calen and Koby waited several minutes after Sophie left her room to go to the dining room for breakfast before they went to her door. Natasha and Simon were already seated in the dining room when Sophie arrived.

Calen had the ring of keys that Natasha had stolen. He tried one in the lock without success, then a second key. When he inserted the third key, the locking mechanism released and he was able to push the door open. Calen and Koby entered the room, Calen started to search through Sophie's things as Koby watched the hallway. The room was neat and orderly. Sophie was filling up the closet and dresser drawers with clothing she was purchasing on her daily shopping trips.

"This room seems staged," Calen said as he was looking through her closet. "Something is not right here." Calen felt the carpet for any indications it could be concealing a trap door, he checked the walls for secret passages. He moved the furniture but found nothing. Calen was being careful as he conducted his search; he did not want Sophie to know anyone had been in her room.

Meanwhile in the dining room, Sophie suddenly stood up and appeared to be looking for something she may have dropped. Sophie was checking her clothing, then her small purse. She moved the chair and looked under the table. Natasha grabbed Simon's hand as she was watching Sophie, "We can't let her go back to the room now," Natasha whispered.

Simon stood up and walked over to Sophie's table. "Might I be of service My Lady," he offered. Sophie was clearly startled by Simon's sudden presence.

"I am sorry I did not mean to give you a fright," Simon said smiling. "I could not help but notice that you appear to be looking for something. And from the look on your face I am assuming it is something of importance to you."

Sophie smiled at the handsome man who was offering to help her. She unconsciously patted her hair to make sure it was in place, then she said, "If you would be so kind, I just realized I am not wearing my ring. I never take it off, it is a family heirloom."

"What does it look like," Simon asked.

"It is silver with a large ruby stone in the middle."

Simon knew instantly Sophie was taking about a blood ring. The members of the Insidiae who had sworn allegiance to Omnibus, wore these rings to identify each other. As Simon searched the floor, he engaged Sophie in conversation. The older woman was flattered by Simon's attention. Seeing that Simon was keeping Sophie distracted, Natasha left the table and quickly walked up the stairs to Sophie's room.

"What's wrong?" Koby asked as Natasha slipped into the room.

"She appears to have lost a ring and may return to the room to look for it," Natasha said. "Have you found anything?"

"I have now," Calen said as he lifted the mattress and saw two books hidden in the bedding. Natasha quickly grabbed the books as Calen put the bedding back in place. "Quickly we must leave," Natasha said as she spied a silver ring on the carpet. Natasha grabbed the ring and the three of them left Sophie's room.

Simon was talking loudly as he and Sophie walked up the stairs. Calen, Koby and Natasha could hear Simon's voice as they entered Simon's room and closed the door. Simon stood with Sophie in front of the door to her hotel room for several minutes talking. He grasped Sophie's hand and kissed it then turned and walked back down the stairs to the dining room.

Natasha handed Calen the books and the ring. "You must leave now," she said and kissed him on the lips. Both Calen and Koby left through the balcony doors. Natasha waited several minutes then left the room and joined Simon in the dining room. Sophie had not returned to her table.

231

"Simon you can be so charming," Natasha said teasingly as she sat across from him at the small table.

"Did they find anything?" Simon asked in a whisper.

"Two books hidden under the mattress and I picked a ring up from the floor," Natasha said as she lifted her veil enough to sip some coffee. "Do you think we should stay here or go?"

"I would like to see what she was hiding," Simon said. "Let's leave." Simon motioned for the waiter to come to their table so he could pay their bill. Natasha took Simon's arm as the two casually walked out of the hotel.

Sophie desperately searched her hotel room for her missing ring, as Simon and Natasha returned to the abandoned hotel their team was staying at. It would be two days before Sophie realized that someone had been in her room. But for now the woman was consumed with finding her blood ring.

When Simon and Natasha walked into the kitchen of the abandoned hotel they found Koby and Calen reading the books they had taken from Sophie's room. Sophie's ring was lying on the table. Simon picked up the ring and examined it. He explained its significance to the others.

"Simon, you said this ruby is to turn into blood when Omnibus ascends," Natasha said. "Then this is our first sign that the ascension has not taken place; that we are not too late. This is very good," she said with excitement. Then as an afterthought Natasha looked at Calen and asked, "Calen, Koby did you eat anything?"

"No," Calen replied. "And we are starving."

Natasha prepared breakfast as the three men looked through the books. "You are all so quiet; what are you reading?" Natasha asked.

"We were very lucky," Simon said. "One of these books appears to have spells and all sorts of information about dark magics and the other book is her diary."

"Oh, I want to read her diary," Natasha said. "I want to know why a woman would want to unleash such horror upon this world."

Gabriel and Hannah spent almost every moment together of Gabriel's first five days in Nora. She showed him the entire City of Nora and introduced Gabriel to everyone she could. Gabriel thought it might be easier for people to trust him if they believed that he and Hannah were lovers. Gabriel's plan did work in many cases although he learned little information of significance during this time.

Gabriel asked Hannah to set up additional meetings with the people who she referred to as her 'eyes and ears.' Gabriel hoped to gain the trust of these people so they would come to him with information instead of Hannah. Gabriel feared for Hannah's safety and wanted to protect her.

The more Hannah learned about Gabriel the more she became intrigued by this handsome, exciting man who did not fit any of her stereotypes. Having a house full of guests made both Hannah and Marcia realize how lonely and scared they had been. Both women enjoyed taking care of and talking with their new found friends. And these bonds of friendship were strengthened by the respect and adoration that Lakin, Raul and the other house guests felt for Hannah and Marcia.

"This has really been fun," Hannah said as she and Gabriel rode into Nora on the morning of the sixth day.

Gabriel was lost in thought as he drove the small boca. "I am sorry what did you say?" Gabriel asked as he turned and looked at Hannah.

"I just said that I have really enjoyed these roles we are playing. I have not had this much fun in a very long time." Hannah had been looking at the landscape and now turned to Gabriel. "You never talk about yourself, is that because you still don't trust me?"

"It's because I don't talk about myself," Gabriel replied with a grin. Hannah was staring at him, so Gabriel asked, "Alright, what do you want to know?"

233

"Are you married, where do you live, why do you hunt demons?" she asked with a laugh.

"Do I get a choice of which of those questions I answer?" Gabriel asked teasingly.

"No."

"I have never been married, I live in a castle near the monastery at Philiste in Wetpr and I hunt demons because it needs to be done."

"I am not sure which of those answers surprises me the most," Hannah said as she was trying to read the expression on Gabriel's face. "A handsome and charming man like you who has never married. A priest who lives in a castle or a selfless man who destroys the nightmares of others."

"My family is wealthy but my parents died when I was nineteen. My sister was only nine and I was not going to raise her in a monastery so we kept our family's castle. And as for being selfless and destroying the nightmares of others, well I guess that is left to interpretation," Gabriel said with a chuckle.

"I have heard the others speak of your sister Natasha; they say wonderful things about her. She sounds like the perfect woman, beautiful, a great cook and a courageous warrior. Rabi was telling me that she just married one of the Ruala warriors you work with. I would say you did a fine job of raising her."

"Thank you but it wasn't always easy, Natasha is very headstrong," Gabriel said, then his voice softened. "Natasha has followed me everywhere and fought at my side. That is no life for a young girl. I am glad she fell in love with a good man. Calen is very protective of her, perhaps he can persuade her to get out of the demon hunting business."

"There is a sadness in your voice," Hannah said. "You are happy for her but letting go of her has not been easy for you."

"Hannah you didn't tell me you were a mind reader too," Gabriel said with a self-conscious laugh. "But it's not like I am losing her. She and Calen are going to take over one of the wings of the castle when they live here and they want me to stay with them in their house in the Ice Caves."

"Are you going to?"

"I think so," Gabriel replied.

"Well, I think it all sounds very exciting," Hannah said. "And changing the subject for a moment; Rabi has been asking me a lot of questions about Marcia. I think he is quite taken with her."

"How does she feel?"

"I haven't talked to her about him yet but I do see the way she looks at him."

Hannah was watching Gabriel, trying to get the nerve up to tell him something, when he started to speak. "I want to go back to the Endleson Hotel and try to find your friend Miriam, do you think she will go to work today?"

"I really don't know."

"I have not found anyone who is willing to talk about that cook disappearing from the hotel."

"Or perhaps no one knows anything."

"Someone knows what happened and I am going to find out."

"Miriam, could we have a word with you about Jorge's disappearance?" Gabriel asked kindly. The woman appeared nervous as she met with Gabriel and Hannah in the alley behind the Endleson Hotel.

"I cannot speak with you here," Miriam said. "I will meet you at Hannah's office in a few moments."

Hannah took Gabriel's arm and the two strolled down the streets of Nora smiling and speaking with those they met. Lloyd walked up to the young couple and kissed Hannah's hand. "Gabriel I must say I have not seen Hannah smile in a very long time. You are good for her; I hope you plan to stay for a while."

"I am enjoying my visit and the company," Gabriel said and kissed Hannah on the cheek. "I do plan on extending my time here."

"Excellent," Lloyd said with a large smile. "And we will see you at the ball?"

"Yes, we will be there," Gabriel said then the two continued their walk to Hannah's office.

"Why are you so quiet?" asked Gabriel.

"Lloyd is right, I have not been happy since Laurabelle was murdered. Gabriel I know this is all a game but I have greatly enjoyed the time we have spent together."

"It's a very dangerous game," Gabriel said. "And I would like to minimize your role in it."

Hannah quickly swung around and looked at Gabriel. "Why?" she demanded.

Gabriel smiled at Hannah's confrontational manner. "Because I don't want you to get hurt. You have done a great deal to help us; I shouldn't be asking you to put yourself at risk."

"If I remember correctly, you did not ask me, I volunteered. And as long as I can be of use, I will continue to do my part." Hannah was clearly insulted by Gabriel's statement.

Gabriel laughed and took Hannah's hand. "For just a moment there I thought I was being yelled at by Natasha," he said kiddingly.

No sooner had Gabriel and Hannah entered her office then there was a knock at the door. Hannah opened the door and Miriam entered. Miriam nervously clung to the shawl she had wrapped around her shoulders as she took a seat in Hannah's sitting room.

"I was working the day that Jorge disappeared," Miriam said. "The kitchen of the hotel is very large and many people work there. On that day Jorge was supposed to buy produce. Farmers come to the back of the restaurant with all manner of meats, fruits and vegetables. Whoever is assigned to buy the produce, must inspect it and make sure Mr. Endleson is paying a fair price."

"The staff are saying that Jorge walked out of the back door, as he would to meet the farmers. After about twenty minutes Mr. Jasper comes walking in the back door asking why he has been kept waiting. Mr. Jasper is a farmer. Jasper said he had been outside of the restaurant for ten minutes and had not seen any sign of Jorge. A couple of the other cooks went outside and they found one of Jorge's shoes lying in the alleyway. And someone said there was blood. Understand I did not see any of this."

"And what time of day was this?" Gabriel asked.

"I don't know, around ten in the morning." Miriam replied fearfully.

"That seems like a busy place for someone to be attacked without witnesses," Gabriel said. "Did Jorge have enemies?"

"No, he was a gentle man and well liked."

"Miriam I want you to think hard about the next question I am going to ask," Gabriel said. "In the past few weeks have you noticed any unusual people at the hotel, or perhaps people acting strangely?"

Miriam was quiet for a couple of moments as she thought about his question. "There are always a lot of people at the Endleson but it is expensive to stay there so most of the guests are wealthy." She paused for a moment. "Well, there are those priests, at least one of the maids said they were wearing priest's robes the day they arrived. They certainly don't act like any priests I have ever heard of, what with all those women coming and going and all the drinking."

Gabriel's face did not betray the surge of adrenaline that ran through him as he listened to Miriam's words. "Tell me more about these priests."

"Well there was three of them but one left after a week. They all have rooms on the fourth floor, next to each other."

"Do these rooms have balconies to the front of the building or to the back?" Gabriel asked.

Miriam thought for a moment, "To the back, in fact they would be above the alleyway where Jorge disappeared."

237

Suddenly Miriam gasped loudly. "Oh, you don't think they did something to Jorge do you?"

"Miriam if they are priests they probably had nothing to do with Jorge's disappearance," Gabriel said in an effort to calm the woman's fears.

"All I can tell you is that when I clean the rooms they are gone but the rooms are always a mess, bottles of whiskey and such all over." Miriam lowered her voice. "And sometimes there is woman's clothing lying around."

"Miriam what days do you clean their rooms?" asked Hannah.

"Mondays, Wednesdays and Fridays; unless of course the guests request extra cleaning."

"Today is Thursday," Hannah said. "So what time do you plan to clean their rooms tomorrow?"

"They are not early risers, so I usually clean their rooms around eleven in the morning."

"Miriam I will meet you at ten tomorrow morning; I will clean their rooms," Hannah said as Gabriel quickly gave her a disapproving look.

"I don't want to get into trouble," Miriam said fearfully.

"I will pay you a week's wages," said Hannah. "Which door should I enter?"

"Come in the back kitchen door but Hannah you will have to dress very differently," Miriam warned. "I will be waiting for you."

"And Miriam, no one should be told about this," Hannah said.

"I wouldn't tell no one," said Miriam. "I could lose my job."

Gabriel waited until after Miriam left before he spoke to Hannah. "Hannah I am running this mission," he said angrily. "I will decide what needs to be done."

"Gabriel what were you going to do; ask that poor frightened woman to search through their things? And what if she got caught?" Hannah boldly stared Gabriel in the eyes as she spoke. "You know this is our best chance of getting into their rooms." Gabriel was so angry he couldn't speak so Hannah continued. "So do you have any better ideas?" Gabriel glared at Hannah, he knew she was right. "Gabriel why are you so angry? Is it because I didn't ask your permission?"

"Hannah I don't want you to get hurt; you are not trained for these things."

"How do you know what I can and cannot do?" Hannah asked angrily. "You would let Natasha do this wouldn't you?"

"Yes but she has trained as a warrior since she was a child. And I still would worry about her."

"Gabriel I am going to do this; now it would help if you would tell me what I should be looking for. But since you seem too mad to talk to me; I am going to buy a disguise." Hannah said and started to walk past him. Gabriel grabbed Hannah's arm and turned her around so she was facing him.

"Hannah we both need to calm down before we walk out that door."

"We could just pretend we are having a lover's quarrel," Hannah said sarcastically.

Gabriel stared at Hannah intensely for several moments then said in a hoarse voice, "The problem is; I think we are."

Hannah stopped talking, she felt as if Gabriel had just discovered her secret and she wasn't sure how he was reacting to it. Fear surged through her as she searched Gabriel's eyes. "I should go shopping," Hannah said softly. But Gabriel did not let go of her arm; Hannah suddenly felt like she wanted to run away. She really did not want to hear Gabriel tell her that he didn't have feelings for her. Hannah's voice was shaking as she whispered, "Gabriel, I really should go."

"I'll go with you," Gabriel said as he let go of Hannah's arm. Gabriel's revelation was such a surprise that it over shadowed his anger. The two barely spoke as they walked down the streets of Nora.

Gabriel and Hannah returned to her home after they bought her disguise. There was still silence between them which was immediately noticed by Raul, Lakin and Luca. Hannah went to the kitchen and started to prepare dinner, without speaking to anyone. Gabriel joined the others in the parlor. He poured himself a glass of whiskey and sat down without saying a word.

"Did you two get into a fight or something?" asked Luca.

"I really don't want to talk about it," Gabriel said gruffly. Luca, Lakin and Raul all looked at each other but none of them spoke. Hannah walked into the parlor with a large tray that appeared heavy. Raul quickly jumped out of his chair and took the tray from her.

"I should probably have waited until after dinner," Hannah said. "I found these bottles of brandy in the wine cellar. My father always had these shipped here; he said it was the finest quality brandy. He would always have a glass of brandy and a cigar or pipe every evening. I don't know if any of you smoke but I bought you some tobacco and cigars to have with your brandy. There are a variety of pipes in that cabinet," Hannah said and nodded at a cupboard behind where Luca was sitting. Hannah turned and was walking out of the room when Lakin spoke.

"Hannah thank you," Lakin said. "This was very generous of you." Hannah smiled and returned to the kitchen without saying a word. Lakin stood up and walked over to the door of the parlor and closed it. "Gabriel what is going on here?"

"It really is none of your business," said Gabriel.

"During the years we have worked together," Lakin said. "How many times have I heard you say we cannot have dissension in the team or we will lose focus? Now you and Hannah are both acting like you are focused on something else. Will the two of you be able to work together?"

"I think so," Gabriel replied with a growl.

240

"She is such a lovely woman, what could she have done to make you so angry Gabriel? I can't remember the last time I saw you angry," Lakin asked.

"I believe I know what is going on," Luca said as he lit a cigar. "Hannah is clearly in love with Gabriel and I think he has feelings for her also and they both just realized it."

Gabriel sat motionless for a moment, then he asked Luca, "Do you really think she is in love with me?"

"We all do," Raul said. "We were wondering how long it would take for you to realize it."

"Gabriel as long as I have known you, you are always keenly perceptive of others," Luca said. "How can you not see this?"

"I don't know," Gabriel answered as he stared at the floor. "This is not good."

"Why not?" Lakin asked. "I think she is perfect for you. And if I wasn't married I would most definitely pursue her."

"The only thing that keeps me from pursuing her," Luca said with a grin. "Is that both of you clearly have feelings for each other."

"This is not good, not at this time, not on this mission," Gabriel muttered more to himself than to the others.

After dinner, Hannah's houseguests went to the parlor to talk and drink, as was becoming their nightly ritual. This night Raul asked Hannah to join them. Hannah declined but Raul said he had something for her and wanted her to join them.

Hannah deliberately took a long time cleaning the kitchen and preparing bread dough and potatoes for the morning breakfast. She felt humiliated and awkward around Gabriel. Hannah felt that he did not return her affections and she thought Gabriel felt uncomfortable now that he realized she cared for him.

"Well, it's about time," Raul said as Hannah entered the parlor.

"I was preparing breakfast," she said meekly.

"You know Hannah, you can join us any time," Lakin said. "We do not mean to exclude you."

"Oh no, I don't feel like that," Hannah said as she took a seat near Raul. "I just have work to do."

"Today when I received my letter from Vitomas, she included a gift and a letter for you," said Raul.

"What is it?" Hannah asked with surprise as Raul handed her a small pouch and an envelope.

"I don't know," Raul replied.

Hannah opened the pouch and a pearl necklace and earrings fell onto her lap. "There are light blue sapphires between the pearls," she gasped. "I love them, they are so beautiful."

"I told her you often wear light blue, she had them made for you."

"Why?"

"Because you are protecting and helping us," said Raul. "I hope you don't mind but I also told her about what Roch did to your sister."

"No," Hannah said in a whisper as she opened the envelope. The men watched in surprise as tears started to stream down Hannah's face as she read the letter which was several pages long.

"Raul I would very much like to meet your wife someday, she is a lovely woman," Hannah said as she stood up and walked over to the fireplace.

"Why are you burning the letter?" Raul asked.

"Because if someone found it, you would all be exposed and I cannot let that happen," Hannah said as she was trying to compose herself.

"Hannah we have all been talking," Gabriel said. "You cannot stay here after we leave. We would like you to return to Wetpr with us."

"Or you can come to the Ice Caves," Lakin offered. "They are a beautiful place to live."

"Well, I don't know what to say. Thank you all for your concern; it is very gracious of you," Hannah put the necklace and earrings back into the pouch. "Now My Lords, if you don't mind I am going to retire."

Luca stopped Hannah as she was starting to walk out of the parlor. "Rabi is in your room with Marcia. Let me go up there and tell him to leave," Luca said as he quickly stood up.

"No Luca, Marcia has had a hard life, let her have her moment of happiness," Hannah sounded exhausted as she spoke.

"Where will you sleep?" Luca asked.

"In one of these chairs; I have before."

"Hannah take my bed and I will sleep on the floor," Raul said.

"Certainly not Raul, I will not have the Prince of Wetpr sleeping on my floor," Hannah said sharply.

"Take my bed," Gabriel said. "I will take the floor."

"No, none of you will shame me by sleeping on the floor, that is final," Hannah said and walked out of the parlor.

Lakin and Raul both looked at Gabriel, who stood up and followed Hannah into the hallway. "Hannah," Gabriel called. She stopped walking and turned around. Gabriel waited to speak until he was near her. "If you won't let me sleep on the floor, then share my bed. I will keep my clothes on; you will have nothing to worry about."

"Gabriel you are always the perfect gentleman, I fear nothing like that from you," Hannah said as she looked into his eyes. The beds that you and Raul have are very small; there is not room for two people. I will be just fine in a chair."

"Hannah you will shame me if you sleep in a chair," Gabriel said softly. "There is plenty of room for the two of us." Then he added with a grin. "You are pretty small."

Hannah lowered her voice so the others would not hear, "Gabriel I don't think this is a good idea. You aren't comfortable with my feelings for you and this could make everything much worse."

"I want you to," Gabriel said. Hannah did not answer. "Let me tell Raul that you are staying with me."

"Do you think he will mind?"

Gabriel laughed, "No, I am telling him so he keeps his clothes on. He always sleeps naked. My bed is the one closest to the window; I will be up in a few minutes."

"I am going back to the mines tomorrow," Raul said as Gabriel entered the room. "Something is not right there. I have been to the mines in Wetpr and they are busy, noisy places. The mines here seem abandoned."

"Many of the people believe Rogetts are behind the disappearances," said Gabriel. "Which is a good reason for them to stay out of the mines."

"I am still going," Raul said. "Sooner or later I will find something."

"Hannah is sleeping in my bed," Gabriel said to Raul, then he grinned and added, "So you will need to keep your pants on."

"Do you want me to sleep someplace else?" Raul offered.

"No that is not necessary," Gabriel said and finished his drink.

When Gabriel walked into his room, Hannah was not there. Although he was not surprised, Gabriel found himself feeling disappointed. He closed the door and took off his shirt and boots; he was just about to take his pants off when he heard a soft knock at the door.

"Come in," Gabriel said. "I didn't think you were coming."

"I didn't want to sleep in that dress, it was dirty, so I changed," Hannah said shyly. Gabriel could see that she was wearing a white silk nightgown; most of which was covered with a shawl. Hannah closed the door but stood with her back against it.

244

"Gabriel I have to tell you, I feel so awkward, I know it's silly we are both adults."

"I haven't seen you with your hair down before," Gabriel said. "It's beautiful. You should wear it down more often." Hannah didn't say anything nor did she move from the door. "Hannah you look scared, it's going to be alright, we are just going to sleep," Gabriel said and held out his hand to her. Hannah nervously walked up to Gabriel, all the while clutching her shawl tightly.

"Take that thing off and climb under the covers, its cold in here," Gabriel said as he removed the shawl from Hannah's shoulders and dropped it on a chair. Gabriel caught his breath as he looked at Hannah. The nightgown had a plunging neckline which exposed a great deal of her breasts. The thin material was not only transparent but clung suggestively to her body.

"Oh I knew I shouldn't have put this on," Hannah said nervously as she reached for her shawl. "I am sorry I didn't mean to embarrass both of us." Hannah looked like she was going to cry.

Gabriel took Hannah's hand, stopping her from picking up the shawl. "No, I like it. I just wasn't expecting it. And you didn't embarrass both of us. Well at least not me," Gabriel said with a grin.

"Gabriel I," Hannah stopped talking as she searched his eyes.

"You what?"

"I shouldn't have come here; this is not a good idea."

"Why do you say that?"

"Gabriel I have never met a man like you before. I have very strong feelings for you and..." Hannah started to cry.

"And what?" Gabriel asked as he put his arm around Hannah and the two sat down on the bed.

"And I think that if I sleep in here with you that I will just want you more and it is obvious you don't have feelings for me."

"I need to go." Hannah attempted to stand but Gabriel pulled her closer to him.

"I never said I didn't have feelings for you Hannah. I think that you are an exceptionally beautiful and amazing woman. Please stay. You are shivering; let's get under the covers and talk."

Gabriel kept his trousers on and the two of them crawled under the blankets. "Don't be afraid to lie in my arm, this bed is small," Gabriel said and extended his arm. Hannah huddled up against him. Gabriel was lying on his back and Hannah laid her head on his chest. The two were silent for several moments.

"Hannah look at me," Gabriel said softly. "I don't live a normal life, I am always traveling and it is dangerous." Hannah now rose up on her elbow so she could look into his face.

"And yet you raised your sister and it sounds like you did a wonderful job." When Gabriel did not say anything Hannah continued. There was sadness in her voice as she spoke. "Gabriel you don't have to want me but don't close yourself off to everyone. There is more to life than hunting demons." Then Hannah lay back down with her head on Gabriel's chest and her face turned away from his. Hannah was trying very hard not to cry; she felt as if there was a great weight in her chest.

"Hannah look at me," Gabriel whispered. She did not move. "Hannah please." She still did not move. Gabriel put his arms around her and rolled both bodies over as one. Hannah was now lying on her back and Gabriel was on top of her. Before Hannah could say anything, Gabriel kissed her lips. A kiss that took them where there were no demons, no horror, no fright. They were both so lost in their emotions they did not hear Raul knocking at the door.

When Gabriel and Hannah did not respond, Raul opened the door, "Hannah some people just brought a badly injured man here."

"Raul take him to the room that's off the parlor, it's another office. I will be right there," Hannah said as she jumped out of bed and started to run towards the door. Gabriel grabbed her arm. "You can't go down there like that," Gabriel said as he picked up his shirt and put it on her.

"Hannah we are so sorry to bother you," the woman said as Hannah ran into the office. "But me and Henry were riding home when we saw this poor soul lying by the road."

"Alice you did the right thing by bringing him here," Hannah said as she started to examine the man who was lying on her table. "Raul will you get Marcia? Gabriel please help me get his clothes off. There is so much blood on him; I don't know where all of his wounds are."

"He's been talking crazy," Alice said as she and her husband were leaving the room. "He keeps saying there are demons in the mines."

The wounded were many, as the warriors of Sendra carried their comrades, both those alive and dead from the caverns of the damned. Sorren was instrumental in getting the dead out of the caverns; he did not want to dishonor their memories by sealing them in a grave with demons. The Sanuri told Matthew to lead the warriors back to the campsite they had established several nights before. "Matthew take them to safety," the Sanuri ordered. "Under no circumstances do any of you come back here. I will meet you at your campsite."

Although the warriors were injured, exhausted and hungry their spirits soared; for only in myths and legends had such battles been spoken of. This small band of men and women from different tribes and races stood against the armies of hell and won. Everyone who could walk was carrying someone who was greatly injured or dead. Sorren started to sing loudly and voice after voice joined in as they sang a song of victory.

Matthew led the warriors to the site of their former camp. Although the warriors had left many of their belongings at this site because they did not want to carry them into battle; Matthew now rearranged the areas.

Galen and Sasha were put in charge of an area to treat the wounded. Stephan and Sorren were in charge of taking care of the dead. Thaos and Thedes established a guarded perimeter.

Any warrior who was still able but not assigned to one of these groups was getting water, fixing food and moving the campsites. There was not a warrior among them who was not injured.

Matthew was now glad that Angelina had forced him to bring extra bags of bandages, herbs and other medical supplies. He went to his campsite and grabbed the four large bags and ran to the area that Galen and Sasha were setting up. "I told Angelina she was worrying too much," Matthew said as he handed them the bags. "Turns out she knew exactly what we faced."

"I wish Angelina or Shara were here now," Sasha said. "They are both great healers."

"Tell me what you need me to do," said Matthew.

Suddenly the earth shook with such great fury that trees toppled down. Huge plumes of smoke and dust rose high into the sky from the areas where the hills once stood. The warriors had moved far enough from the hills that the shower of stones and debris did not fall upon them. Then there was silence. They all knew the battle was over.

The hills near Sendra collapsed as the last of the demons were defeated. For the rest of time the people of Zorta would tell a story of how an entire range of hills was swallowed by an earthquake of unimaginable proportions. The Lion made sure that the faithful warriors who fought at his side, escaped from the caverns before they were swallowed by the earth.

Two hours later the Sanuri was walking among the wounded warriors of Sendra. He was blessing and healing the beings who so bravely stood against the hell beasts. "You all need sleep," the Sanuri said to Matthew.

"We will sleep in shifts," Matthew said. "We need to guard the camp and care for the wounded."

"Because you fought at the side of The Lion, he will guard your camp this night and I will care for the wounded. Go Matthew and tell your people to sleep," the Sanuri said.

Sleep came immediately to all for their exhaustion was great. As the warriors slept the Sanuri laid his hands upon each and every one of them. He gave them some of his own life force to help them heal. As the Sanuri was walking among the sleeping warriors The Lion walked into the camp.

"The children have done well," The Lion said to the Sanuri. "And Matthew has passed his tests but he has some dark days to come and you will need to be there for him."

"Is it another test?" asked the Sanuri.

"No, it is his life that must be played out," The Lion said then disappeared into the night.

Chapter XVII
Healing

Hannah worked diligently trying to save the life of the badly tortured man who had been brought to her home.

"Look at these wounds," Hannah said to Gabriel and Raul as she cleaned the blood off from the man's skin. "It looks like symbols are cut into his flesh. Have you ever seen anything like this?"

Raul put his face close to that of the injured man and asked, "Did Hutas do this to you? Please can you tell me?"

"Yes," the man whispered. "Water, I need some water."

Marcia left the room to get water as Hannah continued to clean the man's wounds and try to stop his bleeding. "We are getting you water," Raul said. "Can you tell me where the Hutas are?"

"Everywhere, they are everywhere."

Marcia helped the man drink a cup of water. He started to gurgle and choke as he drank the liquid. "What are the Hutas doing?" Raul asked since normal behavior for the Hutas would be to attack everything in their path.

"The demon, they are raising a demon."

"Which mines are they in?" Raul asked.

"I don't know, they took me from Nora," the man coughed several times as he spoke.

"What is your name?" asked Gabriel.

"Jorge."

"Jorge why did they take you?" Gabriel asked as he walked closer to hear Jorge's faint voice.

Jorge coughed a couple of times before he spoke, "I don't know, I walked out the backdoor of the hotel and saw a Huta in the alley talking to one of the priests. I was so shocked I just stood there and stared at them."

"The priests staying at the hotel?"

"Yes, the large man with the pock marked face."

"You did all you could do," Gabriel said as Hannah pulled a sheet over Jorge's body.

"It just kills me every time I cannot save a patient," Hannah said sadly. "But it might be a blessing; he was so damaged that if he lived he would have been in constant pain. So you and Raul think those priests are responsible for what happened to Jorge?" Hannah was cleaning her instruments as she talked. When Gabriel did not answer she turned around and realized he was praying over Jorge's body. Hannah waited for Gabriel to finish then she walked up and kissed him on the cheek.

"Yes, those priests have been responsible for many horrible things; that is why I don't want you going into their rooms."

"Gabriel that is exactly why I have to, you know that," Hannah said softly. "Besides you and Raul will be at the hotel if I need help. Hannah walked past a mirror as she was putting her medical instruments away. "Oh Gabriel, your shirt is covered in blood, I will buy you another."

"I have plenty of shirts," Gabriel said as he put his arm around Hannah's shoulders. "I have to admit I was impressed with how hard you were trying to save that man's life. I'll bet in most cases you are successful."

"I have not lost many patients; thank The Great Ruler."

"Let's go to bed and try to get a couple of hours of sleep, the sun will be up soon," Gabriel said as they walked to the bedroom, with their arms around each other.

As they tried to enter the room quietly, Hannah saw that Raul's bed was empty. "Where is Raul?"

"I think he thought we might want to be alone," Gabriel said as he helped Hannah take off the bloody shirt. Gabriel bent down and kissed Hannah on the lips; she stretched upwards and put her arms around his neck. They kissed hungrily for several minutes before there was a knock on the bedroom door.

"I don't believe this," Hannah whispered, then giggled.

"Come in," Gabriel said although he did not let go of Hannah.

Rabi entered the room and smiled when he saw Gabriel and Hannah still in an embrace. "I have some bad news. As soon as Raul realized that man was tortured by Hutas he sent some of us to look for the people who brought him here. Raul was afraid the Hutas would be hunting the man."

Hannah now dropped her arms from Gabriel's neck and turned to face Rabi, whose eyes grew wide when he saw her nightgown. Hannah was so focused on Rabi's words that she forgot what she was wearing. Gabriel quickly grabbed a blanket off from the bed and put it over Hannah. "Rabi what are you saying?" she asked

"We found that man and woman and they are dead."

"Alice and Henry," Hannah gasped. "I have known them my entire life. Where did you find them?"

"Lying alongside the road a few miles from here."

"So you are saying there is a party of Hutas tracking Jorge here?" Gabriel asked.

"There was but we killed them and hid the bodies," Rabi said. "There were eight of them. Right now Raul, Luca and some of the others are wiping away any trail that could lead here."

No one slept in Hannah's house that night. Half of the Ruala warriors were looking for Hutas and the rest were protecting the house. "I will have warriors watching over you as you ride into Nora today," Lakin said as Hannah was serving them breakfast.

"Hannah, Raul is going to sit in the lobby and watch for the priests, Enrops will be on the outside of the hotel to warn us if they return. I am going to try to get a room on the fourth floor; if there aren't any available I will be in the hallway. And I want to help you get ready for the role."

"What do you mean?" Hannah asked as she was putting platters of ham and bacon on the table.

252

"Natasha has become very clever with hiding weapons in her clothes and hair; I want to show you a few of her tricks. Did you mean it when you told us you weren't afraid to use a weapon?"

"Of course I did, I wasn't lying to you," Hannah said with some indignation. "But after hearing the stories about Natasha I will tell you I am not that talented."

"It just takes training," Gabriel said. "But for today, I don't want you to take any unnecessary risks. Just search the rooms and get out of there."

"But if I find any maps or information about demons you want me to take it don't you?"

"Only if you can hide it well," Gabriel said.

"I was already thinking about that," Hannah said. "My father used to wear this, actually I am not sure what it is called. It is like a huge belt with compartments in it. He used to wear it under his shirt when he traveled. He would hide his money and important papers in it. I got it out of his room this morning; I was going to wear it under my blouse. His room is the one Lakin and Luca are sharing. All of Father's things are in that huge closet and that trunk on the floor, you are all welcome to use any of his things for disguises or I guess just to keep them; I have no use for them."

"Did he have any hats?" Raul asked.

"Dozens of them, seriously help yourselves. And Gabriel, Miriam has a cart filled with cleaning supplies and fresh linens that she takes to the rooms; we should be able to hide things in that."

Lakin looked at Gabriel and smiled, "Hannah is cut out for this kind of life."

When Matthew, Stephan, Sorren, Thaos and Thedes awoke the next morning they found the Sanuri sitting at their campfire cooking breakfast.

"Did you do this?" Stephan asked in amazement.

"Do what?" the Sanuri asked.

"My wounds are healing so quickly," Stephan said. "I can move my left arm again."

As Matthew was listening to Stephan; he stood up and put pressure on his right leg that had an axe wound. "I can stand on my leg with little pain. Whatever you did, I thank you."

"You healed us all, didn't you?" Sorren asked.

"It was my gift to all of you, for the choices you made," the Sanuri said as he poured coffee into their cups. Soon their campsite was filled with warriors as they came to thank the Sanuri for the miracle. When Bac and Calla walked into the campsite to speak with the Sanuri, Calla kept looking around suspiciously.

"If you're looking for Lazo, we haven't seen him," Sorren said to Calla.

"Why would you be looking for Lazo?" Bac asked Calla.

Calla looked at Sorren but did not speak. "Because when you were fighting Calla and I saw Lazo coming up behind you with a knife. She was on top of him with her dagger drawn, when the white light blinded us all," Sorren said.

"Calla why didn't you tell me this?" asked Bac.

"Because you needed your rest and I didn't want to upset you."

"Have any of you seen him?" Bac asked.

As the men thought about his question they all realized the last time they saw Lazo was in the caves. "Did he die in the caves?" Sorren asked the Sanuri.

"No." Before anyone could say a word, the Sanuri looked at Bac and Calla. "Did you have a question for me?" The young couple looked at each other with surprise. "Yes we do," Bac said. "We were wondering if you would marry us while you are in the camp."

"When would you like the ceremony?" the Sanuri asked.

"Would sunset be alright?"

"That would be fine. It is good that we are doing something wonderful after so much devastation."

"Sorren would you walk Calla down the aisle?" Bac asked.

"I would be proud to," Sorren said with a big smile.

Both Calla and Bac were visibly excited. "We will leave you to your breakfast," Bac said. "We'll come back later."

"I like those two kids," Sorren said after they left.

Matthew looked at Sorren and grinned. "I keep telling you, Ruala baby named Sorren."

Sorren smiled. "I would be honored if that happened," he said, then he became very serious. "Now that we are alone I can tell you what happened in the cavern before you got there."

As Sorren told of the events in the cave, Matthew and Stephan were filled with fear for their families. "This is like a nightmare that will not end," Matthew said. "There are assassins after our families and we don't know how many or who they are. And now that those demons are destroyed there will be no one to call them off."

"There never was a plan to call them off," the Sanuri said as he lit his pipe. "And those demons never planned to pay the bounty. They were getting humans to do their dirty work, then they were going to kill them."

"How do you know this?" Sorren asked.

"I read the mind of one of the demons before the caverns were destroyed. This entire thing was a trap. Juleta had a calculating mind; she knew you would go after the demons once you found those dolls."

"How did she know we would find the dolls?" Stephan asked.

"I am just guessing that she knew how greedy Lazo was and figured he would return to the castle," the Sanuri said.

"Juleta's plans have played out perfectly," Matthew said. "She must have had a back-up plan, to make sure one of us found those dolls."

"The reason that demon threw the knife at Lazo was to cut off his ear," the Sanuri explained. "What you didn't see was that there was a doll of him and also of you Sorren. She planned it out very carefully."

"Now I am wondering if this entire thing was set up to get us out of our homes so our families would be vulnerable," Matthew said.

"Mathas and Claudius have thought of that also, they are prepared for anything," said the Sanuri. "I am surprised that none of you have asked me if I know who the assassins are."

"Did you see that?" Stephan asked quickly.

"Yes, the only men who took part in the draw were the ones you met in Langer. They were sent to either kill you or tell you about the draw so you would walk into Juleta's trap."

"So this is over?" Matthew asked. An Enrop landed next to Matthew and handed him a letter, which he did not open immediately.

"I believe the lower level demons in that cave only had knowledge of this particular trap. But that doesn't mean Juleta hasn't set up others."

"Lower level demons, what do you mean?" asked Sorren.

"The demons you were fighting with were mere foot soldiers of the Old Ones; that is why you could kill them. The Old Ones are the original demons who came to mankind, they are very powerful, I cannot even kill them."

"And you said The Lion was fighting five of them?" Thedes asked as he poured more coffee into everyone's cups.

Matthew was reading the letter and before the Sanuri could speak Matthew said, "I have two letters here one from my wife and one from yours, Stephan.

"What!" Stephan said with surprise. "Why would Ingr write to you?"

"She is so afraid of distracting you in battle that she wants me to give this to you when you are safe," Matthew said with a grin.

"Did she have the baby?" Stephan asked excitedly as he grabbed the letter from Matthew's hand. "Matthew did you read all of this?"

"Yes," Matthew said as he stood up and started walking to his saddlebags.

"I'm a father," Stephan announced proudly. "Of a boy and a girl, can you believe that?"

"She had twins?" asked Thaos.

"Yes, and Nikki is staying with her, helping with the babies," Stephan said then handed the letter to Thaos.

"What are their names?" Sorren asked.

"Marcus Stephan and Sicily Bella," Stephan said with a proud smile that consumed his entire face.

"Sicily is one of Shara's middle names," Sorren said. "She will be very pleased."

Thaos passed the letter to Sorren. "She says the babies both look like Stephan," Thaos said as he suddenly felt the impact of his own pending fatherhood.

"I thought you would become a father during this trip," Matthew said. "So I raided Father's wine cellar and grabbed a couple of bottles of his finest whiskey. I know it's early but this deserves a toast." As Matthew was pouring whiskey into their cups he said, "You can all read my letter too. Angelina is talking about the delivery and of how they were all worried about Ryan because they thought he was going to faint."

"Faint," Stephan asked. "Was he there for the delivery?"

"He was waiting in the parlor with everyone else, but he was in the kitchen with the girls when Ingr's water broke. The letter is pretty funny, you should read it," Matthew said. When everyone had a cup of whiskey Matthew made a toast, "To Stephan, Ingr and their babies; may they all have long and happy lives."

Suddenly Stephan turned to the Sanuri. "You said we were having a son, you didn't say anything about a daughter."

"Didn't want to ruin the surprise," the Sanuri said with a grin. "Besides after watching how Ingr reacted to the news of one baby, what do you think she would have done knowing she was going to have two; when your relationship was in such turmoil at that time?"

All morning warriors from both the Nordes and Ruala tribes prepared for the wedding of Bac and Calla. Preparing for such a happy event took their minds off from their wounds and the horror they had witnessed in the caves of Sendra. The female warriors gathered what they could to make arrangements of flowers and ferns. The warriors consolidated their food supplies to try and make a banquet for them all. Unknown to the rest of the warriors; Matthew, Stephan and Thaos took the Sanuri's boca into Sendra to buy food and medical supplies.

Bac and Calla had asked Galen and Sasha to stand up for them in the wedding, so the Sanuri took over the care of the wounded. It was late morning when Matthew, Stephan and Thaos returned to camp. All three men were feeling jubilant over the birth of Stephan's children and the end to the most recent threat against their families. Shortly after arriving in camp, Matthew called a meeting, which he held near the area where the warriors with the most serious wounds were being treated.

"We can never thank you for the sacrifices you have made and the courage and skill you have shown in battle. You risked your lives to protect our families and for that we will always be in your debt. When we return to Lentz we will have a formal banquet and bestow more appropriate gifts upon you." As Matthew spoke, Stephan, Thaos and Sorren were unloading all of the items that were purchased in Sendra.

Matthew continued speaking to the group, "In addition to celebrating your bravery and the wedding of Bac and Calla this day we are also celebrating the news that Stephan's wife delivered twins while we were engaged in battle. Stephan is now the father of both a son and a daughter." Many of the warriors applauded when they heard this news. "Sendra is a small town so we could not find some of the things we sought to purchase but hopefully we can put together a feast befitting this occasion."

"We have two pigs to roast, kegs of wine and ale, baskets of breads, fruits and vegetables and other supplies." The warriors yelled and applauded. "Where is Calla?" Matthew asked. Calla walked up to Matthew.

"Our wives would kill us if we did not get you something for the wedding," Matthew said with a grin. "But I will be honest the three of us are not very good at picking out women's clothing; so we bought some bolts of material and lace and some dresses and thought perhaps you could put something together." The entire crowd broke into laughter when they saw Stephan and Thaos carrying two huge baskets filled with material and dresses.

"You must have bought everything in the store," Calla gasped.

"Pretty close," Thaos said with a grin.

Everyone was filled with joy as they worked on the preparations for the wedding and banquet. Sorren took charge of roasting the pigs; telling everyone he had an old family recipe that they would love. Even in the primitive conditions, the warriors started making delicacies of their tribes. The Sanuri watched with pleasure as the fear and pain of these people were replaced with happiness. Sorren led the people in song as they all worked together like one large family.

Raul entered the front lobby of the Endleson Hotel and sat in one of the overstuffed chairs near the front desk. He had brought a book from Hannah's house and read it as he kept a watchful eye on his surroundings. Raul was wearing a large coat and a wide brimmed hat; both had belonged to Hannah's father. About twenty minutes later Gabriel entered the hotel. He walked directly to the front desk, pretending not to know Raul.

Raul was sitting close enough to the front desk that he could hear Gabriel's conversation with the clerk. Gabriel was able to get one of the three available rooms on the fourth floor. "Room 424," Gabriel said loudly. "Thank you." Gabriel walked up the stairs with a suitcase he was using as part of his disguise. Gabriel did not see Hannah in the hallway as he entered his room.

A few minutes later Gabriel heard a woman humming and peeked out of his door. He saw Hannah pushing a cleaning cart down the long hallway. She was dressed in an oversized brown tattered blouse with an equally tattered brown skirt; both were covered with an old stretched-out green sweater. She was wearing her hair in two braids with a brownish scarf covering the crown of her head.

Hannah saw Gabriel peeking through his door; she did not speak as she walked past him but she dropped a piece of paper on the floor then entered room 423. "Gabriel picked the paper up after she entered the next room; *Meekos 419, Pravis 421, Tenebrae 423* were the only words written on the note. "Thank you," Gabriel whispered for now he had confirmation that they were investigating the right men.

"What a mess!" Hannah said out loud when she entered Tenebrae's room. Trash, food and whiskey were everywhere. His clothes were thrown on the floor and over furniture, and just as Miriam had said, there was a woman's stocking lying on the floor. Hannah opened the balcony doors not only to let air into the room that smelled like stale smoke and whiskey but to let the Enrops in if she needed help. These hotel rooms were more like chambers, there was a separate bedroom, a parlor and a bathing area.

Hannah started to pick up the clothing as she walked through the rooms, making sure no one else was there. She searched the pockets and linings of the clothing without finding anything of interest. When Hannah opened the closet she saw a small suit case pushed far in the back. Hannah pulled it out and opened it. She let out a loud gasp when she saw its contents. Hannah took everything out of the suitcase and returned it to its hiding place. She quickly walked into the parlor and hid the items in the cleaning cart.

Hannah had never cleaned so quickly in her life; she couldn't wait to show Gabriel what she had found. As she cleaned she searched the drawers, bookshelves and other suitcases. Hannah looked under the mattresses and bedding as she made the bed. She found a stack of papers under a pile of clothing. She grabbed all of the papers and hid them in her cleaning cart.

Then just as Hannah was starting to leave she spied a small book under one of the chairs, she grabbed it and left the room. Gabriel was waiting and quickly opened the door to his room. Hannah handed him the things she had stolen from Tenebrae's room and quickly left.

Next Hannah entered Pravis' room. She was once again appalled by the mess. As with the first room Hannah checked to make sure she was alone. This time Hannah went straight to the closet and found four suitcases. She searched them all. Hannah took many items from the suitcases; she wasn't sure what they were but she thought they were used for unholy ceremonies.

Hannah saw a stack of crumpled up papers near one of the tables, without reading them she scooped them all up and hid them in her cleaning cart. Hannah found large sums of money which she did not take. She left Pravis' room and again went to Gabriel's room and gave him the items.

When Hannah entered Meekos' room something made the hair on the back of her neck rise. She immediately opened the doors to the balcony so the Enrops could have access if needed. Meekos' room was clean and orderly. There were no suitcases to search. As Hannah walked through the rooms she felt as if she was being watched.

Hannah found nothing of interest in the bedroom or parlor. When she opened the door to the bathing room she had to stop herself from screaming because the bathtub and floor were full of snakes. And there appeared to be some type of altar built next to one of the walls. Hannah quickly left the room. The hallway was empty so she entered Gabriel's room. "Are you alright?" Gabriel asked with concern when he saw the look on Hannah's face.

"Yes," she whispered. "When I was in Meekos' room I kept feeling like I was being watched but I didn't see anyone; then I went into the bathing room and it is filled with snakes and there is some kind of altar in there."

Gabriel went to his balcony, "Is there any sign of the priests?" he asked one of the Enrops.

"Not yet."

"There are serpents and possibly a demon in Meekos' room, I am going in there," Gabriel said to both Hannah and the Enrops. Hannah started to follow Gabriel, when he turned and said angrily, "Hannah you aren't coming."

"Yes I am and I don't think you want to waste time fighting about this."

Gabriel entered Meekos' chambers first; he instantly felt the diabolical presence that Hannah had sensed. Gabriel walked to the bathing room and opened the door. A large snake that was in the bath tub hissed at him while the other snakes moved towards the intruders.

"You have no power here!" Gabriel said loudly to the unseen demon.

"Well, well, what do we have here?" asked a malicious voice that seemed to fill every room of the chambers. Hannah looked around as Gabriel stayed focused on the snakes and the altar. Gabriel started to pray out loud but softly.

"You amuse me priest," the voice said tauntingly. "And this female is she an offering for me?"

Gabriel did not fall to the taunts of the demon. Gabriel continued to pray and as he did the room slowly filled with smoke. The floor started to shake, causing the makeshift altar to wobble and collapse. Hannah pulled out two knives that were hidden in her braids, as she watched the snakes coming towards them. The demon laughed. "Little girl you only have two knives against all those snakes," the voice taunted.

The snakes started to wrap around Gabriel's feet as he prayed. Gabriel did not move as he called forth the power of The Great Ruler to cleanse the evil from this place. The smoke that was getting thicker was caused by the demon, not from Gabriel's prayers. Hannah bent down and repeatedly stabbed the snakes that were crawling on Gabriel.

"Leave this place," Gabriel said with authority.

"You have no power little man."

"It is not my power you should fear," Gabriel said. Suddenly fire rained down upon the snakes in the bathing room. The fire was not of the world of man. The demonic serpents dissolved into puddles of black goo when the holiness of the flames touched them. The unholy altar vanished.

The demon roared with fury. Suddenly Hannah was picked up and thrown against a wall by an unseen force. She hit the wall with such a jolt that she dropped her knives. Instantly the two knifes flew through the air towards Hannah, Gabriel jumped in front of her and one of the knives impaled his left shoulder. The second knife suddenly fell to the floor and the presence of evil was gone.

"Don't pull the knife out until I can look at it," Hannah scolded as she grabbed Gabriel and took him to his room. She opened Gabriel's shirt and examined the wound. "Gabriel I am concerned because I used this knife to cut those snakes. I am going to pull the knife out and bandage it but we need to get to my office. Do you think you can make it?"

"Yes, just get this thing out of me."

Hannah grabbed clean towels and a sheet from the cleaning cart. She tore the sheet into strips and put them on Gabriel's lap. Hannah pulled the knife from his shoulder and instantly pressed a towel against the wound to try and contain the bleeding. She pressed a second towel on top of the first and told Gabriel to hold them in place as she wrapped his shoulder with the strips of torn sheet. Hannah took off the clothing she was wearing as a disguise. She was wearing a white blouse and dark skirt underneath the tattered clothing. Hannah buttoned Gabriel's shirt and put his coat over his shoulders.

"Hand me that suitcase," Gabriel said. "Everything you took is in there."

"I will carry the suitcase," Hannah said as she put one arm around Gabriel's waist. "We need to get out of here before the priests return." They walked down the four flights of stairs. Although Gabriel was in great pain he said nothing.

Raul knew something was wrong when he saw the look on Hannah's face. He waited until Gabriel and Hannah walked out of the hotel before he stood up and left the lobby.

"He's been stabbed, we need to get him to my office," Hannah said. The boca they had ridden in was hitched a block away. Gabriel managed to walk the block but started to lose consciousness as they helped him into the boca.

"I was stabbing demon snakes with the knife the demon used on Gabriel, I am afraid he has poison in his system," Hannah cried as she and Raul placed Gabriel in a lying position in the back of the boca. Raul took off a necklace he was wearing and handed it to Hannah. "Place this on his wound; it is a piece of crystal from the Ice Caves. The crystals have special healing powers from The Great Ruler. You stay back here with Gabriel and I will drive us home."

Hannah took the bandages off from Gabriel's shoulder and placed the crystal directly on the knife wound. "Raul the crystal is turning black and pulsating," Hannah said. "Should I keep it on him?"

"It might be drawing the poison out of his body," Raul said as he flicked the reigns. "Lakin should have more; his sister is a great healer among her tribe."

Raul was still driving the boca through the streets of Nora when Hannah said fearfully, "Raul, I think he is getting worse."

"As soon as we get out of the city; I will have the Rualas fly both of you back to your house."

By sunset an area had been set up for the wedding of Calla and Bac. A makeshift altar was made for the Sanuri and the couple. Although the altar was crude it was filled with flowers, ferns and candles which transformed it into a thing of beauty. A small area was cleared for the aisle and lined with wild flowers. The camp was filled with the wonderful smells of the roasting pigs and other delicacies being prepared for the feast. Many warriors had started to drink the wine and ale before the ceremony so joviality filled the camp.

When the preparations were completed, the Sanuri took his place on the altar facing the small crowd of wounded warriors who had gathered on either side of the aisle. Bac's warrior robe, still had bloodstains even though he had tried to clean them off. Bac walked up to the altar with Galen at his side.

"We don't have rings yet," Bac whispered to the Sanuri.

"That is quite alright," the Sanuri said with a warm smile.

Although there was no music to announce the bride, everyone became quiet when Sorren walked up with Calla on his arm. Several of the Nordes women had transformed one of the dresses that Matthew and the others bought; with the bolts of lace and silk materials. Instead of wearing her warrior's robe, Calla now walked down the aisle in a white lace dress with a high waist. A long lace veil covered her dark curly hair. Bac's heart leaped in his chest when he saw her.

Even though Sorren had not known Calla or Bac long; he was filled with pride as he walked the young warrior down the aisle to her waiting husband. The Sanuri began the ceremony. Everyone's attention was on the young couple and the words of the Sanuri. No one heard the crashing sounds in the forest.

Fear of his blindness filled Lazo with rage as he stumbled through the forest, following a smell of roasting pigs. His knees and forearms were bleeding and bruised from falling over tree limbs and rocks. About midafternoon, Lazo realized he could see a hazy outline of what he thought was a tree. Lazo suddenly fell again; cursing all that was holy he pulled himself back on his feet. Lazo did not understand what happened in the caves after he was blinded by the white light, or how he got out. All Lazo remembered was running in terror until he fell into the river.

Now as Lazo was trying to make his way through the forest, he wondered why he had felt so terrified as he was running from the caves. Lazo's head throbbed in pain but the bleeding had stopped. The side of Lazo's head felt crusty from the dried blood.

The smell of cooking food was getting stronger as the afternoon wore on. Lazo was so focused on his anger that he failed to realize the haziness of his sight was clearing.

As the sun was setting, Lazo stumbled out of the forest and into a clearing. He stared in disbelief at the scene before him. Lazo was standing behind the crowd of warriors and the wedding party. Only the Sanuri saw Lazo as he emerged from the forest. Lazo's sight had returned but now his rage blinded him as he pulled a large knife out of the sheath on his belt and ran towards Bac.

The Sanuri held up his hand and Lazo was thrown onto his back. Lazo struggled with the unseen force which was holding him down. "Matthew you have a prisoner," the Sanuri said calmly.

The warriors closest to Lazo, took his weapons. Lazo screamed, "Calla ya are mine," as he was dragged into the woods and tied to a tree. Bac started to move towards Lazo when the Sanuri put his hand on Bac's shoulder. "Do not let darkness touch your marriage. We will finish the ceremony."

"It's a good thing I like Simon," Calen said kiddingly. "Because my wife sure is spending a lot of time with him."

"Your wife would rather be spending the time with you," Natasha said as she sat on Calen's lap at the kitchen table. The newlyweds kissed passionately for several minutes until they heard Koby loudly clear his throat. Natasha started to laugh and got off from Calen's lap. "I should finish dinner," she said without looking at Koby, Simon and Dagon, who were standing in the kitchen.

"You know if you guys really are planning on living with us, you're going to have to get used to this," Calen said with a grin.

"We have some news," Dagon said. "The Enrops have been watching the caves where the ascension was supposed to take place. They said today four men went into the caves, one was Cerephus and his two wizards but the fourth man wore the robes of a high priest."

"Meekos," Natasha gasped. "Has he met up with Sophie?"

"It appears he is staying at the castle," Koby said. "He may not know she is here."

"I am going back to the hotel," Simon said.

"Should I come?" Natasha asked.

"No, I will probably stay the night."

"We'll join you after it gets dark," Calen said. "I'll write a note and send it to Gabriel."

Chapter XVIII
Beasts

For the next two days Malus, Erebus and Meekos did little besides research spells. They did all of their work in the war room. The three sorcerers filled the table with books and scrolls and they read everything they had available to them. Cerephus joined them but did little besides listen to the sorcerers and keep their glasses filled with whiskey.

Meekos, Erebus and Malus understood that Ahriman was no ordinary demon; these men were searching for extraordinary enchantments. Once they made their decisions, they had to gather the necessary ingredients for the spells. The four men decided to return to the caves late the next morning.

Marcia walked into Hannah's bedroom where Gabriel was recovering from his wounds. Hannah was sitting in a chair next to the bed, reading and watching over Gabriel.

"Hannah I can watch him, you need a break," Marcia said. "When did you eat last?"

"I am fine Marcia, thank you," Hannah said wearily. "And thank you for moving to Rabi's room, I hope it wasn't a great inconvenience."

"Hannah I have something to tell you, although I feel guilty saying it," Marcia knelt down by Hannah. "Rabi asked me to marry him. I know we haven't known each other long but he is so wonderful."

"You said yes, didn't you?" Hannah asked happily and hugged Marcia. "When are you planning on the wedding?"

"Rabi wants Gabriel to perform the service when he is up to it," Marcia said. "Has he awakened at all?"

"No, and in a way I feel very helpless," Hannah said sadly. "My training and medicine had no effects on the poisons of the demon. Lakin's crystals and medicines seem to be more effective. But I am not really sure what I am dealing with."

"Hannah, I am going to move to the Ice Caves with Rabi. I don't want to leave you alone in this awful place. Rabi said you could come with us."

Hannah smiled; an exhausted smile. "Thank you but I don't really know what I am going to do yet and I just can't think about that now."

Marcia stood up. "I am going to bring you a meal and a pot of coffee," she said and started to walk towards the door.

"Marcia wait," Hannah said and jumped out of her chair. Hannah walked inside of her closet and rummaged around for several minutes. When she walked out, she was holding two beautiful white dresses. "Why don't you try these on for your wedding dress? If you like one of them, I can make any necessary adjustments."

Prince Lakin walked into Hannah's bedroom, where he found Hannah still sitting in the chair next to Gabriel's bed. "Have you had anything to eat today?" he asked with concern.

"I'm alright," Hannah replied wearily.

"Hannah you are not going to do Gabriel any good if you get rundown and sick," Lakin scolded. "Get some breakfast; I will sit with him."

"Lakin, Gabriel is deeply unconscious and it scares me; he may not come back," Hannah said fearfully.

"Hannah, he has both the poisons of the demon and the healing of The Great Ruler at war with each other in his body; who knows what he is experiencing."

Hannah looked up at Lakin, "Would you teach me the medicines of your people?"

"Yes, under one condition Hannah," Lakin said with a fatherly voice. "You get something to eat and some sleep. You know you cannot learn when your mind is exhausted."

"Actually what I would really like is a long hot bath," Hannah said. She was so exhausted she could barely speak.

"Then take a bath, I will stay with him until you return." Lakin said as he took Hannah's arm and lifted her out of the chair. As the two faced each other, Lakin said, "Hannah it is obvious to many of us, that you are in love with Gabriel. I have known him for many years. Gabriel is a good man and worth waiting for. But you have to understand how dedicated he is to The Great Ruler and to the missions. Gabriel does have feelings for you; he is just not allowing himself to recognize them."

"Thank you," Hannah said and kissed Lakin on the cheek. "I really needed to hear that. Gabriel has me so confused, I don't always know if he cares about me or is just acting the roles we play."

"Trust me Hannah; Gabriel stopped acting a long time ago."

Cerephus, Erebus, Meekos and Malus returned to the caves midmorning; accompanied by twenty Taperian soldiers. The soldiers remained outside of the main entrance to the caves, while Cerephus and the sorcerer's walked through the caverns until they were in the specific cave where they saw the door to the underworlds appear.

Malus and Erebus strategically placed a variety of bones, blood, candles and herbs in a large circle that surrounded the area that they determined was the door. When they had finished, Meekos started to read a spell in the language of the Old Ones. Malus and Erebus walked to Meekos and each stood on either side of him. When Meekos finished reading the first spell, all three of the sorcerers read a second spell in unison.

Nothing happened. So the three sorcerers read a third spell in unison. Still nothing happened. As they proceeded to read a fourth spell a giant bolt of lightning flashed in the center of the circle and just as quickly the head and long neck of a monster jutted out of the invisible doorway. The monster clenched Malus between its huge teeth and pulled the screaming sorcerer into hell.

"How is he?" Hannah asked when she returned to her bedroom after a bath.

"The same," Lakin replied as he stood up. "I changed his bandage and put more crystals on him." Lakin was looking intently at Hannah's face as he spoke. "Now you need to sleep, you can't keep your eyes open."

As Hannah started to sit in the chair, Lakin gently grabbed her arm. "No in the bed, you can't get any rest in the chair." Hannah did not move. "Do I have to put you into bed?" Lakin asked.

"No," Hannah replied wearily; and turned and crawled under the covers next to Gabriel.

"I will check on you," Lakin said. "So don't worry that you might not wake up if he needs you."

As soon as Hannah's head touched the pillow she was asleep. Lakin walked out of the room and was closing the door behind him when Luca came up to him with a letter in his hand. "There is a note from Calen," Luca said and the two men walked to the parlor, where Raul was sitting at a table sorting through the many things Hannah had removed from the hotel rooms of the high priests.

"That bastard," Raul growled as Luca and Lakin entered the room. "Look at these," Raul said and handed some crumpled pieces of paper to them.

"These are letters to the kidnappers," said Luca as he sat down to read them.

"These are the ones that didn't get sent, I wonder what the other letters said," Raul said angrily.

"Did you read this note from Calen?" Lakin asked.

"Not yet," said Raul.

"The Enrops have seen Meekos at Roch's castle with King Cerephus and his two sorcerers. But Meekos and Sophie have not seen each other yet. Calen says they believe neither is aware of the other's presence in Taperia," Lakin was summarizing the letter for Raul and Luca.

"Also they searched Sophie's room and found a book of dark magic and her diary. They also took her blood ring. They haven't read the books yet but will let us know what information they find. They are now going back to the hotel to watch Sophie."

Erebus, Meekos and Cerephus shrank back in horror as they watched Malus being devoured by the hell beast. Suddenly anger consumed Meekos and he screamed towards the door to hell. "What is the meaning of this, we come to you with offerings and all we want is answers and you attack us?" Then Meekos started muttering a dark spell and soon lightning bolts were attacking the hell door. Suddenly Meekos was thrown violently against one of the stone walls of the cavern.

"Have you learned nothing my little hypocrite?" Ahriman yelled sarcastically. "You have no power compared to me. I am the Power."

"Ahriman," Meekos gasped.

"Why are you attacking these men?" Cerephus yelled into the darkness on the other side of the door.

"The hypocrite knows," Ahriman said then laughed. "I thought you were bringing me the Sanuri."

"We are," Meekos said. "We have kidnapped King Sudfad's youngest son as bait. The Sanuri cares for the child greatly and is looking for him."

"You bumbling fool, you think you can raise Omnibus from The Abyss and you can't even accomplish the kidnapping of a child," Ahriman screamed.

"But, we have the boy."

"You had the boy," Ahriman corrected loudly. "He was returned to his family days ago and you, my arrogant hypocrite aren't even aware of it."

"What!" yelled Meekos. "How?"

"There were many seeking that boy besides the Sanuri and some much smarter than the men you paid," Ahriman bellowed. "You had better come up with another plan."

Hannah wasn't sure what woke her until she turned and saw Gabriel violently thrashing around and foaming at the mouth. Hannah jumped out of bed and ran to the door, "Lakin, Lakin come quickly," she screamed as Hannah returned to Gabriel's side. Gabriel was drenched with sweat and his eyes were rolling back into his head. "What is happening to him?" Hannah cried as Lakin, Luca, Raul and Rabi all ran into the room.

Lakin quickly unwrapped Gabriel's bandages and looked at the crystals which were black and starting to smoke. "Hannah leave," Lakin said.

"I will not."

"Raul, you hang on to her," Lakin ordered. "And the rest of you get back." Lakin opened the large leather pouch that he had earlier placed on the table next to Gabriel's bed. Lakin took out a white cloth that he carefully unfolded and placed on top of Gabriel's wounds. Then Lakin placed some new crystals on top of the cloth. He took a bottle of a clear liquid from the pouch and sprinkled it over Gabriel's body, which started to smoke where ever the liquid touched.

"Great Ruler help Gabriel in his fight against the darkness," Lakin prayed. "Release the demons inside of him and destroy them. Help Gabriel overcome that which is trying to take him. Release, release, release," Lakin yelled.

Suddenly a great wind filled the bedroom, knocking things over with its force. Gabriel's thrashing became more violent as the on-lookers saw a cloud of smoke start to form above Gabriel's head. The ominous form started to take shape. Lakin stared at the form, "You have no power here, be gone demon," he yelled with authority. The dark form started to growl and hiss. Lakin reached into his pouch and pulled out a hand full of a fine white powder, which he threw upon the dark figure. The figure screamed a deafening scream and disappeared.

Lakin instantly felt Gabriel's chest to determine if his heart was beating. Lakin could not hear the pounding of life force within his friend. He reached into his bag and brought out another small bottle of clear liquid which he poured down Gabriel's throat. Then Lakin pulled a large knife out of the sheath on his belt. He made a deep cut on his forearm and then did the same to Gabriel. Lakin rubbed the cuts together as he prayed.

Everyone waited breathlessly for Gabriel's life signs to return. The minutes ticked by and nothing happened. Suddenly Hannah started to fight Raul's hold on her. "Raul, let me go I can see where he is," Hannah screamed. Raul let go of her arms and Hannah jumped onto the bed and knelt next to Gabriel, on the opposite side from where Lakin was standing.

Hannah placed the palms of her hands on his cheeks. "Gabriel follow my voice, I can see where you are, just keep following my voice, the battle is over, you must come back now," Hannah repeated these phrases several times as Lakin watched closely.

Gabriel's chest started to heave as he took in deep breaths. Hannah removed her hands from Gabriel's face. Gabriel's eyes shot wide open as his spirit returned to his body. He quickly sat up and looked at the people around him, as if he didn't immediately recognize them.

"Welcome back old friend," Lakin said with a feeling of relief flooding his body.

"You will never believe where I have been," Gabriel said. "Thank you both for helping me back." Hannah threw her arms around Gabriel's neck and started crying. He hugged her tightly.

"I don't understand at all, what just happened?" Raul asked in disbelief.

"Most people call to darkness and that is how they get on that path," Lakin explained. "But sometimes the darkness attacks the innocents and drags them into hell. The demon poison that entered Gabriel's body took him on a horrible journey; he had to make a choice and he chose to fight the darkness. The battle of the spirit was more than his body could contain."

"Did you destroy that demon?" Rabi asked.

"No, I made it leave," Lakin said. "The water and the dust are blessed with holiness."

Hannah let go of Gabriel's neck and was wiping the tears from her face, "I don't understand what happened to me. I could see Gabriel in this kind of darkness and somehow I knew he had to follow my voice to get back."

"You were given a great gift Hannah," Lakin said. "Our Chief Healer has such visions when he is saving others. Hannah you want to learn our medicines. After what just happened I think I should take you to the Ice Caves and have Mateo himself teach you."

Meekos wanted to leave the caverns but Cerephus and Erebus wanted answers from Ahriman.

"Do you have Roch?" Cerephus yelled.

"Yes," Ahriman said with great self-satisfaction.

"Is he returning to this world?" asked Erebus.

"Well now that is the question," Ahriman said. "And in what manner would he return?" Ahriman was deliberately trying to increase their anxieties with his evasiveness.

"What is it you really want?" asked Cerephus.

"Now here is a man who wants to deal with the devil," Ahriman said tauntingly. "I like that in a human."

"I am assuming you are here for a reason," Cerephus said.

"I am here for many reasons," said Ahriman. "And some of them might be boredom."

"Why did you create this door in between the worlds?" Erebus asked.

"You are not ready for that answer yet."

"You taunt us with questions but you don't give us any answers," Cerephus said.

"My answers come with a price." Ahriman said loudly. "Are you prepared to pay the price?"

Suddenly Meekos became suspicious. "Ahriman, how can you have Roch if he was touched by holiness?"

"Many turn to me after they have been touched by holiness; you certainly did."

"You wanted me to get the Sanuri and force him to reverse the effects of The Lion," Meekos said. "But if you have Roch, all that is futile. So my question is; are you sabotaging Omnibus' ascension?"

Ahriman laughed loudly. "I can put Roch back into your world at any time. And secondly do you really think you could help Omnibus escape from The Abyss?"

"Yes," Meekos said.

"I don't want Roch back in this world as either a man or a beast," Cerephus said with authority. "And I have no reason to believe that you have him. Prove that you have him and I will talk about paying a price."

"As you wish," Ahriman said and in less than an instant another hell beast jutted through the devil's door and grabbed Cerephus, pulling him into hell.

To everyone's surprise, Gabriel returned from his spiritual battle with darkness in good physical shape. The crystals and medicines of the Ruala's healed and fortified Gabriel's body. He left the bed he had been in for two days and walked without assistance to the dining room for a meal.

"It was like I was in two places at the same time," Gabriel was trying to explain to his friends, who were seated around the table. "I was on a battlefield and for some reason I knew it was very old. I was fighting demons and monsters. But the battle was more than just for me, it was for others also."

"Yet, I was aware of everything that went on in my room. I knew when Hannah and Lakin were there." Gabriel turned to Marcia who was bringing bowls of food to the table. "I heard you tell Hannah that you and Rabi were getting married and you asked her to move to the Ice Caves with you."

"Yes, we had that conversation," Marcia said in amazement. "But how could you have heard us, you appeared almost dead?"

"I do not understand it," Lakin said. "But I have heard of such things before."

"When you were on that battlefield, was it like a dream?" asked Raul.

"No, it was very real; it was like my body had been transported to another world."

"Were you alone in this other world?" Rabi asked.

"I suddenly found myself in some mountains, surrounded by demons and monsters. I had a sword, a dagger and a shield and I was fighting with all of the creatures at the same time. The battle seemed like it would last forever because every time I killed a demon or monster another one would take its place. Time seemed different there, because it seemed like years passed instead of days," Gabriel explained. "But I could hear all of your voices in the bedroom and I knew I was not alone."

Gabriel was sitting next to Hannah and he now took her hand into his and squeezed it. "Hannah kept talking to me the entire time I was gone. At one point, the monsters almost killed me and suddenly I heard Hannah's voice and I was transported from that battlefield to a very dark place. I could not see my surroundings, then I heard her voice again and suddenly a bright star appeared and I followed it for a long time. I just kept following that light and then I woke up in the bedroom."

Everyone sat in silence for a few moments after Gabriel stopped talking. "During those days Hannah only left your side once and that was shortly before you returned. I forced her to take a break," Lakin said. "She took a bath and returned to your room. I made her lie down in the bed and get some sleep. An hour later she was screaming for us."

Lakin continued, "As soon as I saw you I knew you were on a dark journey. I poured some blessed water on you and your skin started to smoke, like a demon would. I was praying over you and commanding the demons to leave, when Hannah started screaming that she could see you and you had to follow her voice. She kept telling you to follow her voice and come back to us and you did."

"I did talk to you great deal while you were unconscious," Hannah said. She was overwhelmed and drained from exhaustion yet filled with gratitude for Gabriel's return.

"I could feel your presence with me the entire time," Gabriel said and kissed Hannah's hand.

"I am still having difficulty understanding all of this," Raul said. "Was there a part of him on that battlefield or was it a dream?"

"According to the Sanuri there are many worlds or realities besides this one," Lakin explained. "His spirit was transported from his body by the demons. At some point Gabriel decided to fight them, that is how he ended up on that battlefield. But The Great Ruler was watching over him or Hannah would not have had the vision and Gabriel would not have heard her voice."

"Then why didn't The Great Ruler stop the demon from taking him in the first place?" asked Raul.

"I can give you that answer," Gabriel said. "It is well known that The Great Ruler tests all of us. That is how we grow and advance spiritually. Just like you are tested at the university to get to the next level of your studies. Somehow I understood the journey I was on; although I appeared to be alone I never felt alone. And I realized there was a reason that it was Hannah's voice I heard; she had been sent to me in both worlds to help me and to love me. I believe I was supposed to understand that she is meant to be my wife."

Horrified, Erebus and Meekos ran out of the caverns and to the Taperian soldiers who were waiting outside. "Out of here quickly," Erebus yelled to the soldiers. "Demons are dragging the others into hell." The soldiers simply sat on their horses and watched the two terrified men mounting their own horses. Suddenly loud laughter was heard echoing in the caves.

The soldiers realized Erebus and Meekos were telling the truth; all the men turned their horses and rode as fast as they could to the castle.

Erebus and Meekos both ran into the war room and sat down; their heads were spinning from their fear. After a few minutes, Erebus poured them each a large glass of whiskey which they both drank down to calm themselves. Neither man talked as they thought about their fates. Finally Erebus asked, "Ahriman said he could send Roch back into this world at any time; do you think we can get Cerephus and Malus back?"

"I don't know," Meekos answered in a hoarse whisper. "I have to think."

"Why do you think Ahriman is sabotaging Omnibus' ascension?" Erebus asked. "You would think he would want to help?"

Meekos sat quietly for a few moments, "Erebus, do you and Malus have many books here?"

"Yes, a small library."

"I may have been looking at this the wrong way," Meekos said. "I need to find out everything I can about the history of Ahriman and Omnibus. And I need to let Pravis and Tenebrae know what is happening."

There was a knock at the door. "Come in," called Erebus.

A huge burly man entered the room angrily. "Erebus what is going on here?"

"General Hamond this is High Priest Meekos from the monastery at Malga. Meekos this in Hamond, King Cerephus' second in command," said Erebus as he poured the General a drink. "Meekos was visiting Cerephus," Erebus explained. "When Malus told us of strange events in the caves near here. We all went to the caves and suddenly lighting was flashing and you will never believe what I am to say Hamond. But a type of doorway opened before us. Creatures came out and demons spoke to us. Monsters grabbed Cerephus and Malus and dragged them into hell."

Hamond stared at both Erebus and Meekos as he listened to the story. He would have laughed at Erebus's ramblings had not both men looked so terrified. Hamond did not know all of the concerns about Roch but he knew a lot because he had lived on the castle grounds for over thirty years. Hamond was a ruthless man who had conspired with Cerephus to take Roch's throne.

"Well General Hamond," Meekos said. "Unless we can find a way to bring Cerephus and Malus back; I believe you are now King. And you will want to hear what we have to tell you."

Hannah sat silently staring at Gabriel in disbelief; although others at the table started to smile.

"Hannah will you marry me?" Gabriel asked. Hannah immediately started to cry; she could not speak so she nodded her head in affirmation. Gabriel pulled her to him and hugged her tightly.

"Well," Lakin asked with great pleasure. "When do you want me to perform the ceremony?"

Hannah continued to cry, after a few moments she looked up at Gabriel. "I am sorry; I don't know why I am crying so much; perhaps it is because I am so tired." As Hannah was wiping the tears from her eyes she asked, "Lakin can perform the ceremony?"

"Yes," Gabriel said. "I would like to say our vows today. How about after lunch?"

Hannah again stared at Gabriel in disbelief. "Gabriel, that is fine but I would like to change into something nicer and stop crying first." Gabriel did not say anything but he pulled Hannah to him again and kissed her on the lips. As they embraced they did not see Raul leave the table. Raul returned a few moments later holding a large leather pouch, which he placed on the table.

"Hannah and Marcia, my family sent gifts to Gabriel, Rabi and the others as a small token of our appreciation for them bringing Petra back to us. My mother sent along this pouch of engagement and wedding rings when she heard that Natasha and Calen were so busy helping us that they did not take the time to prepare for their own wedding."

"My mother would be overjoyed if she could also share these with you." Raul poured the contents of the pouch onto the table. "Please if you find any you like, take them."

Both Hannah and Marcia stared at the pile of beautiful jewels before them. "Are you serious?" Hannah asked.

"Most definitely," Raul responded. "We would all rather have you wearing them than to have them sitting in the vault."

"Lakin, do you want to marry us both today?" asked Rabi.

"Do you mean a double ceremony or two separate ones?"

Hannah, Marcia, Rabi and Gabriel all looked at each other, then said almost in unison, "A double wedding." The four picked out their rings with great excitement; then Marcia and Hannah left the table to prepare for their weddings.

"Do you want to talk business while we wait, you certainly don't have to?" Lakin asked.

"Might as well," Gabriel replied.

"We have not finished going through all of the things that you and Hannah took from the rooms," Lakin explained. "But Raul found crumpled letters to the kidnappers and we have found many receipts for tools, explosives and hardware. There was also a receipt from Nora Stone Works for a huge stone tub. We found out that the men who delivered that tub have disappeared."

"I believe the priests are recreating the same chambers in the mines here as they had built near Roch's castle. But we still don't have a lead as to which mines. There are 'no trespassing' signs and armed guards in front of most of the mines; so we have not entered any. Also there is a book written in a language that none of us can translate. I was hoping you would understand it."

"Do we know who the owners of the mines are yet?" Gabriel asked.

"No," said Raul. "I went into Nora one of the days that you were unconscious."

Gabriel interrupted Raul, "That probably wasn't wise, you could have been recognized."

"Honestly Gabriel, we did not know if you would live," Raul said. "And my beard is getting thick enough that it is hiding my face. I went to the Land Title Company and to the Register of Deeds and neither place had the information I wanted; either that or they just wouldn't give it to me."

"They have to have the information," Gabriel said. "But why would they be hiding it?" The voices of Hannah and Marcia could be heard as they returned to the kitchen. "Rabi and I will be taking the rest of the day off," Gabriel said with a grin.

"I should hope so," Lakin said and smiled as the two brides entered the kitchen.

General Hamond sat silently as Meekos and Erebus told him about the Insidiae, Omnibus and Roch being the Vessel for the transformation. Hamond still did not speak as they explained about The Lion putting an affliction on Roch and Ahriman's involvement with sabotaging the accession and trying to lure the Sanuri into a trap.

"Cerephus knew that if Roch returned as a man or demon he would try and kill Cerephus first and possibly all of us," Erebus said. "Meekos and I are going to research some spells to try and bring Cerephus and Malus back."

"I don't think that is necessary," Hamond said. "I will announce myself as King tonight. And I want both of you out of my castle by morning." Hamond stood up and walked out of the room without saying another word.

"I cannot say I am surprised by his actions," Meekos said as he poured himself another drink. "Where will you go Erebus?"

"I came here to help Cerephus; I believe I will return to Ryed," Erebus said. "But, I don't like leaving my friends in that hell dimension."

"Ahriman will expect you to try and release them; you will be pulled through the door next. I understand why you would want to return to Ryed. But I could use your help," Meekos said as he poured more whiskey into Erebus' glass."

"It is very dangerous to be with you," Erebus said with a sly grin.

"And yet I pay very well," Meekos replied.

The warriors who fought at the caves of Sendra spent two more days at their campsite. The Sanuri stayed with them during this time, helping them to heal from their wounds. Lazo's interruption had little impact on the wedding of Bac and Calla and the feast and celebrations that followed. Lazo remained a prisoner, tied to a tree. The night before they planned to start their return trip to Lentz; Matthew called a meeting with the Sanuri, Sorren, Thaos, Stephan and Thedes.

"I didn't know if we should invite Bac or not," Matthew said as the men sat around a large campfire. "I want your suggestions as to what we should do with Lazo."

"He did save my life in the caves," Sorren said.

"And he has fought at my side in the past," added Thaos.

"But he is a great risk to Bac and Calla," Thedes said.

"I could have him locked up at the fort," Matthew suggested. "But he has not committed a crime that I know of; it would be for prevention."

"Sanuri what do you think?" Thedes asked.

"The Rualas can leave tomorrow and fly back to the Ice Caves, they will be healthy enough," the Sanuri said. "Lazo cannot get to them there. Lazo is not a good man but he has a part in all of this with Juleta that is not clear to me yet."

"So you think that we should spare his life?" Stephan asked.

"In this time and place, yes," the Sanuri responded. "He did intend to steal the bounty and take Calla for his own."

"Actually I told him he could have the bounty if he helped us," Stephan said. "Sanuri you have such an unusual look on your face, what are you thinking?"

The Sanuri smiled, "When I get visions, sometimes they are just fragmented images that I do not initially understand. And sometimes The Great Ruler blocks things from my sight until he feels that I am ready for the information. I told you that I looked into Juleta's mind before I vanquished her to The Abyss. I saw that she had great hatred for Lazo as she has for you Thaos, but she also had a fear of him."

"Juleta fear Lazo," Matthew said incredulously.

"I think it was a fear of something he knows about her or her plans," the Sanuri said. "All I can tell you, is that he has a part to play yet and it may be beneficial for you to keep him somewhat near you."

"Please don't tell me that means we have to let him around our families," Stephan said.

"No, you don't have to pretend to like Lazo or to invite him into your homes," the Sanuri said. "But I don't think any of us here believe that this thing with Juleta is over, even though we won this battle."

"So what do you think we should do?" Sorren asked the Sanuri.

"Release him after the Rualas leave and at that time we will have a talk with him," the Sanuri answered. "If he wants to ride with us to Lentz, I would suggest we let him."

Matthew stood up, "I am going to get Bac. He needs to hear what you just said."

"Bring Calla too," the Sanuri said.

"Sanuri you know how much I respect you," Bac said angrily "But this man has tried to kill me and to take Calla more than once. I have no reason to believe he will not try again."

"I understand how you feel," the Sanuri said. "And there isn't a man among us, who does not feel the same." As the Sanuri spoke he looked at the faces of Sorren, Matthew, Thaos, Stephan and Thedes. "Your friends here; and they are your friends, have come to me with their concerns for your safety."

"But Bac, what they do not know which you do, is that no one can enter the Ice Caves without my permission. Lazo will never get to you or Calla there. You rarely leave the Ice Caves, and now when you do, you have family in many different places because of this mission. As deplorable as Lazo's actions have been; he really is no longer a threat to you and your family."

"I do not need to hide behind others," Bac said defiantly.

"And you aren't but don't you see that the bonds of love and friendship that have been forged here, cannot be broken by one as weak as Lazo," the Sanuri said warmly. "Now I know that you and Calla care for these people too. Their nightmares are not over concerning Juleta; Lazo can be of help to them as difficult as that may be to believe. I know you want to help them, or you would not have come on this journey and risked your lives."

Bac was silent as the anger was leaving his body. Calla took Bac's hand. "You know the Sanuri speaks the truth," she said and kissed Bac on the cheek.

"Sanuri I am sorry that I doubted you," Bac said. Then he turned to the others. "We will continue to help you; just call us when you need us." Then Bac walked up to each man and shook his hand. Calla followed Bac but she kissed each man on the cheek and thanked them.

After Bac and Calla walked away, Sorren said, "Yeah, I really do like those kids."

Chapter XIX
To Reveal

Gabriel and Hannah did not leave their room until well into dinner time. They walked into the dining room hand in hand and saw that everyone was already eating. Hannah let go of Gabriel's hand and walked up to Raul and kissed him on the cheek, "Thank you so much for the beautiful rings."

"You are most welcome. You both look very happy," Raul said as he saw that they seemed radiant from their love making.

"We have some news," Lakin said. "Do you want to hear about it now or wait until tomorrow; after all it is your wedding night."

"Now," Gabriel said as he was pulling Hannah's chair out for her. Lakin left the table and returned a few moments later with a letter. "The Enrops intercepted some ravens that were taking this to the high priests at the hotel." Gabriel unfolded the letter.

Pravis and Tenebrae

I have some very bad news. One of the sorcerers at Cerephus' castle discovered well, basically a door to the hell dimensions in the caves near Cerephus' castle; in fact in the same chamber where the ascension was to take place. Cerephus, Erebus, Malus and I went to the caves. Ahriman created the doorway. He said that he had Roch and that he could return him to this world at any time. He also said that Petra had been rescued and returned to King Sudfad.

Have you heard from Vardin? Hopefully they did not reveal us. Ahriman said we had better devise another plan to lure the Sanuri to him. Ahriman sent hell beasts through the doorway and they dragged Cerephus and Malus into the hell dimension. Erebus and I do not know if we can get them back. Although the citizens of Stordt do not yet know it, they have a new king. A man named Hamond who was second in command under Cerephus.

Without going into all that was said and done in that cave; some questions were raised. We need to find out the history of Ahriman and Omnibus. Ahriman is deliberately sabotaging the ascension. Also I think that it is time we tell Omnibus what is going on.

I still have not found Sophie, although she left me a letter saying she had spoken to a powerful being in the caves who said he had Roch. Sophie left for the monastery at Malga weeks ago. I think it is time you came to Taperia.

Meekos

"Well, this is certainly interesting," Gabriel said as he handed the letter to Hannah.

"We copied the letter and sent it to the Sanuri, Father and to Calen," Raul said. "We also asked the Sanuri what he would have us do."

"Without Roch there is no ascension but then will Pravis and Tenebrae unleash the Hutas on Nora?" Lakin asked. "And why would Ahriman prevent the ascension unless he has other plans for Roch?"

"Show me that book you spoke of," Gabriel said. "Perhaps we will find some answers in there."

Rabi left the table and returned with the book, as he was handing it to Gabriel, Hannah said, "I found that lying on the floor, under a chair. I don't know if they were trying to hide it."

Gabriel opened the book and looked at a couple of pages, "I can read this language. It is called the Tongue of the Dead. It is writings about the Old Ones. It was believed that whoever exposed the Old Ones would die a horrible death. So various holy men came together to warn the world about the Old Ones and they made up this language to protect themselves."

"How can you read that?" Hannah asked.

"My specialty is ancient languages," Gabriel said. "Hannah forgive me but I want to start reading this tonight, it may be very important."

287

"Could you read it out loud to us?" asked Hannah.

"Wonderful idea," Lakin said. "After dinner anyone who wants to hear this will meet in the parlor."

Gabriel read long into the night. He translated the book out loud to Raul, Hannah, Rabi, Lakin, Luca and Marcia. The ancient manuscript had sat on a shelf in the Hall of Antiquities in the monastery at Malga for hundreds of years until Tenebrae stole it. As Gabriel turned the fragile pages, dust fell onto his lap. The book had no title, but the leather cover had a face of a demon carved into it.

The holy men who compiled the writings wanted to warn future generations of the unimaginable evil of the Old Ones, the original demons that came to this world. According to the authors, the first humans were ill prepared to deal with such horrors and seductions. The fears of the people empowered the dark ones as they fed off the energy. The Great Ruler sent emissaries to mankind, to teach them how they could conquer the demons that existed both inside and outside of the humans. But few listened and the darkness grew.

Then The Great Ruler sent a special emissary, whose light broke through the darkness and the humans started to listen. It was because of this special emissary that the Old Ones withdrew into the darkness of the hell regions; for the special emissary was strong enough to destroy them with but a glance. But men tend to cling to their fears, so they kept feeding the demons.

And many men are defined by the darkness within them, so they kept calling to the demons. And many men desire such power that they pay and barter with the demons. The authors of the book, wanted to warn mankind that they were bringing their own destruction upon themselves.

The original thirteen demons that came to the World of Nunc were: Ahriman, Omnibus, Petorus, Thanatoes, Fatronas, Dael, Lucifer, Baal, Khryriss, Maligma, Zehmann, Chaladrone and Nieatzae. When they discovered what a rich feeding ground this world provided, they called to others and demons of all natures flocked to this world.

Stolas, Satan, Zede, Ael, Damas, Asmodeus, Bentra, Opago, Abaddon, Jinn, Moloch, Ipos and Raum were the second group of thirteen Old Ones to invade this world. These demons bred with humans creating inferior demons. Of all the creatures in this world only humans would lay with demons.

The Great Ruler was not going to turn His back on His children, even if they called to demons in their ignorance. He sent many emissaries to this world; including a warrior Angel, whose courage was legendary. The warrior Angel walked among the humans and other races often; but they were not prepared to view such holiness as was his. So this Angel assumed the image of a lion; a powerful and noble beast.

The following morning the Ruala warriors who had fought at the caves of Sendra left for the Ice Caves. Strong friendships had been formed during this journey. Members of all the tribes promised to see each other again. Thedes decided to stay with Matthew and the rest as he was finally getting use to riding a horse and liked the experience.

Thedes was surprised at how at home he was among these humans; all courageous warriors and good men, Thedes developed a strong kinship with Matthew, Stephan, Sorren and Thaos. And they in turn, regarded Thedes as family; a concept that filled Thedes with pride when he was told this.

Matthew, Sorren, Stephan, Thaos and Thedes decided to speak with Lazo as a group. The Sanuri accompanied them to the forest where Lazo was bound to a tree.

"Lazo the Rualas have left for the Ice Caves," Matthew said as he cut the ropes on Lazo's feet and wrists. "We are letting you go. But know there is not a warrior here, who believes you to be an honorable man. Your behavior has been despicable. And we will no longer protect you from the others."

"Don't see as I need protection," Lazo said as he rubbed the circulation back into his wrists. "So can someone explain to me what the hell happened at the caves?"

"Up with you," Sorren said as he helped Lazo to his feet. "We will tell you over breakfast, there are things you should know."

289

"I was blinded for a while," Lazo said.

"We all were," Sorren replied as he led Lazo to their fire.

When they reached the campsite, Thaos handed Lazo back his knife. "You know Calla was never interested in you, she has been in love with Bac for a long time."

"Didn't really matter to me," Lazo said as he poured himself a cup of coffee.

"Why am I not surprised?" Stephan said sarcastically.

The Sanuri had been silent but watching Lazo intently. "Lazo would you mind if I looked into your eyes, I will not hurt you?" the Sanuri asked.

"Why?" Lazo asked suspiciously.

"Because I have been having visions of something that I do not understand; visions of you. I was hoping that if I looked into your eyes I would find some answers."

It was obvious to everyone that Lazo was uncomfortable with the idea, "Have at it," he replied with a halfhearted grin.

The Sanuri walked up to Lazo and placed his hands on Lazo's head. The Sanuri stared deeply into Lazo's eyes for several minutes. He saw Lazo's life flashing before him, the dark deeds, the loneliness and the fears. Then he saw Lazo's desires and what the Sanuri thought were glimpses of Lazo's future. Without saying a word, the Sanuri let go of Lazo's head and walked over to the fire and poured himself some coffee.

Everyone was silent as they expected the Sanuri to speak. Finally Lazo said, "Well ain't ya gonna tell us something?"

"No," the Sanuri replied.

"Well now ya are just giving me the willies," Lazo said with fear in his voice.

"You may not want to hear what I have to say," the Sanuri said as he stared at Lazo.

Lazo was silent for a while then said, "Probably not but I want to hear it any way."

"I saw your life, all of your deeds, and desires," the Sanuri said. "And I saw the possibilities of your future."

"What ya saying, possibilities of my future?"

"Every man has free will," the Sanuri explained. "Your choices determine your future. Look at Thaos, he was on the same path as you; but he decided to change his life and look at what a wonderful life he has now."

"What exactly are ya saying?" Lazo asked nervously.

"Think of everyman's life as a journey and every time that man has to make a choice, no matter how small, it is like he is at a crossroads. You have traveled greatly you know what can happen if you take the wrong road." Lazo looked very confused as the Sanuri spoke. "Lazo you usually take the wrong road but you will have some very important choices to make in your future and some of these choices have horrendous outcomes."

"Can ya tell me what they are?" Lazo asked fearfully.

"No but I can tell you that I kept seeing Juleta's face as I looked into your future, which makes me believe this is not over."

The others sat in silence as they listened to the words of the Sanuri. Lazo looked around the campfire at the faces that were now staring at him. He saw the seriousness in their looks. Lazo did not believe in The Great Ruler, he had only believed in what he saw with his own eyes. But both the Sanuri and Juleta made Lazo realize there was more in the world than what he could see.

"Lazo I have a question for you," the Sanuri said. "You do not have to answer it if you don't want but it may be very important. When I see Juleta's face I sense both hatred towards you and fear, fear that you will reveal something. What is it that Juleta fears?"

Lazo was quiet for a moment. "I was always watching her, at first it was partially because I thought she was an attractive woman, now Matthew don't get all angry with me for saying this."

"I'm not," Matthew said.

"But the more I got to know her; she was so ugly inside that even I couldn't stand her," Lazo continued. "She always acted so suspicious and paranoid that I was curious what she was up to, which by the way was a lot." Lazo turned to Thaos, "Thaos I know you hated her and you were gone a lot but didn't ya ever notice how her size changed?"

Thaos thought about it for a while, "I did notice that she was wearing baggy clothing at times."

"She had a baby, a little girl; don't know who the father was. It could have been a damn demon; but I know she took the baby to the monastery at Leven. The priests there are raising her."

Matthew's face turned white at the revelation. "Sanuri will the baby be evil too?" Matthew asked but before the Sanuri could answer Matthew said. "My parents will want to raise that baby."

The Sanuri looked at Lazo, "Making the choice to tell us that, was taking the right road Lazo." The Sanuri looked at Matthew. "I will part company with you today. Matthew lead your people back to Lentz, I will go to the monastery and get the baby. Tell your parents everything. If your family does not want the child, send an Enrop to me with the message."

"What if the baby is a demon?" Matthew asked.

"I will remove the evil from it," the Sanuri said. "And if your family does not want her, I will find the baby a good home."

"Marcia had nightmares about demons last night," Rabi said as they were all sitting in the kitchen eating breakfast.

"I am sorry, I may not want to come to the reading tonight," Marcia said.

"That is alright Marcia; no one is expecting you to listen to that," Gabriel said. "And on a different note Marcia, I already told Hannah; but when we leave Nora, it may be very quickly. You girls should start sorting through your things and decide what you want to take because I doubt if we will be returning here."

"We have many warriors to carry your things," Lakin said. "So bring what you want."

"I really want to bring my medical instruments and supplies," Hannah said.

"Of course," Lakin said. "Hannah, seriously bring what you want."

"I just haven't been thinking straight," Hannah said with embarrassment. "What with Gabriel getting hurt and then our marriage." Hannah looked at Gabriel, "We have to go to the bank, my father has money and papers and I don't know what all in safes there. And there is a safe in the study." Then she looked around the table, "Have any of you been in Father's study?"

"We will go to the bank this morning, we also have to pick up our clothes for the ball," Gabriel said after everyone had indicated they had not been in the study.

"Now that Gabriel and I are married, everything here belongs to him too but Gabriel said I could do whatever I wanted with my family's things," Hannah said as she placed a large leather pouch on the table. She continued to speak as she opened the pouch and took out four smaller pouches.

"My family is very wealthy and my father had these made for my mother." Hannah handed three pouches to Raul. They are made from the gold from the mines and the jewels are from a land across the Sea of Grevtd. I have never seen jewels like these before. Raul I am sending one pouch for your mother for giving us our rings and another to Vitomas, for her kindness. And the third pouch is for Simon's wife."

Raul poured the contents of the pouches on the table. Each pouch contained a necklace with matching earrings, although all three sets were different designs.

"Are these pink diamonds?" Raul asked. "They're beautiful. Hannah are you sure you want to part with these?"

"Yes Raul, I want your family to have them. I really don't know what they are; I just know they are very expensive because my sister and I were never allowed to touch them."

"Thank you," Raul said. "They will love them."

Hannah handed the fourth pouch to Lakin. "This is for your wife. It must be very difficult for her when you are gone for such long periods of time." Lakin opened the pouch which also contained a necklace and earrings made of gold and pink diamonds.

"Hannah, pink is Zada's favorite color, she will love these, thank you. You are too generous."

"Also I would like all of you to follow me into my father's study," Hannah said as she stood up at the table. "My father was a collector of many fine things. I would be honored if you would choose anything you want from this home and take it. And then bring the other warriors in and let them choose anything they would like."

"Hannah are you sure you want to do this?" Raul asked.

"Raul I cannot take all of these things with me, nor would I want to. And who knows what will happen to this house after we leave. I would very much like good friends to have my family's belongings."

Hannah opened two large wooden doors and they walked into a room that was lavishly decorated. Once inside of the study, Hannah walked to her right and opened another door. "My father's weapon collection is in here." Then she walked across the room and opened another set of double doors. "This was Father's library, he collected rare books. Raul I was wondering if your father would like any of these."

"I see your father collected pipes too," Luca said as he was looking at one of the many wooden shelves that was filled with pipes.

294

"Hannah these paintings are wonderful," Gabriel said as he looked at a collection of original paintings that adorned the walls of the study. "You don't want to part with these."

"Gabriel how would we get them to Wetpr?"

"I have connections," Gabriel said. "I will pack them and ship them home."

"Good, I do love those paintings," Hannah said as she started looking through the drawers of the enormous wooded desk that sat in the middle of the study. Hannah was pulling stacks of papers out of the drawers and piling them on the top of the desk until she found what she was looking for. Hannah walked up to Gabriel and handed him a small piece of paper. "The safe is behind that door," Hannah said as she pointed to a panel in the wall that did not look like a door. "Here is the combination. I have no idea what is in there."

"Your father was cunning," Gabriel remarked as he ran his fingers along the panel looking for a release to open the door. "Found it," he said as he pulled the large wooden panel open; exposing a closet that appeared to contain only a very large safe.

"Hannah did your father own any holdings in the mines?" Raul asked.

"I really don't know; we will need to go through all of his papers."

"If he owned any of the mines, we could go onto those lands without trespassing," Raul said. "Would you mind if I looked through his paperwork?"

"It's certainly alright with me if Gabriel agrees," Hannah said and looked towards Gabriel who was opening the safe.

"Raul, you would be helping us greatly if you could start to organize this paperwork. Here are some ledgers," Gabriel said as he placed five large books on top of the desk," Gabriel turned back to the safe and brought out two armfuls of papers, which he placed on top of one of the tables; since the top of the desk was now filled with papers and books because Hannah was emptying all the drawers.

Under the papers Gabriel found two large leather pouches in the safe. "These are filled with gold nuggets," Gabriel said as he showed them to the others.

"I will help Raul," Lakin offered. "It's the least I can do."

Rabi walked out of the weapons room, holding several items. "Hannah are you sure you want to give these away?"

"Rabi, for all we know the Hutas may burn down this house, yes, please take anything you want." Hannah turned to Gabriel as an afterthought. "I am sorry Gabriel I should have let you in there first."

"Hannah I have a huge weapons room at home, it is the library that interests me," Gabriel said and kissed her on the cheek.

Hannah turned back to Rabi, "Rabi I don't know if Marcia has said anything to you but there are some quilts she would really like to have. I hope you can find a way to transport them."

Rabi smiled, "Thanks for telling me; Marcia is rather shy."

Luca was walking around the study looking at the items displayed on the many sets of shelves that lined the walls. "Hannah would I be too bold if I asked if we could take some things for the others who are in Taperia?"

"No Luca, I think that is a wonderful idea," Hannah said. "In fact I would like some suggestions of gifts for Natasha."

Before Luca could answer, Lakin opened the doors to a large cupboard. "This is filled with maps," he said as he took out a large stack and carried it over to one of the many tables in the room. Lakin was quickly sorting through the maps until he found what he was looking for. "And here are maps of some of the mines."

"When Hannah finished cleaning out the desk drawers, she looked up and saw Gabriel, Lakin and Raul all sitting around one of the tables studying the maps. "Hannah I would not be surprised if your father didn't own some of the mines," Gabriel said.

"I never paid attention to my father's business dealings. Now I realize I should have." Hannah said. "Gabriel I will bring you all some coffee, then I am going to prepare for our trip to the bank."

"What do you mean?" Gabriel asked.

"I need to find cases to carry all of the things we will be bringing home."

Matthew was quiet for a while after hearing that his sister had a baby. Stephan and Sorren tried to cheer him up, without success. As everyone was packing up their camps, Matthew decided to find the Sanuri, he asked Stephan to come with him.

The Sanuri was tending to some of the wounded, when Matthew and Stephan approached him. "Sanuri, none of this makes any sense to me," Matthew said with despair in his voice. "I can understand her not telling our family she had a baby because she hated us all. But she was a witch, why would she take the child to a monastery?"

"Perhaps she wanted to protect it from the life she was leading," the Sanuri suggested. "She did have some humanity in her until the end."

"I would like to go with you," Matthew said.

"Matthew your family needs you now. You have a beautiful wife and son who miss you. And this news will greatly sadden your parents. You must be there for them."

"What if they want the baby and it turns out to be pure evil like Juleta?" Stephan asked. "Juleta broke Mathas' heart; can she do it a second time now?"

"And you are all afraid to have this baby around your children and your wives. That is why I must go alone. If the baby is demonic I will be able to tell," the Sanuri said.

"How could it not be?" asked Matthew.

"Juleta chose darkness; that was the life she desired. The fact that she put the child in a monastery does give me hope," the Sanuri replied.

297

"So where are you heading?" Thaos asked.

"I'm thinking about hanging around Langer for a while and making me some money playing cards," Lazo replied. "Another job will turn up, they always do. I'd ask ya to ride with me if ya weren't settled down," Lazo said with a grin, then he paused before adding, "I never figured ya for a family man but it suits you Thaos."

"I am happy and very fortunate," Thaos said then grinned. "You could settle down yourself, of course it would help if you found a girl who wanted to be with you."

Lazo laughed, "Suppose ya are right."

"You're not thinking of going after Calla and Bac are you?"

"Well from what I heard it sounds like ya have to have special permission from the Sanuri to get into those caves," Lazo said sarcastically. "Don't think he'd give it to me."

"I'll look you up in Langer and we can have a drink."

"I'd like that."

"Lazo I have to ask you, is that baby yours?"

"No, never thought I would say this but I almost wish it was. I saw her with the baby and she threatened to kill me if I told anyone. It looked like a regular baby; it didn't have horns coming out of its cheeks or nothing. Since I knew about it, she had me ride with her to the monastery. She actually seemed sad to leave it there."

"Do you think George was the father?"

"Did ya see how old he was? But I suppose anything is possible. Maybe she didn't know who the father was."

"Do you think it is possible she could have had a baby with a demon?"

"If ya would have asked me that question two years ago I would have thought ya were drunk," Lazo said with a laugh. "But after all the things we've seen, I am beginning to think anything is possible. Are ya thinking that baby is another one of her curses?"

"I really don't know what to think. You know you are welcome to ride with us." Thaos said as he watched Lazo saddle his horse.

"Thanks, but I think it's time to part ways," Lazo said sarcastically. "I may have worn out my welcome here. Besides every time your friend Stephan looks at me, I see death in his eyes; it's time for me to go."

Marcia rode into Nora with Gabriel and Hannah so she could start to pack up the medical office and apartment. As always they were escorted by Ruala warriors, who did not enter the City of Nora but stayed on the outskirts so as not to be seen.

"Lloyd is our banker," Hannah said. "You have met him before."

"Yes, a friendly man," Gabriel replied.

"A man who has made a fortune cheating people," Hannah said. "Please do not trust him, Gabriel."

When they reached Hannah's office Gabriel searched the building before he let Marcia work in it alone. "Do not open the door for anyone," Gabriel said. "We will return as soon as we can but it might take a while."

"Gabriel, I don't think you realize how wealthy Hannah's family is, I am sure it will take a while. And believe her warnings about Lloyd. Whatever he shows you, always know there is more that he has not revealed," Marcia said. Gabriel kissed her on the cheek and returned to Hannah who was sitting in the boca.

"Gabriel you worry so," Hannah said. "Marcia and I have been working in the city for a long time."

"I am sure you have my dear but I believe things are changing here and not for the better."

Gabriel and Hannah spent two excruciating hours with Lloyd; who seemed to be deliberately stalling when Hannah would ask for items. Finally Gabriel demanded that Lloyd bring them the contents of all Hannah's family safes immediately. Gabriel was becoming angry which greatly intimated Lloyd who started to bring carts full of items into the small room that Hannah and Gabriel were seated in.

"Gabriel we must take the money with us," Hannah whispered. "I do not trust Lloyd to transfer it to your bank."

Gabriel ordered Lloyd to produce all of her family's financial records that were at the bank. Gabriel carefully examined them as Hannah opened boxes of jewels and sorted through papers. Hannah had brought four large suitcases with her and filled them all with money, jewels and papers.

"Hannah you have now closed out all of your family's accounts," Lloyd said. "I am sorry to lose you as a customer."

"Thank you Lloyd," Hannah said politely. "But Gabriel and I will be moving from here, you can certainly understand."

As Gabriel and Hannah walked out of the bank, they both felt paranoid. "We can pick up our clothes tomorrow," Gabriel said. "I think we should return home right away."

Gabriel hid the suitcases under the front seat of the boca. When they reached Hannah's office, she ran inside and got Marcia. "Marcia, get in the back and get down," Hannah said as she covered Marcia with a blanket. Hannah then climbed into the front seat of the boca, next to Gabriel and the three quickly rode through the city. They felt relieved when they found their friends at the edge of town. Gabriel gave the suitcases to two Ruala warriors; telling them to take the cases to the house.

"Gabriel, there are some men riding this way quickly," Rabi said. "Do you want us to hide?"

"I think it is time we stopped hiding," said Gabriel.

"I was hoping you would say that," Rabi said with a grin.

Six masked men were riding hard trying to catch up with the boca. "Lloyd sent them," Hannah said. "I am sure of it." Hannah loaded her small crossbow.

"Where did you get that?" Gabriel asked with a grin.

"Dear, you don't expect me to give up all of my secrets do you?" Hannah asked and kissed Gabriel on the cheek. The Ruala warriors were staying out of sight until the riders closed the distance to the boca. A masked rider shot ahead of the others and soon came along the passenger side of the boca.

Hannah waited until he got close enough then she shot an arrow through his heart. As the bandit was falling from his horse, his foot became entangled in the stirrup. The horse ran for almost a half mile, dragging the bandit's lifeless body before the foot was freed from the stirrup.

The other five bandits were momentarily distracted by their gang member falling from his horse; they did not see the Ruala warriors who were descending upon them. The Rualas had the advantage and the battle was short lived. The Rualas hid the bodies of the bandits and set their horses free.

"Gabriel, you have no idea how wealthy you are now," Lakin said as Gabriel, Hannah and the others entered the house.

"I know," Gabriel said. "Six bandits just tried to steal our money."

"How did they know you had it?" Raul asked.

"Hannah believes Lloyd, the banker, sent them after us," Gabriel replied.

"What happened?" asked Lakin.

"They caught up with us just after we left the city," Gabriel said. "Your men killed them and hid the bodies."

Rabi grinned, "Hannah killed the first one, shot him through the heart with an arrow."

"I guess you are the perfect wife for Gabriel," Lakin said with a grin. "Now we have some important things to show you." Lakin handed Gabriel a large stack of papers. "Hannah's father owned a great deal of the City of Nora and the surrounding areas, including some of the gold mines. He and Endleson were partners on many ventures. These are all deeds which you and Hannah need to have put in your names immediately."

"I didn't know that," Hannah said with surprise.

"Hannah no wonder some of the people were worried about you making trouble," Raul said. "You own both property and businesses in Nora; you have enough power to make others nervous. And I will bet there are a lot of people who realize that. I think we should go back into Nora and get these titles transferred today. I will ride with you."

"I agree," Gabriel said. "But give me a moment to review these first."

Raul waited for Gabriel to read the deeds before he spoke again. "We have been going through the ledgers that were in the safe. It appears your father and Endleson spent large sums of money on dealings but did not indicate what they were."

"That was probably the protection money they paid to Roch," Hannah replied with disgust.

"No, there are entries for the protection money. Your father kept very detailed books, except for those unnamed expenditures."

"Lakin would you put the money that's in the suitcases in the safe. And would you mind sorting through the papers we brought back?" Gabriel asked.

"Certainly."

"As soon as we get these titles in our names, we are going to start searching the mines," Gabriel said.

Gabriel, Hannah and Raul were all sitting in the front seat of the boca as they drove to Nora. Ruala warriors flew overhead.

"While you two are getting the deeds changed why don't you drop me off at a tailor shop?" Raul said "I think I will go to the ball with you. Perhaps if you can keep Endleson distracted I can look around."

"Do you want to see if Rabi will let Marcia be your escort?" Hannah asked.

"No, they are newlyweds," Raul replied. "Besides it might be dangerous and she is not a fighter like you Hannah."

Hannah smiled at his comment. "So that means I will be attending the ball with the two most handsome men in the kingdom," Hannah said and squeezed both of their hands. "Gabriel, if there is no trouble, can we stop at my office and get the things that Marcia packed?"

"Of course dear."

"Gabriel I was thinking," Hannah said. "Now that I know how wealthy my father was. Well, when we move to Wetpr I would very much like to be a benefactor for the orphanage in Salar."

Gabriel turned and looked at Hannah as a broad smile took over his face. "I think that is a wonderful idea, Hannah."

Hannah turned to Raul, "I met your mother at that orphanage once. When I was in college I would donate hours of medical service to the orphans. One day Queen Renya came with money and an entire boca filled with supplies. She stayed and played with all of the children. The priests introduced us. Your mother is so gracious and well I don't know how to explain it; I was just in awe of her."

"I plan to write a couple of letters and send your gifts to my family tonight, I will mention that," Raul said.

"Oh, I would doubt if she would remember me; but I will never forget her."

"Raul, we will stop at the tailor first, then go to the Register of Deeds. After that I thought the three of us should have lunch at the Endleson Hotel, just to make our presence known. Then we can pick up Hannah's dress and some of the items at her office," Gabriel said.

303

Gabriel and Hannah decided to stay with Raul as he was fitted for a suit; in case Raul was recognized. Gabriel paid for his suit and put it into the back of the boca.

"I can't believe the tailor will have your suit made by the end of the day," Hannah said in astonishment.

"For what I am paying, he better," Raul said with a laugh.

"This should be interesting," Gabriel said sarcastically as he hitched the boca in front of the Register of Deeds office. There was no one in the office but a clerk when they entered. The old clerk knew Hannah and was helpful and efficient with the paperwork, something that Gabriel did not expect. Raul walked around the small office looking at maps which were displayed on the walls; while Gabriel and Hannah completed the paperwork.

"Excuse me sir," Raul said to the clerk. "This map with the names of all the landowners and their parcels, is it for sale?"

The clerk left his desk and walked over to the map that Raul was looking at. The clerk put on his spectacles and read the map number. "I have some in the back, I will get you one," the man said and left the office. He returned in a few moments with a large rolled up map and handed it to Raul. "The map is free," the clerk said and returned to the pile of deeds that Gabriel had handed to him. It took a little over two hours for all the deeds to be put into Gabriel's and Hannah's names.

"You are now landowners," the clerk said with a toothless smile as he handed the last deed to Gabriel. While Gabriel reviewed the paperwork, the clerk said. "Hannah I am happy for you, you have had a rough time of it." Then the clerk looked at Gabriel, "You're a lucky man, your wife is a great physician. She saved the life of my Rita when she got bite by a snake."

"I know, thank you," Gabriel said. Then he handed the clerk two gold coins.

"What's this for?" the man asked in surprise.

"All your hard work," Gabriel replied. Then he, Hannah and Raul walked out of the office and onto the sidewalk.

"We weren't alone in there," Raul said. "When I walked near the back room, I could smell cigarette smoke."

"I suspect Lloyd has been watching us," Hannah said. "I don't know if my father had any business dealings with him other than having him as our banker."

"Let's have some lunch and we can see what Lloyd has planned for us next," Gabriel said sarcastically as he helped Hannah into the boca. They slowly drove through the business district looking at the properties.

"How does it feel to know you own a lot of these places?" Raul asked.

"I am not sure yet," Gabriel said. "If I was in Wetpr I would be very happy but this is such a place of darkness, I just don't know."

"Should we sell everything?" Hannah asked.

"We need to wait before deciding that dear. Some of these places may end up being important to the mission," Gabriel said as they pulled up in front of the Endleson Hotel. When they entered the dining room they saw Lloyd sitting at a table with two other men. Lloyd's eyes widen when he saw Gabriel and Hannah.

"Raul would you take Hannah to a table," Gabriel asked and walked over to Lloyd's table.

"Gentlemen, would you please excuse us for a moment, Lloyd and I have some business to attend to," Gabriel said to the two men who were sitting at Lloyd's table. Lloyd clearly did not want to leave with Gabriel, so Gabriel took Lloyd's right arm and literally lifted him out of his seat. Gabriel maintained his grip on Lloyd's arm as the two men walked out of the dining room.

"What do you think Gabriel is going to do?" Hannah asked.

"I don't know but I rather wish I could watch," said Raul.

"Well go Raul, you don't need to sit here with me," Hannah said. "And besides Lloyd might have some of his hired men around."

"Are you sure you will be alright?"

"Raul, I have weapons on me, now go."

Raul walked out of the hotel and stood on the sidewalk. There was no sign of Gabriel or Lloyd; so Raul decided to look in the alleyways on the sides of the building. Raul was starting to walk to his right when he heard a loud sound coming from his left. Raul turned and ran to that side of the hotel and found Gabriel fighting with three men, while Lloyd stood and watched. The four men were fighting with their fists. Gabriel was not an easy victim for the hired killers. Not only was Gabriel a large and powerful man but he was well trained in combat.

One of the men pulled a knife out of his boot and lunged at Gabriel; who grabbed the man's arm and twisted it so hard the bone snapped. Gabriel then picked the man off the ground and threw him against the side of the building. Raul walked up behind one of the attackers and snapped his neck; as Raul threw the man's body down he saw Lloyd start to run.

Raul quickly grabbed Lloyd and threw him against the outside wall of the hotel. Lloyd hit his nose on the wall with such force that it broke; causing blood to spurt onto the wall and Lloyd's clothing. Lloyd tried to run again and Raul punched him in the stomach, Lloyd fell to his knees gasping for air.

When Gabriel and Raul did not return, Hannah left the hotel to look for them. She followed the sounds of fighting until she found them in the alley. Just as Hannah entered the alley, Gabriel hit the last attacker with a right uppercut to the jaw; that knocked the man unconscious.

"I thought as much," Hannah said with disgust to Lloyd. Suddenly Hannah pulled a small knife out of her cape and held it to Lloyd's throat. "Lloyd you stood by while Laurabelle was raped and murdered and now you attack my family."

"No Hannah!" Gabriel yelled. "Let's take him to your office so we can talk to him in private."

Raul threw Lloyd in the back of the boca and covered him with a blanket. Then Raul sat in the back with Lloyd, to prevent him from escaping. After a short drive through Nora, Gabriel and Raul walked Lloyd into Hannah's office and tied him to a chair.

"Are you going to kill me?" Lloyd asked fearfully.

"I wasn't planning on it but who can say what my wife or friend might do," Gabriel replied. "Lloyd I need some questions answered and the more cooperative you are with us, the better it will be for you; do you understand me?" Gabriel asked. "Why did you send those killers after us when we left your bank?"

"To rob you," Lloyd replied hesitantly.

"Is that the only reason?" Lloyd did not answer. "I said is that the only reason?" Gabriel repeated.

"You haven't read the paperwork I gave you, have you?"

"No, so why don't you fill us in." As Gabriel interrogated Lloyd, Hannah watched out the windows for more of Lloyd's hired men.

"Hannah's father, Arthur owned as much of Nora as the Endleson family does, that includes holdings in my bank." Lloyd looked at Hannah then back to Gabriel and Raul. "It is no secret that Hannah hates us all for what has happened to her family. She has owned ruling shares in many of the large businesses here without knowing it; that is until you came along."

"So, you tried to kill us because you are afraid of Hannah's revenge?" Gabriel asked dubiously.

"Well that and the money. Gabriel you and Hannah own enough of Nora to shut the city down."

"Is anyone else planning on killing us because of this?"

"Not that I know of," Lloyd said with his voice shaking.

"We've been going through Arthur's ledgers," Raul said. "His bookkeeping is meticulous but it appears that he and Endleson have been giving large sums of money to something or somebody that he would not identify. Do you know where that money was going to; every month?"

307

Lloyd suddenly looked terrified, "Gabriel they will kill me if I tell you."

"I'll kill you if you don't," Raul threatened. Lloyd squirmed in his chair as the sweat started to run down his face. "Lloyd!" Raul yelled.

"Arthur and Endleson and some of the others, they belong to this secret society, that's how they gained their wealth."

"Go on," Gabriel said.

"Years ago Arthur asked me to join, I went to a few of the meetings but..."

"But what?" demanded Raul.

"But I was so scared for me and my family," Lloyd was getting emotional as he spoke. "I wouldn't join so Arthur was going to kill me; he was afraid I would tell others about the meetings. I begged him to let me live. You see Arthur took me to those meetings and everyone wears masks so the others didn't know my identity. Arthur let me live for sixty percent of the bank."

As Lloyd spoke Hannah was walking towards him. She was staring at Lloyd intently. "What is the name of this society?" Hannah asked through clenched teeth.

"Hannah, I can't tell you."

"Lloyd you do understand how much I hate you, don't you?" Hannah asked in a threatening tone. "Now tell us."

"The Insidiae."

"What!" Hannah gasped. "No, it can't be true."

"Hannah look at his books, every month each of the members of the organization pay eighteen thousand dollars as dues. Raul you read the ledgers, isn't that the amount of the payments to an unnamed person?"

"Hannah, he is right," Raul replied.

308

Gabriel put his arm around Hannah's shoulders as he continued to question Lloyd. "Lloyd where were the meetings held?"

"In the mines."

"Who owned those mines?"

"Mostly Endleson but sometimes in the ones that Arthur owned."

"Three high priests are building something in one of the mines; do you know where?" Gabriel asked.

Lloyd suddenly looked suspiciously at Gabriel. "How is it that you know about the Insidiae and the priests?"

"Just answer the questions, Lloyd," Raul barked.

"All I know is that Endleson sold some of his property in the mines to the priests, shortly before the disappearances started."

"Can you show us were?" Gabriel asked.

"No, honestly I don't know," Lloyd said fearfully.

"Can you show us on a map where the meetings were held?"

"Yes, yes, but please let me go. I promise I won't say anything."

"Lloyd you just betrayed the Insidiae," Raul said. "If you do say anything, you have them to fear." Gabriel untied Lloyd as Hannah got some paper and a pen.

Chapter XX
Letters

Gabriel and Raul let Lloyd go free although they both had misgivings about doing so. Gabriel, Raul and Hannah filled the boca with medical supplies and other things from Hannah's office and apartment. Then the three walked around the streets of Nora for an hour before picking up Hannah's dress and Raul's suit. They saw nothing suspicious during this time.

"I suppose it will be like last time and the attack will come as soon as we leave the city," Gabriel said as they drove to the outskirts of Nora. Ruala warriors were waiting for them but the journey home was uneventful.

"Something really does not feel right about this," Raul said as they were driving down the roadway to Hannah's front porch. "Rabi, you are sure no one is following us?"

"The only things we can see are some deer and turkeys," Rabi replied.

Once they reached the house, Hannah and Marcia started cooking dinner while the men unloaded the boca. Afterwards the men gathered in the study to scrutinize the deeds, maps and other paperwork.

"Since we missed lunch, I am bringing some things for you to nibble on until dinner is ready," Hannah said as she carried a large tray into the study. Gabriel jumped up and took the tray from her. "Marcia is roasting a couple of turkeys and they won't be done for a while," Hannah said as she took platters of cheeses, sausages, smoked fish, pickles and biscuits from the tray and set them on the table that the men were sitting at. "Would anyone like ale?" Hannah asked. "I found quite a few bottles in the wine cellar."

"Sounds great to me," said Raul.

"I'll help you," Luca said and started to escort Hannah out of the room. Hannah stopped and turned around.

"Lakin, if you want to take any of the medical supplies that we brought home to the Ice Caves; you are more than welcome," Hannah offered.

Lakin smiled, "Thank you Hannah, I will do that."

Luca and Hannah walked down the old cellar steps. "Hannah, Gabriel told us about your father being a member of the Insidiae. I am sorry to hear that," Luca said.

"I still don't know if I believe it," Hannah said as she lit some of the torches that were along the stone wall. "Luca, walk past the wine casks and turn right; there is a wooden shelf full of bottles of ale. I'll get a basket to put them in."

Luca was carrying a torch, which he set in a metal holder fastened to the wall, when he found the shelf of dusty bottles. Luca started to empty one of the shelves when he saw something in the back of it. He grabbed his torch and examined the shelf and wall more closely. Then he moved the heavy wooden shelf just enough to allow him to crawl behind it.

"What are you doing?" Hannah asked as she walked towards Luca, carrying a large basket.

"There is a door behind this shelf. Do you know why it would be concealed?"

"I didn't know there was a door back there," Hannah said as she watched Luca open the door and walk into the room. He stepped out of the room quickly and shut the door.

"Hannah get Gabriel and Lakin."

"Luca what is it?"

"Hannah please just do as I ask."

Hannah turned and ran up the stairs, she returned in a few moments with Gabriel, Lakin, Raul and Rabi. Luca stood outside of the secret door, as the others approached.

"What is it?" Gabriel asked.

311

Luca looked at Hannah then turned to Gabriel, "I wish I didn't have to say this in front of her. There's an altar in there and the remains of humans, one skeleton still has shackles on."

"Hannah stay here," Gabriel said. "Until I see if it is safe." Gabriel took Luca's torch and walked into the dark room with Lakin behind him. After a couple of minutes Gabriel called out, "You can enter." When Raul, Hannah, Rabi and Luca entered the room, it was well lit because Gabriel had ignited all the torches along the walls.

The room was small with an altar against the far wall. The other three walls had shackles affixed to the stone. In the center of the room, in front of the altar was a large fire pit which was filled with bones. The altar held bones, blood stained bowls and a large knife. Hannah gasped and grabbed Raul's arm as the significance of the scene before her exploded in her consciousness. Gabriel was standing at the altar and quickly turned around when he heard Hannah.

"I'm alright," Hannah said with tears filling her eyes. "To think this was going on underneath us; and my own father." Hannah started to cry.

"Raul would you take Hannah upstairs, we will be up in a few minutes," Gabriel asked.

Raul took Hannah's arm and escorted her out of the cellar; to his surprise she did not protest about leaving. "Raul I think I could use a little whiskey," Hannah said as she sat down in one of the large overstuffed chairs in the study. Raul poured some whiskey into a glass and handed it to her. She rarely drank whiskey and winced and choked as she swallowed it. Gabriel walked up to Hannah and kissed her on top of her head.

"Are you alright?" Gabriel asked as he noticed she was holding a glass containing whiskey.

"I'm not sure," Hannah replied with tears running down her cheeks. "I never would have believed that my father could be capable of such things."

The first day of their journey back to Lentz, Matthew had the warriors make an early camp so the wounded could rest. As always Matthew, Sorren, Stephan, Thaos and Thedes made their fire away from the others. Thaos was gathering wood while Sorren was starting dinner.

"Look," Stephan said and pointed to a flock of Enrops flying towards them. "There are so many, I wonder if something is wrong."

The men all watched as the Enrops landed among them. "Napo is there anything wrong?" Matthew asked when he recognized the leader of the flock.

"No, we are just bringing you many things from your families," Napo said as the birds started to drop the envelopes on the ground, in a sort of pile. Each envelope had a name written on it. Thaos knelt down and started to sort the envelopes into five piles.

"Why so many?" Matthew asked Napo.

"Your wives said they did not want to distract you while you were in battle," Napo replied. "Now that they know you are returning they gave us all of the letters they have been writing."

"How do they know we are returning?" Sorren asked.

"Some of the Ruala warriors visited your families on their journey back to the Ice Caves."

Simon and Natasha spent several days watching Sophie with little of consequence. Sophie spent her time eating, walking the streets of Taperia and shopping. She did not receive any messages or visitors during this time.

"I am getting really bored," Natasha complained as she and Simon sat in the dining room of the Taperian Imperial Hotel.

"I will bet she is getting bored too," Simon said. "Perhaps she will make some type of move."

"Perhaps we can force her to," Natasha whispered.

"What do you mean?"

"She does not realize that Meekos is at the castle perhaps we should encourage an encounter."

"I think you should run that past Gabriel first."

"He hasn't written in a couple of days, I hope he is alright," Natasha said as she hid her face under her black mourning veil. "I wonder if Sophie has realized her books are missing yet?" Natasha became very serious. "I looked through her diary Simon. She talks mostly about Roch; I cannot believe what a monster he is. But there are also entries about Vitomas and Annabelle. I don't think you should read that book."

"Calen told me the same thing," Simon was quiet for a few moments. "What sort of things does she write about them?"

"Mostly how Roch treated them. He hurt them a lot, especially Vitomas. She writes a lot about Roch's actions. Perhaps this isn't her diary but more of Roch's."

"What do you mean?"

"Well she was sent there to watch him, maybe she had to document how evil he was so they would know if their plans were working."

"Natasha you are brilliant. I think we have been looking at this all wrong. Come on let's go back to the others," Simon said as he stood up and escorted Natasha out of the hotel.

Once they were in the boca and riding out of the city, Natasha asked, "Ok, so why am I brilliant?"

"We have been focusing on the players of the Insidiae but their focus has always been on Roch," Simon explained. "People establish set patterns of behavior; perhaps that book will reveal some things about Roch that we do not know."

Natasha put her hand on top of Simon's. "Simon I believe you may be on to something but I warn you that book contains a great deal of horror. There are also entries about Raul and your father and mother."

314

"To find what you are looking for you will have to separate yourself from your emotions. Perhaps you and Calen should read it together."

Simon smiled and looked at his friend, "Now for a minute there I thought you were going to offer to read it with me."

"I cannot, I have not finished it because it makes me cry. I would be upset reading that book if I didn't know any of the people involved. But you and Raul have become like brothers and your family seems wonderful; that book both breaks my heart and fills me with anger."

After Thaos sorted the envelopes into piles, he handed the appropriate envelopes to each man. "Want to have a drink while we read these?" Sorren asked, then poured five cups of whiskey. In all the years that Matthew and Stephan had been friends, Matthew had never seen Stephan cry because of pain or sadness. But now he saw tears in the eyes of his old friend, as Stephan took two tiny swatches of dark baby hair from an envelope.

"Look these are from my babies," Stephan said with awe. Each swatch had the tiniest of bows, one blue and one pink. "These are for my locket."

"I didn't think babies had hair that long," Thaos said as he looked at the swatches. Stephan proudly showed them to each of his friends.

"Their hair is the same color as yours," Matthew said.

After Sorren looked at Stephan's gift, he opened a larger envelope from Angelina. A letter and a small package fell out. "Matthew open your big envelope," Sorren said with excitement. "Angelina had lockets made for us too."

Sorren read a little more of his letter before opening his locket, which had the King's crest on the front. Sorren spoke again and the others could clearly hear the emotion in his voice.

"Those girls," Sorren said lovingly. "Angelina put some of Jacob's hair in here and Ingr put some of the twin's hair in the locket. They said these are from my grandbabies."

315

Matthew's locket, which was identical to Sorren's contained a swatch of Jacob's hair. Matthew became homesick as he read Angelina's letter. "Sorren, you know Jacob doesn't talk much so Angelina and Ibula have been teaching him words. Angelina says that whenever anyone says Sorren or Mathias that Jacob now says 'Grandpa.'" Everyone smiled as they heard Matthew's words. "She says that when someone says my name, Jacob says "Papa.'" Matthew stopped reading out loud for a few moments.

"Nikki says that Claudius hasn't stopped smiling since the babies were born," Thaos said. "And that he wants to hold them all of the time, even when they cry." Thaos read silently for a few moments then spoke again, "Nikki said she is really getting big and wonders if we calculated her time right." Thaos smiled as he spoke, "Nikki said she hopes I recognize her when I get home because she is wearing some of Ingr's maternity clothes now but not to worry because no one has ever had twins in her family. I wouldn't worry," Thaos said. "In fact I think it would be great."

"Nikki wasn't that big when we left," Stephan said. "And Ingr was huge, how can she get so big in a matter of weeks?"

"Don't look at me, I have no idea," Thaos said with a grin.

"Matthew, Ibula says that she and Angelina have become very close friends and she has enjoyed her stay," Thedes said. "And she has a surprise for me, when we get to Lentz."

Matthew looked up from his letter and grinned. "I know what that surprise is, if you want to hear it. Angelina told me."

Thedes looked at Matthew as he was trying to decide if he wanted Matthew to tell him; finally Thedes' curiosity got the better of him. "Oh Matthew, Ibula will kill me but tell me what it is."

"You're sure you want to know?" Matthew asked with a broad smile.

"Now you really have my curiosity up, tell me."

"Thedes you are going to be a father too."

"Really?" Thedes asked in disbelief. "Matthew let me see that letter. We have been trying to have a baby for some time."

316

Matthew handed Thedes Angelina's letter and smiled as he watched the look of joy on Thedes' face.

"Congratulations," Stephan said and shook Thedes' hand. Each man around the campfire stood up and shook Thedes' hand. None of them had ever seen Thedes overwhelmed before.

"We have much to celebrate," Sorren said and poured more whiskey into everyone's cups.

"Angelina said that we have to let everyone know when we are a day away because Bella and Claudius are planning a big celebration for our return," Matthew said then he looked at Stephan. "Apparently my parents wanted to have the celebration but the twins are too little to travel."

Stephan had been reading his letters in silence as he was surprised at the emotions they evoked in him. "Ingr just asked me if I wanted to sleep in another room because the babies are awake all night feeding," Stephan said then he looked at Thaos. "Nikki has been up every night helping Ingr. We are lucky our wives are such good friends."

"Matthew, before we get to your castle, can we stop and buy our wives some gifts?" Thedes asked.

"Seriously Simon I don't think you should read this book," Calen said gravely. "It was difficult for me to read."

"Natasha warned me," Simon said. "Calen, every man establishes patterns of behavior. If you study them you can predict how they will act in the future. If Sophie chronicled everything that Roch did and said, it might help us to find answers for this mission. Did you find such patterns?"

"Simon, I became so filled with rage that I had to keep putting the book down. I couldn't finish it," Calen said. "I am telling you as a friend, you don't want to read this."

"You are both right," Natasha said. "So how are we going to get through this book without getting caught up in our emotions?"

"Do you think that if we read it out loud as a group, that at least one of us could see past the crimes?" Dagon asked.

317

"That may be the only way," Calen said. "But it should be Simon's decision; several of his family members are victims in this book. He may not want everyone to hear those passages."

"Simon, you could write down the names of your family that might be the victims and when one of us gets to a part with their names we can ask you before proceeding," Natasha suggested.

"Koby what do you think?" Simon asked.

"I really don't want to hear what is in that book. Simon I have stayed at your home and I have a lot of respect for your family. In a way I feel like we are intruding in your family secrets," Koby said soberly. "But I think you are correct about getting insight into Roch; as horrible as it sounds I think we have to read it. But at least one of us should take notes."

"I can take the notes," Natasha said. "What sort of things are we looking for?"

"Roch's weaknesses, how he responds under duress, things about his personality, how he thinks," Simon said. "We know he is cruel but he may come out of this transformation a very powerful being and we may need to understand his weaknesses to destroy him."

"When do you want to start?" Calen asked.

"Now would be fine," Simon said.

"Well, in that case I am going to pour us some drinks," Calen said. "While Natasha gets some paper and pen." Then Calen looked at Natasha, "You better get a handkerchief too, and if you can't listen, there is no shame in leaving the room."

Simon, Calen, Dagon, Koby and Natasha took turns reading from Sophie's diary. Once they made the decision to look past the horror, they realized what the book really was. Sophie had been analyzing and documenting Roch's behavior for years. She described the most horrific situations in great detail, but with the dispassionate eye of a trained observer.

They realized that Sophie's role was to determine if Roch was ready and capable of being the Vessel for such a powerful demon as Omnibus. Realizing this, made it easier for the team to get through the hundreds of pages of documentation of the most inhumane treatment of mankind.

After they had been reading for several hours, Calen decided the group needed a long break. It was obvious to Calen that Simon was greatly affected by the book, although Simon did not want to take a break.

"This beast has been trying to murder my family for years," Simon said. "This may be the only way we can stop him."

"Simon we understand," Calen said. "But the contents of this book are weighing heavily on everyone right now. We need a break to be able to analyze it logically."

Simon was silent for a few moments. "When Roch dies, Raul is next in line to inherit the throne of Stordt. When we got news that Cerephus was King, Raul was weighing his options as to whether he wanted to take that throne. It is the only time Raul and I have really fought with our wives. They did not want to return here or raise our families here; now I understand why."

"Stordt is a large and rich kingdom," Koby said. "It might be worth the fight."

"There is something about this place that calls to evil men," Natasha said. "If Raul took the throne, he would always be at war."

The next morning an Enrop arrived with the first light of dawn to deliver a letter to Calen. No sooner had that bird left then a second Enrop arrived with another letter for Calen. He brought them to the kitchen table and read them as Natasha was preparing breakfast.

"Anything interesting?" Natasha asked as she was kneading the bread dough.

"Yes, but I will wait until everyone is here and share them with you all at once," Calen said.

Suddenly fear gripped Natasha's heart, "Calen did something happen to Gabriel? Is he alright?"

"He is fine," Calen assured her. "He asked that I read one of the letters to all of you as a group.

Simon, Koby and Dagon all entered the kitchen within minutes of each other. Once they all were seated Natasha put platters of ham, fried potatoes, eggs and pancakes on the table. Next she put biscuits and a large jar of honey on the table.

"Natasha I believe I am gaining weight on this mission," Simon teased.

Natasha filled everyone's cups with coffee then sat at the table. "We received two letters this morning," Calen said. He proceeded to read a copy of the letter that Meekos had written to Pravis and Tenebrae.

"So the witch doesn't know Meekos is here yet," Natasha said. "But why would Ahriman try to stop the ascension?"

"That's a good question," Simon said.

Before anyone else could speak Calen opened the second envelope. "This is from Gabriel and he wanted me to read it to you all at the same time." Gabriel wrote about their mission to search the hotel rooms of the high priests. Gabriel described everything in great detail, including the encounter that he and Hannah had with the demon.

Then Gabriel described the journey that his spirit took as the demon tried to drag him into hell. He told of Hannah's vision and how Hannah and Lakin brought him back." Calen stopped reading at this point and looked at Natasha. "Are you alright?" he asked.

Natasha did not speak, she merely nodded. Calen returned to the letter which ended with Gabriel telling them about the two weddings. Suddenly Natasha began to cry, she put her face against Calen's chest and sobbed. Calen put his arms around her.

"Natasha are you crying because Gabriel almost died or because he is married?" Calen asked

"I don't know," Natasha said and continued to cry. As Simon watched her.

"Well Hannah certainly sounds like a wonderful woman," Calen said.

"Actually she sounds a lot like you Natasha," Koby said trying to cheer her up.

"I know, she sounds exactly like the woman I would have picked out for him," Natasha said between sobs. "And I have no idea why I am crying like this."

Simon started to smile. "When Annabelle was pregnant with the twins, she would cry uncontrollably for no apparent reason. At first I thought I was doing something wrong, but then Mother explained to me it was because she was pregnant."

Natasha quickly lifted her head from Calen's chest and spun around so she could look at Simon. "Simon what are you saying?" Natasha asked as she was wiping the tears from her eyes.

"I am just saying you are reminding me of Annabelle."

"You think I am pregnant?" Natasha asked. "Wouldn't I know if I was?" Then Natasha turned to Calen. "Calen wouldn't we know?"

Calen put his arms around Natasha and hugged her tightly as his face beamed with the possibility that they might be having a baby. "Well, maybe we are finding out now," he said.

Natasha looked into Calen's eyes. "How would you feel about it if I was pregnant?"

"It's hard for me to think I could be happier than I already am with you," Calen said warmly. "But the idea that you might be pregnant just filled my heart with warmth." Natasha smiled at his words and kissed Calen on the lips.

"You have a sister-in-law who is a physician," Dagon said. "Why don't you write to Hannah and ask her about these things. I am sure she wants to get to know you."

Natasha was quiet for a few moments as she was trying to compose herself. "Dagon that is a very good idea, I will," Natasha said. Then she turned to Simon. "Let's go into the city today so I can buy things to fix up Gabriel's room for when he brings Hannah here." Simon smiled.

"Get some things for Rabi and Marcia too," Calen said. "We will have much to celebrate when we all get together."

"Three marriages in one mission," Koby said with a shake of his head. "That is unheard of."

"It just means you two and Luca are next," Natasha said with a smile. "And if you don't get married you can live with us. Calen's parents are building rooms for you in our house."

"Really?" Dagon asked.

"I was going to keep it as a surprise, but yes," Calen said with a grin. "I thought you could help Natasha try to chase the babies around as they fly through the air."

Calen, Simon, Dagon, Koby and Natasha had barely finished breakfast when a third Enrop arrived at the hotel. This bird was not delivering a letter but a very important message. "Meekos and the sorcerer have left the castle and are heading to Taperia. Without saying a word, Simon and Natasha both bolted from the table and ran to their rooms to change into their disguises.

"Have the Enrop wait," Natasha called from her bedroom. "Neither of us knows what they look like."

Koby hitched the horses to the boca and in less than ten minutes Simon and Natasha were driving towards Taperia. Oja the Enrop was sitting on the front seat of the boca with Natasha and Simon. "Meekos is tall and slender with short straight grayish hair. He is wearing the robes of a high priest," Oja explained. "The sorcerer is shorter with brown hair that touches his shoulders, his eyes are black and his eyebrows are very, very large; he is wearing a red robe with blue stripes. They are riding in a boca and the back of it is filled with things."

"What sort of things?" Simon asked.

"We flew over them and looked into the boca; there were suitcases, books and clothing," Oja replied.

"Sounds like they are moving out of the castle," Simon said. "I wonder if they are leaving because their friends were dragged into hell or if something else is going on."

As Simon drove down the main business street of Taperia, Oja watched for Meekos' boca. "There it is," the Enrop said.

"Just as I thought, it's in front of the Taperian Imperial Hotel," Natasha said. "Things should start getting interesting now."

Simon hitched the horses to a railing near the hotel and helped Natasha down. "Oja would you stay in the area, in case we need to get a message to Calen and the others quickly?" Simon asked.

"Certainly."

Simon and Natasha walked into the hotel and saw Meekos and Erebus checking in at the front desk. "Honey would you get a table while I check for messages?" Simon said loudly to Natasha. Then he walked up to the desk and stood behind Meekos and Erebus. After Meekos and Erebus signed the guest register the clerk turned the book around and read their names.

"Meekos," the young clerk said. "There is a lady staying here who has been asking about a man named Meekos."

Meekos was filled with excitement, "Would her name be Sophie by chance?"

"Yes, that's her," the clerk said. "She will be very happy you are here."

"Tell me, what room is she in?" Meekos asked happily.

"Her room is 517, but My Lord, she is not in there."

"Where is she?" Meekos asked with concern.

"Oh, no need to worry, she goes shopping every day after breakfast and she always returns by noon," the clerk explained. "Would you like rooms on the same floor as Sophie?"

"Yes."

Simon watched as the clerk gave Meekos the key for room 519 and Erebus the key to room 521. "We have a lot of things in our boca," Meekos said. "Is there a man who could carry them to our rooms?"

"Yes My Lords, I will get someone right away," the obliging clerk said.

"Let's go to the dining room after we get our things into our rooms," Meekos said to Erebus as they were walking up the stairs.

Simon joined Natasha in the dining room and told her the things he had overheard. They ordered food from the menu and waited for Meekos and Erebus to come to the dining room. Within fifteen minutes the two sorcerers entered the dining room and looked around at the guests before choosing a table. Meekos chose a table near the window, so he could watch for Sophie. Simon and Natasha could not hear what Meekos and Erebus were saying because of the distance between the tables.

"I still have that ring of keys to all the hotel rooms," Natasha whispered to Simon.

"You heard Gabriel's letter, what if Meekos has another demon in his room?" Simon asked.

With indignation Natasha replied, "Simon do you think I have learned nothing from my brother. I too can vanquish a demon."

"You are not going into those rooms without Calen's permission and that is final, Natasha," Simon said with authority. "If something happens to you like it did to Gabriel, I don't think Calen or any of us would know how to bring you back."

Simon and Natasha remained in the dining room of the Taperian Imperial Hotel waiting for Sophie to arrive. Almost an hour and a half later, Sophie walked into the lobby of the hotel. The young desk clerk told her that Meekos was in the dining room waiting for her.

Breathlessly Sophie ran into the dining room, searching the faces of the guests, when she heard her name called. "Sophie," Meekos said happily as he stood up at the table and waved to her. For a woman of her age and size Sophie quickly moved through the dining room and embraced her brother. Then to the surprise of Simon and Natasha they saw Sophie embrace the wizard and kiss him passionately on the lips.

"Well, they certainly look happy to see each other," Natasha said as she and Simon watched from across the room. "Simon, Meekos wasn't in his room long enough to set up an altar or call a demon. Please let me search the rooms while they eat lunch," Natasha begged. "I promise I will leave if anything strange happens."

"Somehow I don't believe you would," Simon said with a smile. "I promised Calen I would protect you and especially now that you might be pregnant, I can't let you take chances. I'll go."

"And Simon, can you please tell me how you would know if a demon was in that room?" Natasha quipped.

"Well you have got me there," Simon replied.

"Why don't you tell Oja to watch them for us and we will both go into the rooms," Natasha suggested. "If there is a demonic presence we will leave right away. And I mean that Simon because I don't want anything to happen to you either."

It was clear to Simon and Natasha that Sophie, Meekos and Erebus were going to have a meal, which meant they would be in the dining room for a while.

Simon and Natasha left the dining room. Natasha walked up the stairs to the room Simon had rented, while he walked outside to talk with Oja. By now, several other Enrops had joined Oja in Taperia.

"We will warn you if they leave the table," Oja promised and Simon entered the hotel and walked up to his chambers.

"They are still looking at the menus," Simon told Natasha when he entered the sitting room. Natasha had removed her disguise and was dressed in a dark blue dress. She grabbed an empty basket that she had previously put into the room.

After checking the hallway Simon and Natasha entered Erebus' chambers; which was in a shambles because all of his property had been piled up in the center of the sitting room.

"There's no presence of evil in here," Natasha said as she quickly started to sort through Erebus' belongings. "They found little of interest, except that Erebus had taken a suitcase full of jewels and gold coins from the secret treasure room in what was once Roch's bedroom chambers. "I'm grabbing these books," Natasha said as she filled her basket.

Simon looked through the other rooms, but Erebus hadn't had time to move in; so they left and went back to Simon's chambers. Natasha emptied her basket while Simon checked the hallway; everything was quiet so they entered Meekos' chambers.

Meekos had four suitcases that were set in the middle of the sitting room. "Ouch," yelled Natasha as she quickly pulled her hand back from a suitcase. Simon reached forward to open the same suitcase and felt a hot pain shoot up his arm. Then he touched a second suitcase and once again received a severe shock. "He put a spell on these," Natasha said. "We should leave." They left Meekos chambers and walked across the hallway to Simon's chambers.

"Natasha," Simon yelled as she suddenly collapsed on the floor. Simon turned Natasha over, she was breathing but unconscious. As he looked at her, Simon's vision was becoming blurry, his head was spinning. He stood up and walked towards the balcony door. Simon pushed the door open and collapsed half in the room and half on the balcony.

"Come quickly," Oja screeched as he approached the abandoned hotel where the Ruala warriors were. "Calen, Calen, come quickly."

Koby was the first one out of the door, followed by Dagon and Calen. Oja circled around them screaming, "Follow me something is wrong with Simon and Natasha, hurry." The Rualas took to the air. "They are lying on the floor, they look like they are dead," Oja screamed, as the four flew to Simon's chambers. Fear so gripped their hearts that none of them spoke until they got to the balcony of Simon's sitting room.

Dagon turned Simon over. "He's breathing," Dagon said as he examined Simon for wounds.

"Where is Natasha?" Calen cried as he entered the hotel room. He found her lying in the middle of the room near a stack of books on black magic. "She's breathing too," Calen said with relief as he looked her over for wounds.

"There are no wounds on Simon," Dagon said.

"I can't find any on Natasha either," said Calen.

"Look at these books, I'll bet they went into the rooms of the sorcerers," Koby said.

"Oja do you know where Gabriel is living?" asked Calen.

"Yes, we can take you."

"Koby bring those books we might need them," Calen said and flew off the balcony holding Natasha. Dagon followed, carrying Simon. Koby was putting all of the books into Natasha's basket, when he heard voices in the hallway. He quickly flew out the balcony doors.

Calen, Koby and Dagon were flying as fast as they could to Nora; a strong wind was at their backs which helped them greatly. Neither Natasha nor Simon had regained consciousness although it had been five hours since they left Taperia. After the first two hours of flight, Koby remembered the other Ruala warriors at the abandoned hotel.

Calen sent an Enrop to these warriors with a message telling them to stay at the hotel while Calen and the others flew to Nora. "Oja," Calen called out. "Fly ahead and tell Gabriel and Lakin we are coming, perhaps they will meet us half way." Oja could hear the fear in Calen's voice.

"I will stay with you and the others will fly ahead," Oja said. Since Enrops can fly faster than Rualas the large birds quickly disappeared from view. The three Ruala warriors continued their fearful journey westward.

Chapter XXI
Gathering

Meekos, Sophie and Erebus enjoyed a long and leisurely lunch. Meekos and Sophie were overjoyed to be reunited. Erebus could clearly see the happiness in their faces. But it was the love in the eyes of Sophie and Erebus that greatly agitated Meekos.

"When we are done eating, why don't both of you join me in my room," Sophie suggested. "I have been here for several weeks and have quite made myself at home. I have some fine whiskey and brandy in my room, in addition to wines and chocolates."

"That sounds fine," Meekos said. "But first I would like to change into something a little more comfortable. I will meet you in your room."

Erebus and Sophie entered her room. She opened the balcony doors to allow the fresh air in. What would you like to drink?" Sophie asked. Erebus did not answer. He turned Sophie around and kissed her passionately on the lips.

"I have been so worried about you," Erebus whispered and kissed Sophie again. Meekos entered the room wearing a shirt and trousers, he looked angry. "What is the matter?" Erebus asked him.

"Someone has touched my suitcases," Meekos growled.

"Well of course, we paid to have them carried up here," Erebus said sarcastically.

"I have a spell on the locks," Meekos explained. "If anyone tries to open them they will die."

"Did you find a dead person in your room?" Erebus asked somewhat cynically.

"No, but the locks were glowing red, so I know they were touched," Meekos said angrily. "I wonder if that man who carried them up tried to steal anything."

"Let's go down to the desk and see if he is still alive; that should give you an answer," Erebus suggested.

Sophie stood in silence as the two men spoke. The color was draining from her face. "I should tell you something," she said seriously. "I don't remember the exact day but within my first two weeks here I lost my blood ring, then some days later I realized I was missing a couple of books which I had hidden under my mattress."

"What sort of books?" Meekos asked suspiciously.

"My chronicles of Roch and a book of spells."

"What!" Meekos yelled. "What did you do?"

"I searched everywhere of course," Sophie replied with indignation. "I figured if there is a thief in this hotel, they would not know what to do with these items anyways."

"Well, I think it is a little too coincidental that all this is happening," Meekos snapped.

"Meekos, who would be targeting us?" Sophie asked. "No one really knows us here and certainly no one knows what we are doing."

"Well, Cerephus and Malus knew about Meekos and Roch, although they didn't know that Sophie had returned. And now King Hamond knows about Roch but does he know you are here?" Erebus asked Sophie.

"General Hamond is king now," Sophie said with disgust. "I have no idea if he knows I am here."

"The Sanuri," Meekos said. "I will bet he is behind all of this."

Matthew led the warriors across the border into the Kingdom of Lentz; where they made an early camp just outside of Fort Castor.

"Why are we stopping when there is still so much day light?" Sorren asked.

"Because I am taking you shopping in Castor," Matthew said with a grin. "So just stay on your horses."

329

Thedes, Thaos, Stephan, Sorren and Matthew left the campsite and rode into Castor. A large city that was built on the shores of the Sea of Grevtd. They could see the masts of huge ships as they neared the docks. The ships brought treasures from other worlds that were sold in the shops in Castor. The five men hitched their horses on a busy street that was lined with businesses.

"Are you going to visit Isabella while we are here?" Stephan asked with a sarcastic grin.

"I'm just hoping we don't run into her," Matthew replied.

"Who is Isabella?" Thaos asked.

"One of my father's sisters, she is married to Joseph who is the commander of Fort Castor," Matthew said.

"And you don't like her?" asked Thedes.

"You would have to meet her to understand," Matthew said. "She has the exact opposite personality from Aunt Renya and our wives for that matter. Personally I can't stand being around her."

Stephan was laughing, "Isabella has the ability to make you feel like the weight of the world is piled on your shoulders when you are with her. I try to avoid her when they come for visits."

"Let's go in here," Matthew suggested as they entered an elegant jewelry store. The store was extremely large and the men all went their own ways as they were searching for gifts.

Within minutes a man's raised voice was heard throughout the store, "Get out! We don't allow Shettees in here."

Sorren quickly stepped beside Thedes. "What is going on here?" Sorren demanded.

"And you, who are you?" loudly demanded the pretentious clerk. "I told him we don't take Shettee money here; it is worthless in this kingdom. And if you are a friend of his you can leave too."

"Do you ever want to take the King's money again?" Matthew asked loudly as he walked towards the clerk.

"Why Prince Matthew; I did not see you here," the clerk said in a considerably lower voice.

"The Shettee you are insulting is my cousin and Chief Sorren of the Nordes Tribe is my father-in-law," Matthew said angrily. "So you have greatly insulted two members of the Royal Family."

"Chief Sorren is my father-in-law also," Stephan said as he joined the group.

"Master Stephan, I am so sorry I didn't realize," the clerk explained. "Please, please, all of you buy anything you want; I will give you all discounts for the misunderstanding."

"We don't need discounts," Matthew said. "But we will not spend money here until you apologize to Thedes and Sorren in a voice as loud as when you insulted them. All the customers in the store were now gathering around to see what was going on.

"I am truly sorry for being so rude," the old clerk said apologetically.

"And in the future will you turn away Shettee customers?" Stephan demanded.

"No, My Lords, never again."

"Whatever they want goes on my bill," Matthew said.

"Matthew I protest," Thedes said.

"It's the least I can do since you risked your life to save our families," Matthew said loud enough for all to hear.

"Whatever they want, split the costs between my bill and Matthew's bill," Stephan ordered.

Thaos walked up to Thedes and handed him a small leather pouch. "What is this?" Thedes asked.

"Gold coins, the money everyone will take," Thaos said with a grin.

"You were awfully quiet during dinner. Are you sure you are alright?" Gabriel called to Hannah as he sat on the edge of their bed and removed his boots.

"I will be fine," Hannah said loudly from the closet. "It's unbelievable when you think you know someone so well and then you find out he was a monster. He really did seem like a good father and husband."

"He may have been those things but that doesn't mean he was a good man," Gabriel said. "Try to hold on to the good memories." Hannah did not respond. "I don't know why you are changing in the closet," Gabriel said with a smile. "You know I will have that nightgown off from you as soon as you get out here."

Gabriel removed the rest of his clothing and turned around when he heard Hannah. "You look absolutely beautiful," Gabriel said as he watched her walking towards him. Hannah was wearing a pale yellow lace nightgown, her long blonde hair was cascading over her shoulders and she smelled like roses.

"I want to look nice for you," Hannah said as she stretched up and put her arms around Gabriel's neck.

Gabriel bent down and the two kissed passionately for several minutes. Then he stopped and looked at her. "Hannah, would you have used that knife on Lloyd today?"

Hannah's voice became emotional. "Gabriel I don't know, I just don't know. I have lost my entire family and I just love you so much, I, I didn't want them to hurt you too." Hannah squealed and giggled as Gabriel suddenly picked her up and started walking towards the bed.

"I love you too," Gabriel said as he softly lowered Hannah onto the bed. Gabriel lowered himself on top of her as they became lost in their embrace.

"Gabriel, Hannah," Luca yelled as he burst into their room. "Get dressed. Natasha and Simon are hurt, the others are bringing them here; they want us to meet them."

Calen, Koby and Dagon were becoming exhausted; they had been flying as fast as they could for almost twelve hours.

They had a strong wind at their back which helped them greatly in covering distance but the speed and the weight they carried were taking their toll. They stopped once so that Koby could take Simon from Dagon. The Ruala warriors were following the River Nebu southwest to Nora; the full moon helped them maintain their course.

"Calen, we will need to rest for a short while or we will never make it," Dagon said.

"I know, let's go just a little further," Calen pleaded. His heart felt like it was crumbling inside of him. Natasha was breathing but had not moved in any way for the twelve hours they were in flight.

"Look, I see a clearing near the river," Koby said. "We will just stop for a short while."

Downward the warriors soared. Unbeknown to them, they were but two hours north of Hannah's home. Oja did not land but continued towards Nora; he knew the situation was becoming increasingly desperate and he wanted to get help. Calen gently laid Natasha on the grass, which was wet with dew.

"I wish we had some blankets," Calen said as he stroked her hair. "How is Simon?"

"He is breathing and he is warm," Koby said.

Dagon had a water pouch draped across his chest. He filled it with cold water from the river and brought it to the others. Each man drank of the water, the only sustenance they had. The warriors were exhausted, hungry and dehydrated. Dagon and Koby lay down on the wet grass, while Calen sat next to Natasha, holding her hand. No one spoke; sadness filled them all.

Koby was drifting into sleep; thoughts and sounds were racing through his mind as the weariness took control.

"Koby, Dagon wake up," Calen yelled. "They're here."

Koby opened his eyes and saw the outlines of Ruala warriors and Enrops against the backdrop of the full moon. Oja was the first to land.

"They were almost here when I found them," Oja said excitedly.

Within moments, Lakin landed; he was carrying Raul. Luca was behind them carrying Gabriel and they were followed by Rabi who held Hannah. Ten other Ruala warriors and three more Enrops landed.

"Build a fire," Lakin ordered as his feet touched the ground. "We have blankets; let's put them next to each other on top of some of the blankets, near the fire." Lakin saw Calen pick Natasha up. "Calen, you Dagon and Koby, cover yourselves with some of the blankets and get some rest, we may be here for a while. You all look exhausted."

Raul and Gabriel each ran to their sibling. "Please stay back unless I ask for your help," Lakin said. "We don't know what we are dealing with yet. Calen walked up to Gabriel and patted his shoulder as if to reassure him.

"Oja told us what happened," Gabriel said as he saw the look of utter sadness on Calen's face.

"Gabriel, you should know, Natasha might be pregnant," Calen said emotionally.

"Lakin did you hear that?" Gabriel asked with fear in his voice.

"Yes, we both did," Lakin replied as he and Hannah were examining the patients.

"Calen come here," Hannah called.

"I am Hannah, I'm a physician. Tell me did Natasha have these burns on her fingers before?"

Calen looked at the tips of Natasha's fingers on her right hand. "I didn't notice them. She didn't say anything about getting burned. But she does a lot of cooking."

"Simon has them too," Lakin said. "They must have touched something in the sorcerer's room. Oja do you know what they were doing in those rooms?"

"Meekos and the other sorcerer had just entered the hotel, then went down to the dining room and waited for the witch to join them. A man from the hotel carried all of their bags to the rooms. Simon and Natasha were going to search the bags," Oja explained.

"Natasha had stolen a ring of keys to all of the hotel rooms, so she could enter any of them," Calen said wearily.

Hannah looked up at Gabriel and saw such despair on his face that it brought tears to her eyes. "Gabriel we will bring them back," she said sweetly. Gabriel did not respond. Hannah realized Gabriel was crippled by his grief. "Gabriel," Hannah said loudly. "You are the expert on demons. What could they have touched that would do this to them? Gabriel we need you to help us." Hannah's words brought Gabriel back from his despair. He bent down and examined the burns on both of their hands.

"I'll bet there was some kind of spell put on the bags as a security measure," Gabriel said.

"You mean so only the owners could open them?" Raul asked as he knelt near Simon.

"Yes," Gabriel replied. "Everyone grab one of those books they brought from the hotel and look for protection spells."

Lakin and Hannah tended to Simon and Natasha while the others looked through the books. Lakin put some of the blessed water on their bodies but it did not smoke like it had with Gabriel. "Well, they have no demons in them," Lakin said.

"Dip their burned fingers in that water," Hannah suggested. Lakin dipped Simon's fingers into the blessed water and within moments, Simon's hand started to jerk, then his entire arm. "Look, there is something moving under his skin," Hannah gasped.

"Hannah grab a handful of crystals and that large bottle of blessed water," Lakin said as he quickly ran to the fire and thrust the blade of a ceremonial knife into the flames.

"Raul, Gabriel hold Simon down," Lakin yelled. Raul held Simon's shoulders while Gabriel held his legs.

"Hannah, as soon as I pull that thing out of his arm, pour the water into the wound, then cover it with crystals," Lakin said.

Lakin said a prayer then dipped Simon's fingers into the blessed water again. Simon's hand and arm jerked dramatically like they had previously. Then they all saw something moving under the skin of Simon's right arm. With the precision of a surgeon, Lakin sliced open Simon's arm and pulled a small red snake out. "Kill this," Lakin said and handed the snake to Gabriel. Hannah poured blessed water into the wound but they saw no other signs of movement. Lakin examined the arm. "Hannah put the crystals on him. I don't see any other snakes."

"But he needs stitches," Hannah said.

"No, just put the crystals in the wound and bandage his arm tightly," Lakin said. "Raul help me with Natasha. I want you to do the same thing that Hannah did." Lakin thrust his knife back into the flames of the fire. Raul was dipping Natasha's burned fingers into the blessed water when Lakin returned to her.

Like Simon, Natasha's hand and arm became spasmodic, then something appeared to move under her skin. Lakin sliced open Natasha's arm and pulled out another red snake which he handed to Calen, who cut its head off. By the time Raul finished pouring water into Natasha's wound Hannah was next to him. Hannah put the crystals into the wound and wrapped Natasha's arm.

"Calen, help Hannah pour some blessed water down Natasha's throat," Lakin said. "Raul you help me with Simon."

Neither Natasha nor Simon regained consciousness. Lakin waited for a few minutes then looked under their bandages and saw that the crystals were turning black. "The crystals and water are drawing the poison out," Lakin said. "Let's take them back to the house. Ty, Kev and Gabi carry Calen, Dagon and Koby; I don't think they can make the rest of the trip."

Simon was put into the spare bed in Raul's room. Raul and Luca moved some of the large overstuffed chairs from the parlor into that bedroom for Lakin and Luca to sleep in.

Natasha was put in one of the other bedrooms that contained two beds, one for Calen. Several large chairs were brought to this room also, for Hannah and Gabriel to sleep in.

Dagon and Koby moved into one of the other bedrooms and the Ruala warriors who had been staying in that room moved to the bunk house. The night was long for everyone, as they waited to find out if Simon and Natasha would survive their wounds.

Lakin changed the bandages and crystals every couple of hours during the night; each time he cleaned the wounds with more blessed water. Neither patient moved as their bandages were changed; nor did they respond when people were talking to them. The hours wore on.

As Angelina had requested, Matthew sent an Enrop ahead to announce that the warriors were but a day's ride from Claudius' castle. Bella, Rosa, Ibula, Angelina, Nikki and Ingr worked at a records pace to finalize the preparations for the huge homecoming celebration they had organized. Besides, many residents of Lentz, all of the Nordes Tribe were invited to the celebration.

Invitations were sent to the Ice Caves of Mordv as well as to the Sanuri. Rosa and Bella forced Isadore to help with the festivities as a way of getting her out of the castle. Both Fahron and Isadore had become reclusive after the scandal and imprisonment of their son Timothy. Now the night before the celebrations, sleep did not come to Ingr, Nikki, Angelina or Ibula as they anxiously awaited the arrival of their husbands.

The Sanuri received his invitation the morning he left the monastery at Leven with baby Sarah. He prayed to The Great Ruler to give him guidance as to what to do with her. The baby appeared normal in all respects. The Sanuri did not see the darkness of her mother in Sarah's soul, nor did he see any demon's commanding her spirit.

The child was almost one year old; she was chubby with curly black hair and blue eyes. Sarah was a happy baby, who had been well cared for by the priests at the monastery.

The Sanuri drove his boca and team of white horses northward towards Lentz, while he waited for The Great Ruler to tell him where he should take little Sarah.

The smell of breakfast cooking woke most of the people in Hannah's house. Marcia had gotten up before sunrise to start preparing food. As she cooked, Rabi told her about all the things that had occurred the night before.

"Rabi, I will be glad when we move to the Ice Caves," Marcia said as she was setting the table. "There is so much darkness here. Hannah's father worshipping demons, demons trying to drag Gabriel into hell and now demonic snakes inside of Natasha and Simon. It all really scares me."

Rabi stood up and put his arms around Marcia. "Don't worry, I won't let anything happen to you," he said and kissed her forehead. Marcia always felt safe in Rabi's strong arms. He was tall, as were all Ruala's with reddish brown hair and large brown eyes. Marcia loved his eyes; she kept telling Rabi she would get lost in those eyes.

"You always make me feel so safe," Marcia said and stretched up and kissed Rabi on the lips. "I don't know what I did before I met you Rabi." He leaned down and kissed her. They held their embrace until they heard the others walking around. Marcia returned to the stove, "I am making soup for Simon and Natasha; I'm not sure what we should feed them," Marcia said with her back to the doorway of the kitchen.

"Soup is fine," Lakin said as he entered the room. "But they haven't woken yet." Lakin did not stay to talk; he quickly walked out of the kitchen carrying three cups of coffee.

"They're coming," someone in the crowd yelled; announcing the arrival of the warriors of Sendra to Claudius' castle. All of the warriors still wore dirty, blood stained clothing as they dismounted amidst cheers. Some of the soldiers stationed at the castle, took the horses as the weary riders dismounted. As tired as they were, the excitement of being home surged through them; reviving their energy.

Husbands and wives of Nordes' warriors ran to their spouses as Matthew, Stephan, Thaos, Thedes and Sorren entered the castle. Ingr squealed with delight and ran across the long room, jumping into Stephan's arms. He picked Ingr up and hugged her tightly as they kissed again and again. They were both laughing and Ingr was crying, they tried to talk as they kissed.

"Stephan I missed you so much."

"I missed you too," Stephan said and kissed Ingr repeatedly. "Ingr I am so sorry I wasn't here when the babies were born. I felt awful."

"That's alright; you will be surprised to know how many people were here."

"How was it?"

Ingr didn't say anything for a moment then she admitted, "I was scared about giving birth and it was actually worse than I imagined. But it was worth it Stephan. You need to meet your children."

Stephan was so focused on Ingr that he didn't see his parents walk up to them, each holding a baby. Stephan was speechless as he stared at Bella who was holding a dark haired baby wrapped in a pink blanket. Then he heard Claudius laugh and Stephan saw that his father was holding his son who was wrapped in a light blue blanket.

"Well aren't you going to say anything?" Claudius asked teasingly as he saw the look of awe on his son's face.

Bella laughed as she handed Stephan the baby, "Hold your daughter."

"They're so little, I am almost afraid to touch them," Stephan said as his mother put Sicily into his arms.

"They may seem little to you Stephan," Ingr said with a laugh. "But they are actually big babies."

Stephan stared at his baby daughter, overwhelmed by the miracle of life. Then he looked behind him and saw Matthew and Angelina hugging and Thaos and Nikki hugging and kissing.

He couldn't see Sorren and Thedes. "Matthew, Thaos come here," Stephan called.

Nikki was crying as she and Thaos walked up to Stephan. "Here," Claudius said and handed baby Marcus to Thaos, who was as uncomfortable holding the baby as Stephan.

"Oh Thaos," Ingr said kiddingly. "You need to do better than that; you're going to be a father soon too."

Nikki adjusted the baby in Thaos' arms. While Matthew walked up with Jacob in his left arm and his right arm around Angelina. Matthew smiled when he saw Stephan's babies. "They're beautiful," Matthew said as he handed Jacob to Angelina so he could hold Sicily.

"Where are Sorren and Thedes?' Stephan asked. Claudius saw them in the crowded room and called them over.

Sorren gave Ingr a hug, "Look at them," Sorren said with a huge grin on his face. Thaos handed Marcus to Sorren, who was a natural at holding babies. Thedes and Ibula walked up to the group hand in hand with broad smiles on their faces.

"Thedes do you want to hold one?" Matthew asked and handed baby Sicily to him. Ibula showed Thedes how to hold the infant. Ibula smiled as she watched the look of awe that overtook Thedes' face.

"Just think, we'll have a little one like that soon," Ibula said softly and kissed Thedes on the cheek.

Tears and laughter filled the castle as the warriors and their friends and families were reunited. After Matthew, Stephan and Thaos had greeted many of the guests, they decided to sneak away from the party and change into some clean clothes. Angelina had brought several things for Matthew to wear, being an experienced warrior herself; she knew the condition he would be returning in. Nikki and Thaos went to their chambers so he could change. While Matthew and Stephan walked into Stephan's and Ingr's home.

"When are you going to tell them?" Stephan asked.

"I don't know, I am dreading the entire thing," Matthew said as he dressed. "I should wait until after the banquet tonight, so I don't spoil their celebration."

"I am surprised that we haven't heard from the Sanuri," Stephan said. "I don't know if that is a bad sign."

"I know, I wish I knew if the baby was a demon or not before I get my parent's hopes up," Matthew said with distress in his voice.

Hannah left Natasha's room to get some coffee, when she returned she saw that Gabriel was awake. He was kneeling beside his sister praying. Tears came to Hannah's eyes as she watched him. Hannah heard a groan and saw that Calen had finally passed out from exhaustion, in one of the chairs. Hannah quietly walked into the room and set three cups of coffee on a table.

Gabriel prayed over Natasha for some time; when he finally stood up, Hannah could see that he had been crying. She walked up to Gabriel and the two hugged tightly without speaking. "Go down stairs and have some breakfast, I will stay with her," Hannah said softly. "Please Gabriel; you're still healing from your experience."

"Alright, but I won't be gone long. When I return then you eat." Gabriel said sadly and walked out of the room.

Hannah took a quilt off from the extra bed and covered Calen with it. Then she put a pillow behind his head. When she turned around she saw Natasha sitting up in bed and smiling at her. "You must be Hannah," Natasha said quietly, so as not to wake Calen. Hannah flew to Natasha's side and first felt her head for a fever, then looked at her arm. As Hannah was examining Natasha she said, "Oh Natasha we have been so worried, how do you feel? Do you have pain anywhere?"

"I feel nauseous and like someone beat me up," Natasha whispered with a grin. "But I think I am alright. What happened to me? And where are we?"

"You are in Nora, this is my family's home," Hannah said with a warm smile then she kissed Natasha on the forehead.

341

"Let me get Gabriel and he can explain the rest. And Calen would never forgive me if I didn't wake him." Hannah walked over to Calen and gently shook him. "Natasha is awake," Hannah said softly. Calen jumped out of the chair before he was completely awake and ran over to Natasha. When Hannah left the room, the two were embracing."

Within minutes Natasha's room filled up with people. After Gabriel hugged her; Natasha said, "Calen told me what happened. How is Simon; he touched more bags than I did?"

"He's still not awake," Lakin said.

"Gabriel pray over him," Natasha urged. "I heard your voice; I could hear what you were saying." Gabriel quickly left the room. Lakin started to unwrap the bandages on Natasha's arm.

"The crystals are black and her arm is flesh colored again," Hannah said. "I just looked at it."

"You pulled a demon snake out of me?" Natasha asked with disgust.

"Yes, I have never seen anything like that before," Lakin replied as he took the crystals off from Natasha's wound. "Look Hannah the wound is almost healed."

"I find your medicines so amazing. I am looking forward to studying under you."

"After last night, I believe the studies have already begun," Lakin said. "And you did very well."

"If she is pregnant, would that poison affect the baby?" Calen asked.

"There is no way we can know that now," Lakin replied.

A shadow hung over Matthew as he joined in the festivities. His little sister Margarit and Jacob were both vying for Matthew's attention and Angelina did not let go of his arm. Matthew spoke with both of his parents briefly, which filled him with guilt but he was afraid they would know something was wrong. And Matthew was not yet prepared to tell them about Juleta's baby.

Nikki and Thaos did not return to the party for some time. They stayed in their chambers and made love. Both of them were overwhelmed by how much they had missed the other.

"I wish I could tell you, never to leave again," Nikki said through tears. "I thought my heart was going to burst, I missed you so much."

"I know," Thaos said and kissed Nikki on the lips. "I couldn't stop thinking about you. I have never felt like this before. I couldn't concentrate on anything."

"We should get back to the party before someone comes looking for us," Nikki said with a laugh. They both got out of bed and started to dress. As Thaos was helping Nikki button the back of her dress she said, "I almost forgot, your friend Lazo stopped by yesterday. I invited him to the party."

Gabriel prayed over Simon for a long time, as Raul sat next to Simon's bed. Simon did not wake up. "Simon you have a beautiful wife and three children who need you," Gabriel said. "You have to come back." Gabriel turned to Raul. "Raul talk to him, when I was unconscious I could hear everything that was being said." Gabriel walked out of the room to leave the two brothers alone. Gabriel walked back into Natasha's room and shook his head from side to side as everyone looked at him expecting an answer about Simon.

Natasha started to cry. "If he dies it is my fault. I talked him into going into those rooms. He didn't want to after hearing about what happened to Gabriel." Natasha looked at Calen, "Simon kept scolding me and saying he promised you he would keep me safe, now I got him hurt." Calen put his arms around Natasha as she cried. Calen sat in silence as he held her.

Suddenly Hannah spun around and looked at Lakin. "This Meekos almost killed my family isn't there something we can do against his magic, instead of just picking up the pieces after people are hurt?"

"We will have to call the Sanuri here," Gabriel said.

"Well then please do it before Simon dies or anyone else is hurt," Hannah begged.

343

"Thaos I don't understand what is wrong," Nikki said as he hurried her back to the party. "I will tell you everything later but Lazo did some horrible things while we were gone and he is a danger to some who may be attending this party." Thaos saw Sorren first and told him of Lazo's visit. Sorren stood on top of a chair and yelled for everyone to be quiet.

"We have just learned that Lazo is aware of this celebration and may attend. For those of you who rode to Sendra I don't need to tell you what that means."

Before Sorren could continue, Thedes called out. "Ibula says that Bac and Calla are coming here."

"Has anyone seen them?" Matthew yelled. No one answered. Both Matthew and Stephan ran outside to alert the soldiers.

Thaos walked up to Claudius. "Nikki you stay with Claudius, until I get back," Thaos said then he pulled Claudius aside and said in a low voice. "Lazo tried several times to rape one of the young Ruala girls and to kill her husband. We kept Lazo tied up just to protect the others. He talked about our wives also. Please watch over the girls, they don't know anything about this yet." Sorren and Thedes waited for Thaos and the three left through the balcony doors to search the area.

"Ingr, Angelina and Ibula come here," Claudius called as his face became red with anger. "Bella you too." They came and formed a group around Claudius and Nikki. "Claudius told them everything that Thaos had said.

"He was in our home yesterday," Bella gasped.

Raul sat close to the side of Simon's bed. "Simon," Raul said with tears running down his face. "You have to come back; I don't know what I would do without you. You're not only my brother you are my best friend. Please Simon, we have faced worse than this; you can beat this sorcerer."

"Annabelle won't be able to live without you. And it sounds like you have another baby on the way Simon." Raul put both of his hands over his face and sobbed.

His tears fell onto Simon's left hand and arm. Simon started to move the fingers of his left hand, then his hand and wrist. Raul did not see that where ever his tears fell, they brought life back to his brother.

"Why are you crying?" Simon asked softly.

Raul suddenly looked up, "Simon, I thought you were dying," he whispered.

"No I had to stay there longer, I was looking for answers," Simon said. "Is Natasha alright?"

"Simon I don't understand what you are talking about but Natasha woke up just a little while ago."

"Raul, get the others and bring Natasha in here, it's important."

Matthew, Stephan, Thedes, Sorren and Thaos all returned to the celebration at different times. It was just after noon and in the full light of the sun, they did not see any sign of Lazo. The soldiers had been given orders to stop Lazo and to bring him to the castle.

"Sicily is hungry," Ingr said as she took the baby from Bella. "I'm going to feed her and I will be right back."

Stephan walked over to Thaos, "You want to take another look outside? I just have a bad feeling about this. Thedes said he sent some Enrops to warn Bac and Calla."

As the two men walked outside Thaos said, "I think I scared Nikki, I got so mad when I found out that Lazo was here. She thought I was mad at her; I just couldn't stand the idea of that animal near my wife."

"Father told them what is going on," Stephan said. "Nikki will understand. She's a warrior too. What are you doing?"

"I am trying to figure out where I would hide if I wanted to ambush someone who could fly away," Thaos said as he tried to get into the mind of Lazo.

"If he grabs Calla, he will have to restrain her and have a quick way to get out of here. Let's look in the barn; it would be like him to hide his horse in plain sight."

Calen carried Natasha into Simon's room and set her on the bed next to Simon. The others gathered around as Lakin examined Simon's arm. Hannah walked into the room with a pitcher of cold water, which she poured into a glass and gave to Simon.

"Natasha do you remember where you were?" Simon asked.

"You mean when I was unconscious?"

"Yes."

"I was dreaming that I was in a huge labyrinth, but it was underground; somehow I knew that. It was dark but I could see my way, I don't know how?"

"Did you see the number thirteen?"

"Why yes, I saw it everywhere, it was like signs on the walls of the labyrinth."

"Simon, when I was on my dark journey, I saw the number thirteen also and I was always fighting thirteen foes," Gabriel said as he started to realize they all had been sent messages.

"Do either of you remember anything else?" Simon asked.

"I kept hearing screaming, like people were in great pain," Natasha said. "I was trying to find them to help them but I kept getting lost in the labyrinth. I kept taking wrong turns. I felt the presence of evil and I felt like something was watching me."

"I heard people screaming also," Gabriel remembered. "I knew that when I was fighting the demons I was fighting for more than just me."

"Simon what did you see?" Natasha asked.

"I too was lost in a dark place but it was like an underground city. I also heard people screaming and I thought I heard my name called. I felt the evil and I heard it speak. It taunted me and that made me angry. So angry that Gabriel, when you were praying over me, I felt myself being pulled back here; but I fought it because I wanted to find the source of the voice," Simon explained.

"Then I prayed to The Great Ruler to tell me why I was in this place," Simon continued. "And suddenly The Lion appeared to me. He said that we would have to go to the demon to stop it. Then he said 'Thirteen levels into hell, thirteen doors.' Then he was gone and I woke up."

Baby Marcus would not stop crying so Claudius carried his beloved grandson to Stephan's chambers where Ingr was feeding Sicily. Sorren called after him. Claudius stopped and turned around.

"Claudius there is something you need to know," Sorren said.

"Let me take him to Ingr first."

"I will walk with you," Sorren said and proceeded to tell Claudius about Juleta's daughter.

"Well ain't ya just about the prettiest thing I have ever laid my eyes on," Lazo said as he grabbed Ingr from behind and pressed a large knife against her throat.

"Don't hurt my baby," Ingr begged.

"I have no intentions of hurting the baby, now ya just put her in that cradle like ya were starting to do." Lazo had his left hand around Ingr's waist as he held the knife with his right hand. "Now, I know ya are too smart to scream for that husband of yours. Cause if ya do, well then the baby is all mine. Your husband don't like me too much, I bet it would just kill him to lose ya and the baby."

Ingr carefully placed Sicily in her cradle and covered her with a blanket. Ingr's mind was racing as she quickly surveyed the room to see what she could use as a weapon.

"Now I know ya are into fighting," Lazo said suggestively. "Which is how I like my women; I already searched this room for weapons while I was waiting for ya. Now step back from the cradle little lady and ya and me are going to have some fun."

"You must be crazy," Ingr said with disgust. "The castle is filled with people and someone will look for me if I am gone too long."

"Oh, I figured that," Lazo said as he pulled her tightly against him. "I didn't say we were going to have fun right here."

"And if I don't go with you?"

"I guess that depends on how badly ya want your baby to live."

Suddenly, Ingr heard Marcus crying.

"Here let me take the little guy," Sorren said as he took Marcus from Claudius. "Babies like me."

Claudius smiled at Sorren's comment but not at the topic of their conversation. "When is Matthew planning on telling Mathas?"

"Tonight after the banquet."

"And no one has heard from the Sanuri? So we don't know if the baby is a demon or..." Claudius did not finish his sentence. As he and Sorren walked into the parlor of Ingr's and Stephan's chambers they could hear the sounds of a fight in the bedroom.

"Get help!" Ingr screamed as she thought Bella was bringing Marcus into their chambers.

Both Claudius and Sorren ran to the bedroom door which was locked. Claudius kicked the door open, shattering it with his power. Ingr was laying on the bed, covered in blood and fighting with Lazo who was on top of her holding a bloody knife.

Claudius grabbed Lazo and threw him against the wall with such force that the pictures fell to the floor. Lazo's head bounced against the wall a couple of times but he did not drop the knife.

Lazo looked at Claudius and smiled, then charged at him welding the bloody knife. Claudius grabbed Lazo's arm and twisted it until he dropped the knife. Then Claudius punched Lazo in the face, the stomach and the kidneys until Lazo fell on the floor. Claudius jumped on top of Lazo and punched him over and over until Lazo's face was unrecognizable. Claudius kept punching Lazo as he was dying. Claudius kept punching Lazo long after he was dead.

A crowd now gathered in Stephan's and Ingr's bedroom but no one tried to stop Claudius from killing Lazo. Sorren had placed Marcus in a cradle. "Get Angelina and Shara," Sorren yelled as he held his hand over the gushing wound in Ingr's stomach.

"Ingr!" screamed Stephan as he pushed through the crowd to get to his wife.

"He was going to kill the baby," Ingr whispered. Stephan grabbed Ingr and hugged her tightly.

"Get out of our way," Angelina screamed as she and Shara ran to Ingr.

"Please everyone get back and give us some room to work," Shara yelled.

"Stephan you need to let go of her," Angelina said. He did not respond. "Stephan!" He still did not move. "Father, Matthew get Stephan out of here so we can work on Ingr," Angelina screamed. Although a trained healer she was feeling the stress and shock of seeing her friend so badly wounded.

Matthew and Sorren each took one of Stephan's arms. "Son, let go of her so they can help her," Sorren said softly.

Both of the babies were screaming. "Will someone take these children out of here?" Shara asked loudly.

Bella and Nikki ran into the room, both of them started to cry when they saw Ingr and Claudius who was covered in Lazo's blood.

"The babies," Shara yelled again.

349

"Nikki grabbed the baby closest to her, which was Marcus. Bella started to pick up Sicily. "She is bleeding, the baby is bleeding," Bella screamed hysterically. Thaos pushed through the crowded room and picked Sicily up.

"Bella, she's alright, it's not her blood," Thaos said as he handed the baby to Bella. Thaos put his arms around Bella and Nikki and escorted them out of the room and to his and Nikki's chambers. Then he returned to Stephan and Ingr's bedroom.

Stephan tried to fight with Sorren and Matthew as they pulled him away from his dying wife. Suddenly everything seemed dreamlike to him. He watched the people who were moving and talking in slow motion. Stephan looked at his father, who was covered with Lazo's blood.

There was blood splattered on the walls and furniture, then Stephan looked up and realized blood was dripping from the ceiling. Stephan stared at Lazo's body which seemed surreal because he was no longer recognizable. Stephan looked at Ingr who was covered in blood. The bed she was lying on was soaked with her blood. He saw the anxiety and fear on the faces of Angelina and Shara as they tried desperately to save Ingr.

Stephan was not a praying man but this day he prayed, "Please God don't let her die."

Chapter XXII
The Shadow of Death

"It is clear that we all received messages from The Great Ruler," Gabriel said. "And I will bet there is more. Calen take Natasha back to your room. Natasha try to remember every little detail of your dreams or journey and Calen you write them down. Simon you do the same and Raul would you write them down?"

"Of course," Raul said.

"I will also write down my experiences," Gabriel said. "And remember there is no detail that is too small."

"Gabriel you seemed delirious and talked in your sleep is that important?" Hannah asked.

"Right now I think everything is important. Please everyone write down anything we may have said or done," Gabriel said. We will compare our notes, then it will be time for some research."

Thedes and Ibula were trying to make their way through the crowd to Stephan and Ingr's chambers. Ibula saw a woman running towards them, who was crying hysterically. Ibula grabbed the woman by the shoulders. "What is it? What has happened?" Ibula asked.

The woman was screaming as she talked, "A man cut up Stephan's wife and she is dying."

"Lazo," Thedes spat.

"Thedes give me your crystal," Ibula said as she took off her own blessed crystal necklace that all Rualas wear. Ibula flapped her wings and raised herself above the crowd. "All Rualas I need your crystals now."

"I'll gather them, go!" Thedes said.

Ibula flew above the crowd and momentarily hovered over Ingr, Angelina and Shara. "Great Ruler we need your presence here," Ibula said as she landed in the room.

Thedes was a monster of a man and he literally pushed everyone who was in his way, aside to get to the bed. "Here," Thedes said. Both of his hands were filled with crystal necklaces.

"Angelina, Shara," Ibula said sharply. "Your medicine can no longer help her. Move and let me take care of her." Neither of the women moved. Ibula looked up and saw Bac and Calla enter the room with looks of horror on their faces. "Bac," Ibula said with authority. "Take Angelina to her home and get my medical pouch." Then Ibula looked at Angelina. "Angelina please go now." Without saying a word Bac grabbed Angelina and lifted her above the crowd and they left the castle.

Ibula put the crystals in and around Ingr's wound. Ingr screamed with pain. "Shara make one of your special tonics to ease her pain," Ibula said.

Calla found Stephan sitting in the parlor with Matthew and Sorren standing over him. "I am so sorry," Calla said as she put her arms around Stephan and leaned her head against his and both of the brave warriors cried.

"We aren't strong enough to fight Ahriman," Meekos said as he was trying to persuade Sophie and Erebus that the three of them should contact Omnibus and tell him of all that was happening. "Our only hope is that Omnibus will stand up to Ahriman; once he understands what Ahriman is doing."

"I am greatly confused," Erebus said. "How can Omnibus be a threat to Ahriman or to us if he is a prisoner in The Abyss?"

"He is very powerful," Sophie said.

"Yes, I understand that," Erebus continued. "But his prison must be strong or Omnibus would have escaped long ago."

"He has many of us who work for him," Meekos said. "Who will do his bidding."

"I know that," Erebus said. "But what exactly can Omnibus do from his prison besides call to others in this world?"

Sophie and Meekos both looked at each other, then Meekos spoke. "He must be able to do some things because those of us who have sold him our allegiance have lived hundreds of years."

"And you are sure that Omnibus is responsible for that and say not another demon?" Neither Sophie nor Meekos responded to Erebus' question. "I am just saying that Ahriman certainly does not seem to fear Omnibus and perhaps you don't need to be so afraid of him either, at least not while he is still a prisoner in The Abyss."

"So you are agreeing with Meekos?" Sophie asked. "And you think we should tell Omnibus?"

"Perhaps you should have someone else tell him and see what happens," Erebus said. "You still haven't heard from your two friends in Nora. How well do you trust them?"

Claudius stood in the doorway between the parlor and the bedroom. The huge man was crippled by despair. He watched as Ibula was trying to stop Ingr's bleeding, it all seemed so hopeless. Then Claudius looked in the parlor and saw Stephan, his only son, the courageous warrior, crying. For just a moment Claudius thought he must be dreaming.

"Claudius," Shara said. "Let me tend to your hands." Claudius seemed confused as he looked down at his large hands which were covered in blood and still bleeding. His knuckles were raw and open from the powerful blows he had administered to Lazo.

"Later," Claudius said softly. "Help Ingr."

"Ibula has stopped the bleeding," Shara said. "Although I don't really understand how. And I just gave her a tonic for the pain."

"Claudius, Shara, we need to get past you," Thaos said since the two were standing in the doorway of the bedroom. "We want to get that body out of there."

Claudius appeared dazed as he slowly looked at Thaos and Matthew but did not move. "Claudius please, let us do this," Matthew said.

"Ok course," Claudius said as he and Shara moved into the parlor. "That piece of filth will not get a burial," Claudius yelled angrily. "Throw him outside for the birds to tear apart."

"Tenebrae, Pravis and I swore our oaths to Omnibus together," Meekos said. "I think it is preposterous that you are suggesting that I not trust them."

"I clearly did not say you shouldn't trust them," Erebus corrected. "I asked if you did trust them. Are they as fearful of Omnibus as you and Sophie? And if so do you think they would sell you out to save themselves?"

Meekos glared at Erebus but did not speak. "Meekos his question is valid," Sophie said.

"Truly Meekos I am only trying to understand what is going on here," Erebus said. "Ever since we arrived in Taperia, you and Sophie have talked constantly about all that has gone wrong with the plans for Omnibus' ascension. And the way you are describing things, it sounds like someone has to be very knowledgeable about the plans to sabotage them. Yet you say these plans have been a guarded secret for hundreds of years, a secret shared with few. So who is responsible for all of these problems?"

"You think there is a spy among us?" Meekos asked.

"I have no idea," Erebus responded. "All I am saying is that you said you contacted Ahriman because there were already problems. Now we all agree that Ahriman has greatly added to the problems but who was responsible for the sabotage before you contacted Ahriman?"

"Well, didn't it start when The Lion gave Roch that affliction?" Sophie asked.

"Are you sure?" Erebus questioned. "I think you need to look into this a bit more."

"Erebus are you trying to cause dissension between the members of the Insidiae?" Meekos asked angrily.

"No, not at all. You two are so closely involved with these issues that I don't believe you are looking at things in an objective manner. And since I am now working with you; I don't want to die because someone is setting you up."

"Make way, make way," a Nordes warrior yelled as he pushed through the crowd. "Make way I tell you, the Sanuri is here!" The hundreds of guests who crowded into the hallways outside of Stephan's and Ingr's chambers moved as quickly as they could in the congestion.

The Sanuri ran through the crowd. He stopped when he saw Matthew, Thaos, Sorren and Stephan all covered in blood and Stephan crying. "Matthew take your niece," the Sanuri said as he thrust Sarah into Matthew's arms." What has happened here?"

Suddenly Stephan stood up, "Come, Ingr is dying. Lazo tried to kill her and the babies." Stephan pushed ahead, leading the Sanuri into the bedroom. Although the Sanuri was moving quickly he was not blind to the looks of stunned horror on the faces of all. When the Sanuri entered the bedroom, he saw that it had become a slaughter house.

"Sanuri, thank The Great Ruler," Ibula said as she was bending over Ingr. "I've been able to stop the bleeding but she has lost so much blood."

"Everyone out of this room but Stephan and Ibula," the Sanuri ordered.

Simon and Natasha felt good enough to come down to the dining room for lunch, although they were both still very weak. All morning they had been trying to recall their experiences in the dark worlds. Raul and Calen had copied down everything that Simon and Natasha could remember.

"We will compare our notes after lunch," Gabriel said as he was the last one to be seated at the table.

"I am not sure how some of the things I remembered can be of use," Natasha said. "So much of my dreams seemed to be me searching for the voices I heard."

"I am hoping that once we compare all of our notes, we will see some kind of pattern emerge," Gabriel replied. "Although the circumstances have been horrific, it is nice to have us all together again."

Natasha sat quietly as she watched everyone who was sitting around the table. The closeness and affection shared was obvious. The warriors were glad to be reunited with their brothers and comrades. Marcia and Rabi reminded Natasha of her and Calen, so young and so in love. And then there was Gabriel and Hannah, who were both radiant. They too seemed very much in love but there was something different about their demeanors that Natasha could not quite put words to.

Hannah was twenty-two years old, a year younger than Calen. Although Gabriel was only twenty-seven, he always seemed much older than his age. Natasha never remembered a time when her brother was not protective and responsible. Gabriel had not only dedicated his life to her but to his work for The Great Ruler. Now, Natasha saw a softness to Gabriel and a light in his eyes that she had never seen before. Although it was obvious to her that there was great passion between Gabriel and Hannah, there was also a quiet contentment; that Natasha did not quite understand.

"You're so quiet Natasha," Gabriel said with a soft smile.

"I just realized something," Natasha said with emotion in her voice. "For so long it has been just Gabriel and me. But as I look around this table, I realize we have all become family. Who would have thought that something so wonderful could come out of such a dangerous and horrible mission?"

Mathas pushed through the crowd until he found Matthew. "I took your mother, Jacob and Margarit to Thaos' chambers to be with Bella and Nikki. Is there anything I can do?"

"The Sanuri is in there with Stephan and Ibula," Matthew said as he nodded towards the bedroom door.

"Where is Angelina?" Mathas asked.

"One of the Ruala warriors took her home so she could retrieve Ibula's medical bag," Matthew said then paused for a few moments. "Father we need to talk."

Mathas saw the look on Matthew's face, which he at first attributed to the attack on Ingr. Although Mathas saw the baby girl that Matthew was holding he did not comment until now. "Matthew whose child is that?"

"Father that is what I need to talk with you about."

"Is she yours?"

"Mine!" Matthew said incredulously. "No, she's not mine," then Matthew paused again. "Father while we were in Zorta we discovered that Juleta had a baby that she took to the monastery in Leven. The Sanuri just brought her back. This is your granddaughter," Matthew said as he handed the smiling baby to Mathas. Before his father could speak, Matthew continued, "The Sanuri was going to determine if she was a demon baby, I don't know what he found out because he immediately ran to Ingr. I don't even know the child's name."

Mathas held the little girl out in front of him so he could look at her. The baby smiled and clapped her hands. "There is no demon in this child," Mathas said as his heart melted. "Why, she is adorable."

"Father you were blind to the darkness in Juleta for a long time, what makes you think this child is not like her? I was afraid to tell you about her because I didn't want your heart broken again."

Mathas looked deeply into his son's eyes with a look of pure love. "Matthew you are right and my blindness caused pain to many others. And I pray to The Great Ruler that I never act like that again. I know you want to protect me and your mother, but this baby is our flesh and blood and should be with our family."

"Father it killed me to see you in so much pain because of Juleta," Matthew said emotionally. "I don't want to see you hurt like that again."

"This child is so young, perhaps if there is some evil in her, the Sanuri can heal her; which is probably what I should have tried with Juleta."

"Father you are not responsible for how she turned out. You and Mother were wonderful parents to her. Juleta was an intelligent person who knowingly made her own choices."

Angelina and Bac ran to the closed bedroom door. "The Sanuri is in there now," Claudius yelled. Angelina knocked on the door. "Ibula I have your medical pouch."

"She will not need it now," the Sanuri called through the closed door.

Angelina turned around and saw Matthew and Mathas talking seriously. She walked up to them and put her hand in Matthew's. "What a cute baby, whose is she?" Angelina asked as she touched the baby's hand.

"Juleta's," Matthew answered.

"What!"

"I will have to think on your words," Meekos said irritably to Erebus. Meekos did not want to consider the idea that Pravis or Tenebrae might not be trustworthy, yet Erebus made some valid points.

"I have listened to you and Sophie talking for the last two days," Erebus said. "You both have sent dozens of messages to each other by Ravens; yet none of them arrived at their destinations. Have you not questioned who is in possession of those messages?"

Meekos stared at Erebus in horror, "You are right. I have been so worried about Sophie and these problems with the ascension; that never entered my mind."

"This is what I mean," Erebus continued. "You are both highly intelligent people but you are so emotionally involved with this thing you really aren't seeing the big picture."

"He's right Meekos," Sophie gasped.

"And what do you think the big picture is?" Meekos asked sincerely.

"I don't know, but I will bet you have many more saboteurs than Ahriman."

Stephan felt such pain in his heart when he looked upon Ingr that his knees started to buckle. "Please can you help her?"

"Stephan would you be willing to give of your blood to save her?" the Sanuri asked.

"Of course," Stephan said without hesitation. "How do I do such a thing?"

The Sanuri smiled, "Give me your knife and roll up your sleeve."

Stephan was in such a hurry to take his knife out of its sheath that he almost dropped it. He handed the knife to the Sanuri and rolled up both of his shirt sleeves. Stephan walked up closer to the Sanuri and held out both of his arms to be cut.

"Most of your life you did not want a wife or family Stephan and now you would give of yourself to save Ingr?" the Sanuri asked.

"Of course I would," Stephan said. "How could you even question how much I love her?"

"I have always known; it is you who has questioned it. Stephan do you now understand what your wife and family means to you?"

Stephan looked shocked that the Sanuri had known of his fears. "Yes, I understand now. Please Sanuri do whatever needs to be done to save her. Give her all that I have."

The Sanuri took Stephan's left hand and made a small incision on the palm. Then the Sanuri placed the palm of Stephan's hand over Ingr's wound. Ingr was unconscious. The Sanuri held his left hand on the back of Stephan's left hand. The Sanuri placed the palm of his right hand on Ingr's forehead and began to pray.

As the Sanuri prayed miracles started to happen. The Sanuri became lighter and lighter until he was almost transparent. The room warmed greatly. Ibula started to cry as she was overwhelmed by what she had been allowed to witness.

Stephan felt as if an energy was surging through him, he did not understand what it was; but he questioned how enough blood could come out of such a small incision. "Is this room becoming lighter?" Stephan asked.

"Yes," Ibula uttered in a whisper.

Stephan suddenly found himself crying and he did not know why.

Raul and Simon sat next to each other at the lunch table. "Hannah has given me some extravagant gifts to send to Mother and the girls," Raul said to Simon. "I haven't had a chance to write the letters yet, so would you like to send Annabelle her gift?"

Simon turned to Hannah, "Why are you sending them gifts?"

"Gabriel and I are wearing rings that your mother sent along," Hannah said as she held her hand up so Simon could see her rings. "And Vitomas sent me a wonderful letter and had a beautiful gift made for me. And I certainly couldn't send them gifts and not Annabelle."

"Simon, Hannah is one of the most generous people you will ever meet," Lakin said fondly of his friend. "She gave me a gift for my wife also. Not only has she treated all of us like royalty but she has told us repeatedly to take anything from her properties that we want before we leave."

"Why are you giving everything away?" Natasha asked.

"I can't imagine that Gabriel and I will ever return here and I would much rather have my friends enjoy these things then to leave them to thieves and Hutas," Hannah said. "In fact I have some gifts for you and Calen and if there is anything at all that you want for your new home, please take it."

"As you can see from the house, Hannah's family is wealthy," Luca said. "But her father has some extraordinary collections. We already took some things for all of you." Luca said as he looked at Dagon, Koby and Calen.

"Hannah, Gabriel this is such a beautiful home, you don't think you will ever come here again?" Natasha asked.

"The home is beautiful," Gabriel said. "But Nora is a place of great darkness. As it turns out, we have recently found out that Hannah inherited a majority of the city. People have already tried to kill us because of that."

"What!" gasped Natasha.

"We have much to tell you but that can wait," Gabriel said.

"It may be none of my business," Simon said. "But I sense there is something more. I still don't understand why Vitomas had a gift made for you. I know she is a generous person also but Hannah your expression changed when you spoke of it."

"Hannah attended Cicero College, she was in the crowd when our oldest boys were christened," Raul said trying to change the subject.

"What Raul and Gabriel don't want to tell you is that I had a baby sister who favored Vitomas greatly in appearance. While I was in Wetpr one night there was a grand ball at the Endleson Hotel. King Roch showed up." Hannah paused. "He pulled Laurabelle into the street and raped her and murdered her before the eyes of many and no one lifted a finger to help her."

"My own father stood in that crowd and watched. He later committed suicide and Mother died shortly afterwards. Now we have discovered that Father was a member of the Insidiae and had done horrible things." Natasha saw that Gabriel held Hannah's hand as she spoke. "Raul told all of this to Vitomas and she sent me a letter of healing."

"You never did tell us what she wrote," Raul said. "Did it help you?"

"Yes, because I had let myself become filled with hatred and resentment for the people of Nora. Vitomas must be a very strong person. She told me that Roch embodied all that was dark and evil. Vitomas said that if I let myself be consumed with such dark emotions as hatred that I was allowing him to win; because I was allowing the darkness to control me too. She said the best way that I could beat Roch was to open myself up to love."

"What do you mean this is Juleta's baby?" Angelina asked. She was obviously shaken by the news.

"When we were in Zorta we learned that Juleta had a baby that she took to the monastery at Leven for the priests to care for. The Sanuri got her and brought her back here," Matthew explained. "We were all concerned that she might be a demon baby but the Sanuri said he would be able to tell."

"So he said the baby isn't evil?" asked Angelina.

"He didn't say anything, he ran into the bedroom to help Ingr," Matthew answered.

"Angelina hold her and look into her eyes," Mathas said as he handed baby Sarah to Angelina. "Tell me you see evil in this child?"

Angelina stared at Sarah who was laughing and trying to play with Angelina's long hair. "She certainly doesn't seem evil but I will feel better after we talk to the Sanuri."

Mathas took the baby from Angelina, "I am going to take her to Rosa," he said with a proud smile.

"Father I don't think that is a very good idea," Matthew protested. "You know Mother will fall in love with her then what if the Sanuri says the baby is evil?"

"Well, we will deal with that if it happens. Matthew it is only fair that Rosa meet her granddaughter. Put yourself in your mother's place."

"Your father is right," Angelina said. "Actually you are both right. Mathas you know Matthew is just afraid of you and Rosa being so hurt again."

"I know, he is a good son," Mathas said affectionately. Then he turned to walk to Thaos' chambers.

"Matthew you should go with your father. I am going to wait here for news about Ingr," Angelina said.

Gabi walked into the dining room of Hannah's house while everyone was still eating lunch. A broad smile consumed his face when he saw Simon and Natasha sitting at the table. "You two had us all pretty scared," Gabi said. "I am sorry I didn't realize you were eating, I will come back."

"Nonsense," Hannah said. "Please join us; I will be right back with a place setting for you. While Hannah was in the kitchen Rabi put another chair near the table.

"Some of us have been reading the books you took from the sorcerers," Gabi said as he walked up to Gabriel. "Here read this and see what you think." Gabi handed Gabriel a large thick book, which was opened to a particular page. Then Gabi walked around the table and sat down. Hannah set dishes and silverware in front of him, as Gabriel read.

After Gabriel read the page he looked at the cover and front page of the book. "The contents of this book are old but it has been translated many times, which means sometimes things can be misinterpreted. Gabi found a protection spell that is designed to kill anything or anyone who comes into contact with the object the spell was put on. According to this, the victim's body is attacked from the inside by a demon snake; that eats the victim's heart and other organs. But this says that death usually comes within minutes after the victim touches the object."

"So why were we spared?" Natasha asked.

"I don't believe anyone at this table can answer that question, but instead of letting you die; The Great Ruler sent you messages to help this mission," Gabriel said. "Gabi we all realized we had received messages so we wrote our experiences down and we are going to compare them after lunch. You are welcome to join us."

"I would like that," Gabi said as he filled his plate with food.

"I may be an awful person," Hannah said. "But can't we find some type of reversal spell and send all of this evil back to that sorcerer. After all he almost killed three of you."

"I like her idea," Natasha said enthusiastically.

"I don't think that is the way it works," Gabriel said.

"Well how does it work?" Hannah asked. "Do you have to be evil to work a spell? I am just feeling frustrated because I feel we are just responding to their attacks. Perhaps we should change things around and put them on the offensive. If we aren't strong enough to kill a demon; well can't we confuse them and have them attack each other? Or trick them into giving us information?" Hannah realized that everyone at the table was looking at her and smiling. "Are you all just laughing at me?"

"No," Raul said with a grin. "I like your idea about putting them on the offensive. I wonder what would happen if we turned the three priests against each other."

"We saw Meekos and Sophie together and I think they are too close to try to turn against each other. But I wonder how close Meekos and that sorcerer from Roch's castle are," Simon said.

"Gabriel, we have been intercepting all of their messages," Natasha said. "Couldn't we send some messages of our own?"

Gabriel was smiling as he was listening to everyone's ideas. "We certainly could send some well thought out messages, but they use ravens for their messengers, we will have to contact the Sanuri for help."

"Honey I still have keys to their hotel rooms," Hannah said. "Couldn't we put something into their rooms that will make them suspicious of each other?"

Natasha looked at Gabriel and winked, "I really like her," Natasha said. "I also have keys to the rooms of Meekos and the others."

"That might be more of a problem," Gabriel said. "According to what I just read about that protection spell, it alerts the sorcerer that someone has touched their things, so they may be expecting us."

"Can we send an Enrop in?" Calen asked.

"These are all good ideas," Gabriel said. "Tomorrow night is the grand ball at the Endleson Hotel, I expect the priests to attend. Raul, Hannah and I will be there. Perhaps we can put something in their rooms then. We will need to plan out a strategy."

"I will go too," Simon said, "But I need a dress suit."

"My father has several in his closet," Hannah offered. "Perhaps one will fit you."

"Can I go to?" Natasha asked Calen.

"No, you have almost died twice just since we have been married. I don't want you doing this anymore."

Calen's answer did not surprise Natasha; she did not argue with him, although she planned to bring the subject up again when they were alone.

"You know I am not as brave as the rest of you," Marcia said, to everyone's surprise. "But I have gone to those balls before and both Raul and Simon will stand out if they do not have escorts. Perhaps Natasha and I could go with them, only to dance; I mean so they don't look suspicious."

As Mathas and Matthew walked down a hallway heading towards Thaos' and Nikki's chambers they heard crying. They stopped and listened. Matthew opened a door to one of the guest bedrooms and saw Ryan sitting on a bed crying. Matthew walked over to the bed and put his hand on Ryan's shoulder as Mathas stood in the doorway holding baby Sarah. Ryan looked up at Matthew. "I saw her, I saw what he did to her," Ryan said. "I promised Thaos I would watch over Nikki and Ingr and now she is dying."

"The Sanuri is with her now," Matthew said soothingly. "He will save her. And besides Ryan, we were all home when it happened, so it was no longer your responsibility to keep them safe."

"She was my friend," Ryan sobbed. "Ingr was like a sister to me."

"Come with us son," Mathas said as Matthew took Ryan's arm and pulled him to his feet. The three men walked down the long hallway in silence.

After lunch Lakin said to Gabriel, "I know you are anxious to compare everyone's notes but as I look around this table I see only exhausted faces. Gabriel perhaps everyone should get a couple of hours sleep; I know Natasha and Simon certainly need some."

Gabriel looked at the faces before him, "You are right Lakin. Perhaps we should compare the notes after dinner."

"I'm the only one here who got some sleep last night," Marcia said. "All of you go to bed, I will take care of the dishes and prepare dinner."

"I can help," Hannah said.

"No," Lakin said. "You need to sleep too."

Everyone slowly left the lunch table and returned to their rooms. Gabriel and Hannah walked with Calen and Natasha. "Gabriel would you mind helping me push these two beds together?" Calen asked as they entered the room that Natasha and Calen shared. Hannah stood with Natasha as the men moved the large rug and nightstand that were between the beds.

"You're worried about the baby, aren't you?" Hannah asked Natasha.

"I don't even know if I am pregnant," Natasha said. "So far the only symptom I have had is that I am very emotional. Simon said I reminded him of his wife when she is pregnant and you should have seen the look on Calen's face; I have never seen him look so happy."

"Those demon snakes did not get far in your bodies. Lakin took them out of your forearms so hopefully the baby wasn't touched," Hannah said as she saw the look of distress on Natasha's face. Hannah put her hands on Natasha's shoulder and turned her around so the two women were facing each other.

"Lakin and I have two very different types of medicine and we both will take care of you. Now you have to promise me that you will tell us whenever you feel something is different, both good and bad. Do you promise?"

"Yes," Natasha whispered.

Gabriel and Calen finished moving the furniture and turned towards Hannah and Natasha. "Is anything wrong?" Gabriel asked.

"No, Natasha is worried that if she is pregnant that the demon snake may have damaged the baby." Hannah said then she turned to Calen. "Calen I told Natasha that both Lakin and I will take care of her but both of you must tell us if there are any problems."

"We will," Calen said as he walked to Natasha and put his arm around her shoulders.

"Calen I don't care what time of the day or night, you come to me or Lakin immediately with anything," Hannah said.

"Hannah is a great physician," Gabriel said as he took her hand into his. "I have seen her work. Now you two need to get some sleep."

Gabriel and Hannah left Calen's and Natasha's bedroom and walked into their own. "I didn't want to say anything in front of them," Hannah said. "But neither Lakin nor I had ever seen anything like those demon snakes before."

"I think they probably realize that," Gabriel said and kissed Hannah on the forehead. "Why don't you change?" Hannah walked into the closet as she liked to prepare for her husband. Gabriel removed his clothing and pulled the blankets back on the bed. "You know we have never talked about children," he said.

"Honey there are a great deal of things we have never talked about," Hannah called out from the closet. "Our lives are crazy right now."

"Do you want children?"

"Oh course, how can you even ask?" Hannah asked.

"I have been thinking and I would like to start a family right away. What do you think?" Gabriel asked then turned as he heard Hannah behind him. "You always take my breath away," Gabriel said. Hannah was walking towards him wearing a pale pink silk nightgown.

"And you take my breath away," Hannah whispered as she stretched upwards and put her arms around Gabriel's neck. "I like your idea but that would mean we would need some uninterrupted time together," she said with a giggle.

"I am thinking that we just make more time to be together," Gabriel said and put his arms around Hannah's waist.

"I love that idea," Hannah said as she kissed Gabriel on the lips.

The door to Ingr's bedroom opened and all the people waiting outside of the room stood in silence. Everyone afraid of the answer to the question in their thoughts. No one moved towards the open door.

"Claudius, please come in here," the Sanuri called. "Angelina we need you too."

Both Claudius and Angelina walked towards the door with a mixture of dread and hopefulness in their beings. After they entered the room the door closed again.

Chapter XXIII
A Second Chance

The door to Ingr's room opened again and this time Claudius stepped out and spoke with his normal voice of authority. "Please everyone out, except for close friends and family. Please return to the Great Hall for we now have another reason to celebrate. Thanks be to The Great Ruler, the Sanuri is healing our Ingr, she will live but we need to move her to a different room and she needs rest." As Claudius spoke, Angelina quickly walked to the next bedroom and started to prepare it for Ingr.

The people crowded in Ingr's and Stephan's chambers did not immediately move. So great was their shock and grief that the news that she would recover did not enter their realities. "Folks, please do as Claudius asks, for Ingr's sake," Sorren said as he turned and faced the crowd. Mumblings could be heard in the crowd then voices and soon clapping, as the guests left the chambers.

"They're gone," Thaos said as he looked in Ingr's bedroom. She was still unconscious but they had changed her into a clean nightgown. Without saying a word, Stephan picked Ingr up and carried her into the next bedroom. He carefully placed her on the sheets that Angelina had just put on the bed. "Is there anything I can do?" Thaos asked.

"Yes, put some chairs and at least one small table in that bedroom," Angelina said. "I am going to clean up their room, I don't want Ingr to see that when she wakes."

"Please let us help also," Calla said. "We have to do something. Lazo probably hurt Ingr because Stephan helped us."

"Lazo hurt Ingr because he knew that Stephan saw him for what he really was," Thaos said with disgust.

Angelina turned to Claudius and said, "Bella, Matthew and the others are with Nikki in their chambers; please tell them that Ingr will be alright and that I am staying here to clean."

"I'll go with you," Thaos said to Claudius. "I want to check on Nikki." Then he turned to Bac. "I'll be back; we are going to have to throw that mattress out and that big rug."

Stephan was oblivious to the commotion in the parlor, his focus was on Ingr. He sat next to her bed in silence and watched her sleep.

Ibula waited until she and the Sanuri were alone in the blood soaked bedroom. "I want to thank you for allowing me to witness such a miracle," Ibula said emotionally. "But may I ask a question?"

"Of course."

"Why did you ask Stephan to give his blood because you certainly didn't use it?"

"Stephan is a complicated man. He is often conflicted about his feelings; especially for Ingr and now the babies."

"But he certainly seems to love them."

"Yes, he does. But there are times when he himself does not realize that. As much as he loves her; he loved his wild and independent life that he gave up. And as much as he wanted the babies, at times he felt like they would be more nails in his coffin."

Ibula was silent for a moment. "Sanuri when you were healing Ingr; I saw how Stephan reacted. Were you healing him also?"

"Yes. You see with Stephan, his conflict was causing fear and guilt within him and he could not forgive himself for his own thoughts. I did not want that darkness to take seed in him."

As Thaos and Claudius were leaving the parlor, Angelina called out, "Please take the Sanuri with you; he needs to talk to Matthew's family."

"Mathas what are you saying?" Rosa asked in disbelief. Rosa searched Mathas' face then Matthew's as if she was expecting to uncover a cruel joke.

Mathas knelt down by Rosa, who was sitting in an overstuffed chair. "I said, this is our granddaughter; Matthew said the Sanuri brought her back from a monastery, where Juleta had left her."

Margarit ran to her parents and stared at the baby. "She looks like Juleta; she's not evil too is she?"

"The Sanuri will be able to tell us that," Matthew said solemnly. "But he is taking care of Ingr now. Mother we all found out about this baby when we were in Zorta. I did not want to get yours or father's hopes up until we heard what the Sanuri had to say."

"Look at her Honey," Mathas said as he handed the baby to Rosa. "Does she look evil to you?"

Rosa picked up the happy little girl, then started to cry. Rosa hugged and kissed the baby. "Mathas I feel like we have been given a second chance." Mathas hugged both Rosa and the baby, while the others in the room watched in silence. Claudius, Thaos and the Sanuri entered the room about twenty minutes later. Their arrival was barely noticed, by the room full of people as everyone's attention was drawn to the drama of their King and Queen.

"Her name is Sarah," the Sanuri said. "And she is a normal little baby girl. There is no demon in her."

"Oh thank you," Rosa gasped and hugged Sarah again.

"Thank you for bringing the baby home," Mathas said as he extended his hand to the Sanuri. "Once again we are in your debt."

"Before we go further about other matters," Claudius said loudly. "The Sanuri has saved Ingr, she will live. But of course she has quite a bit of healing ahead of her."

Bella covered her face with both of her hands and cried with joy. Nikki had not stopped crying and now smiled as the tears rolled down her face.

"Where are the babies?" asked the Sanuri.

"They are in the bedroom, a couple of women who are guests have recently had babies and offered to feed the twins," Shara said. "I examined both of them and they are fine, they were hungry and scared but fine."

"Sanuri tell them what happened," Claudius said.

"Lazo was waiting for Ingr in their chambers, he intended to rape and kill her then kill the babies. Ingr was talking to him trying to stall while she figured out a plan but then she heard baby Marcus crying and she thought Bella was bringing the baby to her. Ingr was afraid of what Lazo might do, so she attacked him with her bare hands. She fought him even after he had stabbed her several times; she was trying to protect the children and Bella."

"How do you know all of this?" Bella asked.

"I looked into her mind," the Sanuri replied.

"When I broke the door down, Ingr was lying on the bed covered in blood but still fighting with Lazo," Claudius said as tears came to his eyes again. "I couldn't love that little girl more if she was my flesh and blood daughter." Bella stood up and walked over to Claudius; the two leaned against each other, arm in arm.

"Sanuri when you read Lazo's thoughts that day, you said you saw some of his future. Did you see any of this?" Matthew asked.

"Matthew I would have stopped him, if I had seen this. When I see things sometimes they appear as disconnected fragments. I saw what Thaos and Stephan were suspecting, that Lazo was a rapist and had been his entire life. That was one reason he was following Juleta. That is until he realized she was too powerful for him."

"Every person's life is filled with choices; that is part of our tests in these worlds," the Sanuri explained. "And every choice no matter how small has a reaction of some kind. Think of throwing pebbles into the water and watching the ripples that are created. Our choices are like that, some make small ripples and touch few while others make huge ripples that affect many. What I saw of Lazo's future was him dying violently in a variety of different ways. I did not see the choices that he made that led to his death."

"What of Juleta and the baby?" Matthew asked.

"He was telling us the truth about that, but what he didn't tell us; was that there was a specific reason he took shelter in the monastery at Leven when he was being pursued by demons. He was going to use the baby as leverage against Juleta."

"Do you know who the baby's father is?" Thaos asked. "I tried to stay away from her but I never really saw her with any men besides George."

"All I can tell you is I do not believe George is the father of this baby."

"Why?" Matthew asked.

"Because I saw brief glimpses of another face," the Sanuri explained. "The face of a man I have never seen before. I saw glimpses of him and Juleta together. I believe Juleta cared for him very much."

"Should we try to find him?" Rosa asked.

"I would not," the Sanuri advised. "I said Juleta cared for him; I did not say he was a good man. Little Sarah is better off with all of you." Then the Sanuri turned to Matthew and Thaos, "To answer your unspoken fears, it is safe to let your children be with Sarah. She is not her mother."

Although the Sanuri knew exactly what Matthew and Thaos were thinking, Thaos felt guilty and sought to change the subject. He looked at Bella, "Angelina and some of the others are cleaning Stephan's and Ingr's bedroom. She has been moved to another room. I am going back to help, but that mattress and the rug are soaked with blood. Where should we throw them and do you have any others to replace them with?"

"Oh, I didn't even think about that," Bella said and started walking towards Thaos. "I will go with you and help."

"Wait," Claudius said and took Bella's arm to stop her. "Sanuri, we are all so grateful that you came but how did you know we needed you?" Claudius asked. With his words everyone turned and looked at the Sanuri in wonder.

373

"When I arrived at the monastery at Leven, I wanted to speak with every one of the priests who had contact with either Juleta or Lazo. I will tell you that although many of the priests were happy that I was reuniting Sarah with her family; their hearts were also saddened because she had brought so much life and love to them all."

"I ended up staying there a couple of days longer than I had originally planned. I received my invitation when I was already on the road, coming here. This morning I was still about two days ride away. I was driving my boca when I heard the voice of The Lion, the emissary to The Great Ruler. He said my friends were praying for help and in that very instant my boca stopped at the front door of your castle, Claudius. I grabbed Sarah and ran into the crowd."

"From the looks on everyone's faces I knew something awful had happened but it wasn't until Stephan took me into the bedroom and I saw Ingr that I understood. Claudius I hope your family realizes how it has been blessed, most people never have the realization that their prayers have been answered."

Four hours of sleep rejuvenated everyone in Hannah's household. As they awoke from their naps, they started to gather in the parlor.

"It smells wonderful in here," Hannah said as she entered the kitchen, where Marcia was preparing dinner.

"I have two roasts in the oven and I made some apple pies," Marcia said as she was washing dishes. "Do you feel better?"

"Yes and thank you for taking care of things," Hannah said as she started to fill plates with cheeses, fruits, nuts and sausages to take into the parlor. "Marcia, I am really going to miss you when we all leave here."

"I know. But Rabi said that once you and Gabriel see how beautiful the Ice Caves are that you will want to build a home there."

"Perhaps he is right," Hannah said smiling. "Isn't it amazing how our lives have changed Marcia? I mean we are both married now and happy. I never would have dreamed this could happen?"

"Why not?"

Hannah paused as she was thinking about her answer, "Because I think part of me died when Laurabelle did. I guess I stopped thinking that I had a future." When Marcia turned around to hug Hannah she saw Natasha standing in the doorway.

"I am sorry I didn't mean to eavesdrop," Natasha apologized. "I just wanted to see if you needed any help."

"Natasha it's alright," Hannah said sweetly. "How are you feeling?"

"Surprisingly well, although I am still disgusted at the thought that a demon snake was inside of me," she said with a shudder.

"Natasha we have heard so much about you from the men, they all say what a wonderful cook you are and what a brave warrior," Marcia said. "I feel like I already know you."

Natasha blushed at Marcia's comments. "They are being kind. I am looking forward to us all getting to know each other. I will say that both Gabriel and Rabi are so happy. I only met Rabi on this mission and he is such a nice man. And Hannah, I just keep looking at Gabriel. He actually seems different but I can't put my finger on it yet."

"Different in a good way?"

"Oh yes, I's obvious that he is very much in love with you but there is something else too. It's almost like he is content," Natasha said. "And from his letters you sound exactly like the woman I would have picked out for him. I know that may sound crazy but Gabriel and I have been taking care of each other since we were young. I felt guilty falling in love with Calen and I prayed that Gabriel would meet someone wonderful. I do believe my prayers were answered," Natasha said with a smile.

Hannah walked over to Natasha and hugged her. "Thank you for telling me that. I think Gabriel is the most wonderful man I have ever met."

"I fell in love with him right away and when he realized I had feelings for him it made him so uncomfortable that I, well, I didn't think he cared about me at all. I really don't know what changed?"

"Hannah, we all could see that Gabriel cared for you too; almost from the beginning," Marcia said. "Rabi said that Gabriel was so focused on the mission that he wasn't going to allow himself to have feelings for you, at least until the mission was over."

"Hannah, what Marcia just said, sounds exactly like Gabriel. He puts so much thought and planning into the missions and he doesn't want anyone to be distracted for fear they will get hurt. That is why this mission is so unusual," Natasha said.

"What do you mean?" Hannah asked.

"Well this is a very dangerous mission, I heard Gabriel and Lakin talking and they fear we may not all make it home. Yet we've had three marriages. I couldn't believe Gabriel would allow all of this."

"Has your love for Calen distracted you?" Marcia asked.

Natasha smiled, "I think about him every moment I am awake. But when I am working on the mission, I can maintain my focus. I only made one big blunder but fortunately it turned out alright."

"What did you do?" asked Hannah.

"I just wanted to do something for Calen so badly, that I left the hotel where we are staying and went into Taperia to buy him a gift. I didn't tell anyone where I was going and Sophie could have seen me. I was so focused on Calen that I didn't even realize that I could have compromised the mission until Calen pointed it out to me."

"You see Gabriel set up a situation where he and I helped Sophie to gain her trust. She was allowed to escape from some members of the Patronus. Sophie would not give them any information about Meekos so Raphael, he is a great leader in the Patronus, thought she might lead them to her brother."

"Gabriel pretended that he just came upon Sophie as she traveled. He brought her to a house we were using. I cooked for her and he helped her get a carriage. As we chatted Sophie gave us a great deal of information; we spent some time together so she would recognize us."

Hannah was captivated by Natasha's narrative but before she could speak Rabi walked into the kitchen. "So this is where you are all hiding," he teased. Then he walked over to Marcia and kissed her on the cheek. "Gabriel is looking for you; he wants to compare the notes."

"Rabi will you help take some of this food into the parlor?" Hannah asked as she handed him two large platters. "Please tell him we will be just a few minutes." As Hannah spoke both Natasha and Marcia started cutting fruit and cheeses and putting them on the platters. Hannah sliced two loafs of bread and within five minutes all three women carried filled platters into the parlor. Luca and Dagon had brought ale, wine and whiskey from the wine cellar. They all filled their glasses and plates and waited for Gabriel to start the review.

"Raul is going to take notes of this meeting. Natasha, Simon and I will each read our own notes. Please stop us at any time if you notice a similarity, pattern or anything of interest. When we are done reading, I would like our caretakers to talk about words that we uttered or things that we did when we were unconscious."

"I remember Simon and me walking into his hotel room," Natasha said as she started to read her notes. "I don't remember falling on the floor but I remember hearing Simon call my name. Because I remembered thinking that he sounded scared. I was not aware of Calen and the others taking us out of the hotel and flying. But I do remember feeling Calen's presence all of the time."

"I felt in a way like I was dreaming except that during the dream I kept thinking this seems so real. I was in a cave with many tunnels. Even though it was dark, for some reason I could see my way. For some reason I didn't think I was lost. I thought I was looking for someone, so I wasn't afraid. And since I kept feeling Calen's presence I thought at first that I was looking for him in the cave," Natasha continued.

377

"There were many tunnels and as I would come upon a new one I would look for some kind of markings so I could find my way back but all I saw was either the number thirteen written on a wall or thirteen objects shown on the wall. The objects were things like dots and lines, and when I saw them I instantly knew there were thirteen of them. Although I kept seeing that number, it did not really dawn on me it was a message or even anything peculiar until Simon later mentioned seeing that number."

"After what seemed like a very long time of walking through the tunnels I started to hear screams, like people were in great pain. I started walking faster until I was running trying to find those people. Since I still felt Calen's presence I was afraid that he was being hurt. And that is really the last thing I remember is running through the tunnels looking for the people who needed help."

"Do you remember what you were wearing?" Simon asked.

Natasha immediately said, "No." But after a moment her eyes grew wide, "Yes, yes I do, it wasn't the clothes I was wearing in the hotel room. I was dressed in all white. Now that I remember, what I was wearing was glowing and that was providing the light for me to see. It was kind of like a dress, or more like a sheet wrapped around me and over one of my shoulders. Simon I had forgotten that."

"Calen did Natasha say anything while she was unconscious?" Gabriel asked.

"Until we came back here, she had not moved or uttered a word, it was as if she was dead. But when she was in bed in our room here; she started tossing and turning. The sound of her movements woke me. I looked over and Gabriel was sleeping in a chair and Hannah was not in the room. I got out of my chair and kneeled beside her. I held her hand and she seemed to know it was me because she started saying, 'Calen I can see them. We need to help them.' Then she was asleep again."

"I don't remember any of that," Natasha said.

"My experience did not seem like a dream at all," Gabriel explained. "I actually felt as if I had been transported to another world."

"I found myself on a barren mountain range surrounded by demons and monsters. I was wearing a variety of weapons and I was fighting thirteen of them at a time. When I would kill one, another different looking creature would appear in its place so the count was always the same. Also as I fought my weapons would keep replenishing. There was something vaguely familiar about the place I was in, I mean the mountain range and as I fought I tried to remember if I had been there before."

"Although I could hear all of the conversations that were going on in the bedroom, I could only feel Hannah's presence. At times I was listening to the conversations here at the house and they were distracting me from my adversaries. Now that I think about it, I too was wearing white but it was not glowing. Even though I didn't hear or see anyone else in the mountain range besides the demons and monsters I somehow knew that my battle was to save many more than me. I heard Hannah telling me she loved me and that seemed to renew my strength." Gabriel looked at Hannah and smiled.

"You didn't tell me that," Hannah said softly.

"It was like I had no sense of time in that world; I didn't know how long I had been gone. I was holding my own in the battle for a very long time. Then all the demons were on top of me at the same time and I could feel their weapons piercing me. Suddenly I heard Hannah screaming to me and my location changed."

"I found myself on a very small rocky cliff in the same barren mountains. I was alone and it was very dark. Hannah kept screaming for me to follow her voice and a star appeared high in the sky. The light from the star illuminated my path. It was as if her voice was coming from that star. I followed it and woke up here."

"Hannah tell the others what happened," Lakin said.

"I had been sitting with Gabriel for days, I wouldn't leave him. Lakin came into the room and persuaded me to take a break. Lakin sat with Gabriel while I took a bath. When I returned to the bedroom, Lakin told me to lie down and get some sleep. I laid next to Gabriel and fell asleep instantly. I don't think I had been sleeping long before I woke up because Gabriel was thrashing around and foaming at the mouth. I called for Lakin. Do you want to tell the rest?" Hannah asked Lakin.

"I had known all along that Gabriel was on a dark spiritual journey. But when I saw him in the state that Hannah described I believed he was battling a great demon. I put blessed water on his skin and it started to smoke which only happens when it touches a demon. I feared Gabriel was losing the battle. I told everyone to stand back and for Raul to hold Hannah so she wouldn't run forward."

"I was putting crystals on Gabriel's wound and praying when Hannah started to scream that she could see where Gabriel was and he needed to follow her voice. Hannah jumped on the bed and kept telling Gabriel to follow her and he woke up in a matter of minutes without any injuries. Gabriel's knife wound was healed."

"What does all this mean?" Natasha asked as she was overwhelmed by the story.

"Hopefully we will be able to figure that out," Gabriel said. "Now does anyone remember me saying or doing anything during the time I was unconscious?"

"At times you would start moving, not as bad as when you were thrashing around and you would mumble words in a language I didn't understand," Hannah said.

"One night Hannah called me into the bedroom to help her hold you down," Luca explained. "Because you were moving so wildly she was afraid you would fall out of bed. You were talking but I didn't understand the language. We both thought you were delirious."

"I don't remember that," Gabriel said thoughtfully.

"I do remember a couple of words you kept repeating but I don't know what they mean," Hannah said. "You said Anga Manya or something like that many times."

Gabriel looked solemnly at Hannah, "Angra Mainya is another name for Ahriman."

When Bella and Thaos walked out of his chambers they saw hundreds of guests standing around and looking lost. "Oh my Thaos, I forgot about them."

"Please go back and tell Claudius to change out of those bloody clothes, we have a home filled with people. I will meet you back in Stephan's and Ingr's chambers. As Bella walked through the crowd she saw horror and fear on the faces of many. She walked into the Great Hall and told the musicians to start playing music.

Then Bella thought better of that idea and she walked up on the stage and spoke to the guests. "If you have not already heard, the Sanuri has saved Ingr from this horror that was inflicted upon her. My husband killed the attacker, who we have learned meant to rape and kill Ingr and our sweet grandbabies. As you can imagine, Stephan and Nikki both are overwhelmed with grief. Thaos, Angelina and some others are kindly cleaning up that room," as Bella spoke tears came to her eyes.

"I feel awful that such evil has touched our family and all of you. But now we are not only celebrating the return of our fine warriors but the miracle of life that the Sanuri has returned to us. Please enjoy yourselves." As Bella spoke, one of her cooks walked up to her and whispered a few words. "I have just been told that the banquet is prepared, if you would all like to step into the dining area."

Bella got off the stage and walked directly to Stephan and Ingr's chambers. There were about twenty people helping to clean the master bedroom. When Angelina saw Bella she pointed to a closed bedroom door, indicating that Ingr and Stephan were in that room. Bella knocked softly on the door then entered the room.

The look of utter despair on her son's face broke Bella's heart. Stephan was sitting in a large chair next to Ingr's bed. Ingr was asleep. Bella thought that Ingr looked like a little Angel, so peacefully sleeping. All the blood had been washed from Ingr's body and she was wearing a clean nightgown. The image of Ingr now gave no hint of the awful scene that Bella had witnessed earlier. Without speaking, Bella pulled a chair next to Stephan's and sat with him.

"My experience was somewhat similar to Natasha's at first," Simon said. "But for some reason I knew it was not a dream, I felt like I suddenly found myself in a series of caves and tunnels."

"Like Natasha's experience I was wearing white clothing that were aglow with a white light that allowed me to see in the darkness of the caverns."

"I too saw the number thirteen written on the walls as well as sets of thirteen objects everywhere. I heard people screaming and crying and I was trying to make my way to them when I heard the voice of a demon. It was loud and taunting. The demon said he knew who I was, that I was one of The Seven Sons that the prophecy spoke of. He said I would never live long enough to fulfill the prophecy. He said the seventh son was being tortured by demons and would not survive and without him we could not stand against the Old Ones."

"Simon what are you talking about?" asked Natasha.

"It is one of the secrets of our family," Simon said as he looked at Raul, waiting for him to protest the fact that Simon was exposing this secret. "There is a prophesy about Seven Sons of Light that defeat the dark ones of the night."

"I have read that prophesy," Gabriel said. "Have you?"

"No, the Sanuri told us about it," Simon said.

"Raul, the prophesy says the sons are of The Great Ruler, not necessarily of a human father, are you too, one of these sons?" Gabriel asked.

"Yes."

"Then I need to show you this prophesy," Gabriel said. "But you have shared a dangerous secret with us. We shall not speak more of this in front of the others." Gabriel turned to the group. "None of you can tell anyone this secret; you will put Simon and Raul in great danger."

"Or it sounds to me that they are more powerful allies than we realized," Lakin said.

"So that is why The Lion came to you?" Gabriel asked. "I envy you; I have devoted my life to The Great Ruler and would be most honored to once meet His emissary. Tell us the rest of your journey."

"The demon kept telling me that I would not make it out of the caves and would not be able to fulfill the prophesy. He said he knew who the other sons were and after he finished with me he would go after them. I got angry. But this is when I started to hear Gabriel calling me back to this world. I could feel myself leaving the caves. Then I fought against Gabriel's voice and I called out to The Great Ruler to tell me why I was in the caves, because on some level I realized I was receiving messages that I did not understand."

"Suddenly the cave was filled with intense light. I heard the roar of a lion which caused the demon's voice and presence of evil to leave. The Lion asked if we truly had the courage to stop the demons. I said we did. He said, 'Even if it means you enter hell to do it.' I said yes, tell us what we need to know. He said 'thirteen levels into hell, thirteen doors.' Then he was gone and I woke up."

Chapter XXIV
Visions

Bella sat with Stephan for almost two hours without either of them speaking. In the silence, the horror of what happened and what could have happened was sinking into their beings. Finally Bella decided she should check on the rest of the family. She tried to persuade Stephan to eat but he told her repeatedly that he was not hungry. Bella kissed Stephan on the forehead and walked out of the bedroom, softly closing the door behind her.

"Bella come here," Angelina called when she saw Bella come out of Ingr's room. "We didn't want to bother you, so we asked Claudius what rug and mattresses we should put in here. I just want to make sure, you are fine with the ones we took."

Bella got tears in her eyes when she walked into the bedroom. Ruala and Nordes warriors were helping Thaos and Angelina clean and decorate the room. "I can't believe what you have done, thank you all so much," Bella said as she put both of her hands to her cheeks.

"Claudius told us which rug to take but as we cleaned we realized the curtains had blood on them too. So we took a different rug and set of curtains from one of your guest rooms. Is that alright?" Angelina asked.

"Of course it is alright, you are all so considerate."

"We picked flowers from your garden," Calla said. "We have some for the other room also but we don't want to bother Stephan."

"That is probably wise but thank you for the thoughts."

"Bella we couldn't get all of the blood stains off the wall," Thaos said. "Claudius showed us where the paint was, so we repainted two of the walls."

"Bella, we know they may not want to use this bedroom again after what happened," Angelina said. "We just didn't want anything to keep reminding them of the attack."

Bella put her arm around Angelina and kissed her on the forehead. "You are all such good friends."

"How is she doing?" asked Ibula.

"Sleeping very soundly," Bella answered. "Its miraculous that she has color back in her face, I mean if you didn't know what happened to her you wouldn't guess to look at her now."

"And Stephan?" Ibula asked.

"He isn't talking. He just sits there and stares at her."

"Thaos, Thaos, is Thaos in here?" Ryan yelled frantically as he ran into the parlor.

Thaos was kneeling down, as he finished painting the lower part of a wall. He jumped up when he heard the concern in Ryan's voice. "Ryan what is the matter? Is Nikki alright?"

"Well, I guess she is," Ryan said nervously. "Shara said to get you because Nikki is starting to have the baby."

"Thaos the shock of all this probably affected her," Bella said. "Nothing to worry about." Thaos did not speak as he ran out of the room with Ryan behind him.

"Ibula, do you want to help deliver a baby?" Angelina asked with a big smile.

"We'll finish up here," Calla said. "Go."

Ibula smiled, set aside her scrubbing brush and followed Angelina out of the chambers. Bella returned to Stephan and told him the news. Then she too, walked to Thaos' and Nikki's chambers.

Raul read his notes back to the group. "Any one care to voice an opinion about the meaning of these experiences?" asked Gabriel.

"Gabriel you said that you were also dressed in white but your clothing did not glow; was there enough light for you to see?" Rabi asked.

"Yes, we were outside and now that you bring it up; it was daylight always, until I was alone on that cliff."

"I think the white clothing represents The Great Ruler," Natasha said. "And I think He is trying to tell us that He will give us what we need to see the things that are important for this mission."

"Does anyone else have an opinion about the white clothing?" Gabriel asked. "Remember we are trying to sort a puzzle, so throw your ideas out."

"You were all trying to help others or sensed you were helping others," Luca said. "I think that reinforces our fears that many people will be in danger if Omnibus ascends."

"Were any of you afraid?" Hannah asked. "Because it sounds like each of you went to some kind of hell world yet you weren't afraid, I think that is significant."

"How so?" asked Lakin.

"Well, perhaps the message is The Great Ruler and The Lion are with us or that we are strong enough to fight these demons, but maybe we didn't realize that," Hannah said. "Since I am new to this group, I have another question. Gabriel you said that you envied Simon because The Lion appeared to him. Have you ever actually asked The Lion to appear to you?"

"No, I do not feel worthy."

"Well perhaps that is part of the message. As soon as Simon asked, The Lion appeared. Perhaps we should all be asking for more direct guidance in this mission," Hannah said. "Gabriel I think you should ask The Lion to appear to you sometime, I mean if he does not, what have you lost?"

Gabriel smiled lovingly at his wife, "I will try to get an audience with him."

"Something bothers me about all of this and I cannot put my finger on it," Calen said. "You all saw the number thirteen in some form so many times. Then The Lion himself says it not once but twice, thirteen levels; thirteen doors."

"I think that either that number has more significance than the obvious or we need to add or multiply the numbers. You are all smart people, how many times did you need to see that number?"

"Simon, Natasha I think the three of us need to remember how many times we encountered that number," Gabriel said.

"The Great Ruler saved all of you from great evil, He sent you on journeys or gave you visions, which to my people are considered the height of our spiritual awakening. He used these awful experiences to send you messages. Personally I think there is a whole lot more to all of this than we realize," Lakin said.

Late that afternoon, when Stephan could hear silence in his home, he felt a sense of relief. Although Stephan was very grateful to his friends for their help; he just wanted to be alone. Stephan continued to sit next to the bed and stare at Ingr. He did not realize that the Sanuri had sent healing energy into his body also; Stephan barely realized that he felt different.

Stephan kept looking at his beautiful wife lying in bed sleeping. The images of her stomach cut open and the room drenched in her blood kept flooding his mind. Stephan thought little about the babies; in fact he had forgotten about them until Bella told him where they were.

Stephan kept thinking about the Sanuri's words; that Lazo planned to kill Ingr and the children because of his hatred for him. Stephan thought about the demon attacks that Juleta had sent against him and Ingr. And he remembered Ingr fighting at his side at the battle at Juleta's castle. In the short time they had been together there had been so much danger and conflict. Yet Ingr never complained, she just wanted Stephan to love her. And he wept.

"Just one more thing before we end this meeting," Gabriel said. "Have any of you had a chance to start reading Sophie's diary?" Calen, Natasha, Koby, Simon and Dagon all looked at each other, no one spoke; no one wanted to tell Raul about the contents of the book. "What is wrong?" Gabriel asked.

"Natasha you have that guilty look on your face that you used to get when you were a child. Did you lose the book?"

"No," Natasha whispered and looked at Simon. "Gabriel perhaps we should discuss this in private."

"Natasha is right," Calen said. "The book isn't exactly what we at first thought."

As Gabriel looked around the table no one who had read the book would look him in the eyes, acts that did not go unnoticed by Raul, Lakin and the others.

"Natasha," Gabriel said in a stern and fatherly tone.

"Please Gabriel don't make me tell you in front of the others."

Raul suddenly swung his head around and looked at Simon, who would not meet his gaze. "Is the book about Vitomas?" Raul gasped in horror.

No one responded to his question for a few moments then Calen said, "Not all of it."

"Simon tell me," Raul almost yelled.

Dagon took the book from a pocket in his warrior's robe and placed it on the table. "No one wants to talk about this book because it is the most horrible thing we have ever read. Simon is the one who figured out what it really was. This is not Sophie's diary but a chronicle of Roch's life. She was sent to observe him, to ensure Roch would be a worthy vessel for the demon Omnibus."

"Sophie writes of many of your family members including you, Raul. We told Simon not to read it but in his genius he realized we could learn enough about Roch to find his weaknesses and to determine his behavior if we could get past our horror and emotions. So we have been reading the book out loud and together and taking notes. We have not finished it yet."

"Raul, please don't read this book," Natasha said softly. "I can't get through it without crying."

"This book makes us understand why we have to stop the ascension at all costs," Koby said adamantly.

Raul reached across the table to pick up the book. Simon grabbed Raul's outstretched hand. "Raul there is no need for you to read that. I will be honest there were parts that made me cry."

"I have to," Raul said in a whisper.

"Raul, there were parts that made us all cry or filled us with such anger that we could barely contain ourselves," Calen said. "I understand that you feel a need to read that book, I believe I would in your place also. But don't read it just to torture yourself. It worked for us to read it as a group because with every passage there would be one of us who could look at the information logically. There is information in that book we need to obtain, we will resume our group and you can join us."

"Alright," Raul said hoarsely. "But I will need to read the beginning to catch up with you."

"Perhaps we should start at the beginning again," Simon said. "Raul has been in that castle and has met Roch. Perhaps he will know things that we missed."

"Does she write about Laurabelle?" Hannah gasped.

Calen reached over and patted Hannah's hand. "We are not that far in the book, it is written chronologically."

"I will join your group," Gabriel said.

"As will I," Lakin added. "Perhaps between all of us we can find a way to bring the demon down."

"Roch's cruelty is beyond comprehension," Dagon said. "If this is what he is like as a human, God help us if he becomes the Vessel for Omnibus."

"Thaos, Nikki wants to see you," Shara said as she walked into the parlor. "She's alright, you don't have to look so nervous," Shara said as she patted Thaos' arm. Thaos hurried into the bedroom. Shara looked at the parlor full of people. "Look at all of these grandpas," she said with a laugh.

Claudius was sitting in a chair holding Marcus, Sorren was sitting in another chair holding Sicily and Mathas was sitting on the floor with Margarit, Sarah and Jacob. Rosa, Bella and Ryan were sitting together at one of the tables.

"Where's Matthew?" Angelina asked as she and Ibula walked into the parlor so they could give Nikki and Thaos some time alone.

"He went with Thedes and the Sanuri to check on Ingr and Stephan," Mathas said.

Angelina stared at Jacob playing with Sarah. "Did the Sanuri tell you anything about her?" Angelina asked with concern in her voice.

"Yes my dear," Rosa said happily. "There is no demon in her. He said she is a normal baby girl."

"Angelina I asked the same thing when I saw her," Margarit said without looking up from her toys. Angelina laughed at Margarit's comments.

"May I see the baby?" Ibula asked as she walked up to Sarah. "Oh she is beautiful," Ibula added as Mathas put Sarah into Ibula's arms. Ibula stared into the baby's eyes. "She has no darkness in her." Ibula said as she walked over to Angelina. "I'm sorry Mathas and Rosa; I just had to be sure."

"We understand," Rosa said. "We had our concerns also."

Angelina turned around and looked at her father and Claudius, they both looked so happy and content holding the grandbabies. "You two aren't going to have enough arms," Angelina teased. "Nikki is having her baby tonight and I am not far behind."

"Claudius that sounds like quite the predicament that we are going to be in," Sorren said with a hearty laugh.

"Well we have to keep up with Mathas," Claudius said cheerfully.

Angelina looked at these three mighty warriors; who were so happy to have grandchildren and her heart warmed.

The rest of that afternoon and late into the night everyone in Hannah's home gathered in her father's study; except for Hannah and Marcia. Neither woman wanted to hear Sophie's words and both of their husbands were glad they did not want to participate.

"Natasha you don't have to be here," Gabriel said. "You have already said this book upsets you."

"Truly Gabriel I don't want to read any more of this book but we are looking for answers. I am the only woman in here and we all know that men and women tend to see things differently. I think it unwise not to have one of us in this group."

Gabriel looked proudly at his sister then at Calen, who was not making her leave. "Very well but don't be afraid to leave if you feel the need."

"I really can't, I am the note taker," Natasha responded with a slight smile.

Lakin picked up the book and began reading Sophie's words. *On this most wondrous day I have arrived at the castle of Roch, soon to be the vessel for our lord Omnibus. His task, his destiny, his gift has never before been bestowed on any mortal being. The Insidiae are quite concerned that Roch may not be worthy or ready for his role, a role that will change this world.*

Centuries we have prepared the path to have the perfect human hold the essence of Omnibus. No mere mortal will do; for pure evil of this magnitude needs a body of like kind to sustain it. And that now is my assignment. To observe Roch as he grows into a man; to determine if he is capable of being the vessel. My heart sings as I prepare for this most honorable task.

Roch has recently murdered his parents for the power of the throne. He has ordered the staff of his parents to leave the castle and Roch is replacing them with his own staff. Arrangements were made, through the Insidiae that I will be Roch's cook. As I write I sit in my room, I have not yet met the young king but I am impressed with him thus far. I believe he has a future as the Vessel.

"The next three pages is just Sophie continuing to say how excited she is for her assignment and complaining about her trip from Ryed. She is from the Village of Benjem," Calen said. "Start again on page four. Sophie spent a great deal of time talking with the staff to find out what Roch said and did before she arrived. She has the details of how he murdered his parents. I find it curious that she never asked Roch about it."

"Maybe she was afraid of exposing herself," Lakin said.

"When I was there, Annabelle and Vitomas warned me that Sophie was a spy for Roch," Raul said. "The girls tried to keep her away from me."

"Well, she watched you whether you realized it or not," Simon said. "She saw you and Vitomas kissing. The strange thing was, she hoped Vitomas would run off with you because she mentions several times that she believed Vitomas was Roch's weakness and the one thing that could keep him from his destiny."

"I don't believe that to be totally true," Raul said. "Sophie came into my room to visit me several times. The first time she started out by asking me questions in a manner that I found very suspicious. But something changed. The girls told me they thought that I reminded Sophie of someone because they had never seen her treat anyone as nicely as she did me. Sophie started to warn me that I needed to leave the castle, she even told me about a secret entrance and brought me crutches."

"Just as I was preparing to leave, Roch bursts into the room. He and I had words and then he dragged Vitomas out. Sophie later commented to me about the look on my face and that I needed to hide my feelings or Roch would use them to hurt Vitomas and me. But it was after that she said something to me I can't remember her exact words, but it was something like, 'don't ever let go of someone you love.'"

"Raul you reminded Sophie of someone she either loved or lost or both," Natasha said. "It is hard to remember she is a person, when you read that book."

"Raul your relationship with Sophie may be something that could be useful to us. You are making it sound like you were her weakness," Gabriel said.

Ingr opened her eyes, she did not recognize where she was at first. The flickering lights of candles gave a warm glow to the bedroom. Ingr looked to her left and saw Stephan sleeping in a chair next to the bed. She smiled, seeing Stephan always made her smile. Every time Ingr looked upon his face, she was in awe of how handsome he was. Ingr tried to sit up and a sharp pain shot through her body. She was suddenly thrust back into reality and remembered the attack.

"Stephan, Stephan." Instantly Stephan's eyes opened and he knelt beside her. "Stephan the babies, did he hurt the babies or your mother?" Stephan took Ingr's left hand in both of his and kissed it.

"Mother and the babies are fine. Fortunately it was Father who was bringing Marcus to you. Father killed Lazo and the Sanuri saved you."

"Oh, now I remember seeing Claudius but things were so blurry. Did he kick the door down?"

"Yes, he and Sorren came here together. Sorren was trying to take care of you while Father beat the hell out of Lazo."

"How did the Sanuri know to come?" Ingr asked weakly.

"I really don't know. I didn't think to ask," Stephan said. "How are you feeling?"

"When I tried to sit up I had an awful pain in my stomach but I am feeling better than I should. It's amazing. Stephan I know this may should crazy but I think I died. I remember walking down this path; or more like I was dancing. Everything was filled with this brilliant white light. I felt so warm and loved. I was looking for you and the babies. And suddenly I heard you calling from behind me and I turned and came back to you."

Stephan kissed Ingr's hand again. "Ingr I am so sorry I didn't protect you from him. All during our trip I had this overpowering feeling like I should kill him; maybe on some level I knew what a threat he was. I should have known he would try something like this."

Ingr tried to sit up again but winced in pain. "What can I do to help you?" Stephan asked.

"Would you help me sit up? I am very thirsty and would like some water."

Stephan helped Ingr to a sitting position, even though it caused her great pain, then he poured her a glass of water, which Ingr drank down. "Stephan did Lazo threaten to hurt our family?"

"No but he tried to hurt Calla and Bac."

"And you and the others stopped him, correct?"

"Yes."

"Stephan there is no way you could have known what he was going to do, so don't torture yourself. We are all going to be fine," Ingr said with a conviction that made Stephan smile.

Stephan leaned forward and kissed Ingr on the lips. When she reached up to put her arms around his neck, she winced in pain again. "Angelina made some pain tonic for you," Stephan said and walked over to one of the tables, where Angelina had placed a large pitcher of tonic and several glasses. Stephan brought a full glass back to Ingr.

"Stephan you should get the babies, they need to be fed," Ingr said as she took the tonic.

"The babies are alright. There are some women from your tribe who are feeding them. They are all over with Nikki and Thaos. Nikki was so upset about you that she started to go into labor. The baby hasn't come yet."

"I hope she will be alright," Ingr said with concern. "The baby isn't due yet. You will let me know when it is born, won't you?"

"Honey it's you that I am worried about. Now you need to get some sleep. Please drink that tonic down."

Ingr did not say anything for a few moments then she drank the glass of tonic. "Stephan I want you to come to bed with me. I don't want you sleeping in that chair."

"Ingr I am afraid I might hurt you if I move too much."

"Stephan I sleep better when you are with me. If I am in a lot of pain I will tell you. Besides I want to lie in your arms."

Stephan took his clothes off and slid under the quilts next to Ingr. She painfully moved up against him, so she could lie in his arm. "I love you Stephan," Ingr said.

"I love you too." As Stephan said these words he realized it was the first time he uttered them without fear.

"I need a break from this," Simon said to the group of warriors reading Sophie's book. "Can someone show me where Hannah's father's clothes are kept? I want to see if I can find something to wear to the ball tomorrow night."

"Marcia and I have talked," Rabi said. "I will let her go to the dance with you but please keep her safe."

"Rabi, you and Marcia don't have to do this," Raul said.

"She is really afraid that you and Simon will be exposed which will lead to Gabriel and Hannah. And you know how close she and Hannah are. Marcia said you need escorts for your disguise."

Natasha turned and looked at Calen to see if he had changed his mind but the look on his face told her he had not. Natasha understood Calen's position on the matter and knew she would feel the same if their roles were reversed. But Natasha also agreed with Rabi and Marcia. Natasha looked down at the table without speaking.

"You really want to go, don't you?" Calen asked sternly.

"Calen I don't want to go because it is a dance," Natasha said. "I agree with every word that Marcia said. I want to go to help protect the others while they look for information."

"Simon don't take this wrong," Calen said with an edge to his voice. "Because of this mission I cannot go out in public with my own wife. You have done more with her than I have. I had really hoped that the first ball we went to, we could attend together."

"Why don't you come too," Raul suggested. "In fact seeing Ruala warriors might be the diversion we need."

"If Tenebrae and Pravis see them at the dance, they will suspect something is going on," Gabriel said. "The dark lords know the Rualas work on behalf of The Great Ruler. But having them at the hotel is a good idea. And perhaps a distraction might be in order. "

"You don't have to be so quiet, I am awake," Hannah said as she sat up in bed.

"We stopped reading so Simon could go through your father's clothes to find a suit for the ball," Gabriel said as he disrobed.

"I can help him with a fitting, we don't have enough time to take the suit to a tailor," Hannah said as she watched Gabriel. "I am sorry that I couldn't read that book with you,"she said sincerely.

"Hannah I am very glad you didn't want to," Gabriel said as he slid under the covers. "You have to apologize for nothing."

"I just feel so bad because Natasha is able to do it."

"It bothers her greatly but she feels it is necessary to have at least one woman in the group, just for a different point of view." As Gabriel said this he saw the dejected look that came across Hannah's face. Gabriel put the palm of his hand gently against her cheek. "Honey the book is difficult for all of us but we must go through it for the mission. You lost your entire family because of Roch and the wounds are still fresh, it would not be a good idea for you to be a part of this."

Hannah kissed Gabriel on the lips. "Gabriel, I disagree. I think I have to join you, otherwise I feel like Roch is intimidating me. I don't want him to have any power over me."

The sun was starting to rise when the cry of a new born infant awoke almost everyone in Thaos' and Nikki's home. Thaos spent the night pacing back and forth as the others slept in the parlor and guest rooms.

Now Thaos' heart felt like it was going to leap out of his chest. Matthew was now standing beside Thaos with his hand on Thaos' shoulder. Ibula opened the bedroom door just a crack and said with a big smile, "Thaos you have a son. Both the baby and Nikki are fine. Just give us a few minutes to clean everyone up and you can come in." Then she disappeared behind the door.

"A son," Thaos repeated. "Matthew I have a son." Thaos was exhausted, excited and completely overwhelmed. "Claudius did you hear? We have a boy." When Claudius stood up, baby Marcus started to cry, so one of the Nordes women took the baby into a bedroom to feed him.

"Where's Bella?" Claudius asked.

"She's sleeping in that room," Thaos said as he pointed to one of the guest rooms.

"She will never forgive us if we don't wake her now," Claudius said as a grin consumed his face. "I will be right back."

Just as Bella and Claudius walked into the parlor, Angelina opened the door to the bedroom. "The baby is early but he is still a good size and looks very healthy," Angelina said happily. "You can come in now." Nikki was sitting up in bed holding her son and smiling. Thaos ran to Nikki's side and stared at the baby in awe. Claudius, Bella, Sorren and Matthew followed Thaos into the room as others crowded in the doorway.

"Meet Titus Derek," Nikki said. "Here Thaos take him."

"He's so little," Thaos said as Ibula put the baby into his arms. "Look," was all Thaos could say as he walked up to Claudius and Bella. Matthew walked over and kissed Angelina then they both walked up to see the baby, arm in arm. Sorren waited for Shara to return to the room, as she was discarding the soiled linens. Then they walked together to see the baby.

"Look at all that black hair," Matthew said in awe. "I didn't know babies were born with that much hair."

Bella had tears in her eyes as Thaos handed her the baby. "Claudius now you have two boys named after you," she said warmly. Claudius beamed proudly as he looked at Titus.

Nikki's mother pushed through the crowd that was outside of the bedroom. "Gladys come hold your grandson," Bella said happily.

Thaos was kneeling next to the bed kissing Nikki when Claudius and Bella walked up to them.

"Son there was something that Bella and I had planned on talking to you about when you first came home. But yesterday took on a life of its own. So this may be a bad time or the perfect time. As Claudius spoke he took a folded piece of paper out of his shirt pocket and handed it to Thaos. Bella and I asked you to live here as family. We never realized how much a part of our family you and Nikki would become."

"Thaos what is it?" Nikki asked when she saw the shocked look on Thaos' face.

"Its adoption papers," Thaos said in disbelief.

"Adoption papers for who?" Nikki asked.

"For me."

Before Thaos could say anything else, Claudius said. "Bella, Stephan and I have discussed this. And Thaos if you would be so inclined we would like to legally adopt you as a member of this family. Think about it. If you don't want to, nothing will change but if you do want to be our adopted son, then you will need to sign that paper."

Thaos was speechless as he signed the adoption paper and handed it to Claudius. Since the age of nine Thaos had greatly desired to have a family again. That hope kept him alive as he lived the dangerous life of an unwanted orphan. But as with many things the heart longs for, repeated pain and disappointments sends such desires to the hidden chambers of the being. Then one loses hope until the thought of such desires brings only pain. Now as a grown man Thaos' hopes and dreams were finally coming true. On this night his beautiful wife gave him a son and Claudius gave him a family and a heritage.

Chapter XXV
The Ball

The next night Hannah's house was bustling as everyone was preparing to go to the grand ball at the Endleson Hotel. Raul, Simon and Gabriel were dressed and in the parlor with Lakin, Calen, Rabi, Luca, Koby and Dagon as they devised various strategies. The men planned to search the rooms of Pravis and Tenebrae as well as the office of Endleson.

"You are never going to get there on time if the girls don't come down pretty soon," Calen said. "I'll see what is keeping Natasha." After Calen exited the parlor, Gabriel and Rabi decided they should check on their wives.

"Oh Calen there you are," Natasha said when he walked into their bedroom. "Would you help me with the back of this dress?" Natasha stood in front of Calen with her back turned to him.

"I never thought I would be helping you get ready to go to a dance with another guy," Calen said sarcastically.

"Calen, you know this doesn't count, it's a mission," Natasha said and started to turn towards him.

"Honey hold still, these buttons are really tiny."

"Calen I have been thinking," Natasha said seriously. "After this mission I would like to take a break. I am so excited about our home that your parents are building and the home here; that Gabriel will have built for us. I want to work on our homes and spend more time with you; that is unless you work on another mission."

Calen smiled as he listened to Natasha then he bent down and kissed her on her bare shoulder. "I have been thinking the same thing. Have you told Gabriel yet?"

"No, I wanted to discuss it with you first."

"You can turn around now," Calen said as he finished with the last of the buttons. His eyes grew wide as he looked at Natasha in the low cut dark blue gown which exposed both of her shoulders.

"You look beautiful." Calen leaned down and kissed Natasha on the lips.

"After Hannah made the adjustments she said I should keep this dress. I feel like a princess in it."

"You look like a princess in it. I think you should keep the dress," Calen said admiringly. "Hannah is a very generous person."

"I really like her," Natasha said with a sly smile. "Calen if I tell you something, promise you won't tell Gabriel."

"What is it?" he asked with a grin.

"I am so happy that Gabriel found a wonderful woman to fall in love with but, oh this is going to sound so childish, but I just can't imagine them making love. I mean I don't think of my brother doing, well, I don't know what I am trying to say."

"You aren't going to tell me that Gabriel hasn't been with other women, are you?"

"Oh no, as handsome as he is, women have been chasing him his entire life," Natasha said. "I've just never seen him look at anyone like he looks at Hannah."

"I'm not really sure I understand what you are saying," Calen said.

Natasha sighed loudly and rolled her eyes, "You know how you and I look at each other when all we can think about is tearing each other's clothes off; well they look at each other the same way."

Calen's laughter roared through the small bedroom; when he composed himself he said, "You know it was difficult for Gabriel when you and I married and started making love. The two of you have devoted your lives to each other. He will always see you as his baby sister and you will always see him as, well, kind of a father figure. You may not realize what big adjustments you two are going through."

"Oh Gabriel you are so handsome," Hannah gushed, as she looked at him dressed in his black suit for the ball. "I am the luckiest woman in the world."

"You look incredible," Gabriel said admiringly. Hannah was wearing a light blue and silver gown that had the tiniest of silver straps. The form fitting, low cut gown greatly accented her curvaceous figure. "I see you are wearing the jewelry that Vitomas sent you. It's beautiful. I didn't really look at it before."

"I have something for you," Hannah said and handed Gabriel a velvet jewelry box. As he opened the box Hannah continued to talk. "I don't know if you like rubies but I bought a red rose for each of you to wear in your lapels, so I thought these would match."

Gabriel leaned down and kissed Hannah on the lips. "They are perfect, help me put them on." Hannah picked up the cufflinks that had gold as the base with a large ruby in the center, surrounded by tiny diamonds. As she fastened his cuffs, Gabriel said. "Thank you, they are wonderful gifts. When did you find time to buy them?"

"When I was supposed to be packing up my office," Hannah said with a laugh. "Here, let me put your tie clasp on," Hannah said. The stones in the tie clasp were considerably larger than the ones in the cufflinks. "The roses are in a vase in the kitchen. We can get them before we leave."

"I am sorry Hannah; I don't have a gift for you."

"Gabriel this evening is going to be a gift. This is the first ball I have attended since Laurabelle was murdered. I do love to dance," Hannah stopped talking and seemed to drift to other thoughts. Gabriel put his arm around her, "Come on pretty lady, let's get the others."

"Marcia you look so beautiful," Natasha said when she entered the parlor. Marcia was wearing a purple silk gown that had a strap on only one shoulder.

"You all look beautiful," Lakin said. "Now you will be driving a large boca with several rows of seats. There are weapons and shields hidden under each of the seats."

"Calen and Rabi will be keeping an eye on all of you while you are in the ball. Koby is leading one group of warriors who will be watching the grounds and Luca will be leading another group to watch the rooms as you search them."

"You're coming!" Natasha said with a little squeal and threw her arms around Calen's neck. Marcia was also very happy and turned and kissed Rabi.

Simon looked at Raul and said softly, "I have a plan."

The ride to Nora was uneventful. Gabriel waited until all of the Ruala warriors were in place before he drove the boca to the front of the hotel. Gabriel and Hannah entered the ballroom first, followed by Raul and Marcia and Simon and Natasha. Lloyd and his wife were standing near the doorway of the ballroom, helping the Endleson family greet the guests. Lloyd was filled with fear when he saw Gabriel and Raul enter the hotel.

"Hannah we are so glad to see you here," said an elegant woman with gray hair who came up to Hannah and hugged her.

"Thank you Edith, I would like to introduce you to my husband Gabriel. Gabriel this is Edith, Lloyd's wife. You remember Lloyd don't you dear?"

"Why yes," Gabriel said and took Edith's hand and kissed it. Lloyd's voice and demeanor betrayed his uneasiness. Gabriel shook hands with Lloyd and whispered, "We are just here to dance." Raul on the other hand, was less charming when he shook hands with Lloyd. "We meet again," Raul said in a manner that greatly intimidated Lloyd.

"Lloyd you have met my cousin Raul and Marcia, let me introduce you to my sister Natasha and her husband Simon." To everyone's surprise Natasha walked up to Lloyd and Edith and hugged them both. "I am thrilled to be here," Natasha said.

As Natasha and Edith chatted, Hannah took Gabriel's arm, "Gabriel I would like you to meet Augustus Endleson and his wife Beatrice."

It was the first time that Gabriel had ever shaken hands with a member of the Insidiae. Endleson had a weak and sweaty handshake, which only reinforced Gabriel's opinion of the type of man who hides behind a mask. Gabriel made sure he introduced Raul and Simon to Endleson, because he wanted them to remember Endleson's face. And once again Natasha hugged Augustus and Beatrice.

After they finished the official greetings, Gabriel, Hannah and the others, walked to the edge of the dance floor. Gabriel stopped a waiter, "Excuse me sir, but we need a table for six and a bottle of your finest wine."

"Yes sir, follow me." The waiter gave them the choice between several tables. Gabriel chose one that gave them the best view of the doors and hallways.

"So what was with all the hugging?" Simon asked Natasha as he slid her chair up to the table.

"Oh dear husband, hold my hand," Natasha replied sarcastically.

"If I know my sister, you better take her hand under the table," Gabriel said with a grin.

Simon sat down and reached his hand to Natasha, under the table. She dropped two rings of keys into his hand. "The smaller ring I took off Lloyd," Natasha said with a mischievous smile. Simon laughed and kissed her on the cheek. "Gabriel your little sister is something," Simon said then turned to Raul and showed him the two key rings.

Hannah leaned forward since she was sitting across the table from Natasha, "You have to teach me some of your tricks," Hannah whispered. Natasha grinned and winked at Gabriel.

"Simon and I will be back momentarily," Raul said and the two left the table. Their wine was served. As they waited for Raul and Simon to return to the table, Marcia and Hannah were pointing out many of the people at the ball to Gabriel and Natasha.

"They have been gone for half an hour," Natasha said with concern in her voice. "Do you think something happened to them?" Gabriel shrugged his shoulders and smiled.

"You know what they are doing, don't you?" Natasha asked of her brother. "Are they searching the rooms?" she whispered.

"Why don't you ask them yourself," Gabriel said as Raul and Simon returned to the table. Neither man sat down but instead offered his arm to his escort. "My Ladies, will you come with us?" Raul asked. Marcia took Raul's arm and Natasha took Simon's; both couples walked across the large ballroom and disappeared.

"Where did they go?" Hannah asked.

"Let's find out," Gabriel said as he stood up and pulled her chair out.

"What are you two up to?" Natasha asked with a laugh as Raul opened a set of double doors that led to a stone patio outside of the ballroom. In the middle of the patio was a table that was draped with a white linen cloth and filled with lit candles. A bottle of wine and four glasses were on the table. Simon closed the door behind them. "I don't understand," Natasha said. "Is this for us?"

"Well it's for you," Simon said and kissed Natasha on the cheek. "Have the first dance with your husbands, we will guard the door." With these words Calen and Rabi walked out of the garden and towards their smiling wives. Raul kissed Marcia on the cheek and gave her hand to Rabi.

"Thank you" Natasha said to Simon as Calen took her into his arms and started to dance to the music which could be heard from the ballroom. The door opened and Gabriel and Hannah stepped onto the patio. Tears came to Hannah's eyes as she watched the two young couples dance. Their faces beamed with love and happiness.

"That was so sweet of you two," Hannah said and stretched up and kissed both Simon and Raul on their cheeks.

"You two should go back inside," Raul said. "We will guard the door for them."

404

After an hour, Natasha and Marcia returned to the ball with Raul and Simon. If anyone had noticed that the two Princes of Wetpr were acting as door guards for an hour, Raul and Simon did not realize it. Gabriel and Hannah did their best to keep Lloyd, Endleson and several others occupied during that time. Hannah smiled proudly as Gabriel's charm and good looks captivated the wives of these powerful and dangerous men; because the wives forced the husbands to remain in the company of Gabriel and Hannah.

Upon leaving Calen and Rabi, Raul and Simon immediately took their escorts to the dance floor where they glided across the entire distance of the room. Both of the Princes were excellent dancers but this night their focus was on the crowd. Simon and Natasha danced on one side of the massive ballroom while Raul and Marcia danced on the other side.

Beatrice Endleson took Gabriel by the arm and led everyone to their private table, which was in a beautifully decorated small room off from the dance floor. When Raul saw this, he danced over to Simon. "It's time," Raul whispered. Since Calen and Rabi were now at the ball, they were allowing their wives to participate with the mission more than originally planned. Natasha and Marcia were not going to enter the rooms as Raul and Simon searched them but rather they planned to stand in the hallway and distract anyone who might come upon them.

Luca had divided his warriors into four groups, all of whom were watching Raul and Simon through various windows. The Endleson Hotel was the most luxurious hotel in all of Stordt. There were no single rooms in this hotel but all lavish chambers. The ground floor chambers had doors that led out to private patios and gardens. And the upper floors had grand balconies attached to them. Each balcony was decorated with furniture, statues and plants.

The plan was for Simon and Raul to open the balcony doors to any room they were searching. For expediency the Ruala warriors were going to assist with the search and carry away any items they would confiscate. Calen and Rabi insisted their wives stand near windows so they could watch them. Endleson had an office on the first floor and a suite on the top floor of the hotel.

Simon and Raul easily found the office which had a large gold sign over the door. They gained access with the stolen set of keys. Both Raul and Simon were happy to discover that Endleson had a fire going in the fireplace and all of the candles lit in his office. Raul opened the balcony doors while Simon unlocked the desk drawers.

"Dagon bring that bag over here," Simon whispered loudly, then proceeded to empty the contents of several drawers into the bag. "I'm not going to take the time to sort through all of these papers and ledgers now," Simon said. Raul, Luca and two other warriors were searching the bookshelves, walls and floor for hidden compartments. Any books or items that they thought might be important they threw into a bag. Raul opened a door and found a huge safe. He tried to open it by guessing at combinations.

"I would call Natasha in here," Luca suggested. "She might have the skills to open it."

Simon opened the door to the hallway and called to Natasha. "Do you think you can open a safe?" Marcia stayed in the hallway as Natasha grabbed a clean glass from Endleson's private bar and held one end to her ear and the other to the safe. She skillfully worked the dial and within minutes opened the safe. She smiled at the men proudly and quickly returned to the hallway. "That girl is something," Luca said with a grin.

There were ledgers and bags of gold in the safe. "We should take some of the money, so they think this was a robbery," Raul said. "They will get suspicious if they see that only their paperwork is missing. No secret compartments were found in Endleson's office. It took the group ten minutes to search the office and return things to their previous condition. Simon and Raul returned to the dance floor with Natasha and Marcia. They wanted to be seen dancing so as not to draw suspicion.

After twenty minutes the group went to the top floor of the hotel and searched Endleson's suite. Besides jewels and money, which they did not take, the group found little of interest. Once again they returned to the dance. Gabriel was still at the Endleson's private table but he was watching for Raul and Simon. Raul nodded to Gabriel, who then left the table and walked up to the two couples.

"We searched Endleson's office and chambers," Raul whispered to Gabriel. "We didn't take the time to read anything we just gave everything of interest to Luca and his men. Do we know if Pravis and Tenebrae are here so we can search their rooms?"

"Yes," Gabriel said and nodded to a table where two drunken older men were seated with four younger women.

"Those are high priests!" Raul whispered in astonishment as they watched Pravis spill his glass of wine on the table. Hannah joined Gabriel and the others as they were looking at the high priests.

"I will go with you," Gabriel said. "In case there are demons in those rooms."

"Do either of you want to help me distract a couple of old drunks for a while?" Natasha asked Hannah and Marcia.

"I will," Hannah said. "I can ask them if they know Padre Octavos from the orphanage in Salar."

"I want both of you to be careful," Gabriel said sternly.

"Gabriel, we know what we are doing," Natasha said with a sweet smile.

"We'll be careful dear," Hannah said and kissed Gabriel on the cheek.

"I will watch the hallway," Marcia said. Hannah and Natasha waited until Gabriel and the others were out of the ballroom before they approached the table of the two priests.

"Excuse me," Hannah said. "But I was told that you were priests and I wondered if either of you know Padre Octavos from the orphanage in Salar."

"I certainly do, my dear," Pravis answered as he stared at Hannah amorously. "Please join us." Tenebrae did not immediately speak, but he boldly stared at Natasha who smiled at him flirtatiously. Tenebrae turned to the two women who were sitting on either side of him and said, "Girls why don't you find something to do for a while." When they stood up to leave, Pravis said the same thing to the women who were with him.

"Goodness you didn't have to send your friends away," Hannah said.

"We don't even know their names," Pravis said and leaned close to Hannah. "So tell me how do you know Padre Octavos?" Hannah's eyes started to water from the powerful smell of whiskey on Pravis' breath. Hannah proceeded to tell them about her work at the orphanage in Salar. Natasha flirted with Tenebrae who seemed to be considerably drunker than Pravis.

Calen watched them through one of the open balcony doors, he didn't know who Natasha and Hannah were flirting with but he guessed they were the two high priests. Even though Calen knew that Natasha and Hannah were attempting to distract the men, he could feel the anger rising within him. Calen was getting tense and he found himself clenching his fists.

Calen almost entered the ballroom, when Tenebrae tried to put his arm around Natasha, but she quickly put an empty wine bottle into Tenebrae's hand. Fortunately for the two women they did not have to endure the company of the two drunken men for long; within twenty minutes Gabriel walked up to Hannah.

"My dear we have been looking for you," Gabriel said and kissed her on the cheek.

Pravis kept staring at Simon and Raul as they approached the table. "I know you, both of you," Pravis said with slurred speech. Gabriel quickly said this is my cousin Robert and my sister's husband Travis.

"Your husband!" Tenebrae said with obvious disappointment.

Pravis kept staring at the two Princes. "Your names are not familiar but I know; I know you from someplace."

"I don't think we have ever met," Raul said and extended his hand to Pravis, who shook it.

"Travis I would love to dance," Natasha said and quickly stood up and took Simon's arm, the two walked over to the dance floor. "I think we should leave soon," Natasha said. "Did you get everything?"

"We grabbed what we could from the rooms," Simon said as he whirled Natasha around. "I don't really know what we got." Raul and Marcia joined them on the dance floor.

"Pravis is the priest that Vitomas saw at our castle," Raul said to Simon. The two couples danced as Gabriel and Hannah continued to talk with Pravis and Tenebrae. Suddenly Raul said to Simon, "Take care of Marcia, I have a plan." And he turned and walked off the dance floor. Ten minutes later, six young women approached Pravis and Tenebrae, at which time Gabriel and Hannah left the table and joined the others. When Raul rejoined the group Simon asked, "Did you send those girls over?"

"Yes, that should keep them distracted for a while; I also sent over two more bottles of wine."

"Let me have one more dance with my beautiful bride," Gabriel said. "Then I think we should leave."

Gabriel was helping Hannah into the front seat of the boca when Calen suddenly landed among them.

"Sorry Simon but I need to talk to my wife," Calen said angrily and before anyone could speak he picked Natasha up and ascended into the dark sky.

"Is he mad Gabriel?" Hannah asked with concern. "He sounded mad. Why would he be mad? Natasha didn't do anything wrong."

Raul helped Marcia into the boca; Simon was the last to be seated. "If I had to guess it was because you two were sitting with those priests," Simon said.

"But we were keeping them distracted so you could search their rooms," said Hannah.

"We know," Simon said. "And we appreciated what you did but..."

"But what Simon?" Hannah asked defensively.

"But they were looking at you and Natasha like they were going to jump on you any second," said Simon.

Hannah turned to Gabriel. "Are you mad at me?" she asked.

"No but I will admit I didn't like you two being with them but it had to be done."

"Natasha and I both have weapons hidden on us, so if they tried anything we were prepared."

Gabriel put his arm around Hannah and asked suggestively, "So you have weapons hidden on you?"

"Guess you will have to try to find them when we get home," Hannah said flirtatiously then kissed Gabriel on the lips.

"Calen you said you wanted to talk but you won't speak to me now," Natasha said as they flew through the night sky. "What are you so mad about?" Calen did not answer her, nor did he look at Natasha. "Calen what did I do wrong?" He still did not answer her questions. "Please will you just tell me? Calen please."

Without looking at Natasha Calen said, "I'm not even sure if I am mad at you, I am just mad."

Natasha was quiet for several moments as she reviewed the events of the night in her head. "It's because Hannah and I talked to the high priests, isn't it?" Calen did not answer. "Calen we were just trying to distract them while the others searched their rooms."

"I know."

"Then why are you mad?"

"Natasha, you and I met and got married on this mission. I can't ever be seen with you for fear of compromising the mission. So every day I watch you go out with Simon, I know there is nothing between you two, but I want to be with you. I want to be the one who dances with you and shops with you and protects you. And tonight, Natasha I know what you were doing and it had to be done but the way those two pigs were looking at you and Hannah, I just wanted to punch them both."

Natasha heard the intensity of Calen's voice as he spoke. "Calen I love you and I know this has been difficult on you and I am sorry. If you want us both to pull out of this mission now and go to the Ice Caves, I will go because I don't want to jeopardize our relationship. But before you make a decision I want you to think about what will be jeopardized if this mission fails. If Omnibus ascends what kind of world will we be bringing our children into?" Calen did not say anything for several moments and when he finally spoke her blood ran cold.

"Hutas."

"Where?" she whispered.

"Don't speak I am going closer to see what they are doing," Calen whispered. Instead of crossing the bridge outside of Nora and following the road to Hannah's house, Calen had been flying along the River Nebu which took them closer to the gold mines. The darkness of the night was thick; there was no moon and few stars in the sky. Natasha looked down and saw a huge fire and men dancing around it.

There were men carrying torches who were going in and out of a cave. Calen landed on a small hill that overlooked the scene. He put his finger against Natasha's lips to reinforce to her that she should not speak. The top of the hill was heavily wooded, Calen and Natasha hid behind a large tree as they watched the Hutas below.

They could hear screams but could not see who was screaming, then they saw him. The Hutas carried a man out of the caves, his arms and legs were bound and they threw him into the fire. Natasha put her own hand over her mouth so that she would not make a sound when she saw this grisly sight. Natasha had never heard anything like the screams of that man as he was being burned alive, this moment would stay with her forever. Calen and Natasha watched the Hutas for several hours and left just before sunrise.

As soon as Gabriel and the others got home that night they proceeded to inspect the items they had taken from the hotel. Endleson's books revealed the same secret monthly payment to the Insidiae that they had seen in the ledgers of Hannah's father. Raul was scrutinizing the ledgers looking for the sale of a gold mine to one of the high priests.

After two hours Raul called Gabriel over to him. "I think I found it," Raul explained. "He didn't sell the mine he gave it to them, that's why I couldn't find it in the regular ledger. The ledger says' he donated parcel thirteen to the church. The deed was made out to High Priest Tenebrae. They all looked over maps of the mines and surrounding areas without finding anything labeled parcel thirteen. It was close to sunrise when the men decided to get some sleep.

Calen and Natasha arrived at Hannah's home shortly after everyone had gone to bed. Calen knocked on Gabriel's bedroom door first. After Calen told Gabriel about the Hutas, Gabriel decided they should wake up everyone in the house and have a meeting. Natasha was already in the kitchen making coffee and starting breakfast as the members of the household made their way down to the dining table.

Even in the thick darkness of the previous night, Calen meticulously identified land marks so he could find that cave again. Gabriel brought maps to the dining table as Calen drew his own map. Hannah and Marcia joined Natasha in the kitchen and by time they served breakfast, the men had identified parcel thirteen and were making arrangements to go to the cave after breakfast.

Chapter XXVI
Jared

Another night sleep did not come easily for Meekos. For days Sophie, Meekos and Erebus had been discussing and debating the situation with the plans for Omnibus' ascension. Erebus' words and questions only fed into Meekos' paranoid and fearful demeanor. Meekos was not a person who let others close, only his beloved sister Sophie knew the real Meekos; a boy who was always bullied by others.

Meekos grew up as an extremely intelligent boy in a village of barbarians. He could not outfight the other boys but he learned at an early age that he could outwit them. A skill he nurtured as he grew older. Like many men who have a fearful spirit, Meekos sought power, power beyond that of others. And his appetite for power consumed him. Power made Meekos feel safe, power made Meekos feel free and above all else power allowed Meekos to become the bully.

"Sophie are you awake?" Meekos called through her door as he stood in the hallway of the hotel. Meekos knocked loudly several times before he heard movement in her room.

"Meekos is something wrong?" Sophie asked as she answered the door in her nightgown.

"I need to talk," Meekos said as he walked into her sitting room. "I am truly sorry for waking you."

"You are disturbed by Erebus' questions aren't you?" Sophie asked as she poured two small glasses of whiskey. "I too keep thinking about the things he has said." Sophie handed Meekos his drink and sat down in a chair across from his.

"And what did you come up with?" Meekos asked.

"I think Erebus is absolutely right when he said we are too close to this mission to see everything clearly. And I think there is something else that you and I need to discuss. Meekos you know how much I love you. I cannot tell you how betrayed and angry I felt when Erebus and I learned you had destroyed our relationship."

"Meekos you saw the pain I went through. My life fell apart after that. Erebus and I are back together and you are just going to have to accept that."

"You already told me this," said Meekos angrily.

"I know but Erebus pointed out that my anger towards you and your emotions about him and I being back together are just making things worse. Our emotions are distracting us. Meekos for all of our sakes we both have to try and see more clearly," Sophie said. "Let's agree to put all of this aside. We have so many other things to focus on now."

"I agree," Meekos said with relief. Both Sophie and Meekos sat quietly for a few moments before Meekos spoke. "The reason I came here was to ask you if you thought there is a possibility that Pravis and Tenebrae could sell me out to save themselves."

"Meekos my dear brother open your eyes, of course they would. And you would do the same also."

Meekos sat quietly as he thought about Sophie's words. "Tonight I will send a message, telling them to contact Omnibus and tell him that Ahriman is sabotaging the ascension."

"And how will you explain that you will not be joining them?"

"Ahriman broke my arm once, I will tell them he has broken my leg and time is of the essence with this matter."

"Are you sure they will even get your message?" Sophie asked.

"I have figured that out," Meekos said. "This time I will send it by rider."

Meekos returned to his room and spent the rest of the night composing a letter to Pravis and Tenebrae. Letter after letter Meekos started then discarded until he had a small pile of crumpled papers scattered on the floor around his writing table. In part Meekos felt guilty trying to deceive his friends yet 'friends' was the word that he questioned. Meekos wrote that he believed their correspondence were being intercepted but he did not have any suspects as to who was taking the messages or why.

He wrote about Roch's disappearance and Sophie's experience with Ahriman. Meekos described in length the events which occurred in the caves that led to the deaths of Cerephus and Malus. But this is where Meekos changed the story. He wrote that he was hurt in the caves and was recuperating in Taperia with Sophie as his nurse.

Meekos described his fears that Ahriman was sabotaging the ascension and their inability to stop him. He requested Pravis and Tenebrae summon Omnibus and tell him about Arhiman's actions because he believed only Omnibus had the power to stop Ahriman. Meekos finished the letter by suggesting they start sending their letters by a rider instead of ravens.

Meekos re-read his letter with satisfaction. He sealed the envelope with wax and placed it on this writing table. Meekos noticed it was almost sunrise, so he decided to shave and dress for the day. Meekos realized he was whistling as he shaved; something he had not done for many years.

At sunrise, Meekos went to the front desk of the hotel and asked the two clerks to find him a rider, who could take a very important message to Nora.

"You will have to pay him," one clerk said.

"Of course I will pay him," Meekos said with annoyance. "In fact I will pay him very well. And if he can assure me he will get to Nora quickly there will be a bonus in it for him also. Do you know anyone who might be interested?"

The two clerks looked at each other as they were thinking. Then the older man said, "Jared might do it."

"Yes Jared," said the younger clerk. "I will go get him."

"Where is he?" asked Meekos.

"I will find him in one of the taverns," the young clerk responded.

"I don't want a drunk," Meekos snapped.

"Oh no, he's not a drunk, he's a hired fighter."

415

"That might be exactly what I need," Meekos said. "Bring him here to me. I will be having coffee in the dining room. If Jared works out there will be a bonus for both of you."

Meekos liked to sit at the dining tables near the windows so he could watch the bustling streets of Taperia. Even at this early hour people filled the streets. Meekos had just poured his second cup of coffee when he saw the young clerk walking towards the hotel; he was accompanied by a monster of a man.

Meekos estimated the man to be six foot nine or ten inches. He had long scraggly black hair that appeared to be partially in a ponytail. The man wore a long dangling earring in his left ear because his right ear had been cut off. As the two walked closer to the hotel, Meekos could see three scars on the man's right cheek. They were long, straight and parallel to each other as if they were made by claws.

"My Lord this is Jared," the young clerk introduced the man to Meekos.

"Thank you," Meekos said to the clerk. "You may leave us now." Then Meekos turned his attention to Jared. "Please have a seat," Meekos said as Jared sat down at the table.

Jared sat back in his chair and stared at Meekos. Jared was studying Meekos appearance and demeanor. Meekos suddenly felt like a boy again in the presence of a bully. "So young Ben tells me you need a job done," Jared said with half a sneer. "Let me guess, you need protection."

Meekos was intimidated by Jared but he was used to covering his fear. "I can protect myself," Meekos said as he stared Jared in the eyes. "What I need is a letter delivered to someone in Nora as quickly as possible. And I will pay you very well."

"What do you mean by very well?"

Meekos dropped a leather pouch of gold coins in front of Jared, who opened the bag and inspected its contents. "If you can get it there in less than three days there will be a bonus for you."

"Must be some letter," Jared said sarcastically.

"You have no idea," Meekos said with a grin. "Do we have a deal?"

"So how will you know if I get the letter to Nora in less than three days?" Jared asked.

"My friends will inform me," replied Meekos.

Jared left for Nora within the hour after his encounter with Meekos. What Jared did not know was that Meekos sent ravens to follow him. The two men did not trust each other; Meekos sent the ravens along as a means to keep tabs on Jared. What Meekos did not know, was that Jared had already been hired by Pravis and Tenebrae to spy on him.

Both Tenebrae and Pravis were concerned since they had not heard from Meekos in weeks. Because of the darkness of their souls, their concerns turned to paranoia and fear. Out of the three of them, they considered Meekos the most powerful dark lord. And they believed Meekos would turn against them in a moment to save himself or Sophie.

Jared was an intelligent and worldly man. He knew full well he had been hired by dark lords. But his assessment of the three men was that they were pretentious cowards. Jared despised weak people, he did not fear these dark lords, on the contrary; he expected to make a great deal of money from them.

Jared did not notice the five ravens that were following him and neither he nor the ravens realized a small flock of Enrops were following both of them. Jared rode quickly, but a voice in his head kept telling him to open the letter. Jared knew he would have to make a fire so he could steam the envelope open, all of which would take time and time was money for him in this job.

Jared had always considered himself a good judge of people; as he would often say, he had to be to survive. He saw the extravagant and expensive jewels the three high priests wore. Their skin was almost sickly white and their hands were soft and clean, which made Jared believe these men hired all of their work done. Jared laughed to himself as he thought about his first meeting with Tenebrae and Pravis and the airs they put on. "Weak, pretentious, hypocrites," Jared thought. "I will kill them all after I bleed them dry."

417

Jared traveled almost four hours when he stopped at a farm. He gave his horse to the farmer and took one of the farmer's horses. The farmer had no choice in the matter. Jared planned to keep switching to fresh horses on this journey. After two more hours of traveling, Jared decided to take a break from the midday sun. He stopped in a wooded area near the bank of the River Nebu. The canopy of the old trees provided cool shade for Jared and his horse.

As Jared sat near his campfire cooking his lunch, he suddenly felt like he was being watched. A man who lived by his instincts, Jared sat motionless, concentrating on locating the presence of the spy. Suddenly the large man grabbed a throwing star from his shirt and hurled the razor sharp projectile at a bush behind him. He heard a thud.

Jared grabbed a second star from his shirt as he listened for another intruder. There was movement in a bush to his right, he threw the second star and heard a strange squawk as it met its mark. A small flock of ravens flew into the air and disappeared.

"That bastard," Jared said as he pulled the sharp blades out of two dead ravens. "He's having me watched." Jared knew that ravens were the messengers of the dark lords. The revelation that Meekos had sent ravens to follow Jared; did not really surprise him but it did anger him. And Jared was not a man one wanted to anger. "Well let's see what that old bastard is so worried about," Jared said out loud.

Jared returned to his fire and placed a cup of water on the embers. As the water heated Jared took Meekos' letter from his pocket and examined it. Once the liquid started to boil, Jared skillfully loosened the seal of the wax stamp without damaging the envelope. After he read the letter he carefully resealed it. Within an hour Jared was back on the road.

Jared traveled hard for the next three hours; he stopped at the Village of Jarta and forced a blacksmith to give him a horse. As Jared rode he watched for ravens, a few were following him but they kept their distance and Jared was aware of their presence. The ravens were now aware that a flock of Enrops were following them. The Enrops greatly outnumbered the ravens. Jared too saw the Enrops but he did not make the connection, since he did not know that Enrops were the messengers for The Great Ruler.

Jared knew little about The Great Ruler because he had no time for a god.

Shortly after breakfast Lakin left six Ruala warriors to protect the women, everyone else left for parcel thirteen. Calen and Natasha had seen at least two hundred Hutas the night before; Lakin's warriors numbered much less. Gabriel, Raul and Simon stood on the same small hill that Calen and Natasha had used as an observation point. After almost an hour a group of twenty Hutas left the cave, they appeared to be a hunting party.

Lakin had his warriors wait until the Hutas were a good distance from the cave before he ordered the attack. The Rualas flew over the Hutas and showered them with arrows; many of the Hutas died before they realized they were being attacked. The Rualas hid the bodies of the Hutas and returned to the woods overlooking the cave.

It was almost two hours before another group of Hutas came out of the cave. These men were covered in war paint and were heading towards Nora. There were many farms between the caves and the City of Nora. Gabriel and the others believed this band of about thirty five warriors were seeking more victims for their unholy sacrifices. Ruala warriors attacked this group in the same manner, an aerial attack. After the bodies were hidden, the Rualas returned to their hiding places.

Gabriel and Lakin did not want the dark lords to know that Rualas were in the kingdom because that would expose the fact that followers of The Great Ruler were at hand. So Lakin ordered his warriors to pull their arrows out of the Huta bodies as they discarded them. No other Hutas were seen that morning.

By midday Gabriel decided that they should return to the house and get some sleep. Lakin left fifty of his warriors to patrol the area. Many of the Ruala warriors who had been staying in the bunkhouse and camping on Hannah's land had become quite bored and now anxiously took on this new assignment.

The Ruala people had not always been a race of warriors. For centuries their kind lived in the Kingdom of Norkv as farmers and hunters.

The Hutas, long being a tribe of demon worshipers with a sense of racial superiority sought to enslave and destroy all who were not of their race. The Hutas had always been a race of well trained and vicious warriors.

In the beginning, the Rualas were no match for the Hutas militarily. The Hutas would have killed the entire race of Rualas had the Sanuri not intervened and taken the Ruala survivors to the safety of the Ice Caves of Mordv. The Rualas healed and grew in numbers. They swore never again to be the victims of demons. The gratitude of the Ruala people to The Great Ruler and to the Sanuri knew no bounds. The Rualas swore a covenant with The Great Ruler that they would always work on His behalf, a covenant that lasted through eternity.

Over the next few days Ingr and Nikki both improved greatly. Thaos had little experience with babies and at first was reluctant to hold his small son; but his confidence grew quickly and after two days, Thaos did not want to put the baby down. Stephan's focus was on Ingr. He barely left her side. Ingr was not yet feeding the babies and Stephan did not leave her to spend time with the twins.

Shara and Sorren stayed at the castle and helped Bella and Claudius with the babies. Claudius hired several women as nursemaids until Ingr was well enough to feed her children. Nikki's mother came to the castle every day to help both Nikki and Ingr. The friendships among all of these people turned into a deep sense of family; something that Bella cherished greatly.

That night as Jared made camp he thought he heard a voice. With the skill and silence of a warrior, Jared searched the wooded area surrounding his campsite. He did not find anyone or even see any footprints that were not of wild animals. Jared returned to his fire. While his dinner was frying, Jared opened a bottle of whiskey and filled his cup. As Jared was putting the cup to his lips, he froze.

Once again Jared heard a voice, faint as it was; he recognized it as a man's voice. Jared got up a second time and searched the area around his campsite. This time he paid special attention to the areas above him, but again he saw no one.

Jared sat down again at his fire. He pulled the frying pan off from the flames and set it on the ground to cool. It was then that Jared's life would change. In the flames of the fire Jared clearly saw the face of a man, a man he did not recognize.

The man had dark skin and straight black hair that was pulled back into a ponytail. He wore both a mustache and a goatee that had highlights of gray, and the man's eyes were as black as the night. The man was screaming in pain and with rage. Jared could not believe is eyes and for just a moment he thought he was dreaming. Jared sat at the fire mesmerized; watching this man and trying to figure out what Roch was saying.

The Rualas had worked in shifts over the last couple of days as they spied upon the Hutas. During this time the Rualas led three more raids on Hutas warriors. The raids were well planned and organized. The Hutas realized their men were disappearing but they did not know how or why since the Rualas were careful to cover any sign of the conflicts. The Hutas started to wonder if their men were missing do to supernatural enemies. It was at this time they sent a warrior into Nora to find Pravis and Tenebrae.

Misha was a lieutenant in the Ruala army and was cousin to Lakin and Ibula as well as an adopted brother to Calen and Luca. Misha was put in charge of the warriors who were watching the cave. Lakin's orders were merely to observe the cave as he was awaiting word from the Sanuri about how they should proceed. The Rualas had fought men and low level demons before but the ascension of an Old One was a realm none of them had ever entered. Both Lakin and Gabriel were concerned that they might only get one change at stopping the ascension and they did not want anything to go wrong.

At sunrise Misha and the others saw a single Huta warrior on horseback, heading towards Nora. "Should we kill him?" Kev asked.

"No, this is most unusual," Misha said. "Kev, take four others and follow him. I will bet he is going to meet the high priests, so make sure you are not seen."

Fortunately for Kev and the other Ruala warriors the Huta was riding on a path that went through a forest. The Rualas concealed their presence behind the tree tops. But entering the City of Nora was more difficult. Even though it was barely past sunrise, there were many people on the streets. The Huta warrior seemed experienced in the city as he took a series of alleys to the Endleson Hotel. The Rualas tried to conceal themselves on rooftops as they followed him.

The Huta stopped at the alley outside of the kitchen in the Endleson Hotel. He remained on his horse and emitted a raspy hissing screech like a raven. The Huta repeated the screech three more times before High Priest Pravis stepped out on his balcony. When Pravis saw the Huta warrior, he returned to his room, got dressed and went to the alley.

The Ruala warriors could not hear what Pravis and the Huta were saying and if they could they would not have been able to understand the Huta dialect. The Huta remained in the alley as Pravis went to a stable and rented a horse, then the two men traveled back to the cave.

Misha had always had an adventurous personality. The previous night Misha had flown closer to the cave than any of the other Rualas. He was examining the top of the hill for openings into the cave. He found an opening at the very top, it was surrounded with brush. Misha didn't realize it was there until he accidently kicked a stone that fell through the brush and down into the bowels of the hill.

Misha cleared the brush away that exposed an opening barely big enough for a man to get through. In the darkness Misha could see little inside of the cave, except for the faint flickering of torches. Misha took the brush and concealed the opening before he left.

Now, after watching the Huta rider and the high priest disappear into the cave, Misha flew to the top of the hill. Three other Ruala warriors accompanied him as he took them to the pile of brush, which concealed the opening to the cave.

The hill was heavily wooded with large trees which prevented a great deal of sunlight from reaching the ground. This worked in the favor of the Rualas, because little sunlight entered the cave when they removed the brush.

Misha lay on his stomach and peered into the opening. The inside of the cave was now brightly lit with torches and a huge fire in a pit. Misha held his breath as he viewed the horrid sight below. Misha estimated there were two thousand Hutas gathered in the cave. They surrounded the high priest who was talking to them. Misha saw human bodies shackled to the stone walls, some of the bodies looked like they had been dead for weeks.

The walls of the cave had symbols painted all over them, symbols that were painted in blood. Misha continued to spy on the Hutas until Pravis left the cave and rode back to Nora. Then Misha covered the opening and he and the three Rualas returned to their observation hill. Misha wrote down everything he saw and gave the note to Ty. "Take this to Lakin and Gabriel as fast as you can, I am not sure what is going on but I fear the ascension is close at hand." Ty left immediately for Hannah's house.

Jared entered Nora early on the morning of the third day after he left Meekos in Taperia. Jared traveled on little sleep; partly because he wanted to get to Nora quickly and earn his bonus and partly because he found himself haunted by the face and voice of Roch. Jared could hear Roch's voice screaming but he could not make out the words that Roch said. The first two nights, Jared saw Roch's face in the flames of his fire. But on this morning of the third day, Jared heard Roch's screams as he rode into Nora.

Kev and two other Rualas followed Pravis back to Nora. The high priest was oblivious to their presence. They followed him into the city. Pravis took his horse back to the stable and walked to the hotel. Just as he was about to enter the lobby a large man rode up to the hotel and called Pravis by name. Pravis turned and greeted the man and they both entered the hotel.

As soon as these men were out of sight the Rualas heard the sounds of battle as the Enrops attacked the ravens that had been following Jared. The screeching was loud in the early morning hours but no one seemed to notice except for the Ruala warriors. When the battle was over, the Enrops flew to the Rualas and told them they had been following a rider sent by Meekos. Kev sent the Enrops to Lakin and Gabriel and he and the other warriors returned to Misha.

Everyone was seated at the breakfast table when Gabriel walked into the room carrying two large envelopes. "I no sooner asked an Enrop to deliver a letter to the Sanuri when these arrived," Gabriel said as he handed the envelopes to Raul and Simon. Each envelope was addressed to both brothers. Raul opened the largest one first and immediately started to laugh.

"This is to us both," Raul said. "It's from Mother and she has written in huge words to read this letter before handing out the other envelopes. Raul looked inside of the large envelope and found four smaller ones. Raul started to read the letter to himself, then announced that he was going to read it out loud.

My dear sons, we miss you greatly. We all enjoy your letters and have come to feel as if we know the people you are living and working with. I was shocked when you told me that Hannah was that beautiful young physician that I had met at the orphanage. She was so loving with the children and devoted many hours caring for them. The priests and the children loved her and please tell her they still speak of her. I guess I was shocked because once again the utter cruelty of Roch was thrust upon me. I am so sorry that a member of our family has destroyed so many others.

But on a brighter note, the girls and I were overwhelmed to receive the beautiful pink diamonds that Hannah sent to us as gifts. And your father loves the books that you sent from her father's collection. But I must explain something here. As all children would be, Petra was rather disappointed that he did not receive a gift. Sudfad told him that instead of sending Petra something that Hannah had asked Sudfad to buy him a puppy. The reason I am telling you this is because Petra sent a thank you letter to Hannah and she will have no idea why unless you explain it to her."

"Now I feel awful," Hannah said. "I forgot about the boy, Gabriel you all saved him, how could I forget about him?"

"Hannah don't feel bad," Simon said. "Petra loves animals more than anything else. The best gift he could receive would be another pet."

"In fact we are beginning to suspect that Petra can communicate with animals like the Sanuri does," Raul said as he handed an envelope to Hannah. Her name was written in a childish scrawl and there were drawings of flowers and butterflies on the envelope. Hannah opened it and started to laugh "He wants to thank me for his German shepherd puppy which he named Max and he drew me a picture of the dog." Hannah handed the letter to Gabriel.

Raul continued to read the letter from Renya. *"Hannah certainly did not have to send us gifts because of the rings. Sudfad and I are just happy that your friends chose those rings for their weddings. And this my sons brings me to the additional three envelopes with this letter. We all look forward to your daily letters and as I said, we feel as if your friends have become a part of our family. I know that people can feel intimidated to tell the King and Queen no, so I want you to ask your friends if they will allow us to have a wedding celebration in their honor, when you all come to the castle.*

This will be a separate event from the one Sudfad has organized to honor the brave warriors who saved our son. I have included an envelope for each couple. *I would like them to provide me with guest's lists of family and friends who they would like to attend the ceremony. We will make travel and lodging accommodations for everyone. There are also other questions that I need answered. We will not be offended if they turn down our offer because we realize they may not want to celebrate their weddings with strangers."*

Simon distributed the envelopes as Raul read the letter. Both Raul and Simon were smiling as this letter was so typical of their mother.

"Is your mother serious?" Natasha asked in disbelief.

"Oh yes," Simon said. "Mother loves to have celebrations."

"I am afraid that my guest list will be very small," Hannah said with a warm smile. "My only family is sitting at this table."

"Mine too," Gabriel said as he held Hannah's hand.

"Well, Calen's family will make up for it, I'll bet we have a hundred cousins," Luca said with a chuckle.

425

"Is he telling the truth?" Natasha asked as she looked at Calen; who smiled and nodded his head.

"My parents will be so honored when they hear this," Calen said.

"Mother is serious, tell her what you want," said Raul. "You were at the celebration she had when we came home; you saw how much she loves to organize things."

Calen looked at Natasha, "The celebration lasted for two weeks; there were all kinds of entertainment and competitions and dances. It was great fun."

"Calen I don't know what to ask for," Natasha whispered.

Calen smiled, "We can talk about it later."

"You can always just tell Mother you don't know what to ask for," Simon said. "Believe me she will come up with something great."

Raul waited for everyone to stop talking before he finished reading the letter to them. *"I understand that none of you know when you will be coming to Wetpr, so I am wondering do all of their families know they are on a mission? If not, how would they like me to explain the possible short notice before the event? Also before you come to the castle I want to share something with your friends.*

Petra appears to have been more overwhelmed by his rescue than we originally thought. He keeps asking us the names and descriptions of the people who rescued him because he wants to thank them all. He remembers Prince Lakin because Lakin flew him home. And he remembers a large Ruala warrior who saved him and was married to the pretty lady who gave him cookies. So as not to offend anyone please explain this to your friends.

And before closing I have a message I want you to give to Hannah. I can't believe she would think that I would not remember her. Please tell her that her dream house is now vacant. Madam Grenda has recently died and has no family to leave the house to. Hannah longed to look at the inside of that house and now she can when she comes to Wetpr.

426

"I cannot believe the Queen remembers our conversation about that house," Hannah said emotionally.

"What is she talking about?" asked Gabriel.

"Oh you will think it is foolish but when I would go to the orphanage I would pass this incredible house that I just fell in love with. It is in Salar and backs up to the River Nebu. It's surrounded with fruit trees and gardens and has a huge horse stable."

Simon started to laugh, "Both Raul and I have spent a great deal of time in that house helping Madam Grenda. We were always getting into trouble and to teach us responsibility..."

"And humility," Raul interrupted with a laugh.

"Our parents would send us out to help other people, we picked Madam Grenda's fruit crops every year and she would make us the best pies. It is a beautiful home."

"Remember how mad she got when she caught us chasing the swans in her pond?" Raul asked as the memory made him laugh. "I thought she was going to beat the tar out of us."

"Gabriel can we look through the house when we are in Wetpr? I know you must think me silly."

"Of course we can. This is the first time you have ever talked about anything you wanted," Gabriel said as he watched the expression on Hannah's face. Gabriel turned to Raul and Simon. "Do you know how much land is with this house?"

"I don't know, twenty or thirty acres," Raul said. "There is also a large pier on the property because the river is very deep there."

"And how many rooms?" Gabriel asked.

"How many did we paint?" Simon asked Raul with a grin.

"I'd say that house is at least as big and nice as this one," Raul said.

"Hannah you have given me so many gifts and I have yet to give you one," Gabriel said. "Would you like that house?"

"We may not live there year round but it can be one of our homes." Hannah stared at Gabriel in disbelief then she started to cry. "I will take that as a yes," Gabriel said as he put his arms around her. Natasha smiled and squeezed Calen's arm as she watched Gabriel and Hannah.

"Raul, Simon do you think I could impose upon your parents to purchase that house for us if I send them the money?"

"I think they would do it gladly," Raul said.

"You don't know our mother and wives yet, not only will they purchase the house they will clean it and have your first dinner on the table," Simon said with a grin. "But seriously it would be nice if you lived in Salar. I believe our families would really enjoy each other. Except for one small thing, I did not tell them that Natasha and I almost died from those demon snakes; that is a conversation I will have when we get home."

"So was it a coincidence that Meekos hired you to deliver this letter?" Tenebrae asked as the three men sat down in his chambers.

"Not at all," Jared said. "I paid the hotel staff to get me if Meekos started looking for anything or anyone."

"You're a smart man," said Tenebrae.

Jared watched as Pravis opened the sealed envelope. Pravis had no inkling that Jared had tampered with it. Tenebrae and Jared watched Pravis as he read the letter. Pravis' eyes grew wide and the color left his face; by the time Pravis finished the last page, Jared could see Pravis' left eye was twitching. Pravis handed the letter to Tenebrae without saying a word. Pravis walked across the room and poured three glasses of whiskey then returned to the others. Terror consumed Tenebrae as he read the letter. He gulped his glass of whiskey down and looked at Pravis.

"I don't know what's in that letter but Meekos looked as scared as you two," Jared said as he sipped his whiskey. "Do you want me to take a note back to him?"

"Jared, we need some time to discuss this, could you meet us in the dining room at noon?" Pravis asked.

"Sure, but I need to get a couple of hours of sleep. Meekos said he would pay me a bonus if I got this to you in less than three days."

"Come, let's go downstairs," Pravis said. "I will pay for your room and we will give you a bonus too. That letter is very important."

Jared turned and looked at Tenebrae as he was leaving the room. Tenebrae was refilling his glass with whiskey and his hands were shaking so badly he was spilling the liquid onto the floor.

Jared ate breakfast in the dining room of the Endleson Hotel before he went to his room. He noticed the stares he was getting from people. Some men would be self-conscious by such behavior but not Jared, he liked to disturb people. Jared laughed to himself when he thought about how frightened the dark lords were. "Those fools pretend they are priests but they work for demons, they deserve whatever they get," he thought.

But the more Jared thought about the situation of the priests the more he realized he could find a way to profit from it. Jared was feeling rather smug when he left the dining room and entered his lavish chambers. His room was on the second floor so he had a large balcony off from his parlor. Jared looked through the rooms, then pulled off his boots and jacket and lay on the bed. No sooner had he closed his eyes than he heard that screaming voice again. Jared sat up in bed, feeling annoyed.

"I don't know what is going on here," Jared said out loud. "I know I'm not crazy, so if you are a ghost or demon who is screaming at me; I can't understand a damn thing you are saying. So either shut the hell up or say something I can understand." Jared lay back down and pulled the covers over him.

Lakin, Gabriel and the others were still sitting at the breakfast table when Ty ran into the house. He handed Misha's letter to Lakin who read it then handed it to Gabriel. "Ty tell Misha I don't want our warriors to engage the Hutas, they should just observe. I will be sending this note to the Sanuri," Lakin said.

"Ty wait a minute," Hannah called from the kitchen as she and Natasha quickly packed up a large basket of food for the warriors.

Within moments from Ty's departure a small flock of Enrops landed at Hannah's house. Three of them flew in through an open kitchen window. They told Gabriel and the others about Jared and the high priests. Gabriel added a few lines at the bottom of Misha's note.

"Can you take this to the Sanuri or do you need to rest from your journey?" Gabriel asked.

"We can take it, we rested when the rider did," the Enrop said and grabbed the note.

"Misha discovered an opening in the top of the hill that contains the cave. This morning he was watching almost two thousand Hutas with one of the high priests. He said there were dead bodies shackled to the walls of the cave." Lakin explained somberly.

"Two thousand," Natasha gasped.

During the breakfast meal, Raul had opened the first envelope from their family and read Renya's letter to everyone. Simon had opened the second envelope which contained letters from their wives and a packet from Sudfad. Before anyone else could comment about Misha's discovery, Simon turned to Gabriel. "Fathers papers arrived." Gabriel looked at Hannah then at Calen.

"I have a couple of things to say then Raul, Simon and I have to go into Nora," Gabriel said.

"Can I go with you?" Natasha asked. "I need to buy some clothes; I have been wearing Hannah's."

"Natasha I want you to stay here today," Gabriel replied solemnly. "I don't think Hannah minds and besides, her clothes look great on you," Gabriel added with a smile. "As many of you who have been on missions before know, sometimes we spend weeks waiting then things suddenly turn into a mad rush and we have to leave quickly. I expect that will be the same on this mission."

"I know many of you, including myself want to take things from this house, so I hired some men who I often use for odd jobs. They will be arriving here in three days with several large covered bocas. I don't believe there will be time to take things back to the Ice Caves, so I want everyone to fill the bocas with the things you choose."

"The men will drive the bocas to Sudfad's castle. Raul and Simon suggested we leave the bocas at the castle since we will all be going there after the mission." Gabriel turned to Hannah, "Dear this is your home that is filled with memories; please take everything you want. I am expecting three to four bocas so there will be room for furniture, carpets, just anything you want to take."

Gabriel turned back to the group. "Also, we have some business in the city that I expect will stir up a lot of trouble, so that is another reason everyone should be prepared to leave."

"Gabriel what is going on?" asked Natasha.

"As you know Hannah and I own a great deal of the property and businesses in Nora; or at least the managing shares of businesses. We own gold mines and this beautiful property. But neither Hannah nor I have any desire to stay here or even to be attached to this city."

"So we are selling everything to King Sudfad. He will control the largest and richest city in this kingdom. Raul, Simon and I will be going into Nora to put the deeds into the King's name. Since men tried to kill us when the deeds were put into Hannah's and my names, we are expecting a fight today. Lakin and many of his warriors will be coming with us."

"But you will be exposing Raul and Simon's identities," Natasha said with concern.

"Yes and we may be exposing the Rualas today also," Gabriel replied. "Luca, Rabi and a few others are going to stay here for protection and to help you pack. I would suggest you spend the day preparing for our departure."

Chapter XXVII
Betrayer

The Sanuri had just finished christening babies Marcus, Sicily, Titus and Sarah all in one ceremony. Ingr could not get out of bed so they held the ceremony in her bedroom. Ingr wanted the twins christened as soon as possible. She knew she was too weak to leave her room so she had asked Bella to take her place. Ingr was happily surprised when the families brought the ceremony to her. As everyone was leaving the bedroom Ingr asked the Sanuri to stay. Stephan turned to her and asked, "Do you want me to stay also?"

Ingr hesitated, "I really would like to speak with him alone, I hope you aren't mad."

"Of course not," Stephan said and leaned down and kissed Ingr on the forehead. Then he walked out of the room holding his son.

"Sanuri I want to thank you for saving my life," Ingr said. "But I have some questions and something I should probably tell you."

The Sanuri sat down in one of the chairs near her bed. "Ask me whatever you like."

"Will I be able to have more children after he cut me up like this?"

"Let me touch your head, it won't hurt." The Sanuri put the palms of his hands on both sides of Ingr's head. After several minutes he removed his hands and sat back in the chair. "When I heal someone the healing is actually done by The Great Ruler I am merely the instrument. From what I can tell he is healing you completely. I believe you will have many more children."

"Oh thank you," Ingr said with a sigh of relief. "You know I really didn't plan to have the twins, but once they were born everything changed. I am so happy with them. Sanuri did I die and come back to life?"

"I was wondering if you would remember that."

"I remembered dancing down a path and I was surrounded by an intense light. I felt warm and loved and very happy. I was looking for Stephan and the babies when I suddenly heard his voice and I came back. Did you see all of that?"

"I did not see the vision you had but I knew you had died just before I started to heal you."

"If you didn't see that well then you didn't see the other thing did you?"

"Ingr I don't know what you are talking about."

"Sanuri will you hand me that paper and pencil that's on the table?"

The Sanuri brought Ingr the items she requested and waited in silence as she drew some pictures. Ingr worked intently for almost twenty minutes, then she looked up from her work. "Sanuri I told you that I turned back when I heard Stephan's voice. But in a brief moment it seemed like I was between worlds. I was no longer in the light but I wasn't back here. And in those moments I think I went to hell or someplace really dark."

"Ingr you are such a good and faithful person, you don't have to worry that you will go to hell," the Sanuri said warmly.

"No Sanuri you don't understand, something stopped me, something really evil and told me to give you a message. Well I forgot about it, then I started to see it in my dreams." Ingr handed the Sanuri the two sheets of paper. "Do you know them?" she asked.

"Yes, what did they say?"

"Those two on the first page didn't say anything, they were both screaming or they looked like they were screaming but I couldn't hear their voices. Who are they?"

"This one is King Roch, at least how he used to look several years ago and the other is Cerephus; he declared himself King of Stordt some months ago. You say they appeared to be screaming, like they were angry or in pain?"

"It seemed like both, but I remembered seeing terror in their eyes. Then I heard a voice laughing. It was an evil voice that scared me. He said for me to tell you that he was waiting for you. He said thirteen levels; thirteen doors. He said you would understand."

The Sanuri suddenly thought about the test The Great Ruler had put him through, he descended thirteen levels to a room with thirteen doors but he could not see how this was connected. "Did he say anything else?" the Sanuri asked.

"He said he knew who The Seven Sons were and he planned to kill them all. I don't know what he was talking about do you?"

"Yes, I do." The Sanuri looked at the second sheet of paper. "I don't know this man, was he screaming like the others?"

"No, I think he is in this world, I saw him riding a horse. I know the picture looks strange but he only had one ear and those big scars on his face."

"Ingr you say you have been seeing these in your dreams too?"

"Yes and I hear the voice, it tells me to give you the message."

The Sanuri stood up and raised his hands towards the heavens. As he prayed the room was filled with light. "That darkness will not touch you again," the Sanuri explained. "It's like a door was open; that allowed him to talk to you."

"Sanuri, the voice was coming from an open door in a cave; or rather it looked like a big hole."

Jared was sitting in the dining room of the Endleson Hotel waiting for his noon meeting with Pravis and Tenebrae. Both priests were late when they joined Jared at his table. "Are you gents feeling better?" he asked sarcastically.

"Not really," Pravis replied. "We still are going over our options. You said that Meekos seemed scared?"

"Meekos seems like the kind of man that would be scared of his own shadow," Jared replied.

434

"Actually Meekos isn't that kind of man at all," Tenebrae said. "That's what worries us."

"Jared, this matter we are dealing with is very dangerous and very delicate. Would you mind staying in town for a day or two until we figure out what we are going to do?" Pravis asked as he put a pouch of gold coins in front of Jared. "Your room, meals and bar bill are on my bill, this is just extra expense money."

Suddenly the hair on the back of Jared's neck started to rise; he was getting a bad feeling in the pit of his stomach. "So why are you being so generous?" Jared asked skeptically.

"Because we might need your services at a moment's notice," Pravis replied.

Jared did not believe what Pravis said. "Well, if this deal you all are mixed up in is that dangerous, maybe you should start paying me in advance," Jared said as he sipped his coffee.

When the Sanuri walked out of Ingr's bedroom, Claudius handed him two pieces of paper. "They weren't delivered together," Claudius said.

The first note was from Gabriel and Lakin. They briefly wrote about the experiences that Simon, Natasha and Gabriel had. They ended the letter with information about parcel thirteen, which they had not yet identified. The second letter was from Sudfad, asking the Sanuri to return to the castle immediately, there was no explanation. The Sanuri walked into the dining room to tell the families he was leaving.

"Will you give this to Aunt Renya," Matthew said as he handed a large envelope to the Sanuri. "I usually write to her every week but I haven't written since we left for Sendra; there was a lot to tell her."

The Sanuri smiled as he took the letter, "I will do my best to fill them in also." Then he searched the crowded room for Stephan. "Stephan you should speak with Ingr."

"Is something wrong?" Stephan asked with great concern.

"Not like you are thinking. She will explain."

435

"Sanuri tell us," Claudius said with fear in his voice.

"Ingr died just before I started to heal her. She had an experience of going to The Great Ruler, then she heard Stephan's voice and came back."

"Yes, she told me about that," Stephan said. "I thought it was a dream."

"It was not," the Sanuri continued. "In a brief moment when she was between the two worlds she had an encounter with a powerful demon, I believe it was Ahriman. The demon wanted Ingr to give me a message. She forgot so he has plagued her dreams. I believe I have closed the door that allowed him to communicate with her but if it continues I want you to contact me immediately."

"Is she in danger?" Bella gasped.

"I would say no. The demon is taunting me. But he showed her these faces," the Sanuri said as he handed the drawings to Stephan. "Ingr did not know who they were but that is Roch and Cerephus, the third man I don't know. I don't understand the message behind these."

As soon as the men left for Nora, Hannah, Natasha and Marcia quickly cleared the morning dishes then started on the enormous job of packing. There was a large covered porch on the back of the house, which Rabi and Luca cleared, so they could store the packed items on it. Luca brought dozens of wooden crates from the wine cellar, while Rabi carried in more crates from the bunk house. Luca was carrying some empty crates to the second floor where the women were starting. As Luca walked past one of the bedrooms he saw Natasha doubled up on a bed.

"Natasha are you alright?" Luca asked as he ran to her side.

"Yes, it's nothing, I'm fine," Natasha replied as she sat up.

"You don't look fine; you're white as a ghost, I getting Hannah."

"No Luca," Natasha said as she grabbed his arm. "Really I am fine."

"Hannah," Luca yelled. "We need you in Natasha's bedroom."

"Luca don't," Natasha pleaded. "I don't want to bother her."

"What is it?" Hannah asked as she ran into the room, followed by Rabi and Marcia.

"I found her doubled up on the bed and she is really pale," Luca said with concern.

"I am fine, I was just nauseous," Natasha said with embarrassment.

"How long have you been like this?" Hannah asked as she felt Natasha's forehead and examined her eyes.

Natasha hesitated, "A couple of weeks."

"Natasha I thought you said your only symptom was being overly emotional," Hannah said. "Well at least you know the demon snake didn't kill the baby. What is it Natasha you don't look happy, is something wrong?" Natasha did not answer. "Does Calen know?' Hannah continued.

"No, I am afraid he will send me away and I don't want to leave," Natasha said almost crying. "That's why I haven't said anything."

"Are you pregnant?" Luca asked with relief.

Natasha nodded her head, "I know he will be excited but he already told me I had to stop working on missions when I got pregnant."

"Gabriel said the same thing," Luca said. "But that doesn't mean Calen will send you away, he's just not going to let you participate."

"You think so?" Natasha asked with tears in her eyes.

"Honey where would Calen send you anyways?" Luca asked.

"I don't know, the Ice Caves. I don't know anyone there. And all I would do is worry about the rest of you."

Hannah sat on the bed next to Natasha and put her arm around Natasha's shoulders. "You have to tell him, the symptoms are only going to get worse," Hannah explained. "And besides you don't want Calen to think you are keeping things from him."

"She's right," Rabi said. "You should tell him when he returns today. I know how I would feel if Marcia kept something like that from me."

Natasha leaned her head against Hannah and cried.

Hannah's office and apartment in Nora were almost empty but the rooms were large enough to hide Lakin's warriors. The office was but a few blocks from the Land Title Company and the Register of Deeds office where Gabriel, Raul and Simon were headed. A dozen Ruala warriors were stationed on various roof tops watching for signs of trouble. Lakin and his men were prepared for battle. The old clerk nervously prepared the paperwork. "Is there anyone hiding in the back room today?" Raul asked.

"No and I had nothing to do with that before," the clerk replied. "That was one of Lloyd's men. They told me they would kill me if I said anything." When the last of the paperwork was signed and sealed the clerk handed everything to Raul and said, "Well I'll be damned the King of Wetpr owns Nora. Maybe we will get some law here now."

Gabriel, Simon and Raul left the Title Office and rode to the Endleson Hotel. Jared was still in the dining room and watched them dismount and enter the hotel. Pravis and Tenebrae were sitting at the table with their backs to the window. Jared recognized the two Princes of Wetpr but did not say anything to the priests. Gabriel, Simon and Raul walked directly into Endleson's office and closed the door.

"What is the meaning of this?" Augustus Endleson demanded as he stood up at his desk.

"Augustus allow me to introduce Prince Raul and Prince Simon of the Kingdom of Wetpr," Gabriel said with a satisfied grin. Hannah and I have sold King Sudfad all of our holdings in Nora, which means he owns sixty-five percent of your hotel."

"We know you are a member of the Insidiae and donated a mine to Pravis and Tenebrae for the ascension of Omnibus. You will give us maps of that mine and tell us what you know."

Endleson almost collapsed into his seat. His face turned red then white and he started to sweat profusely.

"We are waiting," Gabriel said sternly.

"In that case on the chair," Endleson stuttered and pointed to a small suitcase. Simon picked up the suitcase and put it on the desk. Gabriel opened it; the case contained only papers and maps, no weapons. Gabriel shoved the suitcase at Endleson, who nervously shuffled through the papers. He picked up a series of small maps that were fastened together. "Here, turn to page thirteen," Endleson said and handed the maps to Gabriel.

"Are these maps accurate?" demanded Simon.

"They were accurate up until the priests took over control of the mines, I don't know what changes they have made."

"Now start talking," Gabriel said.

"You're right I am a member of the Insidiae and I have been for a long time. But I am not part of the group that is trying to raise Omnibus; in fact I think they are insane. That demon will destroy this world. Just so you know only a small portion of the members of the Insidiae are involved with that plot. The three of you met my dear wife the other night, she knows nothing of this."

"I have secretly been trying to sell our holdings so that I can move her from here," Endleson continued. "Even if the ascension is not successful those crazy priests have brought hundreds of Hutas here and who knows what they will do. Please I beg of you; I will gladly sign all of my holdings over to King Sudfad if you allow my wife and me to leave this place. We will be of no trouble to you, I promise."

"Where will you go?" asked Raul.

"Her sister lives in the Kingdom of Gandt; I thought we would go there first."

"We will consider it, let me speak with my brother," Raul said and he and Simon walked several feet from Endleson's desk and spoke in whispers. When they returned to the desk Raul said, "Unless Gabriel is against it, we will make that deal with you. But you sign everything over to us now."

Endleson had a pleading look on his face as he looked at Gabriel. "Alright," Gabriel said. "But tell us everything you know about the ascension."

Endleson quickly wrote some numbers on a small piece of paper and handed it to Simon. "That's the combination for the safe, all of the deeds are in there, help yourself." Then he turned to Gabriel. "Thank you we will leave this day."

"The ascension," Raul said.

"I am not friends with those two priests so I rarely talk to them about this. I know they came here terrified because the original location for the ascension had been destroyed by the emissaries of The Great Ruler. They have had a lot of work done in those caves to prepare for Omnibus, but I cannot tell you what all they have had done. Most of the time when I see them they are drunk and with prostitutes; they disgust me."

Simon had organized the deeds and now placed them in front of Endleson, who grabbed a pen and started to sign them. "Your father now owns the majority of the gold mines in Nora, a few are owned by private investors," Endleson said as he divided the deeds into groups and was handing each group to Simon.

"Don't get those deeds confused with these," Endleson said. "These are for the Tange mines outside of Tanger. You now own a third of those mines. Here are the titles for two transportation companies. I move some of the gold over land and some by water. Here are the deeds for my businesses, which include a refinery as well as this hotel. I have been buying land on the outskirts of the city with the idea of building new businesses, those are the remaining deeds."

"Why are you giving all of this up so easily?" Raul asked suspiciously.

"Because if those fools are successful Omnibus will destroy all of it anyway and if they aren't successful I fear they will unleash the Hutas upon us. I had already resigned myself to the fact I was going to lose everything. My wife and I have considerable savings we can start over someplace else."

"Back to the ascension," Gabriel said.

"Now mind you I am not part of that group but I had heard from other members of the Insidiae that the timing had to be perfect for Omnibus to be able to escape from The Abyss. He will have to leave his body or form behind so he needs one in this world that is evil enough to contain his essence. That is why they have spent generations creating Roch."

"One night when Tenebrae was drunk he was bragging that Meekos had left to get Roch but that was weeks ago and he has not returned. And those two drunks out there have been acting really nervous. That is why they hired that mean looking guy sitting at the table with them now, he is supposed to spy on Meekos."

"Why do they want to spy on Meekos?" asked Simon.

"Because they sold their souls to Omnibus, if anything goes wrong he is going to collect with a vengeance."

"But how can he collect when he is imprisoned in The Abyss?" Gabriel asked.

"I know and no demon has ever been able to escape from The Abyss. Personally I think there is more going on here than perhaps even those priests know."

"What do you mean?" asked Gabriel.

"From what I have heard, no demon has ever been able to reach out from their prison in The Abyss, which means there must be other powerful demons, probably Old Ones working with Omnibus or impersonating him."

"Impersonating him, why would they do that?" Raul asked.

"The Old Ones have been around since time itself. Who knows what plans or vendettas they have." Endleson said.

441

"So is it correct that to become a member of the Insidiae you have to make a pact with a demon?" Gabriel asked.

"Yes but not all pacts require one to sell their soul."

"Who did you make a pact with?" asked Gabriel.

Endleson hesitated, "Petorus, I pay him homage in a variety of ways but I have not sold my soul."

"Not Ahriman?"

"Ahriman, no, why do you ask?"

"Because I encountered him in Meekos' hotel room."

Endleson stared at Gabriel suspiciously. "You tell me you encountered Ahriman and you live to talk about it, just who are you?"

"I am High Priest Gabriel of the Patronus and I work on behalf of The Great Ruler."

"Well, he must protect you greatly because Ahriman is said to be the most powerful of the Old Ones. But why would Ahriman be in one of these hotel rooms?"

"There was also an unholy altar in there."

"Perhaps but we all pay homage at unholy altars and rarely does a demon speak to any of us, or acknowledge us for that matter. So I take it you are going to try and stop the ascension. You may not believe this but I wish you luck. I like this world just the way it is."

"There are rumors that Ahriman is trying to sabotage the ascension. Do you know anything about that?" Gabriel asked.

"I had not heard that but I am not really surprised. Demons treat each other as badly as they treat humans. They are nothing but arrogance, hatred and jealousy and they all desire ultimate power. There aren't as many allegiances among them as some people think. If Omnibus returns he will be competition for the other demons; they may not be welcoming him back."

"I don't understand," said Raul.

442

"Ok, I am just going to explain it as I see it," Endleson said. "It all reminds me of a giant board game and the demons are playing against each other and at least in their minds against The Great Ruler. All of us people are nothing more than pawns. So some demons may try to help Omnibus because it somehow benefits them while others may try to stop him."

When Gabriel, Raul and Simon walked out of the hotel they all looked into the dining room at Jared, who was staring back at them. Jared continued to watch them through the window, when he caught a movement out of the corner of his eye. It was then that Jared saw a Ruala warrior on a roof top across the street from the hotel.

"Excuse me gents," Jared said as he stood up. "I believe I just saw someone I know." Before Jared had moved from the table he was stopped abruptly by the sound of a blood curdling scream.

As soon as the door closed behind Gabriel, Simon and Raul; Endleson jumped up and quickly threw the money from the safe into the suitcase on his desk.

"So you think we are all filled with arrogance, jealousies and hatred," a voice said. "Betrayer, there is a special place in hell for your treachery."

Endleson was frozen in place. His heart was pounding so hard he felt that he couldn't think. "Who are you?"

"What does it matter, you betrayed us all."

"Please let me make it up to you," Endleson pleaded. "What do you need me to do?"

"You gave our secrets to the emissaries of The Great Ruler. You broke your covenant."

"Please, I didn't know who they were at first. Besides I didn't tell them much."

"You told them more than you realize."

"Well if you knew who they were, why didn't you stop them from coming here?" Endleson snapped. "I thought you were supposed to be stronger than The Great Ruler."

Pravis and Tenebrae jumped up from the table. They watched as hotel staff ran to Endleson's office. Then they heard a woman scream. Pravis, Tenebrae and Jared pushed their way through the crowd and peered into Endleson's office. On the carpet was the silhouette of a man made from shouldering ashes. Jared looked at the faces of his two companions; both Pravis and Tenebrae were shaking and sweating.

"Was he a friend of yours?" Jared asked.

"A business acquaintance," Pravis answered in a hoarse whisper.

"The same business you and Meekos are in?"

Before he could stop himself, Pravis nodded.

"I guess you weren't lying about it being dangerous," Jared said and returned to the dining room.

Gabriel, Raul and Simon were all riding their horses side by side. "It's too quiet," Raul said.

"I don't think Endleson would send anyone after us," Gabriel said. "I believe he wants to get as far away from here as possible."

The three warriors kept looking up at their Ruala friends for information that they were being followed. They were all surprised and suspicious that the journey to Hannah's house was uneventful.

"You're back so soon," Hannah said as she ran up to Gabriel as he and some of the others entered the parlor. "How did everything go?"

Gabriel kissed Hannah then said, "No one tried to attack us, which makes me wonder what is going on. We confronted Endleson. He was so afraid of Omnibus and the Hutas that he signed all of his holdings over to King Sudfad in exchange for us letting him and his wife leave."

"Twenty-seven more deeds," Simon said as he held up two large pouches of papers.

"Boy you have really been packing," Calen remarked as he and Lakin walked into the parlor.

"Lakin could we send some of your warriors to deliver these deeds to Father?" Raul asked. "I think they are too heavy for the Enrops to carry."

"Certainly," Lakin replied. He turned and walked out the door to get some warriors.

Natasha walked into the room; Luca kept staring at her, which made Natasha feel uncomfortable. Natasha did not want to tell Calen she was pregnant and she did not want Luca to pressure her. Finally Natasha looked at Luca and shook her head from side to side, to indicate she wasn't going to say anything.

"I've got some saddle bags we can put those pouches in," Gabriel said as he started to leave the room.

"Calen your wife needs to talk to you," Luca said sternly. Everyone in the room stopped and turned to Natasha.

"Is something the matter?" Calen asked but Natasha did not answer him. Calen saw the looks on Rabi's and Hannah's faces, as did Gabriel.

"What is going on here?" Gabriel asked.

"Natasha needs to talk with Calen," said Hannah.

Calen looked at Natasha, he was growing concerned and the tears in her eyes scared him. "Natasha tell me what is going on."

Natasha started crying harder, Gabriel took a step towards Natasha but Luca grabbed his arm to stop him. Natasha could barely speak, "Calen, I'm, I'm, we're going to have a baby."

445

All of the fear left Calen's body. "Honey that is wonderful," Calen said happily then he paused. "But why are you crying?"

"Because I don't want you to send me away. I want to stay here with you and the others. I don't know anyone in the Ice Caves yet." By the time Natasha finished the last sentence she was sobbing. Calen grabbed Natasha and hugged her tightly.

"Honey I'm not sending you away, why would you think that?" Now everyone's looks of concerns were turning into smiles.

"Because you said I had to stop working on the missions when I got pregnant," Natasha said.

"As of this moment you aren't working on this mission any longer, but you are staying here with me," Calen said and kissed Natasha on the forehead. "Gabriel do you have anything you want to say?" asked Calen.

"I agree with Calen's decisions," Gabriel said as he warmly smiled at Natasha.

"Really? I don't have to go?"

"You're not going anywhere without me," Calen said as he was beaming with the news that he was going to be a father.

"That's why I didn't tell you before Calen," Natasha said. "I'm sorry."

"How far along are you?" asked Calen.

"I don't know," Natasha said and started to sob again.

Raul turned to Simon. "This is just like watching you and Annabelle," Raul said with a grin.

Chapter XXVIII
Heritage

Jared pushed his way through the crowd that had gathered outside of Endleson's office. He walked through the lobby of the hotel and out the front door. "What would bring the Princes of Wetpr to Stordt and why did a demon kill Endleson as soon as they left his office?" Jared thought as he walked down the street looking for the Princes. "And why would Ruala warriors be here and sneaking around rooftops?" Many questions filled Jared's head as he searched the streets.

That bad feeling in the pit of Jared's stomach was getting stronger. Jared was beginning to wonder if Pravis and Tenebrae were setting him up, but for what he had no idea. When Jared returned to the hotel Pravis and Tenebrae were no longer in the crowd. Jared looked for them in the dining room and the lobby; finally he went to their rooms but they did not answer their doors.

Jared returned to his room, grabbed his gear and left the hotel. He got a room at a boarding house that was behind the hotel. The window in Jared's new room gave him a view of the priest's balconies. Jared moved the bed so he could lay in it and watch Pravis' and Tenebrae's rooms. As Jared was falling asleep he heard Roch's muffled screams. "You are just damn annoying," Jared said to his ghost.

After lunch Gabriel asked Calen to meet him in the study. When Calen walked into the room he found Gabriel sitting behind Hannah's father's desk.

"You look natural there," Calen said.

Gabriel smiled, "It's a nice desk; I'm trying to decide if we should take it with us. Calen will you shut the door?"

Calen closed the door to the study and sat in a chair that was directly across from Gabriel. "Calen I should have done this a while ago but I've been preoccupied," Gabriel said as he handed Calen a piece of paper. "Please sign the bottom of that paper," Gabriel said as he handed Calen a pen.

"That now puts half of everything that Natasha's and my parents left us in your name and Natasha's name."

"I have made two copies of each of these forms, one for you and one for me." Gabriel continued, "These are the locations of the family money." Gabriel said as he handed Calen another sheet of paper. "Now this sheet is basically my will, which I will update if I live through this mission. I am leaving you and Natasha half of what I have and Hannah the other half. This does not include Hannah's family money."

"But this form does," Gabriel said as he handed another document to Calen. "If Hannah and I both die, everything we have goes to you and Natasha with the exception that Hannah added at the bottom that she wants to go to the orphanage in Salar."

Gabriel paused to give Calen a chance to read all of the documents. "Gabriel I must admit I am a bit overwhelmed by all of this," Calen said as he signed the papers.

"I want to get this done now, so I can send my papers to King Sudfad for safe keeping," Gabriel said. "Now I have a favor to ask you. If things get ugly here I want you to leave with Natasha, but I would also ask that you take Hannah too. You cannot carry both of them so I would ask that you have Luca carry Hannah. I know they have become good friends and I can trust him to watch over her also."

"Of course Gabriel and you know I will take care of Hannah until you can join her."

"Thank you Calen, I am trusting you with the two most important people in my life. But you and I know what we are facing here. If I don't make it, can I trust you to still watch over Hannah?"

"Gabriel you don't even need to ask, she is my family too."

"Thank you," Gabriel said as he handed Calen another document. "Hannah is a brilliant woman but she has no interest and she says no talent for finances. I would like you to help her with that, this form gives you authority over our finances in the event of my death."

Lakin knocked on the door to the study. "Come in," Gabriel called. "Good it's you. Lakin I would like you to sign as witness on these documents."

"What are they?" Lakin asked as he walked towards the desk.

"Gabriel has just given me a fortune and that doesn't count his wills," Calen said.

"I just made him a part of the family business," Gabriel said. "I should have done this before now. Lakin if things get really bad here, I have asked Calen that he leave with Natasha and I would like Luca to carry Hannah to the Ice Caves. Calen will take care of both of them for me."

"Of course, does Luca know yet?"

"No but I will speak with him next," Gabriel said.

"He is right outside the door," Lakin said. "I just sent Betu to the Ice Caves to get more warriors. Riftca and Kev are ready to leave for Wetpr they just need the rest of your documents."

"Would you please give them these two additional sets of saddlebags also; they contain some of Hannah's family's money, I need to start getting that out of here too." Gabriel said. "And here is another letter for Sudfad; he did offer to provide us with troops if we needed. I have just requested the assistance."

Jared slept for an hour, then sat on his bed and watched the rooms of Pravis and Tenebrae for another hour. There were no signs of movement in the chambers. Jared left his room and returned to the Endleson Hotel. He walked directly to the desk clerk and asked if Pravis and Tenebrae were in the hotel. He was told the priests had left a couple of hours earlier and had not yet returned. When the desk clerk became distracted by other people, Jared ran up the stairs to the fourth floor.

The hallway was empty. Jared pulled some small tools out of the pocket of his leather vest and opened the lock to Pravis' chambers. Jared quickly looked through the rooms, finding little of interest. He looked under the bed and saw a suit case. When Jared opened it, a great smile filled his face. The case was full of bags of gold coins.

Jared grabbed as many bags as he could hide in his clothes then walked out of the room and locked the door behind him.

Jared heard voices in the hallway and ran down the hallway in the opposite direction of the voices; taking shelter in a cleaning closet. He saw Tenebrae and Pravis walking down the hallway. Their voices were raised and they appeared to be arguing although Jared could not make out what they were saying. Each priest entered his room then appeared back in the hallway minutes later. They were both carrying satchels and proceeded to walk down the stairs of the hotel.

Jared waited ten minutes then unlocked the door to Tenebrae's room. In his haste to pack, Tenebrae left his hood lying on the bed. Jared picked it up. The hood looked like it was made out of a sack; it had two holes cut in it for his eyes and one for his mouth. Jared sneered. "I'm not surprised," Jared thought to himself. "He's too much of a coward to show his face." Jared quickly searched Tenebrae's chambers. He found a suitcase filled with pouches of gold coins hidden in the back of the closet.

Jared did not want to remove the suitcase from the room so he looked around until he found a leather backpack in the same closet. This discovery surprised Jared because he could not imagine either of the priests carrying a backpack. When Jared opened the pack it contained four candles, a small black book and a map. Jared left these items in the pack and put as many pouches of gold coins into the pack as it would hold.

Jared was feeling particularly lucky. He returned to his room in the boarding house and proceeded to pull up two of the floorboards. He hid most of the money he had stolen from the priests in the floor then covered the area with a rug and a chair.

Jared went to a stable and bought himself two fine horses; one for riding and the other to carry the gold coins and provisions. Next Jared went to a saddle shop and bought himself two new saddles and bridles for his horses, he paid the man extra to deliver them to the stable; an act of extravagance that Jared was unaccustomed to.

Jared bought himself some badly needed boots, pants and shirts. He ended his shopping trip at a store that specialized in fine weapons.

Jared ate a late lunch in the dining room of the Endleson Hotel, put two bottles of whiskey on Pravis' bill and returned to his room in the boarding house. Jared lay down and took a midday nap.

Pravis and Tenebrae left Nora and rode towards the cave. Each man terrified of what they were planning to do. The sun was hot and was beating down on the two men who were already sweating out of fear. They talked little, both consumed with their private thoughts. Their preoccupations prevented them from seeing the Enrops and the Ruala warriors who watched them.

One of the Enrops flew ahead of the others and told Misha that the high priests were coming. Misha asked the bird to give his message to Gabriel and Lakin. Misha made sure his warriors stayed out of sight, as they waited for the arrival of the priests.

Misha watched as Tenebrae and Pravis were greeted by Huta warriors outside of the cave. The two priests dismounted and left their horses to graze. They took their satchels and walked into the cave with their Huta comrades.

Misha was about to fly to the top of the hill so he could spy on them through the secret opening but just as he was coming out of the concealment of the trees; he saw four groups of armed Hutas station themselves around the front entrance of the cave. Misha stepped back into the shelter of the trees and waited.

Prior to this moment, Pravis and Tenebrae had this cave with its series of tunnels and smaller caverns transformed to the specifications necessary for the ascension. Like the caves that were originally chosen for the ascension, this cave had a large cavern with a huge fire pit in the middle and a large unholy altar built along one wall. This was the area that was exposed by the opening that Misha had discovered in the top of the hill.

Further in the cave was the cavern that held the huge stone tub that Roch would lie in for the transformation. This area also held an unholy altar. Three smaller caverns were turned into prisons or storage areas for the victims who would provide Omnibus with his first meal in this realm.

It was believed that Omnibus would need to eat immediately after the transformation to gain his strength. The other caverns became the living areas for the Hutas. Thousands of sets of iron shackles had been affixed to the various walls of the caverns and tunnels to hold the anticipated number of victims.

But unlike the caves which were located near Roch's castle, the Insidiae did not have centuries to work on these caves near Nora. There were no staircases to descend into lower levels of the ground. Everything here was on one level.

The two high priests ordered the Hutas to build a huge fire in the first room of the caverns. Four Huta warriors dragged a screaming man from one of the prisons to the cavern where the priests were going to summon Omnibus. The man was shackled to the wall. One of the Hutas cut a deep incision in the man's upper arm and used the man's blood to paint unholy symbols on the Huta's skin. The other three Hutas did the same. It was these warriors with the painted symbols who would throw the sacrifices into the flames.

The warriors bled the victim, filling bowls with his blood, they did not have the mercy to kill him first. The man died watching his blood pour into wooden vessels. One of the warriors carried a bowl of warm blood to the high priests who painted their faces and arms with it. The bowl was then placed before the unholy altar. When they were prepared, Pravis and Tenebrae called for the sacrifices.

The Hutas dragged men and women into the large cavern and threw them into the great fire. The screams of the victims did not penetrate the stone walls. The Ruala warriors who were outside the caves never heard the cries of the citizens of Nora who were being murdered inside.

Misha had already sent a second Enrop to tell Lakin and Gabriel that the high priests were inside of the cave. Misha's instincts were telling him that something was wrong; so he requested that Lakin and Gabriel gather some warriors and come to the cave. Misha had but a few warriors on the wooded hill observing the caves of death. Lakin had given him specific orders to only watch the caves and not to take any action.

Pravis and Tenebrae both read out loud from books of the darkest magics as the victims were cast into the fire one by one. The first passages that the high priests read gave praise to the demon Omnibus. More screaming and crying victims were dragged into the cavern and thrown alive into the great fire. After thirteen victims were murdered, the priests read passages that summoned the ancient demon. Omnibus could not hear the summons in his prison in The Abyss, but others did.

"Sudfad I came as soon as I got your message," the Sanuri said as he took a seat in Sudfad's office. Before Sudfad could speak there was a knock on the door, then Renya walked into the room with a tray containing coffee and apple pie.

"I won't be long," Renya said. "I just wanted to greet the Sanuri." The Sanuri stood up and hugged the Queen. "I have something for you Renya," the Sanuri said as he took a large envelope out of his pocket. "It's from Matthew explaining all the things that have involved his family in the last couple of months."

"Are they alright?" Renya asked as she took the envelope.

"Everyone is now but I can explain more later."

Renya kissed Sudfad on the cheek then left the study. "Raul and Simon write every day and they say you have been sent messages about what is going on in Nora, is that correct?" Sudfad asked.

"Yes, in fact I received a message this morning."

"Have they told you very much about Gabriel and Hannah?"

"No," replied the Sanuri as he poured himself a cup of coffee.

"I will try to give you the short version," Sudfad said. "The first day that Raul and Gabriel were in Nora, a young woman ran up to them because she recognized Raul. She told them it was not safe for Raul to be seen on the streets and she has been hiding them and all of the Ruala warriors at her home. The woman's name is Hannah."

"Renya knows Hannah because she attended college here and is a physician who worked at the orphanage. While Hannah was here, Roch raped and killed her little sister as her family and many others watched. Hannah's father committed suicide a short time later, and her mother died shortly after that."

"It's all so tragic," the Sanuri said.

"Hannah hates Roch and his men, so she has been extremely generous and helpful to our people. She and Gabriel fell in love and have recently married and now we are getting to the part that I may need your help with. Since Hannah is a physician she earns her own money and had never paid attention to her father's business dealings. After she and Gabriel married they started to have her families properties put into both of their names."

"Raul rode into Nora with them that first day and they were attacked by a group of hired killers. What they have uncovered is that Hannah's father was a member of the Insidiae and had incredible wealth. He owned the managing shares of most of the businesses in Nora besides great land holdings, including gold mines. Hannah was not aware of this previously and that is why men were sent to kill them."

"Raul has the upmost respect for Gabriel and adores Hannah. He said that neither of them want to live in Stordt or have any business there; so Gabriel has sold me all of their holdings and properties. In fact they should receive my papers today."

The Sanuri smiled as he listened to Sudfad speak. "So you now own a great deal of wealth and important land in Stordt, what are your plans?"

"Apparently the Insidiae is active in Nora whether it is the same branch of that organization that is trying to help Omnibus ascend is unclear at this point. But Raul and Simon believe the ascension is planned to take place somewhere in the gold mines. At this point, my plans are to stop the ascension and the Insidiae. But I need your advice. You understand the political problems associated with this; I would prefer not to go to war with the Kingdom of Stordt."

"Sudfad you are a brilliant man. I am always proud to call you my friend. But today I must say you remind me of Hannah."

454

Sudfad gave the Sanuri a dubious look. "I have absolutely no idea what you mean."

"When was the last time you read your fathers will? I am talking about King Jaretta your blood father not King Alexandras your adoptive father. When Jaretta and Lillian sent you to Alexandras and Sumona it was to save your life because they saw the evil in Roch. Your father sent a copy of his will along with other papers to Alexandras; Roch also had a copy of these things. Do you know where these papers are?"

Sudfad stared at the Sanuri in disbelief. "I never thought about father leaving a will, I just assumed Roch took control of everything. I have never seen these papers. I can tell you they aren't in the safe or the family vault."

"I have seen them and I believe I know where they are," the Sanuri stood up. "We need to go down to the holy vault. The Great Ruler has sent me numerous visions of King Sharonne, your great, great grandfather sitting in the holy vault. This made no sense to me since Sharonne was an evil man who should not have known about the existence of this vault."

Sudfad unlocked the secret door in the wall of his study and the two men proceeded to walk down the seven flights of stairs to the vault. Sudfad and the Sanuri searched in the holy vault for almost an hour before they found Jaretta's will. It was folded inside of a dust covered lambskin pouch. They decided to read it in Sudfad's study since the light was better in that room.

Sudfad was quiet as they ascended the seven flights of steps. He was surprised at the emotions that were surging within him by holding something that had belonged to his father. When Jaretta first sent Sudfad to live with his aunt and uncle, Sudfad was but nine years old. He could not understand why his parents sent him away; Sudfad always felt that he had done something to displease them.

It was not until Sudfad became a teenager that he learned the truth. Roch had stabbed Sudfad and that was not the first violent attack by Roch. Sudfad's parents sent him to a safe home while they tried to heal their other son; the son who would eventually murder them.

When they entered the study, the Sanuri turned and saw the look on Sudfad's face and the emotions in his eyes. "Perhaps I should get Renya," the Sanuri offered. "She should be here for this."

"Yes, yes of course," Sudfad said as he sat down at his desk, clutching the pouch.

Sudfad carefully opened the pouch as if he was afraid it would break. Renya entered the room and she and the Sanuri took seats across the desk from the King. Sudfad pulled out a packet of papers that were folded and tied together with a leather string that had a medal hanging from it. The medal had the image of King Jaretta with his name on the front and an outline of the Kingdom of Stordt on the back.

Sudfad handed the packet to Renya so she and the Sanuri could look at the medal as he reached back into the pouch. Now Sudfad pulled out a rolled piece of paper that had a light blue ribbon tied around it. He removed the ribbon and unrolled the paper. As he read in silence, tears came to his eyes.

"Sudfad would you like me to read that out loud?" Renya asked. Without saying anything Sudfad handed the letter to her.

My dearest son,

Where does a father begin to explain why he abandoned his child? Your mother and I can only hope that someday you have children and can even remotely understand what we are trying to do. You Sudfad; have always been a perfect child in our eyes. And with the innocence of a child you cannot see the pure evil that exists in your brother Roch. It is as if he is not part of us. Your brother has slaughtered all of your pets. How can a child of six be capable of such actions?

We would not believe at first that it was him. But his behavior becomes more cruel everyday and his temper more explosive. Roch has hurt you many times, but last week he stabbed you. Had the nurse not taken the knife from his hands he certainly would have killed you my son. We have seen the evil in his eyes and many people have warned us about him. Your mother has had dreams about a messenger of The Great Ruler warning her that he will surely kill us. But what are we to do; he is our six year old son.

456

We fear for your safety since his hatred for you seems to have no bounds. We are sending you to live with my brother Alexandras and his wife Sumona in Wetpr until we feel it is safe to bring you home. We are sending you away because we love you. I only hope that someday you can understand that and find it in your heart to forgive us.

With all of our love

Papa

Both Renya and Sudfad had tears in their eyes as she read the letter. When Renya was done, Sudfad said in almost a whisper, "I wish I would have found that letter when I was a boy."

After Sudfad composed himself he opened his father's will. As he read the papers a confused scowl came across his face. "This is most unusual, there is more than one will here." Sudfad handed one will to Renya to read and another to the Sanuri.

"I believe your father feared what Roch would do to the family as well as to the kingdom, so he was trying to prepare for a variety of situations," the Sanuri said.

"The will that I am holding names me as king and divides the kingdom equally between Roch and me," Sudfad said.

"What is the date on that will?" the Sanuri asked.

"He wrote it right after Roch was born."

"The will I am holding says that in the event you and your parents are killed that Roch would be King and inherit all the Royal Families' lands and wealth," Renya said. "And if Roch dies first you inherit everything."

The Sanuri looked at the signature on the will that Renya was holding. "These two documents were written on the same day. I am assuming he wrote these just before he sent you to Wetpr," the Sanuri said and started to read the will out loud.

In the event that Roch kills us and takes the kingdom by force, I hope and pray that someday Sudfad will return and take control of the throne. But he cannot do that without my help.

457

Our ancestors were warriors and fought great battles on the soil of this kingdom. When the castle was built two secret underground passages were constructed in case the King's people needed to escape. There is a map of the castle with the locations of these passageways on the last page of this will.

As a means of protecting our people from invaders and the murderous Hutas my father built a series of underground shelters which he had connected by passageways. These shelters run across the kingdom. He told few of these shelters as he did not want invaders to find out about their existence and use them against our people. I have removed all references to these shelters from the official and private chronicles of the castle. The only map of the shelters and passageways is with this will. It is never to fall into Roch's hands.

Sudfad my son, if my worst fears come to fruition and Roch controls the kingdom our people will suffer as never before. Please try to help them and The Great Ruler be with you.

There was a knock on the door to Sudfad's study. "Not now," Sudfad called out as he, Renya and the Sanuri had just finished reading the wills and he was still feeling emotional.

"My Lord, I am sorry to disturb you," Marie called through the closed door. "But the Enrops brought messages for you and the Sanuri and they said they are very important."

The Sanuri opened the door and took the two notes from Marie. "Thank you my dear," he said and closed the door. The Sanuri handed one note to Sudfad and opened his. "Sudfad, Gabriel and your boys have found the location planned for the ascension and they say at least two thousand Hutas are gathering. I must leave at once."

"Sanuri wait," Sudfad said as he put down his note. "I might have a plan."

The Sanuri left Sudfad's castle and traveled along the River Nebu which ran through several kingdoms and was the most direct route from Salar to Nora; but this meant he would have to stop at the border of Stordt.

Roch always had guards along his borders, strangers were usually allowed to enter the kingdom but the people of Stordt could not leave the kingdom without written permission from the King.

Now that General Hamond had taken over the throne, the Sanuri would see if any changes had taken place. It would have been dangerous for the Sanuri to be caught in Stordt under King Roch's rule, as Roch had all holy men killed.

But now time was everything. The Sanuri had to stop the ascension and he had to protect his friends. The Sanuri prayed for guidance, he prayed for help and he prayed for speed.

Chapter XXIX
Fire and Smoke

Pravis and Tenebrae called to Omnibus for over three hours but the demon did not give them a sign that he heard them. So the high priests ordered the Hutas to throw thirteen more victims into the fire. The stench of burning flesh filled the still air of the cavern as the priests tried to summon the great demon of old.

Two more hours passed, then suddenly one of the Huta warriors who had been bestowed with the honor of throwing the sacrifices into the fire, screamed; a blood curdling scream. Pravis and Tenebrae looked up from their books and saw all four of the Huta warriors act as if they were being pulled into the fiery pit. The priests jumped back from the fire in horror.

"What is the meaning of this?" Tenebrae yelled but no answer came. The two priests looked fearfully at each other. Then Pravis started to read again. The book that Pravis was reading from was torn from his hands and flung into the fire.

"Who are you?" Pravis called.

"Hypocrites," was the only word spoken.

When Jared awoke from his nap he watched the hotel rooms of the priests for a while but he saw no movement through the windows. He remembered the items that he found in the backpack in Tenebrae's room. Jared grabbed the pack which was lying on the floor next to his bed. He took the four candles out and looked at them. They were unused but black in color; Jared had never seen candles that weren't white or yellow before. He looked them over carefully then threw them on the bed.

Next Jared took the small black book out of the pack. Jared could read but not the language this book was written in, so he threw the book on the bed, next to the candles. Jared found the map more interesting. He studied it for a while, then decided to take a walk to the Land and Title Company.

As Tenebrae and Pravis stood in the silence of the cavern their fears overwhelmed them. Finally Tenebrae could not take the silence anymore. "Ahriman is that you?" he whispered.

"Don't tell me that I'm not the only one who calls you hypocrites?" Ahriman bellowed.

"Ahriman why are you trying to stop the ascension?" Pravis asked meekly.

"Who says I am?"

"Do you have Roch?" Tenebrae asked.

"Omnibus has more friends than just you; let's just say Roch is in safe keeping."

"So are his friends going to bring Roch here for the ascension?" Tenebrae asked. "Or are we to prepare another place?"

"Why don't I ask the questions," Ahriman bellowed. "I told you to bring me the Sanuri, where is he?"

"I thought we were supposed to get the Sanuri to help reverse the affliction that was put upon Roch," Tenebrae answered. "With Roch gone, what is the purpose?"

"The purpose is that I want the Sanuri and you are going to bring him to me."

"But how?" Pravis whined.

"He is on his way to Nora now; think of something."

"Do you mean you want him in this cave" Tenebrae asked.

"Yes."

"Is he coming to stop the ascension?" Pravis asked fearfully.

"He will try."

"Why can't we speak with Omnibus?" Pravis asked.

"You've never spoken with Omnibus, you fools. He is in The Abyss. As I said he has friends, who have spoken to you on his behalf."

"All we want to know is how can we make the ascension go as planned," Tenebrae said.

"Oh it will," Ahriman said. "It will."

"Calen, good you are here," Natasha said as she was sorting items in one of the bedrooms. "I really wish you would let me know what things you would like us to take."

"I want to show you something," Calen said. He walked up to Natasha and handed her the stack of papers that Gabriel had given to him." As Natasha was reading Calen continued to talk, "Gabriel gave me orders that if things get really bad here that I am to take you and Hannah and go to the Ice Caves. He wants Luca to carry Hannah." When she finished reading all of the papers Natasha handed them back to Calen. He was surprised at the worried look on her face. "What's the matter?" Calen asked.

"Calen I just don't like the sound of this," Natasha said. "I don't think Gabriel expects to survive this mission."

As Jared walked down the streets of Nora, he kept hearing Roch's muffled voice. Jared had never been one to care about what others thought of him so he was talking to Roch out loud. "I don't know who you are or why you are haunting me. But this really is damn annoying. Can't you speak so I can understand what you are saying?" Suddenly a man who had been sitting on a barrel basking in the warm sun, stood up and walked to Jared. The man stood in front of Jared with a vacant look in his eyes.

"Move," Jared ordered. The man did not.

"Are you drunk I told you to move?" Just as Jared was about to shove the man out of his way; the man spoke.

"He is trying to tell you he needs help," the man said in an almost dream like manner. "He is scared and in great pain and he needs your help."

Jared stared at the man, now realizing that he was in some kind of a trance. "Who needs help?"

"King Roch, the demons have him."

"And why should I help him?" Jared asked with a sneer.

"He says your life depends on his; that is how he can connect with you."

"What does that mean?" Jared asked, then caught the man as he suddenly collapsed. The man was dead. Now Jared was taking that voice seriously.

"Calen," Luca called in the hallway.

"We're in here," Calen yelled as he finished rolling up a large carpet.

"We need to go," Luca said. "Misha sent word that the priests are at the cave and something is wrong."

"Be careful," Natasha said and kissed Calen before he ran out the door.

Ruala warriors were carrying Raul, Simon and Gabriel as they headed to the caves. Six Ruala warriors had stayed behind to protect Hannah, Natasha and Marcia. All three of these women were worried about their husbands and their friends so they first intensified their efforts at packing to keep distracted. Lakin had given orders that if Hutas came to the house, the Ruala warriors were to take the women to the Ice Caves.

But the women had other ideas, none of them wanted to leave their husbands. Between Natasha's ingenuity and Hannah's knowledge of the sciences they went to work. The first thing they did was to take weapons from Hannah's father's collection and hide them around the house. Then Marcia and Natasha gathered empty jars from the wine cellar and carried them into the kitchen. As Hannah was carrying boxes of medical supplies and setting them on the kitchen table.

"Tell us what you need us to do," Natasha said enthusiastically.

463

"I haven't mixed some of these chemicals since I was in college," Hannah said. "I hope I can remember all of the ingredients."

"Well, we will just keep experimenting until we get it right," Natasha said. Then she gave Hannah a hug. "You are the perfect sister-in-law."

"Marcia would you find paper, pen and wax?" Hannah asked. "We will have to identify these jars. Natasha have one of the warriors help you set up some tables outside of the house. Don't put them too close to any of the buildings in case something goes wrong. Then have the warrior bring buckets of water in here. If anything goes wrong I may start a fire in the house."

"How do you even know about some of these things?" Natasha asked.

Marcia laughed, "We grew up in a mining city. How do you think the miners break through the stone walls? Natasha, I am certainly not the physician but I don't know if you should be breathing in some of these chemicals once they start to boil," Marcia said.

"She's right," said Hannah. "It might be better for you to stay outside of the house. Have you searched the bunkhouse or other buildings for things you might want? There is a carpenter's workshop out there among other things."

Jared dropped the dead man on the street and continued walking to the Land and Title Company. He was not the kind of man to be shaken, even by supernatural threats but now he wanted answers. Against the wishes of the clerk who worked at the Land and Title Company, Jared took several maps then walked back to the Endleson Hotel. He planned to search the rooms of the high priests again and this time Jared was looking for more than money.

"They will see us if we try to get to the opening," Misha said as Lakin, Gabriel, Raul, Calen, Luca and Simon walked up to him. "It's been like this since the two priests arrived."

Misha was referring to the army of Hutas who were standing in a semi-circle guarding the entrance to the cave. Lakin and Gabriel did not want the presence of their small band of warriors to be known yet, so they stayed hidden in the trees watching the cave; unaware of the horrors that were being unleashed inside.

Jared searched the rooms of Pravis and Tenebrae again. He could not help himself and stole more of their pouches of gold coins. Jared did a more thorough search this time and other than the letter from Meekos he could not find anything that was written in a language he could understand. Jared returned to his room at the boarding house. He sat on his bed, poured himself a large glass of whiskey and waited for the priests to return to their rooms.

Gabriel and the others had been watching the caves for almost four hours. Little had changed since their arrival other than Enrops occasionally telling them that there were no riders or Hutas on the roads. A loud explosion was heard, this in itself was not unusual in a mining area.

"Where did that come from?" Raul asked. "It couldn't have been from the cave because the Hutas aren't paying any attention to it."

Luca had walked through the trees so he could have a clear view of the other side of the hill, now he ran to the men. "There is a big cloud of black smoke in the direction of the house." Half of the Ruala warriors were told to stay with Misha while the others returned to Hannah's house.

"We're in back," a Ruala warrior yelled as Gabriel and the others approached the house.

"What is going on here," Gabriel demanded as they found Hannah, Natasha, Marcia and the six Ruala warriors standing around a huge, smoldering hole in the ground.

"Hannah made up some chemicals for you to use against the Hutas," Natasha said with a grin.

"What!" Gabriel said.

"When you grow up in a mining city everyone knows how to make explosives," Hannah said. "I just mixed the same chemicals that the miners use to blow up the stone." Gabriel and the others stared at Hannah in disbelief; so she continued talking. "We have two tables set up behind the house, one is filled with jars of this explosive and they are labeled 'fire'. The other table is filled with jars of chemicals that will create huge clouds of dark smoke and those jars are labeled 'smoke'."

"And there are barrels of nails in the carpenters shed," Natasha said. "I thought we could put them in the jars of fire so they would shoot out at the Hutas when you drop the jars on the cave."

"How did you three come up with this?" Gabriel asked with a proud grin.

"Well, none of us want to be sent away and we know you are greatly outnumbered, so we wanted to help," Hannah said.

"And we hid weapons in every room just in case we get attacked," Marcia added proudly.

"I'm sorry friends," Raul said. "But I just have to kiss your wives." He kissed Hannah, Marcia and Natasha on their cheeks. "Right now you are my three favorite women," Raul joked.

"How many jars did you drop to create this hole?" Lakin asked.

"I dropped one jar of fire from about fifty feet," Eli said. "They told me to fly high so I wouldn't get injured. Then I dropped one jar of smoke over there," Eli continued and pointed to an area about a hundred yards to the west."

"One jar did this?" Calen asked with surprise.

"The smoke won't injure anyone but it is so thick it will blind them for a while," Hannah said.

"And do the miners use that too?" asked Lakin.

"No I learned that at school," Hannah replied with a coy smile. "Although truthfully our teacher wasn't happy when he found out that some of us had made the smoke."

Gabriel got a broad grin on his face. "This changes everything," he said and picked Hannah up and kissed her.

"How much did you make?" Simon asked.

"There are about thirty jars of each," Hannah replied. "And I still have ingredients so I can make more. But you have to be careful with these jars so they don't blow up in your hands." The group turned and walked towards the back of the house, where the two tables were set up.

"Let's move these farther away from the house," Gabriel said. Then he turned to Hannah. "How many more of these do you think you could make?"

"I don't know, maybe another twenty or thirty jars of the fire and less of the smoke."

"Why don't you show us how to make this stuff," Gabriel said.

"Well, we have dinner cooking now, so you will have to wait." Hannah replied without seeing the irony in her statement. Gabriel smiled and shook his head.

It was still daylight when the Sanuri approached the border between the Kingdoms of Wetpr and Stordt. He pulled the boca off from the road so he could watch for border guards. After a few minutes he saw them; six soldiers from the Taperian Army riding along the border. "I guess nothing has changed," he thought to himself.

He was trying to decide if he should try crossing the border now or wait until after dark. The Sanuri was not afraid of the border guards but he was concerned that they might detain him and time was very important right now. The Sanuri watched for a couple of more minutes then decided to move forward. "I could certainly use some help down here," the Sanuri prayed as he neared the border.

"Stop right there old man," one of the guards called gruffly. "What is your business here?"

"Augustus Endleson has invited me for a visit," the Sanuri said. "I am on my way to Nora to see him." Being one of the wealthiest men in the kingdom, the Sanuri knew there was some power associated with using Endleson's name.

"Be that as it may, we will have to look in your boca," the same guard said. Two of the soldiers rode to the back of the boca; one got off his horse and climbed into the back of the wagon.

"Ain't nothing good back here," the soldier called out and mounted his horse. The two soldiers returned to the front of the boca where the other soldiers were blocking the Sanuri's horses. One of the soldiers; the man wearing sergeant's stripes had been staring at the Sanuri but had not spoken until now.

"I know that I know you from some place, where are you from?"

"Well I don't really have a home," the Sanuri said. "You see I am a physician of sorts and I travel all around healing people."

"What does that mean, a physician of sorts?" the sergeant asked.

"It means I practice the medicine of the old ways, which I much prefer to the newer theories that are taught."

The sergeant stared at the Sanuri suspiciously. He was about to order his men to search the boca again when in the distance the sound of the Horn of Ire could be heard. The Horn of Ire had been used for centuries by the Taperian Armies as a means of communicating; it was usually used when soldiers were calling for help. "Which way did that come from?" the sergeant barked as his horse reared up.

"From the west," a soldier replied and in a moment all six of the soldiers rode west as fast as their horses could run. The Sanuri too left that area quickly, only he was heading southwest towards Nora. The Sanuri drove off the road and into the wooded areas that ran parallel to the river. The travel would be slower but he would be concealed from the eyes of the Taperian soldiers.

468

"You're welcome," the voice of The Lion could be heard saying. The Sanuri smiled.

After dinner the men watched with fascination as Hannah and Marcia showed them how to make fire and smoke. Simon copied down the directions and ingredients to take back to Wetpr. They had enough ingredients to make twenty-seven more jars of fire and fifteen jars of smoke. The jars were carefully taken outside and hidden. Then the men met in the study and discussed battle strategies. The women were cleaning the kitchen and preparing food for breakfast.

Hannah, Natasha and Marcia all felt proud that the men were so happy with their ideas. Natasha in particular felt a sense of relief. She had not wanted to say anything to Hannah, but she was afraid that Gabriel would sacrifice himself for the mission. Soon they heard the men's voices; Gabriel came into the kitchen and pulled Hannah to the side of the room. He talked to her in whispers then left the kitchen.

"What was that all about?" asked Natasha.

"He is going to our room and try to get an audience with The Lion; he does not want me to come up there until he is done."

"He looked worried," Marcia said.

"I know," Hannah replied. "They all do."

Gabriel knelt down beside the bed in the room that he and Hannah shared. "Oh Great Ruler, your servant feels unworthy for what I am about to ask. But the lives of many hinge on the decisions I must make this night. I beseech an audience with your emissary The Lion that I might receive guidance in the matters at hand. I long to hear your voice and his. This is an important mission and I must stop the ascension of the demon Omnibus."

"You have been hearing our voices all your life Gabriel, you just didn't realize it." Gabriel turned around and saw a huge male lion standing behind him. "The voices you have heard in your heart have been ours and I must say you have done well in following them. Did you not ever wonder whose voices those were?"

"I thought it was just my feelings," Gabriel stammered in awe.

"Most people do, few ever recognize our voices in this lifetime. Gabriel why do you look so shocked to see me?"

"I just never thought you would come if I asked."

"I have been waiting a long time for you to ask Gabriel. I have been dropping breadcrumbs along your path waiting for you to recognize their significance. But we will finish this discussion another time. The matter at hand is the Hutas and demons in that cave. The Hutas number many more than two thousand. You are greatly outnumbered. Sudfad is sending an army to help you but they will not get here in time. The Sanuri is on his way, but he has a distance to travel and demons lie in wait for him. Tell me Gabriel do you and your men want to flee?"

This question brought Gabriel out of his stunned silence; in fact it angered him. "I did not ask you here because we are going to flee; I called upon you to give me guidance in how I can stop this darkness."

"Now that is the Gabriel I know and love," The Lion said. "In the forest behind this house there are three large oak trees. Cut them down now, while there is still light. Raul and Simon designed and built trebuchets for their forts; I am surprised they have not thought about using them here. Build one trebuchet from each tree. You will find the materials you need in the carpenter's shed."

"Work through the night. Move all three trebuchets to your observation hill. Pravis and Tenebrae will unleash the Hutas upon Nora tomorrow. Ahriman is demanding the sacrifices because those hypocrites have not led the Sanuri to his slaughter. I want you to attack the caves before the Hutas leave. Use the trebuchets to launch your jars, then have the Rualas do what they do best, aerial attacks. More Rualas will arrive by dawn. I started them before your messenger reached the Ice Caves."

"Thank you," Gabriel said as he started to stand up.

"Also Gabriel I know what is in your heart," The Lion continued. "The Great Ruler does not ask for human sacrifice, as the demons do. This is one battle in many. You will do extraordinary things in your lifetime; do not throw everything away on one battle." The Lion turned and took two steps as if to walk away, then he turned back to Gabriel. "Sometimes the greatest miracles are seen when all seems hopeless, have faith my friend." And with these words The Lion disappeared.

Gabriel ran out of the bedroom and down the stairs to the parlor. He called everyone together and told them the words of The Lion. Lakin immediately called his warriors together and had a group of them cut down the oak trees.

Simon and Raul started drawing their designs for the trebuchets. Marcia and Natasha went back into the kitchen and started to make coffee and food for the men who would be working all night. Gabriel walked up to Hannah and kissed her. "I never would have asked for an audience with The Lion had it not been for you."

"Well, it sounds like he plans on talking to you again," Hannah said with a loving smile.

"Why don't you try to get some sleep," Gabriel said softy.

"No, I am going to prepare bandages and medicines. I am sure many will be hurt tomorrow."

Chapter XXX
The Caves of Death

Everyone at Hannah's house worked through the night and to the amazement of all, they completed the trebuchets two hours before dawn. These weapons were mounted on platforms with wheels. Raul, Simon and Gabriel each drove a team of horses that pulled a trebuchet. The jars were carefully wrapped in cloth and packed in crates.

Twenty Ruala warriors carried crates of explosives and smoke to the observation hill. True to The Lion's word; almost one thousand Ruala warriors arrived at Hannah's house before dawn. Lakin divided his warriors into battalions. Each battalion had its orders. Natasha, Marcia and Hannah stood outside looking up at the sky in awe, as over one thousand Ruala warriors flew in silence.

The few remaining victims in the cave had been murdered and drained of their blood. The Hutas painted themselves and drank what they could of the human blood. Pravis and Tenebrae watched as over seven thousand Huta warriors danced around the fires.

"I will admit I wish we didn't have to do this," Pravis said. "I like Nora."

"You fool; when Omnibus rises he will destroy the city anyways," Tenebrae snapped. He did not want to admit that he shared Pravis' sentiments.

The Huta warriors screamed and hit each other as they worked themselves up to a frenzy. Calen and Misha were on top of the hill, peering into the cave through the secret opening. Their eyes grew wide as the saw the numbers of Huta warriors below. It was at that moment that Calen realized he might never see Natasha again. As one Calen and Misha dropped four jars of smoke into the cave, followed by three jars of explosives.

Both Rualas flew as fast as they could to the observation hill; but the power of the blasts almost knocked them out of the sky. Calen and Misha were severely cut and bleeding from flying debris.

As soon as the first three jars exploded; three, then six, then nine more jars of fire were launched by the trebuchets, followed by three more jars of smoke.

The caverns were collapsing upon the Hutas who were trampling each other in their efforts to get out of the caves. Two battalions of Ruala archers stood ready and showered their arrows upon the first fifty Hutas who were trying to flee the cave. In the thickness of the smoke the Hutas did not realize they were being attacked by arrows. The archers were given an order to stand back, then six more jars of explosives were launched upon the caves, followed by three more jars of smoke. The archers flew forward attacking any fleeing Hutas they could see.

Parts of the hills were collapsing so Lakin ordered two more battalions to cover the back and sides of the hills but in the destruction and chaos the Hutas were running out of the front entrance. Pravis and Tenebrae were terrified but they alone sought to escape the barrage of fire by a tunnel in the rear of the hill. They ran and tripped and ran and tripped in the darkness of the tunnel, the intensity of their fear seemed to give them wings.

"Light, I can see light," Pravis gasped. Tenebrae too, could see the first light of dawn before them. Suddenly the light disappeared. Both men stopped in their tracts.

"Where do you think you are going my little hypocrites?" a voice bellowed from the darkness.

"Ahriman, please let us leave," Pravis pleaded.

"Oh my fools, it is not Ahriman," said The Lion as he walked toward them. An intense white light consumed The Lion and illuminated the entire tunnel. The priests stared in horror.

"You two have spent your lives mocking The Great Ruler. You claim to be His servants when you plot against Him and bring only horror and pain to His children. Ahriman was right when he told you there was a special place in hell for such as you."

The two priests turned and started to run back toward the large cavern. As they ran the stone floor beneath their feet started to disappear. Pravis' left leg fell through the floor. He called to Tenebrae to help him but Tenebrae kept running.

473

Pravis was able to pull his leg out of the hole, only to see Tenebrae trip and fall in front of him.

Tenebrae started to sink into the floor as if it was quicksand; soon only his right wrist and hand were exposed as the rock swallowed his body. Pravis watched in horror, then carefully tried to walk around the area that had consumed Tenebrae. Pravis took two steps toward what he thought was freedom when he heard his own voice screaming and realized he was falling.

The last of the fire and smoke had been launched. The explosions had killed thousands of Hutas but the Rualas were still greatly outnumbered. Most of the archers were out of arrows; as hordes of Hutas poured out of the cave. The Hutas now realized where the attacks were coming from and they charged toward the observation hill.

Raul, Simon and Gabriel drew their swords and started down the hill to meet their destinies. The Ruala warriors who had run out of arrows now landed and ran toward the charging throngs of Hutas. Two of the most feared armies in Opots were charging towards each other in a battle for mankind.

Suddenly the world turned black. The darkness was so intense that some men thought they had been blinded. No one could see, no one could hear. And out of the darkness a single lion roared. The badly bombarded hill now exploded completely; propelling tons of rock into the air. Hot molten lava erupted from the ground under the hill, shooting high into the sky and flooding the ground. Bone chilling screams could be heard as Hutas were burned alive in the liquid fire.

Raul, Simon and Gabriel could all feel themselves being lifted up by their Ruala comrades, who flew them back to the top of the observation hill. The molten lava flooded the area with the intensity of a river that had broken through its dam. The world was still dark but the heat of the lava gave off great light.

"I think our work here is done," Gabriel said. "Let's gather everyone and go back to the house."

"I need help," Dagon yelled as he carried Koby to the top of the observation hill. "Where's Lakin?"

474

Koby was bleeding profusely from multiple knife wounds. The warriors did not have medical bags with them. Simon, Raul and Gabriel all took off their shirts and tore them into pieces of various sizes, some to use as bandages and some as strips to hold the bandages in place.

Lakin quickly joined the men, when he heard them calling his name. Lakin placed crystals in the most severe wounds, bandaged as many as he could and told Dagon to get Koby to Hannah's home as soon as possible. Lakin, Gabriel, Raul and Simon stayed at the battle site until all of the wounded were gathered.

Earlier that morning, after all the warriors left to do battle at the caves, Hannah, Natasha, Marcia and the Ruala warriors who were guarding them went to work to prepare a makeshift hospital. They cleared most of the furniture out of three large rooms. The warriors carried in mattresses from the bunkhouse and placed them on the floors of these rooms. Natasha and Marcia covered the mattresses with bedding while Hannah set up a medical area in each room, and stocked her office.

The women had a large kettle of boiling water on the stove as well as a stock pot of soup started. They hurried, almost running at times to prepare for the wounded warriors. When their work was completed Hannah, Natasha and Marcia waited; waited to see if anyone would make it back to the house.

Hours passed before Hannah and the others had their first glimpse of hope. They heard Dagon calling Hannah's name. Within moments Dagon was in the kitchen with a bloody and unconscious Koby.

"Take him to my office," Hannah said as she led the way. Dagon laid his friend on the medical table.

"I want to stay with him," Dagon said.

"That is fine," Hannah did not finish her sentence because she heard voices yelling.

"We have wounded," a male voice yelled as Ruala warriors were carrying their wounded comrades into the house.

Marcia and Natasha could tend to the minor wounds; the seriously hurt warriors would have to wait for Hannah or Lakin to help them. As the wounded warriors were being placed on the beds, their unwounded comrades also helped with medical care.

"Where's Koby?" yelled Lakin as he pushed through the crowd.

"In her office," Natasha yelled as she was cleaning a wounded warrior's arm.

As Lakin ran toward Hannah's office Marcia called out fearfully, "Lakin, Lakin this man is bleeding too badly for me to stop." Lakin ran to her side and helped with the warrior. As busy as Natasha and Marcia were, they were painfully aware that they had not yet seen their husbands return from battle. Dagon ran out of Hannah's office and took a pile of towels from the kitchen table and filled a large bowl with boiling water then returned to help her.

"Someone help me hold this man," Natasha yelled. "His leg is broken." Before the words were out of her mouth four Ruala warriors were at Natasha's side. The smell of burning flesh started to fill the air as warriors were burning the wounds of others in order to stop the bleeding. The first hour went by quickly and yet seemed to take forever. Marcia and Natasha became more concerned for the safety of their husbands as time passed.

"Natasha," Marcia called, "They're home." Marcia was stitching a wound close and could not leave her patient.

"Calen," Natasha screamed as she saw Rabi help Calen into the house.

"I'm alright," Calen said as Natasha ran up to him.

"Alright, you are not alright you are covered in blood. Rabi please sit him next to this table." Natasha cradled Calen's face in her hands and kissed him on the lips.

"Now tell me what happened." Natasha said as she started to take his warrior's robe off from him. "Calen the back of your robe is ripped to shreds."

"I threw some jars of fire into the cave and couldn't get away fast enough," Calen said in obvious pain. "Where is Misha he was with me?"

Natasha looked around the room, "It looks like they are taking him to Marcia now." There was so much dried blood and dirt on Calen that Natasha could not clearly see his wounds. She started to wash him, "Calen you have small stones embedded in your skin and in your head." Then Natasha turned and called to Marcia, "Check Misha's head he might have stones lodged there." Natasha turned back to Calen. "Have you seen Gabriel?" she asked fearfully.

"Yes, they were still there when we left."

The door to Hannah's office opened, Dagon walked out and talked to several other Ruala warriors who returned to her office. The men carried Koby upstairs to his bed. Dagon promised to sit with Koby since Hannah had so many other wounded warriors to care for. Hannah walked up to Calen and Natasha.

Hannah was covered with Koby's blood. "He will make it," she assured them. "But someone needs to be with him to make sure he doesn't open any of those wounds. Dagon is with him now." As Hannah spoke she was examining Calen. "You've done a fine job with his wounds," Hannah said to Natasha.

"He was hit by rocks after he threw jars of fire," Natasha said.

"I figured as much," Hannah said as she examined his back. "Most of the cuts are minor but you are going to have some good bruising. You may not want to sleep on your back for a while." Hannah had Calen stand up so she could examine the back of his legs and feet. Then she walked in front of him and examined his eyes. "As I thought, you have a mild concussion." Hannah walked over to the medical table and picked up a small jar. "Natasha put him in bed and put this on his wounds. He needs to rest but someone needs to check on him often."

"Misha was with him," Natasha said as she nodded towards the man who Marcia was working on. "You might want to check him too." Two warriors helped Natasha get Calen into his bed. After she had applied the medicine to his wounds; Natasha walked down the stairs to help Hannah.

Natasha stopped before she reached the last steps and looked at the rooms filled with the wounded. Natasha had been so focused on individual patients that she had not realized the enormity of the situation. Tears came to her eyes as her heart went out to all those brave warriors who willingly went to battle, knowing they were incredibly outnumbered.

Natasha took a deep breath and walked down the rest of the steps. She saw two Rualas helping Misha to a bed on the floor. "No," Natasha said as she quickly walked up to them. "Put him in bed with Calen, they both need the same treatment it will be easier that way." Then she led the men up the stairs.

Hannah mournfully searched the faces of the warriors in her house for Gabriel. "We haven't seen him yet," Marcia said, knowing who Hannah was looking for. Marcia put her arm around Hannah's shoulders and said, "I will call you when he comes." Then a voice cried out of the throng, "Hannah over here, we need you."

As the darkness over the battlefield was lifting the Rualas had worked quickly to gather their dead and wounded comrades before the lava engulfed them. Gabriel, Raul and Simon watched as the last Ruala's were flying back to the house.

"After all of this and we don't even know if we stopped the ascension," Gabriel said gravely. Suddenly he remembered the words of The Lion; 'That this was but one battle of many.' And Gabriel feared that the threat still existed.

Raul, Simon and Gabriel were monitoring the lava flow because they had to drive the trebuchets back to the house. Although the lava initially spread quickly it had greatly slowed its pace and appeared to be confined to the battlefield. When the men felt the road was safe to travel, they hitched the teams of horses to the trebuchets and started the drive to the house.

"Well, well, well," Ahriman said with pleasure as Pravis and Tenebrae suddenly appeared before him. "I do believe I have been sent gifts." The two men had been hurled through time and space to the hell dimension of Ahriman.

The priests found themselves lying in a retched smelling tar-like substance. Plums of steam billowed upwards from the waste of hell. They could not see Ahriman at first but they could hear his voice. Tenebrae started to cry. "Where are we?" he called out.

"You're in my realm now," Ahriman's voice seemed to echo in the darkness. Then he started to laugh and laugh and laugh. The more Ahriman laughed the more frightened Pravis and Tenebrae became.

"I told you there was a special place in hell for hypocrites," Ahriman said.

The two priests looked around quickly as Ahriman's voice was sounding louder and closer. Suddenly out of the muck before them; a form started to take shape. Pravis and Tenebrae were frozen with fear as they watched the great demon materializing. Pravis started to puke from the stench that Ahriman emitted. The dark figure kept growing until it reached the height of a great mountain. The priests could not see Ahriman's face but his body was like nothing they had ever seen before.

Every type of darkness of mankind was displayed on Ahriman's robes; not in designs but in individual scenes that were actually alive. The priests were watching millions of acts of total depravity played out before them; they could hear the screams and cries of the victims. These two men who had caused so much terror in their world were now struck dumb by the horror they saw before them.

"Do my robes scare you?" Ahriman asked in a taunting manner. The priests did not speak so Ahriman continued as if they had. "Good, for you will experience everything you see before you and not once or twice but throughout eternity. I will now read the charges against you my hypocrites." Ahriman was taking delight in his mock trial of the priests. Their fears and anxieties were wetting Ahriman's appetite; as the great demon of old prepared to devour two more of mankind.

Ahriman pretended to read from a list of atrocities, "Murder more times than I can count, mocking your god, rape, betrayal, kidnapping, stealing and from the church, always one of my favorites, lying, cheating, defiling. Have I forgotten anything?" Ahriman asked mockingly. "Now my high priests tell me, was it worth it?" Ahriman's laughter filled all spaces and echoed throughout his realm. The laughter, the laughter, the cries.

Rabi and Eli walked up to Marcia, who was wrapping a warrior's wounds. "Is there anything we can do to help?" Rabi asked as he stroked Marcia's long black hair.

"Rabi we have to feed these people; would you help with that?"

"Of course tell us what you want done?"

"The smokehouse is still half full, please bring in meats and fish and start slicing them. The cellar is full of cheeses, canned foods and the wine, ale and whiskey. In the pantry are bowls of hard boiled eggs, pies, honey and baskets of apples." Marcia paused and a look of concern crossed her face. "But where are we going to put everything?"

"We will line tables up," Eli said. "Is there anything else?"

"Bread and we have soup on the stove and, and dishes. Oh Rabi I don't think we have enough for everyone," Marcia said with panic in her voice.

Rabi put his arm around Marcia's shoulders, "Honey the warriors don't starve when they leave the Ice Caves, they have food and dishes with them. We will feed as many as we can."

Now Marcia started to cry, "Rabi I was so afraid you would be killed." He bent down and kissed her tenderly on the lips. She smiled shyly; she did not want to cry, not now with so many to care for. "I will be in to help you as soon as I can," Marcia said as she wiped the tears from her cheeks.

"Honey just keep taking care of the wounded," Rabi said. "I'm sure we can handle slicing food." They turned and started to walk through the crowded rooms, towards the kitchen. Eli raised his voice above the din and asked for help with preparing the meal; within moments thirty warriors filled the kitchen.

Another hour wore on; Hannah and Lakin were becoming exhausted. They had been treating patients for over three hours; many of whom had serious wounds. When Natasha finished tending to patients she went up the stairs to Koby's room so she could give Dagon a break.

"I'm alright," Dagon said wearily.

"At least go down and eat, you were up all night before the battle, you need your strength," Natasha said. "I will stay with him until you return." Natasha examined Koby's bandages to see if he was bleeding through his stitches. Then she placed a cool wet cloth on his forehead and sat down in the chair that Dagon had pulled up beside the bed.

In the quiet of the room, and away from the chaos and misery; Natasha cried. She wasn't even sure why she was crying. Natasha tried to remember the last time any of them had slept. "No wonder," she said out loud. "I'm just exhausted." As if she had to justify her tears to herself.

Dagon quickly ate one plate of food downstairs and brought a second plate to Koby's room. "Have you eaten?" Dagon asked as Natasha got up to give him his chair.

"Not yet."

"Natasha you look exhausted, you have to take care of yourself Honey, you're pregnant," Dagon said sweetly.

"I will, after I check on Calen and Misha." Natasha left Koby's room and walked down the hallway, suddenly her legs felt very heavy. Both Calen and Misha were sleeping peacefully. She put fresh cool cloths on their foreheads and checked their bandages. Natasha bent down and kissed Calen on the forehead. She had been so afraid that he would be killed that she felt she couldn't breathe at times while she was waiting for him to come home. "Now," Natasha thought fearfully. "Where are Gabriel, Raul and Simon?"

Jared had waited all night for Pravis and Tenebrae to return to their rooms. He ate an early breakfast in the dining room of the Endleson Hotel; sitting at a corner table so he could have his back against a wall. From his table, Jared could watch not only the entire dining room but also part of the lobby. He noticed that both the staff and customers were talking excitedly in low voices. Jared called his waiter back to the table.

"Boy, what is going on? What is everyone talking about?"

"Oh My Lord, all kinds of things are happening. We just learned that King Sudfad of Wetpr has purchased almost the entire City of Nora including the mines. He now owns this very hotel. Then this morning there were many explosions at one of the mines. Some of the men rode out to see what was going on."

The waiter leaned closer to Jared as if he did not want others to hear what he was saying. "They said they saw two armies fighting, Hutas and Rualas. Can you believe either of those tribes were here? Well, they said no one would believe this but suddenly everything became dark; a darkness like they had never seen before. Then they heard a lion roar and the entire hill blew up and started spitting hot lava. Have you ever heard such a thing in all your days?"

"Boy, do you know where this hill is?"

"Yes."

"Can you draw me a map?" Jared asked. The young man left to get some paper; he returned and drew a map at Jared's table. When the waiter left, Jared pulled the map he had stolen from the priests out of his shirt pocket and compared the two maps. "Well I'll be damned," Jared said as he realized the maps showed the same area.

As Raul, Simon and Gabriel drove the heavy trebuchets to the house, they continually looked around the landscape. None of them believed the trouble was over. Not only did they suspect there might be more Huta's in the area but they were still expecting a backlash from some of the people from Nora because Sudfad now owned the city. The men had just crossed one of the bridges over the River Nebu when they saw some Ruala warriors flying towards them.

"We have been scouting the area," Armon said as he landed on the road. "Some men from Nora were out here but they left quickly. They may have just been following the sounds of the explosions."

"Do you think they saw any of the battle?" Gabriel asked.

"They may have," replied Armon.

"I don't think we have to keep your presence a secret anymore," Gabriel said. "Did you see anything else?"

"Well, we aren't really sure," Armon explained. "We flew over the area where the hill was. The lava is cooling and causing steam to rise so that may have affected our vision. We saw shadows, it looked like they were coming out of the hole where the hill had been. But we couldn't see anything that was making the shadows."

"What did they look like?" asked Raul.

"I can tell you what they didn't look like; they didn't look like any kind of human or animal that I have ever seen."

"Are they still there?" Gabriel asked.

"We watched as they walked around the hill and the battleground then they disappeared."

"Some sort of demons, you think?" asked Simon.

"I have no idea," Gabriel said. "I just know this isn't over."

Gabriel was the first to walk in the front door of the house, Raul and Simon followed. All three stopped and stared at the scene before them. The floors were lined with makeshift beds filled with wounded warriors. The rooms were so crowded that only narrow pathways existed between the beds. Those who were not wounded or who had minor injuries were tending to and feeding the others.

"Do you see Hannah?" Gabriel asked as he was visually searching the room.

483

"Marcia is over there," Simon said and pointed into one of the rooms, where they could see Marcia washing the blood off from a warrior's face. The door to Hannah's office opened, they saw her and Lakin come out of the room and call for other warriors to carry a patient to a bed. Both Hannah and Lakin were covered in blood and looked weary.

"Hannah," Gabriel called.

Hannah looked up and stared at Gabriel as if dazed; then she started to cry and run across the large room; Hannah flew into Gabriel's arms. Hannah was crying too hard to speak so she buried her head in Gabriel's chest. Gabriel held Hannah tightly and kissed the top of her head. After several moments Hannah was able to compose herself; she looked up at Gabriel and said in a scolding manner, "Next time you send me a message that you're alive, I have been so frightened."

"I'm sorry," Gabriel said and kissed Hannah on the lips.

"Gabriel," Natasha yelled as she was walking down the steps. Natasha ran to her brother and hugged him. Gabriel had his arms around both Hannah and Natasha. Then Natasha hugged both Raul and Simon, kissing them both on the cheeks.

"How come none of you are wearing shirts?" Natasha asked.

"Used them for bandages," Simon said, then asked, "How's Koby?"

"He will be alright eventually," Hannah said. "Dagon is sitting with him to make sure he doesn't tear any of his stitches open. We put Calen and Misha in Natasha's room they both have concussions and injuries from the explosions. And as you can see there are many wounded, with mostly knife and sword wounds."

"How many did you lose?" Gabriel asked Lakin as he walked up behind Hannah.

"I suppose I should say proudly that we only lost six men." Lakin paused then said with great sadness, "But those six men were friends of mine." Simon put his hand on Lakin's shoulder.

"What can we do?" Raul asked.

"We are going to need more food and there are still medical supplies in my office that we could use here," Hannah said. "And we could use more blankets and towels."

"What do you want for food?" Simon asked.

"Rabi and Eli pretty much emptied the smoke house and most of the cellar so everything. And we will need lots of lard and flour because we don't have any bread."

"You girls have your hands full with the wounded here," Gabriel said. "Don't worry about baking bread. Let me get a shirt on and I'll go to Nora."

"We'll come with you," Simon said. Then as an afterthought he asked, "Lakin do you need anything specific? Or do you want to come with us?"

"We aren't going to hide your presence here any longer," Gabriel said. "So you are welcome to come with us. The people of Nora should be damn grateful that your men saved them from the Hutas."

Hannah looked into the next room and called, "Marcia, they are going for supplies, do you want to go with them and show them where the stores are?"

Marcia stood up and the others could see that her dress was covered in blood. "Just let me change and I will be right with them." Marcia turned and ran up the stairs to her room.

"Why don't you take some of the others with you in case there is trouble," Hannah suggested. "We'll be fine here." Ten minutes later Gabriel, Raul, Simon, Lakin, Marcia and fifty Ruala warriors left for Nora.

Jared finished his breakfast and went to the rooms of the priests, stealing everything of value. He walked down the stairs of the hotel carrying three suitcases. As he was walking past the front desk, Jared paused. Then he walked up to the old clerk.

"Those priests, Pravis and Tenebrae, do they have any mail or items here at the desk?"

485

"Let me check," the clerk said and turned to a large wooden cupboard that contained small baskets for each room. "There are some papers here."

"Anything else?" Jared asked.

"We have a safe here," the clerk explained as he dialed the combination. "We don't keep money in it but items for the guests."

Jared could easily see into the open safe, it contained mostly papers, a couple of pouches and some books. "It looks like they have a couple of books here," the clerk said.

"Let me have all of their stuff, I will take it to them," Jared said with authority.

"Well, I don't know if I can give these things to you," the clerk said.

"You know I work for them, right?"

"Well, yes, but we are only supposed to give items to their owners," the clerk was getting nervous as he talked; the look on Jared's face was scaring him.

"Give me their stuff," Jared demanded.

The clerk's hands were shaking as he handed Jared the books and papers. Jared returned to his boarding room and hid the valuables he had taken from the priests under the floorboards; then Jared went to the stable and got his two horses. Jared hitched them outside of the General Store as he bought provisions. Then Jared rode to the boarding house and got all of his new found riches and packed them on the horses.

As he was leaving Nora, Jared rode past two bocas, the first one was being driven by Gabriel with Marcia in the front seat. The second boca was being driven by Raul with Simon sitting next to him and flying over the two bocas were Ruala warriors. Jared stared at Gabriel, Simon and Raul as he passed them and they stared at him; but not a word was spoken.

"Looks like they're back," Rabi said to Hannah as he saw warriors carrying food into the kitchen through the back door.

"I hope there wasn't any trouble," Hannah said as she ran to the back porch. Hannah stood in the doorway dumbfounded. "What is all this?" she asked in amazement.

"Marcia told everyone that the Rualas stopped an army of Hutas from attacking the city and that our house was full of the wounded," Gabriel said with a big smile. "So some of the good folks are coming out to help."

Hannah stared as seven bocas full of food and supplies were pulling up to the house. "Did you buy all of this?"

"No," Simon said. "Your neighbors were so grateful they gave most of it to us, of course we have to return some of the bocas."

"There's more people coming to help take care of the wounded," Raul said. As he spoke, Hannah watched bocas and carriages of all sizes coming down the road to her house. People were riding horses and carrying baskets. Hannah recognized one of the other physicians from Nora in a boca. Tears came to her eyes. "I'd forgotten how kind people can be," she said as Gabriel put his arm around her.

Chapter XXXI
The Law

Eight women from Nora took over the kitchen in Hannah's and Gabriel's house. Other women went to work washing the bloody bedding and towels. Men carried the supplies and water into the house. Those who did not have tasks helped to tend to the wounded. Two of the physicians from Nora came to the house; each bringing their assistants. With so much additional help, many of the Ruala warriors, who had not slept in days, were able to get some rest.

Hannah, Marcia and Natasha, were standing in the middle of the parlor watching all their new help, in utter amazement. Their lack of sleep and the stress of seeing so much pain and horror; left the women somewhat dazed. Rabi walked up to the women and put his arm around Marcia.

"Some woman just kicked me out of the kitchen," he said with a laugh. "What do you need me to do?"

Before any of the women could answer his question; a small elderly woman walked up to them. "Marcia is this your husband?" the woman asked.

Marcia smiled, "Yes, Rabi this is Bertha, Bertha my husband Rabi."

Bertha looked at Marcia and winked, "He sure is a handsome boy, good for you." Then Bertha turned to Rabi and took his hand in both of hers. "I just want to thank all of you for what you did. Complete strangers and you saved us from those monsters. Yes, we have all been saying that you are our guardian Angels."

Rabi had not heard the term 'guardian Angels' before and did not understand what Bertha meant. "Thank you Bertha but we are Rualas."

Bertha smiled warmly, "I know my son but you are still our guardian Angels."

After Bertha walked away, Rabi turned to Hannah and asked, "Where is Gabriel?"

"Some of the leaders of Nora wanted to meet with him, Raul, Simon and Lakin," Hannah replied. "They are all in the study."

Jared rode out to the location identified on the maps. The steam was still rising from the lava as it cooled. Jared was not familiar with this area but he held two maps that showed him what the terrain used to look like. Jared had spoken to several people before he left Nora and they all repeated the same story of the events that took place on this battlefield. Charred bodies of Huta warriors could be seen but Jared did not see one body of a Ruala warrior.

Being a fighting man, nothing at this location looked right to Jared. He dared not ride closer to the site where the hill used to stand because of the lava; so he remained on his horse and studied the scene for some time. Just as Jared started to ride towards the road, he suddenly stopped and looked around. After a few moments he started to ride again. "I could have sworn I heard whispering," Jared said to himself out loud. "I must be imagining things."

Among the throngs of helpful people who came to the home of Hannah and Gabriel; the governing body of the City of Nora came to talk business. Five men approached Gabriel, Raul and Simon and asked to speak with them in private. Gabriel invited Lakin to join them in the study. No sooner had the men entered the room and taken seats, when there was a knock on the door; and Luca escorted Lloyd into the room.

"Luca please stay," said Gabriel.

"First we would like to thank you for seeing us," a man said kindly. "And before we start, we all want to thank the Rualas for saving our city. If there is anything, anything at all that we can do; please let us know. We will forever be in your debt. My name is Morris; that is Wallis." Morris pointed out the men as he introduced them. "Peters is over there with the gray hat, next to him is Jack, then Carston and Lloyd. When Endleson was alive we made up the seven seats of the city government."

Gabriel introduced, Raul, Simon, Lakin and Luca to the men. "What can we do for you gentlemen?" Gabriel asked.

"Well, now that King Sudfad owns the city, well, I guess we have a great deal to talk about," Morris said. "What changes will occur?"

"I don't think Father has thought about any changes yet," Simon explained. "You see, we have been hunting the men who called the Hutas here to attack you. So we have all been focused on that." Simon and Raul watched the expressions on the faces of the men. Simon deliberately gave this information to see if they could tell if any of these men were members of the Insidiae.

"Oh Morris get to the point," Wallis said irritably then Wallis proceeded to talk. "Most of us are damn glad to now have a King who is a sane and reasonable man. We are sick of paying protection money only to have our own King rape and murder our families and burn our businesses. We want King Sudfad to establish law here. Look," Wallis said as he pulled a large map out of his pocket and opened it.

"We have been talking and in order to have law here, that is strong enough to protect us from the groups of men who have attacked us in the past; you will need a fort. We have taken the liberty of drawing several areas on this map that would be fine locations for a fort," Wallis said as he handed the map to Raul. "And the City of Nora will build it. You just tell us what you want."

"I will admit I am rather surprised by all of this," Raul said. "Especially after the reception parties we have already received."

"I don't understand," Wallis said with a look of confusion. Raul noted that all of the men, except for Lloyd looked confused.

"Well, Lloyd here has twice sent hired killers after Gabriel, Hannah and me."

"What!" Morris yelled. "You Lloyd?"

Simon stood up and walked towards Lloyd. "So this is the one," Simon said just before he punched Lloyd with a right hook to the jaw. Simon punched Lloyd with such force that his chair fell backwards with Lloyd flailing to get out.

"If you want law," Simon said. "It starts here and now. Luca chain him in the barn until the troops arrive." The others watched in silence as Luca dragged Lloyd out of the study.

"You have to know that we did not know anything about that," Wallis said apologetically.

"So there are troops coming?" Morris asked with a sigh of relief.

"Yes," Simon said. "But I am sure Father is having talks with King Hamond. We would like to avoid putting this city in the middle of a war. But troops are on their way."

Now Peters, who had been holding a stack of papers, stood up and walked up to Raul and Simon. "We have heard nothing but wonderful stories about life in Wetpr. If most of us would have been able to leave this kingdom we would have moved our families there. This morning when we had a meeting, we were trying to figure out ways we could help your father because we fear he may have problems with King Hamond."

"We think you have maps of some of the mines but we don't know if you have these." Peters spread an unusual looking map out on top of Gabriel's desk as he spoke. "These are the veins of minerals that run through here. We have paid a lot of money to have these maps drawn up. They may not be one hundred percent accurate. But these are the maps we use to determine where we are going to dig for gold."

"These veins go for miles past the city," Gabriel said as he studied the map.

"Yes and we own all of the rights," Morris added. "Peters show him the rest."

Peters unfolded another map, which showed all of the above and underground water rights in the area. "We own these also. Take these maps. Perhaps your father can use them as leverage with King Hamond. You see gold from our mines supply a great deal to the state of affairs of Stordt. And if all that gold was to now go to Wetpr that would hurt this kingdom. And if someone was to block these waterways, well I guess that would leave some of the kingdom in a bad way too."

"Do you have more of these maps for yourselves?" Simon asked.

"Yes," Peters replied.

"What is it you all want?" Raul asked genuinely.

"We want to live in peace," Carston said. "This is a rich city but money draws the worse of mankind. We are truly sick of living in fear all of the time. We want to run our business and to provide for our families. Actually we would like to become citizens of Wetpr. Is that what will happen now that your father owns this city?"

The meeting with the government of Nora lasted another two hours. The men asked permission to build a school, a monastery and a temple; all things that were forbidden under the rule of King Roch. The two young Princes granted all the requests but warned the men that they should wait until troops were in place to protect them.

"Before we go," Jack said as he walked towards Prince Lakin. "We are trying to figure out how we can repay you and your warriors for saving us. We know this may sound silly but before we came here we had men change the signs coming into the city; they are painting them now. We will do much more; but know that we really mean this." Jack handed Lakin two pieces of paper and the five men walked out of the study.

Lakin unfolded the two sheets of paper, each contained a drawing. He smiled deeply as he looked at them, then Lakin handed the pictures to the others. The caption of the first drawing read: *This is what the sign will read today.* The sign read: *Welcome to the City of Nora, Home of the Rualas.* The caption of the second picture read. *This is what we hope the future holds.* That sign read: *Welcome to the City of Nora in the Kingdom of Wetpr. Home of the Rualas.*

"They certainly seem to be sincere," Gabriel said. "But we have reason to believe there is still a strong presence of Insidiae here; perhaps even in this house. I would suggest we sleep in shifts." Raul and Lakin decided they would sleep now and take the night shift. Simon started a letter to Sudfad, explaining all that had occurred. And Gabriel went to the barn to talk with Lloyd.

King Sudfad sent two thousand troops across the border of Stordt. But the men were ordered to wear civilian clothes and to cross at various points of the border in small groups that would join forces at designated locations. Sudfad knew Hamond would forbid his troops to cross the border, so Sudfad planned to start negotiations after his troops were in place. One thousand soldiers traveled to Nora from Fort Salar; one thousand were dispatched from Fort Nir; while soldiers at Fort Polta were told to prepare for troop movement.

Shortly after discovering his father's wills, Sudfad requested Annabelle to make copies of the maps that were included in the paperwork. Annabelle had great artistic talents; that were often utilized by her family. It took her but a few hours to copy the map of the underground shelters and passageways in the Kingdom of Stordt.

As soon as the first copy was completed, Sudfad gave it to one of his captains with orders to take five hundred soldiers and work his way towards Nora. The captain was to investigate the condition or even the existence of these shelters. A small flock of Enrops was sent with these men, as both Sudfad and the captain knew there was a great possibility that Rogetts could have taken over these underground havens.

The very next morning Riftca and Kev arrived at Sudfad's castle. They briefed the King on everything that had occurred in Nora. They gave him Endleson's twenty-seven deeds and Gabriel's letters, paperwork and money. Both warriors wanted to return to Nora immediately, even though they were exhausted. Sudfad made them eat and get some sleep first, as he reviewed all they had brought to him. None of these men were aware of the battle that had occurred earlier that morning.

Because of the increasing threats to his kingdom and his family; King Sudfad had spent the previous three months preparing for the construction of two additional forts in his kingdom. The manufacturing of the materials and supplies were nearly completed.

Sudfad had chosen two experienced generals, with the skills to lead such enormous projects and to command each fort. As Sudfad read the paperwork that Riftca and Kev had brought to him; he waited for the arrival of these two generals.

"What are you going to do to me?" Lloyd asked fearfully.

"I'm just turning you over to King Sudfad's troops when they arrive," Gabriel replied as he pulled a wooden stool close to the wall that Lloyd was chained to. "You tried to kill the King's son and a high priest, to say nothing of my dear wife, who by the way; is a friend of Queen Renya's. I suspect they will not be lenient with you. Lloyd if you have any information that might help your cause; I would suggest you tell me now. Because no one else is going to listen to you."

Lloyd knew Gabriel was speaking the truth. "What kind of information?" Lloyd asked fearfully.

"Well, are there more Hutas in the area? Who are the members of the Insidiae that you have not told us about? And what do you know about those priests who tried to raise Omnibus?" Gabriel asked. Lloyd squirmed in his chains. He looked scared but said nothing. "Fine," Gabriel said then stood up and started to walk out of the barn.

"Gabriel if I tell you; the same thing will happen to me that happened to Endleson."

"Endleson, what are you talking about?"

"After you, Raul and Simon left his office the other day; his screams could be heard throughout the hotel. People ran into his office and found the outline of a man smoldering on the carpet."

"General Craven and General Farnsworth thank you for coming," Sudfad said graciously as he led the men into his study. "Marie will be bringing in refreshments in just a moment. As we wait I would like you to start reviewing these packets of information." Sudfad handed a stack of papers to each man. Within minutes Marie carried a tray of coffee and cake into the study, then quickly left.

After she shut the door, Craven looked at Sudfad. "Are you giving us new commands?" he asked with pleasant surprise.

"Yes, if you will accept them," Sudfad said as he took a seat behind his desk. "All of my generals are experienced in battle and leadership but I believe that you two also have the necessary skills to oversee the construction of two new forts. Of course you can hand pick your initial teams for these projects."

"Will we command these forts when they are completed?" Farnsworth asked.

"That is my intention unless either of you have opposition to that," Sudfad replied. He could see that the generals were interested in the projects. "Both of these forts are going to be larger than the forts we already have."

"General Craven I would like you to command the fort at Stanus. That will be on the border with Stordt, near the foothills of the Caves of Muldun, close to the same area where my sons were almost murdered. And General Farnsworth I would like you to command the fort near Serpha. We have little protection of our northern borders and the Kozach Tribe is causing problems in that area. Would you like to read those packets before you give me an answer?"

Craven and Farnsworth both looked at each other then turned to Sudfad, "I can tell from my friend's eyes that he is thinking the same thing I am," Farnsworth said. "We would be most honored for these assignments."

"Good," Sudfad said. "Each packet contains all of the plans and information about each of the forts that I have completed thus far. As of this moment these projects belong to you. I know you have both traveled great distances to get here. You will be my guests in the castle for as long as you need."

"Scrutinize those papers, if you want to make changes to anything, let me know as soon as possible. I have included the information about the materials and supplies that I have already ordered. Obviously you will need to order more, so purchase what you need and have the bills sent to me."

Sudfad had known both of these men since they were all young boys; they had fought in battle together. Sudfad trusted these two generals which was important, especially now when Sudfad did not know how many spies he had in his kingdom. Spies had already assumed disguises of men in his military and endangered his family; Sudfad could not afford to let that happen again.

Gabriel spent more than an hour in the barn with Lloyd before he returned to the house. "Did he tell you anything?" Simon asked as Gabriel joined him and Luca in the study.

"He's either really afraid or he is stalling," Gabriel said as he poured himself a small glass of whiskey. "He did say that right after we got done talking with Endleson that people heard screams from his office. And when they rushed in they found the outline of a man made of smoldering ashes on the carpet. What bothers me about that is not only does it appear that the act was retribution by a demon; but that a demon was listening to our conversation without me knowing it. And now Lloyd is afraid of that same fate."

"Endleson was part of the Insidiae and gave us information," Simon said. "If Lloyd is afraid of the same fate he must know more than he is saying. Perhaps I should talk to him."

"I kept telling him that your family was going to punish him severely. I was trying to scare him into talking but he fears the demons more than he fears your family," Gabriel said.

"So I should take the nice approach then, is that what you are saying?" Simon asked with a grin.

"A different approach couldn't hurt," Gabriel said.

Late that afternoon, Calen suddenly woke up. Directly in front of him he saw Natasha curled up in a chair sleeping. He felt a presence in bed and turned and saw Misha laying on the other side of the mattress. Calen took the wet cloth off from his forehead and threw it on the floor. "Natasha," he whispered loudly. "Natasha."

Natasha's eyes popped open the second time Calen called her name. She leaned forward and grabbed his hand. "How do you feel?" Natasha asked.

"Like someone beat the hell out of me but I wouldn't expect anything else."

"Do you want some more pain medicine?"

"No, I want my head to clear a little. Lay down next to me Natasha," Calen said as he moved a little to his right to make more room for her.

"Calen, you have so many wounds, I'll hurt you."

"Honey I want to hold you, please."

Natasha took her shoes off and slid under the covers next to Calen. He put his left arm around her shoulders and the palm of his right hand on her stomach. "Misha and I flew to the top of the hill to throw the jars of explosives down an opening he had found. When we first moved the brush away from the opening and looked into the cave, we saw not two thousand Hutas but three, four times that many."

"And for a moment I thought I would never see you again or get a chance to see my baby; that scared me more than the whole damn Huta Army." Calen started to drift asleep as he was talking. Tears were streaming down Natasha's cheeks as she listened to her husband. He was almost asleep now. Natasha kissed Calen softly on the lips and cuddled up against him; and she continued to cry.

The Sanuri had been traveling as fast as he could for two days; he knew he had to give his horses a long rest, so he reluctantly made camp. It was not yet dark but his horses wouldn't make the trip at the pace they had been traveling. The Sanuri built a fire and made himself a late lunch. After he finished his meal; he walked to the top of a small hill. Silently he raised his arms into the air and stood motionless for several minutes. Soon birds of all manner flew around him, many of them landing on his head and shoulders. The Sanuri spoke with these creatures in the silent language of the mind. They told him of the battle between the Rualas and the Hutas.

497

The birds told the Sanuri of The Lion destroying the hill and the battlefield covered with lava and they told him of the shadows that whisper.

That night Raul and Lakin stayed up to watch the house and all the people in it, while Simon, Gabriel and others got some sleep. Raul and Lakin walked around the outside of the house and other buildings that were being guarded by Ruala warriors. Then they walked through the house. Many of the people of Nora were still there, helping with the wounded. Raul and Lakin took refuge in Gabriel's study, where it was just the two of them. "I got it," Lakin said. "But I still don't think you should read it." Lakin handed Raul Sophie's book.

"That's why I thought we could read it together," Raul said. "I'm hoping you can keep me sane, so we can try and figure this thing out. Gabriel believes we did not stop the ascension; so it might be easier to stop a man than a demon. There has to be something in this book that will help us stop Roch and Omnibus."

Lakin poured two glasses of whiskey and the two friends sat down at one of the tables. Lakin was the first to read out loud, as Raul took notes. The contents of Sophie's book took both of the men to places that humans should not go. Raul remembered Vitomas once telling him that he did not want to know of her nightmares. As Lakin read, Raul started to live his wife's nightmares; something that would change his life forever.

Jared had been traveling eastward all day; trying to figure out what he wanted to do, now that he was a wealthy man. Now, late at night as Jared sat before his camp fire, he decided to go to Port Friada. Jared had always heard it was a great place to start over. Feeling very pleased with his decision, Jared filled his cup with whiskey and took a book out of his saddle bag. It was one of the books that the priests had hidden in the safe at the Endleson Hotel.

This book peaked Jared's interest as it was a ledger of sorts. Thinking he may have stumbled onto more riches, Jared studied the book. Although it was written in a language that he could read, it also appeared to be written in some type of code.

Annoyed, Jared took the second book out of his saddlebag, thinking it might help him decipher the code.

The second book had the image of a demon on the cover. There was no writing on the outside of the book. Jared poured more whiskey into his cup and started to read the history of the Insidiae's work to raise the demon Omnibus from The Abyss. As Jared read, he kept thinking about the cryptic message that Roch had sent him. Then Jared suddenly realized that this was the first night in many that Roch had not tried to communicate with him. Jared got that really bad feeling in the pit of his stomach, the one he always got just before something terrible happened. But that feeling compelled Jared to keep reading.

The sun was barely up the next morning when a Ruala warrior ran into the house. He found Raul and Lakin in the kitchen drinking coffee. "There's riders coming from the north, looks like a lot of them," the warrior announced. Raul and Lakin went upstairs and woke Simon and Gabriel; who quickly joined them outside of the house.

"Are they wearing uniforms of either the Taperian or the Wetprian armies?" Raul asked a second Ruala warrior who flew to the house.

"They aren't wearing uniforms but they must be your father's men because Enrops are flying over them,* the warrior replied. A sense of relief filled everyone. They all knew they were not prepared for another large battle. The dust of two thousand horses on the move; could be seen for quite a distance. Gabriel and the others were not the only ones aware of this advancing army. Within thirty minutes the Enrops led the Wetprian troops to the house of Gabriel and Hannah. Raul, Simon, Lakin and Gabriel met the men as they rode in.

"My Lords, it is good to see you," a young captain said as he dismounted.

"Captain Colter, you have no idea how good it is to see you," Raul said.

"Our uniforms are in our saddlebags," Colter explained. "Your father had us wear civilian clothes and cross the border in small groups. We had no difficulty getting here and we haven't seen any Hutas. The King said that a couple of thousand were gathering here."

"It was seven thousand and we already had that battle," Simon said.

"Seven thousand!" Colter almost yelled. "How many Rualas fought with you?"

"One thousand warriors who knew the odds we faced," Raul said with admiration. "And we won that battle with a lot of help from The Great Ruler."

"I don't understand," said Colter.

"Come in and we will explain everything to you," Simon said. "You have a lot of work to do here."

"First, I have letters for you from your wives," Colter said as he pulled two large envelopes from his shirt pocket. "And we picked up some men who said they were coming here to help High Priest Gabriel. Is he among you?"

"I am Gabriel and I almost forgot about Emmet and Grady," Gabriel said. "They're the men I hired to move our things."

Colter looked at Gabriel. "They're back a ways, there's five of them and each is driving a large boca."

By this time several more Ruala warriors had joined the group. Raul saw Eli and Luca standing near the kitchen door. "Luca, Eli will you show our troops where they can camp?" Raul asked. Then he turned to Colter, "Who is your second in command?"

"Lieutenant Tate, My Lord."

"Have him replace the Ruala guards with our troops," Raul said. "Many of them are wounded and exhausted from battle."

Three hours later the Sanuri drove up to Hannah's and Gabriel's house; which was taking on the appearance of a military outpost. The Sanuri entered the house through the front door which took him into the middle of the makeshift hospital. He paused and looked at all of the wounded Ruala warriors.

"The Sanuri is here," a cry rang out and was echoed by other warriors, as the room filled with people. Many of the patients tried to sit up to greet the holy man.

"Rabi who is that?" Bertha asked as she walked out of the kitchen.

"You do not know the Sanuri?" Rabi asked in amazement. "He is an emissary of The Great Ruler; he is a very powerful and holy man."

The door to Gabriel's study opened. Gabriel, Lakin, Raul and Simon walked out to greet the Sanuri, who looked at them and nodded. "I must treat your men first," the Sanuri said as he knelt down and placed his hand on the forehead of the warrior closest to him.

Hannah ran down the stairs, "Is he really here?" she asked.

Gabriel pointed towards the Sanuri and said, "He is healing men now."

"Do you think it would be alright if I spoke to him?" Hannah asked with a concerned look on her face.

"Of course but is something wrong?" Gabriel asked.

"It's Koby; he seems to be getting worse." Lakin quickly left the group and asked the Sanuri to follow him to Koby's room. Hannah followed them both up the stairs. Both Dagon and Natasha moved away from Koby's bed to make room for the Sanuri and Lakin.

"Please help him," Natasha said with tears in her eyes.

The Sanuri held his hands three inches above Koby's body and moved them in a horizontal motion the entire length of Koby's body. Hannah watched the Sanuri's face as he appeared to receive some unseen information about Koby's wounds.

"Where are my two physicians?" the Sanuri asked.

Prince Lakin stepped forward. Hannah stood back meekly and looked at the Sanuri who turned to her. "Are you Hannah?" he asked.

"Yes," she replied in almost a whisper.

"Come forward," the Sanuri said and took Hannah's right hand. The Sanuri took Lakin's left hand. "You two instruments of The Great Ruler have tried so very hard to save your friend; now we will all do it together." The Sanuri placed the palms of their hands on Koby's body, then he put his own hands upon Koby.

The Sanuri did not say a word but everyone in the room suddenly felt different. Natasha, who started to cry, would later say she felt as if she was 'getting lighter' as the Sanuri healed Koby. Hannah's eyes grew wide as she felt the holy energy surging through Koby. Hannah felt other things too but she did not possess the words to describe them.

"Let him sleep now; he will heal," the Sanuri said. "Are there others up here also?"

"Yes," Natasha said and led the Sanuri to the next room. As they walked together the Sanuri said, "Natasha your baby is fine; the demon snake did not touch her."

"Her, we're having a baby girl?" Natasha asked with excitement. "And she is safe! Thank you so much." The Sanuri smiled and walked into the next bedroom to heal two more Ruala warriors.

Two hours later the Sanuri joined the men in Gabriel's study. They told him of everything which had occurred.

"Has the ascension been stopped?" Gabriel asked.

"I don't know the answer to your question," the Sanuri said. "But there is so much more going on here, it is a possibility that the ascension was a ruse to distract all of us from something else. On my way here, creatures were telling me about seeing shadows that whisper walking around the hill that The Lion had destroyed."

502

"Yes, some of the Rualas said they saw shadows but could not see what made them," said Gabriel.

"They are called Acura," the Sanuri explained. "The hell dimensions are constructed of very strict hierarchies. There are different kinds of demons that fit within the cast systems of hell." "But there is also a sort of ranking system, just as you have in your militaries. The Acura would be the inner circle of demons, so to speak. The ones who directly serve the Old Ones. They are very dangerous beings."

"But what bothers me greatly about all that you have told me; is Ahriman's direct involvement in so many things. That is unheard of. The Old Ones are like the ancient kings of the underworlds, they are waited on constantly; others do their bidding for them. It sounds like Ahriman is taking a more active role in this world and that should scare us all."

Jared never left his campsite that day; he had an overwhelming feeling that he needed to finish reading the book he had stolen from the high priests. Jared was not a man who enjoyed reading books, so this was most unusual behavior for him. It did not go unnoticed by Jared, that Roch's voice had stopped haunting him as he read. At noon he was only half way through the book, although he found it interesting he still did not understand how his life was connected to Roch's or why Roch would come to him for help.

The Sanuri was still in Gabriel's study, talking with the men when they heard a loud scream. They all ran out of the room. "It didn't come from in here," Natasha said as she was feeding one of the wounded warriors. "I think it came from outside." A second scream was heard in the still afternoon air. When Raul, Simon, Gabriel, Lakin and the Sanuri ran outside they saw soldiers running into the barn.

"Lloyd," Simon yelled as they ran towards the barn.

Lloyd was screaming and crying hysterically when the men entered the barn. "Get them away from me," he screamed again and again.

"Who, I don't see anyone?" Simon asked as he knelt down next to Lloyd.

"Can't you hear them? Oh tell me you can hear them," Lloyd cried as he pulled at his shackles.

"Lloyd what do you hear?" asked Raul.

"Whispering, they are whispering all around me."

The Sanuri stepped forward and knelt down by Lloyd. "Lloyd I am the Sanuri of Tabrul. I can sense demons and I believe whatever was scaring you is gone now. Lloyd do you know why those demons were around you?" Lloyd became quiet and stared at the Sanuri.

"He has refused to give us any information," Simon said as he stood up.

"Lloyd, would you allow me to touch your head?" the Sanuri asked in a soft and soothing voice. "It will not hurt." Lloyd didn't speak; he just continued to stare at the Sanuri. The Sanuri repeated his question and Gabriel noticed that Lloyd seemed to be going into a trance.

The Sanuri placed the palms of his hands on either side of Lloyd's head. The first image that the Sanuri saw was that of The Lion roaring. Lloyd sat motionless as hundreds of images flooded the Sanuri's mind. The Sanuri stared into Lloyd's eyes trying to decipher all that he was seeing. Lloyd suddenly fell limp and unresponsive.

"Is he dead?" Gabriel asked.

"No, his fears overwhelmed him and he passed out," the Sanuri responded. "Gabriel there is an unholy altar in your cellar, take me to it."

"We destroyed the altar but the room is still there," Gabriel said as he led the Sanuri and the others to the cellar. "Luca found it," Gabriel explained. "Lloyd told us that Hannah's father was a member of the Insidiae." Gabriel moved the wooden shelves that blocked the doorway to the room. He walked into the enclosure and lit all of the torches that were affixed to the stone walls.

The others followed Gabriel into the room that still had skeletons shackled to the walls. The Sanuri felt along the walls of the room without finding anything. Then he turned his attention to the floor.

"Can we help you?" Lakin asked.

The Sanuri shook his head from side to side to indicate 'no' but he did not speak. The Sanuri stepped down into the huge fire pit that was situated in the middle of the room. He started to throw bones and pieces of lumber out of the pit and onto the surrounding floor. The sides of the fire pit were lined with rocks. The Sanuri found several that were loose; he removed the first three without finding anything but behind the fourth rock was a metal lever.

The Sanuri pushed down on the lever and the floor in front of the remains of the altar started to separate into equal halves that were now receding into the side walls. This area of floor lay between what was once the unholy altar and the fire pit. The stench of stale air and decaying flesh filled their nostrils. When the floor stopped moving the Sanuri grabbed one of the torches from the wall and walked over to the opening. "There are steps," he said and started to descend them. The others each grabbed a torch and followed him.

There was only one flight of steps that took them to another stone chamber where they found the body of a naked young woman shackled to the wall. Gabriel quickly ran over to her to check for signs of life. "She is dead," he said. "But she hasn't been long; how can this be?"

"There's a passageway back here," Raul said as he slid behind a small stone wall. He and Simon walked into the passageway and returned ten minutes later.

"This comes out behind the barn," Simon said as they returned to the others.

"Did you see this in Lloyd's mind?" asked Lakin.

"I saw fragments of it," the Sanuri explained. "Lloyd is a member of the Insidiae, although not the group that was trying to raise Omnibus."

"Since your arrival Gabriel, Lloyd has lost a great deal of money. He brought this girl here as a sacrifice to a demon, so that his wealth will be restored."

"Ahriman?" asked Gabriel.

"No, I saw the face of Stolas but he has been vanquished to The Abyss," the Sanuri explained.

"Well let's bury the poor thing," Gabriel said as he took his shirt off and wrapped it around the girl while Lakin busted her shackles open.

"I know her," Raul said as he held a torch up to her face. "Gabriel she came from Nora to help us, we met her in the General Store."

The men left the cellar by way of the secret tunnel, so they would not have to carry the girl's body past all of the people from Nora. The tunnel led them to within ten feet of the back of the barn. Gabriel placed the girl's body on the ground. "Raul why don't you bring one of the townsfolk out here to identify her?" Gabriel asked.

"I'm going to post some guards at that entrance," Simon said and quickly walked away to find Captain Colter.

Raul returned a few minutes later with one of the older women who was working in the kitchen. "This is Charlene," Raul introduced the woman. Then he turned to her and asked, "Do you know this girl?"

"Oh my," the woman gasped. "That's Margolia. Her father Harold owns the General Store. What happened?"

"We found her like this," Gabriel said softly. "We have reason to believe that Lloyd had something to do with her death."

"Lloyd," Charlene gasped. "He is such a despicable man. Is he still in that barn?" Charlene turned around and boldly marched into the barn with a look of determination. The men followed her in. Charlene marched up to Lloyd and slapped him across the face. "Lloyd did you kill that poor girl?"

506

Simon and Colter now joined the group and stood in amazement as Charlene yelled at Lloyd, who did not answer her question. As Charlene stared at Lloyd a look of guilt filled his countenance.

"Well I am waiting," Charlene said as she put her hands on her hips and stamped her foot on the ground. "You tell me now or I am going straight to your wife, then I am going to tell everyone in Nora what you did. You shameless piece of filth!"

"Yes I did," Lloyd admitted in a whisper.

"Why?" demanded Charlene.

Lloyd looked down at the ground, "I don't know."

"Lloyd don't you lie to me, you know very well why you killed her."

"An offering to a demon," Lloyd said in a guilty whisper.

"I thought so; I always thought you were one of those demon worshipers," Charlene said with disgust then quickly turned around to the group of men behind her, who were trying to conceal the grins on their faces. "You hang him high, he doesn't deserve to live," Charlene said then started to walk out of the barn.

"Charlene," Gabriel called as he ran up to her. "Do you know who the demon worshippers are in Nora?"

"Of course, everyone knows who they are."

"How do you know?" Gabriel asked.

"Because most of them are a bunch of fools," Charlene said with indignation. "They play their secret little games then they get drunk and tell people what they did. And most of them, like Lloyd here, think their wives are so stupid they don't know what their husbands are doing."

"Charlene, we are here to stop them," Gabriel said. "Would you mind coming to my study and talking to us?"

"I would be glad to," Charlene said. "But what about Margolia?"

507

"We will have soldiers take her body to her father."

"Harold is a good man; he will want to kill that despicable Lloyd."

Gabriel held out his arm for Charlene to take and he escorted her into the house. Raul turned to the others and said with a grin, "Boy, I'm glad she's on our side." Then the group started to walk to the house.

"I'll be in later," the Sanuri said as he walked towards Lloyd. "Which demon did you give the girl as a sacrifice to?"

Lloyd did not answer. "I saw Stolas when I looked into your mind, is he the demon you made the pact with? He was vanquished to The Abyss a while ago," the Sanuri explained. "He cannot hear you or see you or help you. So who was the sacrifice for?"

"What do you mean, Stolas is in The Abyss, isn't that like a prison?"

"Yes."

"But how can that be?" Lloyd seemed to ask with genuine confusion. "I have had communication from him."

"Communication, what do you mean?"

"I was praising him at the altar in my house, when I heard his voice," Lloyd said fearfully. "He told me to kill a young girl and to put her body, where you found it."

"In Gabriel's house?"

"Yes, well if that wasn't Stolas who was talking to me?" Lloyd asked with panic in his voice.

When Colter joined the others in Gabriel's study, Charlene was preparing to leave.

"Charlene," Raul said. "This is Captain Colter. He will be in charge of our troops after we leave. We are awaiting word from our father, as to whether we will establish a fort here."

"If we do, Captain Colter will be commanding the installation. I hope you will be as helpful to him as you have been to us. We do appreciate it."

Charlene turned to Raul and said, "Oh, he's a handsome boy." Then she looked at Colter, "Tell me are you married?" Colter was so shocked by Charlene's question that he did not answer. As Charlene watched the look that was crossing Colter's face, she laughed, "Not for me you silly boy. I have my Frank. But I have a granddaughter and a pretty little thing she is."

Simon was trying not to laugh when he turned to Raul and whispered, "We are going to have to promote this poor guy."

Chapter XXXII
Darkness Closes In

Shortly after Farnsworth and Craven left Sudfad's study, Marie knocked at the door again.

"My Lord you are having a busy morning," Marie said as she handed him a large envelope from Simon. "The Enrops that delivered this said you should read it right away, that is was very important. And there are two more men here to see you."

"Who are they?" Sudfad asked as he looked at the thickness of the envelope.

"General Hatus and General Tamour from the Army of Lentz."

"Please show them in immediately," Sudfad said as he shoved Simon's envelope into a desk drawer. Sudfad stood up and shook hands with the two generals who were on loan to him from King Mathas.

"Please sit down," Sudfad said. "Have you found anything?"

"We have not found anything that can directly link your General Kretcher with the Insidiae; nor have we found anything that would cast light on him as a spy," Hatus said as he handed a packet of papers to Sudfad. "But the interesting thing is that it appears that General Cedrick T. Kretcher did not exist until thirty five years ago. And as you read his history, everything is too perfect."

"What do you mean?" asked Sudfad.

"He has no family of any kind that we could find. And well, everyone has made a mistake in their life or has an uncle who drinks too much or some type of vice. But read these papers, he's so perfect he doesn't even sound human," Hatus continued.

"Now on the other hand," General Tamour said as he handed another packet of papers to Sudfad. "We found references to a Cedrick Teivel that went back hundreds of years. The Teivel Clan is a powerful ruling family in Ryed. We heard from several people that King Nehmota is merely a figurehead and the Teivel family actually rules that kingdom."

"We have all heard what a dark and dangerous place Ryed is and our investigations only confirmed that. It is a kingdom that gives shelter to all who practice dark magics and demon worship. Many crimes have been linked to the Teivel family although not all of them could be proven. Witnesses disappear and most people are just plain terrified of the Teivel's."

"I too have been searching our family and military records," Sudfad said as he leaned back in his chair. Kretcher was promoted to general when I was a boy. His military record is without blemish yet it is also lacking a great deal of information. There was nothing in his record that would give any indication as to why he was promoted to general."

Sudfad continued," I could not find any information on him holding other ranks. The more I learn the more suspicious I am of him." Sudfad reached into his desk and pulled out two leather pouches of gold coins, handing one to each man. "I want to thank you for all of your hard work. You understand I had to get someone from the outside to investigate one of my generals. I will send letters to Mathias telling him how pleased I am with your performance. But you understand this is still a secret investigation."

"King Sudfad, it has been our pleasure to help you," Hatus said. "The Insidiae is a threat to all mankind. If we can ever be of service to you, please don't hesitate to contact us again."

"May I ask what you are going to do now?" Tamour asked.

"I have some friends in the Patronus," Sudfad said. "They are experts in these things; I believe I will hand the investigation over to them."

No sooner had Charlene walked out of Gabriel's study than there was a knock at the door. The men could hear Natasha's voice through the closed door as she yelled, "What are you doing out of bed?" The door opened and Calen and Misha limped into the study, holding each other up.

"Are you sure you should be up?" Simon asked. "Neither of you look very good."

"It's getting embarrassing," Calen said with a grin. "Misha and I haven't slept together since we were babies and I would much rather be sharing my bed with my wife."

"No kidding," Misha said smiling. "Natasha is starting to ask me to help with baby names." As soon as Misha said this, both he and Calen started to laugh then immediately winced in pain.

"You two are just too much alike," Natasha said as she grabbed both of their arms. "At least let me help you to some chairs."

Calen winked at the men, "She thinks she can hold us both up if we start to fall." Gabriel and Simon quickly pushed large overstuffed chairs up to Calen and Misha, while Natasha helped her two patients to sit down.

"Actually I wouldn't put too much past Natasha," Simon joked.

"So why are you out of bed?" Lakin asked. "Did you just come downstairs to visit?"

"No," Calen said as he pulled Natasha onto his lap. "Misha and I can't remember if we told you what we saw in the cave before we threw the explosives in."

As the afternoon wore on, Jared found himself dozing off as he read. He would sleep for a few minutes then wake up and continue reading. The warmth of the day was so comfortable that Jared was feeling lethargic. He nodded off again; then quickly awoke but this time when he looked around he did not recognize his surroundings.

Jared was now in the middle of a cave, which was illuminated by a huge fire in a pit in the middle of the room. There was a strange type of altar against one wall. The altar was covered with all types of snakes and bones and appeared to have bowls of blood surrounding it. As Jared stared at the altar he realized he was saying to himself, "This must be a dream."

The altar and snakes had captivated his attention so completely; that at first Jared did not see the giant stone tubs lined up side by side on the right side of the huge cave.

The first tub was the largest and adorned much more artistically than the others. There was a sign made of marble above this tub, the sign read *Our Master Omnibus.*

All the other tubs were the same size with the exact same drawings on them. Jared counted, thirteen, there were thirteen smaller tubs to the left of the large tub. As Jared walked closer he realized that each smaller tub contained a body of a man. Each body was lying on its back and appeared to be dead. Jared got that bad feeling in his stomach again, and remembered thinking, "This never happens in dreams." Jared walked up to the first tub and stared at the man. It was the same image he saw in the fire. "This must be Roch," Jared thought without emotion.

Jared walked up to the second tub and his eyes grew wide and his heart started beating faster as Jared recognized himself in the second tub. His body in the tub was dressed in the exact same clothing that Jared was wearing now. Jared quickly ran to the other tubs. But the faces of each man were indiscernible, as if Jared was trying to look at something through a thick fog.

Jared quickly looked around the cave, trying to figure out if he was dreaming. He saw a tunnel and started to run towards it. He ran as fast as he could towards a small light at the very end of this long tunnel. It was then that he heard a voice, "Listen to me." Then darkness fell upon him.

After Calen pulled Natasha onto his lap, he kissed her several times. "Did you tell them?" he asked her after their third kiss.

Natasha smiled, "No, I thought we could tell them together."

Calen looked at Gabriel and smiled, "The Sanuri said we are having a baby girl and she will be just fine; the demon snake did not harm her." Everyone in the room could see how overjoyed Calen and Natasha were about the news. Gabriel walked forward and hugged Natasha, then he shook hands with Calen. Simon, Lakin, Raul, Luca and Colter all walked up and shook hands with Calen also.

After Colter shook hands with Calen he turned to Raul and asked, "Demon snake, what is he talking about?"

Raul smiled, "We have so much to tell you yet."

Misha turned to Calen and said weakly, "I'm going to have to lie down again soon, hurry up and tell them."

"When Misha and I climbed on top of that hill, it seemed to be vibrating. When we looked down through the opening we saw seven maybe eight thousand Hutas dancing and hitting each other. We saw the two priests; they were standing on a stone outcropping above the Hutas. I could see their faces and they did not look happy, in fact they looked kinda scared."

"I looked away for just a moment as I was taking jars of the smoke out of a sack, when I looked back; there were strange shadows on the walls of the cave that weren't there before. I hesitated because I was trying to figure out what made the shadows, that's when Misha looked down the opening."

"I saw them too, the shadows did not look like the Hutas and besides the Hutas were dancing and the shadows were standing still," Misha explained. And they didn't look like the priests either. There were lots of them, as if an audience was watching the Hutas."

"Most of the shadows were huge, as tall as the cave, but there were some smaller ones too. It was difficult to see the features of their faces," Calen said. "But they all had arms and looked like they were wearing robes. I figured we couldn't waste any more time, so I started throwing jars through the opening."

"Some of the men said they saw strange shadows on the battlefield long after the battle was done and everyone was gone," Lakin said.

"And the Sanuri said that birds were telling him about shadows that whispered that were around the battlefield," Gabriel said. "Must be some type of demon."

Misha suddenly turned white, "Sorry, but I really need to lie down." Luca and Colter both helped Misha out of the chair.

"Put him in my bed," Lakin said.

"Good," Misha said jokingly. "Calen rolled over last night and I thought he was going to kiss me. I had to tell him I wasn't Natasha." Misha winced with pain as he laughed at his own joke.

"Where are you going to sleep?" Simon asked Lakin as Luca, Colter and Misha left the room.

"I suspect Raul and I will be up reading all night," Lakin replied.

After the Sanuri finished talking to Lloyd, he did not join the rest of his friends in the study but instead he walked back into the cellar to more closely examine the torture rooms and altars that Hannah's father had built. The Sanuri was greatly disturbed by Lloyd's words. A demon was pretending to be Stolas and told Lloyd to kill that girl and to put her body in the cellar of Gabriel's house, when they all were present.

As the Sanuri entered the tunnel, the pungent smell of decay filled his nose, something he often experienced in these underground horror chambers. The Sanuri started to whisper out loud to The Lion; as he walked down the dark tunnel towards the room where they found the girl's body. "Old friend, I would appreciate some insight," the Sanuri said. "I fear my friends may have been set up in some kind of trap."

"Your friends are not the only ones who have been set up," The Lion's voice ran out of the darkness. "You are a prize which Ahriman greatly desires, but that is but a very small part of what is going on here." The Sanuri could not see The Lion, until he entered the chamber where the body was found.

"Thank you for saving my friends at that battle," the Sanuri said.

"Gabriel finally asked to see my face, which pleases me greatly," The Lion said. "And all of these men have such faith and integrity it honors me to know them. But their numbers are few and this battle so to speak has taken on many new twists as of late. As you know two groups of thirteen Old Ones originally came to this world. It was and still is a rich feeding ground for them because there are so many people who call to darkness here."

"But now there are Old Ones from other worlds who want to take advantage of this world. So the battle lines and allegiances of the demons are shifting frequently. There may be a war among the demons soon. And in addition to this, Ahriman has maintained his power over the other Old Ones in this world."

515

"They have challenged him, individually and collectively but he reigns supreme over them." The Lion continued, "But there is a hell dimension many worlds away from here, known as Xibalba; which is ruled by many powerful Old Ones. The most powerful demon there is known as Samael and he is challenging Ahriman for this world also. So Ahriman may be facing all sorts of challengers soon."

"So is it the demons from Xibalba who want to take control of this world?" the Sanuri asked.

"No, there are demons in four other worlds that want control of this one. In Xibalba only Samael is challenging Ahriman. But Samael is as strong as Ahriman and Ahriman knows it. But there are other concerns here also. Those fools who were trying to raise Omnibus from The Abyss have caused a lot of disruption in the underworlds."

"All the demons know that Omnibus cannot escape a prison of The Great Ruler. But the idea of putting their essences inside of human forms is very captivating to them with its possibilities. That is why several of them were pretending to be Omnibus to manipulate the Insidiae. And more humans have been identified as suitable vessels besides Roch. But the demons cannot attempt such transformations without the cooperation of humans. That group of Insidiae in their insane depravity just brought a new plague upon mankind."

"So why was Lloyd instructed to put the girl's body here?" the Sanuri asked. "They obviously wanted us to find it."

"You forget what grand prizes you all are to the demons," The Lion stated. "Although not nearly as powerful as you, Gabriel is also an emissary of The Great Ruler. And Raul and Simon are two of The Seven Sons. If the demons were to kill any of you, it would greatly empower them; just think if they could get all of you at once."

"So how was this a trap here?"

"Sanuri if you wanted to confront Ahriman right now, where would you go?"

"That cave near Roch's castle were that hole between dimensions exists."

"Exactly, do you think that information just fell into your hands? Ahriman is very cunning; he has left messages of sorts for you, Gabriel, Raul and Simon. He would hope that you would be so emotional that you would blindly run into that cave and thus into his lair. That is why I have not allowed you to go to that cave yet. I will tell you when it is time. But for now, stay close to your friends, they will need your protection and guidance. You may tell them the words that I have spoken."

When Jared regained consciousness, the sun was just starting to set. The sky was brilliant with orange and purple streaks. Jared found himself lying on his stomach, in the dirt. He pushed himself up with both of his forearms and immediately felt a blinding pain in the back of his head. The pain was so intense that it affected his eyesight and caused him to become dizzy.

Jared sat on the ground and held his head in his hands until the dizziness passed. After some minutes he slowly lifted his head and looked around at his surroundings. He was not at his campsite. "Where the hell am I?" Jared growled out loud. Then he remembered the vision or was it a dream that he had.

Jared suddenly jumped up as he remembered all of the money he had in his packs. In the dimming light, he found his way back to his campsite; which was a couple of hundred yards to the west. Everything appeared to be as he last remembered. Jared quickly looked through his packs and was satisfied that his money had not been stolen. He sat down by his campfire and filled his cup with whiskey.

As Jared was putting the cup to his lips he stared at his fire. It was all but extinguished after lunch and yet now he had a roaring blaze. Jared could see that a considerable amount of wood had been piled with precision in the fire.

He knew someone had been at his campsite. Jared sat motionless, thinking he was probably being watched. He survived this long, by developing a keen sense of awareness of his surroundings; Jared now slowed his breathing as he strained to hear even the tiniest sound.

"What are you two doing?" the Sanuri asked as he walked into Gabriel's study that night. Both Lakin and Raul were sitting at a table with their backs to the door; they both turned and looked at the Sanuri as he entered the room. Raul's face was uncharacteristically white and his eyes were red. "Is something wrong?" the Sanuri asked with great concern and quickly walked to the table.

Lakin handed him a book and explained, "Natasha and Simon stole this from Sophie's room. We thought it was a diary at first; but the Insidiae sent her to Roch's castle to chronicle his behavior to determine if he was a fit vessel for Omnibus. She writes very dispassionately but describes every atrocity that he committed in great detail. And as you know many of the crimes that he committed were against Raul's family members."

"Why are you reading it?" the Sanuri asked as he carefully inspected the leather cover and binding of the book.

"Several of us have tried to read this," Lakin said. "We hope to learn something about Roch that we can use to stop him. But it is difficult reading for us all."

The Sanuri reached out and put his hand on Raul's shoulder, "My son, you don't need to torture yourself with this. You have probably learned more than you should have, about the cruelty he inflicted on Vitomas and Annabelle. Both of you get some sleep; I will look through this."

Raul did not move at first and asked, "We all know that Roch is a monster but what is Sophie that she could calmly stand by and watch him do those things? Seriously Sanuri, is she some type of demon too?"

Gabriel was sitting on the edge of the bed, while Hannah kneeled behind him, on the mattress, and massaged his shoulders. "We managed to fill two of the bocas today," Hannah explained. "I was surprised we could get all of that work done and still take care of all our patients. I must say it has been nice to have so much extra help here; although I would never have believed it, if I didn't see if for myself."

"Honey I think your anger and grief blinded you in some respects," Gabriel said softly.

518

"I think most of the people of Nora are probably good people but they made the choice to let fear control their lives. And they are miserable with the choices that they made."

Hannah did not respond at first. "Gabriel I agree with what you say but I still have grief and anger in my heart."

"And I am sure you will for some time and you have a right to. But Hannah you have to make the choice as to whether you are going to let that anger control your life. And if you let it; you really are no different from them." Gabriel had been speaking softly; now he turned around and took both of Hannah's hands into his. "Hannah you are the most amazing woman I have ever met. I don't think there is anything that you can't do and do it well. You have the heart of an Angel; don't let it be sullied with the dark thoughts you have for those people."

The next morning several Enrops flew into Gabriel and Hannah's house looking for Raul and Simon. At that early hour the only people awake in the house were a few women from Nora who were working in the kitchen and the Sanuri, who had stayed up all night reading Sophie's book.

Clair, one of the women from Nora, knocked on the door to the study. When the Sanuri opened the door he saw a rotund middle aged woman who looked wide eyed and excited. "I am sorry to disturb you My Lord but, but there are talking birds here and they want to see the Princes of Wetpr. I know you must think me crazy but Betty heard them too."

The Sanuri laughed, "My dear those birds are Enrops, and they do speak most languages of man. They are our messengers."

"Oh I am so glad I'm not going crazy," Clair said with a sigh of relief. "I don't know which bedroom the Princes are in, do you?"

"Yes, where are the birds?" the Sanuri asked as he shoved Sophie's book into one of the pockets of his robe.

"In the kitchen, I will get them," Clair said and quickly disappeared.

Within moments the Enrops joined the Sanuri, who led them to Raul and Simon's door. Three of the great birds were carrying large, thickly stuffed envelopes.

"Raul, Simon wake up," the Sanuri called through the door. "There are Enrops here for you."

"Come in, the door's unlocked," Raul said as he stumbled out of bed. Raul grabbed his pillow and threw it at Simon who was still sleeping in the next bed. The three Enrops that were carrying the envelopes landed on a small table in the bedroom and dropped their cargo.

"Your father said you should read these right away," one of the Enrops said and the small flock flew out of one of the open bedroom windows.

As Simon and Raul got dressed, the Sanuri looked around their small bedroom and smiled broadly at all of the childish paintings that were hung on the walls.

"Yes our boys are quite the artists," Raul said with a grin as he walked over to the table and picked up an envelope.

"Of course we can't figure out what they are painting but they sure like to use bright colors," Simon said with a warm smile as he joined Raul and the Sanuri at the small table.

"Well, Colter just got one heck of a promotion," Raul said as he read a letter from Sudfad. "Father is making him a general and having him oversee the construction of a fort here at Nora. After the fort is built Colter will remain and command it. Father wants us to pick the location of the fort before we come home. He is sending another three thousand troops here and these men will be riding in uniform. Father says he and King Hamond actually had a meeting on the border, south of Fort Salar."

"He says the documents that the citizens of Nora provided him along with all the deeds he now owns, helped in negotiations. But he," Raul now looked up at the Sanuri. "Says that thanks to the Sanuri, he has his father's will which included vital paperwork and maps. Father and Hamond are still working out a treaty and will fill us in on the details when we get home. But Father is claiming his rights to Nora and safe passage for our people between here and Wetpr."

"I'm actually surprised that Hamond is avoiding a war," Simon said.

"Your great grandfather had secret underground shelters built throughout this entire kingdom and they were connected by tunnels. Your father has the only map of these shelters and his men are searching through them now. They would be a great advantage in a time of war," the Sanuri said.

"Why did he build them?" asked Simon.

"To protect his people from invaders; but then he became afraid that if word of them got out," the Sanuri explained. "That the tunnels could be used by invaders to attack the kingdom. So King Jaretta destroyed all mention of the underground system except for one map that has been in the Holy Vault all of these years."

Gabriel and Hannah both awoke to a strong knock on their bedroom door. Gabriel always slept on the side of the bed that was closest to the door.

"I'll slip this under the door," Raul called through the closed door.

"What is it?" Hannah asked as Gabriel picked an envelope up from the floor.

"It has the King's official seal," Gabriel said as he opened the envelope and walked back to the bed. Gabriel read the short letter and handed it to Hannah.

"He bought us that house!" Hannah gasped "He said as a small token of his appreciation. Gabriel wait until you see that house; that is no small token." Hannah jumped out of bed because she was so excited she had to move around.

"He has an assignment for me that he says is so sensitive he wants to speak to me in person," Gabriel said. "Now he has my curiosity up."

"Are you going to take it?" Hannah asked as she danced around their small bedroom.

"I want to see what it is first," Gabriel said. "But it is hard to turn down the King, especially since he has been so good to us."

"Gabriel did you read the last line? What a wonderful idea. Turning this house into a headquarters for the Patronus. Should we unpack some of the furniture and leave it for them?"

"He wanted to see how we felt before he contacted Raphael," Gabriel said as he started to dress. "I know Raphael will be very pleased. And as for the furniture; Honey these are your family's things, take them. The Patronus can furnish the house as they please. I am going down to the study and write letters to both Raphael and Sudfad."

"On Honey, make sure you thank Sudfad for the house. I am so happy I can't hold still," Hannah said as she danced up to Gabriel and kissed him on the lips.

"Hannah I will say that if I am to leave soon for another mission; I would feel better with you living in Salar, where Raul and Simon can watch over you, than in our home in Philiste."

Hannah stopped dancing and stared at Gabriel. "This is something we should talk about," she said soberly. "Natasha cannot be a part of your missions anymore because she is expecting a baby, and that is as it should be. Calen and Koby are too injured to join you. And who knows what Rabi will want to do since he just got married. Can't I come along and help? I'll ask Natasha to teach me some of her skills so I can be more useful."

Gabriel smiled proudly and put both of his large arms around Hannah and hugged her tightly. "You were of extraordinary help on this mission with your own skills. Let's see what the assignment is first. I had wanted to take some time off to set up our new home and to start a family." Gabriel kissed Hannah on the forehead. "The same rules go for you as Natasha; you're not working on the missions when you are pregnant."

"I can accept that," Hannah said. "But didn't you and Calen say we could still come along and cook and take care of you?"

Chapter XXXIII
Faces of the Damned

The next three weeks seemed to fly by as Raul, Simon and Gabriel completed their business in Nora and prepared to return to Salar. They chose the location where Fort Nora was to be built. The fort would be constructed five miles south of Nora, near the River Nebu. Sudfad sent them architectural plans for the entire military complex. Morris and Carston, two of the members of the governing body of Nora, volunteered to be liaisons on the project. They formed work groups to clear the land and to prepare lumber for the construction.

Wagon loads of rocks were being hauled to the building site daily, for the wall that would surround the military fortress. Wallis, another member of the governing body, acted as the supply coordinator and worked closely with General Colter in determining the massive amounts of construction supplies, living necessities as well as food and clothing needed for the five thousand Wetprian troops that were now camping outside of Nora.

Many of the businessmen of Nora were initially afraid that King Sudfad would shut down their businesses but now they enjoyed a great boom in business because of the construction of the fort. They realized that having the fort so close to their city would be profitable as well as providing them with much needed protection. But the real surprise came when Raul and Simon held a meeting with the business leaders of Nora. The two Princes listened to both the concerns and suggestions of the business community and the governing body of Nora.

Raul and Simon carefully documented all that was said and told the people they would give the documentation to King Sudfad to review. Then they invited everyone at the meeting to come to Wetpr and meet with King Sudfad on a date two months into the future. The people from Nora would be provided safe escort by Wetprian soldiers and lodging would be provided for them in Salar. This invitation caused a surge of excitement that the community had never before experienced. Hope for a better future inspired them all.

The Sanuri had promised The Lion that he would stay with Raul, Simon and the others until they returned to Wetpr. The Sanuri too, met with many people in Nora who were hungry for the teachings of The Great Ruler. King Roch had killed all of the holy men in the kingdom decades earlier and forbade any type of religious teachings. Now hundreds of people attended the daily lessons that the Sanuri taught. And he was asked to perform dozens of marriages and christenings. The Sanuri greatly enjoyed his experience with the people of Nora and promised that he would be a regular visitor to their community.

Padre Bartholomew and Padre Thomas were living comfortable lives of retirement at the castle in Wetpr until they received a letter from the Sanuri that changed their lives. He told them all that had occurred in Nora. The Sanuri explained the risks of living in the Kingdom of Stordt and he told them that the community was building their first monastery but they had no teachers or priests.

The Sanuri asked his two old friends if they knew any priests who might be willing to come to Nora. The two priests packed their belongings and with a large military escort they left for Nora the same day they received the letter.

Gabriel and Lakin tried to track down the remaining members of the Insidiae in the community. But they discovered that most of them had left Nora after the death of Endleson and the battle between the Rualas and Hutas. Gabriel strongly suspected these members of the Insidiae would return to Nora, so he contacted Raphael several times in an effort to ensure a strong presence of the Patronus in the kingdom. High Priest Raphael; left fifty of his men at the monastery at Malga under the leadership of High Priest Philetus and led the rest to Nora.

"Isn't it nice to have the house back?" Marcia said as she, Hannah and Natasha prepared breakfast.

"Thanks to the Sanuri, the warriors healed quickly," Hannah said. "Or we would still have a house full of people."

"Have they decided when we are going to leave for Wetpr?" Natasha asked as she took two pans of biscuits from the oven. "Because we will need a little time to finish packing."

"Gabriel said he wants to wait until Raphael gets here," Hannah answered. "Everyone has been working so hard to get things set up in Nora, so we can leave. But there is just so much work that still needs to be done."

"Calen said that Raul and Simon hardly sleep anymore," Natasha said. "They are trying to get everything done so they can go home to their families. You know, I have worked on a lot of missions with Gabriel but we have never worked with a group of people who we became so close to before. It's really like we are all family. I am going to miss them."

"Who?" Marcia asked.

"Well, Calen and I will be moving to the Ice Caves, I don't know if I will ever see Raul or Simon again," Natasha said as she fought back the tears. "And, and, I don't know how often we will see Gabriel and Hannah either."

Hannah walked over to Natasha and gave her a hug. "Gabriel and I were just talking about that. He is going to have another wing built onto our house in Salar for you and Calen. And he said we could visit you often in the Ice Caves."

"I'm glad you're both coming to the Ice Caves," Marcia said as she was becoming emotional. "Because I won't know anyone there either."

"Hello, hello," a voice called out before there was a knock on the kitchen door.

"Peters, I must say this is an early visit," Hannah said to one of the governing members of Nora. "Is anything wrong?"

"Not at all," Peters said as he stepped inside of the kitchen. "Rosalie has finished the dresses that you ordered; I have them all in the back of the boca. You girls sure had a lot made."

"We will be staying at the castle in Wetpr for a while," Natasha said with excitement. "And we want to look our best." Marcia and Natasha ran out of the door to get their new dresses.

"You left Nora before sunrise to deliver our dresses?" Hannah asked suspiciously.

525

"I have something else," Peters said with a smile and took a handful of envelopes from his coat pocket. "Now that most of the Rualas have healed, we are having a celebration in their honor. It will be held in the ballroom of the Endleson Hotel in two nights. The entire city has been planning it."

"Are these invitations?" Hannah asked as she took the envelopes.

"Yes. We can never repay all of you for what you have done but this will be a start."

For three weeks Jared was haunted by visions of the bodies lying in the stone tubs in the cave where Omnibus was to transform. Jared had no idea of the location of the cave but the visions he was having were so real that Jared believed that Roch was somehow transporting him to that cave. Several times after a vision Jared would wake and find himself in a different location. Jared was not a man who was accustomed to fear but these strange happenings had him greatly disturbed.

Jared was drinking more and becoming afraid to go to sleep. He had not finished reading the book he stole from the priests. He felt that the book was linked to his visions and he was afraid to read the ending. Every night for three weeks Jared found himself in that cave trying to see the faces of the dead. Every morning he awoke, trying to figure out the meaning of the visions.

Jared continued his journey towards Port Friada, although something in the back of his mind kept telling him to go to Taperia. Since the visions started, Jared stopped hearing the muffled screams of Roch's voice. Now he wished he could talk with Roch. Jared had considered going back to Taperia to find out if Meekos could explain what was happening to him. But a part of Jared wanted to get as far away from Meekos as he could. Two more days and Jared would be in Port Friada. Two more days and he could start over.

"Come in," Gabriel called when he heard a knock on the door to his study.

The Wetprian soldier entered the room and walked up to the table where Raul, Lakin, Simon, Luca and Gabriel were studying maps. "My Lords, I am sorry to bother you but the prisoner says he is ready to talk but he will only speak with the Sanuri."

"The Sanuri is in Nora teaching," Raul said. "How is Lloyd acting?"

"Seems the same to me," the soldier responded. "He talks to himself and claims to hear voices whispering."

"Let me see if I can talk to him," Gabriel said as he followed the soldier to the barn.

"I said I wanted to talk to the Sanuri," Lloyd yelled when he saw Gabriel walk up to him.

"The Sanuri is in Nora, Lloyd," Gabriel said soothingly as he crouched down near the prisoner. "Why do you only want to speak to him?"

"Because I think maybe he can protect me," Lloyd said uneasily.

Gabriel was silent for a moment as he watched how fearful Lloyd was acting. "Lloyd who exactly do you want protection from?"

"The Sanuri knows," Lloyd responded with an almost childish mannerism. "He knows I was tricked by a demon who pretended to be Stolas."

"Was it Ahriman?" asked Gabriel.

"How do you know about Ahriman?" Lloyd asked with surprise in his voice.

"Ahriman tried to kill me but The Great Ruler saved me," said Gabriel.

Lloyd stared at Gabriel in disbelief. "Lloyd you do know that I am a high priest with the Patronus," Gabriel said.
"I hunt demons; that is why I came here."

"I knew you were a high priest," Lloyd said. "Can you protect me from the demons?"

"I can try."

"I lied to you before," Lloyd said. "I am a member of the Insidiae but not the sect that is trying to raise Omnibus. We didn't want those crazy priests here trying to destroy the world. I know what you probably think about us but most of the Insidiae want to live in this world the way it is. But there are other fractions like those who worship Omnibus that are extremists. The Insidiae are highly organized and there is now a secret group that was formed to keep the extremists in line."

"What is the name of this group and am I to assume this is a new group?" Gabriel asked.

"Yes it was established because of the group that worships Omnibus," Lloyd explained. "It is called Nefandus."

"Nefandus, that means 'not to be spoken of' in the old tongue," Gabriel said. "So you are telling me this is a secret group within your secret groups?"

"Yes, Endleson, Fraisier and Tome contacted them when those priests came here; you see we were trying to stop them too," said Lloyd.

"We've been looking for Fraisier and Tome," Gabriel said. "We believe they may have left Nora."

"Some of the members of the Insidiae left this place as soon as they found out that those crazy priests brought thousands of Hutas here and were trying to raise Omnibus; but there is more."

"So are members of the Nefandus here?" Gabriel asked.

"Four of them came to Nora; they were staying at the Endleson Hotel. They were all businessmen besides being members of the Nefandus." Lloyd now looked around fearfully as if he suspected something was in the empty barn besides him and Gabriel. "After we found out what happened to Endleson, some of us went to the rooms of these men and we found the same thing."

"The outlines of their bodies in smoldering ashes on the carpets. That's why all the members of the Insidiae are running from here."

"So you think those men were killed because they were going to try to stop the ascension of Omnibus?"

"I don't know why they were killed, just like I don't know why other demons are pretending to be Stolas."

"So if the Old Ones know that a demon cannot escape from The Abyss; how do they benefit from keeping up this ruse about Omnibus?" Gabriel asked.

Lloyd leaned closer to Gabriel and opened his mouth to speak but no words came out. Lloyd frantically grasped at his throat as if he was trying to remove unseen hands that were choking him. Gabriel quickly stood up. "Let go of this man, you have no power here," Gabriel ordered. "This place is claimed for The Great Ruler; go back to your darkness."

Suddenly Lloyd could breathe again. But a great wind consumed the inside of the barn; which blinded both Gabriel and Lloyd with flying debris. Within moments boards were being blown out of the walls of the barn. "You impress no one with your parlor games," Gabriel yelled as he stood his ground. "Be gone demon."

Ahriman's voice bellowed above the din, "You escaped me once priest, you will not be so lucky again."

Gabriel recognized this voice from his experience with the demon in Meekos' room in the Endleson Hotel. "Ahriman, you may be able to claim those who sell their souls to demons but you will never take one who has willingly given his soul to The Great Ruler."

"Fools," Ahriman screamed angrily.

Raul, Simon, Lakin and Luca ran into the barn with their swords drawn. As his friends gathered around him Gabriel said, "We stand united, we cast our swords down before The Great Ruler, you have no power here." As Ahriman's anger grew so did the intensity of the wind but none of the warriors tried to flee. They stood their ground and faced the darkness before them.

529

"Ahriman, it is me that you want," yelled the Sanuri with a powerful voice as he entered the barn. Fear reigns in your world and you control mankind with their fears but are you so arrogant that you think you can cause darkness in the hearts of the emissaries of The Great Ruler."

Ahriman started to laugh, "Sanuri you know that I have, in fact your brother Sporos was quite a trophy. There was a time when Pravis, Tenebrae and Meekos were on your team, oh so very long ago," Ahriman said tauntingly.

"They were not emissaries," the Sanuri said as he now stood in front of the small group of warriors. "They merely gave lip service. Those of us who stand before you now do not give lip service; you cannot create darkness in our hearts." The Sanuri held up his hands and all of the men in the barn could feel unusual vibrations; soon the barn filled with an unnatural light.

The warriors themselves started to feel as if they were floating and tears came to their eyes. As the light grew the wind ceased its destruction. The great demon of old lost this battle. "This is not the end," Ahriman threatened as his presence shrank before the holy light.

"Is everyone alright?" the Sanuri asked as he turned to his friends; who were unharmed. But as one they all turned to look at Lloyd, who had been reduced to a pile of smoldering ashes on the floor of the barn.

"Sophie, Sophie let me in," Meekos yelled as he pounded on the door to her hotel room.

"Meekos what on earth is going on?" Sophie asked as she opened the door and stepped to the side so her brother could enter.

"I was down at Walt's Tavern," Meekos said as he frantically paced back and forth in her parlor. "And all the men were talking about the happenings in Nora. Sophie this is bad very, very bad."

"Here drink this and sit down," Sophie said as she handed Meekos a large glass of whiskey. "What are you talking about?"

"Riders came in from Nora last night and they are all talking about a huge battle that took place between thousands of Hutas and Rualas. Some of the men from Nora saw the battle; they said everything got black, a blackness like they have never seen before, then they heard a lion roar and a large hill just blew up. They said that when the darkness left, the battleground was covered with Huta warriors who had been killed by boiling lava from the hill."

"They said no bodies of Rualas were seen anywhere," Meekos paused to gulp down his whiskey. "And there is more, Augustus Endleson was killed. People heard him screaming in his office and when they ran in, all they saw was an outline of a man on the carpet; the outline was made of smoldering ashes."

"Meekos..." Sophie said as she sat down. But she did not complete her sentence before Meekos interrupted her.

"Sophie I'm not done," Meekos almost screamed. "Apparently the two Princes of Wetpr are in Nora with the Rualas. King Sudfad has bought almost the entire city and surrounding land. He is having a fort built there and thousands of Wetprian soldiers are already in Nora." Meekos was suddenly aware of Erebus' presence in the parlor. "Did you just come out of my sister's bedroom?" Meekos bellowed.

"Meekos, we are all adults here," Sophie said defiantly. "I can sleep with whomever I please. And that is not the issue here. Now calm down."

"Meekos you can be mad at me later," Erebus said as he poured himself a drink. "You think Pravis and Tenebrae were involved in that battle?"

"I know they were," Meekos snapped. "They're the ones who brought the Hutas to Nora. And do you understand the significance of the Rualas being there?"

"No," Erebus said as he sat down next to Sophie on the couch.

"The Rualas work for The Great Ruler like the Hutas work for the demons. And did you hear the part about a lion roaring. One of the most powerful emissaries of The Great Ruler takes on the form of a lion in this world. No one knows who he really is but it is said that he is a member of The Great Ruler's inner circle."

"So you think The Great Ruler stopped Pravis and Tenebrae?" Erebus asked.

"I am willing to bet my fortune on it." Meekos stared disapprovingly at Erebus and Sophie who were sitting near each other and holding hands. "Aren't you two a little old for that."

"Meekos I know you are upset but you have nothing to say about my life," Sophie said indignantly. "And it wouldn't hurt you to become involved with a woman who wasn't a prostitute for once. It might improve your temperament."

"Meekos what is the significance of the Princes of Wetpr being with the Rualas?" Erebus asked, trying to change the subject.

"Do you know nothing man!" Meekos yelled rudely. "It has long been suspected that generations of the Royal Families of Wetpr work for The Great Ruler; which is why the Sanuri lives at that castle. If that is true, then I am sure that Sudfad's troops are purging the Insidiae from Nora. And I am sure that the hill that blew up contained the cave that we were preparing for the transformation. That is the second site that The Great Ruler has destroyed."

"Have you heard anything from Jared?" Sophie asked.

"No and that concerns me also. If he was killed when that hill blew up, that's another vessel we have lost."

"What are you talking about?" asked Erebus.

"The Insidiae aren't stupid," Meekos said irritably. "We have all kinds of back up plans. There were others identified as possible vessels for Omnibus besides Roch; although Roch was the perfect vessel."

"So it wasn't a coincidence that you sent him to Nora?" Erebus asked.

"By no means, ravens have been following him for a long time. Sophie and I knew he would answer the call and come to Taperia."

"Answer what call?" asked Erebus.

"After The Lion destroyed the first site that was prepared for the ascension of Omnibus; members of the Insidiae sent out a call, or more like a secret signal that seduced the darkness in men. The call told them to come to Taperia. We knew that anyone who had been identified as a vessel for Omnibus would heed the call. This way they came here instead of us trying to hunt them down."

"Are there others besides Jared?" Erebus asked.

"Oh yes," Meekos said with a malicious grin. "We call our little army the faces of the damned. They are the most evil men in this world and not one of them suspects their destiny."

Late that evening Gabriel and Hannah were awaken by a loud knock on their bedroom door. "What time is it?" Hannah asked as she was trying to wake herself up. Gabriel quickly got out of bed and answered the door.

"I am sorry to wake you," the Wetprian soldier said. "But an army of men has arrived here; they say they are the Patronus. They are led by a man named Raphael."

"Splendid," Gabriel said. "Would you show Raphael to my study and have some of the other soldiers show our guests where to settle in. They will be assuming ownership of this house when we leave." When Gabriel turned around he was surprised that Hannah was already out of bed and dressed.

"Do you want me to wake the others?" Hannah asked as she was tying her long hair back into a ponytail.

Gabriel walked behind Hannah; putting his hands on her waist he kissed the nape of her neck. "Yes," he said. "Then I want you to come down to the study so I can introduce you. You will like Raphael, he and I have been friends since we were children. In fact after my parents died he helped me raise Natasha. You might say he is my adopted brother."

"I am very much looking forward to meeting him. Does he hunt demons like you do?" Hannah asked as she turned around and kissed Gabriel.

"Yes, but he has a more traditional role," Gabriel explained. "He leads an army, where my work has always been more covert."

Jared sat near his campfire drinking whiskey; waiting for his nightly vision to occur. He now dreaded every nightfall because he expected to be transported to that cave of the damned in his visions. Every vision was the exact same, but why was he having them? As Jared stared into the fire, he had an overwhelming feeling that he was missing something, something that he should have seen in those visions. Something that was important.

Jared reached into one of his saddlebags and pulled out the book he had stolen from the priests; he knew it was time he finished reading it. Jared poured more whiskey into his cup and opened the book to the page he had turned down. He had read about half the page when suddenly a small wind started to blow the pages back and forth.

Annoyed, Jared set down his cup of whiskey so he could have a better grasp on the book. Suddenly the wind subsided and a new page lay open before him. Jared grabbed the corner of the page to turn back to the page he had been reading, when he felt as if his heart stopped. There before him, he saw his name written in this book of Omnibus. Jared's body became tense as he read the page which listed many more names besides his. "This is impossible," Jared said out loud. "This book was written before I was born."

Yet the passage about Jared was accurate, even to his physical description. Jared and the others were referred to as 'the chosen.' Jared strongly suspected what that phrase meant, but he would not let himself dwell on that horror. He voraciously read the rest of the book. When Jared finished, he set the book on the ground and poured more whiskey into his cup. As Jared stared into the fire, anger consumed him. "I refuse to accept this, I'm going to stop those bastards," he growled out loud. Then Jared looked into the fire and yelled, "Roch get your ass here, I need to talk to you!"

"I'm sorry I'm late," the Sanuri said as he walked into Gabriel's study. High Priest Raphael stood up and shook hands with the Sanuri.

"It is always an honor," Raphael said.

Simon pulled another chair up to the table for the Sanuri to sit on. "We were just filling Raphael in on all of the peculiars of this mission," Gabriel said. "Raphael said he also had an encounter with Ahriman in the basement of the monastery at Malga, where the priests had been offering human sacrifices."

There was a knock at the door before Hannah, Natasha and Marcia entered the study. Each woman carried a large tray of food and cups of hot coffee. Lakin, Luca and Raul quickly stood up and took the heavy trays and placed them on the table.

"Natasha," Raphael said as he stood up with open arms to hug her. "Let me look at you. Not only are you married but you're going to have a baby. My little sister is all grown up," he said with a laugh and hugged Natasha again. Then Raphael explained to the others, "Gabriel and I have been close friends for years and little Natasha was always with us. I often felt like her older brother."

"Natasha are you ever going to tell him?" Gabriel asked with a grin. Natasha just laughed so Gabriel continued. "The reason she was always with us is because she had a crush on you."

Natasha walked over to the chair where Calen was sitting and sat on his lap. "Yes, I thought the two of you were the most handsome men in all the world, I just loved following you around," Natasha said with a laugh.

Raphael laughed loudly, then said, "I am honored. But honestly I couldn't be more pleased with your choice for a husband. Gabriel tells me it was love at first sight." Calen and Natasha looked at each other and smiled. "Gabriel I am suddenly feeling old," Raphael said jokingly. "I must say for such an arduous mission you all seem to have been blessed with many miracles; in addition to three loving marriages."

Raphael turned to Hannah and Marcia; he had previously been introduced to both women. "I have worked with your husbands for many, many years. They have always been highly dedicated to the missions; I am glad to see they are taking some time to enjoy life now." Raphael paused then said, "Well, I suppose we should get back to work."

The Sanuri waited until Raphael stopped speaking, then he stood up and addressed the group. "Raphael I am so very glad that you have decided to make a headquarters here. I believe your presence is greatly needed in Stordt. I understand that Gabriel and the others still have much to tell you but I have come across some new and very disturbing information that I want to share with all of you." The Sanuri took Sophie's book from a pocket in his robe and handed it to Raphael.

"Simon and Natasha took this book from Sophie's hotel room. The Insidiae sent Sophie to Roch's castle to observe his behavior to ensure he was the perfect vessel for Omnibus. She recounts his crimes in great detail and because many of the horrors Sophie writes about were committed against Raul and members of his family, it has been very difficult for the men and women here to read. They have been trying to read this book to learn information about Roch. I just finished this book," the Sanuri paused and turned to Raul.

"Raul it will be no surprise to you that Vitomas appears to be the only person he has ever cared about, besides himself."

"Sanuri how can you say he cared about her," Natasha asked. "After all the times he tortured her and humiliated her."

"I know it is difficult to understand; how do you explain the mind of a madman? But Raul must know this; because as long as Roch is alive he will be a threat to Vitomas," the Sanuri said. "But there was so much more in that book. Raphael turn to the last five pages and show the others. The Insidiae did not groom just one person to be a vessel but many. Roch was chosen as the primary vessel but that group is so determined to raise Omnibus that they chose many others in case something went wrong and Roch could not perform his mission. All of the men named on those pages are second sons of second sons of second sons."

"So what are you saying?" Lakin asked in disbelief. "Our entire focus has been on Roch, was he just a diversion?"

"I believe Roch really is the one they intended to be the vessel but I think you may also be correct and he has been a diversion for all of us. The Lion told me that the Insidiae have garnered much attention from demons in many worlds because of their idea of using a human to house the essence of a demon."

"The Lion said a demon cannot use a human as a vessel without the help of other humans. Now it appears there are many potential vessels walking among us. Perhaps that is why other demons seem to be interfering with or manipulating the Insidiae. Raphael you will need to send men out to locate the names on those pages. We will need to monitor them."

"I have already sent men to Taperia," Raphael said as he paged through the book. "They will stay at the abandoned hotel where Gabriel and the others made camp and monitor Meekos and Sophie."

"This may be nothing," Gabriel said. "But it has been nagging at the back of my mind for some time now. I wrote to you about the incident where a group of men tried to attack Natasha. We kept one alive for a while and interrogated him. He said something to the effect; that he and his men had no intention of coming to Taperia but it was almost like something was calling them. In addition one of the shop owners told Natasha that recently all sorts of really evil men were arriving in Taperia. I think we need to concentrate recourses there."

The next day Hannah, Marcia and Natasha finished most of the packing, so that members of the Patronus could start moving into rooms of the house. Gabriel, Raul, Simon, Lakin and Colter took Raphael and some of his men into Nora. The Sanuri was already in the city teaching when he saw his friends riding down the street.

The Sanuri waved them over so he could introduce Raphael and some of the other priests; the Sanuri did not divulge that they were members of the secret army of Patronus. The Sanuri showed Raphael the site where the citizens of Nora were building a monastery and another site where construction of a temple was soon to start.

"These people are also drawing up plans for schools," the Sanuri explained. "They are thirsty for knowledge and the Word of The Great Ruler because for decades they have been denied these basic rights. My two close friends Padre Thomas and Padre Bartholomew are on their way here, as we speak. They will be the first teachers in the monastery. Please Raphael protect them and nourish this little flame of light in this dark kingdom."

Chapter XXXIV
Trials

The next evening General Colter assigned patrols to monitor both the City of Nora and the house of Gabriel and Hannah. This was the evening that the citizens of Nora were hosting a celebration for the Rualas and all who participated in the battle which saved the city from the Hutas. The Sanuri, General Colter and High Priest Raphael also planned to attend the function.

Although this was an evening of festivities all of the battle experienced warriors knew that a distraction like this would provide an excellent situation for an attack. In addition, Gabriel, Raul, Simon and the others all planned to start their journey to Wetpr the following morning; which meant this would be the last night their enemies in Nora would have access to these men.

Koby, Calen and Misha were still healing from their injuries and rode in bocas to the celebration. Many of the other wounded warriors, who were too weak or injured to fly, were carried by their comrades; no one was left behind. Raul was driving the boca that carried, Natasha, Calen, Misha, Koby and Simon.

"Calen," Raul said loudly. "We got a letter from Mother today. She said your family has been at the castle for almost a week helping them with preparations. Does your family know you were wounded?"

"Yes, Lakin sent messages to all of our families," Calen said as he put his arm around Natasha.

"Good," Raul said. "Simon and I told our parents that many of you were seriously injured and to plan the ceremonies accordingly. So they are planning more informal activities the first day that we arrive, so everyone can get rested and moved into their quarters. The next day Father will honor all of you who rescued Petra. And the following night will be the formal ball to celebrate all of your weddings."

Simon was riding in the front seat next to Raul; he now turned to the others. "I would expect all of these activities to be huge gatherings and to last a long time; do not be afraid to leave or sit down if you are not up to it."

"Both Father and even our Mother have fought in battles and have taken care of wounded soldiers; they are realistic about your needs and will not be offended if you cannot attend some of the functions."

"I am so excited and nervous," Natasha said. "Not only am I meeting the King and Queen but this will be the first time that I meet Calen's family."

"Honey you have been writing back and forth so it's not like you are total strangers," Calen said.

"That's different," Natasha said. "What if they don't like me?"

"Natasha they are going to love you," Misha said. "Trust me. Besides, Emeral had all but given up hope that Calen would settle down and marry. All of his sisters have been married for years."

Calen started to laugh, "Yeah, now they can stop nagging me and nag the hell out of Luca."

"Luca is such a wonderful man," Natasha said with a sly smile. "Maybe we can find him someone at the celebrations."

"Honey don't try to set him up," Calen said seriously. "There is more going on here than you know."

"What do you mean?" Natasha asked as she turned to look Calen in the face.

Calen didn't answer. "You might as well tell her," Simon said. "All the rest of us know, well except for the girls."

"Know what Calen? What is going on here?" Natasha asked sharply.

"Luca was very interested in Hannah until he realized that she and Gabriel were falling in love," Calen said.

"He was more than interested in her," Koby said.

"Yeah, I know," Calen replied.

"Luca is in love with Hannah!" Natasha gasped. "Does she know?"

"No and don't tell her," Calen said. "Luca respects Gabriel too much to ever act on his feelings for Hannah and besides it's obvious to everyone how much Hannah loves Gabriel."

"Does Gabriel know?" asked Natasha.

"Of course he does, Luca told him," Calen said. "Why do you think Gabriel chose Luca to take Hannah away from here if we were losing the battle with the Hutas? Gabriel knew that if he died, Luca would take care of her."

"This is the last time we will ever dance here," Hannah said as she and Gabriel glided across the ballroom at the Endleson Hotel.

"Are you sad that we are leaving?" Gabriel asked.

"I am beginning to feel a little sad," Hannah admitted. "But I am so excited about our new life together and moving to Wetpr. Natasha, Marcia and I were talking the other day. What makes us all sad is, well, we have all gotten so close on this mission and now we will all be going our separate ways. Is it always like this?"

Gabriel kissed Hannah on the forehead. "This was an unusual mission and yes many of us became very close. But Hannah, we will have a home in Salar so we can stay in contact with Raul and Simon. And Calen's parents already built a wing for us in Calen's and Natasha's home in the Ice Caves. And perhaps if we really want to stay in the Ice Caves, we will build a home there also. So it's not like we aren't going to see these people again."

"I know; you are right. It's just, well Natasha said it best. We have all been living so closely together we have become family and things will change once we leave here."

"Well, we still have a long ways to travel and I suspect we will all be staying at the castle in Wetpr for a week or two, so don't get melancholy yet," Gabriel said as he bent down and kissed Hannah on the lips. The music stopped and Gabriel guided Hannah off the dance floor towards a table. But before they could sit down, Raul called to Gabriel.

When Gabriel saw that Simon and Raul were standing with Beatrice Endleson, he quickly walked towards them. "I would like to speak with all of you in my husband's office," Beatrice said solemnly and turned and walked out of the ballroom. No one spoke until they were in the office with the door closed. Beatrice turned to the men with tears in her eyes. "Since Augustus died, I have heard many rumors about him and some of the other men in Nora. I do not want to believe them, yet how does someone explain his manner of death?"

Beatrice paused to compose herself. "I have been searching through our home, I guess I wanted to prove all of those awful rumors wrong, but..." Beatrice started to cry as she walked over to the desk and grabbed two large baskets that were sitting on the floor. "Would you please help me?" Beatrice asked as she tried to set the baskets on top of the desk. Simon was standing the closest to Beatrice and took both of the heavy baskets from her.

"I don't know what some of these things are but I think you should look at them," Beatrice said as tears ran down her cheeks. "In fact I think you should come to our home, there are more things there. I don't want any of this in my house."

Beatrice had covered the items in the baskets with towels. Simon removed the towels as Gabriel and Raul walked closer. Simon pulled a hood out of the first basket that also contained several books and a dagger, which had ritualistic drawings on the hilt. Raul took a blood stained cloth out of the second basket. "That cloth has the same markings on it as that dagger," Beatrice explained. There were more books and maps in the second basket.

"Beatrice, we are leaving for Wetpr in the morning," Gabriel said soothingly. "I will have some men go to your house tomorrow to remove the things you don't want there."

"No, Gabriel you don't understand," Beatrice cried as she grabbed his forearm. "I don't know if I found everything and I am frightened, very frightened to stay there. You're a priest; can you cleanse my house so I'm protected from demons?"

Gabriel could see the terror in Beatrice's eyes. "Raul would you please get Raphael?" Gabriel asked. As soon as Raul left the office, Gabriel helped Beatrice to a chair.

When the elderly woman was seated, Gabriel kneeled before her and held her hands. "Beatrice tell me what is really scaring you so?"

"I don't know, it's probably just my imagination," Beatrice said then started to cry. Raul, Raphael and the Sanuri quietly walked into the office. Beatrice was sitting with her back turned to them so she did not realize they had entered the room.

Beatrice squeezed Gabriel's hands and started to speak, "You know my Augustus and I have lived in that house for almost forty years. It is a beautiful home and I have always loved being there, that is until recently. I know I must sound like a crazy old woman but Gabriel I have heard voices and laughing this awful, sinister laughing. And it's not at night, so I know I am not dreaming."

"What are the voices saying?" Gabriel asked softly.

"I know you aren't going to believe me, but one of the voices sounds like my Augustus. It's almost like he is trying to talk to me and something is stopping him. Yesterday I called out to him. I said Augustus if you are trying to talk to me, give me a sign. And suddenly a vase flew off the table and smashed into the wall. Augustus' voice sounds really afraid. Gabriel please go to my house and try to help him or if it's a demon; make it go away."

"Beatrice is there anything you haven't told us?" Gabriel asked.

"Yes," Beatrice said and started to cry again. "He had a room in the basement that he never let me go in. I never really thought anything about it until I heard all of those rumors after he died."

Gabriel took a piece of paper and a pen from the desk and handed them to Beatrice. "Please draw me a map so I can find your house," he said. Everyone remained quiet as the woman drew a small map and wrote directions on the paper. When she finished, Beatrice handed the paper to Gabriel. "Beatrice do you have friends that you can stay with tonight?"

"Yes," Beatrice looked up at Simon. "Would you please hand me that bag on the desk?" Simon picked up a small silk bag that was decorated with turquoise stones that matched the color of Beatrice's dress. Beatrice took a key from her bag and handed it to Gabriel. "This key will get you in all of the doors."

543

Simon escorted Beatrice out of the office and to her table in her private dining room, where many of Beatrice's friends were sitting. Raphael and the others looked at the items that Beatrice had brought in the baskets until Simon returned."

As soon as Simon closed the door to the office Raul said, "This smells like a trap."

"I know," Gabriel said. "But that woman is honestly frightened. Sanuri what do you think?"

"It is probably Ahriman and his tricks. I would highly doubt that Augustus is trying to speak to his wife. I am sure we will find an unholy altar in the basement, so that would be a place of power for Ahriman," the Sanuri was quiet for a few moments then he said. "Gabriel, you Raul and Simon are all honored guests here; you must return to the ceremonies. I believe that Raphael and I will pay this house a visit."

"Not by yourselves," Simon said. "You said it yourself that Ahriman wants you."

"I believe we will be in good company," the Sanuri replied.

When Gabriel, Raul and Simon returned to the ballroom they were immediately called to the front of the room by Morris. All of the members of the governing body of Nora were standing in front of the room as was Prince Lakin, Luca, Misha, Calen, Koby, Dagon, Rabi and six other Ruala warriors. The music stopped playing and all eyes were upon Gabriel, Raul and Simon as they joined their friends at the front of the large ballroom.

Morris stood before the audience and was explaining how the Ruala warriors saved the city. As he talked, Wallis became frustrated and interrupted him. "Morris we all know they saved us, get on with it will ya." The audience roared with laughter as six men pulled a large cart into the center of the dance floor. Carston and Peters got on each side of the cart and pulled down the canvas sheets that were covering a seven foot statue of a Ruala warrior.

"This is going to be placed in the center of the city," Morris said with great pride. At the foot of the statue was a plaque that was inscribed with the following words:

544

They came as strangers and saved us all; they leave here as our friends and our heroes. The modest warriors stood speechless as they read the plaque. Prince Lakin stepped forward and thanked everyone on behalf of his people."

When Lakin had finished speaking, Morris stepped forward and said with a grin, "The Prince here is acting like this shin dig is over, heck we're just beginning. With this statement, Morris waved his arm and dozens of men and women from Nora walked into the ballroom carrying two distinctly different types of baskets. "As you know Nora is a city of gold mines, everything is gold here," Morris said as he looked at all the Ruala warriors in the audience.

"The men will be handing each one of you a pouch of gold coins and the women are handing you boxes of gold jewelry for yourselves and your families. Oh there is more," Morris said with enthusiasm and waved his arm again. More citizens of Nora walked into the ballroom carrying baskets and proceeded to hand small golden tubes to each warrior.

"We realize that your homes are in the Ice Caves but if any of you would like to live here in Nora, those tubes contain legal deeds to land. The land descriptions are not filled in yet because we would let you pick out the acreage that you would want."

As Morris continued to speak, three men walked up to the table that Hannah, Natasha and Marcia were seated at. Each woman was handed a large bouquet of red roses. "And now, what do you give men who have everything?" Morris asked. "That was the question that plagued us all."

"Prince Raul, Prince Simon and High Priest Gabriel, we have come to learn that your initial contact with citizens of this city was anything but favorable. And Gabriel your beautiful wife can tell you that many of us have become shameful cowards over the years. This may sound trite to men like you but King Sudfad, you, the Sanuri and the Rualas have given us hope, something that had ceased to exist here for a very long time."

Peters walked up to Morris and handed him a scroll. Morris continued speaking, "Prince Raul and Prince Simon on behalf of the citizens of Nora I give you this scroll which documents our allegiance to King Sudfad and to your family."

"The flag of Wetpr will fly proudly over the statue of the Ruala warrior, in the center of our city." As Morris said this, Carston and Jack carried out a large Wetprian flag to show the audience. "We greatly wish to become citizens of Wetpr. Anything that we can give you, or do for you, please just ask."

Morris walked directly in front of Gabriel. "We understand that you and Hannah have sold all of your interests in Nora and plan to leave soon. We regret that our actions drove you away. But know you will always have a home here." As Morris talked, Gabriel looked at Hannah, who was crying.

"You know," Morris continued. "Members of this city did not always worship demons. We had a beautiful monastery and two temples here, before Roch became king. The priests that lived here heard that Roch was destroying all of the holy places in the kingdom. So before they were murdered by Roch's men, the priests managed to hide what was most sacred to them and this is what we would like to give to you, Gabriel."

While Morris was talking, Carston walked up to Gabriel, carrying a small wooden chest that was adorned with great jewels and gold. Gabriel lifted the lid of the chest and stared at the contents with amazement. He was speechless and his hands started to shake.

"What is it?" Raul asked as his eyes grew wide as he looked inside the chest.

Gabriel closed the lid and took the chest from Carston, "Thank you all but this is such an extraordinary gift that I do not believe it should be owned by one man. I will turn it over to the Sanuri for safe keeping."

Like Gabriel, Raphael had dedicated himself to The Great Ruler at an early age. The two met as boys as they studied at the monastery at Philiste in the Kingdom of Wetpr; after their first week of studies together they were inseparable.

Gabriel and Raphael were both ruggedly handsome with large and powerful bodies. Raphael had straight black hair and large brown eyes. Like Natasha, Gabriel had curly black hair and violet eyes. Their appearances were similar enough that most people mistook Gabriel and Raphael for brothers.

Gabriel's parents were wealthy and owned a castle near the monastery. Raphael was born into a poor family from the small Village of Prohec which was north of Philiste. Near the end of their first year of studies, Gabriel found Raphael crying in one of the gardens that surrounded the monastery. Raphael had always been a popular student because of his positive and robust nature; Gabriel had never seen his friend sad before.

When Gabriel found out that Raphael was going to have to leave the monastery because his father could no longer pay for his education; Gabriel went to his own family. Gabriel did not ask his father for money but rather Gabriel asked his father to release Gabriel's savings so he could pay for his friend's education. Gabriel's parents were so moved by this charitable request that they not only paid for Raphael's education but took the young boy into their home.

Gabriel's parents liked to travel. They often took journeys, leaving Natasha in the care of her older brother. Gabriel was very protective of his little sister and she followed him everywhere. A few years later when Gabriel's and Natasha's parents were killed in an accident; Raphael helped Gabriel immensely. Not only did Raphael help raise Natasha, who he considered his little sister also, but Raphael helped Gabriel with his father's businesses and legal affairs.

"Sanuri stop!" Raphael yelled, as the two men rode towards the Endleson home. The Sanuri's horse was a few steps ahead of Raphael's. The Sanuri turned back towards his friend. "What is it Raphael?"

"We know this is some kind of trap and Ahriman will know that you realize that," Raphael said. "I don't think the trap is at the house, I think it is on the way there."

The Sanuri smiled, "You have learned a great deal my friend. Now I have a gift for you. Raphael you have worked diligently for The Great Ruler these many years. Our friend The Lion says that you have passed many tests."

"But the stronger that you and Gabriel become the more of a threat you become to the dark ones and the more they will seek the two of you out. You and Gabriel both have tests to pass this night; which is why I needed to separate you."

"So this trap with Ahriman is nothing but a ruse?" Raphael asked.

"No, it is a very real threat," the Sanuri said. "You and Gabriel are such intelligent and capable men that even though you have great faith in The Great Ruler you tend to make the same mistake that I often do. The three of us do not call upon The Great Ruler enough to help us in our work for Him. The Great Ruler will rarely speak with you directly but He sends His emissaries into these worlds."

"Gabriel never felt worthy to ask The Lion to come to his aide. The moment Gabriel called out to The Lion, he appeared immediately. You my dear friend need to do the same thing. Dismount from your horse, walk a few steps away and call for The Lion to appear. He always comes to those with pure hearts. Seek his advice on how we should proceed with this situation. This is your journey to take, I will remain here," said the Sanuri.

Raphael did as the Sanuri instructed. Raphael too, had always felt unworthy to call upon the heavens to see the face of holiness.

"Well it's about time Raphael," The Lion said. Raphael quickly turned around towards the voice. The high priest stood speechless in the presence of The Lion. "Raphael I have been with you for a long time and I know that you are rarely without words."

"Forgive me I just never thought you would actually appear to me," Raphael said.

"And that my son is a lesson you have now learned. What is your question?"

"I believe Ahriman is trying to trap the Sanuri. And I believe that Ahriman knows the Sanuri is intelligent and will know this situation is a trap. How can I best accomplish this mission and keep the Sanuri safe?"

"Tell me why are you riding to the Endleson's home?"

"Because we want to protect Beatrice from any demons in her home."

"And you believed her story?"

548

"Yes," Raphael said without hesitation.

"Good," The Lion said. "She was not lying to you; you do well reading human nature. And you are right this is a trap. And you are also right that the danger to you and the Sanuri exists before you arrive at the house. Tell me what were you planning to do?"

"I thought we should approach the house from a different road than Beatrice showed on her map."

"I see; that is good thinking for a normal human. But Raphael neither you nor Gabriel are normal humans. Every time you pass a holy test you come closer to The Great Ruler. Think of it as two worlds that are connected by many roads. The world that you are in is very dark and heavy and the world The Great Ruler is in is filled with light. Now do not get confused, that does not mean that He is not with you here."

"But you see the tests of mankind are to help you leave this world and come closer to Him. Both you and Gabriel are on your journeys towards Him. Wouldn't you think that as you come closer to His world that you would have to expand your way of thinking about this world? The two of you function in realms that are unseen by most humans."

"As you evolve, you must learn to communicate with The Great Ruler much more than you already do. And when I say, communicate I mean you need to ask Him for direct guidance more often, instead of looking for answers in this world of man. There is power in being a child of The Great Ruler because He does help you in ways you could never imagine. Now Raphael, look at this situation with less human eyes and tell me what you would do?"

Raphael smiled. "I would ask to see through the eyes of an Enrop, so we could see precisely were the enemy is."

"And there are but two of you," The Lion challenged. "Tell me how you would defeat that army of demons that is lying in wait for you?"

"I would ask The Great Ruler for help."

"That is the right answer Raphael, now see what happens when you let The Great Ruler lead."

The sound of powerful wings moving in the still night air distracted Raphael. He looked up into the darkness and when he looked back towards The Lion, he saw that the emissary of The Great Ruler was gone.

"Mount him," the Sanuri called. Raphael looked around and realized that a giant blue Henger had landed behind him. The Sanuri now appeared on the back of another of these ancient birds of war. Raphael climbed onto the back of the great Henger and excitement surged through him as he quickly ascended into the night sky. Raphael caught his breath when he realized the sky was filled with Hengers.

"I have heard of these birds but I must admit I didn't know if they really existed," Raphael said loudly as he flew alongside of the Sanuri.

"These are birds of war," the Sanuri yelled. "When we come upon the demons, just hang on tightly. You will not have to direct the birds; they will know exactly what to do." They had traveled less than a mile when the Sanuri said, "We are over them now."

"How do you know, I can't see anything in the darkness," Raphael asked as he strained his eyes to try and see the demons.

"Ask for clear sight."

As soon as Raphael asked The Great Ruler to give him clear sight, he saw the vast army of demons that were hiding alongside the road, waiting to ambush both him and the Sanuri. Raphael caught his breath as the Henger quickly plunged downward to do battle.

Gabriel sat up all night in his study waiting for Raphael and the Sanuri to return. Finally just before morning, Gabriel fell asleep in one of the large, overstuffed chairs; still clutching the precious bejeweled chest he had received as a gift.

Both Raul and Simon recognized the precious gift inside of the chest. Gabriel did not share its secret with anyone else, not even Hannah; because he wanted to speak with the Sanuri first. No sooner had Gabriel fallen asleep, when Raphael and the Sanuri entered the house through the back kitchen door.

Hannah, Marcia and Natasha were already busy in the kitchen preparing breakfast. "Are you alright?" Natasha asked. "Gabriel sat up all night waiting for you."

"We are fine," the Sanuri replied. "Where is Gabriel?"

"In his study," Hannah answered.

Gabriel awoke to find Raphael and the Sanuri standing before him smiling. "Let us tell you about last night," the Sanuri said.

"No Sanuri," Gabriel said as he stood up and thrust the jeweled chest into the Sanuri's arms. "First you must take this. The people of Nora gave it to me as a gift. They said that before Roch destroyed their monastery, their priests hid this. Those people have no idea what it is. I showed it to Raul and Simon because I knew they would recognize it. I hope that was alright. I didn't tell anyone else what it was."

Without opening the chest the Sanuri asked, "Why do you not want your gift?"

"You will see when you open it," Gabriel said. "That should not be owned by a single man. That is a holy gift from The Great Ruler. I want you to take it."

The Sanuri looked at Raphael and smiled. "Tell your friend," said the Sanuri.

"We have both been tested this night and I am assuming that you just passed your test," Raphael said. "For mine, I called to The Great Lion and he appeared and gave me guidance. We defeated an army of demons with The Great Ruler's help."

"Behold my sons; you are about to see one of the most extraordinary gifts from The Great Ruler to His children in this world. Few men have laid eyes on this, yet armies of both men and demons have sought it for centuries." The Sanuri lifted the lid of the chest, exposing its contents.

"The Ruby Scroll!" Raphael gasped in utter amazement.

"Gabriel do you know what information this scroll contains?" the Sanuri asked.

"It is said to contain the secrets of immortality," Gabriel replied. "Sanuri how could such a precious object be here, in this dark kingdom?"

"Waiting for men with pure hearts to find it," the Sanuri said. "There are few men in this world who would not have used this for personal gain. And I am so very proud to say, that all but a couple are in this house this day. Tell me Gabriel did you read it?"

"Of course not!" Gabriel said with indignation.

"Why not?" the Sanuri asked.

Gabriel paused for a moment and looked at Raphael, "Because I don't think I am ready for the truths that scroll holds."

Chapter XXXV
Birthright

Meekos seethed with jealousy about Sophie's romantic relationship with Erebus. For so many years it had been just the two of them; Meekos did not want to share his sister's attention with another. "They're acting like a couple of fools," Meekos mumbled to himself as he walked down the street from the Taperian Imperial Hotel to Walt's Tavern.

Although there were many taverns in Taperia, Meekos became a regular at Walt's. He liked the diverse clientele. Walt's was located on the main business street of Taperia and drew a lot of travelers. Meekos learned a great deal as he sat over his drinks, watching and listening to the other patrons. On this afternoon as Meekos walked down the street, absorbed in his thoughts; he did not realize all the eyes that were upon him.

Five members of the Patronus were on the streets of Taperia that day. The priests did not wear their robes but dressed in a manner that they would not stand out from the other citizens of Taperia. Enrops too, watched Meekos. Jared sat in a wooden chair that was in front of the butcher shop, which was across the street from Walt's Tavern.

Jared had his hat pulled down over his face, pretending to sleep. He hoped that his new clothes and hat would prevent Meekos from recognizing him. Jared watched Meekos as he walked down the street and through the open door of Walt's Tavern. Jared also watched the members of the Patronus watching Meekos, although he did not know who the men were. And the Enrops that circled overhead did not go unnoticed by Jared; he wondered why Meekos was drawing so much attention.

On the night of the fourth day after they left Nora, Raul and Simon were introducing their comrades to the Royal Family of Wetpr. Thanks to the Enrops that flew in advance of the returning warriors, Renya was able to organize a reception in true Wetprian splendor. Honor guards led the Ruala warriors into the Great Hall of the castle, where their families were waiting with great anticipation.

553

Both Vitomas and Annabelle broke from the traditional receiving line to run to their husbands. After reading about the atrocities that had been committed against Vitomas and Annabelle during their captivity in Stordt, Raul and Simon hugged their wives tighter than ever before.

Raul swung Vitomas around in the air as they kissed. He set her feet on the floor, just as Gabriel and Hannah walked up to them. Vitomas initially had her back turned to the couple. "Honey this is Gabriel and Hannah," Raul said. "Gabriel and Hannah this is my beautiful wife Vitomas."

Vitomas turned around slowly; she did not even look at Gabriel but stared at Hannah. Neither woman spoke as they looked into each other's eyes. Both knowing that the other fully understood the horrors they had survived. Vitomas and Hannah hugged each other and cried as their husbands looked on.

Simon and Annabelle kissed hungrily for several minutes. "I missed you so much," Simon said and kissed Annabelle again. "Come, there are some people I want you to meet." Simon and Annabelle held hands as they walked into the Great Hall. "There they are," Simon said as he escorted Annabelle across the floor. "Calen, Natasha, this is Annabelle," Simon said.

Annabelle hugged them both, "I feel like I already know you from Simon's letters. I am so glad to finally meet you in person."

"Natasha is a little unnerved," Calen said and laughed. "She just met my family."

"They seem wonderful," Natasha said nervously. "I was just so afraid they wouldn't like me."

"Emeral and Maxwell have been here for over a week," Annabelle said. "All they have been talking about is how excited they are to meet you and how happy they are about the baby. I am sure they loved you."

"Speaking of babies," Simon said as he jokingly gave Annabelle a suspicious look. "You never answered my questions; are we having another baby?"

Annabelle looked up into Simon's face and smiled, "Yes you are going to be a daddy again." Simon picked Annabelle up and kissed her. "Are the children sleeping?"

"Vitomas and I made them all take long naps, so that we could get them up when you came home," Annabelle said. "Stay with your friends and I'll get them."

"I'll help you," Natasha said and walked across the dance floor with Annabelle. Both women stopped by Vitomas and Hannah.

"Come, we're getting the babies," Annabelle said. Both Vitomas and Hannah turned to leave the Great Hall with Annabelle and Natasha when Hannah heard her name called. Two, three more times Hannah heard someone yelling her name, before Hannah saw Petra in the crowded room. Hannah grabbed Gabriel's arm. "Oh Gabriel, look," she said with a warm smile. They watched as the excited little boy ran up to them. Petra had a young German shepherd dog following him as he carried a German shepherd puppy in his arms.

"Are you Hannah?" Petra asked exuberantly as he walked up to Hannah, Gabriel and Raul.

"Yes," Hannah said and kneeled down so she was at Petra's height.

"This is Max," Petra said and thrust the puppy at her.

"He is beautiful," Hannah said as she hugged the pup. "And what is your other dog's name."

"Argus," Petra said proudly. "He is really friendly; you can pet him."

As Hannah played with both of the dogs, Gabriel said to Petra. "Hannah felt bad that she couldn't send you a gift, when she sent the others. Do you think your parents would let us get you a little sister for those two pups?"

Petra's eyes grew wide with excitement. He looked up at Raul for approval. "Go ask him, I am sure he will say yes," Raul said with a big grin.

Petra grabbed his puppy from Hannah and ran through the crowd yelling, "Papa."

"I know I should have asked your father before I said anything to Petra," Gabriel said to Raul. "The boy will be disappointed if Sudfad says 'no'.

"Trust me, he will let Petra have the puppy," Raul said with a laugh.

Annabelle, Natasha and Vitomas returned to the reception, and drew the attention of many. Vitomas was holding baby Ariel and held little Sudfad's hand. Annabelle was carrying baby Arianna and holding Anthony's hand. Natasha walked between the two Princesses and held the hands of Samuel and Alexander. All of the boys were wearing miniature versions of the Wetprian dress military uniform, while the girls were wearing fancy dresses with bows in their hair.

Samuel was the first to see Raul and started screaming loudly. Natasha let go of his hand as he and little Sudfad ran to their father. Raul picked up his sons and kissed them over and over. Vitomas stayed with Raul, Hannah and Gabriel as Annabelle and Natasha made their way through the crowded room, looking for Simon and Calen.

"There's your papa," Annabelle said to the boys, when they were within a few feet of Simon. "Simon the boys are running to you," she called out.

Simon turned quickly and ran to meet his sons. He picked them both up, hugging and kissing them. When Annabelle was next to Simon again, he bent down and kissed Arianna on the head. "Calen I want you to meet my family," Simon said as he walked up to Calen.

"They are the spitting image of you," Calen said with a laugh as he held his hands out. Anthony went to Calen and kept touching Calen's wings. Calen looked at Natasha, "Honey I know we haven't had much time to talk about our future but I would like to have a lot of children.

556

Natasha squeezed Calen's arm and smiled. She did not want to tell him what was in her heart. Natasha loved Calen dearly and wanted to have a family with him but a large family meant she would not be allowed to work on the missions and that brought her great sadness.

The next morning Sudfad and Renya called Gabriel, Hannah, Raul and Simon into the King's study immediately after breakfast.

"My dear it is so good to see you again?" Renya said as she hugged Hannah. "I am sorry that I didn't get much of a chance to talk to you last night."

"I'm surprised we could talk at all, as busy as you were," Hannah said. "Please Renya allow me to help you while we are staying here."

"I would welcome the help," Renya said with a smile. "But first let's hear what Sudfad has to say."

Sudfad opened his top desk drawer and pulled out a ring of keys. "These are the keys to your new home," Sudfad said as he handed them to Gabriel. "This is our gift to you. Also I took the liberty of having the house cleaned and any repairs that had to be done are taken care of."

"There is a large horse stable on the property that had not been used for some time. Our carpenters had been working on it. When they finished, it just didn't look right standing empty. So you now have twelve fine horses to fill it. The horses are gifts from Raul and Vitomas and Simon and Annabelle."

Just as Gabriel was about to speak, Sudfad handed him a piece of paper. "We took the liberty of hiring some staff for you; of course you can replace them but I think you will be pleased; they have good references and we thoroughly checked their backgrounds so as not to place spies into your home."

Gabriel read the paper which included the names of a house keeper, grounds keeper and stableman, then he handed it to Hannah.

"I don't know what to say, you are so generous, thank you so much," Gabriel said. Hannah was crying; she walked over to the King and Queen and hugged them both.

"We called you in here at this early hour, so you could have a chance to look at your house before the ceremonies start this afternoon," Sudfad said. "And Gabriel, after all the ceremonies are completed I have some business, I would like to talk with you about."

"If you don't mind, I would like to talk to you about that business now," Gabriel said. "You have peeked my curiosity."

"That would be fine," Sudfad said. "Raul and Simon you should be a part of this conversation also."

Gabriel turned to Hannah, "Why don't you get Natasha, Calen and Luca and any of the others who would like to see our house and we will leave when I am done talking with King Sudfad." Gabriel kissed Hannah on the forehead and waited until she closed the door behind her before he turned back to Sudfad.

"I believe you know Padre Bartholomew and Padre Thomas," Sudfad said. "They are very loyal friends of the Sanuri and have helped him immensely. While they were living at the monastery in Malga they did a great deal of research and well, investigating into the Insidiae. They send stacks and stacks of documents and their meticulously detailed notes to the Sanuri. I will let you review all of those things later but right now I want to show you these drawings," Sudfad said as he handed several sheets of paper to Gabriel.

"Meekos, Pravis and Tenebrae tried to recruit some of the other priests into the Insidiae," Sudfad continued. "Apparently they initially tricked the priests as to the nature of this sinister organization. A priest by the name of Padre Dominick attended several of the gatherings and after he realized the Insidiae pledged their allegiance to demons, he drew pictures of everyone he had seen at the gatherings."

"The Sanuri told me that humans would keep the looks they had at the time they sold their souls to demons, no matter how old they were. Simon would you point out the men as I name them?"

Sudfad asked. "Gregory Bancar is a wealthy landowner in Wetpr and has been in our castle on several occasions. There is a man in that picture named Cedrick Teivel. Who is identical to a Cedrick T. Kretcher, Commanding General of Fort Polta in the western portion of Wetpr. That picture is several hundreds of years old and both of those men look identical to those images."

Sudfad let Gabriel look at the drawings for a moment before he continued, "Renya's brother is King Mathas of Lentz. He assigned two of his most trusted generals to assist me. If I have members of the Insidiae in my military I did not want word to get out about internal investigations. General Hatus and General Tamour compiled these folders of information," Sudfad said as he handed two heavy folders to Gabriel. "Raul and Simon have not had a chance to review those yet."

"As you will read, Kretcher did not exist until thirty-five years ago. I have also included his military records in that file," Sudfad continued. "Now they found references to Cedrick Teivel that went back hundreds of years. He comes from the Teivel Clan that virtually owns Ryed. Gabriel I am sure that you heard about the Rualas saving my boys lives."

"Raul and Simon were ambushed several times by Hutas, on that mission and only the commanding generals of each fort knew the itineraries of my sons. I need to find out if Kretcher is a member of the Insidiae or some type of spy. My family has been under direct attack by members of the Insidiae and I need to protect them."

"Father he knows," Simon said softly.

"He knows what?" asked Sudfad.

"Gabriel knows that we are two of The Seven Sons of the ancient prophesy," Raul said. Sudfad sat back in his chair and glared angrily at his sons.

"Mother, Father before you say anything," Simon said. "There is something I have to tell you. I haven't told Annabelle yet and honestly I thought this was something that I should explain in person."

"We did tell the Sanuri," Raul added.

Sudfad and Renya listed with horror as Simon told of the experiences that he and Natasha had with the demon snakes. As soon as Simon finished talking, Gabriel shared his experience after being stabbed by Ahriman."

"Father before you say anything," Raul said. "Our small group was trying to figure out the meanings of the journeys they had taken, and well; they all know."

"Raul and Simon, I know you have shared much with those people and trust your lives to them, but you must realize how you have endangered them by telling our secret. Tell me the names of those who know."

"Gabriel, Hannah, Calen, Natasha, Luca, Lakin, Koby, Dagon, Rabi and Marcia," Simon said. "And Father I am the one who told them."

"And what did the Sanuri say when you told him?" Sudfad asked.

"He said the time is fast approaching when many will know who we are," Raul said.

"King Sudfad," Gabriel said. "There is so very much more that we need to tell you about this mission. But you have to know that Ahriman was striking close to all of us. If in fact he knows or suspects who The Seven Sons are; don't you think it would benefit those of us who have made the same covenants with The Great Ruler as you have, to know these things. The Patronus will protect you with our lives."

Gabriel stopped talking when they heard a knock at the door. "My Lord and My Lady, King Mathas and the others just arrived from Lentz."

"Come in Marie," Renya said excitedly. When Marie entered the room Renya asked, "Did they bring Jacob and Sarah?"

"Yes, and what little darlings they both are. And wait until you see Angelina."

560

"What do you mean Marie?"

"Why that girl looks like she could have that baby any moment now. Matthew is helping her into the castle."

"Please excuse us," Sudfad said. "We will be back momentarily."

As soon as Renya and Sudfad left the study, Raul turned to Gabriel and said. "Don't feel that you have to accept this mission, we know you wanted to take a break and spend some time with Hannah."

Gabriel looked at the large stack of paperwork that Sudfad had handed him. "Raul you and Simon have become as family to me and Sudfad is my King and now to know the two of you will play such an important part in The Great Ruler's plan; how can I not jump at this opportunity."

"We will review that paperwork too," Simon said. "If you are to go to Fort Polta you will need our help, besides," Simon said with his voice lowering. "If Kretcher was behind the attacks on us, I want a piece of him too."

"Gabriel if you are to risk your life to protect our family, well, Father won't approve but," Raul looked at Simon, who knew what Raul was about to say. "Our cousin Matthew, who you will meet shortly is one of The Seven Sons also; as is Petra, Father and the Sanuri. We do not know who the seventh son is yet. I will be honest, I would not have been surprised if the Sanuri told us it was you."

The door to the study quickly opened and Sudfad, Renya, Matthew and the Sanuri walked into the room and shut the door. The Sanuri had just arrived at the castle and was carrying the bejeweled chest that held The Ruby Scroll. Both Raul and Simon stood up and hugged Matthew who shook hands with Gabriel.

"We hadn't gotten around to telling Father about that," Raul said to the Sanuri, who set the chest on the desk and lifted the lid. Sudfad, Renya and Matthew crowded around the chest and stared at the sacred gift in awe.

"Sanuri we told Father that Gabriel knows we are part of The Seven Sons," Raul said.

"And I'll bet he would have spanked you if you were boys," the Sanuri said with a laugh.

"Sanuri we took an oath never to reveal that information, I take this very seriously," Sudfad said with disdain.

"As do I my friend, but time moves on and The Great Ruler's plans slowly unfold before us," the Sanuri explained. "You know how there always seems to be, how should I say it? Multiple meanings to every test and mission The Great Ruler has for us. Well, two of His emissaries have made The Great Ruler very happy and therefore their positions in this world are changing."

"Gabriel and Raphael will be working very closely with your family. So closely that I am about to share another secret that has been kept for hundreds of years." The Sanuri turned to Gabriel. "Behold The Keepers of The Holy Scrolls. The men in this family, their wives and myself have guarded this secret for hundreds of years. Gabriel you will now lay your eyes upon the Holy Vault of The Great Ruler."

Sudfad opened the secret door in his study and the Sanuri led them all down the seven flights of steps to the Holy Vault. No one spoke until they were all inside. "Gabriel I took the liberty of sending Raphael a message to meet with us here." The Sanuri said then he looked at Sudfad.

"Sudfad the armies of darkness are growing at a tremendous rate. There is much I need to tell you after all of your ceremonies are completed. Gabriel and Raphael have now earned the right to stand with your family and to protect these most holy gifts. When Raphael arrives all of us in this room will meet down here again and I will explain their roles."

Gabriel stood in awed silence as he looked around the modest room that held the most valuable and sacred items of their world. Whisperings about such a vault had transcended time but never did Gabriel dream he would be allowed to see such a place. "I am sorry I am just speechless," Gabriel said as his voice choked up.

"To be so close to the actual gifts that The Great Ruler gave to this world, is truly beyond anything that I could have imagined."

The sound of knocking could be heard from Sudfad's study. "Oh Gabriel we forgot to tell you, there are several carriages of people waiting to go to your new home. Go!" Renya said. Gabriel looked at Sudfad as if for approval.

"We will discuss all of this later, go now with your wife and friends but be back by early afternoon for the parade."

"Parade?" Simon asked.

"Yes," Sudfad said with pride. "All the heroes will take part in a parade down the streets of Salar before the ceremony."

Raphael pondered over the strange message he had received from the Sanuri. *Raphael, put your second in command in charge of the Nora site. Pack all of your belongings. Choose one hundred of your best men and come to the castle of King Sudfad in the Kingdom of Wetpr. I will explain when you get here. Sanuri*

Raphael and his men were on the road heading to Wetpr within hours of receiving that message. Raphael was a loyal servant of The Great Ruler. He realized the Sanuri needed him in Wetpr; he never realized the journey would change his life.

Jared had not made contact with Meekos but followed him for several days. Every day and night Enrops flew over or near Meekos and men other than Jared seemed to be watching him. If Meekos was aware of all the eyes upon him, he was not giving any indication. Now that Jared had finished reading the book of the priests, he started to hear Roch's voice again. But as before, the voice was muffled and the words indistinguishable. Jared considered himself a patient man but his inability to understand Roch greatly annoyed him.

Jared had a corner room in the Sunrise Hotel, which was across the street and one building to the west of the Taperian Imperial Hotel. Like Meekos, Sophie and Erebus, Jared got a room on the fifth floor of his hotel. This was not an accident.

From his room Jared could see into Sophie's chambers and he could see through several of the windows in the hallway on that floor. Sophie was an early riser and a creature of habit. Every morning she went shopping. This morning Jared decided to follow her.

Sophie spent a great deal of time in two dress shops which had recently opened. Jared followed Sophie to a hat shop and a jewelry store. Then for the first time Sophie acted suspiciously. When Sophie walked out of the jewelers, she looked up and down the busy street then quickly darted into an alley. Fortunately for Jared, there were people walking in that alley so his presence did not stand out. The alley was long and lined with doors to what appeared to be smaller shops.

Sophie once again looked both ways up and down the alley; she looked at Jared but did not act like she really saw him. Sophie walked into a shop that had a large wooden sign that hung out from the stone building. The sign contained the symbols of a crescent moon and a human eye but no business name. Across the alley was a tobacco shop, which Jared browsed in as he kept an eye on the door of the shop Sophie was in.

"That's an unusual sign across the street," Jared said to the store clerk. "Do you know what it means?"

"No," the old man replied with disgust. "I've never been in there but I've heard plenty about that place. It's some kind of a shop for witches. Guess we must have a lot of witches in Taperia," the clerk said with a laugh. "Because there's always people going in there."

"They say they've got a woman in there who can speak with the dead, of course you have to pay her and who knows if she is really talking to the dead or making that crap up," the clerk said as he wrapped up the tobacco that Jared purchased. Sophie left the shop and walked down the alley towards her hotel. Without hesitation, Jared entered the shop without a name.

Mathas pulled Sudfad and Renya into the hallway so he could speak with them privately. "Claudius' family could not attend. We wrote to you about the brutal attack on Ingr. She is healing but was not up to a trip such as this."

564

"And with three new babies in the house, they have their hands full. Claudius and Bella asked me to give you this." Mathas handed a small envelope with the seal of the house of Claudius on the back, to Sudfad. "Also, you were so gracious to invite Fahron and Isadore. They are wonderful people who rarely leave their home anymore because they are so humiliated by the actions of their son. Rosa and I practically forced them to come along. I believe they may ask you if they can visit Timothy in prison."

"We are glad they came," Sudfad said. "We have certainly learned that you cannot judge an entire family by the actions of one member. And I would expect they want to visit their son, but Mathas you must prepare them. Timothy seems to have gone quite mad during his imprisonment. He has not been hurt by my men, but he has started fights with other prisoners and always lost. Because of that we usually keep him in a cell by himself. Although you would think he is with someone because he seems to be talking always to an imaginary person."

Jared stood by the door for a moment as his eyes became accustomed to the dim lights in the shop.

"Can I help you?" a woman asked him. Jared looked at the clerk and thought her a very normal looking woman of middle age. He wondered if she was a witch.

"I heard there is a woman here who can speak with the dead," Jared said nonchalantly. "Would you be her?"

"No, no, you're looking for Zoya, just walk through that door," the clerk pointed to a wooden door on the far side of the small shop. "She doesn't have any customers now."

When Jared walked through the door, he entered a room with a large hearth and a table with six chairs around it. There were a variety of smaller tables in the room that were covered with many lit candles which gave the room a warm glow. A slender woman was standing at the hearth with her back to him.

"Please have a seat, would you like a cup of tea?" she asked without turning around.

"No thanks," Jared said as he took his hat off and placed it on one of the chairs. Jared walked around the long table until he found a seat where he could watch the door he had entered and the door he saw in the back of the room.

Zoya turned around and put a cup of steaming tea on the table. She looked at Jared and smiled. "I see you found the spot that affords you the best means of escape. Do not worry, I will not hurt you."

"I wasn't really worried about that," Jared said with a grin. He found Zoya to be very attractive, something that he was not expecting. She was in her early twenties with long brown hair and large hazel eyes. "You don't look like a witch," Jared said kiddingly. Jared found himself surprised that Zoya was dressed like any other Taperian woman. She wore a long sky blue skirt, a white blouse with long sleeves and a short blue and brown embroidered jacket.

"I'm not but tell me, would you know a witch if you saw one?"

"I'm not sure," Jared said with a laugh. His demeanor was softening because of his attraction to Zoya.

"Who would you like me to contact for you?"

"His name is Roch and I'm not sure if he is dead or not, but I believe he is trying to contact me. If I tell you how, you will just think that I am crazy but, well, all I want to know is, what is he trying to say to me."

Zoya sat down in a chair that was very close to Jared's. She stared at him without speaking for several minutes as if she was reading his face. Then she softly grasped both of his large hands in hers. "Are you talking about King Roch?" Zoya asked.

"Yes."

"The underworlds have been exploding for some time, there are great wars among the demons and demons from other, darker worlds are coming here. I have heard that Roch was taken alive and is a prisoner of a great demon. If this is true, it may be very dangerous for me to attempt to contact him."

566

"Dangerous for you or for me?"

"Perhaps for both of us," Zoya replied softly. "The decision is yours but I wanted you to know the risks."

"I don't want to put you in any harm," Jared said. "But I will pay you very well for this."

"You seem very conflicted," Zoya said. "Would talking with Roch bring you peace or greater agitation?"

"I don't know," Jared said as he stared into Zoya's large eyes. Jared was taken by surprise with her question. "Listen I don't want you to get hurt, you don't have to do this," Jared said softly.

"No I will do this, on one condition," Zoya said.

"And what is that?"

"You look like a man who is capable of taking care of just about anything. But this is my realm. Please once we start, do exactly as I tell you, do you promise me?"

"Yes," Jared said. "By the way my name is Jared."

"Yes I know, the spirits told me." Zoya extinguished all of the candles in the small room except for the ones in the middle of the large table. She sat down at the table and appeared to be putting herself into a trance. Before his experiences with Roch, Jared would have never come to a woman like Zoya. But now Jared realized there was more to this world than he could see with his eyes. Suddenly Zoya spoke with a man's voice.

"Finally, you're thinking here Jared, smart move coming to her."

"Well don't kill her," Jared said.

"I won't, she's stronger than that man was. Now listen to me. Those visions I showed you are real. There's a bunch of insane people called the Insidiae and they are grooming bodies for demons to take over."

"I was being groomed but another demon grabbed me before it could happen. I need you to help me escape, then we have to figure out a way to stop this."

"Where are you and how can I help you escape? And how can you be contacting me and showing me visions?"

"I'm in some kind of hell world but these worlds are so close that things seem to seep through. And the demon that is holding me is putting holes in the walls of these worlds."

"How do you know this?"

"Because I'm not the only one here," Roch snapped impatiently. "We don' have much time. That book you stole, do you still have it?"

"Yes."

"Take it to the castle at Wetpr and give it to the Sanuri."

"What! Who are you really?"

"Roch, you fool! Now will you listen to me? I have no time for holy men but this demon is really worried about the Sanuri finding out what he is doing. So I figure, that's who should have that book. Tell the Sanuri about the visions and what I have told you. He should know how to get me out of here."

"And if I don't?"

"Then you will be here with me."

Suddenly Zoya came out of her trance and grabbed Jared's hand. "He was not alone, there was something of great evil listening to the two of you. This might be a trap."

"How do you know this?"

"I could see a dark form and I could hear him laughing. It was as if he wanted Roch to tell you those things."

Jared placed a handful of gold coins in front of Zoya. "Thank you," he said as he walked around the table and got his hat. Jared walked over to the door, then stopped and turned back to Zoya.

"Come with me," he said. "I could use someone with your abilities, I will pay you well." Zoya stared at Jared with a mixture of fear and disbelief. "I won't harm you, I promise. If there's a way your spirits can tell you that I am telling the truth then ask them. Just come with me to Wetpr and then I will bring you back here." Jared walked up to Zoya and put his hand on her cheek. "You heard what Roch said. This could be dangerous, I won't let anything happen to you."

Gabriel, Hannah and the others returned to the castle only to be told they had minutes to dress before they were to ride in open carriages in the parade. The women frantically changed their clothing and were whisked into open carriages. Two hundred Wetprian horsemen led the parade through the crowded streets of Salar.

Queen Renya, Petra and King Sudfad rode in the first open carriage with King Mathas, Rosa, Margarit and baby Sarah. Princes Raul, Simon and Matthew and their families rode in the next carriages followed by Gabriel and Hannah, who were riding in the same carriage as Prince Lakin, his wife Zada and their small son Jacot.

Natasha rode in the next carriage with Calen, Luca and Koby. Rabi and Marcia followed in a carriage with Dagon and Misha. Dozens of carriages carried Ruala warriors and their families. The crowds cheered and threw flowers to the brave men and women who rescued their young prince. There were banners displayed on many of the buildings, thanking the warriors for saving Petra. People stood on balconies and threw flower petals on the people in the carriages as they passed.

"Calen, I feel like a princess," Natasha said with excitement. Calen looked across the carriage at Luca and Koby, who were quite overwhelmed by the reception. The two hour parade ended back at the castle.

A stage had been erected on the massive front lawn of the castle. Long red carpets were laid between rows upon rows of chairs, which were filled with the family members of the Ruala warriors.

Huge platforms had been erected on the outside of the wall that surrounded the castle so spectators could watch the ceremonies. Everywhere there were tables of refreshments and bouquets of flowers. Soldiers were wearing their dress military uniforms and groups of musicians played in various areas of the castle grounds.

The entire Royal Family of Wetpr were seated on the stage as was the Royal Family of Lentz, including Sorren, Shara and their sons. Fahron and Isadore were also asked to sit on the stage, a request they complied with reluctantly. Gifts of great extravagance were bestowed upon Petra's rescuers as Sudfad called them up individually to stand before the stage.

The citizens of Wetpr now learned the names of these brave warriors. When the last of the gifts had been given, Sudfad told the warriors to turn around and face the citizens of Wetpr. The roar of the crowds was deafening; so many people were clapping and stomping their feet that the earth shook.

Now Sudfad addressed the audience. "As you can see many of these warriors are wounded. Just weeks ago they battled a large army of Hutas to protect the citizens of Nora in the Kingdom of Stordt. So you see being heroes is in their nature."

"Normally I would open the gates so you, the good citizens of Wetpr could shake hands with these fine men and women. But as we all can see, fatigue is taking its toll on many of them. Please bear with us as these warriors and their families go inside of the castle. Then the gates will be opened for you to listen to music and enjoy refreshments."

Jared left the shop and went to the General Store and bought provisions. After he packed his horses with all of his belongings he returned to the shop to get Zoya's answer. To his surprise she was waiting for him in the alley. Zoya was sitting on top of a chestnut mare; her two saddlebags were bulging.

"I really didn't think you would come," Jared said.

"Jared, I hope you don't make me regret this," Zoya said with trepidation. "I trust you are a man of your word."

"Zoya I promise you I will not hurt you and I will not let any harm come to you," Jared said with conviction.

Meekos walked out of Walt's Tavern and stood on the sidewalk as he eyes became accustomed to the bright afternoon light. Jared and Meekos stared into each other's eyes as Jared and Zoya rode past him. Neither man spoke, but the look in Jared's eyes filled Meekos with fear. In his semi drunken state, Meekos was so focused on Jared that he did not notice Zoya who was riding behind him.

Meekos hurried back to his hotel to tell Sophie and Erebus that Jared was in the city. Meekos had become a slave to his own fears after hearing about the battle between the Hutas and Rualas and the destruction of the caves in Nora. He was drinking a great deal, which was uncharacteristic for him.

Neither Sophie nor Erebus were in their rooms. Meekos searched the lobby and dining room of the hotel without finding them. He returned to his room, poured himself a glass of whiskey and sat on the edge of his bed.

"The way he looked at me, he must know something but how?" Meekos thought. "If Jared is alive perhaps Pravis and Tenebrae are alive also." This last thought made Meekos feel hopeful. "I need to pull myself together," he said out loud and loudly. Then he threw his glass against the wall, smashing it into tiny pieces.

Meekos started to pace back and forth in his room. He talked out loud to himself thinking it would help clear his head. "I don't really know what happened in Nora; perhaps it isn't what I think." He stopped his pacing and pulled the curtains away from the window so he could look down at that street. "Where are they?" he asked angrily, referring to Sophie and Erebus.

Meekos started pacing again as he considered his options; he could try a spell and see if something in the underworld was still blocking him, he could try to find Jared and ask him about Nora. Then Meekos remembered the look in Jared's eyes and fear filled him again. He could send a message to Pravis and Tenebrae, then Meekos thought about all of the messages that he had sent that never made their destinations.

Meekos stopped pacing and walked over to the table in his room. He took a pen and paper and wrote a quick letter, then he packed his suitcases and left the hotel.

Jared kept looking behind them, as he and Zoya rode out of Taperia. "Do you expect to be followed?" she asked.

"I expect just about anything these days." Jared paused for a few moments. "Zoya I can't really say that I understand what you can do. I guess I should be asking, what exactly can you do?"

Zoya laughed, Jared liked the sound of her laughter. "It is kind of hard to explain," she said. "Ever since I was a small child I would have visions; not when I was asleep but awake. And always these visions would come true. I didn't ask for them they would just happen to me. I know that is probably hard to believe."

"Actually it isn't," Jared said dryly. "Go on."

"Then, as I got older I would hear things or feel things that weren't happening in this world. At first I was so scared and I thought I was going crazy. But then strange things would happen, like I would hear voices that were warning me about things."

"You mean threatening you?"

"Oh no, I mean, well like one time I was traveling with my husband and I keep hearing this voice telling me that we should get off the road and camp on high ground. Finally we did and late that night there was a storm and a flash flood washed out the road we had been traveling on."

"Wait," Jared said as he stopped his horse and turned around and looked at Zoya. "You have a husband? Does he know you're traveling with me?"

"Thomas is dead," Zoya said with sadness in her voice. "Some drunken men in Taperia beat him to death with bull whips a year ago."

"I'm sorry," Jared said as he could see she was upset. "So are you alone?"

Zoya stared at Jared suspiciously. "Why is that of any matter; I thought this trip was purely business?"

"It is," Jared said. "I didn't lie to you. But I don't want a jealous boyfriend hunting us down."

"You don't have to worry, there is no boyfriend."

"Really?" Jared said quizzically.

"Why do you say it like that?"

"Well, you're such a pretty girl I would think all kinds of men would be after you. So what, do your spirit friends chase them away?"

Zoya laughed loudly, "Sometimes they do."

Jared turned around in his saddle and started riding again. "So finish telling me about whatever it is that you do."

Zoya found Jared's mannerisms amusing and surprisingly nonjudgmental. "After the spirits warned me about a couple of other things I started to feel like they were protecting me. That's when I started talking to them. You know there are all kinds of things happening around us that we can't see but most people won't believe that."

"I believe it; that's why I came to you," Jared said. "So tell me more about that demon that was listening to me and Roch. And why do you think it is some kind of trap?"

"Jared is Roch a friend of yours?"

573

"No, you might say he is a spirit that has been trying to talk to me of late."

"I have never had a reading like the one I did for you. Roch made it sound like he was alive and taken prisoner by a demon; which is what I had heard. But I couldn't tell if he was dead or alive. And the entire time I could see this vast darkness and feel how cold and sinister it was. Jared I'm not sure Roch was the one talking to you."

Chapter XXXVI
Angry Souls

"He's gone," Sophie said in disbelief as she read a letter that the hotel clerk handed to her.

"What do you mean he is gone?" Erebus asked with concern. "Where did he go to?"

Sophie handed the letter to Erebus, "He said he saw Jared riding down the street and knew from the look in Jared's eyes that he knew something. Meekos said he is tired of sitting around here wondering what is going on so he left for Nora. Erebus I am worried. Meekos has not been acting like himself lately and to leave like this without even saying 'good bye', well it just isn't him."

"Do you think it is because we are seeing each other?" Erebus asked.

"I am sure that is part of it," Sophie answered. "But Meekos has always been the one who strategizes and plans out every long-term detail because it gives him control of situations. I think he feels like he has lost control of everything and that is why he is going to Nora. But that truly may be the last place he should go to."

Erebus leaned close to Sophie to talk because he did not want the other people in the hotel lobby to hear them. "Let's go back out to that field and try some more spells. Perhaps if we try to get information about Pravis and Tenebrae instead of Roch the demons won't block us."

That evening Jared and Zoya made their first camp. Zoya was cooking over the fire as Jared took care of the horses and brought more wood to their campsite. He hoped that he would not have another vision while they were together. Then Jared realized it might be a good thing if Zoya was there, perhaps she could help him understand the visions. Jared stacked the last load of fire wood and poured himself a cup of whiskey. "Whatever you are cooking sure smells good."

"It's just stew; while you were getting wood I found some herbs and mushrooms that I put in it," Zoya said. "It's going to need to cook for a while, though. I made some biscuits, if you're hungry now why don't you have some," Zoya said as she handed him a plate containing three biscuits.

"These are great," Jared said as he devoured the pastries. "Zoya I have to tell you some things but first I want to know why you came with me. Spirits or not, you just don't seem like the kind of girl who would leave with a strange man, especially one who looks like me."

Zoya picked up her cup of tea and sat down near Jared. She looked him in the eyes as she spoke. "Do you mean because you look like a hired fighter?"

"Well that and some people think I look scary what with my missing one ear and these scars."

"Jared, you don't look scary but you do look like you could handle just about anything and honestly that is why I came with you. I have been so frightened living in Taperia, even before my husband was murdered. If anyone could get past the border guards I think it would be you. I just want to leave Stordt. I will help you like I promised, then when it's over; I don't want you to bring me back here. You can leave me in Wetpr."

Jared watched Zoya as she spoke and believed she was sincere. "Do you have family or friends in Wetpr?"

"No, but I have heard it is a wonderful place to live. And I just want to be someplace where I can feel safe for once."

"Now don't start giving me that suspicious look of yours again but when I leave Wetpr I am going to Port Friada to start a new life, you are welcome to come with me."

"How do you mean?" Zoya asked skeptically.

"Now there you go again, looking at me like you think I'm going to do something to you. I just meant you could ride along. I have heard that it's a great place to start over. And besides its kind of nice having company."

"Can I think it over before I give you an answer?"

"You can think it over until our business is done in Wetpr." Jared paused, took a drink of his whiskey and looked at Zoya for a few moments before he continued. "Now I have to tell you that almost every night Roch shows me a vision, it's always the same vision and it happens when I am awake. But after the vision sometimes I wake up away from the campsite. I have always been alone when it happens so I wanted to warn you that I might act strangely."

"What do you see in the vision?"

"It might scare you if I tell you."

"Just tell me."

"You know how Roch said there was a bunch of crazy people grooming humans so demons could take over their bodies?" Jared waited for Zoya to nod before he continued. "Well in the vision I am in a cave and there is a large stone tub that has a sign that says it belongs to the demon Omnibus. Next to this tub is a row of smaller tubs that all contain dead human bodies. Roch is in the first tub and I am in the second. I can never see the faces of the others."

"Does this scare you?"

"Hell ya, especially when I wake up some place else after the vision."

Zoya moved closer to Jared and took his hand. "Jared I believe you are in very great danger. Another human being cannot transport you through visions. I told you I wondered if Roch was really talking to you. Now I am convinced that demon is doing this to you."

"Then why would he send me to the Sanuri to give him the book?"

"Perhaps this is a trap for the Sanuri. Jared I don't know what you have done in your past but to help a demon trap a holy man is about the worst thing you could do. The Great Ruler will punish you severely. Please don't do this thing."

577

Jared stared at Zoya for a few moments as he thought about her words. "If this demon is so powerful why does he need me to set a trap for the Sanuri?"

"The Sanuri is a very powerful being," Zoya said. "I think we should give him that book and tell him everything, including that we think it is a trap for him. In fact Jared, now that you told me this; if you don't warn the Sanuri I will."

"I always love being here," Angelina said as she and Matthew danced in the Great Hall. "I know I have told you this before but I admire Renya so much. I would like to be just like her someday."

Matthew looked down at Angelina and smiled. "Honey I don't think you realize how much you are like her already. And when you become Queen, I will bet you do the same things she does."

Angelina smiled warmly at Matthew's words. "You know when I was growing up; Father was so suspicious and disapproving of your father and well, I guess you could say all royal families. And now I look at him and he is not the same person. He and Mother love your parents and they love coming here as much as I do. And Father and Claudius, well you can't tear them apart anymore, especially with Ingr's and Nikki's babies. I think it is so cute."

"I'm sorry Ingr and Stephan and the rest couldn't come," Matthew said. "But I am truly amazed that Ingr can get around as well as she does. Are you alright?" Matthew asked as he could feel Angelina tensing up.

"Yes, it's just labor pains," Angelina said as she winced in pain.

"What! How long have you been having them?"

"All day."

"All day! Angelina why didn't you say anything?" Matthew asked nervously.

"Because I didn't think you would let me go to the parade and ceremonies," Angelina said as she started to bend over with pain. "Besides the baby wasn't ready to come then."

"How about now?" Matthew asked as he looked around the room nervously for Shara.

"It may be time," Angelina said as she gritted her teeth and tried to smile.

"Raul, Raul," Matthew yelled over the dance floor as he saw Raul and Vitomas dancing a few feet away. When Raul and Vitomas looked at Matthew he waved his arm frantically and yelled, "The baby's coming." Raul and Vitomas ran over to them, as did others who heard Matthew yelling. "We need Shara," Matthew yelled frantically.

"I'm a physician," Hannah said as she ran up to the young couple. "I can help."

"Raul take care of Matthew," Angelina said as she tried to laugh. "He's in much worse shape than I am."

"Can you walk?" Matthew asked nervously.

"Yes, and it's good for me to walk, you stay with Raul," Angelina said as Vitomas, Annabelle and Hannah escorted her down the hallway towards Matthew's wing of the castle. Within minutes the news spread through the dance room. Soon all of Angelina's and Matthew's family were making themselves comfortable in Angelina's and Matthew's parlor.

Hannah walked out of the bedroom and announced, "It will be a while yet but she is doing fine. Has anyone seen her mother?"

"She's in the kitchen making some tonics for pain," Sorren said. "I am Angelina's father."

"I am Hannah and I am a physician, you can go in and visit her if you want." Both Sorren and Matthew quickly entered the bedroom where Vitomas and Annabelle were keeping Angelina company.

"All of you should change out of your ball gowns so they don't get soiled," Angelina said.

Neither Vitomas nor Annabelle moved. Sorren looked at them both and nodded. "Go we will stay with her."

Vitomas walked up to Hannah, "We're going to change then come right back."

"That sounds like a good idea," Hannah said then turned to Gabriel. "Honey you don't have to stay here, it will be a while."

"If you don't mind, Sudfad gave me several large stacks of paperwork to read. I'll be in our chambers if you need me."

"Jared are you a hired fighter?" Zoya asked as she ladled hot stew onto a plate for him.

"I have been several times," Jared said as he took the plate of food.

"Do you like that life?"

This question took Jared by surprise. "Well it pays the bills."

"That's not what I asked."

Jared looked seriously at Zoya, "You probably want me to say that is not who I am but it is. Does that make a difference to you?"

"I really don't know. Would you like more stew?" Zoya asked as she noticed that Jared hungrily devoured his food. Jared handed her his plate without saying anything.

"Jared are you married?" Zoya asked as she handed him a second plate of food.

"This is very good," he said. "No, I was but I wasn't a very good husband."

"What do you mean? Did you beat your wife?"

"Oh no, I would never hurt Mary, at least not like that," Jared said with regret in his voice. Both Zoya and Jared were quiet for a few moments before he continued.

"We had a small place near Danner in the Kingdom of Puntd. I spent more time in the city drinking and playing cards than I did at home."

"One day I promised her I would come home early, only I got involved in a card game and well…" Jared paused. "I saw the smoke and flames long before I found her. Mary's body was a couple of hundred yards behind the house. She was naked and…" Jared sighed loudly. "The Hutas had skinned her alive. It took me six months but I tracked them all down and…"

"And what Jared?"

"And I skinned each one of them when they were alive. That's how I lost my ear, fighting with one of those Hutas."

Meekos was able to hire a carriage and was already on his way to Nora before Sophie and Erebus knew he was gone. "I hope she feels bad," Meekos thought. Then he recognized how immature he was acting. "What has happened to me? I've got to pull myself together. I need to think this thing through." The rocking of the carriage lulled Meekos to sleep. But there were a lot of ruts in the dirt road they were traveling on. Meekos awoke several times when one of the carriage wheels hit a rut.

"Can't you avoid those damn things?" Meekos yelled out the window of the enclosed carriage, at the two men who rode up front. One man was driving the carriage and the other was a guard.

The two men smiled at each other when they heard Meekos yelling. "I don't know Chance, I think you could manage to hit a couple more if you really try." The man acting as a guard said to the driver with a laugh.

"These ruts are going to be the least of his problems," the driver said. "I know Raphael is on his way to Wetpr but see if you can get a message to him too. He will want to know we're bringing Meekos back to Nora."

"Do I scare you?" Jared asked.

"A little," Zoya replied. "But you have been honest with me and so far you have been kind and I appreciate that."

"I don't want to scare you," Jared said softly. Zoya didn't respond.

"When we first met you said the spirits told you what my name was," Jared continued as he wanted to change the subject. "What else did they tell you?"

Zoya smiled, "When the spirits talk to me it's not always like having a conversation with another person. Sometimes I am flooded with images and feelings as well as hearing words. I saw that you were a dangerous man and that you, yourself were in a great deal of danger, although at the time I didn't know from what. And I saw that I would go on a journey with you."

"Really?" Jared asked with great surprise. Zoya nodded. "Well it doesn't sound like your spirits are protecting you too damn much if they tell you to go on a journey with a dangerous man who is in trouble," Jared said sarcastically.

Zoya laughed. "Do you want me to sit up with you to see if you have a vision?"

"No, get some sleep."

"I will sit up with you if you want."

Jared threw some more wood on the fire, "Maybe we should both try to get some sleep."

Marie brought refreshments into the parlor for everyone who was waiting for the birth of Angelina's and Matthew's baby. Abigail and Gabriella, the two nannies of the Royal Family, were watching all of the children, who had been put to bed in two large bedrooms in the wing of the castle that Raul and his family shared. That wing was the closest to the wing built for Matthew. Only Petra sat up with the adults, although sleep was overtaking him as he sat in a chair trying to watch a family card game.

"They're laughing, I just heard laughter in there," Matthew declared with astonishment as he nervously paced outside of the bedroom door. "Do you think that means the baby is here?"

"Dear, they will let us know when the baby is born," Renya said lovingly.

"Matthew, join us in cards," Simon said. "It will get your mind off the baby."

"I don't know if I can sit still," Matthew replied.

Raul walked up to Matthew and slapped him on the back, "Now you understand why I always get so nervous."

"Matthew, both Shara and Hannah are in there as well as Annabelle and Vitomas; she really couldn't be in better hands," Rosa said soothingly.

"I know Mother but it doesn't really help."

Laurel walked into the parlor carrying a large basket. "I am sorry I wasn't here sooner but I had to finish the quilt." Laurel walked up to Matthew and handed him the basket. "Here are some things I made for your baby."

"Thank you Laurel," Matthew said sincerely. Then his eyes grew wide. "We never thought to bring anything for the baby."

"We have some gifts for you too," Renya said. "You will have enough to take the baby home in."

"Let's see what you made," Rosa said as she took the basket from Matthew. "Laurel, these are beautiful," Rosa gushed as she held up a baby's quilt with matching sheets. Then Rosa took a knitted cap and matching booties out of the basket and showed Mathias. Rosa took several embroidered nightgowns out of the basket and held them up for everyone to see. "Matthew why don't you take these beautiful things in and show Angelina," Rosa suggested.

Mathas laughed as he watched his son. Matthew had always been a confident, decisive man and now, anticipating the birth of his first child, it appeared that Matthew couldn't think clearly. Rosa returned all of the items to the basket then knocked on the bedroom door. "Can Matthew come in and show you the beautiful gifts that Laurel made for the baby?" Annabelle opened the bedroom door with a big smile on her face.

Gabriel became so immersed in the files that Sudfad had given him, that he lost all concept of time. He did not want to mark the papers he was reading so he made notes on separate sheets.

Gabriel first started reading the documentation that Padre Bartholomew and Padre Thomas had uncovered and sent to the Sanuri. Gabriel was impressed with the thoroughness of their work. But the knowledge that such atrocities occurred in a monastery dedicated to The Great Ruler filled Gabriel with both horror and sadness.

"Gabriel you're still up," Hannah said when she walked into their bedroom.

"Yes, what time is it?" Gabriel asked as he set the papers he was reading on the small table in their room.

"It's almost dawn," Hannah said as she pranced over to Gabriel and kissed him on the cheek. "Angelina and Matthew have a beautiful baby girl. I love delivering babies."

Gabriel pulled Hannah onto his lap and kissed her passionately on the lips. "I'll be glad when we start having our own babies." He said then proceeded to kiss the side of her neck.

"So tell me my husband, are you going to keep working?" Hannah asked with a coy smile. Gabriel laughed as he closed the file of papers, picked Hannah up and carried her to their bed.

"We've been traveling all night," Meekos yelled out of the window of his carriage. "Stop at the next village or town where we can get something to eat."

"Yes My Lord," Eldridge yelled back to Meekos.

"Kendra is coming up soon," Chance said. "We can stop there. Hopefully the men are in place."

As the morning sun was rising in the sky, two Enrops landed on the front seat of the carriage next to the two members of the Patronus. Eldridge took a note from the beak of one of the great birds and read it.

"It's from Ruben; he wants us to take Meekos straight to the headquarters. Ruben says he will be sending some Salts of Envoy to put Meekos to sleep. We'll have to slip it into his food or water. Within moments a third Enrop landed on the front seat of the carriage with a small pouch in its beak.

Jared awoke to the smell of coffee brewing and bacon frying. When he opened his eyes he saw Zoya kneeling next to the fire and stirring something in a pan. "I can't believe you got up and I didn't hear you," he said in disbelief as he sat up.

Zoya quickly poured Jared a cup of coffee and carried it over to him. "Did you have your vision last night?"

Jared stopped and thought momentarily. "No, no I didn't. You must bring me good luck."

"I don't think I bring anyone good luck," Zoya said soberly as she returned to the fire.

"What do you mean?"

"Thomas and I were run out of Jarta because people were afraid of my visions and thought I was a witch. How could I be a witch, I pray to The Great Ruler? Then when Thomas was murdered, the spirits never said anything; they never warned us."

"Zoya you can't blame yourself for any of that. I am sure you were a wonderful wife to Thomas and that's the best you can do."

"Oh I was a good wife but these visions, I don't know if they are a blessing or a curse. And if they are a blessing; wouldn't you think I could do more with them?"

"Alexas Rose," Sorren announced proudly as he showed his sleeping granddaughter to Prince Lakin and his family. "Alexas is one of my wife's middle names and Rose is Matthew's mother."

"She's absolutely beautiful," Zada said admiringly. "And look at all of that red hair for such a little baby. What color are her eyes?"

"From what we can tell they are brown but Shara says that might change later on," Sorren was so happy he felt like his heart was going to explode. "Everyone was up all night, so I took her, so Angelina and Matthew could get a little sleep."

585

Lakin patted Sorren on the shoulder. "Well that little one couldn't be in better hands. I have a feeling you are going to be a very doting grandpa."

"Honey can't we do this later, I'm tired," Simon asked kiddingly.

"No," Annabelle said in a loud whisper. "We want to surprise them when they wake up."

Raul and Simon were removing furniture from the bedroom that was nearest to Matthew's and Angelina's room. Annabelle and Vitomas were hanging new drapes that had pictures of baby animals on the material. Raul started to carry a rocking chair into the room when Renya stopped him. "No we have to pick up this carpet and put down a new one," she whispered.

"Wouldn't you think we would have help that could do this?" Simon asked Raul with a grin.

"Oh Honey, we'll make it up to you," Annabelle said with a flirtatious smile.

"Our wives know us so well," Raul said with a chuckle.

Raul and Simon put the new carpet down and started carrying furniture into the baby's room. As soon as they would set a piece of furniture down, Renya, Rosa and Laurel would fill the drawers with baby things and cover the top with toys.

"They are going to be so surprised," Rosa said as the group stood back to admire their work.

"Rosa, you aren't going to travel back to Lentz right away with a new baby are you?" Vitomas asked.

"I think we will be staying a little longer than we originally planned," Rosa said smiling.

Later that afternoon, Jared and Zoya stopped for lunch just north of where the River Neior intersects with the River Nebu.

"You're awfully quiet," Zoya said. "What is wrong?"

"I'm just thinking about the border guards," Jared said. "We should be at the border in a couple of hours. I expect there will be a fight, so be prepared for anything. Show me your hands." Zoya held her hands out so Jared could look at them. "It would probably be safer for you if we told people you were my wife, at least until we get to Wetpr. Do you still have your wedding rings?"

Zoya was quiet for a few moments. "No, I sold them for food," she said in a hoarse whisper.

Jared walked over to his saddlebags and returned to the campfire with a medium sized pouch. He poured the contents on the ground. "See if any of these fit you."

Zoya's eyes grew wide with disbelief as she looked at the pile of rings that now lay before her. "Jared did you steal these?" she asked in a scolding manner.

"Yes, but the guys I took them from were already dead and well, I'm sure they had stolen them." Jared was talking about the jewels he had taken from the hotel rooms of Pravis and Tenebrae.

"Jared, I can't wear something that's stolen."

"It's up to you," Jared said as he shrugged his shoulders. "But we have all heard what the soldiers of Taperia do to women. I think you should just wear one until we get across the border. Do you have any weapons on you?"

Zoya walked over to her bedroll and pulled a large knife out of the rolled blankets. "That's fine," Jared said but you need something smaller so you can hide it on your body; something that will be easier for you to reach if you need to." He stood up and took a sheath containing a dagger off from his belt and handed it to Zoya. "Do you have a belt in your saddlebags?" Jared asked. Zoya walked over to her saddlebags and took out a narrow leather belt; Zoya threaded it through the sheath and put it on. She was now realizing the seriousness of their situation.

The castle at Wetpr was filled with activity as everyone prepared for the celebration of the weddings of Gabriel and Hannah, Rabi and Marcia and Calen and Natasha.

Renya only slept for two hours before she went to work on the decorations. Many of the guests were sorting through the items that Emmet, Grady and their men had just delivered from Nora. Other guests were visiting the large City of Salar and a few guests were helping with the preparations for the Grand Ball.

"Gabriel, Emmet and Grady arrived a little while ago with our things," Hannah said as she walked into their chambers and found Gabriel reviewing paperwork. "They want to know if they should just drive some of the bocas to our house."

"Do you want to start moving in?" Gabriel asked with a broad smile.

"Yes," Hannah said excitedly. "Should I see if some of the others want to come with us?"

"Of course; I will meet you downstairs in a few moments."

After Hannah left the room, Gabriel picked up one of Padre Dominick's drawings and stared at it again. There was a face of a man, in the back of a gathering of Insidiae that Gabriel recognized. Gabriel had been staring at the man's face for some time, trying to remember how he knew the man. Finally he placed the drawing on top of the stack of papers and closed the file.

Jared watched the border guards for several minutes before approaching them. From what he could see there were eight men on horseback. As Jared approached the men, he held the reigns of his horse in his left hand and two razor sharp throwing stars in his right.

"Stop right there," one of the men yelled. "Where do you think you are going?" The man who was talking and another man rode up to Jared and Zoya.

"Well we were planning on going to Wetpr," Jared said confidently as he looked into the eyes of the guards.

"What business do you have in Wetpr?"

"Not that it's any of your business but my wife's mother is dying."

"Do you have written permission from the King to leave?"

"We're not citizens of Stordt," Jared said with conviction. "I didn't need paperwork to get in this damn kingdom and I sure as hell don't need paperwork to leave." Zoya slowly moved her right hand and grasped the hilt of the dagger on her belt, as Jared talked. She could see that his challenging attitude was making the guards angry.

Jared and the guard who had been doing all the talking stared into each other's eyes. Jared saw a movement in the corner of his right eye. Before Zoya realized what had happened the two guards closest to them fell from their horses. Each man had a metal star embedded between his eyes.

Jared's attack happened so quickly that it took the other guards by surprise momentarily. And in that brief moment, Jared pulled a knife from a sheath on the back of his neck and threw it into the heart of another soldier. Jared pulled two swords out of sheaths on his saddle as the five remaining guards charged at him.

Jared charged forward brandishing his weapons in what seemed to Zoya to be wild movements but as soon as Jared was close enough; he thrust both of the swords into the stomachs of two of the soldiers. Jared never stopped his horse as he pulled the swords out of the bodies. He kept riding for several more feet, then turned his horse around and charged again.

Zoya held her breath as she watched Jared charging at the two Taperian soldiers. She was so focused on him that she did not realize one of the men had ridden up beside her.

The man grabbed Zoya by the waist and was pulling her off from her horse, towards him. "Well aren't you a pretty little thing," she heard the man say. Zoya already had her hand on the hilt of her dagger, now she pulled it from its sheath and plunged it into the man's forearm.

"You bitch!" the man yelled and dropped Zoya on the ground. Zoya's horse was frightened and immediately reared on its hind legs.

Being an experienced rider, Zoya rolled to her side, so as not to be struck by the horse's hooves. The man jumped off from his horse and ran towards Zoya as she jumped up and ran to her horse. As Zoya was pulling her large knife out of her bedroll, she heard Jared yell her name, Zoya saw Jared look at her and in that moment one of the soldiers stabbed Jared in the side with a dagger.

Zoya now realized that her attacker had one of his arms around her waist and the other around her shoulders. Everything slowed down for Zoya as she turned and thrust her knife into the man's stomach. She pushed him away as she pulled her knife out of him. Suddenly Zoya found herself running towards Jared who was rolling on the ground with the remaining soldier.

The ground where the two men were fighting was covered in blood. Jared saw Zoya standing near them with her knife posed to strike. Jared threw his weight so his back was on the ground and the Taperian soldier was on top of him. Jared held the soldier's arms while Zoya stabbed him in the back. Jared pushed the dying soldier off from him and quickly got up, "Are you alright?" he asked.

"Yes, but you are bleeding badly," Zoya said as she looked at the wound on this left side.

"Get on your horse and let's get across the border now," Jared said.

"But your wound."

"We can deal with that later," Jared said as he pulled himself up on his horse. "If more soldiers come we may not be so lucky, ride!"

Chapter XXXVII
To Begin

"I can't believe I am so nervous," Hannah said as she clutched Gabriel's right arm. The three couples who were being honored at the Grand Ball were given instructions to line up outside of the ballroom. When the doors opened and the music started to play, they were to proceed down the red carpet.

Gabriel and Hannah were first in line, followed by Natasha and Calen and Marcia and Rabi. To the surprise of Natasha and Marcia their husbands were not wearing the traditional white warrior's robe of that tribe. Both men were wearing black suits that were similar to Gabriel's; except of course, for the openings for their wings.

"I just can't believe how handsome you look," Natasha said to Calen. "Is this how you dress in the Ice Caves?"

"We have to wear the robes for flying but at home we can wear whatever we want. When we go out on missions we travel light. Our families brought our clothes here," Calen replied.

"I just can't stop staring at Rabi," Marcia said with a giggle.

Gabriel turned around and said, "Well, all of you ladies look incredibly beautiful tonight." All three of the women were wearing long white gowns of different designs. Renya talked them into wearing wedding dresses for the ball since they weren't able to wear wedding dresses for their actual weddings. Hannah squeezed Gabriel's arm tightly as the double doors to the ballroom opened. All three couples gasped at the splendor before them.

The long red carpet ran through the entire ballroom. There were arbors of white flowers of every variety along the carpet and in between the arbors stood Wetprian soldiers in their dress uniforms. The soldiers had their swords raised to form archways. Everything in the ballroom was decorated in white and silver except for the head table which contained huge bouquets of red roses. The guests stood up and clapped as the three couples walked down the red carpet and the brides cried.

When Meekos awoke, he found himself tied to a chair in the basement of the home that Hannah grew up in; although he did not know his location. The chair he was tied to was set in the room that contained the unholy altar that was built by Hannah's father. There was no fire in the huge pit but the torches that were fastened to the stone wall were lit. The room was cold, very cold.

Meekos' head ached and his mouth was so dry he could not call out; both of these conditions were side effects from the numerous doses of Salts of Envoy that he had been given.

As Meekos looked around he realized he was wearing clothing that did not belong to him. He wondered why someone would take his clothing. Meekos was still groggy from the potion. The dancing flames of the torches were causing shadows on the stone walls. He strained his eyes to see if any of the shadows were demons.

Meekos' arms were tied behind the wooden chair and his legs were bound together at the ankles and the knees. He had never been a man of strength and his attempts to pull at his restraints were futile.

As his head started to clear, Meekos became consumed with anger. He concentrated on starting the ropes that bound him on fire, a spell of minor consequence for Meekos but nothing happened. He mumbled a spell to call forth a demon snake but no snake materialized. Fear started to rise within Meekos. What was blocking his spells?

Meekos looked at the unholy altar and whispered, "Omnibus I am your loyal servant, I beseech you, help me from these restraints." Meekos waited but there was no response from the ancient demon. In an act of desperation Meekos called out for Ahriman to help him. But the holiness that now engulfed this house prevented the great demon from entering. Meekos the powerful dark lord, sat alone in the stone cellar, thirsty, cold and afraid.

The morning after the Grand Ball, the castle of Wetpr was bustling with activity. Although Simon and Raul enjoyed the ceremonies they were becoming a little overwhelmed by all of the people and commotion so they decided to take an early morning ride.

"We used to do this all of the time," Raul said as he enjoyed the sensation of freedom. "Why did we give it up?"

"Because we got married and started having babies," Simon said with a grin. "You know Annabelle is pregnant again, you're going to have to catch up Brother."

Raul laughed then said, "Speaking of wives and babies, we should probably head back pretty soon."

They turned back towards the castle and had only ridden for ten minutes before they heard loud voices coming from the road, which they were riding parallel to. The road was only a few yards to their left but was not visible because of a small tree line. Raul and Simon could hear a woman's voice that sounded frantic, so they quickly rode through the trees and brush and came out onto the road near a group of their soldiers.

"What is going on?" Raul asked as he and Simon rode closer to the group.

Zoya was almost in tears. "Please won't you help us?" Zoya had no idea she was speaking to the Princes of Wetpr. "My friend is seriously injured; we risked our lives to deliver something to the Sanuri of Tabrul. Please the Sanuri may be in trouble, we have to warn him and my friend needs a physician badly."

Both Simon and Raul recognized Jared who was barely able to sit on his horse. "What happened to him?" Simon asked.

"He fought eight Taperian border guards to get here; please I am telling the truth. See we have to deliver this book to the Sanuri." Zoya pulled the book out of a pouch that she had hanging from the front of her saddle and handed it to Raul. "Please will you ask the King's family if we can see the Sanuri?"

Raul looked at the book and handed it back to Zoya, "Here, we are the King's sons, follow us."

"Help that man stay on his horse," Simon ordered some of his soldiers. Within minutes they were entering the front door of the castle. Four soldiers were carrying Jared, who was now unconscious.

"My Lords," Marie gasped as she saw them enter.

"Marie get Hannah, we're going to put him in this first bedroom down here," Raul said as he walked ahead of the others so he could open the door.

"I'll get the Sanuri and Father," Simon said and walked to the study. When Simon entered the room he found Gabriel, Raphael, and the Sanuri with Sudfad. Simon closed the door behind him. "Gabriel do you remember that big man who was sitting with the priests in Nora, the one that Endleson said was working for them?"

"The guy with the scars and no ear?" Gabriel asked.

"Yes, Raul and I just found him and a woman along the road. He is injured; we just put him in one of the bedrooms on this floor."

"Why is he here?"

"The woman he is with seems sincere. She said they battled border guards to come here and warn the Sanuri that he might be in danger. She showed us a book that looks like it belongs to the Insidiae; she said they were bringing it to the Sanuri."

"That man looks like a hired killer and he is trying to help the Sanuri," Gabriel said in disbelief. "Something isn't right here."

The Sanuri smiled as he stood up, "Things are not always as they appear, Gabriel, you know that."

Simon led the men into the bedroom where Hannah and Marcia were taking off Jared's shirt and examining his wound. "Please everyone leave here," Hannah said as the room was filling up. "This man is badly injured, we need room to work."

Raul led Zoya into the hallway. "Do you think he will live?" she asked with tears in her eyes.

"My wife is a great physician," Gabriel said. "He is in good hands."

"This is the Sanuri," Raul said. "I'm sorry but you didn't tell us your name."

Zoya turned and looked at the Sanuri and instantly fell to her knees. "My name is Zoya."

"Zoya, please stand up," the Sanuri said. "Don't bow before me."

"But I have never been in the presence of a holy man before."

"You are in the presence of a man," the Sanuri said and taking Zoya's arm he lifted her to her feet. "I hear you have a message for me?"

"Yes, but I have more than a message, I have a great deal to tell you and I think you are in grave danger."

"Let's go into my study," Sudfad said. After everyone entered the study, Raphael closed the door. "Please take a seat," Sudfad offered.

"Zoya this is our father King Sudfad," Raul said.

Zoya's eyes grew wide and she looked visibly shaken. "You're the King, oh forgive me," Zoya said and bowed before him.

"You don't have to bow before me either," Sudfad said with a smile. "These are my sons, Raul and Simon, and High Priest Gabriel, and High Priest Raphael."

Zoya looked flustered as she clutched the book tightly. The Sanuri touched her hand and said soothingly, "Zoya, you don't have to be afraid, just tell me what it is you want to say."

"I'm sorry; I'm just not used to being in the presence of so many important men." Zoya took a couple of deep breaths to calm herself. "I'm not sure where to begin," Zoya said as she handed the book to the Sanuri. "I am from Taperia, I am a seer, but I never made money from my abilities until my husband was murdered last year. Sanuri when we are done here maybe you could explain to me why I see these visions."

595

"Yes, of course."

"I help people communicate with loved ones who have died. Most of the spirits I talk with are kind and gentle and want to speak with their families. But the spirits have been taking about the upheaval in the dark worlds. They say that demons are waging wars against each other and I was told that King Roch was taken alive by a powerful demon and is being held captive. All of this I had heard before Jared walked into my shop a few days ago. He said he would pay me to contact Roch."

"When I asked him why, Jared seemed nervous. He said that I would think he was crazy but that Roch had been trying to contact him. Jared said he couldn't understand what Roch was trying to say and wanted me to find out."

"Sanuri I never had a session like that before. The voice that said it was Roch, well I couldn't tell if it was a spirit or a living person and the whole time it talked there was this dark, horrible presence that kept laughing and I told Jared later I think it was the dark presence that was actually doing the talking."

Zoya continued, "The voice said that he was Roch and that he was being held prisoner by a demon. He asked Jared if he still had the book that he stole from the priests in Nora. He told Jared to bring it to you."

"When Jared asked why, the voice said the demon seemed to be worried about you finding out his plans so he, that is the voice, thought that the demon was afraid of you. The voice said that you would be able to figure out how to get him out of his prison. Jared asked what would happen if he didn't deliver the book and the voice said Jared would end up in that prison with Roch."

Zoya seemed to relax as she was talking. "Jared said he would pay me to come here with him. He said he might need my skills. Sanuri, don't think badly of me but I have been so terrified living in Stordt. I thought if anyone could get me over the border it would be Jared. I know he's a hired fighter, but he has been very kind to me." The Sanuri did not respond.

"The first night that we camped out, Jared said he had to tell me something. He said that every night for weeks Roch has been showing him the same vision."

596

"He has these visions when he is awake but after the visions he often finds himself in different places. Jared said the visions are so real that he believes Roch is really taking him to a cave."

Zoya continued, "Jared said that in the cave is a huge stone tub with a sign that says Omnibus. There is a row of thirteen tubs next to the big one and each smaller tub contains the dead body of a man. Jared said he saw Roch in the first tub and himself in the second tub. Jared said that every night he would try to see the faces of the men in the other tubs but he couldn't."

"Sanuri tell me if I am wrong but I don't think a man can transport another man in a vision. I think it's that demon doing it. Jared and I talked about why the demon might be doing all of this and we think he is trying to lure you into a trap."

"Did Jared want to warn the Sanuri?" Simon asked.

"Not at first but I told him that he may have done some bad things but to help a demon trap a holy man would be the worst thing he could do in this world and The Great Ruler would punish him severely." Both Gabriel and Raphael smiled at her words; which made Zoya come to the defense of her friend.

"I know Jared is probably a bad man but he really is trying to warn you. Zoya put her hand into her pocket and brought out a piece of paper. "Last night, Jared said that if he died I was to tell you this. And I wrote down the names so I would remember. He said these two men, Pravis and Tenebrae were in Nora and they hired him to go to Taperia to watch this other man, Meekos."

"Jared paid the staff at the hotel that Meekos was staying at, so if Meekos asked for anyone to hire they would suggest Jared. Meekos hired Jared to take a letter to Pravis and Tenebrae. Jared will be able to tell you better if he makes it."

"But he told me he had a really bad feeling about Meekos so he stopped and read the letter. Jared said Meekos' letter said another demon pulled some men through some kind of hole in a cave and killed them. Meekos wanted the men in Nora to contact Omnibus and tell him what was going on."

"Jared said that Meekos wrote in the letter that he couldn't join them because he had a broken leg but Jared said there wasn't anything wrong with Meekos' leg when he saw him."

"But Jared said that Pravis and Tenebrae acted really scared when they read the letter. Then they gave Jared a lot of gold and paid for a fancy hotel room and told him to stay in Nora in case they needed him."

"Jared thought they were setting him up for some kind of trap so he got a room in a boarding house and started watching those two priests. Jared said that after he thought they had been killed he stole all of the things out of their hotel rooms, that's how he got this book." Zoya handed the piece of paper to the Sanuri.

Everyone in the room sat in silence and looked at Zoya. "I am telling you the truth," Zoya said. "Really."

"Oh we believe you," the Sanuri said. "You see Zoya, we have been trying to figure out a puzzle and you just gave us a piece of it."

"Oh, I almost forgot to tell you," Zoya said anxiously. "I haven't looked at that book but Jared said he read it and in the back he found his name listed with a lot of others. He said this scared him because the book was written a long time ago and it describes Jared as he looks now."

The Sanuri had previously handed the book to Gabriel, who now flipped through the back pages. After a few moments Gabriel said, "I found it," and showed the passage to the others.

"Sanuri please be careful," Zoya said sincerely. "And if you could, would you help my friend, he really was trying to warn you."

The Sanuri smiled, "And what of you Zoya, what are you going to do now?"

Zoya turned to Sudfad, "My Lord would it be alright if I lived in this kingdom, I really don't want to go back to Stordt, it is such a horrible place."

"Zoya you are free to live anywhere you would like in Wetpr," Sudfad said.

"Is Jared planning on living here too?" Raul asked.

"No, he is going to Port Friada; he said he wants to start a new life."

"I will go with you," Mathis said to Fahron and Isadore. "Sudfad said it was perfectly fine for you to visit Timothy. But he said that Timothy has gotten mouthy with some of the other prisoners and that leads to fights and well, Timothy always loses the fights. So they moved him to a cell by himself. Be prepared for anything my friends, being in prison can change a man."

Isadore clung to her husband as Mathis told the soldier to open the door that would lead them to the hallway were Timothy was imprisoned. They heard Timothy's voice before they saw him in the dimly lit cell.

"Well, if it isn't my loving parents," Timothy said sarcastically. "Are you finally getting me out of here? And I hope you told that King Sudfad who is boss."

"Show yourself son," Fahron said as he held his wife.

Isadore had been crying softly but now she gasped as she looked at Timothy, who walked up to the bars. Timothy was filthy and his hair was wild and disheveled. He had a long beard which he had braided into dozens of tiny braids. Some of the braids looked like they had small bones tied at the ends.

"Timothy are you alright?" Isadore asked in almost a whisper.

"Timothy are you alright?" Timothy mimicked his mother sarcastically. "No Mother I am not alright, I want to get the hell out of here."

"Don't talk to your mother like that," Fahron snapped.

"Well why the hell haven't you gotten me out of here?" Timothy screamed.

Fahron was furious, he walked up to the bars and said through clenched teeth, "Well why the hell did you attack the King's daughter?"

"Oh hell if it was any other girl no one would care," Timothy said disgustingly. "So what are you waiting for, tell them to open the door."

Isadore gathered all of the courage she had and walked closer to the bars, "Timothy I cannot believe what you just said. Have you attacked other girls?"

Timothy got a smug look on his face and said sarcastically, "Mother you don't really want me to answer that question."

Something died inside of Isadore in that moment. It was as if her attachment to her son was severed. "You're right; I don't want to hear the answer because it will confirm something I have suspected for a long time. You're a monster Timothy and to see you act so smugly about what you have done. Have you learned nothing being in prison?"

"Well are you going to get me out of here?" Timothy demanded again.

Isadore grabbed Fahron's arm, "Let's go."

"Go, what the hell, get me the hell out of here, it's the least you can do," Timothy screamed.

Fahron moved closer to the bars. "The least that we can do," he said angrily. "You lived a pampered life, you never worked a day in your life and you certainly never became a man. Tell me Timothy do you attack girls to make you feel like more of a man. I think the world is better off with you in here." Fahron, Isadore and Mathas turned around; as they were walking away they could here Timothy yelling.

"Not a man, well I will show you. If I ever get out of here I will kill you all."

Terror filled his soul, as Roch ran aimlessly through the forest. The burning in his body made him want to scream out in pain; but no sound came. Dazed and confused Roch had no idea where he was or how he had arrived at such a place. He just kept running to escape the nightmare he had been in. Roch's body did not feel like his own; he felt as if he was somehow changing.

Roch did not understand the way he was feeling or the thoughts in his head. All he could think of was escape.

He had the sensation of flying. He knew he was moving quickly but he did not feel his feet touching the ground. Roch's heart was pounding wildly and he felt as if his entire body was in a panic. Part of Roch's brain kept telling him to stop but he couldn't, he couldn't run fast enough to escape the nightmare. As beams from the rising sun started to filter to the forest floor, Roch finally collapsed in exhaustion. He fell onto the ground, face first with his arms extending over his head.

Roch did not open his eyes for a long time because he was afraid to look at himself. He realized he was crying as he lay on the ground gasping for air. He could hear voices in his head that terrified him but Roch did not know who was speaking. "Shut up, shut up," he screamed as he covered his ears with his hands.

Fearfully Roch slowly opened his eyes and stretched his arms out in front of him. Roch watched with horror as his arms and hands seemed to change shapes before his eyes. At times his arms appeared almost transparent, then they would look solid and human again, then they would darken and appear to grow and to lose their definition.

Roch the powerful warlord who had terrorized all kingdoms for decades was now on his knees, alone, in a deep forest screaming. "What is happening to me?" he screamed to the dark lords, he screamed to the demons and finally he screamed to the heavens.

I spoke with a soldier yesterday

Eyes that would reveal

The trauma of a soul

The wounds that would not heal

A Celebration Of Angels © 2008

By

Sandra J Year man

Glossary of Characters

Aaryan: a male Grand Master of the Insidiae

Abaddon: an ancient demon/one of the Old Ones

Abella: daughter of Prince Lakin and Princess Zada/Ruala

Abigail: sister of Marie/ nurse for grandchildren of King Sudfad

Adi: son of Elen and Batya/ Ruala

Adrone: youngest son of Joshua and Iris/younger brother of Vivian/Clan of Gesmal

Adwell: Prince/ son of King Zachariah and Queen Noella of New Samona/husband of Nada/father of Misha/ Adwell was killed in battle leaving Nada to raise ten children/Ruala/

Ael: an ancient demon/ one of the Old Ones

Ahriman: an ancient demon/ one of the Old Ones

Akasha: former king of Ryed/grandfather of Nehmota

Alexander: former servant of King Roch's parents/ father of Annabelle

Alexander: one of the twin sons of Simon and Annabelle

Alexandras: King of Wetpr/brother of Jaretta/uncle of Sudfad and Roch

Alexas Rose: daughter of Matthew and Angelina

Alexis: son of Usman, the leader of the Valdore Tribe

Alice: and her husband find Jorge near death in Nora

Ana: Princess/daughter of Zeman and Oda/niece of King Manu of New Samona/Ruala

Anda: one of Chief Romogi's three wives/Huta

Andres: Princess of Ryed/daughter of Oren and Astrel/ has twin sister Jorga

Andrew: jeweler in Salar

Andrus: father of Rabi/Ruala

Angelina: daughter of Sorren, Chief of the Nordes Tribe/female warrior

Annabar: daughter of King Sharonne

Annabelle: handmaid and best friend to Queen Vitomas of the Kingdom of Stordt

Anthony: one of the twin sons of Simon and Annabelle

Arca: Enrop leader who protects King Mathas' family

Archetenus The Brave: Captain in the Taperian Army

Arianna: daughter of Simon and Annabelle

Ariel: daughter of Raul and Vitomas

Armstrong: soldier and scout in the army of Wetpr

Arthur Marcus: father of Hannah

Asher: male Ruala warrior

Asmodeus: an ancient demon/ one of the Old Ones

Astrel: former princess of Ryed/daughter of Akasha and Norah

Atomos: Elder of the Centras and Keeper of the Box of Itifer

Augustus Endleson: a wealthy businessman who owned part of the City of Nora

Baal: an ancient demon/ one of the Old Ones

Babu: Enrop

Bac: male Ruala warrior

Bachnenus: warrior guarding refugees/Shettee

Bali: Enrop leader of the flock that does battle at Juleta's castle

Balin: Prince of Norkv/son of Thaddius and Omara/grandson of Benjeman and Esther

Banacus: General in the army of King Tobias of Puntd

Banaka: a female Grand Master of the Insidiae

Barak: Prince of Norkv/grandson of Benjeman and Esther

Barak: Prince/son of King Neputa and Queen Tiara/Shettee

Barid: Prince of Ogg

Barid: Prince of Ryed/son of Nehmota and Vasart

Bastra: Huta captain

Batya: wife of Elen/Ruala

Beatrice Endleson: wife of Augustus

Becca: Princess of Norkv/daughter of Thaddius and Omara/granddaughter of Benjeman and Esther

Behtay: Princess/daughter of Segal and Cahina/niece of King Manu of New Samona/Ruala

Bekka: female Ruala warrior

Bella: wife of Claudius and mother of Stephan

Benedict: Prince of Norkv/son of Benjeman and Esther

Benjeman: vicious rebel leader who overthrew the government of Samona

Bentra: an ancient demon/ one of the Old Ones

Berta: Queen of Stordt/wife of Micha/grandmother of Roch and Sudfad

Bertha: an elderly woman from Nora

Betty: a woman from Nora

Betu: male Ruala warrior

Black Jack: a regular patron at the Ghost Ship Tavern in Port Friada

Brik: son of Prince Lakin and Princess Zada /Ruala

Brina: Princess of Norkv/daughter of Valor and Cai/granddaughter of Benjeman and Esther

605

Cabal: son of Karzman and Nadia

Cacu: Enrop leader that joined Raul and Simon on a mission

Cade: son of King Pergo and Queen Vinus/ Kingdom of Gandt

Cadi: daughter of Prince Hadar and Princess Paj/ granddaughter of Manu/Ruala

Cael: Shettee boy who is adopted by Thedes and Ibula

Cahina: Princess/ married to Segal son of King Zachariah and Queen Noella of New Samona/Ruala

Cai: Princess of Norkv/wife of Valor who was the son of Benjeman and Esther

Calen: male Ruala warrior/cousin of Luca/son of Maxwell and Emeral/

Calla: female Ruala warrior

Calvin: a desk clerk at The Captain's Retreat Hotel in Port Friada

Campbell: one of the spies at the Castle at Wetpr

Canton: Cisero's second in command

Cara: Princess of Ogg

Carlsman: a Lieutenant in the Army of Lentz

Carson Dormors: a wealthy landowner in the Kingdom of Ganz

Carston: member of the governing body of Nora

Casey: male Ruala warrior/father of Melanie/husband of Tasha

Cassandra: daughter of King Friada and Queen Marla of the Kingdom of Ganz

Cassandra: female Ruala warrior

Cedrick Teivel: a ruthless, powerful man in the Kingdom of Ryed

Celo: Prince of Ryed/son of Oren and Astrel

Cere: daughter of Tristt/Shettee

Cerephus: General in the Taperian Army

Cerey: orphan girl/sister of Nicholas

Ceria: Princess/daughter of Gunnel and Uma/niece of King Manu of New Samona/ sister of Elan/Ruala

Chaez: son of Fahron

Chaladrone: an ancient demon/ one of the Old Ones

Chalta: daughter of King Pergo and Queen Vinus/ Kingdom of Gandt

Chance: works with the Patronus

Charlene: a woman from Nora

Charles: hired farmhand of Arthur Marcus

Chief Romogi: leader of the Hutas/ Kingdom of Marba

Christopher: six year old boy who Luca saves from the Hutas/brother of Lila

Ciao: female Ruala warrior

Cisero: a member of the Insidiae

Clair: a woman from Nora

Claudius: General in the Army of Lentz

Cleo: a man who works for Cicero/a vessel

Cobren: Prince of Norkv/son of Grace and Makalo/Grandson of Benjeman and Esther

Compro: Taperian soldier injured at Wall of Dorath

Corwin: son of King Fahra and Queen Sitha of Zorta

Crater: a soldier in the army of Wetpr

Crispus: a guard at King Roch's castle

Dack: male Ruala warrior

Dacron: former prince of Ryed/is murdered by his younger brother Nehmota for the throne

607

Dael: an ancient demon/ one of the Old Ones

Dagon: a male Ruala warrior

Dagor: son of King Fahra and Queen Sitha of Zorta

Dai: son of Gael, grandson of Manu/Ruala

Damas: an ancient demon/ one of the Old Ones

Danar: a man created to be a vessel for demons

Daniel: an emissary of The Great Ruler who takes on the disguise of a human man

Danilla: mother of King Mathas

Darius: Prince of Samona/son of Thomas and Rewel/brother of Varden

Delilah: wife of Dieter

Delilia: Queen of New Samona/mother of Ibula, Lakin, Gael and Hadar/ wife of King Manu/Ruala

Demanko: a demon

Demetries: a demon

Denise Froush: wife of Martin who is a wealthy ship builder in Port Friada

Denks: a soldier in the army of Wetpr

Denton: one of the spies at the Castle in Wetpr

Derek: friend of Thaos

Derlock: Huta warrior

Dieter: member of the Insidiae

Dion: Princess of Samona/wife of Yorggi who was the son of Thomas and Rewel/brother of Varden

Dixon: a Taperian soldier

Dominic Petlov: was the senior High Priest at the monastery at Malga before he was murdered

Dorme: Prince of Ogg

Doros: works for High Priest Meekos

Douma: King of Ogg

Duncan: Chief of the Clan of Gesmal in Ryed/ husband of Liza

Duran: father of Nikki/Nordes Tribe

Edith: wife of Lloyd a banker in Nora

Elan: male Ruala warrior/son of Gunnel and Uma/

Eldridge: works with the Patronus

Elen: son of Andrus and Naomi/ brother of Rabi/ Ruala

Elexas: a female Nordes warrior

Elsa: female Ruala warrior/mother of Mia/wife of Tyron

Emeral: mother of Calen/Ruala

Emeric: a male Grand Master of the Insidiae

Emmet: worker for Gabriel

Emon: a male Grand Master of the Insidiae

Erebus: sorcerer from Ryed

Esser: Prince/son of Segal and Cahina/nephew of King Manu of New Samona/Ruala

Esteban: a member of the Insidiae

Esther: Queen of New Norkv/wife of rebel leader Benjeman

Fabron: Prince of Ogg

Fadil: a male Grand Master of the Insidiae

Fahra: King of Zorta

Fahron: General in the Army of Lentz

Fala: female Ruala warrior

Farnsworth: General in charge of building Fort Serpha in Wetpr

Fatima: Prince of Ryed/ son of Oren and Astrel

Fatronas: an ancient demon/one of the Old Ones

Fengu: Enrop leader who helps Gabriel and his group against Omnibus

Ferguson: a Sergeant in the Army of Lentz

Fraisier: a businessman and member of the Insidiae in Nora

Friada: King of the Kingdom of Ganz

Gabriella: sister of Marie/nurse to grandchildren of King Sudfad

Gad: male Ruala warrior

Gael: Prince/son of King Manu and Queen Delilia/Ruala

Gala: a healer from the Kingdom of Stordt

Galen: male Nordes warrior

Geoff: Prince of Lentz/son of Princess Isabella and Captain Josef

Geoff: Prince of Norkv/son of Benedict and Sasaha/grandson of Benjeman and Esther

George: an advisor for King Fahra of Zorta

George: middle son of Chief Duncan and Liza of the Clan of Gesmal in Ryed

Gita: wife of Hadi/ Ruala

Gladys: member of Nordes Tribe/ mother of Nikki

Glenda: great, great, great grandmother of Gala/ a healer from the Kingdom of Stordt

Grace: Princess of New Norkv/daughter of Benjeman and Esther

Gracie: cook for the Arthur Marcus family

Grady: worker for Gabriel

Great Ruler: God

Gregory Bancar: a wealthy landowner in the Kingdom of Wetpr and member of the Insidiae

Gunnel: Prince/ son of King Zachariah and Queen Noella of New Samona/husband of Uma/father of Elan/Ruala

Hadar: Prince/son of King Manu and Queen Delilia/Ruala

Hadi: son of Andrus and Naomi/brother of Rabi/Ruala

Hadu: female Ruala warrior

Hamon: one of the members of the Nordes Tribe who was injured in an attack at Snakes Crossing

Hamond: General of the Taperian Army who declares himself king

Hanger: one of the spies at the Castle at Wetpr

Hannah: physician in Nora/ Roch murdered her sister

Harold: owner of the general store in Nora

Harriet Marcus: mother of Hannah and Laurabelle/wife of Arthur

Hatus: General in the Army of Lentz/on loan to Sudfad

Hector: fighter hired by Juleta

Hector: Prince of Samona/son of Varden

Henry: and his wife Alice find Jorge in Nora

Henry: husband of Noreen/father of Jacob

Hermanas: second in command to Archetenus at Wall of Dorath

High Priest Aaron: member of the Patronus

High Priest Amos: a member of the Patronus

High Priest Barnabas: most Senior High Priest of the monastery at Leven

High Priest Caleb: member of the Patronus

High Priest Ephraim: a member of the Patronus

High Priest Gabriel: member of the Patronus/demon hunter

High Priest Gideon: a member of the Patronus

High Priest Gregory: member of the Patronus

High Priest Joseph: member of the Patronus, in charge of the Cicero Headquarters

High Priest Josiah: member of the Patronus

High Priest Meekos: priest at the monastery at Malga

High Priest Nicholas: most Senior High Priest of the monastery at Philiste and most Senior High Priest of the Patronus

High Priest Paulas: member of the Patronus

High Priest Phanuel: member of the Patronus

High Priest Philetus: member of the Patronus in charge of Malga Headquarters

High Priest Pravis: priest at the monastery at Malga

High Priest Raphael: a leader of the Patronus

High Priest Rueben: member of the Patronus in charge of Nora Headquarters

High Priest Silas: a member of the Patronus

High Priest Tenebrae: priest at the monastery at Malga

High Priest Timothy: was murdered by Meekos, Pravis and Tenebrae

High Priest Tyrus: a member of the Patronus

High Priest Uriel: member of the Patronus

High Priest Vincent: assigned to the monastery at Malga before he was murdered

High Priest Zophar: priest at monastery at Malga/ trained as a healer

Hores: son of Chief Romogi and Anda, Kingdom of Marba/Huta

Horta: Prince/son of Gunnel and Uma/nephew of King Manu of New Samona/brother of Elan/Ruala

Hunter: Prince of Samona/son of Varden

Ian: husband of Mia/ brother-in-law of Calen/ Ruala

Ibula: warrior princess and healer of the Ruala Tribe/daughter of King Manu and Queen Delilia/

Iden: warrior guarding refugees/Shettee

Igor: brother of King Sharonne

Imad: a male Grand Master of the Insidiae

Ina: daughter of Mia and Ian/ Ruala

Ingr: female warrior of Nordes Tribe

Inon: one of Cisero's men/a vessel

Ipos: an ancient demon/ one of the Old Ones

Iris: mother of Vivian/wife of Joshua/Clan of Gesmal in Ryed

Irit: daughter of Hadi and Gita/ Ruala

Isabella: Princes of Lentz, sister of Mathas, Renya and Tasha, married to Captain Josef

Isadore: wife of Fahron

Isla: female warrior of Nordes Tribe

Isla: daughter of Prince Lakin and Princess Zada/Ruala

Ivan: youngest son of Chief Duncan and Liza of the Clan of Gesmal in Ryed

Jace: husband of Oda/ brother- in-law of Calen/Ruala

Jack: member of governing body of Nora

Jackson: a private in the Army of Lentz

Jacob: boy who Angelina found in the woods

Jacot: son of Prince Lakin and Princess Zada/ grandson of King Manu/Ruala

Jaden: Sergeant in the Army of Lentz

Jago: son of Elen and Batya/ Ruala

Jake: works for Talverson Transport Company in Port Friada

Jakiv: Prince/son of Segal and Cahina/nephew of King Manu of New Samona/Ruala

Jama: Enrop leader who protects Chief Sorren's family

James: Taperian soldier

Janja: Princess/daughter of Gunnel and Uma/niece of King Manu of New Samona/ sister of Elan/Ruala

Jared: hired fighter

Jaretta: King of Stordt/husband of Queen Lillian/ father of Roch and Sudfad

Jarrod: works for Pravis/leads attack on castle in Wetpr

Jasper: Prince of Lentz/son of Princess Isabella and Captain Josef

Jatu: Enrop leader who protects Fahron's family

Jeb: friend of Thaos

Jeb: one of Cisero's men

Jela: Queen of Samona/wife of Varden

Jeremy: cousin of Andrew the jeweler in Salar

Jerik: a male Grand Master of the Insidiae

Jess: a soldier of Wetpr

Jillian: Queen of Ogg/wife of King Douma

Jinn: an ancient demon/ one of the Old Ones

Joao: male Ruala warrior

Jonas: Captain in the Taperian Army

Jorga: Princess of Ryed/daughter of Oren and Astrel/ has twin sister Andres

Jorge: a cook who is kidnapped from Endleson Hotel in Nora

Josef: Captain in the Lentz military/ married to Princess Isabella, sister of King Mathas

Joshua: father of Vivian/husband of Iris/Clan of Gesmal in Ryed

Juleta: cousin to Raul and Simon/daughter and oldest child of King Mathas and Queen Rosa

Kadin: a member of Valdore Tribe

Kagen: a man who kidnaps and exploits children

Karta: male Ruala warrior

Karzman: leader of Kozach Tribe/ stepfather of Michael

Kasper: Prince/son of Zeman and Oda/nephew of King Manu of New Samona/Ruala

Kata: Princess/daughter of Gunnel and Uma/niece of King Manu of New Samona/ sister of Elan/Ruala

Khryriss: an ancient demon/ one of the Old Ones

Kiana: Princess/daughter of Gunnel and Uma/niece of King Manu of New Samona/ sister of Elan/Ruala

Klass: Lieutenant in the Wetprian Army

Koby: male Ruala warrior

Koh: son of Prince Gael and Princess Mada/grandson of King Manu/Ruala

Kora: Princess/ married to Raphael son of King Zachariah and Queen Noella of New Samona/ mother of Luca/ Raphael and Kora were killed in battle when Luca was a small boy/Ruala

Korth: son of Tristt/Shettee

Kraus: hired fighter and intended vessel, works for Dieter

Kretcher: Commanding General of Fort Polta in Wetpr

Krister: Princess of Samoan/daughter of Thomas and Rewel

Kyra: young sister of Marie/ friend of Petra

Laban: Prince of Samona/son of Yorggi and Dion/grandson of Thomas and Rewel

Lael: daughter of Nina and Rhea/ Ruala

Lakin: Prince/son of King Manu and Queen Delilia/husband of Zada/Ruala

Lala: Princess/daughter of Adwell and Nada/niece of King Manu of New Samona/ sister of Misha/Ruala

Lana: female warrior of the Nordes Tribe

Lana: Princess/daughter of Segal and Cahina/niece of King Manu of New Samona/Ruala

Lani: daughter of Mia and Ian/Ruala

Lara: one of Usman's wives

Larson: a fighter hired by Juleta

Laurabelle: Hannah's sister who was murdered by Roch

Laurel: Annabelle's mother and former servant of King Roch's parents

Lazo: fighter hired by Juleta

Lea: Princess/daughter of Adwell and Nada/niece of King Manu of New Samona/ sister of Misha/Ruala

Leo: Prince of Samona/son of Darius and Rebek/grandson of Thomas and Rewel

Lila: seventeen year old girl who Luca saves from the Hutas/sister of Christopher

Lilian: female warrior of the Nordes Tribe

Lillian: Queen of Stordt/wife of Jaretta/ mother of Roch and Sudfad

Lily: daughter of Calen and Natasha/Ruala and human

Liza: wife of Duncan the Chief of the Clan of Gesmal in Ryed

Lloyd: banker in Nora

Loftus: Commanding General of Fort Styls

616

Loni: daughter of King Friada and Queen Marla of the Kingdom of Ganz

Louie: works for Talverson Transport Company in Port Friada

Luca: male Ruala warrior

Lucifer: an ancient demon/ one of the Old Ones

Luque: Prince/son of Segal and Cahina/nephew of King Manu of New Samona/Ruala

Mab: a female Grand Master of the Insidiae

Mabon: warrior guarding refugees/Shettee

Mada: Princess /wife of Prince Gael/Ruala

Madam Bular: owner of a dress shop in Port Friada

Maggie: elderly store owner in Salar

Mahon: son of King Neputa

Makalo: Prince of Norkv/husband of Grace who was the daughter of Benjeman and Esther

Malana: daughter of King Neputa

Mali: Princess of Norkv/daughter of Makalo and Grace/granddaughter of Benjeman and Esther

Maligma: an ancient demon/ one of the Old Ones

Malik: member of the Insidiae

Malus: sorcerer from Ryed

Mandrake: Taperian soldier

Manu: King of New Samona/The Chief of the Grand Council made up of Rualas and Shettees/ father of Ibula, Lakin, Gael and Hadar/husband of Delilia

Marcia: friend of Hannah's/ Roch's men murdered her family

Marcus Stephan: son of Stephan and Ingr

Margarit: daughter of King Mathas and Queen Rosa of the Kingdom of Lentz/ cousin of Raul and Simon

Margolia: girl from Nora who was sacrificed to a demon

Marie: a cook for King Sudfad and Queen Renya

Markus: a soldier in the Army of Wetpr

Marla: High Priest Meekos' housekeeper

Marla: Queen of the Kingdom of Ganz

Martha: a cook for Cerephus

Martin Froush: wealthy ship builder in Port Friada/husband of Denise

Mary: Jared's young wife who was brutally murdered by Hutas

Mata: Igor's wife

Mateo: Chief Healer of the Ruala Tribe

Mathas: King of Lentz/ brother to Queen Renya

Matilda: one of Usman's wives

Matthew: son of King Mathas and Queen Rosa of the Kingdom of Lentz/ cousin of Raul and Simon

Maxwell: father of Calen/ Ruala

Maxwell: infant son of Nina and Rhea/grandson of elder Maxwell/Ruala

Melanie: female Ruala warrior/daughter of Casey and Tasha

Melina: mother of Thaos

Melinda: grandmother of Misha

Mia: daughter of Maxwell and Emeral/ Ruala

Mia: female Ruala warrior/daughter of Tyron and Elsa

Mica: Princess of Norkv/daughter of Benedict and Sasaha/granddaughter of Benjeman and Esther

Micha: oldest son of Joshua and Iris/older brother of Vivian/Clan of Gesmal

Micha: son of King Sharonne/ grandfather of Sudfad and Roch

Michael: ancient king of Wetpr/father of Queen Sumona

Miranda: emissary of The Great Ruler who takes on the disguise of a human seer

Miriam: a friend of Hannah's/works at Endleson Hotel in Nora

Misha: male Ruala warrior/lieutenant

Molach: a member of the Insidiae

Moloch: an ancient demon/one of the Old Ones

Morris: member of governing body of Nora

Myla: wife of the owner of the Dragons Inn in Salar

Naal: warrior guarding refugees/Shettee

Nabi: male Ruala warrior

Nada: Princess/ married to Adwell son of King Zachariah and Queen Noella of New Samona/ mother of Misha/ Adwell was killed in battle leaving Nada to raise ten children/Ruala

Nadia: wife of Karzman

Naomi: mother of Rabi/ Ruala

Napo: Enrop leader who protects Claudius' family

Natasha: sister of High Priest Gabriel

Nathaniel: Sorren's oldest son/ Nordes Tribe

Nebula: son of Chief Romogi and Anda/ Kingdom of Marba/Huta

Nehmota: King of Ryed

Neputa: leader of the Shettee Tribe when it was conquered by the Hutas

Nestor: a demon that specializes in procuring things for a price

619

Nica: Enrop leader who protects Sudfad's family

Nicholas: orphan boy /brother of Cerey

Nicolas: Prince of Puntd/son of King Tobias and Queen Tasha

Nieatzae: an ancient demon/ one of the Old Ones

Nikki: female warrior of Nordes Tribe

Nina: daughter of Maxwell and Emeral/Ruala

Nina: youngest daughter of Karzman and Nadia

Nita: Princess/daughter of Adwell and Nada/niece of King Manu of New Samona/ sister of Misha/has twin brother Waed/Ruala

Nobel: former prince of Ryed/son of Akasha and Norah/father of Nehmota

Noella: the first Queen of New Samona/wife of King Zachariah/mother of seven sons/Ruala

Norah: former queen of Ryed/grandmother of Nehmota

Noreen: mother of Jacob/ wife of Henry

Norris: hired fighter and intended vessel, works for Dieter

Nyla: oldest daughter of Karzman and Nadia

Oda: daughter of Maxwell and Emeral/ Ruala

Oda: Princess/ married to Zeman son of King Zachariah and Queen Noella of New Samona/Ruala

Odam: male Ruala warrior

Odell: one of the spies at the Castle at Wetpr

Omar: Prince/son of Zeman and Oda/nephew of King Manu of New Samona/Ruala

Omara: Queen of Norkv/wife of Thaddius who was son of Benjeman and Esther

Omnibus: an ancient demon/ one of the Old Ones

Omoria: former queen of Ryed/wife of Nobel/mother of Nehmota

Opago: an ancient demon/ one of the Old Ones

Oren: former prince of Gandt who marries princess Astrel of Ryed

Ottillia: Princess of Lenz/daughter of Princess Isabella and Captain Josef

Padre Augustus: a member of the Patronus

Padre Bartholomew: survives the massacre at the monastery at Avaide

Padre Cornelius: a member of the Patronus

Padre Darius: a member of the Patronus

Padre Dibon: a priest at the monastery at Malga

Padre Dominick: priest at monastery at Malga

Padre Edgar: member of the Patronus

Padre Edward: a member of the Patronus

Padre Francis: priest at monastery at Malga

Padre Joram: member of the Patronus

Padre Lucas: a member of the Patronus

Padre Octavos: runs orphanage in Salar

Padre Philip: a member of the Patronus

Padre Philip: a priest at the monastery at Malga

Padre Simpson: priest at the monastery at Malga

Padre Sorben: a member of the Patronus

Padre Stephens: priest at monastery at Malga

Padre Thomas: priest at the monastery at Malga

Padre Tobias: a member of the Patronus

Padre Xavier: priest at monastery at Malga

Paj: Princess/wife of Prince Hadar/Ruala

Pata: daughter of Chief Romogi and Trina/Huta

Paul: third son of Joshua and Iris/younger brother of Vivian/Clan of Gesmal

Paulas: Sergeant under Archetenus in Taperian Army

Paulas: a man who works for Cicero/a vessel

Paullo: works for High Priest Meekos

Pearl: eldest daughter of King Tobias and Queen Tasha of Puntd

Pergo: King of the Kingdom of Gandt

Peter: Sorren's second son/Nordes Tribe

Peters: member of the governing body of Nora

Petorus: an ancient demon/one of the Old Ones

Petra: peasant boy from Ort who saves Padre Bartholomew

Philip: Prince of Puntd/ son of King Tobias and Queen Tasha

Phillip: Court Physician to the Royal Family of Wetpr

Polgate: one of the men who kidnapped Petra

Potomas: warrior guarding refugees/Shettee

Powell: a lieutenant in the Military of Lentz/stationed at Fahron's castle

Prescott: a hired killer

Rabi: male Ruala warrior

Radnor: a male Grand Master of the Insidiae

Rael: Prince of old Samona/husband of Krister who was the daughter of Thomas and Rewel

Rahi: a female Grand Master of the Insidiae

Rakio: Prince/son of Adwell and Nada/nephew of King Manu of New Samona/brother of Misha/Ruala

Rako: a male Ruala warrior

Raphael: Prince/ son of King Zachariah and Queen Noella of New Samona/husband of Kora/Ruala/father of Luca/ Raphael and Kora were killed in battle when Luca was a small boy/Ruala

Ratri: male Ruala warrior

Raul: Prince/son of King Sudfad and Queen Renya of the Kingdom of Wetpr

Raum: an ancient demon/ one of the Old Ones

Rebek: Princess of Samona/wife of Darius, who was the son of Thomas and Rewel

Renya: Queen of Wetpr/ wife of Sudfad

Rewel: Queen of Samona/wife of Thomas/mother of Varden

Rex: a notorious pick pocket in Port Friada

Rhea: husband of Nina/ brother-in-law of Calen/ Ruala

Riftca: male Ruala warrior

Roch: King of the Kingdom of Stordt/brother of King Sudfad

Rogers: one of the men who kidnapped Petra

Rolif: son of Chief Romogi and Silva/ Kingdom of Marba/Huta

Romale: member of the Insidiae

Romos: an elder of the Centras

Rosa: Queen of Lentz/wife of King Mathas

Rosalie: a dressmaker in Nora/wife of Peters

Ryan: grandson of Jeb/friend of Thaos

Sabot: member of the Insidiae

Sahil: a male Ruala warrior

Samara: wife of Tristt/Shettee

Samat: son of Chief Romogi and Silva/ Kingdom of Marba/Huta

Samos: Prince of Norkv/son of Thaddius

Sampson: oldest son of Chief Duncan and Liza of the Clan of Gesmal in Ryed

Sampson: Sergeant in the Taperian Army

Samuel: a high priest at the monastery at Malga who was murdered

Samuel: Prince of the original Samona/grandson of Thomas and Rewel

Samuel: second son of Raul and Vitomas

Sanuri: a holy man/emissary of The Great Ruler/warrior

Sar: an Enrop

Sar: male Ruala warrior

Sara: daughter of Usman

Sarah: baby granddaughter of Mathas and Rosa

Sarah: housekeeper for Claudius and Bella

Saran: daughter of Karzman and Nadia

Sasaha: Princess of the original Samona/granddaughter of Thomas and Rewel

Sasha: female warrior of the Nordes Tribe/wife of Galen

Satan: an ancient demon/ one of the Old Ones

Saunders: a Taperian soldier

Schroeder: man who works for Insidiae leader Dieter

Segal: Prince/ son of King Zachariah and Queen Noella of New Samona/husband of Cahina/Ruala

Seguna: former princess of Ryed/daughter of Akasha and Norah/ committed suicide

Selen: house keeper for Juleta

Shara: wife of Sorren/Nordes Tribe

Sharonne: King of Stordt; great, great, grandfather of King Roch and King Sudfad

Shon: son of King Fahra and Queen Sitha

Shone: Princess/daughter of Zeman and Oda/niece of King Manu of New Samona/Ruala

Sicily Bella: daughter of Stephan and Ingr

Sila: Princess of Ogg

Silva: one of Chief Romogi's three wives/Huta

Simmons: Commanding General of Fort Nir

Simon: adopted son of King Sudfad and Queen Renya of the Kingdom of Wetpr

Sinclair: King of Lentz/father of King Mathas

Sirius: works for High Priest Meekos

Sitha: Queen of Zorta

Smoking Joe: a regular patron at the Ghost Ship Tavern

Sonja: female warrior of the Nordes Tribe

Sophie: cook and servant of King Roch

Sorren: leader of the Nordes Tribe

Sporos: priest turned demon

Stephan: Captain in Army of Lentz/son of Claudius and Bella

Stiller: a fighter hired by Juleta

Stolas: an ancient demon/one of the Old Ones

Stone: hired fighter and intended vessel, works for Dieter

Sudfad: King of the Kingdom of Wetpr and brother to King Roch of Stordt

Sudfad: little Sudfad is grandson of King Sudfad

Sumona: Queen of Wetpr/wife of Alexandras/aunt of Roch and Sudfad

Syrius: a Bakken hired by Juleta

Tabeth: daughter of Fahron

Tabith: son of Tristt/Shettee

Tabitha: Princess of Lentz/daughter of Princess Isabella and Captain Josef of Lentz

Tadeo: Prince/son of Adwell and Nada/nephew of King Manu of New Samona/brother of Misha/Ruala

Tafer: a warlord who drove the Hutas out of the Kingdom of Norkv after years of wars and rebellions

Tahira: Princess of Samona/granddaughter of Thomas and Rewel

Tahira: a female Grand Master of the Insidiae

Tal: son of Oda and Jace/ Ruala

Talmai: Shettee boy who Thedes and Ibula adopt

Tambor: male Ruala warrior

Tamour: General in the Army of Lentz/on loan to Sudfad

Tanner: a Sergeant in the Army of Lentz

Tapster: a demon who works for Meekos

Tarig: a lieutenant in the Huta army

Tarin: son of King Neputa and Queen Tiara/Shettee

Taron: Prince/son of Adwell and Nada/nephew of King Manu of New Samona/brother of Misha/Ruala

Tasha: Queen of Puntd/ married to Tobias/ sister of Renya and Mathas

Tasha: female Ruala warrior/mother of Melanie/wife of Casey

Tate: a Lieutenant in the Wetprian Army

Tavin: son of Prince Lakin and Princess Zada/Ruala

Tega: housekeeper for the cabins of the captains of the Taperian Army

Tegman: soldier of Wetpr

Temark: villager of Neva

Thadddius: Prince of the new Kingdom of Norkv/son of Benjeman

Thaddies: member of Nordes Tribe/ father of Ingr

Thanatoes: an ancient demon/ one of the Old Ones

Thaos: a hired fighter

Thatcher: Prince/son of Zeman and Oda/nephew of King Manu of New Samona/Ruala

Thatus: Taperian soldier

The Lion: emissary of The Great Ruler who takes on the appearance of a lion when he is in the world of man

Thedes: warrior guarding refugees/Shettee

Thomas: King of the original Kingdom of Samona/father of Varden

Thomas: second son of Joshua and Iris/older brother of Vivian/Clan of Gesmal

Thomas: the young husband of Zoya who was murdered in Taperia

Thompson: Wetprian soldier

Thronson: one of Meekos hired killers

Tiara: Queen of Shettee Tribe when it was conquered by Hutas/wife of Neputa

Timothy: son of Fahron

Tito: member of Valdore Tribe

Titus Derek: son of Thaos and Nikki

Titus: a lieutenant in the Taperian Army

Tobart: a member of the Nordes Tribe

Tobias: King of Puntd.

Tomas: works for High Priest Pravis

Tome: a businessman and member of the Insidiae in Nora

Tomi: son of Usman the leader of the Valdore Tribe

Toomback: Huta warrior

Torance: father of Thaos

Torin: oldest son of Karzman and Nadia

Tratz: one of the men who kidnapped Petra

Travor: Taperian warrior who was injured at the Wall of Dorath

Tresdore: son of King Sharonne

Trevor: Prince/son of Zeman and Oda/nephew of King Manu of New Samona/Ruala

Tria: daughter of Oda and Jace/Ruala

Trina: one of Chief Romogi's three wives/Huta

Trina: Princess/daughter of Zeman and Oda/niece of King Manu of New Samona/Ruala

Trist: a male Ruala warrior

Tristt the Horrible: Shettee warrior

Tye: Prince of Norkv/son of Princess Grace and Prince Makalo

Tyron: male Ruala warrior/father of Mia/husband of Elsa

Tyson: Wetprian soldier

Ulger: a demon

Uma: Princess/ married to Gunnel son of King Zachariah and Queen Noella of New Samona/mother of Elan/Ruala

Umar: Prince/son of Adwell and Nada/nephew of King Manu of New Samona/brother of Misha/Ruala

Uri: son of Nina and Rhea/ Ruala

Usman: leader of the Valdore Tribe

Valor: Prince of the new Kingdom of Norkv/son of Benjeman and Esther

Vandrew: Petra's male tutor

Vania: Princess of Samona/daughter of Yorggi and Dion/granddaughter of Thomas and Rewel

Varden: last king of Samona/he and his family were murdered by rebels

Vardin: one of the men who kidnapped Petra

Vasart: Queen of Ryed/ wife of Nehmota

Vinca: Queen of Stordt, wife of Sharonne

Vincent: Prince of Ryed/son of Nehmota and Vasart

Vinus: Queen of the Kingdom of Gandt

Vitomas: Queen of Stordt

Vivian: a demon hunter from the Clan of Gesmal

Voltar: Prince of Samona/son of Darius and Rebek/grandson of Thomas and Rewel/later becomes King of Wetpr

Waed: Prince/son of Adwell and Nada/nephew of King Manu of New Samona/brother of Misha/has twin sister Nita/Ruala

Wallis: member of governing body of Nora

Wilard: Captain at Fort Polta

Willis: son of King Pergo and Queen Vinus/ Kingdom of Gandt

Xeni: a female Grand Master of the Insidiae

Yara: daughter of Nina and Rhea/Ruala

Yorggi: Prince of Samona/son of Thomas and Rewel/brother of Varden

Yori: son of Usman the leader of the Valdore Tribe

Yuri: Prince/son of Adwell and Nada/nephew of King Manu of New Samona/brother of Misha/Ruala

Zac: one of the men who kidnapped Petra

Zachariah: first King of New Samona/husband of Queen Noella/father of seven sons/Ruala

Zada: Princess/wife of Prince Lakin/Ruala

Zadok: a male Grand Master of the Insidiae

Zede: an ancient demon/ one of the Old Ones

Zehmann: an ancient demon/ one of the Old Ones

Zeman: Prince/ son of King Zachariah and Queen Noella of New Samona/husband of Oda/Ruala

Zorda: Taperian soldier injured in battle at the Wall of Dorath

Zoya: a seer from Taperia

Glossary of Terms

Aboultis: the calling cards of demons

Abyss: a vast void used to imprison demons

Acura: the whispering shadows/are in the inner circle of demons that directly serve the Old Ones

Amark: ancient language of The Great Ruler

Amulth: means filth in the language of demons/these monsters are made out of the waste of tortured souls from the hell dimensions

Anewa: one of seven continents in the World of Nunc

Aplewort: an herb when mixed with water purges poisons from a body

Asherane: ancient Tribe that lived in the northern regions of the Kingdom of Lentz

Astras: the ancient underground city of the Centras

Beltrad: a species of lower level demons

Blood rings: Large red rubies set in silver with markings of the Old Ones

Boca: a covered wagon pulled by horses

Box of Itifer: a gift to the world of man from The Great Ruler; this gift affects the balance of creation

Bozie: a game of skill played by the Nordes Tribe

Cava plant: a poisonous plant that grows freely near bodies of water

Centras: ancient race of creatures who have the responsibility of protecting the Holy Box of Itifer

Chalice of Ascension: a gift from The Great Ruler, this gift contains unimaginable powers

Cicero College: in Wetpr, outside of Salar, where Raul, Simon and Hannah attended college

Clan of Gesmal: a tribe of demon hunters who live in the southern region of the Kingdom of Ryed

631

Crystal pillars: in the Ice Caves of Mordv/are blessed by The Great Ruler and filled with spiritual life force

Czarsta: one of seven continents in the World of Nunc

Demalogs: an inferior species of demons

Demosa: a slow acting poison from the cava plant

Diamond of Cazo: a gift from The Great Ruler, this gift can unleash powers from the center of the world

Durisks: large demonic birds/their elongated beaks contain rows of fangs

Engas: a wild cat that inhabits the Vandrew Mountains

Engor: a small pack animal that lives in trees

Enrop: a large species of bird that can speak many human languages

Farduth: a Shettee necklace that symbolizes a male has completed his rite of passage to become a warrior

Gafet: an ancient Shettee weapon

Gants: large apelike creatures/Watchers of the Caves of Muldun

Gate of Isula: the only opening in the great Wall of Dorath

Gefrey Games: games of sport where men fight each other and great beasts to the death

Grand Masters: the first people to call to the demons and invite them into this world

Great Ruler: God

Hall of Antiquities: a giant hall located in the monastery at Malga/ a sanctuary for holy items and manuscripts

Hall of Light: the Great Hall in the Ice Caves of Mordv

Hengers: giant blue eagles/ birds of war

Highland Pass: the only passage through the Rosu Mountain Range

Holy Scrolls: gifts given to each kingdom by The Great Ruler, these gifts contain powers, wisdom and immortality

Holy Vault: a secret vault under the King's study in the castle in Wetpr designed to protect holy objects

Horn of Asher: a horn used by the Patronus warrior priests to signal each other

Horn of Cass: a horn used by the Wetprian soldiers to signal each other

Horn of Cornwell: a horn used by Dieter's men to signal each other

Horn of Eel: a horn used by the Ruala warriors to communicate with each other

Horn of Esker: a horn used by the Valdore Tribe to communicate with each other

Horn of Ire: a horn carried by the Taperian soldiers to communicate with each other

Horn of Shana: a horn carried by the soldiers of Lentz to communicate with each other

Horn of Tula: a horn used by the members of the Nordes Tribe for communication

Horn of Vamont: a horn used by the Kozach Tribe for communication

Horn of Xepoltr: a horn used by the Shettee warriors to communicate

Huta: a race of humans that is driven by hatred and ideas of racial superiority who live in the Kingdom of Marba

Insidiae: means conspirators/a highly organized secret group of humans who have sold their souls to demons

Jacar: giant leech-like creatures

Jacept Plant: a plant that a powerful poison is made from

Kafer: a small crescent shaped knife carried by the Beltrad

Keepers of the Scrolls: the Royal Family of the Kingdom of Wetpr entered into a covenant with The Great Ruler to protect his gifts until a time when they can be safely given back to the world of man

Kozach: a tribe that lives in the far north central regions of the Kingdom of Wetpr

Lamsman: an ankle bracelet worn by Venatores/stones in the bracelet signify great feats they had to accomplish to become a demon hunter

Linges plant: a plant that grows in damp, swampy regions in Opots/the white berries are used to make the drug Melanwhop

Mark of Satan: a coiled red snake with green eyes and a yellow tongue

Matu potage: a food staple of the Shettee Tribe

Mayka: one of seven continents in the World of Nunc

Melanwhop: a drug made from the linges plant, causes lethargy and apathy

Mordov: the special place in hell for hypocrites

Motfer: the land of the dead

Nefandus: a secret sect within the Insidiae

Nordes: a tribe of fiercely trained warriors who live in the northern region of the Kingdom of Lentz

Nunc: the world where this story takes place

Old Ones: the original demons that came to the World of Nunc

Opatu bread: a food staple of the Shettee Tribe

Opots: one of seven continents in the World of Nunc/the continent where this story takes place

Oran: a tobisk that is filled with a mixture of ramni oil, buruto powder and meno salts, designed to explode on impact

Patronus: an elite group of men who serve as the protectors of the church

Porto: one of seven continents in the World of Nunc

Prostras: an ancient tribe that once inhabited the Ice Caves of Mordv

Raftifa: ancient bat-like creatures that devour human flesh

Ravens: messengers used by the dark lords

Recupero: a sect within the Insidiae that worships the demon Omnibus

Rogetts: a tribe of humans that have digressed into murderous mutant monsters

Rualas: an ancient tribe of warriors said to be half human and half bird

Salszar: one of seven continents in the World of Nunc

Salts of Envoy: a sleeping potion

Scio: a crystal ball

Scroll of Imari: a gift of The Great Ruler, a scroll that unleashes the power of the Box of Itifer

Seal of Natun: a gift from the Holy Ruler that can open doors to other worlds

Serpents of Satan: can only be called forth by dark lords and demons, large red snakes with green eyes and yellow tongues

Seven Sons Prophesy: an ancient prophesy about seven sons who stand up against the demons and dark lords

Shesone: an ancient fighting style of the Shettee Tribe

Shettee: an ancient tribe of warriors said to be half human and half lion

Solv: a specific prison within the Abyss

Song of the Second Son: an ancient prophesy about an evil that is passed between second sons of a family resulting in a monster that brings terror and darkness to the world of man

Sundra Templer: a gift from The Great Ruler that was stolen by dark lords/an orb with extraordinary powers that can be used in multiple ways such as transporting humans through other worlds

Tabutu: an ancient form of fighting developed by the Asherane Tribe of the Kingdom of Lentz

Talisman: an object with magical or supernatural meaning

Talmuth: giant red dragon-like creatures

Tangers: large wild, grazing animals that travel in herds

Tansof: one of seven continents in the World of Nunc

Telgras: a hell beast that looks like it is half wolf and half panther

Teragon: death terror/a monster created as a result of diabolical acts

Terbot bear: a bear that roams in the northern regions of the Continent of Opots

Tervator: fourteen foot monster that walks like a man with long dark hair over its entire body and bull-like horns protruding from its head

Texts of Semalia: ancient texts about demonic language and rituals

The Celebration of Days: an annual celebration of the Centras

The Hall of Understanding: the building in Astras where the history of the Centras is documented in drawings

The Hunters: another name for the Shettee Tribe

The Lion: a very powerful messenger of The Great Ruler assumes the form of a lion when he walks in the worlds of man

The thirteenth color: not seen in the world of man it is the color of horror/hell

Timbar: ghost dragons/ demons that can fly

Tinchure water: an herbal pain remedy used by the Nordes Tribe

Tincture of the Redeti Plant: Hutas dip the tips of their weapons in this insect infested liquid. The insects lay eggs inside of the victim. When the eggs are mature and hatch, two inch worm-like creatures are produced and will eat the organs of the victim causing a long and painful death

Tobisks: sphere shaped objects, metal and hollow inside that are designed to be launched from a Trebuchet

Trebuchets: wooden machines used to catapult objects

Tygrus: a ship that docked in Port Friada

Unholy altar: altar used to worship demons

Valdees: the tribe that lives in the underwater Kingdom of Ogg

Valdore: a tribe of merciless separatists who live in the extreme northern regions of the Kingdom of Lentz

Venator: means hunter in the old language

Venom of the Atha serpent: one of the poisons that Hutas put on their arrows

Vessel of Darkness: a human created from darkness to hold the essence of a powerful demon

Wall of Dorath: a giant wall that separates the Kingdoms of Norkv and Xepoltr from the Kingdom of Marba

Willimonns: small furry creatures that are hunted for food and sport

Xelope: the oneness of spirit with all that lives

Zendoti: demons that are distinguished by the geometrically shaped tuffs of hair that protrude from their heads

Glossary of Maps

The maps are displayed in order of relevance

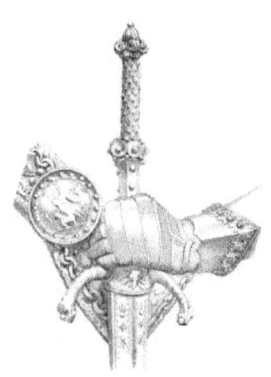

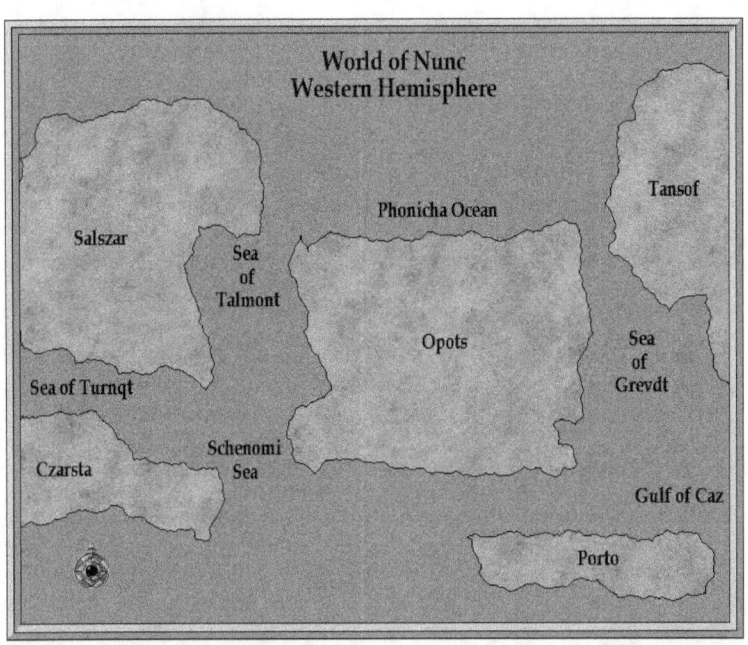

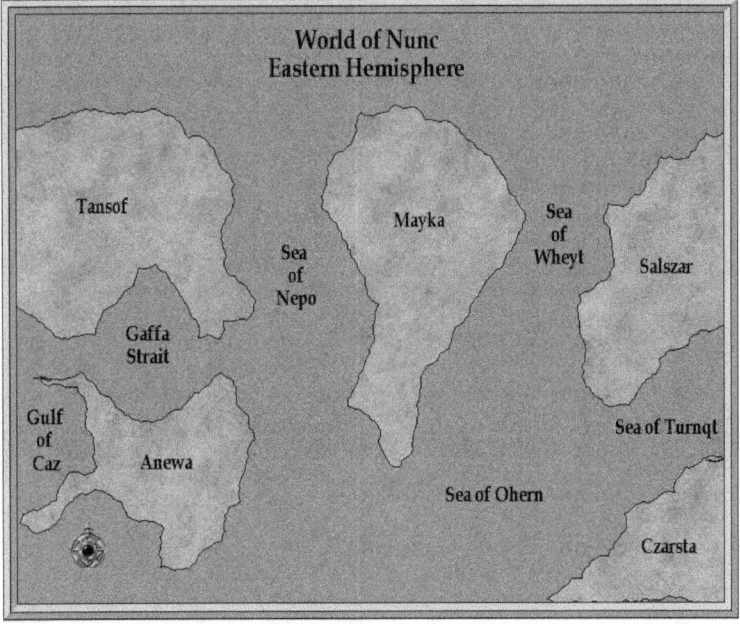

Continent of Opots
With new forts

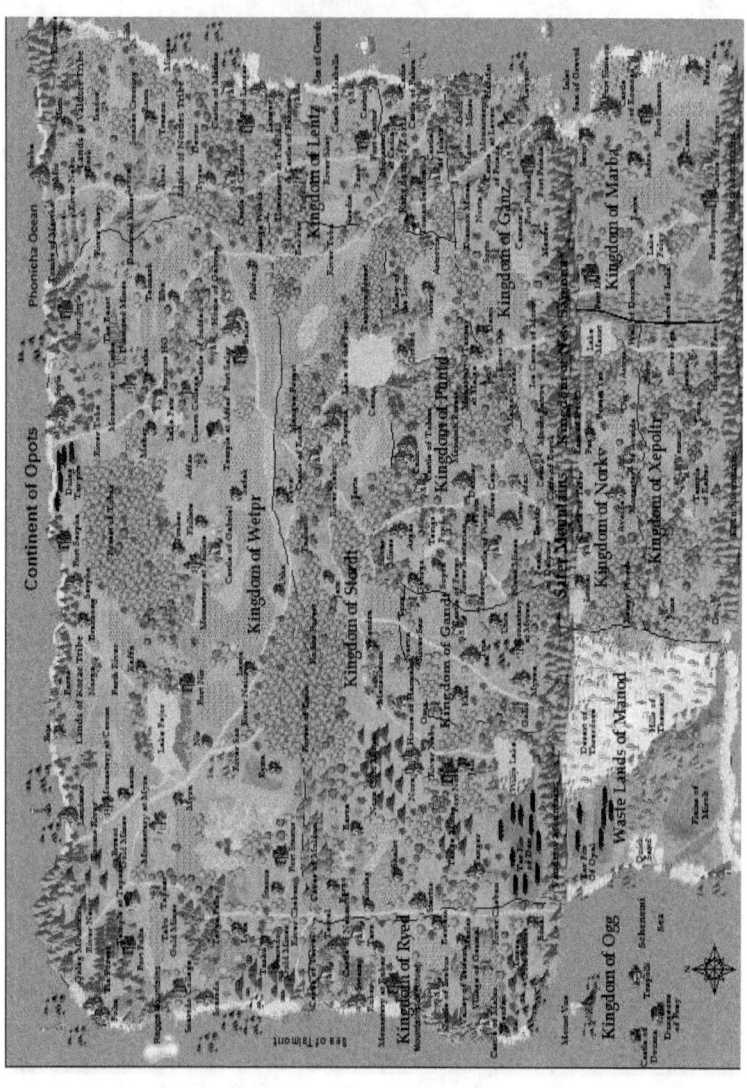

Western Stordt
With Fort Nora

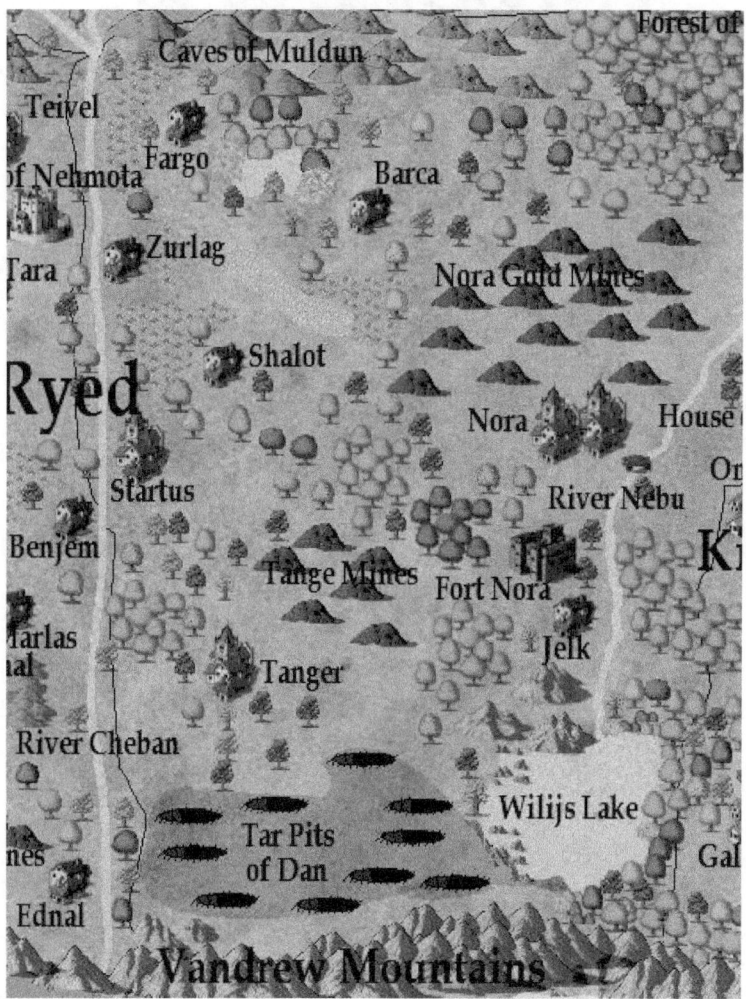

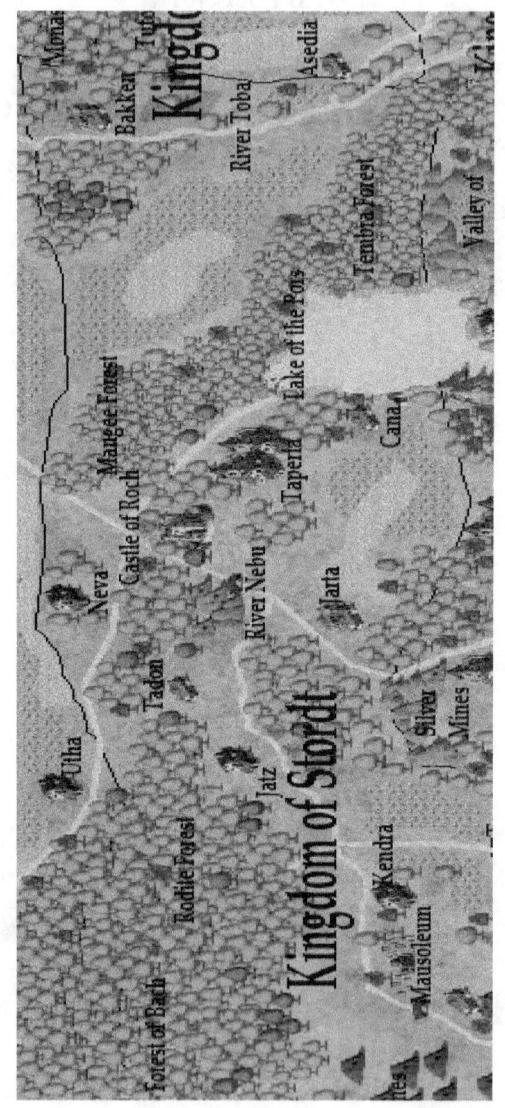

Western Wetpr
With Fort Stanus

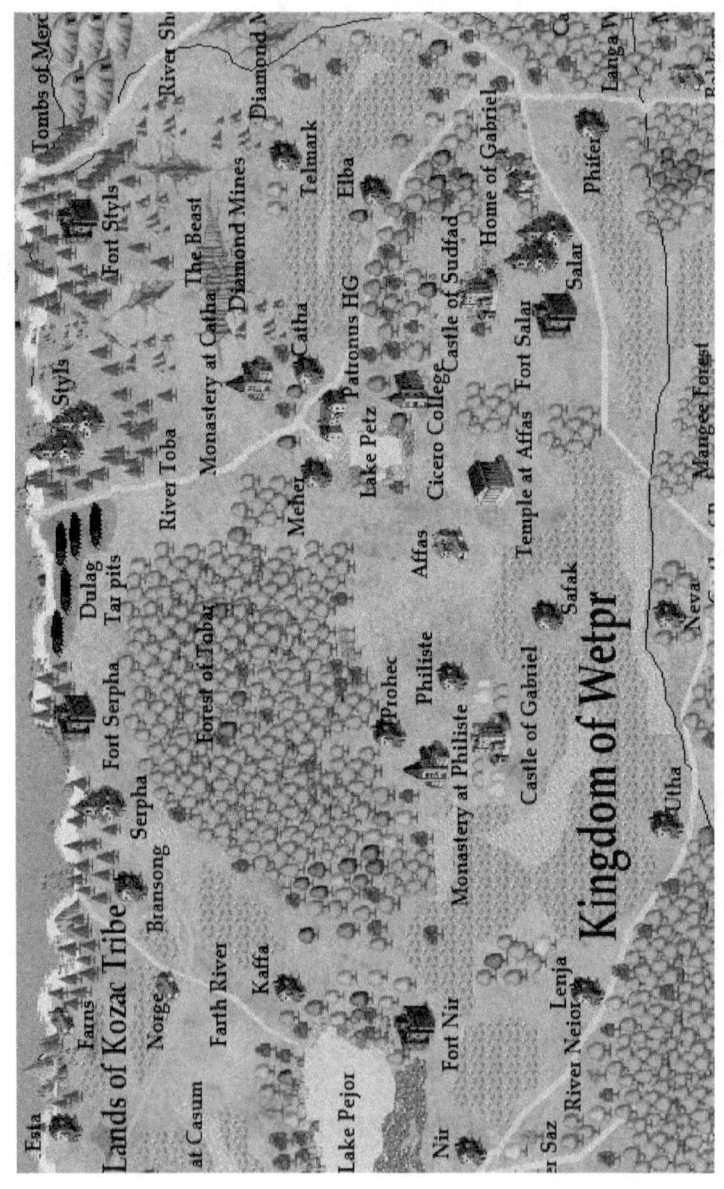

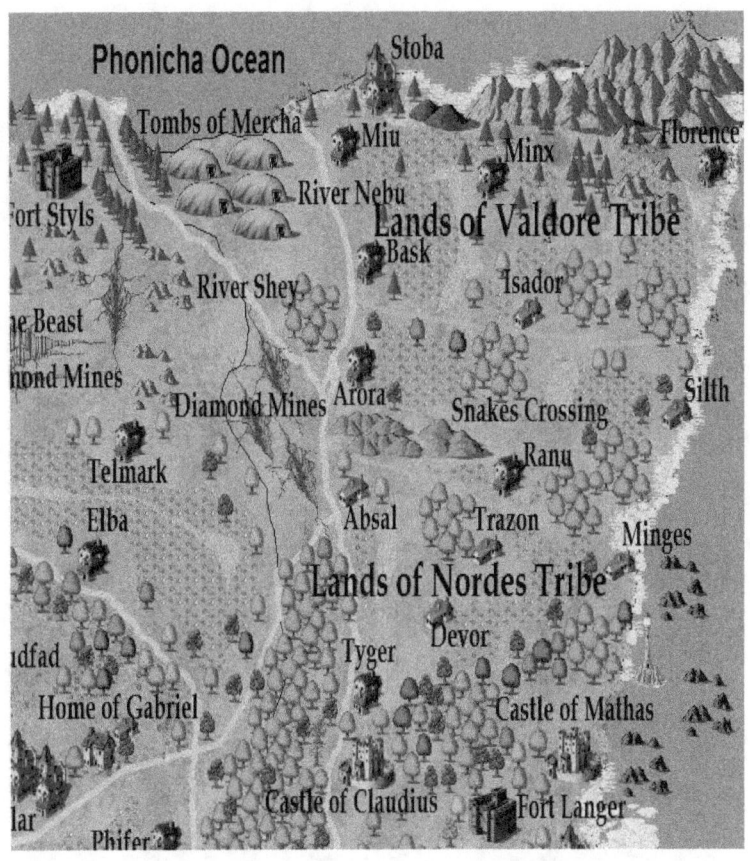

Marba

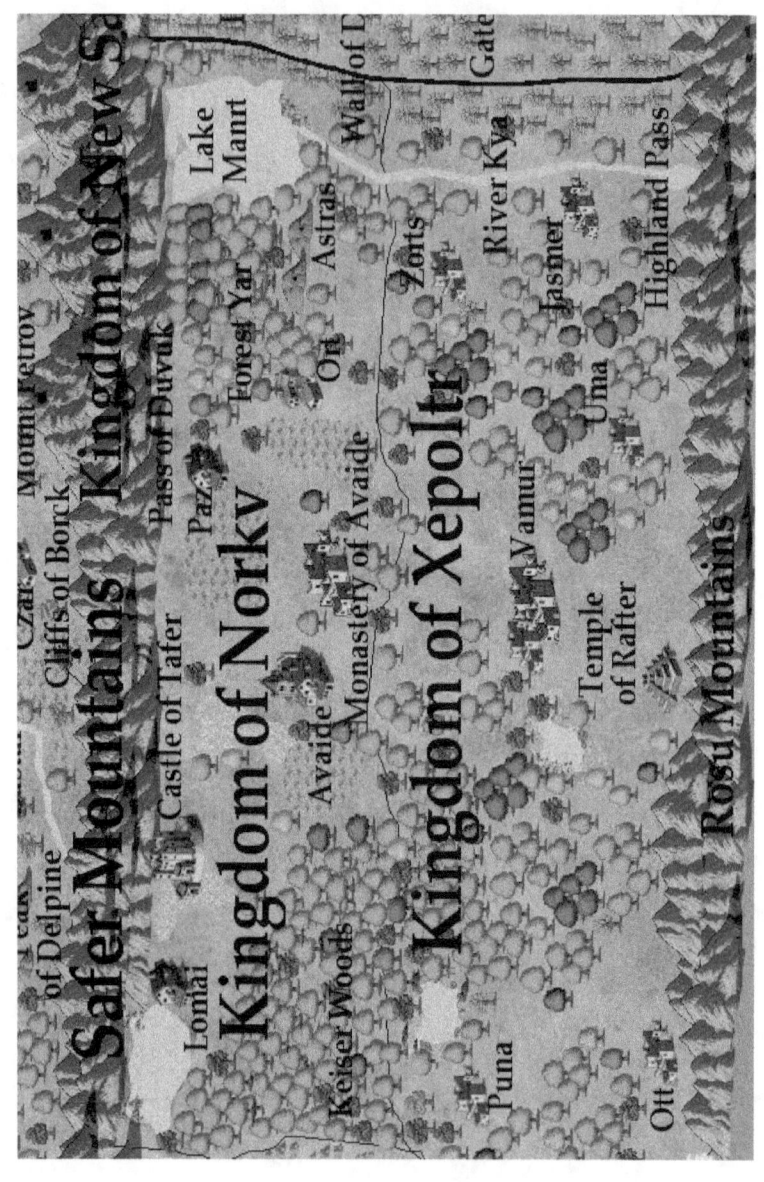

Waste Lands of Manod

Lower Opots

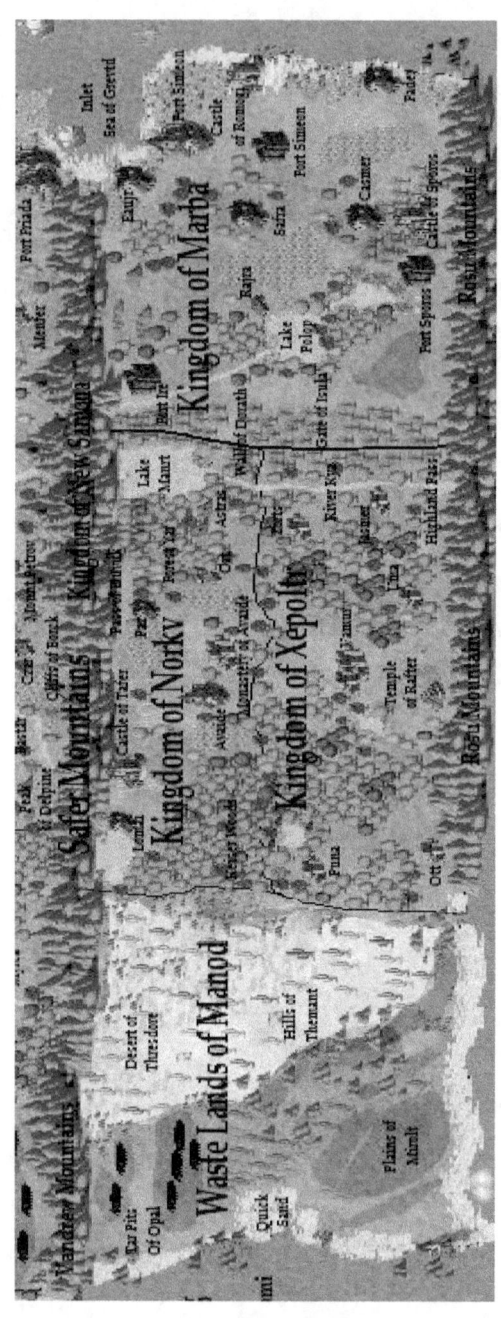

Ganz